Night and Morning by Edward Bulwer-Lytton

Edward George Earle Bulwer-Lytton was born on May 25th, 1803 the youngest of three sons.

When Edward was four his father died and his mother moved the family to London. As a child he was delicate and neurotic and failed to fit in at any number of boarding schools. However, he was academically and creatively precocious and, as a teenager, he published his first work; Ishmael and Other Poems in 1820.

In 1822 he entered university at Cambridge and in 1825 he won the Chancellor's Gold Medal for English verse for Sculpture. The following year he received his B.A. degree and printed, for private circulation, the small volume of poems, Weeds and Wild Flowers.

During his career he was to be extremely prolific and write across a number of genres; historical fiction, mystery, romance, the occult, and science fiction as well as poetry.

In 1828 his novel, Pelham, brought him an income, as well as a commercial and critical reputation. The books intricate plot and humorous, intimate portrayals kept many a gossip busy trying to pair up public figures with characters in the book.

Bulwer-Lytton reached, perhaps, the height of his popularity with the publication of Godolphin (1833), followed by The Pilgrims of the Rhine (1834), The Last Days of Pompeii (1834), Rienzi, Last of the Roman Tribunes (1835), and Harold, the Last of the Saxons (1848).

In 1841, he started the Monthly Chronicle, a semi-scientific magazine. The Victorian era was filled with many magazines and periodicals all of whom had a great fascination to chronicle and publish the many things that the Empire and Industrial Revolution were discovering, inventing and changing.

In 1858 he entered Lord Derby's government as Secretary of State for the Colonies. He took an active interest in the development of the Crown Colony of British Columbia and wrote with great passion to the Royal Engineers upon assigning them their duties there.

In 1866 Bulwer-Lytton was raised to the peerage as Baron Lytton of Knebworth in the County of Hertford but his passion for politics now somewhat dimmed.

Bulwer-Lytton had long suffered with a disease of the ear and for the last two or three years of his life he lived in Torquay nursing his health. An operation to cure his deafness resulted in an abscess forming in his ear which later burst.

Edward George Earle Bulwer-Lytton endured intense pain for a week and died at 2am on January 18th, 1873, in Torquay, just short of his 70th birthday.

Index of Contents

D1521253

PREFACE TO THE EDITION OF 1845

Much has been written by critics, especially by those in Germany (the native land of criticism), upon the important question, whether to please or to instruct should be the end of Fiction—whether a moral purpose is or is not in harmony with the undidactic spirit perceptible in the higher works of the imagination. And the general result of the discussion has been in favour of those who have contended that Moral Design, rigidly so called, should be excluded from the aims of the Poet; that his Art should regard only the Beautiful, and be contented with the indirect moral tendencies, which can never fail the creation of the Beautiful. Certainly, in fiction, to interest, to please, and sportively to elevate—to take man from the low passions, and the miserable troubles of life, into a higher region, to beguile weary and selfish pain, to excite a genuine sorrow at vicissitudes not his own, to raise the passions into sympathy with heroic struggles—and to admit the soul into that serener atmosphere from which it rarely returns to ordinary existence, without some memory or association which ought to enlarge the domain of thought and exalt the motives of action;—such, without other moral result or object, may satisfy the Poet,* and constitute the highest and most universal morality he can effect. But subordinate to this, which is not the duty, but the necessity, of all Fiction that outlasts the hour, the writer of imagination may well permit to himself other purposes and objects, taking care that they be not too sharply defined, and too obviously meant to contract the Poet into the Lecturer—the Fiction into the Homily. The delight in Shylock is not less vivid for the Humanity it latently but profoundly inculcates; the healthful merriment of the Tartufe is not less enjoyed for the exposure of the Hypocrisy it denounces. We need not demand from Shakespeare or from Moliere other morality than that which Genius unconsciously throws around it—the natural light which it reflects; but if some great principle which guides us practically in the daily intercourse with men becomes in the general lustre more clear and more pronounced, we gain doubly, by the general tendency and the particular result.

[I use the word Poet in its proper sense, as applicable to any writer, whether in verse or prose, who invents or creates.]

Long since, in searching for new regions in the Art to which I am a servant, it seemed to me that they might be found lying far, and rarely trodden, beyond that range of conventional morality in which Novelist after Novelist had entrenched himself—amongst those subtle recesses in the ethics of human life in which Truth and Falsehood dwell undisturbed and unseparated. The vast and dark Poetry around us—the Poetry of Modern Civilisation and Daily Existence, is shut out from us in much, by the shadowy giants of Prejudice and Fear. He who would arrive at the Fairy Land must face the Phantoms. Betimes, I set myself to the task of investigating the motley world to which our progress in humanity has attained, caring little what misrepresentation I incurred, what hostility I provoked, in searching through a devious labyrinth for the foot-tracks of Truth.

In the pursuit of this object, I am, not vainly, conscious that I have had my influence on my time—that I have contributed, though humbly and indirectly, to the benefits which Public Opinion has extorted from Governments and Laws. While (to content myself with a single example) the ignorant or malicious were decrying the moral of Paul Clifford, I consoled myself with perceiving that its truths had stricken deep—that many, whom formal essays might not reach, were enlisted by the picture and the popular force of Fiction into the service of that large and Catholic Humanity which frankly examines into the causes of crime, which ameliorates the ills of society by seeking to amend the circumstances by which they are occasioned; and commences the great work of justice to mankind by proportioning the punishment to the offence. That work, I know, had its share in the wise and great relaxation of our Criminal Code—it has had its share in results yet more valuable, because leading to more comprehensive reforms—viz., in the courageous facing of the ills which the mock decorum of timidity would shun to contemplate, but which, till fairly fronted, in the spirit of practical Christianity, sap daily, more and more, the walls in which blind Indolence would protect itself from restless Misery and rampant Hunger. For it is not till Art has told the unthinking that nothing (rightly treated) is too low for its breath to vivify and its wings to raise, that the Herd awaken from their chronic lethargy of contempt, and the Lawgiver is compelled to redress what the Poet has lifted into esteem. In thus enlarging the boundaries of the Novelist, from trite and conventional to untrodden ends, I have seen, not with the jealousy of an author, but with the pride of an Originator, that I have served as a guide to later and abler writers, both in England and abroad. If at times, while imitating, they have mistaken me, I am not answerable for their errors; or if, more often, they have improved where they borrowed, I am not envious of their laurels. They owe me at least this, that I prepared the way for their reception, and that they would have been less popular and more misrepresented, if the outcry which bursts upon the first researches into new directions had not exhausted its noisy vehemence upon me.

In this Novel of Night and Morning I have had various ends in view—subordinate, I grant, to the higher and more durable morality which belongs to the Ideal, and instructs us playfully while it interests, in the passions, and through the heart. First—to deal fearlessly with that universal unsoundness in social justice which makes distinctions so marked and iniquitous between Vice and Crime—viz., between the corrupting habits and the violent act—which scarce touches the former with the lightest twig in the fasces—which lifts against the latter the edge of the Lictor's axe. Let a child steal an apple in sport, let a starveling steal a roll in despair, and Law conducts them to the Prison, for evil commune to mellow them for the gibbet. But let a man spend one apprenticeship from youth to old age in vice—let him devote a fortune, perhaps colossal, to the wholesale demoralisation of his kind—and he may be surrounded with the adulation of the so-called virtuous, and be served upon its knee, by that Lackey—the Modern World! I say not that Law can, or that Law should, reach the Vice as it does the Crime; but I say, that Opinion may be more than the servile shadow of Law. I impress not here, as in Paul Clifford, a material moral to work its effect on the Journals, at the Hustings, through Constituents, and on Legislation;—I direct myself to a channel less active, more tardy, but as sure—to the Conscience—that reigns elder and superior to all Law, in men's hearts and souls;—I utter boldly and loudly a truth, if not all untold, murmured feebly and falteringly before, sooner or later it will find its way into the judgment and the conduct, and shape out a tribunal which requires not robe or ermine.

Secondly—in this work I have sought to lift the mask from the timid selfishness which too often with us bears the name of Respectability. Purposely avoiding all attraction that may savour of extravagance, patiently subduing every tone and every hue to the aspect of those whom we meet daily in our thoroughfares, I have shown in Robert Beaufort the man of decorous phrase and bloodless action—the systematic self-server—in whom the world forgive the lack of all that is generous, warm, and noble, in order to respect the passive acquiescence in methodical conventions and hollow forms. And how common such men are with us in this century, and how inviting and how necessary their delineation, may be seen in this,—that the popular and pre-eminent Observer of the age in which we live has since placed their prototype in vigorous colours upon imperishable canvas.—[Need I say that I allude to the Pecksniff of Mr. Dickens?]

There is yet another object with which I have identified my tale. I trust that I am not insensible to such advantages as arise from the diffusion of education really sound, and knowledge really available;—for these, as the right of my countrymen, I have contended always. But of late years there has been danger that what ought to be an important truth may be perverted into a pestilent fallacy. Whether for rich or for poor, disappointment must ever await the endeavour to give knowledge without labour, and experience without trial. Cheap literature and popular treatises do not in themselves suffice to fit the nerves of man for the strife below, and lift his aspirations, in healthful confidence above. He who seeks to divorce toil from knowledge deprives knowledge of its most valuable property.—the strengthening of the mind by exercise. We learn what really braces and elevates us only in proportion to the effort it costs us. Nor is it in Books alone, nor in Books chiefly, that we are made conscious of our strength as Men; Life is the great Schoolmaster, Experience the mighty Volume. He who has made one stern sacrifice of self has acquired more than he will ever glean from the odds and ends of popular philosophy. And the man the least scholastic may be more robust in the power that is knowledge, and approach nearer to the Arch-Seraphim, than Bacon himself, if he cling fast to two simple maxims—"Be honest in temptation, and in Adversity believe in God." Such moral, attempted before in Eugene Aram, I have enforced more directly here; and out of such convictions I have created hero and heroine, placing them in their primitive and natural characters, with aid more from life than books,—from courage the one, from affection the other—amidst the feeble Hermaphrodites of our sickly civilisation;—examples of resolute Manhood and tender Womanhood.

The opinions I have here put forth are not in fashion at this day. But I have never consulted the popular any more than the sectarian, Prejudice. Alone and unaided I have hewn out my way, from first to last, by the force of my own convictions. The corn springs up in the field centuries after the first sower is forgotten. Works may perish with the workman; but, if truthful, their results are in the works of others, imitating, borrowing, enlarging, and improving, in the everlasting Cycle of Industry and Thought.

Knelworth, 1845.

NOTE TO THE PRESENT EDITION, 1851

I have nothing to add to the preceding pages, written six years ago, as to the objects and aims of this work; except to say, and by no means as a boast, that the work lays claims to one kind of interest which I certainly never desired to effect for it—viz., in exemplifying the glorious uncertainty of the Law. For, humbly aware of the blunders which Novelists not belonging to the legal profession are apt to commit, when they summon to the denouement of a plot the aid of a deity so mysterious as Themis, I submitted to an eminent lawyer the whole case of "Beaufort versus Beaufort," as it stands in this Novel. And the pages which refer to that suit were not only written from the opinion annexed to the brief I sent in, but submitted to the eye of my counsel, and revised by his pen.—(N.B. He was feed.) Judge then my dismay when I heard long afterwards that the late Mr. O'Connell disputed the soundness of the law I had thus bought and paid for! "Who shall decide when doctors disagree?" All I can say is, that I took the best opinion that love or money could get me; and I should add, that my lawyer, unawed by the alleged ipse dixit of the great Agitator (to be sure, he is dead), still stoutly maintains his own views of the question.

[I have, however, thought it prudent so far to meet the objection suggested by Mr. O'Connell, as to make a slight alteration in this edition, which will probably prevent the objection, if correct, being of any material practical effect on the disposition of that visionary El Dorado—the Beaufort Property.]

Let me hope that the right heir will live long enough to come under the Statute of Limitations. Possession is nine points of the law, and Time may give the tenth.

Kenbworth.

NIGHT AND MORNING

BOOK I

"Noch in meines Lebens Lenze
War ich and ich wandert' aus,
Und der Jugend frohe Tanze
Liess ich in des Vaters Haus."

SCHILLER, *Der Pilgrim.*

INTRODUCTORY CHAPTER

"Now rests our vicar. They who knew him best,
Proclaim his life to have been entirely rest;
Not one so old has left this world of sin,
More like the being that he entered in."—CRABBE.

In one of the Welsh counties is a small village called A—. It is somewhat removed from the high road, and is, therefore, but little known to those luxurious amateurs of the picturesque, who view nature through the windows of a carriage and four. Nor, indeed, is there anything, whether of scenery or association, in the place itself, sufficient to allure the more sturdy enthusiast from the beaten tracks which tourists and guide-books prescribe to those who search the Sublime and Beautiful amidst the mountain homes of the ancient Britons. Still, on the whole, the village is not without its attractions. It is placed in a small valley, through which winds and leaps down many a rocky fall, a clear, babbling, noisy rivulet, that affords excellent sport to the brethren of the angle. Thither, accordingly, in the summer season occasionally resort the Waltons of the neighbourhood—young farmers, retired traders, with now and then a stray artist, or a roving student from one of the universities. Hence the solitary hostelry of A—, being somewhat more frequented, is also more clean and comfortable than could reasonably be anticipated from the insignificance and remoteness of the village.

At a time in which my narrative opens, the village boasted a sociable, agreeable, careless, half-starved parson, who never failed to introduce himself to any of the anglers who, during the summer months, passed a day or two in the little valley. The Rev. Mr. Caleb Price had been educated at the University of Cambridge, where he had contrived, in three years, to run through a little fortune of £3500. It is true, that he acquired in return the art of making milkpunch, the science of pugilism, and the reputation of one of the best-natured, rattling, open-hearted companions whom you could desire by your side in a tandem to Newmarket, or in a row with the bargemen. By the help of these gifts and accomplishments, he had not failed to find favour, while his money lasted, with the young aristocracy of the "Gentle Mother." And, though the very reverse of an ambitious or calculating man, he had certainly nourished the belief that some one of the "hats" or "tinsel gowns"—i.e., young lords or fellow-commoners, with whom he was on such excellent terms, and who supped with him so often, would do something for him in the way of a living. But it so happened that when Mr. Caleb Price had, with a little difficulty, scrambled through his degree, and found himself a Bachelor of Arts and at the end of his finances, his grand acquaintances parted from him to their various posts in the State Militant of Life. And, with the exception of one, joyous and reckless as himself, Mr. Caleb Price found that when Money makes itself wings it flies away with our friends. As poor Price had earned no academical distinction, so he could expect no advancement from his college; no fellowship; no tutorship leading hereafter to livings, stalls, and deaneries. Poverty began already to stare him in the face, when the only friend who, having shared his prosperity, remained true to his adverse fate,—a friend, fortunately for him, of high connections and brilliant prospects—succeeded in obtaining for him the humble living of A—. To this primitive spot the once jovial roisterer cheerfully retired—contrived to live contented upon an income somewhat less than he had formerly given to his groom—preached very short sermons to a very scanty and ignorant congregation, some of whom only understood Welsh—did good to the poor and sick in his own careless, slovenly way—and, uncheered or unvexed by wife and children, he rose in summer with the lark and in winter went to bed at nine precisely, to save coals and candles. For the rest, he was the most skilful angler in the whole county; and so willing to communicate the results of his experience as to the most taking colour of the flies, and the most favoured haunts of the trout—that he had given especial orders at the inn, that whenever any strange gentleman came to fish, Mr. Caleb Price should be immediately sent for. In this, to be sure, our worthy pastor had his usual recompense. First, if the stranger were tolerably liberal, Mr. Price was asked to dinner at the inn; and, secondly, if this failed, from the poverty or the churlishness of the obliged party, Mr. Price still had an opportunity to hear the last news—to talk about the Great World—in a word, to exchange ideas, and perhaps to get an old newspaper, or an odd number of a magazine.

Now, it so happened that one afternoon in October, when the periodical excursions of the anglers, becoming gradually rarer and more rare, had altogether ceased, Mr. Caleb Price was summoned from his parlour in which he had been employed in the fabrication of a net for his cabbages, by a little white-headed boy, who came to say there was a gentleman at the inn who wished immediately to see him—a strange gentleman, who had never been there before.

Mr. Price threw down his net, seized his hat, and, in less than five minutes, he was in the best room of the little inn.

The person there awaiting him was a man who, though plainly clad in a velveteen shooting-jacket, had an air and mien greatly above those common to the pedestrian visitors of A—. He was tall, and of one of those athletic forms in which vigour in youth is too often followed by corpulence in age. At this period, however, in the full prime of manhood—the ample chest and sinewy limbs, seen to full advantage in their simple and manly dress—could not fail to excite that popular admiration which is always given to strength in the one sex as to delicacy in the other. The stranger was walking impatiently to and fro the small apartment when Mr. Price entered; and then, turning to the clergyman a countenance handsome and striking, but yet more prepossessing from its expression of frankness than from the regularity of its features,—he stopped short, held out his hand, and said, with a gay laugh, as he glanced over the parson's threadbare and slovenly costume, "My poor Caleb!—what a metamorphosis!—I should not have known you again!"

"What! you! Is it possible, my dear fellow?—how glad I am to see you! What on earth can bring you to such a place? No! not a soul would believe me if I said I had seen you in this miserable hole."

"That is precisely the reason why I am here. Sit down, Caleb, and we'll talk over matters as soon as our landlord has brought up the materials for—"

"The milk-punch," interrupted Mr. Price, rubbing his hands.

"Ah, that will bring us back to old times, indeed!"

In a few minutes the punch was prepared, and after two or three preparatory glasses, the stranger thus commenced: "My dear Caleb, I am in want of your assistance, and above all of your secrecy."

"I promise you both beforehand. It will make me happy the rest of my life to think I have served my patron—my benefactor—the only friend I possess."

"Tush, man! don't talk of that: we shall do better for you one of these days. But now to the point: I have come here to be married—married, old boy! married!"

And the stranger threw himself back in his chair, and chuckled with the glee of a schoolboy.

"Humph!" said the parson, gravely. "It is a serious thing to do, and a very odd place to come to."

"I admit both propositions: this punch is superb. To proceed. You know that my uncle's immense fortune is at his own disposal; if I disobliged him, he would be capable of leaving all to my brother; I should disoblige him irrevocably if he knew that I had married a tradesman's daughter; I am going to marry a tradesman's daughter—a girl in a million! the ceremony must be as secret as possible. And in this church, with you for the priest, I do not see a chance of discovery."

"Do you marry by license?"

"No, my intended is not of age; and we keep the secret even from her father. In this village you will mumble over the bans without one of your congregation ever taking heed of the name. I shall stay here a month for the purpose. She is in London, on a visit to a relation in the city. The bans on her side will be published with equal privacy in a little church near the Tower, where my name will be no less unknown than hers. Oh, I've contrived it famously!"

"But, my dear fellow, consider what you risk."

"I have considered all, and I find every chance in my favour. The bride will arrive here on the day of our wedding: my servant will be one witness; some stupid old Welshman, as antediluvian as possible—I leave it to you to select him—shall be the other. My servant I shall dispose of, and the rest I can depend on."

"But—"

"I detest buts; if I had to make a language, I would not admit such a word in it. And now, before I run on about Catherine, a subject quite inexhaustible, tell me, my dear friend, something about yourself."

Somewhat more than a month had elapsed since the arrival of the stranger at the village inn. He had changed his quarters for the Parsonage—went out but little, and then chiefly on foot excursions among the sequestered hills in the neighbourhood. He was therefore but partially known by sight, even in the village; and the visit of some old college friend to the minister, though indeed it had never chanced before, was not, in itself, so remarkable an event as to excite any particular observation. The bans had been duly, and half audibly, hurried over, after the service was concluded, and while the scanty congregation were dispersing down the little aisle of the church,—when one morning a chaise and pair arrived at the Parsonage. A servant out of livery leaped from the box. The stranger opened the door of the chaise, and, uttering a joyous exclamation, gave his arm to a lady, who, trembling and agitated, could scarcely, even with that stalwart support, descend the steps. "Ah!" she said, in a voice choked with tears, when they found themselves alone in the little parlour,—"ah! if you knew how I have suffered!"

How is it that certain words, and those the homeliest, which the hand writes and the eye reads as trite and commonplace expressions—when spoken convey so much,—so many meanings complicated and refined? "Ah! if you knew how I have suffered!"

When the lover heard these words, his gay countenance fell; he drew back—his conscience smote him: in that complaint was the whole history of a clandestine love, not for both the parties, but for the woman—the painful secrecy—the remorseful deceit—the shame—the fear—the sacrifice. She who uttered those words was scarcely sixteen. It is an early age to leave Childhood behind for ever!

"My own love! you have suffered, indeed; but it is over now.

"Over! And what will they say of me—what will they think of me at home? Over! Ah!"

"It is but for a short time; in the course of nature my uncle cannot live long: all then will be explained. Our marriage once made public, all connected with you will be proud to own you. You will have wealth, station—a name among the first in the gentry of England. But, above all, you will have the happiness to think that your forbearance for a time has saved me, and, it may be, our children, sweet one!—from poverty and—"

"It is enough," interrupted the girl; and the expression of her countenance became serene and elevated. "It is for you—for your sake. I know what you hazard: how much I must owe you! Forgive me, this is the last murmur you shall ever hear from these lips."

An hour after these words were spoken, the marriage ceremony was concluded.

"Caleb," said the bridegroom, drawing the clergyman aside as they were about to re-enter the house, "you will keep your promise, I know; and you think I may depend implicitly upon the good faith of the witness you have selected?"

"Upon his good faith?—no," said Caleb, smiling, "but upon his deafness, his ignorance, and his age. My poor old clerk! He will have forgotten all about it before this day three months. Now I have seen your lady, I no longer wonder that you incur so great a risk. I never beheld so lovely a countenance. You will be happy!" And the village priest sighed, and thought of the coming winter and his own lonely hearth.

"My dear friend, you have only seen her beauty—it is her least charm. Heaven knows how often I have made love; and this is the only woman I have ever really loved. Caleb, there is an excellent living that adjoins my uncle's house. The rector is old; when the house is mine, you will not be long without the living. We shall be neighbours, Caleb, and then you shall try and find a bride for yourself. Smith,"—and the bridegroom turned to the servant who had accompanied his wife, and served as a second witness to the marriage,—"tell the post-boy to put to the horses immediately."

"Yes, Sir. May I speak a word with you?"

"Well, what?"

"Your uncle, sir, sent for me to come to him, the day before we left town."

"Aha!—indeed!"

"And I could just pick up among his servants that he had some suspicion—at least, that he had been making inquiries—and seemed very cross, sir."

"You went to him?"

"No, Sir, I was afraid. He has such a way with him;—whenever his eye is fixed on mine, I always feel as if it was impossible to tell a lie; and—and—in short, I thought it was best not to go."

"You did right. Confound this fellow!" muttered the bridegroom, turning away; "he is honest, and loves me: yet, if my uncle sees him, he is clumsy enough to betray all. Well, I always meant to get him out of the way—the sooner the better. Smith!"

"Yes, sir!"

"You have often said that you should like, if you had some capital, to settle in Australia. Your father is an excellent farmer; you are above the situation you hold with me; you are well educated, and have some knowledge of agriculture; you can scarcely fail to make a fortune as a settler; and if you are of the same mind still, why, look you, I have just £1000. at my bankers: you shall have half, if you like to sail by the first packet."

"Oh, sir, you are too generous."

"Nonsense—no thanks—I am more prudent than generous; for I agree with you that it is all up with me if my uncle gets hold of you. I dread my prying brother, too; in fact, the obligation is on my side; only stay abroad till I am a rich man, and my marriage made public, and then you may ask of me what you will. It's agreed, then; order the horses, we'll go round by Liverpool, and learn about the vessels. By the way, my good fellow, I hope you see nothing now of that good-for-nothing brother of yours?"

"No, indeed, sir. It's a thousand pities he has turned out so ill; for he was the cleverest of the family, and could always twist me round his little finger."

"That's the very reason I mentioned him. If he learned our secret, he would take it to an excellent market. Where is he?"

"Hiding, I suspect, sir."

"Well, we shall put the sea between you and him! So now all's safe."

Caleb stood by the porch of his house as the bride and bridegroom entered their humble vehicle. Though then November, the day was exquisitely mild and calm, the sky without a cloud, and even the leafless trees seemed to smile beneath the cheerful sun. And the young bride wept no more; she was with him she loved—she was his for ever. She forgot the rest. The hope—the heart of sixteen—spoke brightly out through the blushes that mantled over her fair cheeks. The bridegroom's frank and manly countenance was radiant with joy. As he waved his hand to Caleb from the window the post-boy cracked his whip, the servant settled himself on the dickey, the horses started off in a brisk trot,—the clergyman was left alone.

To be married is certainly an event in life; to marry other people is, for a priest, a very ordinary occurrence; and yet, from that day, a great change began to operate in the spirits and the habits of Caleb Price. Have you ever, my gentle reader, buried yourself for some time quietly in the lazy ease of a dull country-life? Have you ever become gradually accustomed to its monotony, and inured to its solitude; and, just at the time when you have half-forgotten the great world—that mare magnum that frets and roars in the distance—have you ever received in your calm retreat some visitor, full of the busy and excited life which you imagined yourself contented to relinquish? If so, have you not perceived, that, in proportion as his presence and communication either revived old memories, or brought before you new pictures of "the bright tumult" of that existence of which your guest made a part,—you began to compare him curiously with yourself; you began to feel that what before was to rest is now to rot; that your years are gliding from you unenjoyed and wasted; that the contrast between the animal life of passionate civilisation and the vegetable torpor of motionless seclusion is one that, if you are still young, it tasks your philosophy to bear,—feeling all the while that the torpor may be yours to your grave? And when your guest has left you, when you are again alone, is the solitude the same as it was before?

Our poor Caleb had for years rooted his thoughts to his village. His guest had been like the Bird in the Fairy Tale, settling upon the quiet branches, and singing so loudly and so gladly of the enchanted skies afar, that, when it flew away, the tree pined, nipped and withering in the sober sun in which before it had basked contented. The guest was, indeed, one of those men whose animal spirits exercise upon such as come within their circle the influence and power usually ascribed only to intellectual qualities. During the month he had sojourned with Caleb, he had brought back to the poor parson all the gaiety of the brisk and noisy novitiate that preceded the solemn vow and the dull retreat;—the social parties, the merry suppers, the open-handed, open-hearted fellowship of riotous, delightful, extravagant, thoughtless YOUTH. And Caleb was not a bookman—not a scholar; he had no resources in himself, no occupation but his indolent and ill-paid duties. The emotions, therefore, of the Active Man were easily aroused within him. But if this comparison between his past and present life rendered him restless and disturbed, how much more deeply and lastingly was he affected by a contrast between his own future and that of his friend! Not in those points where he could never hope equality—wealth and station—the conventional distinctions to which, after all, a man of ordinary sense must sooner or later reconcile himself—but in that one respect wherein all, high and low, pretend to the same rights—rights which a man of moderate warmth of feeling can never willingly renounce—viz., a partner in a lot however obscure; a kind face by a hearth, no matter how mean it be! And his happier friend, like all men full of life, was full of himself—full of his love, of his future, of the blessings of home, and wife, and children. Then, too, the young bride seemed so fair, so confiding, and so tender; so formed to grace the noblest or to cheer the humblest home! And both were so happy, so all in all to each other, as they left that barren threshold! And the priest felt all this, as, melancholy and envious, he turned from the door in that November day, to find himself thoroughly alone. He now began seriously to muse upon those fancied blessings which men wearied with celibacy see springing, heavenward, behind the altar. A few weeks afterwards a notable change was visible in the good man's exterior. He became more careful of his dress, he shaved every morning, he purchased a crop-eared Welsh cob; and it was soon known in the neighbourhood that the only journey the cob was ever condemned to take was to the house of a certain squire, who, amidst a family of all ages, boasted two very pretty marriageable daughters. That was the second holy day-time of poor Caleb—the love-romance of his life: it soon closed. On learning the amount of the pastor's stipend the squire refused to receive his addresses; and, shortly after, the girl to whom he had attached himself made what the world calls a happy match: and perhaps it was one, for I never heard that she regretted the forsaken lover. Probably Caleb was not one of those whose place in a woman's heart is never to be supplied. The lady married, the world went round as before, the brook danced as merrily through the village, the poor worked on the week-days, and the urchins gambolled round the gravestones on the Sabbath,—and the pastor's heart was broken. He languished gradually and silently away. The villagers observed that he had lost his old good-humoured smile; that he did not stop every Saturday evening at the carrier's gate, to ask if there were any news stirring in the town which the carrier weekly visited; that he did not come to borrow the stray newspapers that now and then found their way into the village; that, as he sauntered along the brookside, his clothes hung loose on his limbs, and that he no longer "whistled as he went;" alas, he was no longer "in want of thought!" By degrees, the walks themselves were suspended; the parson was no longer visible: a stranger performed his duties.

One day, it might be some three years and more after the fatal visit I have commemorated—one very wild rough day in early March, the postman, who made the round of the district, rang at the parson's bell. The single female servant, her red hair loose on her neck, replied to the call.

"And how is the master?"

"Very bad;" and the girl wiped her eyes.

"He should leave you something handsome," remarked the postman, kindly, as he pocketed the money for the letter.

The pastor was in bed—the boisterous wind rattled down the chimney and shook the ill-fitting casement in its rotting frame. The clothes he had last worn were thrown carelessly about, unsmoothed, unbrushed; the scanty articles of furniture were out of their proper places; slovenly discomfort marked the death-chamber. And by the bedside stood a neighbouring clergyman, a stout, rustic, homely, thoroughly Welsh priest, who might have sat for the portrait of Parson Adams.

"Here's a letter for you," said the visitor.

"For me!" echoed Caleb, feebly. "Ah—well—is it not very dark, or are my eyes failing?" The clergyman and the servant drew aside the curtains and propped the sick man up: he read as follows, slowly, and with difficulty:

"DEAR, CALEB,—At last I can do something for you. A friend of mine has a living in his gift just vacant, worth, I understand, from three to four hundred a year: pleasant neighbourhood—small parish. And my friend keeps the hounds!—just the thing for you. He is, however, a very particular sort of person—wants a companion, and has a horror of anything evangelical; wishes, therefore, to see you before he decides. If you can meet me in London, some day next month, I'll present you to him, and I have no doubt it will be settled. You must think it strange I never wrote to you since we parted, but you know I never was a very good correspondent; and as I had nothing to communicate advantageously to you I thought it a sort of insult to enlarge on my own happiness, and so forth. All I shall say on that score is, that I've sown my wild oats; and that you may take my word for it, there's nothing that can make a man know how large the heart is, and how little the world, till he comes home (perhaps after a hard day's hunting) and sees his own fireside, and hears one dear welcome; and—oh, by the way, Caleb, if you could but see my boy, the sturdiest little rogue! But enough of this. All that vexes me is, that I've never yet been able to declare my marriage: my uncle, however, suspects nothing: my wife bears up against all, like an angel as she is; still, in case of any accident, it occurs to me, now I'm writing to you, especially if you leave the place, that it may be as well to send me an examined copy of the register. In those remote places registers are often lost or mislaid; and it may be useful hereafter, when I proclaim the marriage, to clear up all doubt as to the fact.

"Good-bye, old fellow,

"Yours most truly, &c., &c."

"It comes too late," sighed Caleb, heavily; and the letter fell from his hands. There was a long pause. "Close the shutters," said the sick man, at last; "I think I could sleep: and—and—pick up that letter."

With a trembling, but eager gripe, he seized the paper, as a miser would seize the deeds of an estate on which he has a mortgage. He smoothed the folds, looked complacently at the well-known hand, smiled—a ghastly smile! and then placed the letter under his pillow, and sank down; they left him alone. He did not wake for some hours, and that good clergyman, poor as himself, was again at his post. The only friendships that are really with us in the hour of need are those which are cemented by equality of circumstance. In the depth of home, in the hour of tribulation, by the bed of death, the rich and the poor are seldom found side by side. Caleb was evidently much feebler; but his sense seemed clearer than it had been, and the instincts of his native kindness were the last that left him. "There is something he wants me do for him," he muttered.

"Ah! I remember: Jones, will you send for the parish register? It is somewhere in the vestry-room, I think—but nothing's kept properly. Better go yourself—'tis important."

Mr. Jones nodded, and sallied forth. The register was not in the vestry; the church-wardens knew nothing about it; the clerk—a new clerk, who was also the sexton, and rather a wild fellow—had gone ten miles off to a wedding: every place was searched; till, at last, the book was found, amidst a heap of old magazines and dusty papers, in the parlour of Caleb himself. By the time it was brought to him, the sufferer was fast declining; with some difficulty his dim eye discovered the place where, amidst the clumsy pothooks of the parishioners, the large clear hand of the old friend, and the trembling characters of the bride, looked forth, distinguished.

"Extract this for me, will you?" said Caleb. Mr. Jones obeyed.

"Now, just write above the extract:

"'Sir,—By Mr. Price's desire I send you the inclosed. He is too ill to write himself. But he bids me say that he has never been quite the same man since you left him; and that, if he should not get well again, still your kind letter has made him easier in his mind."

Caleb stopped.

"Go on."

"That is all I have to say: sign your name, and put the address—here it is. Ah, the letter," he muttered, "must not lie about! If anything happens to me, it may get him into trouble."

And as Mr. Jones sealed his communication, Caleb feebly stretched his wan hand, held the letter which had "come too late" over the flame of the candle. As the blazing paper dropped on the carpetless floor, Mr. Jones prudently set thereon the broad sole of his top-boot, and the maidservant brushed the tinder into the grate.

"Ah, trample it out:—hurry it amongst the ashes. The last as the rest," said Caleb, hoarsely. "Friendship, fortune, hope, love, life—a little flame, and then—and then—"

"Don't be uneasy—it's quite out!" said Mr. Jones. Caleb turned his face to the wall. He lingered till the next day, when he passed insensibly from sleep to death. As soon as the breath was out of his body, Mr. Jones felt that his duty was discharged, that other duties called him home. He promised to return to read the burial-service over the deceased, gave some hasty orders about the plain funeral, and was turning from the room, when he saw the letter he had written by Caleb's wish, still on the table. "I pass the post-office—I'll put it in," said he to the weeping servant; "and just give me that scrap of paper." So he wrote on the scrap, "P. S. He died this morning at half-past twelve, without pain.—M. J.;" and not taking the trouble to break the seal, thrust the final bulletin into the folds of the letter, which he then carefully placed in his vest pocket, and safely transferred to the post. And that was all that the jovial and happy man, to whom the letter was addressed, ever heard of the last days of his college friend.

The living, vacant by the death of Caleb Price, was not so valuable as to plague the patron with many applications. It continued vacant nearly the whole of the six months prescribed by law. And the desolate parsonage was committed to the charge of one of the villagers, who had occasionally assisted Caleb in the care of his little garden. The villager, his wife, and half-a-dozen noisy, ragged children, took possession of the quiet bachelor's abode. The furniture had been sold to pay the expenses of the funeral, and a few trifling bills; and, save the kitchen and the two attics, the empty house, uninhabited, was surrendered to the sportive mischief of the idle urchins, who prowled about the silent chambers in fear of the silence, and in ecstasy at the space. The bedroom in which Caleb had died was, indeed, long held sacred by infantine superstition. But one day the eldest boy having ventured across the threshold, two cupboards, the doors standing ajar, attracted the child's curiosity. He opened one, and his exclamation soon brought the rest of the children round him. Have you ever, reader, when a boy, suddenly stumbled on that El Dorado, called by the grown-up folks a lumber room? Lumber, indeed! what Virtu double-locks in cabinets is the real lumber to the boy! Lumber, reader! to thee it was a treasury! Now this cupboard had been the lumber-room in Caleb's household. In an instant the whole troop had thrown themselves on the motley contents. Stray joints of clumsy fishing-rods; artificial baits; a pair of worn-out top-boots, in which one of the urchins, whooping and shouting, buried himself up to the middle; moth-eaten, stained, and ragged, the collegian's gown—relic of the dead man's palmy time; a bag of carpenter's tools, chiefly broken; a cricket-bat; an odd boxing-glove; a fencing-foil, snapped in the middle; and, more than all, some half-finished attempts at rude toys: a boat, a cart, a doll's house, in which the good-natured Caleb had busied himself for the younger ones of that family in which he had found the fatal ideal of his trite life. One by one were these lugged forth from their dusty slumber-profane hands struggling for the first right of appropriation. And now, revealed against the wall, glared upon the startled violators of the sanctuary, with glassy eyes and horrent visage, a grim monster. They huddled back one upon the other, pale and breathless, till the eldest, seeing that the creature moved not, took heart, approached on tip-toe-twice receded, and twice again advanced, and finally drew out, daubed, painted, and tricked forth in the semblance of a griffin, a gigantic kite.

The children, alas! were not old and wise enough to know all the dormant value of that imprisoned aeronaut, which had cost Caleb many a dull evening's labour—the intended gift to the false one's favourite brother. But they guessed that it was a thing or spirit appertaining of right to them; and they resolved, after mature consultation, to impart the secret of their discovery to an old wooden-legged villager, who had served in the army, who was the idol of all the children of the place, and who, they firmly believed, knew everything under the sun, except the mystical arts of reading and writing. Accordingly, having seen that the coast was clear—for they considered their parents (as the children of the hard-working often do) the natural foes to amusement—they carried the monster into an old outhouse, and ran to the veteran to beg him to come up slyly and inspect its properties.

Three months after this memorable event, arrived the new pastor—a slim, prim, orderly, and starch young man, framed by nature and trained by practice to bear a great deal of solitude and starving. Two loving couples had waited to be married till his Reverence should arrive. The ceremony performed, where was the registry-book? The vestry was searched—the church-wardens interrogated; the gay clerk, who, on the demise of his deaf predecessor, had come into office a little before Caleb's last illness, had a dim recollection of having taken the registry up to Mr. Price at the time the vestry-room was whitewashed. The house was searched—the cupboard, the mysterious cupboard, was explored. "Here it is, sir!" cried the clerk; and he pounced upon a pale parchment volume. The thin clergyman opened it, and recoiled in dismay—more than three-fourths of the leaves had been torn out.

"It is the moths, sir," said the gardener's wife, who had not yet removed from the house.

The clergyman looked round; one of the children was trembling. "What have you done to this book, little one?"

"That book?—the—hi!—hi!—"

"Speak the truth, and you sha'n't be punished."

"I did not know it was any harm—hi!—hi!—"

"Well, and—"

"And old Ben helped us."

"Well?"

"And—and—and—hi!—hi!—The tail of the kite, sir!—"

"Where is the kite?"

Alas! the kite and its tail were long ago gone to that undiscovered limbo where all things lost, broken, vanished, and destroyed; things that lose themselves—for servants are too honest to steal; things that break themselves—for servants are too careful to break; find an everlasting and impenetrable refuge.

"It does not signify a pin's head," said the clerk; "the parish must find a new 'un!"

"It is no fault of mine," said the Pastor. "Are my chops ready?"

CHAPTER II

"And soothed with idle dreams the frowning fate."—CRABBE.

"Why does not my father come back? what a time he has been away!"

"My dear Philip, business detains him; but he will be here in a few days—perhaps to-day!"

"I should like him to see how much I am improved."

"Improved in what, Philip?" said the mother, with a smile. "Not Latin, I am sure; for I have not seen you open a book since you insisted on poor Todd's dismissal."

"Todd! Oh, he was such a scrub, and spoke through his nose: what could he know of Latin?"

"More than you ever will, I fear, unless—" and here there was a certain hesitation in the mother's voice, "unless your father consents to your going to school."

"Well, I should like to go to Eton! That's the only school for a gentleman. I've heard my father say so."

"Philip, you are too proud."—"Proud! you often call me proud; but, then, you kiss me when you do so. Kiss me now, mother."

The lady drew her son to her breast, put aside the clustering hair from his forehead, and kissed him; but the kiss was sad, and the moment after she pushed him away gently and muttered, unconscious that she was overheard:

"If, after all, my devotion to the father should wrong the children!"

The boy started, and a cloud passed over his brow; but he said nothing. A light step entered the room through the French casements that opened on the lawn, and the mother turned to her youngest-born, and her eye brightened.

"Mamma! mamma! here is a letter for you. I snatched it from John: it is papa's handwriting."

The lady uttered a joyous exclamation, and seized the letter. The younger child nestled himself on a stool at her feet, looking up while she read it; the elder stood apart, leaning on his gun, and with something of thought, even of gloom, upon his countenance.

There was a strong contrast in the two boys. The elder, who was about fifteen, seemed older than he was, not only from his height, but from the darkness of his complexion, and a certain proud, nay, imperious, expression upon features that, without having the soft and fluent graces of childhood, were yet regular and striking. His dark-green shooting-dress, with the belt and pouch, the cap, with its gold tassel set upon his luxuriant curls, which had the purple gloss of the raven's plume, blended perhaps something prematurely manly in his own tastes, with the love of the fantastic and the picturesque which bespeaks the presiding genius of the proud mother. The younger son had scarcely told his ninth year; and the soft, auburn ringlets, descending half-way down the shoulders; the rich and delicate bloom that exhibits at once the hardy health and the gentle fostering; the large deep-blue eyes; the flexile and almost effeminate contour of the harmonious features; altogether made such an ideal of childlike beauty as Lawrence had loved to paint or Chantrey model. And the daintiest cares of a mother, who, as yet, has her darling all to herself—her toy, her plaything—were visible in the large falling collar of finest cambric, and the blue velvet dress with its filigree buttons and embroidered sash.

Both the boys had about them the air of those whom Fate ushers blandly into life; the air of wealth, and birth, and luxury, spoiled and pampered as if earth had no thorn for their feet, and heaven not a wind to visit their young cheeks too roughly. The mother had been extremely handsome; and though the first bloom of youth was now gone, she had still the beauty that might captivate new love—an easier task than to retain the old. Both her sons, though differing from each other, resembled her; she had the features of the younger; and probably any one who had seen her in her own earlier youth would have recognized in that child's gay yet gentle countenance the mirror of the mother when a girl. Now, however, especially when silent or thoughtful, the expression of her face was rather that of the elder boy;—the cheek, once so rosy was now pale, though clear, with something which time had given, of pride and thought, in the curved lip and the high forehead. One who could have looked on her in her more lonely hours, might have seen that the pride had known shame, and the thought was the shadow of the passions of fear and sorrow.

But now as she read those hasty, brief, but well-remembered characters—read as one whose heart was in her eyes—joy and triumph alone were visible in that eloquent countenance. Her eyes flashed, her breast heaved; and at length, clasping the letter to her lips, she kissed it again and again with passionate transport. Then, as her eyes met the dark, inquiring, earnest gaze of her eldest born, she flung her arms round him, and wept vehemently.

"What is the matter, mamma, dear mamma?" said the youngest, pushing himself between Philip and his mother. "Your father is coming back, this day—this very hour;—and you—you—child—you, Philip—" Here sobs broke in upon her words, and left her speechless.

The letter that had produced this effect ran as follows:

TO MRS MORTON, Fernside Cottage.

"DEAREST KATE,—My last letter prepared you for the news I have now to relate—my poor uncle is no more. Though I had seen little of him, especially of late years, his death sensibly affected me; but I have at least the consolation of thinking that there is nothing now to prevent my doing justice to you. I am the sole heir to his fortune—I have it in my power, dearest Kate, to offer you a tardy recompense for all you have put up with for my sake;—a sacred testimony to your long forbearance, your unreproachful love, your wrongs, and your devotion. Our children, too—my noble Philip!—kiss them, Kate—kiss them for me a thousand times.

"I write in great haste—the burial is just over, and my letter will only serve to announce my return. My darling Catherine, I shall be with you almost as soon as these lines meet your eyes—those clear eyes, that, for all the tears they have shed for my faults and follies, have never looked the less kind. Yours, ever as ever, "PHILIP BEAUFORT.

This letter has told its tale, and little remains to explain. Philip Beaufort was one of those men of whom there are many in his peculiar class of society—easy, thoughtless, good-humoured, generous, with feelings infinitely better than his principles.

Inheriting himself but a moderate fortune, which was three parts in the hands of the Jews before he was twenty-five, he had the most brilliant expectations from his uncle; an old bachelor, who, from a courtier, had turned a misanthrope—cold—shrewd—penetrating—worldly—sarcastic—and imperious; and from this relation he received, meanwhile, a handsome and, indeed, munificent allowance. About sixteen years before the date at which this narrative opens, Philip Beaufort had "run off," as the saying is, with Catherine Morton, then little more than a child,—a motherless child—educated at a boarding-school to notions and desires far beyond her station; for she was the daughter of a provincial tradesman. And Philip Beaufort, in the prime of life, was possessed of most of the qualities that dazzle the eyes and many of the arts that betray the affections. It was suspected by some that they were privately married:

if so, the secret had been closely kept, and baffled all the inquiries of the stern old uncle. Still there was much, not only in the manner, at once modest and dignified, but in the character of Catherine, which was proud and high-spirited, to give colour to the suspicion. Beaufort, a man naturally careless of forms, paid her a marked and punctilious respect; and his attachment was evidently one not only of passion, but of confidence and esteem. Time developed in her mental qualities far superior to those of Beaufort, and for these she had ample leisure of cultivation. To the influence derived from her mind and person she added that of a frank, affectionate, and winning disposition; their children cemented the bond between them. Mr. Beaufort was passionately attached to field sports. He lived the greater part of the year with Catherine, at the beautiful cottage to which he had built hunting stables that were the admiration of the county; and though the cottage was near London, the pleasures of the metropolis seldom allured him for more than a few days—generally but a few hours—at a time; and he—always hurried back with renewed relish to what he considered his home.

Whatever the connection between Catherine and himself (and of the true nature of that connection, the Introductory Chapter has made the reader more enlightened than the world), her influence had, at least, weaned from all excesses, and many follies, a man who, before he knew her, had seemed likely, from the extreme joviality and carelessness of his nature, and a very imperfect education, to contract whatever vices were most in fashion as preservatives against ennui. And if their union had been openly hallowed by the Church, Philip Beaufort had been universally esteemed the model of a tender husband and a fond father. Ever, as he became more and more acquainted with Catherine's natural good qualities, and more and more attached to his home, had Mr. Beaufort, with the generosity of true affection, desired to remove from her the pain of an equivocal condition by a public marriage. But Mr. Beaufort, though generous, was not free from the worldliness which had met him everywhere, amidst the society in which his youth had been spent. His uncle, the head of one of those families which yearly vanish from the commonalty into the peerage, but which once formed a distinguished peculiarity in the aristocracy of England—families of ancient birth, immense possessions, at once noble and untitled—held his estates by no other tenure than his own caprice. Though he professed to like Philip, yet he saw but little of him. When the news of the illicit connection his nephew was reported to have formed reached him, he at first resolved to break it off; but observing that Philip no longer gambled, nor ran in debt, and had retired from the turf to the safer and more economical pastimes of the field, he contented himself with inquiries which satisfied him that Philip was not married; and perhaps he thought it, on the whole, more prudent to wink at an error that was not attended by the bills which had here-to-fore characterised the human infirmities of his reckless nephew. He took care, however, incidentally, and in reference to some scandal of the day, to pronounce his opinion, not upon the fault, but upon the only mode of repairing it.

"If ever," said he, and he looked grimly at Philip while he spoke, "a gentleman were to disgrace his ancestry by introducing into his family one whom his own sister could not receive at her house, why, he ought to sink to her level, and wealth would but make his disgrace the more notorious. If I had an only son, and that son were booby enough to do anything so discreditable as to marry beneath him, I would rather have my footman for my successor. You understand, Phil!"

Philip did understand, and looked round at the noble house and the stately park, and his generosity was not equal to the trial. Catherine—so great was her power over him—might, perhaps, have easily triumphed over his more selfish calculations; but her love was too delicate ever to breathe, of itself, the hope that lay deepest at her heart. And her children!—ah! for them she pined, but for them she also hoped. Before them was a long future, and she had all confidence in Philip. Of late, there had been considerable doubts how far the elder Beaufort would realise the expectations in which his nephew had been reared. Philip's younger brother had been much with the old gentleman, and appeared to be in high favour: this brother was a man in every respect the opposite to Philip—sober, supple, decorous, ambitious, with a face of smiles and a heart of ice.

But the old gentleman was taken dangerously ill, and Philip was summoned to his bed of death. Robert, the younger brother, was there also, with his wife (who he had married prudently) and his children (he had two, a son and a daughter). Not a word did the uncle say as to the disposition of his property till an hour before he died. And then, turning in his bed, he looked first at one nephew, then at the other, and faltered out:

"Philip, you are a scapegrace, but a gentleman! Robert, you are a careful, sober, plausible man; and it is a great pity you were not in business; you would have made a fortune!—you won't inherit one, though you think it: I have marked you, sir. Philip, beware of your brother. Now let me see the parson."

The old man died; the will was read; and Philip succeeded to a rental of £20,000. a-year; Robert, to a diamond ring, a gold repeater, £5,000. and a curious collection of bottled snakes.

CHAPTER III

"Stay, delightful Dream;

Let him within his pleasant garden walk;
Give him her arm—of blessings let them talk."—CRABBE.

"There, Robert, there! now you can see the new stables. By Jove, they are the completest thing in the three kingdoms!"

"Quite a pile! But is that the house? You lodge your horses more magnificently than yourself."

"But is it not a beautiful cottage?—to be sure, it owes everything to Catherine's taste. Dear Catherine!"

Mr. Robert Beaufort, for this colloquy took place between the brothers, as their britska rapidly descended the hill, at the foot of which lay Fernside Cottage and its miniature demesnes—Mr. Robert Beaufort pulled his travelling cap over his brows, and his countenance fell, whether at the name of Catherine, or the tone in which the name was uttered; and there was a pause, broken by a third occupant of the britska, a youth of about seventeen, who sat opposite the brothers.

"And who are those boys on the lawn, uncle?"

"Who are those boys?" It was a simple question, but it grated on the ear of Mr. Robert Beaufort—it struck discord at his heart. "Who were those boys?" as they ran across the sward, eager to welcome their father home; the westering sun shining full on their joyous faces—their young forms so lithe and so graceful—their merry laughter ringing in the still air. "Those boys," thought Mr. Robert Beaufort, "the sons of shame, rob mine of his inheritance." The elder brother turned round at his nephew's question, and saw the expression on Robert's face. He bit his lip, and answered, gravely:

"Arthur, they are my children."

"I did not know you were married," replied Arthur, bending forward to take a better view of his cousins.

Mr. Robert Beaufort smiled bitterly, and Philip's brow grew crimson.

The carriage stopped at the little lodge. Philip opened the door, and jumped to the ground; the brother and his son followed. A moment more, and Philip was locked in Catherine's arms, her tears falling fast upon his breast; his children plucking at his coat; and the younger one crying in his shrill, impatient treble, "Papa! papa! you don't see Sidney, papa!"

Mr. Robert Beaufort placed his hand on his son's shoulder, and arrested his steps, as they contemplated the group before them.

"Arthur," said he, in a hollow whisper, "those children are our disgrace and your supplanters; they are bastards! bastards! and they are to be his heirs!"

Arthur made no answer, but the smile with which he had hitherto gazed on his new relations vanished.

"Kate," said Mr. Beaufort, as he turned from Mrs. Morton, and lifted his youngest-born in his arms, "this is my brother and his son: they are welcome, are they not?"

Mr. Robert bowed low, and extended his hand, with stiff affability, to Mrs. Morton, muttering something equally complimentary and inaudible.

The party proceeded towards the house. Philip and Arthur brought up the rear.

"Do you shoot?" asked Arthur, observing the gun in his cousin's hand.

"Yes. I hope this season to bag as many head as my father: he is a famous shot. But this is only a single barrel, and an old-fashioned sort of detonator. My father must get me one of the new gulls: I can't afford it myself."

"I should think not," said Arthur, smiling.

"Oh, as to that," resumed Philip, quickly, and with a heightened colour, "I could have managed it very well if I had not given thirty guineas for a brace of pointers the other day: they are the best dogs you ever saw."

"Thirty guineas!" echoed Arthur, looking with native surprise at the speaker; "why, how old are you?"

"Just fifteen last birthday. Holla, John! John Green!" cried the young gentleman in an imperious voice, to one of the gardeners, who was crossing the lawn, "see that the nets are taken down to the lake to-morrow, and that my tent is pitched properly, by the lime-trees, by nine o'clock. I hope you will understand me this time: Heaven knows you take a deal of telling before you understand anything!"

"Yes, Mr. Philip," said the man, bowing obsequiously; and then muttered, as he went off, "Drat the nat'rel! He speaks to a poor man as if he warn't flesh and blood."

"Does your father keep hunters?" asked Philip.

"No."

"Why?"

"Perhaps one reason may be, that he is not rich enough."

"Oh! that's a pity. Never mind, we'll mount you, whenever you like to pay us a visit."

Young Arthur drew himself up, and his air, naturally frank and gentle, became haughty and reserved. Philip gazed on him, and felt offended; he scarce knew why, but from that moment he conceived a dislike to his cousin.

CHAPTER IV

"For a man is helpless and vain, of a condition so exposed to calamity that a raisin is able to kill him; any trooper out of the Egyptian army—a fly can do it, when it goes on God's errand."—JEREMY TAYLOR On the Deceitfulness of the Heart.

The two brothers sat at their wine after dinner. Robert sipped claret, the sturdy Philip quaffed his more generous port. Catherine and the boys might be seen at a little distance, and by the light of a soft August moon, among the shrubs and bosquets of the lawn.

Philip Beaufort was about five-and-forty, tall, robust, nay, of great strength of frame and limb; with a countenance extremely winning, not only from the comeliness of its features, but its frankness, manliness, and good nature. His was the bronzed, rich complexion, the inclination towards embonpoint, the athletic girth of chest, which denote redundant health, and mirthful temper, and sanguine blood. Robert, who had lived the life of cities, was a year younger than his brother; nearly as tall, but pale, meagre, stooping, and with a careworn, anxious, hungry look, which made the smile that hung upon his lips seem hollow and artificial. His dress, though plain, was neat and studied; his manner, bland and plausible; his voice, sweet and low: there was that about him which, if it did not win liking, tended to excite respect—a certain decorum, a nameless propriety of appearance and bearing, that approached a little to formality: his every movement, slow and measured, was that of one who paced in the circle that fences round the habits and usages of the world.

"Yes," said Philip, "I had always decided to take this step, whenever my poor uncle's death should allow me to do so. You have seen Catherine, but you do not know half her good qualities: she would grace any station; and, besides, she nursed me so carefully last year, when I broke my collar-bone in that cursed steeple-chase. Egad, I am getting too heavy and growing too old for such schoolboy pranks."

"I have no doubt of Mrs. Morton's excellence, and I honour your motives; still, when you talk of her gracing any station, you must not forget, my dear brother, that she will be no more received as Mrs. Beaufort than she is now as Mrs. Morton."

"But I tell you, Robert, that I am really married to her already; that she would never have left her home but on that condition; that we were married the very day we met after her flight."

Robert's thin lips broke into a slight sneer of incredulity. "My dear brother, you do right to say this—any man in your situation would say the same. But I know that my uncle took every pains to ascertain if the report of a private marriage were true."

"And you helped him in the search. Eh, Bob?"

Bob slightly blushed. Philip went on.

"Ha, ha! to be sure you did; you knew that such a discovery would have done for me in the old gentleman's good opinion. But I blinded you both, ha, ha! The fact is, that we were married with the greatest privacy; that even now, I own, it would be difficult for Catherine herself to establish the fact, unless I wished it. I am ashamed to think that I have never even told her where I keep the main proof of the marriage. I induced one witness to leave the country, the other must be long since dead: my poor friend, too, who officiated, is no more. Even the register, Bob, the register itself, has been destroyed: and yet, notwithstanding, I will prove the ceremony and clear up poor Catherine's fame; for I have the attested copy of the register safe and sound. Catherine not married! why, look at her, man!"

Mr. Robert Beaufort glanced at the window for a moment, but his countenance was still that of one unconvinced. "Well, brother," said he, dipping his fingers in the water-glass, "it is not for me to contradict you. It is a very curious tale—parson dead—witnesses missing. But still, as I said before, if you are resolved on a public marriage, you are wise to insist that there has been a previous private one. Yet, believe me, Philip," continued Robert, with solemn earnestness, "the world—"

"Damn the world! What do I care for the world! We don't want to go to routs and balls, and give dinners to fine people. I shall live much the same as I have always done; only, I shall now keep the hounds—they are very indifferently kept at present—and have a yacht; and engage the best masters for the boys. Phil wants to go to Eton, but I know what Eton is: poor fellow! his feelings might be hurt there, if others are as sceptical as yourself. I suppose my old friends will not be less civil now I have £20,000. a year. And as for the society of women, between you and me, I don't care a rush for any woman but Catherine: poor Katty!"

"Well, you are the best judge of your own affairs: you don't misinterpret my motives?"

"My dear Bob, no. I am quite sensible how kind it is in you—a man of your starch habits and strict views, coming here to pay a mark of respect to Kate (Mr. Robert turned uneasily in his chair)—even before you knew of the private marriage, and I'm sure I don't blame you for never having done it before. You did quite right to try your chance with my uncle."

Mr. Robert turned in his chair again, still more uneasily, and cleared his voice as if to speak. But Philip tossed off his wine, and proceeded, without heeding his brother,—

"And though the poor old man does not seem to have liked you the better for consulting his scruples, yet we must make up for the partiality of his will. Let me see—what with your wife's fortune, you muster £2000. a year?"

"Only £1500., Philip, and Arthur's education is growing expensive. Next year he goes to college. He is certainly very clever, and I have great hopes—"

"That he will do Honour to us all—so have I. He is a noble young fellow: and I think my Philip may find a great deal to learn from him,—Phil is a sad idle dog; but with a devil of a spirit, and sharp as a needle. I wish you could see him ride. Well, to return to Arthur. Don't trouble yourself about his education—that shall be my care. He shall go to Christ Church—a gentleman-commoner, of course—and when he is of age we'll get him into parliament. Now for yourself, Bob. I shall sell the town-house in Berkeley Square, and whatever it brings you shall have. Besides that, I'll add £1500. a year to your £1000.—so that's said and done. Pshaw! brothers should be brothers.—Let's come out and play with the boys!"

The two Beauforts stepped through the open casement into the lawn.

"You look pale, Bob—all you London fellows do. As for me, I feel as strong as a horse: much better than when I was one of your gay dogs straying loose about the town. 'Gad, I have never had a moment's ill health, except from a fall now and then. I feel as if I should live for ever, and that's the reason why I could never make a will."

"Have you never, then, made your will?"

"Never as yet. Faith, till now, I had little enough to leave. But now that all this great Beaufort property is at my own disposal, I must think of Kate's jointure. By Jove! now I speak of it, I will ride to—to-morrow, and consult the lawyer there both about the will and the marriage. You will stay for the wedding?"

"Why, I must go into —shire to-morrow evening, to place Arthur with his tutor. But I'll return for the wedding, if you particularly wish it: only Mrs. Beaufort is a woman of very strict—"

"I—do particularly wish it," interrupted Philip, gravely; "for I desire, for Catherine's sake, that you, my sole surviving relation, may not seem to withhold your countenance from an act of justice to her. And as for your wife, I fancy £1500. a year would reconcile her to my marrying out of the Penitentiary."

Mr. Robert bowed his head, coughed huskily, and said, "I appreciate your generous affection, Philip."

The next morning, while the elder parties were still over the breakfast-table, the younger people were in the grounds; it was a lovely day, one of the last of the luxuriant August—and Arthur, as he looked round, thought he had never seen a more beautiful place. It was, indeed, just the spot to captivate a youthful and susceptible fancy. The village of Fernside, though in one of the counties adjoining Middlesex, and as near to London as the owner's passionate pursuits of the field would permit, was yet as rural and sequestered as if a hundred miles distant from the smoke of the huge city. Though the dwelling was called a cottage, Philip had enlarged the original modest building into a villa of some pretensions. On either side a graceful and well-proportioned portico stretched verandahs, covered with roses and clematis; to the right extended a range of costly conservatories, terminating in vistas of trellis-work which formed those elegant alleys called roseries, and served to screen the more useful gardens from view. The lawn, smooth and even, was studded with American plants and shrubs in flower, and bounded on one side by a small lake, on the opposite bank of which limes and cedars threw their shadows over the clear waves. On the other side a light fence separated the grounds from a large paddock, in which three or four hunters grazed in indolent enjoyment. It was one of those cottages which bespeak the ease and luxury not often found in more ostentatious mansions—an abode which, at sixteen, the visitor contemplates with vague notions of poetry and love—which, at forty, he might think dull and d—d expensive—which, at sixty, he would pronounce to be damp in winter, and full of earwigs in the summer. Master Philip was leaning on his gun; Master Sidney was chasing a peacock butterfly; Arthur was silently gazing on the shining lake and the still foliage that drooped over its surface. In the countenance of this young man there was something that excited a certain interest. He was less handsome than Philip, but the expression of his face was more prepossessing. There was something of pride in the forehead; but of good nature, not unmixed with irresolution and weakness, in the curves of the mouth. He was more delicate of frame than Philip; and the colour of his complexion was not that of a robust constitution. His movements were graceful and self-possessed, and he had his father's sweetness of voice. "This is really beautiful!—I envy you, cousin Philip."

"Has not your father got a country-house?"

"No: we live either in London or at some hot, crowded watering-place."

"Yes; this is very nice during the shooting and hunting season. But my old nurse says we shall have a much finer place now. I liked this very well till I saw Lord Belville's place. But it is very unpleasant not to have the finest house in the county: aut Caesar aut nullus—that's my motto. Ah! do you see that swallow? I'll bet you a guinea I hit it." "No, poor thing! don't hurt it." But ere the remonstrance was uttered, the bird lay quivering on the ground. "It is just September, and one must keep one's hand in," said Philip, as he reloaded his gun.

To Arthur this action seemed a wanton cruelty; it was rather the wanton recklessness which belongs to a wild boy accustomed to gratify the impulse of the moment—the recklessness which is not cruelty in the boy, but which prosperity may pamper into cruelty in the man. And scarce had he reloaded his gun before the neigh of a young colt came from the neighbouring paddock, and Philip bounded to the fence. "He calls me, poor fellow; you shall see him feed from my hand. Run in for a piece of bread—a large piece, Sidney." The boy and the animal seemed to understand each other. "I see you don't like horses," he said to Arthur. "As for me, I love dogs, horses—every dumb creature."

"Except swallows." said Arthur, with a half smile, and a little surprised at the inconsistency of the boast.

"Oh! that is short,—all fair: it is not to hurt the swallow—it is to obtain skill," said Philip, colouring; and then, as if not quite easy with his own definition, he turned away abruptly.

"This is dull work—suppose we fish. By Jove!" (he had caught his father's expletive) "that blockhead has put the tent on the wrong side of the lake, after all. Holla, you, sir!" and the unhappy gardener looked up from his flower-beds; "what ails you? I have a great mind to tell my father of you—you grow stupider every day. I told you to put the tent under the lime-trees."

"We could not manage it, sir; the boughs were in the way."

"And why did you not cut the boughs, blockhead?"

"I did not dare do so, sir, without master's orders," said the man doggedly.

"My orders are sufficient, I should think; so none of your impertinence," cried Philip, with a raised colour; and lifting his hand, in which he held his ramrod, he shook it menacingly over the gardener's head,—"I've a great mind to—"

"What's the matter, Philip?" cried the good-humoured voice of his father. "Fie!"

"This fellow does not mind what I say, sir."

"I did not like to cut the boughs of the lime-trees without your orders, sir," said the gardener.

"No, it would be a pity to cut them. You should consult me there, Master Philip;" and the father shook him by the collar with a good-natured, and affectionate, but rough sort of caress.

"Be quiet, father!" said the boy, petulantly and proudly; "or," he added, in a lower voice, but one which showed emotion, "my cousin may think you mean less kindly than you always do, sir."

The father was touched: "Go and cut the lime-boughs, John; and always do as Mr. Philip tells you."

The mother was behind, and she sighed audibly. "Ah! dearest, I fear you will spoil him."

"Is he not your son? and do we not owe him the more respect for having hitherto allowed others to—"

He stopped, and the mother could say no more. And thus it was, that this boy of powerful character and strong passions had, from motives the most amiable, been pampered from the darling into the despot.

"And now, Kate, I will, as I told you last night, ride over to — and fix the earliest day for our public marriage: I will ask the lawyer to dine here, to talk about the proper steps for proving the private one."

"Will that be difficult" asked Catherine, with natural anxiety.

"No,—for if you remember, I had the precaution to get an examined copy of the register; otherwise, I own to you, I should have been alarmed. I don't know what has become of Smith. I heard some time since from his father that he had left the colony; and (I never told you before—it would have made you uneasy) once, a few years ago, when my uncle again got it into his head that we might be married, I was afraid poor Caleb's successor might, by chance, betray us. So I went over to A— myself, being near it when I was staying with Lord C—, in order to see how far it might be necessary to secure the parson; and, only think! I found an accident had happened to the register—so, as the clergyman could know nothing, I kept my own counsel. How lucky I have the copy! No doubt the lawyer will set all to rights; and, while I am making the settlements, I may as well make my will. I have plenty for both boys, but the dark one must be the heir. Does he not look born to be an eldest son?"

"Ah, Philip!"

"Pshaw! one don't die the sooner for making a will. Have I the air of a man in a consumption?"—and the sturdy sportsman glanced complacently at the strength and symmetry of his manly limbs. "Come, Phil, let's go to the stables. Now, Robert, I will show you what is better worth seeing than those miserable flower-beds." So saying, Mr. Beaufort led the way to the courtyard at the back of the cottage. Catherine and Sidney remained on the lawn; the rest followed the host. The grooms, of whom Beaufort was the idol, hastened to show how well the horses had thriven in his absence.

"Do see how Brown Bess has come on, sir! but, to be sure, Master Philip keeps her in exercise. Ah, sir, he will be as good a rider as your honour, one of these days."

"He ought to be a better, Tom; for I think he'll never have my weight to carry. Well, saddle Brown Bess for Mr. Philip. What horse shall I take? Ah! here's my old friend, Puppet!"

"I don't know what's come to Puppet, sir; he's off his feed, and turned sulky. I tried him over the bar yesterday; but he was quite restive like."

"The devil he was! So, so, old boy, you shall go over the six-barred gate to-day, or we'll know why." And Mr. Beaufort patted the sleek neck of his favourite hunter. "Put the saddle on him, Tom."

"Yes, your honour. I sometimes think he is hurt in the loins somehow—he don't take to his leaps kindly, and he always tries to bite when we bridles him. Be quiet, sir!"

"Only his airs," said Philip. "I did not know this, or I would have taken him over the gate. Why did not you tell me, Tom?"

"Lord love you, sir! because you have such a spurret; and if anything had come to you—"

"Quite right: you are not weight enough for Puppet, my boy; and he never did like any one to back him but myself. What say you, brother, will you ride with us?"

"No, I must go to — to-day with Arthur. I have engaged the post-horses at two o'clock; but I shall be with you to-morrow or the day after. You see his tutor expects him; and as he is backward in his mathematics, he has no time to lose."

"Well, then, good-bye, nephew!" and Beaufort slipped a pocket-book into the boy's hand. "Tush! whenever you want money, don't trouble your father—write to me—we shall be always glad to see you; and you must teach Philip to like his book a little better—eh, Phil?"

"No, father; I shall be rich enough to do without books," said Philip, rather coarsely; but then observing the heightened colour of his cousin, he went up to him, and with a generous impulse said, "Arthur, you admired this gun; pray accept it. Nay, don't be shy—I can have as many as I like for the asking: you're not so well off, you know."

The intention was kind, but the manner was so patronising that Arthur felt offended. He put back the gun, and said, drily, "I shall have no occasion for the gun, thank you."

If Arthur was offended by the offer, Philip was much more offended by the refusal. "As you like; I hate pride," said he; and he gave the gun to the groom as he vaulted into his saddle with the lightness of a young Mercury. "Come, father!"

Mr. Beaufort had now mounted his favourite hunter—a large, powerful horse well known for its prowess in the field. The rider trotted him once or twice through the spacious yard.

"Nonsense, Tom: no more hurt in the loins than I am. Open that gate; we will go across the paddock, and take the gate yonder—the old six-bar—eh, Phil?"

"Capital!—to be sure!—"

The gate was opened—the grooms stood watchful to see the leap, and a kindred curiosity arrested Robert Beaufort and his son.

How well they looked! those two horsemen; the ease, lightness, spirit of the one, with the fine-limbed and fiery steed that literally "bounded beneath him as a barb"—seemingly as gay, as ardent, and as haughty as the boyrider. And the manly, and almost herculean form of the elder Beaufort, which, from the buoyancy of its movements, and the supple grace that belongs to the perfect mastership of any athletic art, possessed an elegance and dignity, especially on horseback, which rarely accompanies proportions equally sturdy and robust. There was indeed something knightly and chivalrous in the bearing of the elder Beaufort—in his handsome aquiline features, the erectness of his mien, the very wave of his hand, as he spurred from the yard.

"What a fine-looking fellow my uncle is!" said Arthur, with involuntary admiration.

"Ay, an excellent life—amazingly strong!" returned the pale father, with a slight sigh.

"Philip," said Mr. Beaufort, as they cantered across the paddock, "I think the gate is too much for you. I will just take Puppet over, and then we will open it for you."

"Pooh, my dear father! you don't know how I'm improved!" And slackening the rein, and touching the side of his horse, the young rider darted forward and cleared the gate, which was of no common height, with an ease that extorted a loud "bravo" from the proud father.

"Now, Puppet," said Mr. Beaufort, spurring his own horse. The animal cantered towards the gate, and then suddenly turned round with an impatient and angry snort. "For shame, Puppet!—for shame, old boy!" said the sportsman, wheeling him again to the barrier. The horse shook his head, as if in remonstrance; but the spur vigorously applied showed him that his master would not listen to his mute reasonings. He bounded forward—made at the gate—struck his hoofs against the top bar—fell forward, and threw his rider head foremost on the road beyond. The horse rose instantly—not so the master. The son dismounted, alarmed and terrified. His father was speechless! and blood gushed from the mouth and nostrils, as the head drooped heavily on the boy's breast. The bystanders had witnessed the fall—they crowded to the spot—they took the fallen man from the weak arms of the son—the head groom examined him with the eye of one who had picked up science from his experience in such casualties.

"Speak, brother!—where are you hurt?" exclaimed Robert Beaufort.

"He will never speak more!" said the groom, bursting into tears. "His neck is broken!"

"Send for the nearest surgeon," cried Mr. Robert. "Good God! boy! don't mount that devilish horse!"

But Arthur had already leaped on the unhappy steed, which had been the cause of this appalling affliction. "Which way?"

"Straight on to —, only two miles—every one knows Mr. Powis's house. God bless you!" said the groom. Arthur vanished.

"Lift him carefully, and take him to the house," said Mr. Robert. "My poor brother! my dear brother!"

He was interrupted by a cry, a single shrill, heartbreaking cry; and Philip fell senseless to the ground.

No one heeded him at that hour—no one heeded the fatherless BASTARD. "Gently, gently," said Mr. Robert, as he followed the servants and their load. And he then muttered to himself, and his sallow cheek grew bright, and his breath came short: "He has made no will—he never made a will."

CHAPTER V

"Constance. O boy, then where art thou?
What becomes of me"—King John.

It was three days after the death of Philip Beaufort—for the surgeon arrived only to confirm the judgment of the groom: in the drawing-room of the cottage, the windows closed, lay the body, in its coffin, the lid not yet nailed down. There, prostrate on the floor, tearless, speechless, was the miserable Catherine; poor Sidney, too young to comprehend all his loss, sobbing at her side; while Philip apart, seated beside the coffin, gazed abstractedly on that cold rigid face which had never known one frown for his boyish follies.

In another room, that had been appropriated to the late owner, called his study, sat Robert Beaufort. Everything in this room spoke of the deceased. Partially separated from the rest of the house, it communicated by a winding staircase with a chamber above, to which Philip had been wont to betake himself whenever he returned late, and over-exhilarated, from some rural feast crowning a hard day's hunt. Above a quaint, old-fashioned bureau of Dutch workmanship (which Philip had picked up at a sale in the earlier years of his marriage) was a portrait of Catherine taken in the bloom of her youth. On a peg on the door that led to the staircase, still hung his rough driving coat. The window commanded the view of the paddock in which the worn-out hunter or the unbroken colt grazed at will. Around the walls of the "study"—(a strange misnomer!)—hung prints of celebrated fox-hunts and renowned steeple-chases: guns, fishing-rods, and foxes' brushes, ranged with a sportsman's neatness, supplied the place of books. On the mantelpiece lay a cigar-case, a well-worn volume on the Veterinary Art, and the last number of the Sporting Magazine. And in the room—thus witnessing of the hardy, masculine, rural life, that had passed away—sallow, stooping, town-worn, sat, I say, Robert Beaufort, the heir-at-law,—alone: for the very day of the death he had remanded his son home with the letter that announced to his wife the change in their fortunes, and directed her to send his lawyer post-haste to the house of death. The bureau, and the drawers, and the boxes which contained the papers of the deceased were open; their contents had been ransacked; no certificate of the private marriage, no hint of such an event; not a paper found to signify the last wishes of the rich dead man.

He had died, and made no sign. Mr. Robert Beaufort's countenance was still and composed.

A knock at the door was heard; the lawyer entered.

"Sir, the undertakers are here, and Mr. Greaves has ordered the bells to be rung: at three o'clock he will read the service."

"I am obliged to you., Blackwell, for taking these melancholy offices on yourself. My poor brother!—it is so sudden! But the funeral, you say, ought to take place to-day?"

"The weather is so warm," said the lawyer, wiping his forehead. As he spoke, the death-bell was heard.

There was a pause.

"It would have been a terrible shock to Mrs. Morton if she had been his wife," observed Mr. Blackwell. "But I suppose persons of that kind have very little feeling. I must say that it was fortunate for the family that the event happened before Mr. Beaufort was wheedled into so improper a marriage."

"It was fortunate, Blackwell. Have you ordered the post-horses? I shall start immediately after the funeral."

"What is to be done with the cottage, sir?"

"You may advertise it for sale."

"And Mrs. Morton and the boys?" "Hum! we will consider. She was a tradesman's daughter. I think I ought to provide for her suitably, eh?"

"It is more than the world could expect from you, sir; it is very different from a wife."

"Oh, very!—very much so, indeed! Just ring for a lighted candle, we will seal up these boxes. And—I think I could take a sandwich. Poor Philip!"

The funeral was over; the dead shovelled away. What a strange thing it does seem, that that very form which we prized so charily, for which we prayed the winds to be gentle, which we lapped from the cold in our arms, from whose footstep we would have removed a stone, should be suddenly thrust out of sight—an abomination that the earth must not look upon—a despicable loathsomeness, to be concealed and to be forgotten! And this same composition of bone and muscle that was yesterday so strong—which men respected, and women loved, and children clung to—to-day so lamentably powerless, unable to defend or protect those who lay nearest to its heart; its riches wrested from it, its wishes spat upon, its influence expiring with its last sigh! A breath from its lips making all that mighty difference between what it was and what it is!

The post-horses were at the door as the funeral procession returned to the house.

Mr. Robert Beaufort bowed slightly to Mrs. Morton, and said, with his pocket-handkerchief still before his eyes:

"I will write to you in a few days, ma'am; you will find that I shall not forget you. The cottage will be sold; but we sha'n't hurry you. Good-bye, ma'am; good-bye, my boys;" and he patted his nephews on the head.

Philip winced aside, and scowled haughtily at his uncle, who muttered to himself, "That boy will come to no good!" Little Sidney put his hand into the rich man's, and looked up, pleadingly, into his face. "Can't you say something pleasant to poor mamma, Uncle Robert?"

Mr. Beaufort hemmed huskily, and entered the britska—it had been his brother's: the lawyer followed, and they drove away.

A week after the funeral, Philip stole from the house into the conservatory, to gather some fruit for his mother; she had scarcely touched food since Beaufort's death. She was worn to a shadow; her hair had turned grey. Now she had at last found tears, and she wept noiselessly but unceasingly.

The boy had plucked some grapes, and placed them carefully in his basket: he was about to select a nectarine that seemed riper than the rest, when his hand was roughly seized; and the gruff voice of John Green, the gardener, exclaimed:

"What are you about, Master Philip? you must not touch them 'ere fruit!"

"How dare you, fellow!" cried the young gentleman, in a tone of equal astonishment and, wrath.

"None of your airs, Master Philip! What I means is, that some great folks are coming too look at the place tomorrow; and I won't have my show of fruit spoiled by being pawed about by the like of you; so, that's plain, Master Philip!"

The boy grew very pale, but remained silent. The gardener, delighted to retaliate the insolence he had received, continued:

"You need not go for to look so spiteful, master; you are not the great man you thought you were; you are nobody now, and so you will find ere long. So, march out, if you please: I wants to lock up the glass."

As he spoke, he took the lad roughly by the arm; but Philip, the most irascible of mortals, was strong for his years, and fearless as a young lion. He caught up a watering-pot, which the gardener had deposited while he expostulated with his late tyrant and struck the man across the face with it so violently and so suddenly, that he fell back over the beds, and the glass crackled and shivered under him. Philip did not wait for the foe to recover his equilibrium; but, taking up his grapes, and possessing himself quietly of the disputed nectarine, quitted the spot; and the gardener did not think it prudent to pursue him. To boys, under ordinary circumstances—boys who have buffeted their way through a scolding nursery, a wrangling family, or a public school—there would have been nothing in this squabble to dwell on the memory or vibrate on the nerves, after the first burst of passion: but to Philip Beaufort it was an era in life; it was the first insult he had ever received; it was his initiation into that changed, rough, and terrible career, to which the spoiled darling of vanity and love was henceforth condemned. His pride and his self-esteem had incurred a fearful shock. He entered the house, and a sickness came over him; his limbs trembled; he sat down in the hall, and, placing the fruit beside him, covered his face with his hands and wept. Those were not the tears of a boy, drawn from a shallow source; they were the burning, agonising, reluctant tears, that men shed, wrung from the heart as if it were its blood. He had never been sent to school, lest he should meet with mortification. He had had various tutors, trained to show, rather than to exact, respect; one succeeding another, at his own whim and caprice. His natural quickness, and a very strong, hard, inquisitive turn of mind, had enabled him, however, to pick up more knowledge, though of a desultory and miscellaneous nature, than boys of his age generally possess; and his roving, independent, out-of-door existence had served to ripen his understanding. He had certainly, in spite of every precaution, arrived at some, though not very distinct, notion of his peculiar position; but none of its inconveniences had visited him till that day. He began now to turn his eyes to the future; and vague and dark forebodings—a consciousness of the shelter, the protector, the station, he had lost in his father's death—crept coldly, over him. While thus musing, a ring was heard at the bell; he lifted his head; it was the postman with a letter. Philip hastily rose, and, averting his face, on which the tears were not dried, took the letter; and then, snatching up his little basket of fruit, repaired to his mother's room.

The shutters were half closed on the bright day—oh, what a mockery is there in the smile of the happy sun when it shines on the wretched! Mrs. Morton sat, or rather crouched, in a distant corner; her streaming eyes fixed on vacancy; listless, drooping; a very image of desolate woe; and Sidney was weaving flower-chains at her feet.

"Mamma!—mother!" whispered Philip, as he threw his arms round her neck; "look up! look up!—my heart breaks to see you. Do taste this fruit: you will die too, if you go on thus; and what will become of us—of Sidney?"

Mrs. Morton did look up vaguely into his face, and strove to smile.

"See, too, I have brought you a letter; perhaps good news; shall I break the seal?"

Mrs. Morton shook her head gently, and took the letter—alas! how different from that one which Sidney had placed in her hands not two short weeks since—it was Mr. Robert Beaufort's handwriting. She shuddered, and laid it down. And then there suddenly, and for the first time, flashed across her the sense of her strange position—the dread of the future. What were her sons to be henceforth?

What herself? Whatever the sanctity of her marriage, the law might fail her. At the disposition of Mr. Robert Beaufort the fate of three lives might depend. She gasped for breath; again took up the letter; and hurried over the contents: they ran thus:

"DEAR MADAM,—Knowing that you must naturally be anxious as to the future prospects of your children and yourself, left by my poor brother destitute of all provision, I take the earliest opportunity which it seems to me that propriety and decorum allow, to apprise you of my intentions. I need not say that, properly speaking, you can have no kind of claim upon the relations of my late brother; nor will I hurt your feelings by those moral reflections which at this season of sorrow cannot, I hope, fail involuntarily to force themselves upon you. Without more than this mere allusion to your peculiar connection with my brother, I may, however, be permitted to add that that connection tended very materially to separate him from the legitimate branches of his family; and in consulting with them as to a provision for you and your children, I find that, besides scruples that are to be respected, some natural degree of soreness exists upon their minds. Out of regard, however, to my poor brother (though I saw very little of him of late years), I am willing to waive those feelings which, as a father and a husband, you may conceive that I share with the rest of my family. You will probably now decide on living with some of your own relations; and that you may not be entirely a burden to them, I beg to say that I shall allow you a hundred a year; paid, if you prefer it, quarterly. You may also select such articles of linen and plate as you require for your own use. With regard to your sons, I have no objection to place them at a grammar-school, and, at a proper age, to apprentice them to any trade suitable to their future station, in the choice of which your own family can give you the best advice. If they conduct themselves properly, they may always depend on my protection. I do not wish to hurry your movements; but it will probably be painful to you to remain longer than you can help in a place crowded with unpleasant recollections; and as the cottage is to be sold—indeed, my brother-in-law, Lord Lilburne, thinks it would suit him—you will be liable to the interruption of strangers to see it; and your prolonged residence at Fernside, you must be sensible, is rather an obstacle to the sale. I beg to inclose you a draft for £100. to pay any present expenses; and to request, when you are settled, to know where the first quarter shall be paid.

"I shall write to Mr. Jackson (who, I think, is the bailiff) to detail my instructions as to selling the crops, &c., and discharging the servants; so that you may have no further trouble.

"I am, Madam,
"Your obedient Servant,
"ROBERT BEAUFORT.
"Berkeley Square, September 12th, 18—."

The letter fell from Catherine's hands. Her grief was changed to indignation and scorn.

"The insolent!" she exclaimed, with flashing eyes. "This to me!—to me—the wife, the lawful wife of his brother! the wedded mother of his brother's children!"

"Say that again, mother! again—again!" cried Philip, in a loud voice. "His wife—wedded!"

"I swear it," said Catherine, solemnly. "I kept the secret for your father's sake. Now for yours, the truth must be proclaimed."

"Thank God! thank God!" murmured Philip, in a quivering voice, throwing his arms round his brother, "We have no brand on our names, Sidney."

At those accents, so full of suppressed joy and pride, the mother felt at once all that her son had suspected and concealed. She felt that beneath his haughty and wayward character there had lurked delicate and generous forbearance for her; that from his equivocal position his very faults might have arisen; and a pang of remorse for her long sacrifice of the children to the father shot through her heart. It was followed by a fear, an appalling fear, more painful than the remorse. The proofs that were to clear herself and them! The words of her husband, that last awful morning, rang in her ear. The minister dead; the witness absent; the register lost! But the copy of that register!—the copy! might not that suffice? She groaned, and closed her eyes as if to shut out the future: then starting up, she hurried from the room, and went straight to Beaufort's study. As she laid her hand on the latch of the door, she trembled and drew back. But care for the living was stronger at that moment than even anguish for the dead: she entered the apartment; she passed with a firm step to the bureau. It was locked; Robert Beaufort's seal upon the lock:—on every cupboard, every box, every drawer, the same seal that spoke of rights more valued than her own. But Catherine was not daunted: she turned and saw Philip by her side; she pointed to the bureau in silence; the boy understood the appeal. He left the room, and returned in a few moments with a chisel. The lock was broken: tremblingly and eagerly Catherine ransacked the contents; opened paper after paper, letter after letter, in vain: no certificate, no will, no memorial. Could the brother have abstracted the fatal proof? A word sufficed to explain to Philip what she sought for; and his search was more minute than hers. Every possible receptacle for papers in that room, in the whole house, was explored, and still the search was fruitless.

Three hours afterwards they were in the same room in which Philip had brought Robert Beaufort's letter to his mother. Catherine was seated, tearless, but deadly pale with heart-sickness and dismay.

"Mother," said Philip, "may I now read the letter?" Yes, boy; and decide for us all. She paused, and examined his face as he read. He felt her eye was upon him, and restrained his emotions as he proceeded. When he had done, he lifted his dark gaze upon Catherine's watchful countenance.

"Mother, whether or not we obtain our rights, you will still refuse this man's charity? I am young—a boy; but I am strong and active. I will work for you day and night. I have it in me—I feel it; anything rather than eating his bread."

"Philip! Philip! you are indeed my son; your father's son! And have you no reproach for your mother, who so weakly, so criminally, concealed your birthright, till, alas! discovery may be too late? Oh! reproach me, reproach me! it will be kindness. No! do not kiss me! I cannot bear it. Boy! boy! if as my heart tells me, we fail in proof, do you understand what, in the world's eye, I am; what you are?"

"I do!" said Philip, firmly; and he fell on his knees at her feet. " Whatever others call you, you are a mother, and I your son. You are, in the judgment of Heaven, my father's Wife, and I his Heir."

Catherine bowed her head, and with a gush of tears fell into his arms. Sidney crept up to her, and forced his lips to her cold cheek. "Mamma! what vexes you? Mamma, mamma!"

"Oh, Sidney! Sidney! How like his father! Look at him, Philip! Shall we do right to refuse him even this pittance? Must he be a beggar too?"

"Never beggar," said Philip, with a pride that showed what hard lessons he had yet to learn. "The lawful sons of a Beaufort were not born to beg their bread!"

CHAPTER VI

"The storm above, and frozen world below.
The olive bough
Faded and cast upon the common wind,
And earth a doveless ark."—LAMAN BLANCHARD.

Mr. Robert Beaufort was generally considered by the world a very worthy man. He had never committed any excess—never gambled nor incurred debt—nor fallen into the warm errors most common with his sex. He was a good husband—a careful father—an agreeable neighbour—rather charitable than otherwise, to the poor. He was honest and methodical in his dealings, and had been known to behave handsomely in different relations of life. Mr. Robert Beaufort, indeed, always meant to do what was right—in the eyes of the world! He had no other rule of action but that which the world supplied; his religion was decorum—his sense of honour was regard to opinion. His heart was a dial to which the world was the sun: when the great eye of the public fell on it, it answered every purpose that a heart could answer; but when that eye was invisible, the dial was mute—a piece of brass and nothing more.

It is just to Robert Beaufort to assure the reader that he wholly disbelieved his brother's story of a private marriage. He considered that tale, when heard for the first time, as the mere invention (and a shallow one) of a man wishing to make the imprudent step he was about to take as respectable as he could. The careless tone of his brother when speaking upon the subject—his confession that of such a marriage there were no distinct proofs, except a copy of a register (which copy Robert had not found)—made his incredulity natural. He therefore deemed himself under no obligation of delicacy or respect, to a woman through whose means he had very nearly lost a noble succession—a woman who had not even borne his brother's name—a woman whom nobody knew. Had Mrs. Morton been Mrs. Beaufort, and the natural sons legitimate children, Robert Beaufort, supposing their situation of relative power and dependence to have been the same, would have behaved with careful and scrupulous generosity. The world would have said, "Nothing can be handsomer than Mr. Robert Beaufort's conduct!" Nay, if Mrs. Morton had been some divorced wife of birth and connections, he would have made very different dispositions in her favour: he would not have allowed the connections to call him shabby. But here he felt that, all circumstances considered, the world, if it spoke at all (which it would scarce think it worth while to do), would be on his side. An artful woman—low-born, and, of course, low-bred—who wanted to inveigle her rich and careless paramour into marriage; what could be expected from the man she had sought to injure—the rightful heir? Was it not very good in him to do anything for her, and, if he provided for the children suitably to the original station of the mother, did he not go to the very utmost of reasonable expectation? He certainly thought in his conscience, such as it was, that he had acted well—not extravagantly, not foolishly; but well. He was sure the world would say so if it knew all: he was not bound to do anything. He was not, therefore, prepared for Catherine's short, haughty, but temperate reply to his letter: a reply which conveyed a decided refusal of his offers—asserted positively her own marriage, and the claims of her children—intimated legal proceedings—and was signed in the name of Catherine Beaufort. Mr. Beaufort put the letter in his bureau, labelled, "Impertinent answer from Mrs. Morton, Sept. 14," and was quite contented to forget the existence of the writer, until his lawyer, Mr. Blackwell, informed him that a suit had been instituted by Catherine.

Mr. Robert turned pale, but Blackwell composed him.

"Pooh, sir! you have nothing to fear. It is but an attempt to extort money: the attorney is a low practitioner, accustomed to get up bad cases: they can make nothing of it."

This was true: whatever the rights of the case, poor Catherine had no proofs—no evidence—which could justify a respectable lawyer to advise her proceeding to a suit. She named two witnesses of her marriage—one dead, the other could not be heard of. She selected for the alleged place in which the ceremony was performed a very remote village, in which it appeared that the register had been destroyed. No attested copy thereof was to be found, and Catherine was stunned on hearing that, even if found, it was doubtful whether it could be received as evidence, unless to corroborate actual personal testimony. It so happened that when Philip, many years ago, had received a copy, he had not shown it to Catherine, nor mentioned Mr. Jones's name as the copyist. In fact, then only three years married to Catherine, his worldly caution had not yet been conquered by confident experience of her generosity. As for the mere moral evidence dependent on the publication of her bans in London, that amounted to no proof whatever; nor, on inquiry at A—, did the Welsh villagers remember anything further than that, some fifteen years ago, a handsome gentleman had visited Mr. Price, and one or two rather thought that Mr. Price had married him to a lady from London; evidence quite inadmissible against the deadly, damning fact, that, for fifteen years, Catherine had openly borne another name, and lived with Mr. Beaufort ostensibly as his mistress. Her generosity in this destroyed her case. Nevertheless, she found a low practitioner, who took her money and neglected her cause; so her suit was heard and dismissed with contempt. Henceforth, then, indeed, in the eyes of the law and the public, Catherine was an impudent adventurer, and her sons were nameless outcasts.

And now relieved from all fear, Mr. Robert Beaufort entered upon the full enjoyment of his splendid fortune.

The house in Berkeley Square was furnished anew. Great dinners and gay routs were given in the ensuing spring. Mr. and Mrs. Beaufort became persons of considerable importance. The rich man had, even when poor, been ambitious; his ambition now centred in his only son. Arthur had always been considered a boy of talents and promise; to what might he not now aspire? The term of his probation with the tutor was abridged, and Arthur Beaufort was sent at once to Oxford.

Before he went to the university, during a short preparatory visit to his father, Arthur spoke to him of the Mortons. "What has become of them, sir? and what have you done for them?"

"Done for them!" said Mr. Beaufort, opening his eyes. "What should I do for persons who have just been harassing me with the most unprincipled litigation? My conduct to them has been too generous: that is, all things considered. But when you are my age you will find there is very little gratitude in the world, Arthur."

"Still, sir," said Arthur, with the good nature that belonged to him: "still, my uncle was greatly attached to them; and the boys, at least, are guiltless."

"Well, well!" replied Mr. Beaufort, a little impatiently; "I believe they want for nothing: I fancy they are with the mother's relations. Whenever they address me in a proper manner they shall not find me revengeful or hardhearted; but, since we are on this topic," continued the father smoothing his shirt-frill with a care that showed his decorum even in trifles, "I hope you see the results of that kind of connection, and that you will take warning by your poor uncle's example. And now let us change the subject; it is not a very pleasant one, and, at your age, the less your thoughts turn on such matters the better."

Arthur Beaufort, with the careless generosity of youth, that gauges other men's conduct by its own sentiments, believed that his father, who had never been niggardly to himself, had really acted as his words implied; and, engrossed by the pursuits of the new and brilliant career opened, whether to his pleasures or his studies, suffered the objects of his inquiries to pass from his thoughts.

Meanwhile, Mrs. Morton, for by that name we must still call her, and her children, were settled in a small lodging in a humble suburb; situated on the high road between Fernside and the metropolis. She saved from her hopeless law-suit, after the sale of her jewels and ornaments, a sufficient sum to enable her, with economy, to live respectably for a year or two at least, during which time she might arrange her plans for the future. She reckoned, as a sure resource, upon the assistance of her relations; but it was one to which she applied with natural shame and reluctance. She had kept up a correspondence with her father during his life. To him, she never revealed the secret of her marriage, though she did not write like a person conscious of error. Perhaps, as she always said to her son, she had made to her husband a solemn promise never to divulge or even hint that secret until he himself should authorise its disclosure. For neither he nor Catherine ever contemplated separation or death. Alas! how all of us, when happy, sleep secure in the dark shadows, which ought to warn us of the sorrows that are to come! Still Catherine's father, a man of coarse mind and not rigid principles, did not take much to heart that connection which he assumed to be illicit. She was provided for, that was some comfort: doubtless Mr. Beaufort would act like a gentleman, perhaps at last make her an honest woman and a lady. Meanwhile, she had a fine house, and a fine carriage, and fine servants; and so far from applying to him for money, was constantly sending him little presents. But Catherine only saw, in his permission of her correspondence, kind, forgiving, and trustful affection, and she loved him tenderly: when he died, the link that bound her to her family was broken. Her brother succeeded to the trade; a man of probity and honour, but somewhat hard and unamiable. In the only letter she had received from him—the one announcing her father's death—he told her plainly, and very properly, that he could not countenance the life she led; that he had children growing up—that all intercourse between them was at an end, unless she left Mr. Beaufort; when, if she sincerely repented, he would still prove her affectionate brother.

Though Catherine had at the time resented this letter as unfeeling—now, humbled and sorrow-stricken, she recognised the propriety of principle from which it emanated. Her brother was well off for his station—she would explain to him her real situation—he would believe her story. She would write to him, and beg him at least to give aid to her poor children.

But this step she did not take till a considerable portion of her pittance was consumed—till nearly three parts of a year since Beaufort's death had expired—and till sundry warnings, not to be lightly heeded, had made her forebode the probability of an early death for herself. From the age of sixteen, when she had been placed by Mr. Beaufort at the head of his household, she had been cradled, not in extravagance, but in an easy luxury, which had not brought with it habits of economy and thrift. She could grudge anything to herself, but to her children—his children, whose every whim had been anticipated, she had not the heart to be saving. She could have starved in a garret had she been alone; but she could not see them wanting a comfort while she possessed a guinea. Philip, to do him justice, evinced a consideration not to have been expected from his early and arrogant recklessness. But Sidney, who could expect consideration from such a child? What could he know of the change of circumstances—of the value of money? Did he seem dejected, Catherine would steal out and spend a week's income on the lapful of toys which she brought home. Did he seem a shade more pale—did he complain of the slightest ailment, a doctor must be sent for. Alas! her own ailments, neglected and unheeded, were growing beyond the reach of medicine. Anxious— fearful—gnawed by regret for the past—the thought of famine in the future—she daily fretted and wore herself away. She had cultivated her mind during her secluded residence with Mr. Beaufort, but she had learned none of the arts by which decayed gentlewomen keep the wolf from the door; no little holiday accomplishments, which, in the day of need turn to useful trade; no water-colour drawings, no paintings on velvet, no fabrications of pretty gewgaws, no embroidery and fine needlework. She was helpless—utterly helpless; if she had resigned herself to the thought of service, she would not have had the physical strength for a place of drudgery, and where could she have found the testimonials necessary for a place of trust? A great change, at this time, was apparent in Philip. Had he fallen, then, into kind hands, and under guiding eyes, his passions and energies might have ripened into rare qualities and great virtues. But perhaps as Goethe has somewhere said, "Experience, after all, is the best teacher." He kept a constant guard on his vehement temper—his wayward will; he would not have vexed his mother for the world. But, strange to say (it was a great mystery in the woman's heart), in proportion as he became more amiable, it seemed that his mother loved him less. Perhaps she did not, in that change, recognise so closely the darling of the old time; perhaps the very weaknesses and importunities of Sidney, the hourly sacrifices the child entailed upon her, endeared the younger son more to her from that natural sense of dependence and protection which forms the great bond between mother and child; perhaps too, as Philip had been one to inspire as much pride as affection, so the pride faded away with the expectations that had fed it, and carried off in its decay some of the affection that was intertwined with it. However this be, Philip had formerly appeared the more spoiled and favoured of the two: and now Sidney seemed all in all. Thus, beneath the younger son's caressing gentleness, there grew up a certain regard for self; it was latent, it took amiable colours; it had even a certain charm and grace in so sweet a child, but selfishness it was not the less. In this he differed from his brother. Philip was self-willed: Sidney self-loving. A certain timidity of character, endearing perhaps to the anxious heart of a mother, made this fault in the younger boy more likely to take root. For, in bold natures, there is a lavish and uncalculating recklessness which scorns self unconsciously and though there is a fear which arises from a loving heart, and is but sympathy for others—the fear which belongs to a timid character is but egotism—but, when physical, the regard for one's own person: when moral, the anxiety for one's own interests.

It was in a small room in a lodging-house in the suburb of H— that Mrs. Morton was seated by the window, nervously awaiting the knock of the postman, who was expected to bring her brother's reply to her letter. It was therefore between ten and eleven o'clock—a morning in the merry month of June. It was hot and sultry, which is rare in an English June. A flytrap, red, white, and yellow, suspended from the ceiling, swarmed with flies; flies were on the ceiling, flies buzzed at the windows; the sofa and chairs of horsehair seemed stuffed with flies. There was an air of heated discomfort in the thick, solid moreen curtains, in the gaudy paper, in the bright-staring carpet, in the very looking-glass over the chimney-piece, where a strip of mirror lay imprisoned in an embrace of frame covered with yellow muslin. We may talk of the dreariness of winter; and winter, no doubt, is desolate: but what in the world is more dreary to eyes inured to the verdure and bloom of Nature—,

"The pomp of groves and garniture of fields," —than a close room in a suburban lodging-house; the sun piercing every corner; nothing fresh, nothing cool, nothing fragrant to be seen, felt, or inhaled; all dust, glare, noise, with a chandler's shop, perhaps, next door? Sidney armed with a pair of scissors, was cutting the pictures out of a story-book, which his mother had bought him the day before. Philip, who, of late, had taken much to rambling about the streets—it may be, in hopes of meeting one of those benevolent, eccentric, elderly gentlemen, he had read of in old novels, who suddenly come to the relief of distressed virtue; or, more probably, from the restlessness that belonged to his adventurous temperament;—Philip had left the house since breakfast.

"Oh! how hot this nasty room is!" exclaimed Sidney, abruptly, looking up from his employment. "Sha'n't we ever go into the country, again, mamma?"

"Not at present, my love."

"I wish I could have my pony; why can't I have my pony, mamma?"

"Because,—because—the pony is sold, Sidney."

"Who sold it?"

"Your uncle."

"He is a very naughty man, my uncle: is he not? But can't I have another pony? It would be so nice, this fine weather!"

"Ah! my dear, I wish I could afford it: but you shall have a ride this week! Yes," continued the mother, as if reasoning with herself, in excuse of the extravagance, "he does not look well: poor child! he must have exercise."

"A ride!—oh! that is my own kind mamma!" exclaimed Sidney, clapping his hands. "Not on a donkey, you know!—a pony. The man down the street, there, lets ponies. I must have the white pony with the long tail. But, I say, mamma, don't tell Philip, pray don't; he would be jealous."

"No, not jealous, my dear; why do you think so?"

"Because he is always angry when I ask you for anything. It is very unkind in him, for I don't care if he has a pony, too,—only not the white one."

Here the postman's knock, loud and sudden, started Mrs. Morton from her seat.

She pressed her hands tightly to her heart, as if to still its beating, and went tremulously to the door; thence to the stairs, to anticipate the lumbering step of the slipshod maidservent.

"Give it me, Jane; give it me!"

"One shilling and eightpence—double charged—if you please, ma'am! Thank you."

"Mamma, may I tell Jane to engage the pony?"

"Not now, my love; sit down; be quiet: I—I am not well."

Sidney, who was affectionate and obedient, crept back peaceably to the window, and, after a short, impatient sigh, resumed the scissors and the story-book. I do not apologise to the reader for the various letters I am obliged to lay before him; for character often betrays itself more in letters than in speech. Mr. Roger Morton's reply was couched in these terms,—

"DEAR CATHERINE, I have received your letter of the 14th inst., and write per return. I am very much grieved to hear of your afflictions; but, whatever you say, I cannot think the late Mr. Beaufort acted like a conscientious man, in forgetting to make his will, and leaving his little ones destitute. It is all very well to talk of his intentions; but the proof of the pudding is in the eating. And it is hard upon me, who have a large family of my own, and get my livelihood by honest industry, to have a rich gentleman's children to maintain. As for your story about the private marriage, it may or not be. Perhaps you were taken in by that worthless man, for a real marriage it could not be. And, as you say, the law has decided that point; therefore, the less you say on the matter the better. It all comes to the same thing. People are not bound to believe what can't be proved. And even if what you say is true, you are more to be blamed than pitied for holding your tongue so many years, and discrediting an honest family, as ours has always been considered. I am sure my wife would not have thought of such a thing for the finest gentleman that ever wore shoe-leather. However, I don't want to hurt your feelings; and I am sure I am ready to do whatever is right and proper. You cannot expect that I should ask you to my house. My wife, you know, is a very religious woman—what is called evangelical; but that's neither here nor there: I deal with all people, churchmen and dissenters—even Jews,—and don't trouble my head much about differences in opinion. I dare say there are many ways to heaven; as I said, the other day, to Mr. Thwaites, our member. But it is right to say my wife will not hear of your coming here; and, indeed, it might do harm to my business, for there are several elderly single gentlewomen, who buy flannel for the poor at my shop, and they are very particular; as they ought to be, indeed: for morals are very strict in this county, and particularly in this town, where we certainly do pay very high church-rates. Not that I grumble; for, though I am as liberal as any man, I am for an established church; as I ought to be, since the dean is my best customer. With regard to yourself I inclose you £10., and you will let me know when it is gone, and I will see what more I can do. You say you are very poorly, which I am sorry to hear; but you must pluck up your spirits, and take in plain work; and I really think you ought to apply to Mr. Robert Beaufort. He bears a high character; and notwithstanding your lawsuit, which I cannot approve of, I dare say he might allow you £40. or £50. a-year, if you apply properly, which would be the right thing in him. So much for you. As for the boys—poor, fatherless creatures!—it is very hard that they should be so punished for no fault of their own; and my wife, who, though strict, is a good-hearted woman, is ready and willing to do what I wish about them. You say the eldest is near sixteen and well come on in his studies. I can get him a very good thing in a light genteel way. My wife's brother, Mr. Christopher Plaskwith, is a bookseller and stationer with pretty practice, in R—. He is a clever man, and has a newspaper, which he kindly sends me every week; and, though it is not my county, it has some very sensible views and is often noticed in the London papers, as 'our provincial contemporary.'—Mr. Plaskwith owes me some money, which I advanced him when he set up the paper; and he has several times most honestly offered to pay me, in shares in the said paper. But, as the thing might break, and I don't like concerns I don't understand, I have not taken advantage of his very handsome proposals. Now, Plaskwith wrote me word, two days ago, that he wanted a genteel, smart lad, as assistant and 'prentice, and offered to take my eldest boy; but we can't spare him. I write to Christopher by this post; and if your youth will run down on the top of the coach, and inquire for Mr. Plaskwith—the fare is trifling—I have no doubt he will be engaged at once. But you will say, 'There's the premium to consider!' No such thing; Kit will set off the premium against his debt to me; so you will have nothing to pay. 'Tis a very pretty business; and the lad's education will get him on; so that's off your mind. As to the little chap, I'll take him at once. You say he is a pretty boy; and a pretty boy is always a help in a linendraper's shop. He shall share and share with my own young folks; and Mrs. Morton will take care of his washing and morals. I conclude—(this is Mrs. M's. suggestion)—that he has had the measles, cowpock, and whooping-cough, which please let me know. If he behave well, which, at his age, we can easily break him into, he is settled for life. So now you have got rid of two mouths to feed, and have nobody to think of but yourself, which must be a great comfort. Don't forget to write to Mr. Beaufort; and if he don't do something for you he's not the gentleman I take him for; but you are my own flesh and blood, and sha'n't starve; for, though I don't think it right in a man in business to encourage what's wrong, yet, when a person's down in the world, I think an ounce of help is better than a pound of preaching. My wife thinks otherwise, and wants to send you some tracts; but every body can't be as correct as some folks. However, as I said before, that's neither here nor there. Let me know when your boy comes down, and also about the measles, cowpock, and whooping-cough; also if all's right with Mr. Plaskwith. So now I hope you will feel more comfortable; and remain,

"Dear Catherine,
"Your forgiving and affectionate brother,
"ROGER MORTON.
"High Street, N—, June 13."

"P.S.—Mrs. M. says that she will be a mother to your little boy, and that you had better mend up all his linen before you send him."

As Catherine finished this epistle, she lifted her eyes and beheld Philip. He had entered noiselessly, and he remained silent, leaning against the wall, and watching the face of his mother, which crimsoned with painful humiliation while she read. Philip was not now the trim and dainty stripling first introduced to the reader. He had outgrown his faded suit of funereal mourning; his long-neglected hair hung elf-like and matted down his cheeks; there was a gloomy look in his bright dark eyes. Poverty never betrays itself more than in the features and form of Pride. It was evident that his spirit endured, rather than accommodated itself to, his fallen state; and, notwithstanding his soiled and threadbare garments, and a haggardness that ill becomes the years of palmy youth, there was about his whole mien and person a wild and savage grandeur more impressive than his former ruffling arrogance of manner.

"Well, mother," said he, with a strange mixture of sternness in his countenance and pity in his voice; "well, mother, and what says your brother?"

"You decided for us once before, decide again. But I need not ask you; you would never—"

"I don't know," interrupted Philip, vaguely; "let me see what we are to decide on."

Mrs. Morton was naturally a woman of high courage and spirit, but sickness and grief had worn down both; and though Philip was but sixteen, there is something in the very nature of woman—especially in trouble—which makes her seek to lean on some other will than her own. She gave Philip the letter, and went quietly to sit down by Sidney.

"Your brother means well," said Philip, when he had concluded the epistle.

"Yes, but nothing is to be done; I cannot, cannot send poor Sidney to—to—" and Mrs. Morton sobbed.

"No, my dear, dear mother, no; it would be terrible, indeed, to part you and him. But this bookseller—Plaskwith—perhaps I shall be able to support you both."

"Why, you do not think, Philip, of being an apprentice!—you, who have been so brought up—you, who are so proud!"

"Mother, I would sweep the crossings for your sake! Mother, for your sake I would go to my uncle Beaufort with my hat in my hand, for halfpence. Mother, I am not proud—I would be honest, if I can—but when I see you pining away, and so changed, the devil comes into me, and I often shudder lest I should commit some crime—what, I don't know!"

"Come here, Philip—my own Philip—my son, my hope, my firstborn!"—and the mother's heart gushed forth in all the fondness of early days. "Don't speak so terribly, you frighten me!"

She threw her arms round his neck, and kissed him soothingly. He laid his burning temples on her bosom, and nestled himself to her, as he had been wont to do, after some stormy paroxysm of his passionate and wayward infancy. So there they remained—their lips silent, their hearts speaking to each other—each from each taking strange succour and holy strength—till Philip rose, calm, and with a quiet smile, "Good-bye, mother; I will go at once to Mr. Plaskwith."

"But you have no money for the coach-fare; here, Philip," and she placed her purse in his hand, from which he reluctantly selected a few shillings. "And mind, if the man is rude and you dislike him—mind, you must not subject yourself to insolence and mortification."

"Oh, all will go well, don't fear," said Philip, cheerfully, and he left the house.

Towards evening he had reached his destination. The shop was of goodly exterior, with a private entrance; over the shop was written, "Christopher Plaskwith, Bookseller and Stationer:" on the private door a brass plate, inscribed with "R— and — Mercury Office, Mr. Plaskwith." Philip applied at the private entrance, and was shown by a "neat-handed Phillis" into a small office-room. In a few minutes the door opened, and the bookseller entered.

Mr. Christopher Plaskwith was a short, stout man, in drab-coloured breeches, and gaiters to match; a black coat and waistcoat; he wore a large watch-chain, with a prodigious bunch of seals, alternated by small keys and old-fashioned mourning-rings. His complexion was pale and sodden, and his hair short, dark, and sleek. The bookseller valued himself on a likeness to Buonaparte; and affected a short, brusque, peremptory manner, which he meant to be the indication of the vigorous and decisive character of his prototype.

"So you are the young gentleman Mr. Roger Morton recommends?" Here Mr. Plaskwith took out a huge pocketbook, slowly unclasped it, staring hard at Philip, with what he designed for a piercing and penetrative survey.

"This is the letter—no! this is Sir Thomas Champerdown's order for fifty copies of the last Mercury, containing his speech at the county meeting. Your age, young man?—only sixteen?—look older;—that's not it—that's not it—and this is it!—sit down. Yes, Mr. Roger Morton recommends you—a relation—unfortunate circumstances—well educated—hum! Well, young man, what have you to say for yourself?"

"Sir?"

"Can you cast accounts?—know bookkeeping?"

"I know something of algebra, sir."

"Algebra!—oh, what else?"

"French and Latin."

"Hum!—may be useful. Why do you wear your hair so long?—look at mine. What's your name?"

"Philip Morton."

"Mr. Philip Morton, you have an intelligent countenance—I go a great deal by countenances. You know the terms?—most favourable to you. No premium—I settle that with Roger. I give board and bed—find your own washing. Habits regular—'prenticeship only five years; when over, must not set up in the same town. I will see to the indentures. When can you come?"

"When you please, sir."

"Day after to-morrow, by six o'clock coach."

"But, sir," said Philip, "will there be no salary? something, ever so small, that I could send to my another?"

"Salary, at sixteen?—board and bed—no premium! Salary, what for? 'Prentices have no salary!—you will have every comfort."

"Give me less comfort, that I may give my mother more;—a little money, ever so little, and take it out of my board: I can do with one meal a day, sir."

The bookseller was moved: he took a huge pinch of snuff out of his waistcoat pocket, and mused a moment. He then said, as he re-examined Philip:

"Well, young man, I'll tell you what we will do. You shall come here first upon trial;—see if we like each other before we sign the indentures; allow you, meanwhile, five shillings a week. If you show talent, will see if I and Roger can settle about some little allowance. That do, eh?"

"I thank you, sir, yes," said Philip, gratefully. "Agreed, then. Follow me—present you to Mrs. P." Thus saying, Mr. Plaskwith returned the letter to the pocket-book, and the pocket-book to the pocket; and, putting his arms behind his coat tails, threw up his chin, and strode through the passage into a small parlour, that locked upon a small garden. Here, seated round the table, were a thin lady, with a squint (Mrs. Plaskwith), two little girls, the Misses Plaskwith, also with squints, and pinafores; a young man of three or four-and-twenty, in nankeen trousers, a little the worse for washing, and a black velveteen jacket and waistcoat. This young gentleman was very much freckled; wore his hair, which was dark and wiry, up at one side, down at the other; had a short thick nose; full lips; and, when close to him, smelt of cigars. Such was Mr. Plimmins, Mr. Plaskwith's factotum, foreman in the shop, assistant editor to the Mercury. Mr. Plaskwith formally went the round of the introduction; Mrs. P. nodded her head; the Misses P. nudged each other, and grinned; Mr. Plimmins passed his hand through his hair, glanced at the glass, and bowed very politely.

"Now, Mrs. P., my second cup, and give Mr. Morton his dish of tea. Must be tired, sir—hot day. Jemima, ring—no, go to the stairs and call out 'more buttered toast.' That's the shorter way—promptitude is my rule in life, Mr. Morton. Pray-hum, hum—have you ever, by chance, studied the biography of the great Napoleon Buonaparte?"

Mr. Plimmins gulped down his tea, and kicked Philip under the table. Philip looked fiercely at the foreman, and replied, sullenly, "No, sir."

"That's a pity. Napoleon Buonaparte was a very great man,—very! You have seen his cast?—there it is, on the dumb waiter! Look at it! see a likeness, eh?"

"Likeness, sir? I never saw Napoleon Buonaparte."

"Never saw him! No, just look round the room. Who does that bust put you in mind of? who does it resemble?"

Here Mr. Plaskwith rose, and placed himself in an attitude; his hand in his waistcoat, and his face pensively inclined towards the tea-table. "Now fancy me at St. Helena; this table is the ocean. Now, then, who is that cast like, Mr. Philip Morton?"

"I suppose, sir, it is like you!"

"Ah, that it is! strikes every one! Does it not, Mrs. P., does it not? And when you have known me longer, you will find a moral similitude—a moral, sir! Straightforward—short—to the point—bold—determined!"

"Bless me, Mr. P.!" said Mrs. Plaskwith, very querulously, "do make haste with your tea; the young gentleman, I suppose, wants to go home, and the coach passes in a quarter of an hour."

"Have you seen Kean in Richard the Third, Mr. Morton?" asked Mr. Plimmins.

"I have never seen a play."

"Never seen a play! How very odd!"

"Not at all odd, Mr. Plimmins," said the stationer. "Mr. Morton has known troubles—so hand him the hot toast."

Silent and morose, but rather disdainful than sad, Philip listened to the babble round him, and observed the ungenial characters with which he was to associate. He cared not to please (that, alas! had never been especially his study); it was enough for him if he could see, stretching to his mind's eye beyond the walls of that dull room, the long vistas into fairer fortune. At sixteen, what sorrow can freeze the Hope, or what prophetic fear whisper, "Fool!" to the Ambition? He would bear back into ease and prosperity, if not into affluence and station, the dear ones left at home. From the eminence of five shillings a week, he looked over the Promised Land.

At length, Mr. Plaskwith, pulling out his watch, said, "Just in time to catch the coach; make your bow and be off—smart's the word!" Philip rose, took up his hat, made a stiff bow that included the whole group, and vanished with his host.

Mrs. Plaskwith breathed more easily when he was gone. "I never seed a more odd, fierce, ill-bred-looking young man! I declare I am quite afraid of him. What an eye he has!"

"Uncommonly dark; what I may say gipsy-like," said Mr. Plimmins.

"He! he! You always do say such good things, Plimmins. Gipsy-like, he! he! So he is! I wonder if he can tell fortunes?"

"He'll be long before he has a fortune of his own to tell. Ha! ha!" said Plimmins.

"He! he! how very good! you are so pleasant, Plimmins."

While these strictures on his appearance were still going on, Philip had already ascended the roof of the coach; and, waving his hand, with the condescension of old times, to his future master, was carried away by the "Express" in a whirlwind of dust.

"A very warm evening, sir," said a passenger seated at his right; puffing, while he spoke, from a short German pipe, a volume of smoke in Philip's face.

"Very warm. Be so good as to smoke into the face of the gentleman on the other side of you," returned Philip, petulantly.

"Ho, ho!" replied the passenger, with a loud, powerful laugh—the laugh of a strong man. "You don't take to the pipe yet; you will by and by, when you have known the cares and anxieties that I have gone through. A pipe!—it is a great soother!—a pleasant comforter! Blue devils fly before its honest breath! It ripens the brain—it opens the heart; and the man who smokes thinks like a sage and acts like a Samaritan!"

Roused from his reverie by this quaint and unexpected declamation, Philip turned his quick glance at his neighbour. He saw a man of great bulk and immense physical power—broad-shouldered—deep-chested—not corpulent, but taking the same girth from bone and muscle that a corpulent man does from flesh. He wore a blue coat—frogged, braided, and buttoned to the throat. A broad-brimmed straw hat, set on one side, gave a jaunty appearance to a countenance which, notwithstanding its jovial complexion and smiling mouth, had, in repose, a bold and decided character. It was a face well suited to the frame, inasmuch as it betokened a mind capable of wielding and mastering the brute physical force of body;—light eyes of piercing intelligence; rough, but resolute and striking features, and a jaw of iron. There was thought, there was power, there was passion in the shaggy brow, the deep-ploughed lines, the dilated, nostril and the restless play of the lips. Philip looked hard and grave, and the man returned his look.

"What do you think of me, young gentleman?" asked the passenger, as he replaced the pipe in his mouth. "I am a fine-looking man, am I not?"

"You seem a strange one."

"Strange!—Ay, I puzzle you, as I have done, and shall do, many. You cannot read me as easily as I can read you. Come, shall I guess at your character and circumstances? You are a gentleman, or something like it, by birth;—that the tone of your voice tells me. You are poor, devilish poor;—that the hole in your coat assures me. You are proud, fiery, discontented, and unhappy;—all that I see in your face. It was because I saw those signs that I spoke to you. I volunteer no acquaintance with the happy."

"I dare say not; for if you know all the unhappy you must have a sufficiently large acquaintance," returned Philip.

"Your wit is beyond your years! What is your calling, if the question does not offend you?"

"I have none as yet," said Philip, with a slight sigh, and a deep blush.

"More's the pity!" grunted the smoker, with a long emphatic nasal intonation. "I should have judged that you were a raw recruit in the camp of the enemy."

"Enemy! I don't understand you."

"In other words, a plant growing out of a lawyer's desk. I will explain. There is one class of spiders, industrious, hard-working octopedes, who, out of the sweat of their brains (I take it, by the by, that a spider must have a fine craniological development), make their own webs and catch their flies. There is another class of spiders who have no stuff in them wherewith to make webs; they, therefore, wander about, looking out for food provided by the toil of their neighbours. Whenever they come to the web of a smaller spider, whose larder seems well supplied, they rush upon his domain—pursue him to his hole—eat him up if they can—reject him if he is too tough for their maws, and quietly possess themselves of all the legs and wings they find dangling in his meshes: these spiders I call enemies—the world calls them lawyers!"

Philip laughed: "And who are the first class of spiders?"

"Honest creatures who openly confess that they live upon flies. Lawyers fall foul upon them, under pretence of delivering flies from their clutches. They are wonderful blood-suckers, these lawyers, in spite of all their hypocrisy. Ha! ha! ho! ho!"

And with a loud, rough chuckle, more expressive of malignity than mirth, the man turned himself round, applied vigorously to his pipe, and sank into a silence which, as mile after mile glided past the wheels, he did not seem disposed to break. Neither was Philip inclined to be communicative. Considerations for his own state and prospects swallowed up the curiosity he might otherwise have felt as to his singular neighbour. He had not touched food since the early morning. Anxiety had made him insensible to hunger, till he arrived at Mr. Plaskwith's; and then, feverish, sore, and sick at heart, the sight of the luxuries gracing the tea-table only revolted him. He did not now feel hunger, but he was fatigued and faint. For several nights the sleep which youth can so ill dispense with had been broken and disturbed; and now, the rapid motion of the coach, and the free current of a fresher and more exhausting air than he had been accustomed to for many months, began to operate on his nerves like the intoxication of a narcotic. His eyes grew heavy; indistinct mists, through which there seemed to glare the various squints of the female Plaskwiths, succeeded the gliding road and the dancing trees. His head fell on his bosom; and thence, instinctively seeking the strongest support at hand, inclined towards the stout smoker, and finally nestled itself composedly on that gentleman's shoulder. The passenger, feeling this unwelcome and unsolicited weight, took the pipe, which he had already thrice refilled, from his lips, and emitted an angry and impatient snort; finding that this produced no effect, and that the load grew heavier as the boy's sleep grew deeper, he cried, in a loud voice, "Holla! I did not pay my fare to be your bolster, young man!" and shook himself lustily. Philip started, and would have fallen sidelong from the coach, if his neighbour had not griped him hard with a hand that could have kept a young oak from falling.

"Rouse yourself!—you might have had an ugly tumble." Philip muttered something inaudible, between sleeping and waking, and turned his dark eyes towards the man; in that glance there was so much unconscious, but sad and deep reproach, that the passenger felt touched and ashamed. Before however, he could say anything in apology or conciliation, Philip had again fallen asleep. But this time, as if he had felt and resented the rebuff he had received, he inclined his head away from his neighbour, against the edge of a box on the roof—a dangerous pillow, from which any sudden jolt might transfer him to the road below.

"Poor lad!—he looks pale!" muttered the man, and he knocked the weed from his pipe, which he placed gently in his pocket. "Perhaps the smoke was too much for him—he seems ill and thin," and he took the boy's long lean fingers in his own. "His cheek is hollow!—what do I know but it may be with fasting? Pooh! I was a brute. Hush, coachee, hush! don't talk so loud, and be d—d to you—he will certainly be off!" and the man softly and creepingly encircled the boy's waist with his huge arm.

"Now, then, to shift his head; so-so,—that's right." Philip's sallow cheek and long hair were now tenderly lapped on the soliloquist's bosom. "Poor wretch! he smiles; perhaps he is thinking of home, and the butterflies he ran after when he was an urchin—they never come back, those days;—never—never—never! I think the wind veers to the east; he may catch cold;"—and with that, the man, sliding the head for a moment, and with the tenderness of a woman, from his breast to his shoulder, unbuttoned his coat (as he replaced the weight, no longer unwelcomed, in its former part), and drew the lappets closely round the slender frame of the sleeper, exposing his own sturdy breast—for he wore no waistcoat—to the sharpening air. Thus cradled on that stranger's bosom, wrapped from the present and dreaming perhaps—while a heart scorched by fierce and terrible struggles with life and sin made his pillow—of a fair and unsullied future, slept the fatherless and friendless boy.

CHAPTER VII

"Constance. My life, my joy, my food, my all the world,
My widow-comfort."—King John.

Amidst the glare of lamps—the rattle of carriages—the lumbering of carts and waggons—the throng, the clamour, the reeking life and dissonant roar of London, Philip woke from his happy sleep. He woke uncertain and confused, and saw strange eyes bent on him kindly and watchfully.

"You have slept well, my lad!" said the passenger, in the deep ringing voice which made itself heard above all the noises around.

"And you have suffered me to incommode you thus!" said Philip, with more gratitude in his voice and look than, perhaps, he had shown to any one out of his own family since his birth.

"You have had but little kindness shown you, my poor boy, if you think so much of this."

"No—all people were very kind to me once. I did not value it then." Here the coach rolled heavily down the dark arch of the inn-yard.

"Take care of yourself, my boy! You look ill;" and in the dark the man slipped a sovereign into Philip's hand.

"I don't want money. Though I thank you heartily all the same; it would be a shame at my age to be a beggar. But can you think of an employment where I can make something?—what they offer me is so trifling. I have a mother and a brother—a mere child, sir—at home."

"Employment!" repeated the man; and as the coach now stopped at the tavern door, the light of the lamp fell full on his marked face. "Ay, I know of employment; but you should apply to some one else to obtain it for you! As for me, it is not likely that we shall meet again!"

"I am sorry for that!—What and who are you?" asked Philip, with a rude and blunt curiosity.

"Me!" returned the passenger, with his deep laugh. "Oh! I know some people who call me an honest fellow. Take the employment offered you, no matter how trifling the wages—keep out of harm's way. Good night to you!"

So saying, he quickly descended from the roof, and, as he was directing the coachman where to look for his carpetbag, Philip saw three or four well-dressed men make up to him, shake him heartily by the hand, and welcome him with great seeming cordiality.

Philip sighed. "He has friends," he muttered to himself; and, paying his fare, he turned from the bustling yard, and took his solitary way home.

A week after his visit to R—, Philip was settled on his probation at Mr. Plaskwith's, and Mrs. Morton's health was so decidedly worse, that she resolved to know her fate, and consult a physician. The oracle was at first ambiguous in its response. But when Mrs. Morton said firmly, "I have duties to perform; upon your candid answer rest my Plans with respect to my children—left, if I die suddenly, destitute in the world,"—the doctor looked hard in her face, saw its calm resolution, and replied frankly:

"Lose no time, then, in arranging your plans; life is uncertain with all—with you, especially; you may live some time yet, but your constitution is much shaken—I fear there is water on the chest. No, ma'am—no fee. I will see you again."

The physician turned to Sidney, who played with his watch-chain, and smiled up in his face.

"And that child, sir?" said the mother, wistfully, forgetting the dread fiat pronounced against herself,—"he is so delicate!"

"Not at all, ma'am,—a very fine little fellow;" and the doctor patted the boy's head, and abruptly vanished.

"Ah! mamma, I wish you would ride—I wish you would take the white pony!"

"Poor boy! poor boy!" muttered the mother; "I must not be selfish." She covered her face with her hands, and began to think!

Could she, thus doomed, resolve on declining her brother's offer? Did it not, at least, secure bread and shelter to her child? When she was dead, might not a tie, between the uncle and nephew, be snapped asunder? Would he be as kind to the boy as now when she could commend him with her own lips to his care—when she could place that precious charge into his hands? With these thoughts, she formed one of those resolutions which have all the strength of self-sacrificing love. She would put the boy from her, her last solace and comfort; she would die alone,—alone!

CHAPTER VIII

"Constance. When I shall meet him in the court of heaven, I shall not know him."—King John.

One evening, the shop closed and the business done, Mr. Roger Morton and his family sat in that snug and comfortable retreat which generally backs the warerooms of an English tradesman. Happy often, and indeed happy, is that little sanctuary, near to, and yet remote from, the toil and care of the busy mart from which its homely ease and peaceful security are drawn. Glance down those rows of silenced shops in a town at night, and picture the glad and quiet groups gathered within, over that nightly and social meal which custom has banished from the more indolent tribes who neither toil nor spin. Placed between the two extremes of life, the tradesman, who ventures not beyond his means, and sees clear books and sure gains, with enough of occupation to give healthful excitement, enough of fortune to greet each new-born child without a sigh, might be envied alike by those above and those below his state—if the restless heart of men ever envied Content!

"And so the little boy is not to come?" said Mrs. Morton as she crossed her knife and fork, and pushed away her plate, in token that she had done supper.

"I don't know.—Children, go to bed; there—there—that will do. Good night!—Catherine does not say either yes or no. She wants time to consider."

"It was a very handsome offer on our part; some folks never know when they are well off."

"That is very true, my dear, and you are a very sensible person. Kate herself might have been an honest woman, and, what is more, a very rich woman, by this time. She might have married Spencer, the young brewer—an excellent man, and well to do!"

"Spencer! I don't remember him."

"No: after she went off, he retired from business, and left the place. I don't know what's become of him. He was mightily taken with her, to be sure. She was uncommonly handsome, my sister Catherine."

"Handsome is as handsome does, Mr. Morton," said the wife, who was very much marked with the small-pox. "We all have our temptations and trials; this is a vale of tears, and without grace we are whited sepulchers."

Mr. Morton mixed his brandy and water, and moved his chair into its customary corner.

"You saw your brother's letter," said he, after a pause; "he gives young Philip a very good character."

"The human heart is very deceitful," replied Mrs. Morton, who, by the way, spoke through her nose. "Pray Heaven he may be what he seems; but what's bred in the bone comes out in the flesh."

"We must hope the best," said Mr. Morton, mildly; "and—put another lump into the grog, my dear."

"It is a mercy, I'm thinking, that we didn't have the other little boy. I dare say he has never even been taught his catechism: them people don't know what it is to be a mother. And, besides, it would have been very awkward, Mr. M.; we could never have said who he was: and I've no doubt Miss Pryinall would have been very curious."

"Miss Pryinall be —!" Mr. Morton checked himself, took a large draught of the brandy and water, and added, "Miss Pryinall wants to have a finger in everybody's pie."

"But she buys a deal of flannel, and does great good to the town; it was she who found out that Mrs. Giles was no better than she should be."

"Poor Mrs. Giles!—she came to the workhouse."

"Poor Mrs. Giles, indeed! I wonder, Mr. Morton, that you, a married man with a family, should say, poor Mrs. Giles!"

"My dear, when people who have been well off come to the workhouse, they may be called poor:—but that's neither here nor there; only, if the boy does come to us, we must look sharp upon Miss Pryinall."

"I hope he won't come,—it will be very unpleasant. And when a man has a wife and family, the less he meddles with other folks and their little ones, the better. For as the Scripture says, 'A man shall cleave to his wife and—'"

Here a sharp, shrill ring at the bell was heard, and Mrs. Morton broke off into:

"Well! I declare! at this hour; who can that be? And all gone to bed! Do go and see, Mr. Morton."

Somewhat reluctantly and slowly, Mr. Morton rose; and, proceeding to the passage, unbarred the door. A brief and muttered conversation followed, to the great irritability of Mrs. Morton, who stood in the passage—the candle in her hand.

"What is the matter, Mr. M.?"

Mr. Morton turned back, looking agitated.

"Where's my hat? oh, here. My sister is come, at the inn."

"Gracious me! She does not go for to say she is your sister?"

"No, no: here's her note—calls herself a lady that's ill. I shall be back soon."

"She can't come here—she sha'n't come here, Mr. M. I'm an honest woman—she can't come here. You understand—"

Mr. Morton had naturally a stern countenance, stern to every one but his wife. The shrill tone to which he was so long accustomed jarred then on his heart as well as his ear. He frowned:

"Pshaw! woman, you have no feeling!" said he, and walked out of the house, pulling his hat over his brows. That was the only rude speech Mr. Morton had ever made to his better half. She treasured it up in her heart and memory; it was associated with the sister and the child; and she was not a woman who ever forgave.

Mr. Morton walked rapidly through the still, moon-lit streets, till he reached the inn. A club was held that night in one of the rooms below; and as he crossed the threshold, the sound of "hip-hip-hurrah!" mingled with the stamping of feet and the jingling of glasses, saluted his entrance. He was a stiff, sober, respectable man,—a man who, except at elections—he was a great politician—mixed in none of the revels of his more boisterous townsmen. The sounds, the spot, were ungenial to him. He paused, and the colour of shame rose to his brow. He was ashamed to be there—ashamed to meet the desolate and, as he believed, erring sister.

A pretty maidservant, heated and flushed with orders and compliments, crossed his path with a tray full of glasses.

"There's a lady come by the Telegraph?"

"Yes, sir, upstairs, No. 2, Mr. Morton."

Mr. Morton! He shrank at the sound of his own name.

"My wife's right," he muttered. "After all, this is more unpleasant than I thought for."

The slight stairs shook under his hasty tread. He opened the door of No. 2, and that Catherine, whom he had last seen at her age of gay sixteen, radiant with bloom, and, but for her air of pride, the model for a Hebe,—that Catherine, old ere youth was gone, pale, faded, the dark hair silvered over, the cheeks hollow, and the eye dim,—that Catherine fell upon his breast!

"God bless you, brother! How kind to come! How long since we have met!"

"Sit down, Catherine, my dear sister. You are faint—you are very much changed—very. I should not have known you."

"Brother, I have brought my boy; it is painful to part from him—very—very painful: but it is right, and God's will be done." She turned, as she spoke, towards a little, deformed rickety dwarf of a sofa, that seemed to hide itself in the darkest corner of the low, gloomy room; and Morton followed her. With one hand she removed the shawl that she had thrown over the child, and placing the forefinger of the other upon her lips—lips that smiled then—she whispered,—"We will not wake him, he is so tired. But I would not put him to bed till you had seen him."

And there slept poor Sidney, his fair cheek pillowed on his arm; the soft, silky ringlets thrown from the delicate and unclouded brow; the natural bloom increased by warmth and travel; the lovely face so innocent and hushed; the breathing so gentle and regular, as if never broken by a sigh.

Mr. Morton drew his hand across his eyes.

There was something very touching in the contrast between that wakeful, anxious, forlorn woman, and the slumber of the unconscious boy. And in that moment, what breast upon which the light of Christian pity—of natural affection, had ever dawned, would, even supposing the world's judgment were true, have recalled Catherine's reputed error? There is so divine a holiness in the love of a mother, that no matter how the tie that binds her to the child was formed, she becomes, as it were, consecrated and sacred; and the past is forgotten, and the world and its harsh verdicts swept away, when that love alone is visible; and the God, who watches over the little one, sheds His smile over the human deputy, in whose tenderness there breathes His own!

"You will be kind to him—will you not?" said Mrs. Morton; and the appeal was made with that trustful, almost cheerful tone which implies, 'Who would not be kind to a thing so fair and helpless?' "He is very sensitive and very docile; you will never have occasion to say a hard word to him—never! you have children of your own, brother."

"He is a beautiful boy—beautiful. I will be a father to him!"

As he spoke,—the recollection of his wife—sour, querulous, austere—came over him, but he said to himself, "She must take to such a child,—women always take to beauty." He bent down and gently pressed his lips to Sidney's forehead: Mrs. Morton replaced the shawl, and drew her brother to the other end of the room.

"And now," she said, colouring as she spoke, "I must see your wife, brother: there is so much to say about a child that only a woman will recollect. Is she very good-tempered and kind, your wife? You know I never saw her; you married after—after I left."

"She is a very worthy woman," said Mr. Morton, clearing his throat, "and brought me some money; she has a will of her own, as most women have; but that's neither here nor there—she is a good wife as wives go; and prudent and painstaking—I don't know what I should do without her."

"Brother, I have one favour to request—a great favour."

"Anything I can do in the way of money?"

"It has nothing to do with money. I can't live long—don't shake your head—I can't live long. I have no fear for Philip, he has so much spirit—such strength of character—but that child! I cannot bear to leave him altogether; let me stay in this town—I can lodge anywhere; but to see him sometimes—to know I shall be in reach if he is ill—let me stay here—let me die here!"

"You must not talk so sadly—you are young yet—younger than I am—I don't think of dying."

"Heaven forbid! but—"

"Well—well," interrupted Mr. Morton, who began to fear his feelings would hurry him into some promise which his wife would not suffer him to keep; "you shall talk to Margaret,—that is Mrs. Morton—I will get her to see you—yes, I think I can contrive that; and if you can arrange with her to stay,—but you see, as she brought the money, and is a very particular woman—"

"I will see her; thank you—thank you; she cannot refuse me."

"And, brother," resumed Mrs. Morton, after a short pause, and speaking in a firm voice—"and is it possible that you disbelieve my story?—that you, like all the rest, consider my children the sons of shame?"

There was an honest earnestness in Catherine's voice, as she spoke, that might have convinced many. But Mr. Morton was a man of facts, a practical man—a man who believed that law was always right, and that the improbable was never true.

He looked down as he answered, "I think you have been a very ill-used woman, Catherine, and that is all I can say on the matter; let us drop the subject."

"No! I was not ill-used; my husband—yes, my husband—was noble and generous from first to last. It was for the sake of his children's prospects—for the expectations they, through him, might derive from his proud uncle—that he concealed our marriage. Do not blame Philip—do not condemn the dead."

"I don't want to blame any one," said Mr. Morton, rather angrily; "I am a plain man—a tradesman, and can only go by what in my class seems fair and honest, which I can't think Mr. Beaufort's conduct was, put it how you will; if he marries you as you think, he gets rid of a witness, he destroys a certificate, and he dies without a will. How ever, all that's neither here nor there. You do quite right not to take the name of Beaufort, since it is an uncommon name, and would always make the story public. Least said, soonest mended. You must always consider that your children will be called natural children, and have their own way to make. No harm in that! Warm day for your journey." Catherine sighed, and wiped her eyes; she no longer reproached the world, since the son of her own mother disbelieved her.

The relations talked together for some minutes on the past—the present; but there was embarrassment and constraint on both sides—it was so difficult to avoid one subject; and after sixteen years of absence, there is little left in common, even between those who once played together round their parent's knees. Mr. Morton was glad at last to find an excuse in Catherine's fatigue to leave her. "Cheer up, and take a glass of something warm before you go to bed. Good night!" these were his parting words.

Long was the conference, and sleepless the couch, of Mr. and Mrs. Morton. At first that estimable lady positively declared she would not and could not visit Catherine (as to receiving her, that was out of the question). But she secretly resolved to give up that point in order to insist with greater strength upon another—viz., the impossibility of Catherine remaining in the town; such concession for the purpose of resistance being a very common and sagacious policy with married ladies. Accordingly, when suddenly, and with a good grace, Mrs. Morton appeared affected by her husband's eloquence, and said, "Well, poor thing! if she is so ill, and you wish it so much, I will call to-morrow," Mr. Morton felt his heart softened towards the many excellent reasons which his wife urged against allowing Catherine to reside in the town. He was a political character—he had many enemies; the story of his seduced sister, now forgotten, would certainly be raked up; it would affect his comfort, perhaps his trade, certainly his eldest daughter, who was now thirteen; it would be impossible then to adopt the plan hitherto resolved upon—of passing off Sidney as the legitimate orphan of a distant relation; it would be made a great handle for gossip by Miss Pryinall. Added to all these reasons, one not less strong occurred to Mr. Morton himself—the uncommon and merciless rigidity of his wife would render all the other women in the town very glad of any topic that would humble her own sense of immaculate propriety. Moreover, he saw that if Catherine did remain, it would be a perpetual source of irritation in his own home; he was a man who liked an easy life, and avoided, as far as possible, all food for domestic worry. And thus, when at length the wedded pair turned back to back, and composed themselves to sleep, the conditions of peace were settled, and the weaker party, as usual in diplomacy, sacrificed to the interests of the united powers. After breakfast the next morning, Mrs. Morton sallied out on her husband's arm. Mr. Morton was rather a handsome man, with an air and look grave, composed, severe, that had tended much to raise his character in the town.

Mrs. Morton was short, wiry, and bony. She had won her husband by making desperate love to him, to say nothing of a dower that enabled him to extend his business, new-front, as well as new-stock his shop, and rise into the very first rank of tradesmen in his native town. He still believed that she was excessively fond of him—a common delusion of husbands, especially when henpecked. Mrs. Morton was, perhaps, fond of him in her own way; for though her heart was not warm, there may be a great deal of fondness with very little feeling. The worthy lady was now clothed in her best. She had a proper pride in showing the rewards that belong to female virtue. Flowers adorned her Leghorn bonnet, and her green silk gown boasted four flounces,—such, then, was, I am told, the fashion. She wore, also, a very handsome black shawl, extremely heavy, though the day was oppressively hot, and with a deep border; a smart sevigni brooch of yellow topazes glittered in her breast; a huge gilt serpent glared from her waistband; her hair, or more properly speaking her front, was tortured into very tight curls, and her feet into very tight half-laced boots, from which the fragrance of new leather had not yet departed. It was this last infliction, for il faut souffrir pour etre belle, which somewhat yet more acerbated the ordinary acid of Mrs. Morton's temper. The sweetest disposition is ruffled when the shoe pinches; and it so happened that Mrs. Roger Morton was one of those ladies who always have chilblains in the winter and corns in the summer. "So you say your sister is a beauty?"

"Was a beauty, Mrs. M.,—was a beauty. People alter."

"A bad conscience, Mr. Morton, is—"

"My dear, can't you walk faster?"

"If you had my corns, Mr. Morton, you would not talk in that way!"

The happy pair sank into silence, only broken by sundry "How d'ye dos?" and "Good mornings!" interchanged with their friends, till they arrived at the inn.

"Let us go up quickly," said Mrs. Morton.

And quiet—quiet to gloom, did the inn, so noisy overnight, seem by morning. The shutters partially closed to keep out the sun—the taproom deserted—the passage smelling of stale smoke—an elderly dog, lazily snapping at the flies, at the foot of the staircase—not a soul to be seen at the bar. The husband and wife, glad to be unobserved, crept on tiptoe up the stairs, and entered Catherine's apartment.

Catherine was seated on the sofa, and Sidney-dressed, like Mrs. Roger Morton, to look his prettiest, nor yet aware of the change that awaited his destiny, but pleased at the excitement of seeing new friends, as handsome children sure of praise and petting usually are—stood by her side.

"My wife—Catherine," said Mr. Morton. Catherine rose eagerly, and gazed searchingly on her sister-in-law's hard face. She swallowed the convulsive rising at her heart as she gazed, and stretched out both her hands, not so much to welcome as to plead. Mrs. Roger Morton drew herself up, and then dropped a courtesy—it was an involuntary piece of good breeding—it was extorted by the noble countenance, the matronly mien of Catherine, different from what she had anticipated—she dropped the courtesy, and Catherine took her hand and pressed it.

"This is my son;" she turned away her head. Sidney advanced towards his protectress who was to be, and Mrs. Roger muttered:

"Come here, my dear! A fine little boy!"

"As fine a child as ever I saw!" said Mr. Morton, heartily, as he took Sidney on his lap, and stroked down his golden hair.

This displeased Mrs. Roger Morton, but she sat herself down, and said it was "very warm."

"Now go to that lady, my dear," said Mr. Morton. "Is she not a very nice lady?—don't you think you shall like her very much?"

Sidney, the best-mannered child in the world, went boldly up to Mrs. Morton, as he was bid. Mrs. Morton was embarrassed. Some folks are so with other folk's children: a child either removes all constraint from a party, or it increases the constraint tenfold. Mrs. Morton, however, forced a smile, and said, "I have a little boy at home about your age."

"Have you?" exclaimed Catherine, eagerly; and as if that confession made them friends at once, she drew a chair close to her sister-in-law's,—"My brother has told you all?"

"Yes, ma'am."

"And I shall stay here—in the town somewhere—and see him sometimes?"

Mrs. Roger Morton glanced at her husband—her husband glanced at the door—and Catherine's quick eye turned from one to the other.

"Mr. Morton will explain, ma' am," said the wife.

"E-hem!—Catherine, my dear, I am afraid that is out of the question," began Mr. Morton, who, when fairly put to it, could be business-like enough. "You see bygones are bygones, and it is no use raking them up. But many people in the town will recollect you."

"No one will see me—no one, but you and Sidney."

"It will be sure to creep out; won't it, Mrs. Morton?"

"Quite sure. Indeed, ma'am, it is impossible. Mr. Morton is so very respectable, and his neighbours pay so much attention to all he does; and then, if we have an election in the autumn, you see, ma'am, he has a great stake in the place, and is a public character."

"That's neither here nor there," said Mr. Morton. "But I say, Catherine, can your little boy go into the other room for a moment? Margaret, suppose you take him and make friends."

Delighted to throw on her husband the burden of explanation, which she had originally meant to have all the importance of giving herself in her most proper and patronising manner, Mrs. Morton twisted her fingers into the boy's hand, and, opening the door that communicated with the bedroom, left the brother and sister alone. And then Mr. Morton, with more tact and delicacy than might have been expected from him, began to soften to Catherine the hardship of the separation he urged. He dwelt principally on what was best for the child. Boys were so brutal in their intercourse with each other. He had even thought it better represent Philip to Mr. Plaskwith as a more distant relation than he was; and he begged, by the by, that Catherine would tell Philip to take the hint. But as for Sidney, sooner or later, he would go to a day-school—have companions of his own age—if his birth were known, he would be exposed to many mortifications—so much better, and so very easy, to bring him up as the lawful, that is the legal, offspring of some distant relation.

"And," cried poor Catherine, clasping her bands, "when I am dead, is he never to know that I was his mother?" The anguish of that question thrilled the heart of the listener. He was affected below all the surface that worldly thoughts and habits had laid, stratum by stratum, over the humanities within. He threw his arms round Catherine, and strained her to his breast:

"No, my sister—my poor sister—he shall know it when he is old enough to understand, and to keep his own secret. He shall know, too, how we all loved and prized you once; how young you were, how flattered and tempted; how you were deceived, for I know that—on my soul I do—I know it was not your fault. He shall know, too, how fondly you loved your child, and how you sacrificed, for his sake, the very comfort of being near him. He shall know it all—all—"

"My brother—my brother, I resign him—I am content. God reward you. I will go—go quickly. I know you will take care of him now."

"And you see," resumed Mr. Morton, re-settling himself, and wiping his eyes, "it is best, between you and me, that Mrs. Morton should have her own way in this. She is a very good woman—very; but it's prudent not to vex her. You may come in now, Mrs. Morton."

Mrs. Morton and Sidney reappeared.

"We have settled it all," said the husband. "When can we have him?"

"Not to-day," said Mrs. Roger Morton; "you see, ma'am, we must get his bed ready, and his sheets well aired: I am very particular."

"Certainly, certainly. Will he sleep alone?—pardon me."

"He shall have a room to himself," said Mr. Morton. "Eh, my dear? Next to Martha's. Martha is our parlourmaid—very good-natured girl, and fond of children."

Mrs. Morton looked grave, thought a moment, and said, "Yes, he can have that room."

"Who can have that room?" asked Sidney, innocently. "You, my dear," replied Mr. Morton.

"And where will mamma sleep? I must sleep near mamma."

"Mamma is going away," said Catherine, in a firm voice, in which the despair would only have been felt by the acute ear of sympathy,—"going away for a little time: but this gentleman and lady will be very—very kind to you."

"We will do our best, ma'am," said Mrs. Morton.

And as she spoke, a sudden light broke on the boy's mind—he uttered a loud cry, broke from his aunt, rushed to his mother's breast, and hid his face there, sobbing bitterly.

"I am afraid he has been very much spoiled," whispered Mrs. Roger Morton. "I don't think we need stay longer—it will look suspicious. Good morning, ma'am: we shall be ready to-morrow."

"Good-bye, Catherine," said Mr. Morton; and he added, as he kissed her, "Be of good heart, I will come up by myself and spend the evening with you."

It was the night after this interview. Sidney had gone to his new home; they had been all kind to him—Mr. Morton, the children, Martha the parlour-maid. Mrs. Roger herself had given him a large slice of bread and jam, but had looked gloomy all the rest of the evening: because, like a dog in a strange place, he refused to eat. His little heart was full, and his eyes, swimming with tears, were turned at every moment to the door. But he did not show the violent grief that might have been expected. His very desolation, amidst the unfamiliar faces, awed and chilled him. But when Martha took him to bed, and undressed him, and he knelt down to say his prayers, and came to the words, "Pray God bless dear mamma, and make me a good child," his heart could contain its load no longer, and he sobbed with a passion that alarmed the good-natured servant. She had been used, however, to children, and she soothed and caressed him, and told him of all the nice things he would do, and the nice toys he would have; and at last, silenced, if not convinced, his eyes closed, and, the tears yet wet on their lashes, he fell asleep.

It had been arranged that Catherine should return home that night by a late coach, which left the town at twelve. It was already past eleven. Mrs. Morton had retired to bed; and her husband, who had, according to his wont, lingered behind to smoke a cigar over his last glass of brandy and water, had just thrown aside the stump, and was winding up his watch, when he heard a low tap at his window. He stood mute and alarmed, for the window opened on a back lane, dark and solitary at night, and, from the heat of the weather, the iron-cased shutter was not yet closed; the sound was repeated, and he heard a faint voice. He glanced at the poker, and then cautiously moved to the window, and looked forth,—"Who's there?"

"It is I—it is Catherine! I cannot go without seeing my boy. I must see him—I must, once more!"

"My dear sister, the place is shut up—it is impossible. God bless me, if Mrs. Morton should hear you!"

"I have walked before this window for hours—I have waited till all is hushed in your house, till no one, not even a menial, need see the mother stealing to the bed of her child. Brother, by the memory of our own mother, I command you to let me look, for the last time, upon my boy's face!"

As Catherine said this, standing in that lonely street—darkness and solitude below, God and the stars above—there was about her a majesty which awed the listener. Though she was so near, her features were not very clearly visible; but her attitude—her hand raised aloft—the outline of her wasted but still commanding form, were more impressive from the shadowy dimness of the air.

"Come round, Catherine," said Mr. Morton after a pause; "I will admit you."

He shut the window, stole to the door, unbarred it gently, and admitted his visitor. He bade her follow him; and, shading the light with his hand, crept up the stairs. Catherine's step made no sound.

They passed, unmolested, and unheard, the room in which the wife was drowsily reading, according to her custom before she tied her nightcap and got into bed, a chapter in some pious book. They ascended to the chamber where Sidney lay; Morton opened the door cautiously, and stood at the threshold, so holding the candle that its light might not wake the child, though it sufficed to guide Catherine to the bed. The room was small, perhaps close, but scrupulously clean; for cleanliness was Mrs. Roger Morton's capital virtue. The mother, with a tremulous hand, drew aside the white curtains, and checked her sobs as she gazed on the young quiet face that was turned towards her. She gazed some moments in passionate silence; who shall say, beneath that silence, what thoughts, what prayers moved and stirred!

Then bending down, with pale, convulsive lips she kissed the little hands thrown so listlessly on the coverlet of the pillow on which the head lay. After this she turned her face to her brother with a mute appeal in her glance, took a ring from her finger—a ring that had never till then left it—the ring which Philip Beaufort had placed there the day after that child was born. "Let him wear this round his neck," said she, and stopped, lest she should sob aloud, and disturb the boy. In that gift she felt as if she invoked the father's spirit to watch over the friendless orphan; and then, pressing together her own hands firmly, as we do in some paroxysm of great pain, she turned from the room, descended the stairs, gained the street, and muttered to her brother, "I am happy now; peace be on these thresholds!" Before he could answer she was gone.

CHAPTER IX

"Thus things are strangely wrought,
While joyful May doth last;
Take May in Time—when May is gone
The pleasant time is past "—RICHARD EDWARDS.
From the Paradise of Dainty Devices.

It was that period of the year when, to those who look on the surface of society, London wears its most radiant smile; when shops are gayest, and trade most brisk; when down the thoroughfares roll and glitter the countless streams of indolent and voluptuous life; when the upper class spend, and the middle class make; when the ball-room is the Market of Beauty, and the club-house the School for Scandal; when the hells yawn for their prey, and opera-singers and fiddlers—creatures hatched from gold, as the dung-flies from the dung—swarm, and buzz, and fatten, round the hide of the gentle Public. In the cant phase, it was "the London season." And happy, take it altogether, happy above the rest of the year, even for the hapless, is that period of ferment and fever. It is not the season for duns, and the debtor glides about with a less anxious eye; and the weather is warm, and the vagrant sleeps, unfrozen, under the starlit portico; and the beggar thrives, and the thief rejoices—for the rankness of the civilisation has superfluities clutched by all. And out of the general corruption things sordid and things miserable crawl forth to bask in the common sunshine—things that perish when the first autumn winds whistle along the melancholy city. It is the gay time for the heir and the beauty, and the statesman and the lawyer, and the mother with her young daughters, and the artist with his fresh pictures, and the poet with his new book. It is the gay time, too, for the starved journeyman, and the ragged outcast that with long stride and patient eyes follows, for pence, the equestrian, who bids him go and be d—d in vain. It is a gay time for the painted harlot in a crimson pelisse; and a gay time for the old hag that loiters about the thresholds of the gin-shop, to buy back, in a draught, the dreams of departed youth. It is gay, in fine, as the fulness of a vast city is ever gay—for Vice as for Innocence, for Poverty as for Wealth. And the wheels of every single destiny wheel on the merrier, no matter whether they are bound to Heaven or to Hell.

Arthur Beaufort, the young heir, was at his father's house. He was fresh from Oxford, where he had already discovered that learning is not better than house and land. Since the new prospects opened to him, Arthur Beaufort was greatly changed. Naturally studious and prudent, had his fortunes remained what they had been before his uncle's death, he would probably have become a laborious and distinguished man. But though his abilities were good, he had not those restless impulses which belong to Genius—often not only its glory, but its curse. The Golden Rod cast his energies asleep at once. Good-natured to a fault, and somewhat vacillating in character, he adopted the manner and the code of the rich young idlers who were his equals at College. He became, like them, careless, extravagant, and fond of pleasure. This change, if it deteriorated his mind, improved his exterior. It was a change that could not but please women; and of all women his mother the most. Mrs. Beaufort was a lady of high birth; and in marrying her, Robert had hoped much from the interest of her connections; but a change in the ministry had thrown her relations out of power; and, beyond her dowry, he obtained no worldly advantage with the lady of his mercenary choice. Mrs. Beaufort was a woman whom a word or two will describe. She was thoroughly commonplace—neither bad nor good, neither clever nor silly. She was what is called well-bred; that is, languid, silent, perfectly dressed, and insipid. Of her two children, Arthur was almost the exclusive favourite, especially after he became the heir to such brilliant fortunes. For she was so much the mechanical creature of the world, that even her affection was warm or cold in proportion as the world shone on it. Without being absolutely in love with her husband, she liked him—they suited each other; and (in spite of all the temptations that had beset her in their earlier years, for she had been esteemed a beauty—and lived, as worldly people must do, in circles where examples of unpunished gallantry are numerous and contagious) her conduct had ever been scrupulously correct. She had little or no feeling for misfortunes with which she had never come into contact; for those with which she had—such as the distresses of younger sons, or the errors of fashionable women, or the disappointments of "a proper ambition"—she had more sympathy than might have been supposed, and touched on them with all the tact of well-bred charity and ladylike forbearance. Thus, though she was regarded as a strict person in point of moral decorum, yet in society she was popular—as women at once pretty and inoffensive generally are.

To do Mrs. Beaufort justice, she had not been privy to the letter her husband wrote to Catherine, although not wholly innocent of it. The fact is, that Robert had never mentioned to her the peculiar circumstances that made Catherine an exception from ordinary rules—the generous propositions of his brother to him the night before his death; and, whatever his incredulity as to the alleged private marriage, the perfect loyalty and faith that Catherine had borne to the deceased,—he had merely observed, "I must do something, I suppose, for that woman; she very nearly entrapped my poor brother into marrying her; and he would then, for what I know, have cut Arthur out of the estates. Still, I must do something for her—eh?"

"Yes, I think so. What was she?—very low?"

"A tradesman's daughter."

"The children should be provided for according to the rank of the mother; that's the general rule in such cases: and the mother should have about the same provision she might have looked for if she had married a tradesman and been left a widow. I dare say she was a very artful kind of person, and don't deserve anything; but it is always handsomer, in the eyes of the world, to go by the general rules people lay down as to money matters."

So spoke Mrs. Beaufort. She concluded her husband had settled the matter, and never again recurred to it. Indeed, she had never liked the late Mr. Beaufort, whom she considered mauvais ton.

In the breakfast-room at Mr. Beaufort's, the mother and son were seated; the former at work, the latter lounging by the window: they were not alone. In a large elbow-chair sat a middle-aged man, listening, or appearing to listen, to the prattle of a beautiful little girl—Arthur Beaufort's sister. This man was not handsome, but there was a certain elegance in his air, and a certain intelligence in his countenance, which made his appearance pleasing. He had that kind of eye which is often seen with red hair—an eye of a reddish hazel, with very long lashes; the eyebrows were dark, and clearly defined; and the short hair showed to advantage the contour of a small well-shaped head. His features were irregular; the complexion had been sanguine, but was now faded, and a yellow tinge mingled with the red. His face was more wrinkled, especially round the eyes—which, when he laughed, were scarcely visible—than is usual even in men ten years older. But his teeth were still of a dazzling whiteness; nor was there any trace of decayed health in his countenance. He seemed one who had lived hard; but who had much yet left in the lamp wherewith to feed the wick. At the first glance he appeared slight, as he lolled listlessly in his chair—almost fragile. But, at a nearer examination, you perceived that, in spite of the small extremities and delicate bones, his frame was constitutionally strong. Without being broad in the shoulders, he was exceedingly deep in the chest—deeper than men who seemed giants by his side; and his gestures had the ease of one accustomed to an active life. He had, indeed, been celebrated in his youth for his skill in athletic exercises, but a wound, received in a duel many years ago, had rendered him lame for life—a misfortune which interfered with his former habits, and was said to have soured his temper. This personage, whose position and character will be described hereafter, was Lord Lilburne, the brother of Mrs. Beaufort.

"So, Camilla," said Lord Lilburne to his niece, as carelessly, not fondly, he stroked down her glossy ringlets, "you don't like Berkeley Square as you did Gloucester Place."

"Oh, no! not half so much! You see I never walk out in the fields,—[Now the Regent's Park.]—nor make daisy-chains at Primrose Hill. I don't know what mamma means," added the child, in a whisper, "in saying we are better off here."

Lord Lilburne smiled, but the smile was a half sneer. "You will know quite soon enough, Camilla; the understandings of young ladies grow up very quickly on this side of Oxford Street. Well, Arthur, and what are your plans to-day?"

"Why," said Arthur, suppressing a yawn, "I have promised to ride out with a friend of mine, to see a horse that is for sale somewhere in the suburbs."

As he spoke, Arthur rose, stretched himself, looked in the glass, and then glanced impatiently at the window.

"He ought to be here by this time."

"He! who?" said Lord Lilburne, "the horse or the other animal—I mean the friend?"

"The friend," answered Arthur, smiling, but colouring while he smiled, for he half suspected the quiet sneer of his uncle.

"Who is your friend, Arthur?" asked Mrs. Beaufort, looking up from her work.

"Watson, an Oxford man. By the by, I must introduce him to you."

"Watson! what Watson? what family of Watson? Some Watsons are good and some are bad," said Mrs. Beaufort, musingly.

"Then they are very unlike the rest of mankind," observed Lord Lilburne, drily.

"Oh! my Watson is a very gentlemanlike person, I assure you," said Arthur, half-laughing, "and you need not be ashamed of him." Then, rather desirous of turning the conversation, he continued, "So my father will be back from Beaufort Court to-day?"

"Yes; he writes in excellent spirits. He says the rents will bear raising at least ten per cent., and that the house will not require much repair."

Here Arthur threw open the window.

"Ah, Watson! how are you? How d'ye do, Marsden? Danvers, too! that's capital! the more the merrier! I will be down in an instant. But would you not rather come in?"

"An agreeable inundation," murmured Lord Lilburne. "Three at a time: he takes your house for Trinity College."

A loud, clear voice, however, declined the invitation; the horses were heard pawing without. Arthur seized his hat and whip, and glanced to his mother and uncle, smilingly. "Good-bye! I shall be out till dinner. Kiss me, my pretty Milly!" And as his sister, who had run to the window, sickening for the fresh air and exercise he was about to enjoy, now turned to him wistful and mournful eyes, the kind-hearted young man took her in his arms, and whispered while he kissed her:

"Get up early to-morrow, and we'll have such a nice walk together."

Arthur was gone: his mother's gaze had followed his young and graceful figure to the door.

"Own that he is handsome, Lilburne. May I not say more:—has he not the proper air?"

"My dear sister, your son will be rich. As for his air, he has plenty of airs, but wants graces."

"Then who could polish him like yourself?"

"Probably no one. But had I a son—which Heaven forbid!—he should not have me for his Mentor. Place a young man—(go and shut the door, Camilla!)—between two vices—women and gambling, if you want to polish him into the fashionable smoothness. Entre nous, the varnish is a little expensive!"

Mrs. Beaufort sighed. Lord Lilburne smiled. He had a strange pleasure in hurting the feelings of others. Besides, he disliked youth: in his own youth he had enjoyed so much that he grew sour when he saw the young.

Meanwhile Arthur Beaufort and his friends, careless of the warmth of the day, were laughing merrily, and talking gaily, as they made for the suburb of H—.

"It is an out-of-the-way place for a horse, too," said Sir Harry Danvers.

"But I assure you," insisted Mr. Watson, earnestly, "that my groom, who is a capital judge, says it is the cleverest hack he ever mounted. It has won several trotting matches. It belonged to a sporting tradesman, now done up. The advertisement caught me."

"Well," said Arthur, gaily, "at all events the ride is delightful. What weather! You must all dine with me at Richmond to-morrow—we will row back."

"And a little chicken-hazard, at the M—, afterwards," said Mr. Marsden, who was an elder, not a better, man than the rest—a handsome, saturnine man—who had just left Oxford, and was already known on the turf.

"Anything you please," said Arthur, making his horse curvet.

Oh, Mr. Robert Beaufort! Mr. Robert Beaufort! could your prudent, scheming, worldly heart but feel what devil's tricks your wealth was playing with a son who if poor had been the pride of the Beauforts! On one side of our pieces of old we see the saint trampling down the dragon. False emblem! Reverse it on the coin! In the real use of the gold, it is the dragon who tramples down the saint! But on—on! the day is bright and your companions merry; make the best of your green years, Arthur Beaufort!

The young men had just entered the suburb of H—, and were spurring on four abreast at a canter. At that time an old man, feeling his way before him with a stick,—for though not quite blind, he saw imperfectly,—was crossing the road. Arthur and his friends, in loud converse, did not observe the poor passenger. He stopped abruptly, for his ear caught the sound of danger—it was too late: Mr. Marsden's horse, hard-mouthed, and high-stepping, came full against him. Mr. Marsden looked down:

"Hang these old men! always in the way," said he, plaintively, and in the tone of a much-injured person, and, with that, Mr. Marsden rode on. But the others, who were younger—who were not gamblers—who were not yet grinded down into stone by the world's wheels—the others halted. Arthur Beaufort leaped from his horse, and the old man was already in his arms; but he was severely hurt. The blood trickled from his forehead; he complained of pains in his side and limbs.

"Lean on me, my poor fellow! Do you live far off? I will take you home."

"Not many yards. This would not have happened if I had had my dog. Never mind, sir, go your way. It is only an old man—what of that? I wish I had my dog."

"I will join you," said Arthur to his friends; "my groom has the direction. I will just take the poor old man home, and send for a surgeon. I shall not be long."

"So like you, Beaufort: the best fellow in the world!" said Mr. Watson, with some emotion. "And there's Marsden positively, dismounted, and looking at his horse's knees as if they could be hurt! Here's a sovereign for you, my man."

"And here's another," said Sir Harry; "so that's settled. Well, you will join us, Beaufort? You see the yard yonder. We'll wait twenty minutes for you. Come on, Watson." The old man had not picked up the sovereigns thrown at his feet, neither had he thanked the donors. And on his countenance there was a sour, querulous, resentful expression.

"Must a man be a beggar because he is run over, or because he is half blind?" said he, turning his dim, wandering eyes painfully towards Arthur. "Well, I wish I had my dog!"

"I will supply his place," said Arthur, soothingly. "Come, lean on me—heavier; that's right. You are not so bad,—eh?"

"Um!—the sovereigns!—it is wicked to leave them in the kennel!"

Arthur smiled. "Here they are, sir."

The old man slid the coins into his pocket, and Arthur continued to talk, though he got but short answers, and those only in the way of direction, till at last the old man stopped at the door of a small house near the churchyard.

After twice ringing the bell, the door was opened by a middle-aged woman, whose appearance was above that of a common menial; dressed, somewhat gaily for her years, in a cap seated very far back on a black touroet, and decorated with red ribands, an apron made out of an Indian silk handkerchief, a puce-coloured sarcenet gown, black silk stockings, long gilt earrings, and a watch at her girdle.

"Bless us and save us, sir! What has happened?" exclaimed this worthy personage, holding up her hands.

"Pish! I am faint: let me in. I don't want your aid any more, sir. Thank you. Good day!"

Not discouraged by this farewell, the churlish tone of which fell harmless on the invincibly sweet temper of Arthur, the young man continued to assist the sufferer along the narrow passage into a little old-fashioned parlour; and no sooner was the owner deposited on his worm-eaten leather chair than he fainted away. On reaching the house, Arthur had sent his servant (who had followed him with the horses) for the nearest surgeon; and while the woman was still employed, after taking off the sufferer's cravat, in burning feathers under his nose, there was heard a sharp rap and a shrill ring. Arthur opened the door, and admitted a smart little man in nankeen breeches and gaiters. He bustled into the room.

"What's this—bad accident—um—um! Sad thing, very sad. Open the window. A glass of water—a towel."

"So—so: I see—I see—no fracture—contusion. Help him off with his coat. Another chair, ma'am; put up his poor legs. What age is he, ma'am?—Sixty-eight! Too old to bleed. Thank you. How is it, sir? Poorly, to be sure: will be comfortable presently—faintish still? Soon put all to rights."

"Tray! Tray! Where's my dog, Mrs. Boxer?"

"Lord, sir, what do you want with your dog now? He is in the back-yard."

"And what business has my dog in the back-yard?" almost screamed the sufferer, in accents that denoted no diminution of vigour. "I thought as soon as my back was turned my dog would be ill-used! Why did I go without my dog? Let in my dog directly, Mrs. Boxer!"

"All right, you see, sir," said the apothecary, turning to Beaufort—"no cause for alarm—very comforting that little passion—does him good—sets one's mind easy. How did it happen? Ah, I understand! knocked down—might have been worse. Your groom (sharp fellow!) explained in a trice, sir. Thought it was my old friend here by the description. Worthy man—settled here a many year—very odd—eccentric (this in a whisper). Came off instantly: just at dinner—cold lamb and salad. 'Mrs. Perkins,' says I, 'if any one calls for me, I shall be at No. 4, Prospect Place.' Your servant observed the address, sir. Oh, very sharp fellow! See how the old gentleman takes to his dog—fine little dog—what a stump of a tail! Deal of practice—expect two accouchements every hour. Hot weather for childbirth. So says I to Mrs. Perkins, 'If Mrs. Plummer is taken, or Mrs. Everat, or if old Mr. Grub has another fit, send off at once to No. 4. Medical men should be always in the way—that's my maxim. Now, sir, where do you feel the pain?"

"In my ears, sir."

"Bless me, that looks bad. How long have you felt it?"

"Ever since you have been in the room."

"Oh! I take. Ha! ha!—very eccentric—very!" muttered the apothecary, a little disconcerted. "Well, let him lie down, ma'am. I'll send him a little quieting draught to be taken directly—pill at night, aperient in the morning. If wanted, send for me—always to be found. Bless me, that's my boy Bob's ring. Please to open the door, ma' am. Know his ring—very peculiar knack of his own. Lay ten to one it is Mrs. Plummer, or perhaps, Mrs. Everat—her ninth child in eight years—in the grocery line. A woman in a thousand, sir!"

Here a thin boy, with very short coat-sleeves, and very large hands, burst into the room with his mouth open. "Sir—Mr. Perkins—sir!"

"I know—I know—coming. Mrs. Plummer or Mrs. Everat?"

"No, sir; it be the poor lady at Mrs. Lacy's; she be taken desperate. Mrs. Lacy's girl has just been over to the shop, and made me run here to you, sir."

"Mrs. Lacy's! oh, I know. Poor Mrs. Morton! Bad case—very bad—must be off. Keep him quiet, ma'am. Good day! Look in to-morrow—nine o'clock. Put a little lint with the lotion on the head, ma'am. Mrs. Morton! Ah! bad job that."

Here the apothecary had shuffled himself off to the street door, when Arthur laid his hand on his arm.

"Mrs. Morton! Did you say Morton, sir? What kind of a person—is she very ill?"

"Hopeless case, sir—general break-up. Nice woman—quite the lady—known better days, I'm sure."

"Has she any children—sons?"

"Two—both away now—fine lads—quite wrapped up in them—youngest especially."

"Good heavens! it must be she—ill, and dying, and destitute, perhaps,"—exclaimed Arthur, with real and deep feeling; "I will go with you, sir. I fancy that I know this lady—that," he added generously, "I am related to her."

"Do you?—glad to hear it. Come along, then; she ought to have some one near her besides servants: not but what Jenny, the maid, is uncommonly kind. Dr. —, who attends her sometimes, said to me, says he, 'It is the mind, Mr. Perkins; I wish we could get back her boys.'"

"And where are they?"

"'Prenticed out, I fancy. Master Sidney—"

"Sidney!"

"Ah! that was his name—pretty name. D'ye know Sir Sidney Smith?—extraordinary man, sir! Master Sidney was a beautiful child—quite spoiled. She always fancied him ailing—always sending for me. 'Mr. Perkins,' said she, 'there's something the matter with my child; I'm sure there is, though he won't own it. He has lost his appetite—had a headache last night.' 'Nothing the matter, ma'am,' says I; 'wish you'd think more of yourself.'

"These mothers are silly, anxious, poor creatures. Nater, sir, Nater—wonderful thing—Nater!—Here we are."

And the apothecary knocked at the private door of a milliner and hosier's shop.

CHAPTER X

"Thy child shall live, and I will see it nourished."—Titus Andronicus.

As might be expected, the excitement and fatigue of Catherine's journey to N— had considerably accelerated the progress of disease. And when she reached home, and looked round the cheerless rooms all solitary, all hushed—Sidney gone, gone from her for ever, she felt, indeed, as if the last reed on which she had leaned was broken, and her business upon earth was done. Catherine was not condemned to absolute poverty—the poverty which grinds and gnaws, the poverty of rags and famine. She had still left nearly half of such portion of the little capital, realised by the sale of her trinkets, as had escaped the clutch of the law; and her brother had forced into her hands a note for £20. with an assurance that the same sum should be paid to her half-yearly. Alas! there was little chance of her needing it again! She was not, then, in want of means to procure the common comforts of life. But now a new passion had entered into her breast—the passion of the miser; she wished to hoard every sixpence as some little provision for her children. What was the use of her feeding a lamp nearly extinguished, and which was fated to be soon broken up and cast amidst the vast lumber-house of Death? She would willingly have removed into a more homely lodging, but the servant of the house had been so fond of Sidney—so kind to him. She clung to one familiar face on which there seemed to live the reflection of her child's. But she relinquished the first floor for the second; and there, day by day, she felt her eyes grow heavier and heavier beneath the clouds of the last sleep. Besides the aid of Mr. Perkins, a kind enough man in his way, the good physician whom she had before consulted, still attended her, and refused his fee. Shocked at perceiving that she rejected every little alleviation of her condition, and wishing at least to procure for her last hours the society of one of her sons, he had inquired the address of the elder; and on the day preceding the one in which Arthur discovered her abode, he despatched to Philip the following letter:

"SIR:—Being called in to attend your mother in a lingering illness, which I fear may prove fatal, I think it my duty to request you to come to her as soon as you receive this. Your presence cannot but be a great comfort to her. The nature of her illness is such that it is impossible to calculate exactly how long she may be spared to you; but I am sure her fate might be prolonged, and her remaining days more happy, if she could be induced to remove into a better air and a more quiet neighbourhood, to take more generous sustenance, and, above all, if her mind could be set more at ease as to your and your brother's prospects. You must pardon me if I have seemed inquisitive; but I have sought to draw from your mother some particulars as to her family and connections, with a wish to represent to them her state of mind. She is, however, very reserved on these points. If, however, you have relations well to do in the world, I think some application to them should be made. I fear the state of her affairs weighs much upon your poor mother's mind; and I must leave you to judge how far it can be relieved by the good feeling of any persons upon whom she may have legitimate claims. At all events, I repeat my wish that you should come to her forthwith.

"I am, &c."

After the physician had despatched this letter, a sudden and marked alteration for the worse took place in his patient's disorder; and in the visit he had paid that morning, he saw cause to fear that her hours on earth would be much fewer than he had before anticipated. He had left her, however, comparatively better; but two hours after his departure, the symptoms of her disease had become very alarming, and the good-natured servant girl, her sole nurse, and who had, moreover, the whole business of the other lodgers to attend to, had, as we have seen, thought it necessary to summon the apothecary in the interval that must elapse before she could reach the distant part of the metropolis in which Dr. — resided.

On entering the chamber, Arthur felt all the remorse, which of right belonged to his father, press heavily on his soul. What a contrast, that mean and solitary chamber, and its comfortless appurtenances, to the graceful and luxurious abode where, full of health and hope, he had last beheld her, the mother of Philip Beaufort's children! He remained silent till Mr. Perkins, after a few questions, retired to send his drugs.

He then approached the bed; Catherine, though very weak and suffering much pain, was still sensible. She turned her dim eyes on the young man; but she did not recognise his features.

"You do not remember me?" said he, in a voice struggling with tears: "I am Arthur—Arthur Beaufort." Catherine made no answer.

"Good Heavens! Why do I see you here? I believed you with your friends—your children provided for—as became my father to do. He assured me that you were so." Still no answer.

And then the young man, overpowered with the feelings of a sympathising and generous nature, forgetting for a while Catherine's weakness, poured forth a torrent of inquiries, regrets, and self-upbraidings, which Catherine at first little heeded. But the name of her children, repeated again and again, struck upon that chord which, in a woman's heart, is the last to break; and she raised herself in her bed, and looked at her visitor wistfully.

"Your father," she said, then—"your father was unlike my Philip; but I see things differently now. For me, all bounty is too late; but my children—to-morrow they may have no mother. The law is with you, but not justice! You will be rich and powerful;—will you befriend my children?"

"Through life, so help me Heaven!" exclaimed Arthur, falling on his knees beside the bed.

What then passed between them it is needless to detail; for it was little, save broken repetitions of the same prayer and the same response. But there was so much truth and earnestness in Arthur's voice and countenance, that Catherine felt as if an angel had come there to administer comfort. And when late in the day the physician entered, he found his patient leaning on the breast of her young visitor, and looking on his face with a happy smile.

The physician gathered enough from the appearance of Arthur and the gossip of Mr. Perkins, to conjecture that one of the rich relations he had attributed to Catherine was arrived. Alas! for her it was now indeed too late!

CHAPTER XI

"D'ye stand amazed?—Look o'er thy head, Maximinian!
Look to the terror which overhangs thee."
BEAUMONT AND FLETCHER: The Prophetess.

Phillip had been five weeks in his new home: in another week, he was to enter on his articles of apprenticeship. With a stern, unbending gloom of manner, he had commenced the duties of his novitiate. He submitted to all that was enjoined him. He seemed to have lost for ever the wild and unruly waywardness that had stamped his boyhood; but he was never seen to smile—he scarcely ever opened his lips. His very soul seemed to have quitted him with its faults; and he performed all the functions of his situation with the quiet listless regularity of a machine. Only when the work was done and the shop closed, instead of joining the family circle in the back parlour, he would stroll out in the dusk of the evening, away from the town, and not return till the hour at which the family retired to rest. Punctual in all he did, he never exceeded that hour. He had heard once a week from his mother; and only on the mornings in which he expected a letter, did he seem restless and agitated. Till the postman entered the shop, he was as pale as death—his hands trembling—his lips compressed. When he read the letter he became composed for Catherine sedulously concealed from her son the state of her health: she wrote cheerfully, besought him to content himself with the state into which he had fallen, and expressed her joy that in his letters he intimated that content; for the poor boy's letters were not less considerate than her own. On her return from her brother, she had so far silenced or concealed her misgivings as to express satisfaction at the home she had provided for Sidney; and she even held out hopes of some future when, their probation finished and their independence secured, she might reside with her sons alternately. These hopes redoubled Philip's assiduity, and he saved every shilling of his weekly stipend; and sighed as he thought that in another week his term of apprenticeship would commence, and the stipend cease.

Mr. Plaskwith could not but be pleased on the whole with the diligence of his assistant, but he was chafed and irritated by the sullenness of his manner. As for Mrs. Plaskwith, poor woman! she positively detested the taciturn and moody boy, who never mingled in the jokes of the circle, nor played with the children, nor complimented her, nor added, in short, anything to the sociability of the house. Mr. Plimmins, who had at first sought to condescend, next sought to bully; but the gaunt frame and savage eye of Philip awed the smirk youth, in spite of himself; and he confessed to Mrs. Plaskwith that he should not like to meet "the gipsy," alone, on a dark night; to which Mrs. Plaskwith replied, as usual, "that Mr. Plimmins always did say the best things in the world!"

One morning, Philip was sent a few miles into the country, to assist in cataloguing some books in the library of Sir Thomas Champerdown—that gentleman, who was a scholar, having requested that some one acquainted with the Greek character might be sent to him, and Philip being the only one in the shop who possessed such knowledge.

It was evening before he returned. Mr. and Mrs. Plaskwith were both in the shop as he entered—in fact, they had been employed in talking him over.

"I can't abide him!" cried Mrs. Plaskwith. "If you choose to take him for good, I sha'n't have an easy moment. I'm sure the 'prentice that cut his master's throat at Chatham, last week, was just like him."

"Pshaw! Mrs. P.," said the bookseller, taking a huge pinch of snuff, as usual, from his waistcoat pocket. "I myself was reserved when I was young; all reflective people are. I may observe, by the by, that it was the case with Napoleon Buonaparte: still, however, I must own he is a disagreeable youth, though he attends to his business."

"And how fond of money he is!" remarked Mrs. Plaskwith, "he won't buy himself a new pair of shoes!—quite disgraceful! And did you see what a look he gave Plimmins, when he joked about his indifference to his sole? Plimmins always does say such good things!"

"He is shabby, certainly," said the bookseller; "but the value of a book does not always depend on the binding."

"I hope he is honest!" observed Mrs. Plaskwith;—and here Philip entered.

"Hum," said Mr. Plaskwith; "you have had a long day's work: but I suppose it will take a week to finish?"

"I am to go again to-morrow morning, sir: two days more will conclude the task."

"There's a letter for you," cried Mrs. Plaskwith; "you owes me for it."

"A letter!" It was not his mother's hand—it was a strange writing—he gasped for breath as he broke the seal. It was the letter of the physician.

His mother, then, was ill—dying—wanting, perhaps, the necessaries of life. She would have concealed from him her illness and her poverty. His quick alarm exaggerated the last into utter want;—he uttered a cry that rang through the shop, and rushed to Mr. Plaskwith.

"Sir, sir! my mother is dying! She is poor, poor, perhaps starving;—money, money!—lend me money!—ten pounds!—five!—I will work for you all my life for nothing, but lend me the money!"

"Hoity-toity!" said Mrs. Plaskwith, nudging her husband—"I told you what would come of it: it will be 'money or life' next time."

Philip did not heed or hear this address; but stood immediately before the bookseller, his hands clasped—wild impatience in his eyes. Mr. Plaskwith, somewhat stupefied, remained silent.

"Do you hear me?—are you human?" exclaimed Philip, his emotion revealing at once all the fire of his character. "I tell you my mother is dying; I must go to her! Shall I go empty-handed? Give me money!"

Mr. Plaskwith was not a bad-hearted man; but he was a formal man, and an irritable one. The tone his shopboy (for so he considered Philip) assumed to him, before his own wife too (examples are very dangerous), rather exasperated than moved him.

"That's not the way to speak to your master:—you forget yourself, young man!"

"Forget!—But, sir, if she has not necessaries—if she is starving?"

"Fudge!" said Plaskwith. "Mr. Morton writes me word that he has provided for your mother! Does he not, Hannah?"

"More fool he, I'm sure, with such a fine family of his own! Don't look at me in that way, young man; I won't take it—that I won't! I declare my blood friz to see you!"

"Will you advance me money?—five pounds—only five pounds, Mr. Plaskwith?"

"Not five shillings! Talk to me in this style!—not the man for it, sir!—highly improper. Come, shut up the shop, and recollect yourself; and, perhaps, when Sir Thomas's library is done, I may let you go to town. You can't go to-morrow. All a sham, perhaps; eh, Hannah?"

"Very likely! Consult Plimmins. Better come away now, Mr. P. He looks like a young tiger."

Mrs. Plaskwith quitted the shop for the parlour. Her husband, putting his hands behind his back, and throwing back his chin, was about to follow her. Philip, who had remained for the last moment mute and white as stone, turned abruptly; and his grief taking rather the tone of rage than supplication, he threw himself before his master, and, laying his hand on his shoulder, said:

"I leave you—do not let it be with a curse. I conjure you, have mercy on me!"

Mr. Plaskwith stopped; and had Philip then taken but a milder tone, all had been well. But, accustomed from childhood to command—all his fierce passions loose within him—despising the very man he thus implored—the boy ruined his own cause. Indignant at the silence of Mr. Plaskwith, and too blinded by his emotions to see that in that silence there was relenting, he suddenly shook the little man with a vehemence that almost overset him, and cried:

"You, who demand for five years my bones and blood—my body and soul—a slave to your vile trade—do you deny me bread for a mother's lips?"

Trembling with anger, and perhaps fear, Mr. Plaskwith extricated himself from the gripe of Philip, and, hurrying from the shop, said, as he banged the door:

"Beg my pardon for this to-night, or out you go to-morrow, neck and crop! Zounds! a pretty pass the world's come to! I don't believe a word about your mother. Baugh!"

Left alone, Philip remained for some moments struggling with his wrath and agony. He then seized his hat, which he had thrown off on entering—pressed it over his brows—turned to quit the shop—when his eye fell upon the till. Plaskwith had left it open, and the gleam of the coin struck his gaze—that deadly smile of the arch tempter. Intellect, reason, conscience—all, in that instant, were confusion and chaos. He cast a hurried glance round the solitary and darkening room—plunged his hand into the drawer, clutched he knew not what—silver or gold, as it came uppermost—and burst into a loud and bitter laugh. The laugh itself startled him—it did not sound like his own. His face fell, and his knees knocked together—his hair bristled—he felt as if the very fiend had uttered that yell of joy over a fallen soul.

"No—no—no!" he muttered; "no, my mother,—not even for thee!" And, dashing the money to the ground, he fled, like a maniac, from the house.

At a later hour that same evening, Mr. Robert Beaufort returned from his country mansion to Berkeley Square. He found his wife very uneasy and nervous about the non-appearance of their only son. Arthur had sent home his groom and horses about seven o'clock, with a hurried scroll, written in pencil on a blank page torn from his pocket-book, and containing only these words,—

"Don't wait dinner for me—I may not be home for some hours. I have met with a melancholy adventure. You will approve what I have done when we meet."

This note a little perplexed Mr. Beaufort; but, as he was very hungry, he turned a deaf ear both to his wife's conjectures and his own surmises, till he had refreshed himself; and then he sent for the groom, and learned that, after the accident to the blind man, Mr. Arthur had been left at a hosier's in H—. This seemed to him extremely mysterious; and, as hour after hour passed away, and still Arthur came not, he began to imbibe his wife's fears, which were now wound up almost to hysterics; and just at midnight he ordered his carriage, and taking with him the groom as a guide, set off to the suburban region. Mrs. Beaufort had wished to accompany him; but the husband observing that young men would be young men, and that there might possibly be a lady in the case, Mrs. Beaufort, after a pause of thought, passively agreed that, all things considered, she had better remain at home. No lady of proper decorum likes to run the risk of finding herself in a false position. Mr. Beaufort accordingly set out alone. Easy was the carriage—swift were the steeds—and luxuriously the wealthy man was whirled along. Not a suspicion of the true cause of Arthur's detention crossed him; but he thought of the snares of London—or artful females in distress; "a melancholy adventure" generally implies love for the adventure, and money for the melancholy; and Arthur was young—generous—with a heart and a pocket equally open to imposition. Such scrapes, however, do not terrify a father when he is a man of the world, so much as they do an anxious mother; and, with more curiosity than alarm, Mr. Beaufort, after a short doze, found himself before the shop indicated.

Notwithstanding the lateness of the hour, the door to the private entrance was ajar,—a circumstance which seemed very suspicious to Mr. Beaufort. He pushed it open with caution and timidity—a candle placed upon a chair in the narrow passage threw a sickly light over the flight of stairs, till swallowed up by the deep shadow from the sharp angle made by the ascent. Robert Beaufort stood a moment in some doubt whether to call, to knock, to recede, or to advance, when a step was heard upon the stairs above—it came nearer and nearer—a figure emerged from the shadow of the last landing-place, and Mr. Beaufort, to his great joy, recognised his son.

Arthur did not, however, seem to perceive his father; and was about to pass him, when Mr. Beaufort laid his hand on his arm.

"What means all this, Arthur? What place are you in? How you have alarmed us!"

Arthur cast a look upon his father of sadness and reproach.

"Father," he said, in a tone that sounded stern—almost commanding—"I will show you where I have been; follow me—nay, I say, follow."

He turned, without another word re-ascended the stairs; and Mr. Beaufort, surprised and awed into mechanical obedience, did as his son desired. At the landing-place of the second floor, another long-wicked, neglected, ghastly candle emitted its cheerless ray. It gleamed through the open door of a small bedroom to the left, through which Beaufort perceived the forms of two women. One (it was the kindly maidservant) was seated on a chair, and weeping bitterly; the other (it was a hireling nurse, in the first and last day of her attendance) was unpinning her dingy shawl before she lay down to take a nap. She turned her vacant, listless face upon the two men, put on a doleful smile, and decently closed the door.

"Where are we, I say, Arthur?" repeated Mr. Beaufort. Arthur took his father's hand-drew him into a room to the right—and taking up the candle, placed it on a small table beside a bell, and said, "Here, sir—in the presence of Death!"

Mr. Beaufort cast a hurried and fearful glance on the still, wan, serene face beneath his eyes, and recognised in that glance the features of the neglected and the once adored Catherine.

"Yes—she, whom your brother so loved—the mother of his children—died in this squalid room, and far from her sons, in poverty, in sorrow! died of a broken heart! Was that well, father? Have you in this nothing to repent?"

Conscience-stricken and appalled, the worldly man sank down on a seat beside the bed, and covered his face with his hands.

"Ay," continued Arthur, almost bitterly—"ay, we, his nearest of kin—we, who have inherited his lands and gold—we have been thus heedless of the great legacy your brother bequeathed to us:—the things dearest to him—the woman he loved—the children his death cast, nameless and branded, on the world. Ay, weep, father: and while you weep, think of the future, of reparation. I have sworn to that clay to befriend her sons; join you, who have all the power to fulfil the promise—join in that vow: and may Heaven not visit on us both the woes of this bed of death!"

"I did not know—I—I—" faltered Mr. Beaufort.

"But we should have known," interrupted Arthur, mournfully. "Ah, my dear father! do not harden your heart by false excuses. The dead still speaks to you, and commends to your care her children. My task here is done: O sir! yours is to come. I leave you alone with the dead."

So saying, the young man, whom the tragedy of the scene had worked into a passion and a dignity above his usual character, unwilling to trust himself farther to his emotions, turned abruptly from the room, fled rapidly down the stairs and left the house. As the carriage and liveries of his father met his eye, he groaned; for their evidences of comfort and wealth seemed a mockery to the deceased: he averted his face and walked on. Nor did he heed or even perceive a form that at that instant rushed by him—pale, haggard, breathless—towards the house which he had quitted, and the door of which he left open, as he had found it—open, as the physician had left it when hurrying, ten minutes before the arrival of Mr. Beaufort, from the spot where his skill was impotent. Wrapped in gloomy thought, alone, and on foot—at that dreary hour, and in that remote suburb—the heir of the Beauforts sought his splendid home. Anxious, fearful, hoping, the outcast orphan flew on to the death-room of his mother.

Mr. Beaufort, who had but imperfectly heard Arthur's parting accents, lost and bewildered by the strangeness of his situation, did not at first perceive that he was left alone. Surprised, and chilled by the sudden silence of the chamber, he rose, withdrew his hands from his face, and again he saw that countenance so mute and solemn. He cast his gaze round the dismal room for Arthur; he called his name—no answer came; a superstitious tremor seized upon him; his limbs shook; he sank once more on his seat, and closed his eyes: muttering, for the first time, perhaps, since his childhood, words of penitence and prayer. He was roused from this bitter self-abstraction by a deep groan. It seemed to come from the bed. Did his ears deceive him? Had the dead found a voice? He started up in an agony of dread, and saw opposite to him the livid countenance of Philip Morton: the Son of the Corpse had replaced the Son of the Living Man! The dim and solitary light fell upon that countenance. There, all the bloom and freshness natural to youth seemed blasted! There, on those wasted features, played all the terrible power and glare of precocious passions,—rage, woe, scorn, despair. Terrible is it to see upon the face of a boy the storm and whirlwind that should visit only the strong heart of man!

"She is dead!—dead! and in your presence!" shouted Philip, with his wild eyes fixed upon the cowering uncle; "dead with—care, perhaps with famine. And you have come to look upon your work!"

"Indeed," said Beaufort, deprecatingly, "I have but just arrived: I did not know she had been ill, or in want, upon my honour. This is all a—a—mistake: I—I—came in search of—of—another—"

"You did not, then, come to relieve her?" said Philip, very calmly. "You had not learned her suffering and distress, and flown hither in the hope that there was yet time to save her? You did not do this? Ha! ha!—why did I think it?"

"Did any one call, gentlemen?" said a whining voice at the door; and the nurse put in her head.

"Yes—yes—you may come in," said Beaufort, shaking with nameless and cowardly apprehension; but Philip had flown to the door, and, gazing on the nurse, said,

"She is a stranger! see, a stranger! The son now has assumed his post. Begone, woman!" And he pushed her away, and drew the bolt across the door.

And then there looked upon him, as there had looked upon his reluctant companion, calm and holy, the face of the peaceful corpse. He burst into tears, and fell on his knees so close to Beaufort that he touched him; he took up the heavy hand, and covered it with burning kisses.

"Mother! mother! do not leave me! wake, smile once more on your son! I would have brought you money, but I could not have asked for your blessing, then; mother, I ask it now!"

"If I had but known—if you had but written to me, my dear young gentleman—but my offers had been refused, and—"

"Offers of a hireling's pittance to her; to her for whom my father would have coined his heart's blood into gold! My father's wife!—his wife!—offers—"

He rose suddenly, folded his arms, and facing Beaufort, with a fierce determined brow, said:

"Mark me, you hold the wealth that I was trained from my cradle to consider my heritage. I have worked with these hands for bread, and never complained, except to my own heart and soul. I never hated, and never cursed you—robber as you were—yes, robber! For, even were there no marriage save in the sight of God, neither my father, nor Nature, nor Heaven, meant that you should seize all, and that there should be nothing due to the claims of affection and blood. He was not the less my father, even if the Church spoke not on my side. Despoiler of the orphan, and derider of human love, you are not the less a robber though the law fences you round, and men call you honest! But I did not hate you for this. Now, in the presence of my dead mother—dead, far from both her sons—now I abhor and curse you. You may think yourself safe when you quit this room—safe, and from my hatred you may be so but do not deceive yourself. The curse of the widow and the orphan shall pursue—it shall cling to you and yours—it shall gnaw your heart in the midst of splendour—it shall cleave to the heritage of your son! There shall be a deathbed yet, beside which you shall see the spectre of her, now so calm, rising for retribution from the grave! These words—no, you never shall forget them—years hence they shall ring in your ears, and freeze the marrow of your bones! And now begone, my father's brother—begone from my mother's corpse to your luxurious home!"

He opened the door, and pointed to the stairs. Beaufort, without a word, turned from the room and departed. He heard the door closed and locked as he descended the stairs; but he did not hear the deep groans and vehement sobs in which the desolate orphan gave vent to the anguish which succeeded to the less sacred paroxysm of revenge and wrath.

BOOK II

CHAPTER I

"Incubo. Look to the cavalier. What ails he?
Hostess. And in such good clothes, too!"
BEAUMONT AND FLETCHER: Love's Pilgrimage.

"Theod. I have a brother—there my last hope!.
Thus as you find me, without fear or wisdom,
I now am only child of Hope and Danger."—Ibid.

The time employed by Mr. Beaufort in reaching his home was haunted by gloomy and confused terrors. He felt inexplicably as if the denunciations of Philip were to visit less himself than his son. He trembled at the thought of Arthur meeting this strange, wild, exasperated scatterling—perhaps on the morrow—in the very height of his passions. And yet, after the scene between Arthur and himself, he saw cause to fear that he might not be able to exercise a sufficient authority over his son, however naturally facile and obedient, to prevent his return to the house of death. In this dilemma he resolved, as is usual with cleverer men, even when yoked to yet feebler helpmates, to hear if his wife had anything comforting or sensible to say upon the subject. Accordingly, on reaching Berkeley Square, he went straight to Mrs. Beaufort; and having relieved her mind as to Arthur's safety, related the scene in which he had been so unwilling an actor. With that more lively susceptibility which belongs to most women, however comparatively unfeeling, Mrs. Beaufort made greater allowance than her husband for the excitement Philip had betrayed. Still Beaufort's description of the dark menaces, the fierce countenance, the brigand-like form, of the bereaved son, gave her very considerable apprehensions for Arthur, should the young men meet; and she willingly coincided with her husband in the propriety of using all means of parental persuasion or command to guard against such an encounter. But, in the meanwhile, Arthur returned not, and new fears seized the anxious parents. He had gone forth alone, in a remote suburb of the metropolis, at a late hour, himself under strong excitement. He might have returned to the house, or have lost his way amidst some dark haunts of violence and crime; they knew not where to send, or what to suggest. Day already began to dawn, and still he came not. A length, towards five o'clock, a loud rap was heard at the door, and Mr. Beaufort, hearing some bustle in the hall, descended. He saw his son borne into the hall from a hackney-coach by two strangers, pale, bleeding, and apparently insensible. His first thought was that he had been murdered by Philip. He uttered a feeble cry, and sank down beside his son.

"Don't be darnted, sir," said one of the strangers, who seemed an artisan; "I don't think he be much hurt. You sees he was crossing the street, and the coach ran against him; but it did not go over his head; it be only the stones that makes him bleed so: and that's a mercy."

"A providence, sir," said the other man; "but Providence watches over us all, night and day, sleep or wake. Hem! We were passing at the time from the meeting—the Odd Fellows, sir—and so we took him, and got him a coach; for we found his card in his pocket. He could not speak just then; but the rattling of the coach did him a deal of good, for he groaned—my eyes! how he groaned! did he not, Burrows?"

"It did one's heart good to hear him."

"Run for Astley Cooper—you—go to Brodie. Good Heavens! he is dying. Be quick—quick!" cried Mr. Beaufort to his servants, while Mrs. Beaufort, who had now gained the spot, with greater presence of mind had Arthur conveyed into a room.

"It is a judgment upon me," groaned Beaufort, rooted to the stone of his hall, and left alone with the strangers. "No, sir, it is not a judgment, it is a providence," said the more sanctimonious and better dressed of the two men "for, put the question, if it had been a judgment, the wheel would have gone over him—but it didn't; and, whether he dies or not, I shall always say that if that's not a providence, I don't know what is. We have come a long way, sir; and Burrows is a poor man, though I'm well to do."

This hint for money restored Beaufort to his recollection; he put his purse into the nearest hand outstretched to clutch it, and muttered forth something like thanks.

"Sir, may the Lord bless you! and I hope the young gentleman will do well. I am sure you have cause to be thankful that he was within an inch of the wheel; was he not, Burrows? Well, it's enough to convert a heathen. But the ways of Providence are mysterious, and that's the truth of it. Good night, sir."

Certainly it did seem as if the curse of Philip was already at its work. An accident almost similar to that which, in the adventure of the blind man, had led Arthur to the clue of Catherine, within twenty-four hours stretched Arthur himself upon his bed. The sorrow Mr. Beaufort had not relieved was now at his own hearth. But there were parents and nurses, and great physicians, and skilful surgeons, and all the army that combine against Death, and there were ease, and luxury, and kind eyes, and pitying looks, and all that can take the sting from pain. And thus, the very night on which Catherine had died, broken down, and worn out, upon a strange breast, with a feeless doctor, and by the ray of a single candle, the heir to the fortunes once destined to her son wrestled also with the grim Tyrant, who seemed, however, scared from his prey by the arts and luxuries which the world of rich men raises up in defiance of the grave.

Arthur, was, indeed, very seriously injured; one of his ribs was broken, and he had received two severe contusions on the head. To insensibility succeeded fever, followed by delirium. He was in imminent danger for several days. If anything could console his parents for such an affliction, it was the thought that, at least, he was saved from the chance of meeting Philip.

Mr. Beaufort, in the instinct of that capricious and fluctuating conscience which belongs to weak minds, which remains still, and drooping, and lifeless, as a flag on a masthead during the calm of prosperity, but flutters, and flaps, and tosses when the wind blows and the wave heaves, thought very acutely and remorsefully of the condition of the Mortons, during the danger of his own son. So far, indeed, from his anxiety for Arthur monopolising all his care, it only sharpened his charity towards the orphans; for many a man becomes devout and good when he fancies he has an Immediate interest in appeasing Providence. The morning after Arthur's accident, he sent for Mr. Blackwell. He commissioned him to see that Catherine's funeral rites were performed with all due care and attention; he bade him obtain an interview with Philip, and assure the youth of Mr. Beaufort's good and friendly disposition towards him, and to offer to forward his views in any course of education he might prefer, or any profession he might adopt; and he earnestly counselled the lawyer to employ all his tact and delicacy in conferring with one of so proud and fiery a temper. Mr. Blackwell, however, had no tact or delicacy to employ: he went to the house of mourning, forced his way to Philip, and the very exordium of his harangue, which was devoted to praises of the extraordinary generosity and benevolence of his employer, mingled with condescending admonitions towards gratitude from Philip, so exasperated the boy, that Mr. Blackwell was extremely glad to get out of the house with a whole skin. He, however, did not neglect the more formal part of his mission; but communicated immediately with a fashionable undertaker, and gave orders for a very genteel funeral. He thought after the funeral that Philip would be in a less excited state of mind, and more likely to hear reason; he, therefore, deferred a second interview with the orphan till after that event; and, in the meanwhile, despatched a letter to Mr. Beaufort, stating that he had attended to his instructions; that the orders for the funeral were given; but that at present Mr. Philip Morton's mind was a little disordered, and that he could not calmly discuss the plans for the future suggested by Mr. Beaufort. He did not doubt, however, that in another interview all would be arranged according to the wishes his client had so nobly conveyed to him. Mr. Beaufort's conscience on this point was therefore set at rest. It was a dull, close, oppressive morning, upon which the remains of Catherine Morton were consigned to the grave. With the preparations for the funeral Philip did not interfere; he did not inquire by whose orders all that solemnity of mutes, and coaches, and black plumes, and crape bands, was appointed. If his vague and undeveloped conjecture ascribed this last and vain attention to Robert Beaufort, it neither lessened the sullen resentment he felt against his uncle, nor, on the other hand, did he conceive that he had a right to forbid respect to the dead, though he might reject service for the survivor. Since Mr. Blackwell's visit, he had remained in a sort of apathy or torpor, which seemed to the people of the house to partake rather of indifference than woe.

The funeral was over, and Philip had returned to the apartments occupied by the deceased; and now, for the first time, he set himself to examine what papers, &c., she had left behind. In an old escritoire, he found, first, various packets of letters in his father's handwriting, the characters in many of them faded by time. He opened a few; they were the earliest love-letters. He did not dare to read above a few lines; so much did their living tenderness, and breathing, frank, hearty passion, contrast with the fate of the adored one. In those letters, the very heart of the writer seemed to beat! Now both hearts alike were stilled! And GHOST called vainly unto GHOST!

He came, at length, to a letter in his mother's hand, addressed to himself, and dated two days before her death. He went to the window and gasped in the mists of the sultry air for breath. Below were heard the noises of London; the shrill cries of itinerant vendors, the rolling carts, the whoop of boys returned for a while from school. Amidst all these rose one loud, merry peal of laughter, which drew his attention mechanically to the spot whence it came; it was at the threshold of a public-house, before which stood the hearse that had conveyed his mother's coffin, and the gay undertakers, halting there to refresh themselves. He closed the window with a groan, retired to the farthest corner of the room, and read as follows·

"MY DEAREST PHILIP,—When you read this, I shall be no more. You and poor Sidney will have neither father nor mother, nor fortune, nor name. Heaven is more just than man, and in Heaven is my hope for you. You, Philip, are already past childhood; your nature is one formed, I think, to wrestle successfully with the world. Guard against your own passions, and you may bid defiance to the obstacles that will beset your path in life. And lately, in our reverses, Philip, you have so subdued those passions, so schooled the pride and impetuosity of your childhood, that I have contemplated your prospects with less fear than I used to do, even when they seemed so brilliant. Forgive me, my dear child, if I have concealed from you my state of health, and if my death be a sudden and unlooked-for shock. Do not grieve for me too long. For myself, my release is indeed escape from the prison-house and the chain—from bodily pain and mental torture, which may, I fondly hope, prove some expiation for the errors of a happier time. For I did err, when, even from the least selfish motives, I suffered my union with your father to remain concealed, and thus ruined the hopes of those who had rights upon me equal even to his. But, O Philip! beware of the first false steps into deceit; beware, too, of the passions, which do not betray their fruit till years and years after the leaves that look so green and the blossoms that seem so fair.

"I repeat my solemn injunction—Do not grieve for me; but strengthen your mind and heart to receive the charge that I now confide to you—my Sidney, my child, your brother! He is so soft, so gentle, he has been so dependent for very life upon me, and we are parted now for the first and last time. He is with strangers; and—and—O Philip, Philip! watch over him for the love you bear, not only to him, but to me! Be to him a father as well as a brother. Put your stout heart against the world, so that you may screen him, the weak child, from its malice. He has not your talents nor strength of character; without you he is nothing. Live, toil, rise for his sake not less than your own. If you knew how this heart beats as I write to you, if you could conceive what comfort I take for him from my confidence in you, you would feel a new spirit—my spirit—my mother-spirit of love, and forethought, and vigilance, enter into you while you read. See him when I am gone—comfort and soothe him. Happily he is too young yet to know all his loss; and do not let him think unkindly of me in the days to come, for he is a child now, and they may poison his mind against me more easily than they can yours. Think, if he is unhappy hereafter, he may forget how I loved him, he may curse those who gave him birth. Forgive me all this, Philip, my son, and heed it well.

"And now, where you find this letter, you will see a key; it opens a well in the bureau in which I have hoarded my little savings. You will see that I have not died in poverty. Take what there is; young as you are, you may want it more now than hereafter. But hold it in trust for your brother as well as yourself. If he is harshly treated (and you will go and see him, and you will remember that he would writhe under what you might scarcely feel), or if they overtask him (he is so young to work), yet it may find him a home near you. God watch over and guard you both! You are orphans now. But HE has told even the orphans to call him 'Father!'"

When he had read this letter, Philip Morton fell upon his knees, and prayed.

CHAPTER II

"His curse! Dost comprehend what that word means?
Shot from a father's angry breath."
JAMES SHIRLEY: The Brothers.

"This term is fatal, and affrights me."—Ibid.

"Those fond philosophers that magnify
Our human nature......
Conversed but little with the world-they knew not
The fierce vexation of community!"—Ibid.

After he had recovered his self-possession, Philip opened the well of the bureau, and was astonished and affected to find that Catherine had saved more than £100. Alas! how much must she have pinched herself to have hoarded this little treasure! After burning his father's love-letters, and some other papers, which he deemed useless, he made up a little bundle of those trifling effects belonging to the deceased, which he valued as memorials and relies of her, quitted the apartment, and descended to the parlour behind the shop. On the way he met with the kind servant, and recalling the grief that she had manifested for his mother since he had been in the house, he placed two sovereigns in her hand. "And now," said he, as the servant wept while he spoke, "now I can bear to ask you what I have not before done. How did my poor mother die? Did she suffer much?—or—or—"

"She went off like a lamb, sir," said the girl, drying her eyes. "You see the gentleman had been with her all the day, and she was much more easy and comfortable in her mind after he came."

"The gentleman! Not the gentleman I found here?"

"Oh, dear no! Not the pale middle-aged gentleman nurse and I saw go down as the clock struck two. But the young, soft-spoken gentleman who came in the morning, and said as how he was a relation. He stayed with her till she slept; and, when she woke, she smiled in his face—I shall never forget that smile—for I was standing on the other side, as it might be here, and the doctor was by the window, pouring out the doctor's stuff in the glass; and so she looked on the young gentleman, and then looked round at us all, and shook her head very gently, but did not speak. And the gentleman asked her how she felt, and she took both his hands and kissed them; and then he put his arms round and raised her up to take the physic like, and she said then, 'You will never forget them?' and he said, 'Never.' I don't know what that meant, sir!"

"Well, well—go on."

"And her head fell back on his buzzom, and she looked so happy; and, when the doctor came to the bedside, she was quite gone."

"And the stranger had my post! No matter; God bless him—God bless him. Who was he? what was his name?"

"I don't know, sir; he did not say. He stayed after the doctor went, and cried very bitterly; he took on more than you did, sir."

"And the other gentleman came just as he was a-going, and they did not seem to like each other; for I heard him through the wall, as nurse and I were in the next room, speak as if he was scolding; but he did not stay long."

"And has never been seen since?"

"No, sir. Perhaps missus can tell you more about him. But won't you take something, sir? Do—you look so pale."

Philip, without speaking, pushed her gently aside, and went slowly down the stairs. He entered the parlour, where two or three children were seated, playing at dominoes; he despatched one for their mother, the mistress of the shop, who came in, and dropped him a courtesy, with a very grave, sad face, as was proper.

"I am going to leave your house, ma'am; and I wish to settle any little arrears of rent, &c."

"O sir! don't mention it," said the landlady; and, as she spoke, she took a piece of paper from her bosom, very neatly folded, and laid it on the table. "And here, sir," she added, taking from the same depository a card,—"here is the card left by the gentleman who saw to the funeral. He called half an hour ago, and bade me say, with his compliments, that he would wait on you to-morrow at eleven o'clock. So I hope you won't go yet: for I think he means to settle everything for you; he said as much, sir."

Philip glanced over the card, and read, "Mr. George Blackwell, Lincoln's Inn." His brow grew dark—he let the card fall on the ground, put his foot on it with a quiet scorn, and muttered to himself, "The lawyer shall not bribe me out of my curse!" He turned to the total of the bill—not heavy, for poor Catherine had regularly defrayed the expense of her scanty maintenance and humble lodging—paid the money, and, as the landlady wrote the receipt, he asked, "Who was the gentleman—the younger gentleman—who called in the morning of the day my mother died?"

"Oh, sir! I am so sorry I did not get his name. Mr. Perkins said that he was some relation. Very odd he has never been since. But he'll be sure to call again, sir; you had much better stay here."

"No: it does not signify. All that he could do is done. But stay, give him this note, if he should call."

Philip, taking the pen from the landlady's hand, hastily wrote (while Mrs. Lacy went to bring him sealing-wax and a light) these words:

"I cannot guess who you are: they say that you call yourself a relation; that must be some mistake. I knew not that my poor mother had relations so kind. But, whoever you be, you soothed her last hours—she died in your arms; and if ever—years, long years hence—we should chance to meet, and I can do anything to aid another, my blood, and my life, and my heart, and my soul, all are slaves to your will. If you be really of her kindred, I commend to you my brother: he is at —, with Mr. Morton. If you can serve him, my mother's soul will watch over you as a guardian angel. As for me, I ask no help from any one: I go into the world and will carve out my own way. So much do I shrink from the thought of charity from others, that I do not believe I could bless you as I do now if your kindness to me did not close with the stone upon my mother's grave. PHILIP."

He sealed this letter, and gave it to the woman.

"Oh, by the by," said she, "I had forgot; the Doctor said that if you would send for him, he would be most happy to call on you, and give you any advice."

"Very well."

"And what shall I say to Mr. Blackwell?"

"That he may tell his employer to remember our last interview."

With that Philip took up his bundle and strode from the house. He went first to the churchyard, where his mother's remains had been that day interred. It was near at hand, a quiet, almost a rural, spot. The gate stood ajar, for there was a public path through the churchyard, and Philip entered with a noiseless tread. It was then near evening; the sun had broken out from the mists of the earlier day, and the wistering rays shone bright and holy upon the solemn place.

"Mother! mother!" sobbed the orphan, as he fell prostrate before that fresh green mound: "here—here I have come to repeat my oath, to swear again that I will be faithful to the charge you have entrusted to your wretched son! And at this hour I dare ask if there be on this earth one more miserable and forlorn?"

As words to this effect struggled from his lips, a loud, shrill voice—the cracked, painful voice of weak age wrestling with strong passion, rose close at hand.

"Away, reprobate! thou art accursed!"

Philip started, and shuddered as if the words were addressed to himself, and from the grave. But, as he rose on his knee, and tossing the wild hair from his eyes, looked confusedly round, he saw, at a short distance, and in the shadow of the wall, two forms; the one, an old man with grey hair, who was seated on a crumbling wooden tomb, facing the setting sun; the other, a man apparently yet in the vigour of life, who appeared bent as in humble supplication. The old man's hands were outstretched over the head of the younger, as if suiting terrible action to the terrible words, and, after a moment's pause—a moment, but it seemed far longer to Philip—there was heard a deep, wild, ghastly howl from a dog that cowered at the old man's feet; a howl, perhaps of fear at the passion of his master, which the animal might associate with danger.

"Father! father!" said the suppliant reproachfully, "your very dog rebukes your curse."

"Be dumb! My dog! What hast thou left me on earth but him? Thou hast made me loathe the sight of friends, for thou hast made me loathe mine own name. Thou hast covered it with disgrace,—thou hast turned mine old age into a by-word,—thy crimes leave me solitary in the midst of my shame!"

"It is many years since we met, father; we may never meet again—shall we part thus?"

"Thus, aha!" said the old man in a tone of withering sarcasm! "I comprehend,—you are come for money!"

At this taunt the son started as if stung by a serpent; raised his head to its full height, folded his arms, and replied:

"Sir, you wrong me: for more than twenty years I have maintained myself—no matter how, but without taxing you;—and now, I felt remorse for having suffered you to discard me,—now, when you are old and helpless, and, I heard, blind: and you might want aid, even from your poor good-for-nothing son. But I have done. Forget,—not my sins, but this interview. Repeal your curse, father; I have enough on my head without yours; and so—let the son at least bless the father who curses him. Farewell!"

The speaker turned as he thus said, with a voice that trembled at the close, and brushed rapidly by Philip, whom he did not, however, appear to perceive; but Philip, by the last red beam of the sun, saw again that marked storm-beaten face which it was difficult, once seen, to forget, and recognised the stranger on whose breast he had slept the night of his fatal visit to R—.

The old man's imperfect vision did not detect the departure of his son, but his face changed and softened as the latter strode silently through the rank grass.

"William!" he said at last, gently; "William!" and the tears rolled down his furrowed cheeks; "my son!" but that son was gone—the old man listened for reply—none came. "He has left me—poor William!—we shall never meet again;" and he sank once more on the old tombstone, dumb, rigid, motionless—an image of Time himself in his own domain of Graves. The dog crept closer to his master, and licked his hand. Philip stood for a moment in thoughtful silence: his exclamation of despair had been answered as by his better angel. There was a being more miserable than himself; and the Accursed would have envied the Bereaved!

The twilight had closed in; the earliest star—the star of Memory and Love, the Hesperus hymned by every poet since the world began—was fair in the arch of heaven, as Philip quitted the spot, with a spirit more reconciled to the future, more softened, chastened, attuned to gentle and pious thoughts than perhaps ever yet had made his soul dominant over the deep and dark tide of his gloomy passions. He went thence to a neighbouring sculptor, and paid beforehand for a plain tablet to be placed above the grave he had left. He had just quitted that shop, in the same street, not many doors removed from the house in which his mother had breathed her last. He was pausing by a crossing, irresolute whether to repair at once to the home assigned to Sidney, or to seek some shelter in town for that night, when three men who were on the opposite side of the way suddenly caught sight of him.

"There he is—there he is! Stop, sir!—stop!"

Philip heard these words, looked up, and recognised the voice and the person of Mr. Plaskwith; the bookseller was accompanied by Mr. Plimmins, and a sturdy, ill-favoured stranger.

A nameless feeling of fear, rage, and disgust seized the unhappy boy, and at the same moment a ragged vagabond whispered to him, "Stump it, my cove; that's a Bow Street runner."

Then there shot through Philip's mind the recollection of the money he had seized, though but to dash away; was he now—he, still to his own conviction, the heir of an ancient and spotless name—to be hunted as a thief; or, at the best, what right over his person and his liberty had he given to his taskmaster? Ignorant of the law—the law only seemed to him, as it ever does to the ignorant and the friendless—a Foe. Quicker than lightning these thoughts, which it takes so many words to describe, flashed through the storm and darkness of his breast; and at the very instant that Mr. Plimmins had laid hands on his shoulder his resolution was formed. The instinct of self beat loud at his heart. With a bound—a spring that sent Mr. Plimmins sprawling in the kennel, he darted across the road, and fled down an opposite lane.

"Stop him! stop!" cried the bookseller, and the officer rushed after him with almost equal speed. Lane after lane, alley after alley, fled Philip; dodging, winding, breathless, panting; and lane after lane, and alley after alley, thickened at his heels the crowd that pursued. The idle and the curious, and the officious,—ragged boys, ragged men, from stall and from cellar, from corner and from crossing, joined in that delicious chase, which runs down young Error till it sinks, too often, at the door of the gaol or the foot of the gallows. But Philip slackened not his pace; he began to distance his pursuers. He was now in a street which they had not yet entered—a quiet street, with few, if any, shops. Before the threshold of a better kind of public-house, or rather tavern, to judge by its appearance, lounged two men; and while Philip flew on, the cry of "Stop him!" had changed as the shout passed to new voices, into "Stop the thief!"—that cry yet howled in the distance. One of the loungers seized him: Philip, desperate and ferocious, struck at him with all his force; but the blow was scarcely felt by that Herculean frame.

"Pish!" said the man, scornfully; "I am no spy; if you run from justice, I would help you to a sign-post."

Struck by the voice, Philip looked hard at the speaker. It was the voice of the Accursed Son.

"Save me! you remember me?" said the orphan, faintly. "Ah! I think I do; poor lad! Follow me—this way!" The stranger turned within the tavern, passed the hall through a sort of corridor that led into a back yard which opened upon a nest of courts or passages.

"You are safe for the present; I will take you where you can tell me all at your ease—See!" As he spoke they emerged into an open street, and the guide pointed to a row of hackney coaches. "Be quick—get in. Coachman, drive fast to —"

Philip did not hear the rest of the direction.

Our story returns to Sidney.

CHAPTER III

"Nous vous mettrons a couvert,
Repondit le pot de fer
Si quelque matiere dure
Vous menace d'aventure,
Entre deux je passerai,
Et du coup vous sauverai.
....
Le pot de terre en souffre!"—LA FONTAINE.

[*"We, replied the Iron Pot, will shield you: should any hard substance menace you with danger, I'll intervene, and save you from the shock.* .... *The Earthen Pot was the sufferer!*]

"SIDNEY, come here, sir! What have you been at? you have torn your frill into tatters! How did you do this? Come sir, no lies."

"Indeed, ma'am, it was not my fault. I just put my head out of the window to see the coach go by, and a nail caught me here."

"Why, you little plague! you have scratched yourself—you are always in mischief. What business had you to look after the coach?"

"I don't know," said Sidney, hanging his head ruefully. "La, mother!" cried the youngest of the cousins, a square-built, ruddy, coarse-featured urchin, about Sidney's age, "La, mother, he never see a coach in the street when we are at play but he runs arter it."

"After, not arter," said Mr. Roger Morton, taking the pipe from his mouth.

"Why do you go after the coaches, Sidney?" said Mrs. Morton; "it is very naughty; you will be run over some day."

"Yes, ma'am," said Sidney, who during the whole colloquy had been trembling from head to foot.

"'Yes ma'am,' and 'no, ma'am:' you have no more manners than a cobbler's boy."

"Don't tease the child, my dear; he is crying," said Mr. Morton, more authoritatively than usual. "Come here, my man!" and the worthy uncle took him in his lap and held his glass of brandy-and-water to his lips; Sidney, too frightened to refuse, sipped hurriedly, keeping his large eyes fixed on his aunt, as children do when they fear a cuff.

"You spoil the boy more than do your own flesh and blood," said Mrs. Morton, greatly displeased.

Here Tom, the youngest-born before described, put his mouth to his mother's ear, and whispered loud enough to be heard by all: "He runs arter the coach 'cause he thinks his ma may be in it. Who's home-sick, I should like to know? Ba! Baa!"

The boy pointed his finger over his mother's shoulder, and the other children burst into a loud giggle.

"Leave the room, all of you,—leave the room!" said Mr. Morton, rising angrily and stamping his foot.

The children, who were in great awe of their father, huddled and hustled each other to the door; but Tom, who went last, bold in his mother's favour, popped his head through the doorway, and cried, "Good-bye, little home-sick!"

A sudden slap in the face from his father changed his chuckle into a very different kind of music, and a loud indignant sob was heard without for some moments after the door was closed.

"If that's the way you behave to your children, Mr. Morton, I vow you sha'n't have any more if I can help it. Don't come near me—don't touch me!" and Mrs. Morton assumed the resentful air of offended beauty.

"Pshaw!" growled the spouse, and he reseated himself and resumed his pipe. There was a dead silence. Sidney crouched near his uncle, looking very pale. Mrs. Morton, who was knitting, knitted away with the excited energy of nervous irritation.

"Ring the bell, Sidney," said Mr. Morton. The boy obeyed—the parlour-maid entered. "Take Master Sidney to his room; keep the boys away from him, and give him a large slice of bread and jam, Martha."

"Jam, indeed!—treacle," said Mrs. Morton.

"Jam, Martha," repeated the uncle, authoritatively. "Treacle!" reiterated the aunt.

"Jam, I say!"

"Treacle, you hear: and for that matter, Martha has no jam to give!"

The husband had nothing more to say.

"Good night, Sidney; there's a good boy, go and kiss your aunt and make your bow; and I say, my lad, don't mind those plagues. I'll talk to them to-morrow, that I will; no one shall be unkind to you in my house."

Sidney muttered something, and went timidly up to Mrs. Morton. His look so gentle and subdued; his eyes full of tears; his pretty mouth which, though silent, pleaded so eloquently; his willingness to forgive, and his wish to be forgiven, might have melted many a heart harder, perhaps, than Mrs. Morton's. But there reigned what are worse than hardness,—prejudice and wounded vanity—maternal vanity. His contrast to her own rough, coarse children grated on her, and set the teeth of her mind on edge.

"There, child, don't tread on my gown: you are so awkward: say your prayers, and don't throw off the counterpane! I don't like slovenly boys."

Sidney put his finger in his mouth, drooped, and vanished.

"Now, Mrs. M.," said Mr. Morton, abruptly, and knocking out the ashes of his pipe; "now Mrs. M., one word for all: I have told you that I promised poor Catherine to be a father to that child, and it goes to my heart to see him so snubbed. Why you dislike him I can't guess for the life of me. I never saw a sweeter-tempered child."

"Go on, sir, go on: make your personal reflections on your own lawful wife. They don't hurt me—oh no, not at all! Sweet-tempered, indeed; I suppose your own children are not sweet-tempered?"

"That's neither here nor there," said Mr. Morton: "my own children are such as God made them, and I am very well satisfied."

"Indeed you may be proud of such a family; and to think of the pains I have taken with them, and how I have saved you in nurses, and the bad times I have had; and now, to find their noses put out of joint by that little mischief-making interloper—it is too bad of you, Mr. Morton; you will break my heart—that you will!"

Mrs. Morton put her handkerchief to her eyes and sobbed. The husband was moved: he got up and attempted to take her hand. "Indeed, Margaret, I did not mean to vex you."

"And I who have been such a fa—fai—faithful wi—wi—wife, and brought you such a deal of mon—mon—money, and always stud—stud—studied your interests; many's the time when you have been fast asleep that I have sat up half the night—men—men—mending the house linen; and you have not been the same man, Roger, since that boy came!"

"Well, well" said the good man, quite overcome, and fairly taking her round the waist and kissing her; "no words between us; it makes life quite unpleasant. If it pains you to have Sidney here, I will put him to some school in the town, where they'll be kind to him. Only, if you would, Margaret, for my sake—old girl! come, now! there's a darling!—just be more tender with him. You see he frets so after his mother. Think how little Tom would fret if he was away from you! Poor little Tom!"

"La! Mr. Morton, you are such a man!—there's no resisting your ways! You know how to come over me, don't you?"

And Mrs. Morton smiled benignly, as she escaped from his conjugal arms and smoothed her cap.

Peace thus restored, Mr. Morton refilled his pipe, and the good lady, after a pause, resumed, in a very mild, conciliatory tone:

"I'll tell you what it is, Roger, that vexes me with that there child. He is so deceitful, and he does tell such fibs!"

"Fibs! that is a very bad fault," said Mr. Morton, gravely. "That must be corrected."

"It was but the other day that I saw him break a pane of glass in the shop; and when I taxed him with it, he denied it;—and with such a face! I can't abide storytelling."

"Let me know the next story he tells; I'll cure him," said Mr. Morton, sternly. "You now how I broke Tom of it. Spare the rod, and spoil the child. And where I promised to be kind to the boy, of course I did not mean that I was not to take care of his morals, and see that he grew up an honest man. Tell truth and shame the devil—that's my motto."

"Spoke like yourself, Roger," said Mrs. Morton, with great animation. "But you see he has not had the advantage of such a father as you. I wonder your sister don't write to you. Some people make a great fuss about their feelings; but out of sight out of mind."

"I hope she is not ill. Poor Catherine! she looked in a very bad way when she was here," said Morton; and he turned uneasily to the fireplace and sighed.

Here the servant entered with the supper-tray, and the conversation fell upon other topics.

Mrs. Roger Morton's charge against Sidney was, alas! too true. He had acquired, under that roof, a terrible habit of telling stories. He had never incurred that vice with his mother, because then and there he had nothing to fear; now, he had everything to fear;—the grim aunt—even the quiet, kind, cold, austere uncle—the apprentices—the strange servants—and, oh! more than all, those hardeyed, loud-laughing tormentors, the boys of his own age! Naturally timid, severity made him actually a coward; and when the nerves tremble, a lie sounds as surely as, when I vibrate that wire, the bell at the end of it will ring. Beware of the man who has been roughly treated as a child.

The day after the conference just narrated, Mr. Morton, who was subject to erysipelas, had taken a little cooling medicine. He breakfasted, therefore, later than usual—after the rest of the family; and at this meal pour lui soulager he ordered the luxury of a muffin. Now it so chanced that he had only finished half the muffin, and drunk one cup of tea, when he was called into the shop by a customer of great importance—a prosy old lady, who always gave her orders with remarkable precision, and who valued herself on a character for affability, which she maintained by never buying a penny riband without asking the shopman how all his family were, and talking news about every other family in the place. At the time Mr. Morton left the parlour, Sidney and Master Tom were therein, seated on two stools, and casting up division sums on their respective slates—a point of education to which Mr. Morton attended with great care. As soon as his father's back was turned, Master Tom's eyes wandered from the slate to the muffin, as it leered at him from the slop-basin. Never did Pythian sibyl, seated above the bubbling spring, utter more oracular eloquence to her priest, than did that muffin—at least the parts of it yet extant—utter to the fascinated senses of Master Tom. First he sighed; then he moved round on his stool; then he got up; then he peered at the muffin from a respectful distance; then he gradually approached, and walked round, and round, and round it—his eyes getting bigger and bigger; then he peeped through the glass-door into the shop, and saw his father busily engaged with the old lady; then he began to calculate and philosophise, perhaps his father had done breakfast; perhaps he would not come back at all; if he came back, he would not miss one corner of the muffin; and if he did miss it, why should Tom be supposed to have taken it? As he thus communed with himself, he drew nearer into the fatal vortex, and at last with a desperate plunge, he seized the triangular temptation,—

"And ere a man had power to say 'Behold!'
The jaws of Thomas had devoured it up."

Sidney, disturbed from his studies by the agitation of his companion, witnessed this proceeding with great and conscientious alarm. "O Tom!" said he, "what will your papa say?"

"Look at that!" said Tom, putting his fist under Sidney's reluctant nose. "If father misses it, you'll say the cat took it. If you don't—my eye, what a wapping I'll give you!"

Here Mr. Morton's voice was heard wishing the lady "Good morning!" and Master Tom, thinking it better to leave the credit of the invention solely to Sidney, whispered, "Say I'm gone up stairs for my pocket-hanker," and hastily absconded.

Mr. Morton, already in a very bad humour, partly at the effects of the cooling medicine, partly at the suspension of his breakfast, stalked into the parlour. His tea-the second cup already poured out, was cold. He turned towards the muffin, and missed the lost piece at a glance.

"Who has been at my muffin?" said he, in a voice that seemed to Sidney like the voice he had always supposed an ogre to possess. "Have you, Master Sidney?"

"N—n—no, sir; indeed, sir!"

"Then Tom has. Where is he?"

"Gone up stairs for his handkerchief, sir."

"Did he take my muffin? Speak the truth!"

"No, sir; it was the—it was the—the cat, sir!"

"O you wicked, wicked boy!" cried Mrs. Morton, who had followed her husband into the parlour; "the cat kittened last night, and is locked up in the coal-cellar!"

"Come here, Master Sidney! No! first go down, Margaret, and see if the cat is in the cellar: it might have got out, Mrs. M.," said Mr. Morton, just even in his wrath.

Mrs. Morton went, and there was a dead silence, except indeed in Sidney's heart, which beat louder than a clock ticks. Mr. Morton, meanwhile, went to a little cupboard;—while still there, Mrs. Morton returned: the cat was in the cellar—the key turned on her—in no mood to eat muffins, poor thing!—she would not even lap her milk! like her mistress, she had had a very bad time!

"Now come here, sir," said Mr. Morton, withdrawing himself from the cupboard, with a small horsewhip in his hand, "I will teach you how to speak the truth in future! Confess that you have told a lie!"

"Yes, sir, it was a lie! Pray—pray forgive me: but Tom made me!"

"What! when poor Tom is up-stairs? worse and worse!" said Mrs. Morton, lifting up her hands and eyes. "What a viper!"

"For shame, boy,—for shame! Take that—and that—and that—"

Writhing—shrinking, still more terrified than hurt, the poor child cowered beneath the lash.

"Mamma! mamma!" he cried at last, "Oh, why—why did you leave me?"

At these words Mr. Morton stayed his hand, the whip fell to the ground.

"Yet it is all for the boy's good," he muttered. "There, child, I hope this is the last time. There, you are not much hurt. Zounds, don't cry so!"

"He will alarm the whole street," said Mrs. Morton; "I never see such a child! Here, take this parcel to Mrs. Birnie's—you know the house—only next street, and dry your eyes before you get there. Don't go through the shop; this way out."

She pushed the child, still sobbing with a vehemence that she could not comprehend, through the private passage into the street, and returned to her husband.

"You are convinced now, Mr. M.?"

"Pshaw! ma'am; don't talk. But, to be sure, that's how I cured Tom of fibbing.—The tea's as cold as a stone!"

CHAPTER IV

"Le bien nous le faisons: le mal c'est la Fortune.
On a toujours raison, le Destin toujours tort."—LA FONTAINE.

[The Good, we effect ourselves; the Evil is the handiwork of Fortune. Mortals are always in the right, Destiny always in the wrong.]

Upon the early morning of the day commemorated by the historical events of our last chapter, two men were deposited by a branch coach at the inn of a hamlet about ten miles distant from the town in which

Mr. Roger Morton resided. Though the hamlet was small, the inn was large, for it was placed close by a huge finger-post that pointed to three great roads: one led to the town before mentioned; another to the heart of a manufacturing district; and a third to a populous seaport. The weather was fine, and the two travellers ordered breakfast to be taken into an arbour in the garden, as well as the basins and towels necessary for ablution. The elder of the travellers appeared to be unequivocally foreign; you would have guessed him at once for a German. He wore, what was then very uncommon in this country, a loose, brown linen blouse, buttoned to the chin, with a leathern belt, into which were stuck a German meerschaum and a tobacco-pouch. He had very long flaxen hair, false or real, that streamed half-way down his back, large light mustaches, and a rough, sunburnt complexion, which made the fairness of the hair more remarkable. He wore an enormous pair of green spectacles, and complained much in broken English of the weakness of his eyes. All about him, even to the smallest minutiae, indicated the German; not only the large muscular frame, the broad feet, and vast though well-shaped hands, but the brooch—evidently purchased of a Jew in some great fair—stuck ostentatiously and superfluously into his stock; the quaint, droll-looking carpet-bag, which he refused to trust to the boots; and the great, massive, dingy ring which he wore on his forefinger. The other was a slender, remarkably upright and sinewy youth, in a blue frock, over which was thrown a large cloak, a travelling cap, with a shade that concealed all of the upper part of his face, except a dark quick eye of uncommon fire; and a shawl handkerchief, which was equally useful in concealing the lower part of the countenance. On descending from the coach, the German with some difficulty made the ostler understand that he wanted a post-chaise in a quarter of an hour; and then, without entering the house, he and his friend strolled to the arbour. While the maid-servant was covering the table with bread, butter, tea, eggs, and a huge round of beef, the German was busy in washing his hands, and talking in his national tongue to the young man, who returned no answer. But as soon as the servant had completed her operations the foreigner turned round, and observing her eyes fixed on his brooch with much female admiration, he made one stride to her.

"Der Teufel, my goot Madchen—but you are von var pretty—vat you call it?" and he gave her, as he spoke, so hearty a smack that the girl was more flustered than flattered by the courtesy.

"Keep yourself to yourself, sir!" said she, very tartly, for chambermaids never like to be kissed by a middle-aged gentleman when a younger one is by: whereupon the German replied by a pinch,—it is immaterial to state the exact spot to which that delicate caress was directed. But this last offence was so inexpiable, that the "Madchen" bounced off with a face of scarlet, and a "Sir, you are no gentleman—that's what you arn't!" The German thrust his head out of the arbour, and followed her with a loud laugh; then drawing himself in again, he said in quite another accent, and in excellent English, "There, Master Philip, we have got rid of the girl for the rest of the morning, and that's exactly what I wanted to do—women's wits are confoundedly sharp. Well, did I not tell you right, we have baffled all the bloodhounds!"

"And here, then, Gawtrey, we are to part," said Philip, mournfully.

"I wish you would think better of it, my boy," returned Mr. Gawtrey, breaking an egg; "how can you shift for yourself—no kith nor kin, not even that important machine for giving advice called a friend—no, not a friend, when I am gone? I foresee how it must end. [D— it, salt butter, by Jove!]"

"If I were alone in the world, as I have told you again and again, perhaps I might pin my fate to yours. But my brother!"

"There it is, always wrong when we act from our feelings. My whole life, which some day or other I will tell you, proves that. Your brother—bah! is he not very well off with his own uncle and aunt?—plenty to eat and drink, I dare say. Come, man, you must be as hungry as a hawk—a slice of the beef? Let well alone, and shift for yourself. What good can you do your brother?"

"I don't know, but I must see him; I have sworn it."

"Well, go and see him, and then strike across the country to me. I will wait a day for you,—there now!"

"But tell me first," said Philip, very earnestly, and fixing his dark eyes on his companion,—"tell me—yes, I must speak frankly—tell me, you who would link my fortunes with your own,—tell me, what and who are you?"

Gawtrey looked up.

"What do you suppose?" said he, dryly.

"I fear to suppose anything, lest I wrong you; but the strange place to which you took me the evening on which you saved me from pursuit, the persons I met there—"

"Well-dressed, and very civil to you?"

"True! but with a certain wild looseness in their talk that—But I have no right to judge others by mere appearance. Nor is it this that has made me anxious, and, if you will, suspicious."

"What then?"

"Your dress—your disguise."

"Disguised yourself!—ha! ha! Behold the world's charity! You fly from some danger, some pursuit, disguised—you, who hold yourself guiltless—I do the same, and you hold me criminal—a robber, perhaps—a murderer it may be! I will tell you what I am: I am a son of Fortune, an adventurer; I live by my wits—so do poets and lawyers, and all the charlatans of the world; I am a charlatan—a chameleon. 'Each man in his time plays many parts:' I play any part in which Money, the Arch-Manager, promises me a livelihood. Are you satisfied?"

"Perhaps," answered the boy, sadly, "when I know more of the world, I shall understand you better. Strange—strange, that you, out of all men, should have been kind to me in distress!"

"Not at all strange. Ask the beggar whom he gets the most pence from—the fine lady in her carriage—the beau smelling of eau de Cologne? Pish! the people nearest to being beggars themselves keep the beggar alive. You were friendless, and the man who has all earth for a foe befriends you. It is the way of the world, sir,—the way of the world. Come, eat while you can; this time next year you may have no beef to your bread."

Thus masticating and moralising at the same time, Mr. Gawtrey at last finished a breakfast that would have astonished the whole Corporation of London; and then taking out a large old watch, with an enamelled back—doubtless more German than its master—he said, as he lifted up his carpet-bag, "I must be off—tempos fugit, and I must arrive just in time to nick the vessels. Shall get to Ostend, or Rotterdam, safe and snug; thence to Paris. How my pretty Fan will have grown! Ah, you don't know Fan—make you a nice little wife one of these days! Cheer up, man, we shall meet again. Be sure of it; and hark ye, that strange place, as you call it, where I took you,—you can find it again?"

"Not I."

"Here, then, is the address. Whenever you want me, go there, ask to see Mr. Gregg—old fellow with one eye, you recollect—shake him by the hand just so—you catch the trick—practise it again. No, the forefinger thus, that's right. Say 'blater,' no more—'blater;'—stay, I will write it down for you; and then ask for William Gawtrey's direction. He will give it you at once, without questions—these signs understood; and if you want money for your passage, he will give you that also, with advice into the bargain. Always a warm welcome with me. And so take care of yourself, and good-bye. I see my chaise is at the door."

As he spoke, Gawtrey shook the young man's hand with cordial vigour, and strode off to his chaise, muttering, "Money well laid out—fee money; I shall have him, and, Gad, I like him,—poor devil!"

CHAPTER V

"He is a cunning coachman that can turn well in a narrow room."
Old Play: from Lamb's Specimens.

"Here are two pilgrims,
And neither knows one footstep of the way."
HEYWOOD's Duchess of Suffolk, Ibid.

The chaise had scarce driven from the inn-door when a coach stopped to change horses on its last stage to the town to which Philip was, bound. The name of the destination, in gilt letters on the coach-door, caught his eye, as he walked from the arbour towards the road, and in a few moments he was seated as the fourth passenger in the "Nelson Slow and Sure." From under the shade of his cap, he darted that quick, quiet glance, which a man who hunts, or is hunted,—in other words, who observes, or shuns,— soon acquires. At his left hand sat a young woman in a cloak lined with yellow; she had taken off her bonnet and pinned it to the roof of the coach, and looked fresh and pretty in a silk handkerchief, which she had tied round her head, probably to serve as a nightcap during the drowsy length of the journey. Opposite to her was a middle-aged man of pale complexion, and a grave, pensive, studious expression of face; and vis-a-vis to Philip sat an overdressed, showy, very good-looking man of about two or three and forty. This gentleman wore auburn whiskers, which met at the chin; a foraging cap, with a gold tassel; a velvet waistcoat, across which, in various folds, hung a golden chain, at the end of which dangled an eye-glass, that from time to time he screwed, as it were, into his right eye; he wore, also, a blue silk stock, with a frill much crumpled, dirty kid gloves, and over his lap lay a cloak lined with red silk. As Philip glanced towards this personage, the latter fixed his glass also at him, with a scrutinising stare, which drew fire from Philip's dark eyes. The man dropped his glass, and said in a half provincial, half haw-haw tone, like the stage exquisite of a minor theatre, "Pawdon me, and split legs!" therewith stretching himself between Philip's limbs in the approved fashion of inside passengers. A young man in a white great-coat now came to the door with a glass of warm sherry and water.

"You must take this—you must now; it will keep the cold out," (the day was broiling,) said he to the young woman.

"Gracious me!" was the answer, "but I never drink wine of a morning, James; it will get into my head."

"To oblige me!" said the young man, sentimentally; whereupon the young lady took the glass, and looking very kindly at her Ganymede, said, "Your health!" and sipped, and made a wry face—then she looked at the passengers, tittered, and said, "I can't bear wine!" and so, very slowly and daintily, sipped up the rest. A silent and expressive squeeze of the hand, on returning the glass, rewarded the young man, and proved the salutary effect of his prescription.

"All right!" cried the coachman: the ostler twitched the cloths from the leaders, and away went the "Nelson Slow and Sure," with as much pretension as if it had meant to do the ten miles in an hour. The pale gentleman took from his waistcoat pocket a little box containing gum-arabic, and having inserted a couple of morsels between his lips, he next drew forth a little thin volume, which from the manner the lines were printed was evidently devoted to poetry.

The smart gentleman, who since the episode of the sherry and water had kept his glass fixed upon the young lady, now said, with a genteel smirk:

"That young gentleman seems very auttentive, miss!"

"He is a very good young man, sir, and takes great care of me."

"Not your brother, miss,—eh?"

"La, sir—why not?"

"No faumily likeness—noice-looking fellow enough! But your oiyes and mouth—ah, miss!"

Miss turned away her head, and uttered with pert vivacity: "I never likes compliments, sir! But the young man is not my brother."

"A sweetheart,—eh? Oh fie, miss! Haw! haw!" and the auburn-whiskered Adonis poked Philip in the knee with one hand, and the pale gentleman in the ribs with the other. The latter looked up, and reproachfully; the former drew in his legs, and uttered an angry ejaculation.

"Well, sir, there is no harm in a sweetheart, is there?"

"None in the least, ma'am; I advoise you to double the dose. We often hear of two strings to a bow. Daun't you think it would be noicer to have two beaux to your string?" As he thus wittily expressed himself, the gentleman took off his cap, and thrust his fingers through a very curling and comely head of hair; the young lady looked at him with evident coquetry, and said, "How you do run on, you gentlemen!"

"I may well run on, miss, as long as I run aufter you," was the gallant reply.

Here the pale gentleman, evidently annoyed by being talked across, shut his book up, and looked round. His eye rested on Philip, who, whether from the heat of the day or from the forgetfulness of thought, had pushed his cap from his brows; and the gentleman, after staring at him for a few moments with great earnestness, sighed so heavily that it attracted the notice of all the passengers.

"Are you unwell, sir?" asked the young lady, compassionately.

"A little pain in my side, nothing more!"

"Chaunge places with me, sir," cried the Lothario, officiously. "Now do!" The pale gentleman, after a short hesitation, and a bashful excuse, accepted the proposal. In a few moments the young lady and the beau were in deep and whispered conversation, their heads turned towards the window. The pale gentleman continued to gaze at Philip, till the latter, perceiving the notice he excited, coloured, and replaced his cap over his face.

"Are you going to N—? asked the gentleman, in a gentle, timid voice.

"Yes!"

"Is it the first time you have ever been there?"

"Sir!" returned Philip, in a voice that spoke surprise and distaste at his neighbour's curiosity.

"Forgive me," said the gentleman, shrinking back; "but you remind me of-of—a family I once knew in the town. Do you know—the—the Mortons?"

One in Philip's situation, with, as he supposed, the officers of justice in his track (for Gawtrey, for reasons of his own, rather encouraged than allayed his fears), might well be suspicious. He replied therefore shortly, "I am quite a stranger to the town," and ensconced himself in the corner, as if to take a nap. Alas! that answer was one of the many obstacles he was doomed to build up between himself and a fairer fate.

The gentleman sighed again, and never spoke more to the end of the journey. When the coach halted at the inn,—the same inn which had before given its shelter to poor Catherine,—the young man in the white coat opened the door, and offered his arm to the young lady.

"Do you make any stay here, sir?" said she to the beau, as she unpinned her bonnet from the roof.

"Perhaps so; I am waiting for my phe-a-ton, which my faellow is to bring down,—tauking a little tour."

"We shall be very happy to see you, sir!" said the young lady, on whom the phe-a-ton completed the effect produced by the gentleman's previous gallantries; and with that she dropped into his hand a very neat card, on which was printed, "Wavers and Snow, Staymakers, High Street."

The beau put the card gracefully into his pocket—leaped from the coach—nudged aside his rival of the white coat, and offered his arm to the lady, who leaned on it affectionately as she descended.

"This gentleman has been so perlite to me, James," said she. James touched his hat; the beau clapped him on the shoulder,—"Ah! you are not a hauppy man,—are you? Oh no, not at all a hauppy man!—Good day to you! Guard, that hat-box is mine!"

While Philip was paying the coachman, the beau passed, and whispered him—

"Recollect old Gregg—anything on the lay here—don't spoil my sport if we meet!" and bustled off into the inn, whistling "God save the king!"

Philip started, then tried to bring to mind the faces which he had seen at the "strange place," and thought he recalled the features of his fellow-traveller. However, he did not seek to renew the acquaintance, but inquired the way to Mr. Morton's house, and thither he now proceeded.

He was directed, as a short cut, down one of those narrow passages at the entrance of which posts are placed as an indication that they are appropriated solely to foot-passengers. A dead white wall, which screened the garden of the physician of the place, ran on one side; a high fence to a nursery-ground was on the other; the passage was lonely, for it was now the hour when few persons walk either for business or pleasure in a provincial town, and no sound was heard save the fall of his own step on the broad flagstones. At the end of the passage in the main street to which it led, he saw already the large, smart, showy shop, with the hot sum shining full on the gilt letters that conveyed to the eyes of the customer the respectable name of "Morton,"—when suddenly the silence was broken by choked and painful sobs. He turned, and beneath a compo portico, jutting from the wall, which adorned the physician's door, he saw a child seated on the stone steps weeping bitterly—a thrill shot through Philip's heart! Did he recognise, disguised as it was by pain and sorrow, that voice? He paused, and laid his hand on the child's shoulder: "Oh, don't—don't—pray don't—I am going, I am indeed:" cried the child, quailing, and still keeping his hands clasped before his face.

"Sidney!" said Philip. The boy started to his feet, uttered a cry of rapturous joy, and fell upon his brother's breast.

"O Philip!—dear, dear Philip! you are come to take me away back to my own—own mamma; I will be so good, I will never tease her again,—never, never! I have been so wretched!"

"Sit down, and tell me what they have done to you," said Philip, checking the rising heart that heaved at his mother's name.

So, there they sat, on the cold stone under the stranger's porch, these two orphans: Philip's arms round his brother's waist, Sidney leaning on his shoulder, and imparting to him—perhaps with pardonable exaggeration, all the sufferings he had gone through; and, when he came to that morning's chastisement, and showed the wale across the little hands which he had vainly held up in supplication, Philip's passion shook him from limb to limb. His impulse was to march straight into Mr. Morton's shop and gripe him by the throat; and the indignation he betrayed encouraged Sidney to colour yet more highly the tale of his wrongs and pain.

When he had done, and clinging tightly to his brother's broad chest, said—

"But never mind, Philip; now we will go home to mamma."

Philip replied—

"Listen to me, my dear brother. We cannot go back to our mother. I will tell you why, later. We are alone in the world—we two! If you will come with me—God help you!—for you will have many hardships: we shall have to work and drudge, and you may be cold and hungry, and tired, very often, Sidney,—very, very often! But you know that, long ago, when I was so passionate, I never was wilfully unkind to you; and I declare now, that I would bite out my tongue rather than it should say a harsh word to you. That is all I can promise. Think well. Will you never miss all the comforts you have now?"

"Comforts!" repeated Sidney, ruefully, and looking at the wale over his hands. "Oh! let—let—let me go with you, I shall die if I stay here. I shall indeed—indeed!"

"Hush!" said Philip; for at that moment a step was heard, and the pale gentleman walked slowly down the passage, and started, and turned his head wistfully as he looked at the boys.

When he was gone. Philip rose.

"It is settled, then," said he, firmly. "Come with me at once. You shall return to their roof no more. Come, quick: we shall have many miles to go to-night."

CHAPTER VI

"He comes—
Yet careless what he brings; his one concern
Is to conduct it to the destined inn;
And having dropp'd the expected bag, pass on—
To him indifferent whether grief or joy."
COWPER: Description of the Postman.

The pale gentleman entered Mr. Morton's shop; and, looking round him, spied the worthy trader showing shawls to a young lady just married. He seated himself on a stool, and said to the bowing foreman—

"I will wait till Mr. Morton is disengaged."

The young lady having closely examined seven shawls, and declared they were beautiful, said, "she would think of it," and walked away. Mr. Morton now approached the stranger.

"Mr. Morton," said the pale gentleman; "you are very little altered. You do not recollect me?"

"Bless me, Mr. Spencer! is it really you? Well, what a time since we met! I am very glad to see you. And what brings you to N—? Business?"

"Yes, business. Let us go within?"

Mr. Morton led the way to the parlour, where Master Tom, reperched on the stool, was rapidly digesting the plundered muffin. Mr. Morton dismissed him to play, and the pale gentleman took a chair.

"Mr. Morton," said he, glancing over his dress, "you see I am in mourning. It is for your sister. I never got the better of that early attachment—never."

"My sister! Good Heavens!" said Mr. Morton, turning very pale; "is she dead? Poor Catherine!—and I not know of it! When did she die?"

"Not many days since; and—and—" said Mr. Spencer, greatly affected, "I fear in want. I had been abroad for some months: on my return last week, looking over the newspapers (for I always order them to be filed), I read the short account of her lawsuit against Mr. Beaufort, some time back. I resolved to find her out. I did so through the solicitor she employed: it was too late; I arrived at her lodgings two days after her—her burial. I then determined to visit poor Catherine's brother, and learn if anything could be done for the children she had left behind."

"She left but two. Philip, the elder, is very comfortably placed at R—; the younger has his home with me; and Mrs. Morton is a moth—that is to say, she takes great pains with him. Ehem! And my poor—poor sister!"

"Is he like his mother?"

"Very much, when she was young—poor dear Catherine!"

"What age is he?"

"About ten, perhaps; I don't know exactly; much younger than the other. And so she's dead!"

"Mr. Morton, I am an old bachelor" (here a sickly smile crossed Mr. Spencer's face); "a small portion of my fortune is settled, it is true, on my relations; but the rest is mine, and I live within my income. The elder of these boys is probably old enough to begin to take care of himself. But, the younger—perhaps you have a family of your own, and can spare him!"

Mr. Morton hesitated, and twitched up his trousers. "Why," said he, "this is very kind in you. I don't know—we'll see. The boy is out now; come and dine with us at two—pot-luck. Well, so she is no more! Heigho! Meanwhile, I'll talk it over with Mrs. M."

"I will be with you," said Mr. Spencer, rising.

"Ah!" sighed Mr. Morton, "if Catherine had but married you she would have been a happy woman."

"I would have tried to make her so," said Mr. Spencer, as he turned away his face and took his departure.

Two o'clock came; but no Sidney. They had sent to the place whither he had been despatched; he had never arrived there. Mr. Morton grew alarmed; and, when Mr. Spencer came to dinner, his host was gone in search of the truant. He did not return till three. Doomed that day to be belated both at breakfast and dinner, this decided him to part with Sidney whenever he should be found. Mrs. Morton was persuaded that the child only sulked, and would come back fast enough when he was hungry. Mr. Spencer tried to believe her, and ate his mutton, which was burnt to a cinder; but when five, six, seven o'clock came, and the boy was still missing,—even Mrs. Morton agreed that it was high time to institute a regular search. The whole family set off different ways. It was ten o'clock before they were reunited; and then all the news picked up was, that a boy, answering Sidney's description, had been seen with a young man in three several parts of the town; the last time at the outskirts, on the high road towards the manufacturing districts. These tidings so far relieved Mr. Morton's mind that he dismissed the chilling fear that had crept there,—that Sidney might have drowned himself. Boys will drown themselves sometimes! The description of the young man coincided so remarkably with the fellow-passenger of Mr. Spencer, that he did not doubt it was the same; the more so when he recollected having seen him with a fair-haired child under the portico; and yet more, when he recalled the likeness to Catherine that had struck him in the coach, and caused the inquiry that had roused Philip's suspicion. The mystery was thus made clear—Sidney had fled with his brother. Nothing more, however, could be done that night. The next morning, active measures should be devised; and when the morning came, the mail brought to Mr. Morton the two following letters. The first was from Arthur Beaufort.

"SIR,—I have been prevented by severe illness from writing to you before. I can now scarcely hold a pen; but the instant my health is recovered I shall be with you at N —, on her deathbed, the mother of the boy under your charge, Sidney Morton, committed him solemnly to me. I make his fortunes my care, and shall hasten to claim him at your kindly hands. But the elder son,—this poor Philip, who has suffered so unjustly,—for our lawyer has seen Mr. Plaskwith, and heard the whole story—what has become of him? All our inquiries have failed to track him. Alas, I was too ill to institute them myself while it was yet time. Perhaps he may have sought shelter, with you, his uncle; if so, assure him that he is in no danger from the pursuit of the law,—that his innocence is fully recognised; and that my father and myself implore him to accept our affection. I can write no more now; but in a few days I shall hope to see you.

"I am, sir, &c.,
"ARTHUR BEAUFORT.
"Berkely Square."

The second letter was from Mr. Plaskwith, and ran thus:

"DEAR MORTON,—Something very awkward has happened,—not my fault, and very unpleasant for me. Your relation, Philip, as I wrote you word, was a painstaking lad, though odd and bad mannered,—for want, perhaps, poor boy! of being taught better, and Mrs. P. is, you know, a very genteel woman—women go too much by manners—so she never took much to him. However, to the point, as the French emperor used to say: one evening he asked me for money for his mother, who, he said, was ill, in a very insolent way: I may say threatening. It was in my own shop, and before Plimmins and Mrs. P.; I was forced to answer with dignified rebuke, and left the shop. When I returned, he was gone, and some shillings-fourteen, I think, and three sovereigns—evidently from the till, scattered on the floor. Mrs. P. and Mr. Plimmins were very much frightened; thought it was clear I was robbed, and that we were to be murdered. Plimmins slept below that night, and we borrowed butcher Johnson's dog. Nothing happened. I did not think I was robbed; because the money, when we came to calculate, was all right. I know human nature. He had thought to take it, but repented—quite clear. However, I was naturally very angry, thought he'd comeback again—meant to reprove him properly—waited several days—heard nothing of him—grew uneasy—would not attend longer to Mrs. P.; for, as Napoleon Buonaparte observed, 'women are well in their way, not in ours.' Made Plimmins go with me to town—hired a Bow Street runner to track him out—cost me £1. 1s, and two glasses of brandy and water. Poor Mrs. Morton was just buried—quite shocked! Suddenly saw the boy in the streets. Plimmins rushed forward in the kindest way—was knocked down—hurt his arm—paid 2s. 6d. for lotion. Philip ran off, we ran after him—could not find him. Forced to return home. Next day, a lawyer from a Mr. Beaufort—Mr. George Blackwell, a gentlemanlike man called. Mr. Beaufort will do anything for him in reason. Is there anything more I can do? I really am very uneasy about the lad, and Mrs. P. and I have a tiff about it: but that's nothing—thought I had best write to you for instructions.

"Yours truly,
"C. PLASHWITH.

"P. S.—Just open my letter to say, Bow Street officer just been here—has found out that the boy has been seen with a very suspicious character: they think he has left London. Bow Street officer wants to go after him—very expensive: so now you can decide."

Mr. Spencer scarcely listened to Mr. Plaskwith's letter, but of Arthur's he felt jealous. He would fain have been the only protector to Catherine's children; but he was the last man fitted to head the search, now so necessary to prosecute with equal tact and energy.

A soft-hearted, soft-headed man, a confirmed valtudinarian, a day-dreamer, who had wasted away his life in dawdling and maundering over Simple Poetry, and sighing over his unhappy attachment; no child, no babe, was more thoroughly helpless than Mr. Spencer.

The task of investigation devolved, therefore, on Mr. Morton, and he went about it in a regular, plain, straightforward way. Hand-bills were circulated, constables employed, and a lawyer, accompanied by Mr. Spencer, despatched to the manufacturing districts: towards which the orphans had been seen to direct their path.

CHAPTER VII

*"Give the gentle South
Yet leave to court these sails."*
BEAUMONT AND FLLTCHER: *Beggar's Bush.*

*"Cut your cloth, sir,
According to your calling."—Ibid.*

Meanwhile the brothers were far away, and He who feeds the young ravens made their paths pleasant to their feet. Philip had broken to Sidney the sad news of their mother's death, and Sidney had wept with bitter passion. But children,—what can they know of death? Their tears over graves dry sooner than the dews. It is melancholy to compare the depth, the endurance, the far-sighted, anxious, prayerful love of a parent, with the inconsiderate, frail, and evanescent affection of the infant, whose eyes the hues of the butterfly yet dazzle with delight. It was the night of their flight, and in the open air, when Philip (his arms round Sidney's waist) told his brother-orphan that they were motherless. And the air was balmy, the skies filled with the effulgent presence of the August moon; the cornfields stretched round them wide and far, and not a leaf trembled on the beech-tree beneath which they had sought shelter. It seemed as if Nature herself smiled pityingly on their young sorrow, and said to them, "Grieve not for the dead: I, who live for ever, I will be your mother!"

They crept, as the night deepened, into the warmer sleeping-place afforded by stacks of hay, mown that summer and still fragrant. And the next morning the birds woke them betimes, to feel that Liberty, at least, was with them, and to wander with her at will.

Who in his boyhood has not felt the delight of freedom and adventure? to have the world of woods and sward before him—to escape restriction—to lean, for the first time, on his own resources—to rejoice in the wild but manly luxury of independence—to act the Crusoe—and to fancy a Friday in every footprint—an island of his own in every field? Yes, in spite of their desolation, their loss, of the melancholy past, of the friendless future, the orphans were happy—happy in their youth—their freedom—their love—their wanderings in the delicious air of the glorious August. Sometimes they came upon knots of reapers lingering in the shade of the hedge-rows over their noonday meal; and, grown sociable by travel, and bold by safety, they joined and partook of the rude fare with the zest of fatigue and youth. Sometimes, too, at night, they saw, gleam afar and red by the woodside, the fires of gipsy tents. But these, with the superstition derived from old nursery-tales, they scrupulously shunned, eying them with a mysterious awe! What heavenly twilights belong to that golden month!—the air so lucidly serene, as the purple of the clouds fades gradually away, and up soars, broad, round, intense, and luminous, the full moon which belongs to the joyous season! The fields then are greener than in the heats of July and June,—they have got back the luxury of a second spring. And still, beside the paths of the travellers, lingered on the hedges the clustering honeysuckle—the convolvulus glittered in the tangles of the brake—the hardy heathflower smiled on the green waste.

And ever, at evening, they came, field after field, upon those circles which recall to children so many charmed legends, and are fresh and frequent in that month—the Fairy Rings! They thought, poor boys! that it was a good omen, and half fancied that the Fairies protected them, as in the old time they had often protected the desolate and outcast.

They avoided the main roads, and all towns, with suspicious care. But sometimes they paused, for food and rest, at the obscure hostel of some scattered hamlet: though, more often, they loved to spread the simple food they purchased by the way under some thick tree, or beside a stream through whose limpid waters they could watch the trout glide and play. And they often preferred the chance shelter of a haystack, or a shed, to the less romantic repose offered by the small inns they alone dared to enter. They went in this much by the face and voice of the host or hostess. Once only Philip had entered a town, on the second day of their flight, and that solely for the purchase of ruder clothes, and a change of linen for Sidney, with some articles and implements of use necessary in their present course of shift and welcome hardship. A wise precaution; for, thus clad, they escaped suspicion.

So journeying, they consumed several days; and, having taken a direction quite opposite to that which led to the manufacturing districts, whither pursuit had been directed, they were now in the centre of another county—in the neighbourhood of one of the most considerable towns of England; and here Philip began to think their wanderings ought to cease, and it was time to settle on some definite course of life. He had carefully hoarded about his person, and most thriftily managed, the little fortune bequeathed by his mother. But Philip looked on this capital as a deposit sacred to Sidney; it was not to be spent, but kept and augmented—the nucleus for future wealth. Within the last few weeks his character was greatly ripened, and his powers of thought enlarged. He was no more a boy,—he was a man: he had another life to take care of. He resolved, then, to enter the town they were approaching, and to seek for some situation by which he might maintain both. Sidney was very loath to abandon their present roving life; but he allowed that the warm weather could not always last, and that in winter the fields would be less pleasant. He, therefore, with a sigh, yielded to his brother's reasonings.

They entered the fair and busy town of one day at noon; and, after finding a small lodging, at which he deposited Sidney, who was fatigued with their day's walk, Philip sallied forth alone.

After his long rambling, Philip was pleased and struck with the broad bustling streets, the gay shops—the evidences of opulence and trade. He thought it hard if he could not find there a market for the health and heart of sixteen. He strolled slowly and alone along the streets, till his attention was caught by a small corner shop, in the window of which was placed a board, bearing this inscription:

"OFFICE FOR EMPLOYMENT.—RECIPROCAL ADVANTAGE.

"Mr. John Clump's bureau open every day, from ten till four. Clerks, servants, labourers, &c., provided with suitable situations. Terms moderate. N.B.—The oldest established office in the town.

"Wanted, a good cook. An under gardener."

What he sought was here! Philip entered, and saw a short fat man with spectacles, seated before a desk, poring upon the well-filled leaves of a long register.

"Sir," said Philip, "I wish for a situation. I don't care what."

"Half-a-crown for entry, if you please. That's right. Now for particulars. Hum!—you don't look like a servant!"

"No; I wish for any place where my education can be of use. I can read and write; I know Latin and French; I can draw; I know arithmetic and summing."

"Very well; very genteel young man—prepossessing appearance (that's a fudge!), highly educated; usher in a school, eh?"

"What you like."

"References?"

"I have none."

"Eh!—none?" and Mr. Clump fixed his spectacles full upon Philip.

Philip was prepared for the question, and had the sense to perceive that a frank reply was his best policy. "The fact is," said he boldly, "I was well brought up; my father died; I was to be bound apprentice to a trade I disliked; I left it, and have now no friends."

"If I can help you, I will," said Mr. Clump, coldly. "Can't promise much. If you were a labourer, character might not matter; but educated young men must have a character. Hands always more useful than head. Education no avail nowadays; common, quite common. Call again on Monday."

Somewhat disappointed and chilled, Philip turned from the bureau; but he had a strong confidence in his own resources, and recovered his spirits as he mingled with the throng. He passed, at length, by a livery-stable, and paused, from old associations, as he saw a groom in the mews attempting to manage a young, hot horse, evidently unbroken. The master of the stables, in a green short jacket and top-boots, with a long whip in his hand, was standing by, with one or two men who looked like horsedealers.

"Come off, clumsy! you can't manage that I 'ere fine hanimal," cried the liveryman. "Ah! he's a lamb, sir, if he were backed properly. But I has not a man in the yard as can ride since Will died. Come off, I say, lubber!"

But to come off, without being thrown off, was more easily said than done. The horse was now plunging as if Juno had sent her gadfly to him; and Philip, interested and excited, came nearer and nearer, till he stood by the side of the horse-dealers. The other ostlers ran to the help of their comrade, who at last, with white lips and shaking knees, found himself on terra firma; while the horse, snorting hard, and rubbing his head against the breast and arms of the ostler, who held him tightly by the rein, seemed to ask, in his own way, "Are there any more of you?"

A suspicion that the horse was an old acquaintance crossed Philip's mind; he went up to him, and a white spot over the left eye confirmed his doubts. It had been a foal reserved and reared for his own riding! one that, in his prosperous days, had ate bread from his hand, and followed him round the paddock like a dog; one that he had mounted in sport, without saddle, when his father's back was turned; a friend, in short, of the happy Lang syne;—nay, the very friend to whom he had boasted his affection, when, standing with Arthur Beaufort under the summer sky, the whole world seemed to him full of friends. He put his hand on the horse's neck, and whispered, "Soho! So, Billy!" and the horse turned sharp round with a quick joyous neigh.

"If you please, sir," said Philip, appealing to the liveryman, "I will undertake to ride this horse, and take him over yon leaping-bar. Just let me try him."

"There's a fine-spirited lad for you!" said the liveryman, much pleased at the offer. "Now, gentlemen, did I not tell you that 'ere hanimal had no vice if he was properly managed?"

The horse-dealers shook their heads.

"May I give him some bread first?" asked Philip; and the ostler was despatched to the house. Meanwhile the animal evinced various signs of pleasure and recognition, as Philip stroked and talked to him; and, finally, when he ate the bread from the young man's hand, the whole yard seemed in as much delight and surprise as if they had witnessed one of Monsieur Van Amburgh's exploits.

And now, Philip, still caressing the horse, slowly and cautiously mounted; the animal made one bound half-across the yard—a bound which sent all the horse-dealers into a corner—and then went through his paces, one after the other, with as much ease and calm as if he had been broken in at Mr. Fozard's to carry a young lady. And when he crowned all by going thrice over the leaping-bar, and Philip, dismounting, threw the reins to the ostler, and turned triumphantly to the horse-dealer, that gentleman slapped him on the back, and said, emphatically, "Sir, you are a man! and I am proud to see you here."

Meanwhile the horse-dealers gathered round the animal; looked at his hoofs, felt his legs, examined his windpipe, and concluded the bargain, which, but for Philip, would have been very abruptly broken off. When the horse was led out of the yard, the liveryman, Mr. Stubmore, turned to Philip, who, leaning against the wall, followed the poor animal with mournful eyes.

"My good sir, you have sold that horse for me—that you have! Anything as I can do for you? One good turn deserves another. Here's a brace of shiners."

"Thank you, sir! I want no money, but I do want some employment. I can be of use to you, perhaps, in your establishment. I have been brought up among horses all my life."

"Saw it, sir! that's very clear. I say, that 'ere horse knows you!" and the dealer put his finger to his nose.

"Quite right to be mum! He was bred by an old customer of mine—famous rider!—Mr. Beaufort. Aha! that's where you knew him, I s'pose. Were you in his stables?"

"Hem—I knew Mr. Beaufort well."

"Did you? You could not know a better man. Well, I shall be very glad to engage you, though you seem by your hands to be a bit of a gentleman—eh? Never mind; don't want you to groom!—but superintend things. D'ye know accounts, eh?"

"Yes."

"Character?"

Philip repeated to Mr. Stubmore the story he had imparted to Mr. Clump. Somehow or other, men who live much with horses are always more lax in their notions than the rest of mankind. Mr. Stubmore did not seem to grow more distant at Philip's narration.

"Understand you perfectly, my man. Brought up with them 'ere fine creturs, how could you nail your nose to a desk? I'll take you without more palaver. What's your name?"

"Philips."

"Come to-morrow, and we'll settle about wages. Sleep here?"

"No. I have a brother whom I must lodge with, and for whose sake I wish to work. I should not like him to be at the stables—he is too young. But I can come early every day, and go home late."

"Well, just as you like, my man. Good day."

And thus, not from any mental accomplishment—not from the result of his intellectual education, but from the mere physical capacity and brute habit of sticking fast on his saddle, did Philip Morton, in this great, intelligent, gifted, civilised, enlightened community of Great Britain, find the means of earning his bread without stealing it.

CHAPTER VIII

"Don Salluste (souriunt). Je paire
Que vous ne pensiez pas a moi?"—Ruy Blas.

"Don Salluste. Cousin!
Don Cesar. De vos bienfaits je n'aurai nulle envie,
Tant que je trouverai vivant ma libre vie."—Ibid.

Don Sallust (smiling). I'll lay a wager you won't think of me?
Don Sallust. Cousin!
Don Caesar. I covet not your favours, so but I lead an independent life.

Phillip's situation was agreeable to his habits. His great courage and skill in horsemanship were not the only qualifications useful to Mr. Stubmore: his education answered a useful purpose in accounts, and his manners and appearance were highly to the credit of the yard. The customers and loungers soon grew to like Gentleman Philips, as he was styled in the establishment. Mr. Stubmore conceived a real affection for him. So passed several weeks; and Philip, in this humble capacity, might have worked out his destinies in peace and comfort, but for a new cause of vexation that arose in Sidney. This boy was all in all to his brother. For him he had resisted the hearty and joyous invitations of Gawtrey (whose gay manner and high spirits had, it must be owned, captivated his fancy, despite the equivocal mystery of the man's avocations and condition); for him he now worked and toiled, cheerful and contented; and him he sought to save from all to which he subjected himself. He could not bear that that soft and delicate child should ever be exposed to the low and menial associations that now made up his own life—to the obscene slang of grooms and ostlers—to their coarse manners and rough contact. He kept him, therefore, apart and aloof in their little lodging, and hoped in time to lay by, so that Sidney might ultimately be restored, if not to his bright original sphere, at least to a higher grade than that to which Philip was himself condemned. But poor Sidney could not bear to be thus left alone—to lose sight of his brother from daybreak till bed-time—to have no one to amuse him; he fretted and pined away: all the little inconsiderate selfishness, uneradicated from his breast by his sufferings, broke out the more, the more he felt that he was the first object on earth to Philip. Philip, thinking he might be more cheerful at a day-school, tried the experiment of placing him at one where the boys were much of his own age. But Sidney, on the third day, came back with a black eye, and he would return no more. Philip several times thought of changing their lodging for one where there were young people. But Sidney had taken a fancy to the kind old widow who was their landlady, and cried at the thought of removal. Unfortunately, the old woman was deaf and rheumatic; and though she bore teasing ad libitum, she could not entertain the child long on a stretch. Too young to be reasonable, Sidney could not, or would not, comprehend why his brother was so long away from him; and once he said, peevishly,—

"If I had thought I was to be moped up so, I would not have left Mrs. Morton. Tom was a bad boy, but still it was somebody to play with. I wish I had not gone away with you!"

This speech cut Philip to the heart. What, then, he had taken from the child a respectable and safe shelter—the sure provision of a life—and the child now reproached him! When this was said to him, the tears gushed from his eyes. "God forgive me, Sidney," said he, and turned away.

But then Sidney, who had the most endearing ways with him, seeing his brother so vexed, ran up and kissed him, and scolded himself for being naughty. Still the words were spoken, and their meaning rankled deep. Philip himself, too, was morbid in his excessive tenderness for this boy. There is a certain age, before the love for the sex commences, when the feeling of friendship is almost a passion. You see it constantly in girls and boys at school. It is the first vague craving of the heart after the master food of human life—Love. It has its jealousies, and humours, and caprices, like love itself. Philip was painfully acute to Sidney's affection, was jealous of every particle of it. He dreaded lest his brother should ever be torn from him.

He would start from his sleep at night, and go to Sidney's bed to see that he was there. He left him in the morning with forebodings—he returned in the dark with fear. Meanwhile the character of this young man, so sweet and tender to Sidney, was gradually becoming more hard and stern to others. He had now climbed to the post of command in that rude establishment; and premature command in any sphere tends to make men unsocial and imperious.

One day Mr. Stubmore called him into his own countinghouse, where stood a gentleman, with one hand in his coatpocket, the other tapping his whip against his boot.

"Philips, show this gentleman the brown mare. She is a beauty in harness, is she not? This gentleman wants a match for his pheaton."

"She must step very hoigh," said the gentleman, turning round: and Philip recognised the beau in the stage-coach. The recognition was simultaneous. The beau nodded, then whistled, and winked.

"Come, my man, I am at your service," said he.

Philip, with many misgivings, followed him across the yard. The gentleman then beckoned him to approach.

"You, sir,—moind, I never peach—setting up here in the honest line? Dull work, honesty,—eh?"

"Sir, I really don't know you."

"Daun't you recollect old Greggs, the evening you came there with jolly Bill Gawtrey? Recollect that, eh?" Philip was mute.

"I was among the gentlemen in the back parlour who shook you by the hand. Bill's off to France, then. I am tauking the provinces. I want a good horse—the best in the yard, moind! Cutting such a swell here! My name is Captain de Burgh Smith—never moind yours, my fine faellow. Now, then, out with your rattlers, and keep your tongue in your mouth."

Philip mechanically ordered out the brown mare, which Captain Smith did not seem much to approve of; and, after glancing round the stables with great disdain of the collection, he sauntered out of the yard without saying more to Philip, though he stopped and spoke a few sentences to Mr. Stubmore. Philip hoped he had no design of purchasing, and that he was rid, for the present, of so awkward a customer. Mr. Stubmore approached Philip.

"Drive over the greys to Sir John," said he. "My lady wants a pair to job. A very pleasant man, that Captain Smith. I did not know you had been in a yard before—says you were the pet at Elmore's in London. Served him many a day. Pleasant, gentlemanlike man!"

"Y-e-s!" said Philip, hardly knowing what he said, and hurrying back into the stables to order out the greys. The place to which he was bound was some miles distant, and it was sunset when he returned. As he drove into the main street, two men observed him closely.

"That is he! I am almost sure it is," said one. "Oh! then it's all smooth sailing," replied the other.

"But, bless my eyes! you must be mistaken! See whom he's talking to now!"

At that moment Captain de Burgh Smith, mounted on the brown mare, stopped Philip.

"Well, you see, I've bought her,—hope she'll turn out well. What do you really think she's worth? Not to buy, but to sell?"

"Sixty guineas."

"Well, that's a good day's work; and I owe it to you. The old faellow would not have trusted me if you had not served me at Elmore's—ha! ha! If he gets scent and looks shy at you, my lad, come to me. I'm at the Star Hotel for the next few days. I want a tight faellow like you, and you shall have a fair percentage. I'm none of your stingy ones. I say, I hope this devil is quiet? She cocks up her ears dawmnably!"

"Look you, sir!" said Philip, very gravely, and rising up in his break; "I know very little of you, and that little is not much to your credit. I give you fair warning that I shall caution my employer against you."

"Will you, my fine faellow? then take care of yourself."

"Stay, and if you dare utter a word against me," said Philip, with that frown to which his swarthy complexion and flashing eyes gave an expression of fierce power beyond his years, "you will find that, as I am the last to care for a threat, so I am the first to resent an injury!"

Thus saying, he drove on. Captain Smith affected a cough, and put his brown mare into a canter. The two men followed Philip as he drove into the yard.

"What do you know against the person he spoke to?" said one of them.

"Merely that he is one of the cunningest swells on this side the Bay," returned the other. "It looks bad for your young friend."

The first speaker shook his head and made no reply.

On gaining the yard, Philip found that Mr. Stubmore had gone out, and was not expected home till the next day. He had some relations who were farmers, whom he often visited; to them he was probably gone.

Philip, therefore, deferring his intended caution against the gay captain till the morrow, and musing how the caution might be most discreetly given, walked homeward. He had just entered the lane that led to his lodgings, when he saw the two men I have spoken of on the other side of the street. The taller and better-dressed of the two left his comrade; and crossing over to Philip, bowed, and thus accosted him,—

"Fine evening, Mr. Philip Morton. I am rejoiced to see you at last. You remember me—Mr. Blackwell, Lincoln's Inn."

"What is your business?" said Philip, halting, and speaking short and fiercely.

"Now don't be in a passion, my dear sir,—now don't. I am here on behalf of my clients, Messrs. Beaufort, sen. and jun. I have had such work to find you! Dear, dear! but you are a sly one! Ha! ha! Well, you see we have settled that little affair of Plaskwith's for you (might have been ugly), and now I hope you will—"

"To your business, sir! What do you want with me?"

"Why, now, don't be so quick! 'Tis not the way to do business. Suppose you step to my hotel. A glass of wine now, Mr. Philip! We shall soon understand each other."

"Out of my path, or speak plainly!"

Thus put to it, the lawyer, casting a glance at his stout companion, who appeared to be contemplating the sunset on the other side of the way, came at once to the marrow of his subject.

"Well, then,—well, my say is soon said. Mr. Arthur Beaufort takes a most lively interest in you; it is he who has directed this inquiry. He bids me say that he shall be most happy—yes, most happy—to serve you in anything; and if you will but see him, he is in the town, I am sure you will be charmed with him—most amiable young man!"

"Look you, sir," said Philip, drawing himself up "neither from father, nor from son, nor from one of that family, on whose heads rest the mother's death and the orphans' curse, will I ever accept boon or benefit—with them, voluntarily, I will hold no communion; if they force themselves in my path, let them beware! I am earning my bread in the way I desire—I am independent—I want them not. Begone!"

With that, Philip pushed aside the lawyer and strode on rapidly. Mr. Blackwell, abashed and perplexed, returned to his companion.

Philip regained his home, and found Sidney stationed at the window alone, and with wistful eyes noting the flight of the grey moths as they darted to and fro, across the dull shrubs that, variegated with lines for washing, adorned the plot of ground which the landlady called a garden. The elder brother had returned at an earlier hour than usual, and Sidney did not at first perceive him enter. When he did he clapped his hands, and ran to him.

"This is so good in you, Philip. I have been so dull; you will come and play now?"

"With all my heart—where shall we play?" said Philip, with a cheerful smile.

"Oh, in the garden!—it's such a nice time for hide and seek."

"But is it not chill and damp for you?" said Philip.

"There now; you are always making excuses. I see you don't like it. I have no heart to play now."

Sidney seated himself and pouted.

"Poor Sidney! you must be dull without me. Yes, let us play; but put on this handkerchief;" and Philip took off his own cravat and tied it round his brother's neck, and kissed him.

Sidney, whose anger seldom lasted long, was reconciled; and they went into the garden to play. It was a little spot, screened by an old moss-grown paling, from the neighbouring garden on the one side and a lane on the other. They played with great glee till the night grew darker and the dews heavier.

"This must be the last time," cried Philip. "It is my turn to hide."

"Very well! Now, then."

Philip secreted himself behind a poplar; and as Sidney searched for him, and Philip stole round and round the tree, the latter, happening to look across the paling, saw the dim outline of a man's figure in the lane, who appeared watching them. A thrill shot across his breast. These Beauforts, associated in his thoughts with every evil omen and augury, had they set a spy upon his movements? He remained erect and gazing at the form, when Sidney discovered, and ran up to him, with his noisy laugh.

As the child clung to him, shouting with gladness, Philip, unheeding his playmate, called aloud and imperiously to the stranger—

"What are you gaping at? Why do you stand watching us?"

The man muttered something, moved on, and disappeared. "I hope there are no thieves here! I am so much afraid of thieves," said Sidney, tremulously.

The fear grated on Philip's heart. Had he not himself, perhaps, been judged and treated as a thief? He said nothing, but drew his brother within; and there, in their little room, by the one poor candle, it was touching and beautiful to see these boys—the tender patience of the elder lending itself to every whim of the younger—now building houses with cards—now telling stories of fairy and knight-errant—the sprightliest he could remember or invent. At length, as all was over, and Sidney was undressing for the night, Philip, standing apart, said to him, in a mournful voice:—

"Are you sad now, Sidney?"

"No! not when you are with me—but that is so seldom."

"Do you read none of the story-books I bought for you?"

"Sometimes! but one can't read all day."

"Ah! Sidney, if ever we should part, perhaps you will love me no longer!"

"Don't say so," said Sidney. "But we sha'n't part, Philip?"

Philip sighed, and turned away as his brother leaped into bed. Something whispered to him that danger was near; and as it was, could Sidney grow up, neglected and uneducated; was it thus that he was to fulfil his trust?

CHAPTER IX

"But oh, what storm was in that mind!"—CRABBE. Ruth

While Philip mused, and his brother fell into the happy sleep of childhood, in a room in the principal hotel of the town sat three persons, Arthur Beaufort, Mr. Spencer, and Mr. Blackwell.

"And so," said the first, "he rejected every overture from the Beauforts?"

"With a scorn I cannot convey to you!" replied the lawyer. "But the fact is, that he is evidently a lad of low habits; to think of his being a sort of helper to a horse dealer! I suppose, sir, he was always in the stables in his father's time. Bad company depraves the taste very soon; but that is not the worst. Sharp declares that the man he was talking with, as I told you, is a common swindler. Depend on it, Mr. Arthur, he is incorrigible; all we can do is to save the brother."

"It is too dreadful to contemplate!" said Arthur, who, still ill and languid, reclined on a sofa.

"It is, indeed," said Mr. Spencer; "I am sure I should not know what to do with such a character; but the other poor child, it would be a mercy to get hold of him."

"Where is Mr. Sharp?" asked Arthur.

"Why," said the lawyer, "he has followed Philip at a distance to find out his lodgings, and learn if his brother is with him. Oh! here he is!" and Blackwell's companion in the earlier part of the evening entered.

"I have found him out, sir," said Mr. Sharp, wiping his forehead. "What a fierce 'un he is! I thought he would have had a stone at my head; but we officers are used to it; we does our duty, and Providence makes our heads unkimmon hard!"

"Is the child with him?" asked Mr. Spencer.

"Yes, sir."

"A little, quiet, subdued boy?" asked the melancholy inhabitant of the Lakes.

"Quiet! Lord love you! never heard a noisier little urchin! There they were, romping and romping in the garden, like a couple of gaol birds."

"You see," groaned Mr. Spencer, "he will make that poor child as bad as himself."

"What shall us do, Mr. Blackwell?" asked Sharp, who longed for his brandy and water.

"Why, I was thinking you might go to the horse-dealer the first thing in the morning; find out whether Philip is really thick with the swindler; and, perhaps, Mr. Stubmore may have some influence with him, if, without saying who he is—"

"Yes," interrupted Arthur, "do not expose his name."

"You could still hint that he ought to be induced to listen to his friends and go with them. Mr. Stubmore may be a respectable man, and—"

"I understand," said Sharp; "I have no doubt as how I can settle it. We learns to know human natur in our profession;—'cause why? we gets at its blind side. Good night, gentlemen!"

"You seem very pale, Mr. Arthur; you had better go to bed; you promised your father, you know."

"Yes, I am not well; I will go to bed;" and Arthur rose, lighted his candle, and sought his room.

"I will see Philip to-morrow," he said to himself; "he will listen to me."

The conduct of Arthur Beaufort in executing the charge he had undertaken had brought into full light all the most amiable and generous part of his character. As soon as he was sufficiently recovered, he had expressed so much anxiety as to the fate of the orphans, that to quiet him his father was forced to send for Mr. Blackwell. The lawyer had ascertained, through Dr. —, the name of Philip's employer at R—. At Arthur's request he went down to Mr. Plaskwith; and arriving there the day after the return of the bookseller, learned those particulars with which Mr. Plaskwith's letter to Roger Morton has already made the reader acquainted. The lawyer then sent for Mr. Sharp, the officer before employed, and commissioned him to track the young man's whereabout. That shrewd functionary soon reported that a youth every way answering to Philip's description had been introduced the night of the escape by a man celebrated, not indeed for robberies, or larcenies, or crimes of the coarser kind, but for address in all that more large and complex character which comes under the denomination of living upon one's wits, to a polite rendezvous frequented by persons of a similar profession. Since then, however, all clue of Philip was lost. But though Mr. Blackwell, in the way of his profession, was thus publicly benevolent towards the fugitive, he did not the less privately represent to his patrons, senior and junior, the very equivocal character that Philip must be allowed to bear. Like most lawyers, hard upon all who wander from the formal tracks, he unaffectedly regarded Philip's flight and absence as proofs of a reprobate disposition; and this conduct was greatly aggravated in his eyes by Mr. Sharp's report, by which it appeared that after his escape Philip had so suddenly, and, as it were, so naturally, taken to such equivocal companionship. Mr. Robert Beaufort, already prejudiced against Philip, viewed matters in the same light as the lawyer; and the story of his supposed predilections reached Arthur's ears in so distorted a shape, that even he was staggered and revolted:—still Philip was so young—Arthur's oath to the orphans' mother so recent—and if thus early inclined to wrong courses, should not every effort be made to lure him back to the straight path? With these views and reasonings, as soon as he was able, Arthur himself visited Mrs. Lacy, and the note from Philip, which the good lady put into his hands, affected him deeply, and confirmed all his previous resolutions. Mrs. Lacy was very anxious to get at his name; but Arthur, having heard that Philip had refused all aid from his father and Mr. Blackwell, thought that the young man's pride might work equally against himself, and therefore evaded the landlady's curiosity. He wrote the next day the letter we have seen, to Mr. Roger Morton, whose address Catherine had given to him; and by return of post came a letter from the linendraper narrating the flight of Sidney, as it was supposed with his brother. This news so excited Arthur that he insisted on going down to N— at once, and joining in the search. His father, alarmed for his health, positively refused; and the consequence was an increase of fever, a consultation with the doctors, and a declaration that Mr. Arthur was in that state that it would be dangerous not to let him have his own way, Mr. Beaufort was forced to yield, and with Blackwell and Mr. Sharp accompanied his son to N—. The inquiries, hitherto fruitless, then assumed a more regular and business-like character. By little and little they came, through the aid of Mr. Sharp, upon the right clue, up to a certain point. But here there was a double scent: two youths answering the description, had been seen at a small village; then there came those who asserted that they had seen the same youths at a seaport in one direction; others, who deposed to their having taken the road to an inland town in the other. This had induced Arthur and his father to part company. Mr. Beaufort, accompanied by Roger Morton, went to the seaport; and Arthur, with Mr. Spencer and Mr. Sharp, more fortunate, tracked the fugitives to their retreat. As for Mr. Beaufort, senior, now that his mind was more at ease about his son, he was thoroughly sick of the whole thing; greatly bored by the society of Mr. Morton; very much ashamed that he, so respectable and great a man, should be employed on such an errand; more afraid of, than pleased with, any chance of discovering the fierce Philip; and secretly resolved upon slinking back to London at the first reasonable excuse.

The next morning Mr. Sharp entered betimes Mr. Stubmore's counting-house. In the yard he caught a glimpse of Philip, and managed to keep himself unseen by that young gentleman.

"Mr. Stubmore, I think?"

"At your service, sir."

Mr. Sharp shut the glass door mysteriously, and lifting up the corner of a green curtain that covered the panes, beckoned to the startled Stubmore to approach.

"You see that 'ere young man in the velveteen jacket? you employs him?"

"I do, sir; he's my right hand."

"Well, now, don't be frightened, but his friends are arter him. He has got into bad ways, and we want you to give him a little good advice."

"Pooh! I know he has run away, like a fine-spirited lad as he is; and as long as he likes to stay with me, they as comes after him may get a ducking in the horse-trough!"

"Be you a father? a father of a family, Mr. Stubmore?" said Sharp, thrusting his hands into his breeches pockets, swelling out his stomach, and pursing up his lips with great solemnity.

"Nonsense! no gammon with me! Take your chaff to the goslings. I tells you I can't do without that 'ere lad. Every man to himself."

"Oho!" thought Sharp, "I must change the tack."

"Mr. Stubmore," said he, taking a stool, "you speaks like a sensible man. No one can reasonably go for to ask a gentleman to go for to inconvenience hisself. But what do you know of that 'ere youngster. Had you a carakter with him?"

"What's that to you?"

"Why, it's more to yourself, Mr. Stubmore; he is but a lad, and if he goes back to his friends they may take care of him, but he got into a bad set afore he come here. Do you know a good-looking chap with whiskers, who talks of his pheaton, and was riding last night on a brown mare?"

"Y—e—s!" said Mr. Stubmore, growing rather pale, "and I knows the mare, too. Why, sir, I sold him that mare!"

"Did he pay you for her?"

"Why, to be sure, he gave me a cheque on Coutts."

"And you took it! My eyes! what a flat!" Here Mr. Sharp closed the orbs he had invoked, and whistled with that self-hugging delight which men invariably feel when another man is taken in.

Mr. Stubmore became evidently nervous.

"Why, what now;—you don't think I'm done? I did not let him have the mare till I went to the hotel,—found he was cutting a great dash there, a groom, a pheaton, and a fine horse, and as extravagant as the devil!"

"O Lord!—O Lord! what a world this is! What does he call his-self?"

"Why, here's the cheque—George Frederick de—de Burgh Smith."

"Put it in your pipe, my man,—put it in your pipe—not worth a d—!"

"And who the deuce are you, sir?" bawled out Mr. Stubmore, in an equal rage both with himself and his guest.

"I, sir," said the visitor, rising with great dignity,—"I, sir, am of the great Bow Street Office, and my name is John Sharp!"

Mr. Stubmore nearly fell off his stool, his eyes rolled in his head, and his teeth chattered. Mr. Sharp perceived the advantage he had gained, and continued,—

"Yes, sir; and I could have much to say against that chap, who is nothing more or less than Dashing Jerry, as has ruined more girls and more tradesmen than any lord in the land. And so I called to give you a bit of caution; for, says I to myself, 'Mr. Stubmore is a respectable man.'"

"I hope I am, sir," said the crestfallen horse-dealer; "that was always my character."

"And the father of a family?"

"Three boys and a babe at the buzzom," said Mr. Stubmore pathetically.

"And he sha'n't be taken in if I can help it! That 'ere young man as I am arter, you see, knows Captain Smith—ha! ha!—smell a rat now—eh?"

"Captain Smith said he knew him—the wiper—and that's what made me so green."

"Well, we must not be hard on the youngster: 'cause why? he has friends as is gemmen. But you tell him to go back to his poor dear relations, and all shall be forgiven; and say as how you won't keep him; and if he don't go back, he'll have to get his livelihood without a carakter; and use your influence with him like a man and a Christian, and what's more, like the father of a family—Mr. Stubmore—with three boys and a babe at the buzzom. You won't keep him now?"

"Keep him! I have had a precious escape. I'd better go and see after the mare."

"I doubt if you'll find her: the Captain caught a sight of me this morning. Why, he lodges at our hotel. He's off by this time!"

"And why the devil did you let him go?"

"'Cause I had no writ agin him!" said the Bow Street officer; and he walked straight out of the counting-office, satisfied that he had "done the job."

To snatch his hat—to run to the hotel—to find that Captain Smith had indeed gone off in his phaeton, bag and baggage, the same as he came, except that he had now two horses to the phaeton instead of one—having left with the landlord the amount of his bill in another cheque upon Coutts—was the work of five minutes with Mr. Stubmore. He returned home, panting and purple with indignation and wounded feeling.

"To think that chap, whom I took into my yard like a son, should have connived at this! 'Tain't the money—'tis the willany that 'flicts me!" muttered Mr. Stubmore, as he re-entered the mews.

Here he came plump upon Philip, who said—

"Sir, I wished to see you, to say that you had better take care of Captain Smith."

"Oh, you did, did you, now he's gone? 'sconded off to America, I dare say, by this time. Now look ye, young man; your friends are after you, I won't say anything agin you; but you go back to them—I wash my hands of you. Quite too much for me. There's your week, and never let me catch you in my yard agin, that's all!"

Philip dropped the money which Stubmore had put into his hand. "My friends!—friends have been with you, have they? I thought so—I thank them. And so you part with me? Well, you have been very kind, very kind; let us part kindly;" and he held out his hand.

Mr. Stubmore was softened—he touched the hand held out to him, and looked doubtful a moment; but Captain de Burgh Smith's cheque for eighty guineas suddenly rose before his eyes. He turned on his heel abruptly, and said, over his shoulder:

"Don't go after Captain Smith (he'll come to the gallows); mend your ways, and be ruled by your poor dear relatives, whose hearts you are breaking."

"Captain Smith! Did my relations tell you?"

"Yes—yes—they told me all—that is, they sent to tell me; so you see I'm d—d soft not to lay hold of you. But, perhaps, if they be gemmen, they'll act as sich, and cash me this here cheque!"

But the last words were said to air. Philip had rushed from the yard.

With a heaving breast, and every nerve in his body quivering with wrath, the proud, unhappy boy strode through the gay streets. They had betrayed him then, these accursed Beauforts! they circled his steps with schemes to drive him like a deer into the snare of their loathsome charity! The roof was to be taken from his head—the bread from his lips—so that he might fawn at their knees for bounty. "But they shall not break my spirit, nor steal away my curse. No, my dead mother, never!"

As he thus muttered, he passed through a patch of waste land that led to the row of houses in which his lodging was placed. And here a voice called to him, and a hand was laid on his shoulder. He turned, and Arthur Beaufort, who had followed him from the street, stood behind him. Philip did not, at the first glance, recognise his cousin; illness had so altered him, and his dress was so different from that in which he had first and last beheld him. The contrast between the two young men was remarkable. Philip was clad in a rough garb suited to his late calling—a jacket of black velveteen, ill-fitting and ill-fashioned, loose fustian trousers, coarse shoes, his hat set deep over his pent eyebrows, his raven hair long and neglected. He was just at that age when one with strong features and robust frame is at the worst in point of appearance—the sinewy proportions not yet sufficiently fleshed, and seeming inharmonious and undeveloped; precisely in proportion, perhaps, to the symmetry towards which they insensibly mature: the contour of the face sharpened from the roundness of boyhood, and losing its bloom without yet acquiring that relief and shadow which make the expression and dignity of the masculine countenance. Thus accoutred, thus gaunt, and uncouth, stood Morton. Arthur Beaufort, always refined in his appearance, seemed yet more so from the almost feminine delicacy which ill-health threw over his pale complexion and graceful figure; that sort of unconscious elegance which belongs to the dress of the rich when they are young—seen most in minutiae—not observable, perhaps, by themselves-marked forcibly and painfully the distinction of rank between the two. That distinction Beaufort did not feel; but at a glance it was visible to Philip.

The past rushed back on him. The sunny lawn—the gun offered and rejected—the pride of old, much less haughty than the pride of to-day.

"Philip," said Beaufort, feebly, "they tell me you will not accept any kindness from me or mine. Ah! if you knew how we have sought you!"

"Knew!" cried Philip, savagely, for that unlucky sentence recalled to him his late interview with his employer, and his present destitution. "Knew! And why have you dared to hunt me out, and halloo me down?—why must this insolent tyranny, that assumes the right over these limbs and this free will, betray and expose me and my wretchedness wherever I turn?"

"Your poor mother—" began Beaufort.

"Name her not with your lips—name her not!" cried Philip, growing livid with his emotions. "Talk not of the mercy—the forethought—a Beaufort could show to her and her offspring! I accept it not—I believe it not. Oh, yes! you follow me now with your false kindness; and why? Because your father—your vain, hollow, heartless father—"

"Hold!" said Beaufort, in a tone of such reproach, that it startled the wild heart on which it fell; "it is my father you speak of. Let the son respect the son."

"No—no—no! I will respect none of your race. I tell you your father fears me. I tell you that my last words to him ring in his ears! My wrongs! Arthur Beaufort, when you are absent I seek to forget them; in your abhorred presence they revive—they—"

He stopped, almost choked with his passion; but continued instantly, with equal intensity of fervour:

"Were yon tree the gibbet, and to touch your hand could alone save me from it, I would scorn your aid. Aid! The very thought fires my blood and nerves my hand. Aid! Will a Beaufort give me back my birthright—restore my dead mother's fair name? Minion!—sleek, dainty, luxurious minion!—out of my path! You have my fortune, my station, my rights; I have but poverty, and hate, and disdain. I swear, again and again, that you shall not purchase these from me."

"But, Philip—Philip," cried Beaufort, catching his arm; "hear one—hear one who stood by your—"

The sentence that would have saved the outcast from the demons that were darkening and swooping round his soul, died upon the young Protector's lips. Blinded, maddened, excited, and exasperated, almost out of humanity itself, Philip fiercely—brutally—swung aside the enfeebled form that sought to cling to him, and Beaufort fell at his feet. Morton stopped—glared at him with clenched hands and a smiling lip, sprung over his prostrate form, and bounded to his home.

He slackened his pace as he neared the house, and looked behind; but Beaufort had not followed him. He entered the house, and found Sidney in the room, with a countenance so much more gay than that he had lately worn, that, absorbed as he was in thought and passion, it yet did not fail to strike him.

"What has pleased you, Sidney?" The child smiled.

"Ah! it is a secret—I was not to tell you. But I'm sure you are not the naughty boy he says you are."

"He!—who?"

"Don't look so angry, Philip: you frighten me!"

"And you torture me. Who could malign one brother to the other?"

"Oh! it was all meant very kindly—there's been such a nice, dear, good gentleman here, and he cried when he saw me, and said he knew dear mamma. Well, and he has promised to take me home with him and give me a pretty pony—as pretty—as pretty—oh, as pretty as it can be got! And he is to call again and tell me more: I think he is a fairy, Philip."

"Did he say that he was to take me, too, Sidney?" said Morton, seating himself, and looking very pale. At that question Sidney hung his head.

"No, brother—he says you won't go, and that you are a bad boy—and that you associate with wicked people—and that you want to keep me shut up here and not let any one be good to me. But I told him I did not believe that—yes, indeed, I told him so."

And Sidney endeavoured caressingly to withdraw the hands that his brother placed before his face.

Morton started up, and walked hastily to and fro the room. "This," thought he, "is another emissary of the Beauforts'—perhaps the lawyer: they will take him from me—the last thing left to love and hope for. I will foil them."

"Sidney," he said aloud, "we must go hence today, this very hour—nay, instantly."

"What! away from this nice, good gentleman?"

"Curse him! yes, away from him. Do not cry—it is of no use—you must go."

This was said more harshly than Philip had ever yet spoken to Sidney; and when he had said it, he left the room to settle with the landlady, and to pack up their scanty effects. In another hour, the brothers had turned their backs on the town.

CHAPTER X

"I'll carry thee
In sorrow's arms to welcome Misery."
HEYWOOD's Duchess of Sufolk.

"Who's here besides foul weather?"
SHAKSPEARE Lear.

The sun was as bright and the sky as calm during the journey of the orphans as in the last. They avoided, as before, the main roads, and their way lay through landscapes that might have charmed a Gainsborough's eye. Autumn scattered its last hues of gold over the various foliage, and the poppy glowed from the hedges, and the wild convolvuli, here and there, still gleamed on the wayside with a parting smile.

At times, over the sloping stubbles, broke the sound of the sportsman's gun; and ever and anon, by stream and sedge, they startled the shy wild fowl, just come from the far lands, nor yet settled in the new haunts too soon to be invaded.

But there was no longer in the travellers the same hearts that had made light of hardship and fatigue. Sidney was no longer flying from a harsh master, and his step was not elastic with the energy of fear that looked behind, and of hope that smiled before. He was going a toilsome, weary journey, he knew not why nor whither; just, too, when he had made a friend, whose soothing words haunted his childish fancy. He was displeased with Philip, and in sullen and silent thoughtfulness slowly plodded behind him; and Morton himself was gloomy, and knew not where in the world to seek a future.

They arrived at dusk at a small inn, not so far distant from the town they had left as Morton could have wished; but the days were shorter than in their first flight.

They were shown into a small sanded parlour, which Sidney eyed with great disgust; nor did he seem more pleased with the hacked and jagged leg of cold mutton, which was all that the hostess set before them for supper. Philip in vain endeavoured to cheer him up, and ate to set him the example. He felt relieved when, under the auspices of a good-looking, good-natured chambermaid, Sidney retired to rest, and he was left in the parlour to his own meditations. Hitherto it had been a happy thing for Morton that he had had some one dependent on him; that feeling had given him perseverance, patience, fortitude, and hope. But now, dispirited and sad, he felt rather the horror of being responsible for a human life, without seeing the means to discharge the trust. It was clear, even to his experience, that he was not likely to find another employer as facile as Mr. Stubmore; and wherever he went, he felt as if his Destiny stalked at his back. He took out his little fortune and spread it on the table, counting it over and over; it had remained pretty stationary since his service with Mr. Stubmore, for Sidney had swallowed up the wages of his hire. While thus employed, the door opened, and the chambermaid, showing in a gentleman, said, "We have no other room, sir."

"Very well, then,—I'm not particular; a tumbler of braundy and water, stiffish, cold without, the newspaper—and a cigar. You'll excuse smoking, sir?"

Philip looked up from his hoard, and Captain de Burgh Smith stood before him.

"Ah!" said the latter, "well met!" And closing the door, he took off his great-coat, seated himself near Philip, and bent both his eyes with considerable wistfulness on the neat rows into which Philip's bank-notes, sovereigns, and shillings were arrayed.

"Pretty little sum for pocket money; caush in hand goes a great way, properly invested. You must have been very lucky. Well, so I suppose you are surprised to see me here without my pheaton?"

"I wish I had never seen you at all," replied Philip, uncourteously, and restoring his money to his pocket; "your fraud upon Mr. Stubmore, and your assurance that you knew me, have sent me adrift upon the world."

"What's one man's meat is another man's poison," said the captain, philosophically; "no use fretting, care killed a cat. I am as badly off as you; for, hang me, if there was not a Bow Street runner in the town. I caught his eye fixed on me like a gimlet: so I bolted—went to N—, left my pheaton and groom there for the present, and have doubled back, to bauffle pursuit, and cut across the country. You recollect that noice girl we saw in the coach; 'gad, I served her spouse that is to be a praetty trick! Borrowed his money under pretence of investing it in the New Grand Anti-Dry-Rot Company; cool hundred—it's only just gone, sir."

Here the chambermaid entered with the brandy and water, the newspaper, and cigar,—the captain lighted the last, took a deep sup from the beverage, and said, gaily:

"Well, now, let us join fortunes; we are both, as you say, 'adrift.' Best way to staund the breeze is to unite the caubles."

Philip shook his head, and, displeased with his companion, sought his pillow. He took care to put his money under his head, and to lock his door.

The brothers started at daybreak; Sidney was even more discontented than on the previous day. The weather was hot and oppressive; they rested for some hours at noon, and in the cool of the evening renewed their way. Philip had made up his mind to steer for a town in the thick of a hunting district, where he hoped his equestrian capacities might again befriend him; and their path now lay through a chain of vast dreary commons, which gave them at least the advantage to skirt the road-side unobserved. But, somehow or other, either Philip had been misinformed as to an inn where he had proposed to pass the night, or he had missed it; for the clouds darkened, and the sun went down, and no vestige of human habitation was discernible.

Sidney, footsore and querulous, began to weep, and declare that he could stir no further; and while Philip, whose iron frame defied fatigue, compassionately paused to rest his brother, a low roll of thunder broke upon the gloomy air. "There will be a storm," said he, anxiously. "Come on—pray, Sidney, come on."

"It is so cruel in you, brother Philip," replied Sidney, sobbing. "I wish I had never—never gone with you."

A flash of lightning, that illuminated the whole heavens, lingered round Sidney's pale face as he spoke; and Philip threw himself instinctively on the child, as if to protect him even from the wrath of the unshelterable flame. Sidney, hushed and terrified, clung to his brother's breast; after a pause, he silently consented to resume their journey. But now the storm came nearer and nearer to the wanderers. The darkness grew rapidly more intense, save when the lightning lit up heaven and earth alike with intolerable lustre. And when at length the rain began to fall in merciless and drenching torrents, even Philip's brave heart failed him. How could he ask Sidney to proceed, when they could scarcely see an inch before them?—all that could now be done was to gain the high-road, and hope for some passing conveyance. With fits and starts, and by the glare of the lightning, they obtained their object; and stood at last on the great broad thoroughfare, along which, since the day when the Roman carved it from the waste, Misery hath plodded, and Luxury rolled, their common way.

Philip had stripped handkerchief, coat, vest, all to shelter Sidney; and he felt a kind of strange pleasure through the dark, even to hear Sidney's voice wail and moan. But that voice grew more languid and faint—it ceased—Sidney's weight hung heavy—heavier on the fostering arm.

"For Heaven's sake, speak!—speak, Sidney!—only one word—I will carry you in my arms!"

"I think I am dying," replied Sidney, in a low murmur; "I am so tired and worn out I can go no further—I must lie here." And he sank at once upon the reeking grass beside the road. At this time the rain gradually relaxed, the clouds broke away—a grey light succeeded to the darkness—the lightning was more distant; and the thunder rolled onward in its awful path. Kneeling on the ground, Philip supported his brother in his arms, and cast his pleading eyes upward to the softening terrors of the sky. A star, a solitary star—broke out for one moment, as if to smile comfort upon him, and then vanished. But lo! in the distance there suddenly gleamed a red, steady light, like that in some solitary window; it was no will-o'-the-wisp, it was too stationary—human shelter was then nearer than he had thought for. He pointed to the light, and whispered, "Rouse yourself, one struggle more—it cannot be far off."

"It is impossible—I cannot stir," answered Sidney: and a sudden flash of lightning showed his countenance, ghastly, as if with the damps of Death. What could the brother do?—stay there, and see the boy perish before his eyes? leave him on the road and fly to the friendly light? The last plan was the sole one left, yet he shrank from it in greater terror than the first. Was that a step that he heard across the road? He held his breath to listen—a form became dimly visible—it approached.

Philip shouted aloud.

"What now?" answered the voice, and it seemed familiar to Morton's ear. He sprang forward; and putting his face close to the wayfarer, thought to recognise the features of Captain de Burgh Smith. The Captain, whose eyes were yet more accustomed to the dark, made the first overture.

"Why, my lad, is it you then? 'Gad, you froightened me!"

Odious as this man had hitherto been to Philip, he was as welcome to him as daylight now; he grasped his hand,—"My brother—a child—is here, dying, I fear, with cold and fatigue; he cannot stir. Will you stay with him—support him—but for a few moments, while I make to yon light? See, I have money—plenty of money!"

"My good lad, it is very ugly work staying here at this hour: still—where's the choild?"

"Here, here! make haste, raise him! that's right! God bless you! I shall be back ere you think me gone."

He sprang from the road, and plunged through the heath, the furze, the rank glistening pools, straight towards the light—as the swimmer towards the shore.

The captain, though a rogue, was human; and when life—an innocent life—is at stake, even a rogue's heart rises up from its weedy bed. He muttered a few oaths, it is true, but he held the child in his arms; and, taking out a little tin case, poured some brandy down Sidney's throat and then, by way of company, down his own. The cordial revived the boy; he opened his eyes, and said, "I think I can go on now, Philip."

We must return to Arthur Beaufort. He was naturally, though gentle, a person of high spirit and not without pride. He rose from the ground with bitter, resentful feelings and a blushing cheek, and went his way to the hotel. Here he found Mr. Spencer just returned from his visit to Sidney. Enchanted with the soft and endearing manners of his lost Catherine's son, and deeply affected with the resemblance the child bore to the mother as he had seen her last at the gay and rosy age of fair sixteen, his description of the younger brother drew Beaufort's indignant thoughts from the elder. He cordially concurred with Mr. Spencer in the wish to save one so gentle from the domination of one so fierce; and this, after all, was the child Catherine had most strongly commended to him. She had said little of the elder; perhaps she had been aware of his ungracious and untractable nature, and, as it seemed to Arthur Beaufort, his predilections for a coarse and low career.

"Yes," said he, "this boy, then, shall console me for the perverse brutality of the other. He shall indeed drink of my cup, and eat of my bread, and be to me as a brother."

"What!" said Mr. Spencer, changing countenance, "you do not intend to take Sidney to live with you. I meant him for my son—my adopted son."

"No; generous as you are," said Arthur, pressing his hand, "this charge devolves on me—it is my right. I am the orphan's relation—his mother consigned him to me. But he shall be taught to love you not the less."

Mr. Spencer was silent. He could not bear the thought of losing Sidney as an inmate of his cheerless home, a tender relic of his early love. From that moment he began to contemplate the possibility of securing Sidney to himself, unknown to Beaufort.

The plans both of Arthur and Spencer were interrupted by the sudden retreat of the brothers. They determined to depart different ways in search of them. Spencer, as the more helpless of the two, obtained the aid of Mr. Sharp; Beaufort departed with the lawyer.

Two travellers, in a hired barouche, were slowly dragged by a pair of jaded posters along the commons I have just described.

"I think," said one, "that the storm is very much abated; heigho! what an unpleasant night!"

"Unkimmon ugly, sir," answered the other; "and an awful long stage, eighteen miles. These here remote places are quite behind the age, sir—quite. However, I think we shall kitch them now."

"I am very much afraid of that eldest boy, Sharp. He seems a dreadful vagabond."

"You see, sir, quite hand in glove with Dashing Jerry; met in the same inn last night—preconcerted, you may be quite shure. It would be the best day's job I have done this many a day to save that 'ere little fellow from being corrupted. You sees he is just of a size to be useful to these bad karakters. If they took to burglary, he would be a treasure to them—slip him through a pane of glass like a ferret, sir."

"Don't talk of it, Sharp," said Mr. Spencer, with a groan; "and recollect, if we get hold of him, that you are not to say a word to Mr. Beaufort."

"I understand, sir; and I always goes with the gemman who behaves most like a gemman."

Here a loud halloo was heard close by the horses' heads. "Good Heavens, if that is a footpad!" said Mr. Spencer, shaking violently.

"Lord, sir, I have my barkers with me. Who's there?" The barouche stopped—a man came to the window. "Excuse me, sir," said the stranger; "but there is a poor boy here so tired and ill that I fear he will never reach the next town, unless you will koindly give him a lift."

"A poor boy!" said Mr. Spencer, poking his head over the head of Mr. Sharp. "Where?"

"If you would just drop him at the King's Awrms it would be a chaurity," said the man.

Sharp pinched Mr. Spencer in his shoulder. "That's Dashing Jerry; I'll get out." So saying, he opened the door, jumped into the road, and presently reappeared with the lost and welcome Sidney in his arms. "Ben't this the boy?" he whispered to Mr. Spencer; and, taking the lamp from the carriage, he raised it to the child's face.

"It is! it is! God be thanked!" exclaimed the worthy man.

"Will you leave him at the King's Awrms?—we shall be there in an hour or two," cried the Captain.

"We! Who's we?" said Sharp, gruffly. "Why, myself and the choild's brother."

"Oh!" said Sharp, raising the lantern to his own face; "you knows me, I think, Master Jerry? Let me kitch you again, that's all. And give my compliments to your 'sociate, and say, if he prosecutes this here hurchin any more, we'll settle his bizness for him; and so take a hint and make yourself scarce, old boy!"

With that Mr. Sharp jumped into the barouche, and bade the postboy drive on as fast as he could.

Ten minutes after this abduction, Philip, followed by two labourers, with a barrow, a lantern, and two blankets, returned from the hospitable farm to which the light had conducted him. The spot where he had left Sidney, and which he knew by a neighbouring milestone, was vacant; he shouted an alarm, and the Captain answered from the distance of some threescore yards. Philip came to him. "Where is my brother?"

"Gone away in a barouche and pair. Devil take me if I understand it." And the Captain proceeded to give a confused account of what had passed.

"My brother! my brother! they have torn thee from me, then;" cried Philip, and he fell to the earth insensible.

CHAPTER XI

"Vous me rendrez mon frere!"
CASIMER DELAVIGNE: Les Enfans d'Edouard.

[You shall restore me my brother!]

One evening, a week after this event, a wild, tattered, haggard youth knocked at the door of Mr. Robert Beaufort. The porter slowly presented himself.

"Is your master at home? I must see him instantly."

"That's more than you can, my man; my master does not see the like of you at this time of night," replied the porter, eying the ragged apparition before him with great disdain.

"See me he must and shall," replied the young man; and as the porter blocked up the entrance, he grasped his collar with a hand of iron, swung him, huge as he was, aside, and strode into the spacious hall.

"Stop! stop!" cried the porter, recovering himself. "James! John! here's a go!"

Mr. Robert Beaufort had been back in town several days. Mrs. Beaufort, who was waiting his return from his club, was in the dining-room. Hearing a noise in the hall, she opened the door, and saw the strange grim figure I have described, advancing towards her. "Who are you?" said she; "and what do you want?"

"I am Philip Morton. Who are you?"

"My husband," said Mrs. Beaufort, shrinking into the parlour, while Morton followed her and closed the door, "my husband, Mr. Beaufort, is not at home."

"You are Mrs. Beaufort, then! Well, you can understand me. I want my brother. He has been basely reft from me. Tell me where he is, and I will forgive all. Restore him to me, and I will bless you and yours." And Philip fell on his knees and grasped the train of her gown. "I know nothing of your brother, Mr. Morton," cried Mrs. Beaufort, surprised and alarmed. "Arthur, whom we expect every day, writes us word that all search for him has been in vain."

"Ha! you admit the search?" cried Morton, rising and clenching his hands. "And who else but you or yours would have parted brother and brother? Answer me where he is. No subterfuge, madam: I am desperate!"

Mrs. Beaufort, though a woman of that worldly coldness and indifference which, on ordinary occasions, supply the place of courage, was extremely terrified by the tone and mien of her rude guest. She laid her hand on the bell; but Morton seized her arm, and, holding it sternly, said, while his dark eyes shot fire through the glimmering room, "I will not stir hence till you have told me. Will you reject my gratitude, my blessing? Beware! Again, where have you hid my brother?"

At that instant the door opened, and Mr. Robert Beaufort entered. The lady, with a shriek of joy, wrenched herself from Philip's grasp, and flew to her husband.

"Save me from this ruffian!" she said, with an hysterical sob.

Mr. Beaufort, who had heard from Blackwell strange accounts of Philip's obdurate perverseness, vile associates, and unredeemable character, was roused from his usual timidity by the appeal of his wife.

"Insolent reprobate!" he said, advancing to Philip; "after all the absurd goodness of my son and myself; after rejecting all our offers, and persisting in your miserable and vicious conduct, how dare you presume to force yourself into this house? Begone, or I will send for the constables to remove YOU!

"Man, man," cried Philip, restraining the fury that shook him from head to foot, "I care not for your threats—I scarcely hear your abuse—your son, or yourself, has stolen away my brother: tell me only where he is; let me see him once more. Do not drive me hence, without one word of justice, of pity. I implore you—on my knees I implore you—yes, I,—I implore you, Robert Beaufort, to have mercy on your brother's son. Where is Sidney?" Like all mean and cowardly men, Robert Beaufort was rather encouraged than softened by Philip's abrupt humility.

"I know nothing of your brother; and if this is not all some villainous trick—which it may be—I am heartily rejoiced that he, poor child! is rescued from the contamination of such a companion," answered Beaufort.

"I am at your feet still; again, for the last time, clinging to you a suppliant: I pray you to tell me the truth."

Mr. Beaufort, more and more exasperated by Morton's forbearance, raised his hand as if to strike; when, at that moment, one hitherto unobserved—one who, terrified by the scene she had witnessed but could not comprehend, had slunk into a dark corner of the room,—now came from her retreat. And a child's soft voice was heard, saying:

"Do not strike him, papa!—let him have his brother!" Mr. Beaufort's arm fell to his side: kneeling before him, and by the outcast's side, was his own young daughter; she had crept into the room unobserved, when her father entered. Through the dim shadows, relieved only by the red and fitful gleam of the fire, he saw her fair meek face looking up wistfully at his own, with tears of excitement, and perhaps of pity—for children have a quick insight into the reality of grief in those not far removed from their own years—glistening in her soft eyes. Philip looked round bewildered, and he saw that face which seemed to him, at such a time, like the face of an angel.

"Hear her!" he murmured: "Oh, hear her! For her sake, do not sever one orphan from the other!"

"Take away that child, Mrs. Beaufort," cried Robert, angrily. "Will you let her disgrace herself thus? And you, sir, begone from this roof; and when you can approach me with due respect, I will give you, as I said I would, the means to get an honest living."

Philip rose; Mrs. Beaufort had already led away her daughter, and she took that opportunity of sending in the servants: their forms filled up the doorway.

"Will you go?" continued Mr. Beaufort, more and more emboldened, as he saw the menials at hand, "or shall they expel you?"

"It is enough, sir," said Philip, with a sudden calm and dignity that surprised and almost awed his uncle. "My father, if the dead yet watch over the living, has seen and heard you. There will come a day for justice. Out of my path, hirelings!"

He waved his arm, and the menials shrank back at his tread, stalked across the inhospitable hall, and vanished. When he had gained the street, he turned and looked up at the house. His dark and hollow eyes, gleaming through the long and raven hair that fell profusely over his face, had in them an expression of menace almost preternatural, from its settled calmness; the wild and untutored majesty which, though rags and squalor, never deserted his form, as it never does the forms of men in whom the will is strong and the sense of injustice deep; the outstretched arm the haggard, but noble features; the bloomless and scathed youth, all gave to his features and his stature an aspect awful in its sinister and voiceless wrath. There he stood a moment, like one to whom woe and wrong have given a Prophet's power, guiding the eye of the unforgetful Fate to the roof of the Oppressor. Then slowly, and with a half smile, he turned away, and strode through the streets till he arrived at one of the narrow lanes that intersect the more equivocal quarters of the huge city. He stopped at the private entrance of a small pawnbroker's shop; the door was opened by a slipshod boy; he ascended the dingy stairs till he came to the second floor; and there, in a small back room, he found Captain de Burgh Smith, seated before a table with a couple of candles on it, smoking a cigar, and playing at cards by himself.

"Well, what news of your brother, Bully Phil?"

"None: they will reveal nothing."

"Do you give him up?"

"Never! My hope now is in you."

"Well, I thought you would be driven to come to me, and I will do something for you that I should not loike to do for myself. I told you that I knew the Bow Street runner who was in the barouche. I will find him out—Heaven knows that is easily done; and, if you can pay well, you will get your news."

"You shall have all I possess, if you restore my brother. See what it is, one hundred pounds—it was his fortune. It is useless to me without him. There, take fifty now, and if—"

Philip stopped, for his voice trembled too much to allow him farther speech. Captain Smith thrust the notes into his pocket, and said—

"We'll consider it settled."

Captain Smith fulfilled his promise. He saw the Bow Street officer. Mr. Sharp had been bribed too high by the opposite party to tell tales, and he willingly encouraged the suspicion that Sidney was under the care of the Beauforts. He promised, however, for the sake of ten guineas, to procure Philip a letter from Sidney himself. This was all he would undertake.

Philip was satisfied. At the end of another week, Mr. Sharp transmitted to the Captain a letter, which he, in his turn, gave to Philip. It ran thus, in Sidney's own sprawling hand:

"DEAR BROTHER PHILIP,—I am told you wish to know how I am, and therfore take up my pen, and assure you that I write all out of my own head. I am very Comfortable and happy—much more so than I have been since poor deir mama died; so I beg you won't vex yourself about me: and pray don't try and Find me out, For I would not go with you again for the world. I am so much better Off here. I wish you would be a good boy, and leave off your Bad ways; for I am sure, as every one says, I don't know what would have become of me if I had staid with you. Mr. [the Mr. half scratched out] the gentleman I am with, says if you turn out Properly, he will be a friend to you, Too; but he advises you to go, like a Good boy, to Arthur Beaufort, and ask his pardon for the past, and then Arthur will be very kind to you. I send you a great Big sum of £20., and the gentleman says he would send more, only it might make you naughty, and set up. I go to church now every Sunday, and read good books, and always pray that God may open your eyes. I have such a Nice Pony, with such a long tale. So no more at present from your affectionate brother, SIDNEY MORTON."

Oct. 8, 18—

"Pray, pray don't come after me Any more. You know I neerly died of it, but for this deir good gentleman I am with."

So this, then, was the crowning reward of all his sufferings and all his love! There was the letter, evidently undictated, with its errors of orthography, and in the child's rough scrawl; the serpent's tooth pierced to the heart, and left there its most lasting venom.

"I have done with him for ever," said Philip, brushing away the bitter tears. "I will molest him no farther; I care no more to pierce this mystery. Better for him as it is—he is happy! Well, well, and I—I will never care for a human being again."

He bowed his head over his hands; and when he rose, his heart felt to him like stone. It seemed as if Conscience herself had fled from his soul on the wings of departed Love.

CHAPTER XII

"But you have found the mountain's top—there sit
On the calm flourishing head of it;
And whilst with wearied steps we upward go,
See us and clouds below."—COWLEY.

It was true that Sidney was happy in his new home, and thither we must now trace him.

On reaching the town where the travellers in the barouche had been requested to leave Sidney, "The King's Arms" was precisely the inn eschewed by Mr. Spencer. While the horses were being changed, he summoned the surgeon of the town to examine the child, who had already much recovered; and by stripping his clothes, wrapping him in warm blankets, and administering cordials, he was permitted to reach another stage, so as to baffle pursuit that night; and in three days Mr. Spencer had placed his new charge with his maiden sisters, a hundred and fifty miles from the spot where he had been found. He would not take him to his own home yet. He feared the claims of Arthur Beaufort. He artfully wrote to that gentleman, stating that he had abandoned the chase of Sidney in despair, and desiring to know if he had discovered him; and a bribe of £300. to Mr. Sharp with a candid exposition of his reasons for secreting Sidney—reasons in which the worthy officer professed to sympathise—secured the discretion of his ally. But he would not deny himself the pleasure of being in the same house with Sidney, and was therefore for some months the guest of his sisters. At length he heard that young Beaufort had been ordered abroad for his health, and he then deemed it safe to transfer his new idol to his Lares by the lakes. During this interval the current of the younger Morton's life had indeed flowed through flowers. At his age the cares of females were almost a want as well as a luxury, and the sisters spoiled and petted him as much as any elderly nymphs in Cytherea ever petted Cupid. They were good, excellent, high-nosed, flat-bosomed spinsters, sentimentally fond of their brother, whom they called "the poet," and dotingly attached to children. The cleanness, the quiet, the good cheer of their neat abode, all tended to revive and invigorate the spirits of their young guest, and every one there seemed to vie which should love him the most. Still his especial favourite was Mr. Spencer: for Spencer never went out without bringing back cakes and toys; and Spencer gave him his pony; and Spencer rode a little crop-eared nag by his side; and Spencer, in short, was associated with his every comfort and caprice. He told them his little history; and when he said how Philip had left him alone for long hours together, and how Philip had forced him to his last and nearly fatal journey, the old maids groaned, and the old bachelor sighed, and they all cried in a breath, that "Philip was a very wicked boy." It was not only their obvious policy to detach him from his brother, but it was their sincere conviction that they did right to do so. Sidney began, it is true, by taking Philip's part; but his mind was ductile, and he still looked back with a shudder to the hardships he had gone through: and so by little and little he learned to forget all the endearing and fostering love Philip had evinced to him; to connect his name with dark and mysterious fears; to repeat thanksgivings to Providence that he was saved from him; and to hope that they might never meet again. In fact, when Mr. Spencer learned from Sharp that it was through Captain Smith, the swindler, that application had been made by Philip for news of his brother, and having also learned before, from the same person, that Philip had been implicated in the sale of a horse, swindled, if not stolen, he saw every additional reason to widen the stream that flowed between the wolf and the lamb. The older Sidney grew, the better he comprehended and appreciated the motives of his protector—for he was brought up in a formal school of propriety and ethics, and his mind naturally revolted from all images of violence or fraud. Mr. Spencer changed both the Christian and the surname of his protege, in order to elude the search whether of Philip, the Mortons, or the Beauforts, and Sidney passed for his nephew by a younger brother who had died in India.

So there, by the calm banks of the placid lake, amidst the fairest landscapes of the Island Garden, the youngest born of Catherine passed his tranquil days. The monotony of the retreat did not fatigue a spirit which, as he grew up, found occupation in books, music, poetry, and the elegances of the cultivated, if quiet, life within his reach. To the rough past he looked back as to an evil dream, in which the image of Philip stood dark and threatening. His brother's name as he grew older he rarely mentioned; and if he did volunteer it to Mr. Spencer, the bloom on his cheek grew paler. The sweetness of his manners, his fair face and winning smile, still continued to secure him love, and to screen from the common eye whatever of selfishness yet lurked in his nature. And, indeed, that fault in so serene a career, and with friends so attached, was seldom called into action. So thus was he severed from both the protectors, Arthur and Philip, to whom poor Catherine had bequeathed him.

By a perverse and strange mystery, they, to whom the charge was most intrusted were the very persons who were forbidden to redeem it. On our death-beds when we think we have provided for those we leave behind—should we lose the last smile that gilds the solemn agony, if we could look one year into the Future?

Arthur Beaufort, after an ineffectual search for Sidney, heard, on returning to his home, no unexaggerated narrative of Philip's visit, and listened, with deep resentment, to his mother's distorted account of the language addressed to her. It is not to be surprised that, with all his romantic generosity, he felt sickened and revolted at violence that seemed to him without excuse. Though not a revengeful character, he had not that meekness which never resents. He looked upon Philip Morton as upon one rendered incorrigible by bad passions and evil company. Still Catherine's last request, and Philip's note to him, the Unknown Comforter, often recurred to him, and he would have willingly yet aided him had Philip been thrown in his way. But as it was, when he looked around, and saw the examples of that charity that begins at home, in which the world abounds, he felt as if he had done his duty; and prosperity having, though it could not harden his heart, still sapped the habits of perseverance, so by little and little the image of the dying Catherine, and the thought of her sons, faded from his remembrance. And for this there was the more excuse after the receipt of an anonymous letter, which relieved all his apprehensions on behalf of Sidney. The letter was short, and stated simply that Sidney Morton had found a friend who would protect him throughout life; but who would not scruple to apply to Beaufort if ever he needed his assistance. So one son, and that the youngest and the best loved, was safe. And the other, had he not chosen his own career? Alas, poor Catherine! when you fancied that Philip was the one sure to force his way into fortune, and Sidney the one most helpless, how ill did you judge of the human heart! It was that very strength of Philip's nature which tempted the winds that scattered the blossoms, and shook the stem to its roots; while the lighter and frailer nature bent to the gale, and bore transplanting to a happier soil. If a parent read these pages, let him pause and think well on the characters of his children; let him at once fear and hope the most for the one whose passions and whose temper lead to a struggle with the world. That same world is a tough wrestler, and has a bear's gripe.

Meanwhile, Arthur Beaufort's own complaints, which grew serious and menaced consumption, recalled his thoughts more and more every day to himself. He was compelled to abandon his career at the University, and to seek for health in the softer breezes of the South. His parents accompanied him to Nice; and when, at the end of a few months, he was restored to health, the desire of travel seized the mind and attracted the fancy of the young heir. His father and mother, satisfied with his recovery, and not unwilling that he should acquire the polish of Continental intercourse, returned to England; and young Beaufort, with gay companions and munificent income, already courted, spoiled, and flattered, commenced his tour with the fair climes of Italy.

So, O dark mystery of the Moral World!—so, unlike the order of the External Universe, glide together, side by side, the shadowy steeds of NIGHT AND MORNING. Examine life in its own world; confound not that world, the inner one, the practical one, with the more visible, yet airier and less substantial system, doing homage to the sun, to whose throne, afar in the infinite space, the human heart has no wings to flee. In life, the mind and the circumstance give the true seasons, and regulate the darkness and the light. Of two men standing on the same foot of earth, the one revels in the joyous noon, the other shudders in the solitude of night. For Hope and Fortune, the day-star is ever shining. For Care and Penury, Night changes not with the ticking of the clock, nor with the shadow on the dial. Morning for the heir, night for the houseless, and God's eye over both.

BOOK III

CHAPTER I

"The knight of arts and industry,
And his achievements fair."
THOMSON'S Castle of Indolence: Explanatory Verse to Canto II.

In a popular and respectable, but not very fashionable quartier in Paris, and in the tolerably broad and effective locale of the Rue —, there might be seen, at the time I now treat of, a curious-looking building, that jutted out semicircularly from the neighbouring shops, with plaster pilasters and compo ornaments. The virtuosi of the quartier had discovered that the building was constructed in imitation of an ancient temple in Rome; this erection, then fresh and new, reached only to the entresol. The pilasters were painted light green and gilded in the cornices, while, surmounting the architrave, were three little statues—one held a torch, another a bow, and a third a bag; they were therefore rumoured, I know not with what justice, to be the artistical representatives of Hymen, Cupid and Fortune.

On the door was neatly engraved, on a brass plate, the following inscription:

"MONSIEUR LOVE, ANGLAIS,
A L'ENTRESOL."

And if you had crossed the threshold and mounted the stairs, and gained that mysterious story inhabited by Monsieur Love, you would have seen, upon another door to the right, another epigraph, informing those interested in the inquiry that the bureau, of M. Love was open daily from nine in the morning to four in the afternoon.

The office of M. Love—for office it was, and of a nature not unfrequently designated in the "petites affiches" of Paris—had been established about six months; and whether it was the popularity of the profession, or the shape of the shop, or the manners of M. Love himself, I cannot pretend to say, but certain it is that the Temple of Hymen—as M. Love classically termed it—had become exceedingly in vogue in the Faubourg St.—. It was rumoured that no less than nine marriages in the immediate neighbourhood had been manufactured at this fortunate office, and that they had all turned out happily except one, in which the bride being sixty, and the bridegroom twenty-four, there had been rumours of domestic dissension; but as the lady had been delivered,—I mean of her husband, who had drowned himself in the Seine, about a month after the ceremony, things had turned out in the long run better than might have been expected, and the widow was so little discouraged; that she had been seen to enter the office already—a circumstance that was greatly to the credit of Mr. Love.

Perhaps the secret of Mr. Love's success, and of the marked superiority of his establishment in rank and popularity over similar ones, consisted in the spirit and liberality with which the business was conducted. He seemed resolved to destroy all formality between parties who might desire to draw closer to each other, and he hit upon the lucky device of a table d'hote, very well managed, and held twice a-week, and often followed by a soiree dansante; so that, if they pleased, the aspirants to matrimonial happiness might become acquainted without gene. As he himself was a jolly, convivial fellow of much savoir vivre, it is astonishing how well he made these entertainments answer. Persons who had not seemed to take to each other in the first distant interview grew extremely enamoured when the corks of the champagne—an extra of course in the abonnement—bounced against the wall. Added to this, Mr. Love took great pains to know the tradesmen in his neighbourhood; and, what with his jokes, his appearance of easy circumstances, and the fluency with which he spoke the language, he became a universal favourite. Many persons who were uncommonly starched in general, and who professed to ridicule the bureau, saw nothing improper in dining at the table d'hote. To those who wished for secrecy he was said to be wonderfully discreet; but there were others who did not affect to conceal their discontent at the single state: for the rest, the entertainments were so contrived as never to shock the delicacy, while they always forwarded the suit.

It was about eight o'clock in the evening, and Mr. Love was still seated at dinner, or rather at dessert, with a party of guests. His apartments, though small, were somewhat gaudily painted and furnished, and his dining-room was decorated a la Turque. The party consisted—first, of a rich epicier, a widower, Monsieur Goupille by name, an eminent man in the Faubourg; he was in his grand climacteric, but still belhomme; wore a very well-made peruque of light auburn, with tight pantaloons, which contained a pair of very respectable calves; and his white neckcloth and his large frill were washed and got up with especial care. Next to Monsieur Goupille sat a very demure and very spare young lady of about two-and-thirty, who was said to have saved a fortune—Heaven knows how—in the family of a rich English milord, where she had officiated as governess; she called herself Mademoiselle Adele de Courval, and was very particular about the de, and very melancholy about her ancestors. Monsieur Goupille generally put his finger through his peruque, and fell away a little on his left pantaloon when he spoke to Mademoiselle de Courval, and Mademoiselle de Courval generally pecked at her bouquet when she answered Monsieur Goupille. On the other side of this young lady sat a fine-looking fair man—M. Sovolofski, a Pole, buttoned up to the chin, and rather threadbare, though uncommonly neat. He was flanked by a little fat lady, who had been very pretty, and who kept a boarding-house, or pension, for the English, she herself being English, though long established in Paris. Rumour said she had been gay in her youth, and dropped in Paris by a Russian nobleman, with a very pretty settlement, she and the settlement having equally expanded by time and season: she was called Madame Beavor. On the other side of the table was a red-headed Englishman, who spoke very little French; who had been told that French ladies were passionately fond of light hair; and who, having £2000. of his own, intended to quadruple that sum by a prudent marriage. Nobody knew what his family was, but his name was Higgins. His neighbour was an exceedingly tall, large-boned Frenchman, with a long nose and a red riband, who was much seen at Frascati's, and had served under Napoleon. Then came another lady, extremely pretty, very piquante, and very gay, but past the premiere jeunesse, who ogled Mr. Love more than she did any of his guests: she was called Rosalie Caumartin, and was at the head of a large bon-bon establishment; married, but her husband had gone four years ago to the Isle of France, and she was a little doubtful whether she might not be justly entitled to the privileges of a widow. Next to Mr. Love, in the place of honour, sat no less a person than the Vicomte de Vaudemont, a French gentleman, really well-born, but whose various excesses, added to his poverty, had not served to sustain that respect for his birth which he considered due to it. He had already been twice married; once to an Englishwoman, who had been decoyed by the title; by this lady, who died in childbed, he had one son; a fact which he sedulously concealed from the world of Paris by keeping the unhappy boy—who was now some eighteen or nineteen years old—a perpetual exile in England. Monsieur de Vaudemont did not wish to pass for more than thirty, and he considered that to produce a son of eighteen would be to make the lad a monster of ingratitude by giving the lie every hour to his own father! In spite of this precaution the Vicomte found great difficulty in getting a third wife—especially as he had no actual land and visible income; was, not seamed, but ploughed up, with the small-pox; small of stature, and was considered more than un peu bete. He was, however, a prodigious dandy, and wore a lace frill and embroidered waistcoat. Mr. Love's vis-a-vis was Mr. Birnie, an Englishman, a sort of assistant in the establishment, with a hard, dry, parchment face, and a remarkable talent for silence. The host himself was a splendid animal; his vast chest seemed to occupy more space at the table than any four of his guests, yet he was not corpulent or unwieldy; he was dressed in black, wore a velvet stock very high, and four gold studs glittered in his shirt-front; he was bald to the crown, which made his forehead appear singularly lofty, and what hair he had left was a little greyish and curled; his face was shaved smoothly, except a close-clipped mustache; and his eyes, though small, were bright and piercing. Such was the party.

"These are the best bon-bons I ever ate," said Mr. Love, glancing at Madame Caumartin. "My fair friends, have compassion on the table of a poor bachelor."

"But you ought not to be a bachelor, Monsieur Lofe," replied the fair Rosalie, with an arch look; "you who make others marry, should set the example."

"All in good time," answered Mr. Love, nodding; "one serves one's customers to so much happiness that one has none left for one's self."

Here a loud explosion was heard. Monsieur Goupille had pulled one of the bon-bon crackers with Mademoiselle Adele.

"I've got the motto!—no—Monsieur has it: I'm always unlucky," said the gentle Adele.

The epicier solemnly unrolled the little slip of paper; the print was very small, and he longed to take out his spectacles, but he thought that would make him look old. However, he spelled through the motto with some difficulty:—

"Comme elle fait soumettre un coeur,
En refusant son doux hommage,
On peut traiter la coquette en vainqueur;
De la beauty modeste on cherit l'esclavage."

[The coquette, who subjugates a heart, yet refuses its tender homage, one may treat as a conqueror: of modest beauty we cherish the slavery.]

"I present it to Mademoiselle," said he, laying the motto solemnly in Adele's plate, upon a little mountain of chestnut-husks.

"It is very pretty," said she, looking down.

"It is very a propos," whispered the epicier, caressing the peruque a little too roughly in his emotion. Mr. Love gave him a kick under the table, and put his finger to his own bald head, and then to his nose, significantly. The intelligent epicier smoothed back the irritated peruque.

"Are you fond of bon-bons, Mademoiselle Adele? I have a very fine stock at home," said Monsieur Goupille. Mademoiselle Adele de Courval sighed: "Helas! they remind me of happier days, when I was a petite and my dear grandmamma took me in her lap and told me how she escaped the guillotine: she was an emigree, and you know her father was a marquis."

The epicier bowed and looked puzzled. He did not quite see the connection between the bon-bons and the guillotine. "You are triste, Monsieur," observed Madame Beavor, in rather a piqued tone, to the Pole, who had not said a word since the roti.

"Madame, an exile is always triste: I think of my pauvre pays."

"Bah!" cried Mr. Love. "Think that there is no exile by the side of a belle dame."

The Pole smiled mournfully.

"Pull it," said Madame Beavor, holding a cracker to the patriot, and turning away her face.

"Yes, madame; I wish it were a cannon in defence of La Pologne."

With this magniloquent aspiration, the gallant Sovolofski pulled lustily, and then rubbed his fingers, with a little grimace, observing that crackers were sometimes dangerous, and that the present combustible was d'une force immense.

"Helas! J'ai cru jusqu'a ce jour

Pouvoir triompher de l'amour,"

[Alas! I believed until to-day that I could triumph over love.]

said Madame Beavor, reading the motto. "What do you say to that?"

"Madame, there is no triumph for La Pologne!" Madame Beavor uttered a little peevish exclamation, and glanced in despair at her red-headed countryman. "Are you, too, a great politician, sir?" said she in English.

"No, mem!—I'm all for the ladies."

"What does he say?" asked Madame Caumartin.

"Monsieur Higgins est tout pour les dames."

"To be sure he is," cried Mr. Love; "all the English are, especially with that coloured hair; a lady who likes a passionate adorer should always marry a man with gold-coloured hair—always. What do you say, Mademoiselle Adele?"

"Oh, I like fair hair," said Mademoiselle, looking bashfully askew at Monsieur Goupille's peruque. "Grandmamma said her papa—the marquis—used yellow powder: it must have been very pretty."

"Rather a la sucre d' orge," remarked the epicier, smiling on the right side of his mouth, where his best teeth were. Mademoiselle de Courval looked displeased. "I fear you are a republican, Monsieur Goupille."

"I, Mademoiselle. No; I'm for the Restoration;" and again the epicier perplexed himself to discover the association of idea between republicanism and sucre d'orge.

"Another glass of wine. Come, another," said Mr. Love, stretching across the Vicomte to help Madame Canmartin.

"Sir," said the tall Frenchman with the riband, eying the epicier with great disdain, "you say you are for the Restoration—I am for the Empire—Moi!"

"No politics!" cried Mr. Love. "Let us adjourn to the salon."

The Vicomte, who had seemed supremely ennuye during this dialogue, plucked Mr. Love by the sleeve as he rose, and whispered petulantly, "I do not see any one here to suit me, Monsieur Love—none of my rank."

"Mon Dieu!" answered Mr. Love: "point d' argent point de Suisse. I could introduce you to a duchess, but then the fee is high. There's Mademoiselle de Courval—she dates from the Carlovingians."

"She is very like a boiled sole," answered the Vicomte, with a wry face. "Still—what dower has she?"

"Forty thousand francs, and sickly," replied Mr. Love; "but she likes a tall man, and Monsieur Goupille is—"

"Tall men are never well made," interrupted the Vicomte, angrily; and he drew himself aside as Mr. Love, gallantly advancing, gave his arm to Madame Beavor, because the Pole had, in rising, folded both his own arms across his breast.

"Excuse me, ma'am," said Mr. Love to Madame Beavor, as they adjourned to the salon, "I don't think you manage that brave man well."

"Ma foi, comme il est ennuyeux avec sa Pologne," replied Madame Beavor, shrugging her shoulders.

"True; but he is a very fine-shaped man; and it is a comfort to think that one will have no rival but his country. Trust me, and encourage him a little more; I think he would suit you to a T."

Here the attendant engaged for the evening announced Monsieur and Madame Giraud; whereupon there entered a little—little couple, very fair, very plump, and very like each other. This was Mr. Love's show couple—his decoy ducks—his last best example of match-making; they had been married two months out of the bureau, and were the admiration of the neighbourhood for their conjugal affection. As they were now united, they had ceased to frequent the table d'hote; but Mr. Love often invited them after the dessert, pour encourager les autres.

"My dear friends," cried Mr. Love, shaking each by the hand, "I am ravished to see you. Ladies and gentlemen, I present to you Monsieur and Madame Giraud, the happiest couple in Christendom;—if I had done nothing else in my life but bring them together I should not have lived in vain!"

The company eyed the objects of this eulogium with great attention.

"Monsieur, my prayer is to deserve my bonheur," said Monsieur Giraud.

"Cher ange!" murmured Madame: and the happy pair seated themselves next to each other.

Mr. Love, who was all for those innocent pastimes which do away with conventional formality and reserve, now proposed a game at "Hunt the Slipper," which was welcomed by the whole party, except the Pole and the Vicomte; though Mademoiselle Adele looked prudish, and observed to the epicier, "that Monsieur Lofe was so droll, but she should not have liked her pauvre grandmaman to see her."

The Vicomte had stationed himself opposite to Mademoiselle de Courval, and kept his eyes fixed on her very tenderly.

"Mademoiselle, I see, does not approve of such bourgeois diversions," said he.

"No, monsieur," said the gentle Adele. "But I think we must sacrifice our own tastes to those of the company."

"It is a very amiable sentiment," said the epicier.

"It is one attributed to grandmamma's papa, the Marquis de Courval. It has become quite a hackneyed remark since," said Adele.

"Come, ladies," said the joyous Rosalie; "I volunteer my slipper."

"Asseyez-vous donc," said Madame Beavor to the Pole. "Have you no games of this sort in Poland?"

"Madame, La Pologne is no more," said the Pole. "But with the swords of her brave—"

"No swords here, if you please," said Mr. Love, putting his vast hands on the Pole's shoulder, and sinking him forcibly down into the circle now formed.

The game proceeded with great vigour and much laughter from Rosalie, Mr. Love, and Madame Beavor, especially whenever the last thumped the Pole with the heel of the slipper. Monsieur Giraud was always sure that Madame Giraud had the slipper about her, which persuasion on his part gave rise to many little endearments, which are always so innocent among married people. The Vicomte and the epicier were equally certain the slipper was with Mademoiselle Adele, who defended herself with much more energy than might have been supposed in one so gentle. The epicier, however, grew jealous of the attentions of his noble rival, and told him that he gene'd mademoiselle; whereupon the Vicomte called him an impertinent; and the tall Frenchman, with the riband, sprang up and said:

"Can I be of any assistance, gentlemen?"

Therewith Mr. Love, the great peacemaker, interposed, and reconciling the rivals, proposed to change the game to Colin Maillard-Anglice, "Blind Man's Buff." Rosalie clapped her hands, and offered herself to be blindfolded. The tables and chairs were cleared away; and Madame Beaver pushed the Pole into Rosalie's arms, who, having felt him about the face for some moments, guessed him to be the tall Frenchman. During this time Monsieur and Madame Giraud hid themselves behind the window-curtain.

"Amuse yourself, mon ami," said Madame Beaver, to the liberated Pole.

"Ah, madame," sighed Monsieur Sovolofski, "how can I be gay! All my property confiscated by the Emperor of Russia! Has La Pologne no Brutus?"

"I think you are in love," said the host, clapping him on the back.

"Are you quite sure," whispered the Pole to the matchmaker, "that Madame Beavor has vingt mille livres de rentes?"

"Not a sous less."

The Pole mused, and, glancing at Madame Beavor, said, "And yet, madame, your charming gaiety consoles me amidst all my suffering;" upon which Madame Beavor called him "flatterer," and rapped his knuckles with her fan; the latter proceeding the brave Pole did not seem to like, for he immediately buried his hands in his trousers' pockets.

The game was now at its meridian. Rosalie was uncommonly active, and flew about here and there, much to the harassment of the Pole, who repeatedly wiped his forehead, and observed that it was warm work, and put him in mind of the last sad battle for La Pologne. Monsieur Goupille, who had lately taken lessons in dancing, and was vain of his agility—mounted the chairs and tables, as Rosalie approached—with great grace and gravity. It so happened that, in these saltations, he ascended a stool near the curtain behind which Monsieur and Madame Giraud were ensconced. Somewhat agitated by a slight flutter behind the folds, which made him fancy, on the sudden panic, that Rosalie was creeping that way, the epicier made an abrupt pirouette, and the hook on which the curtains were suspended caught his left coat-tail,

"The fatal vesture left the unguarded side;"

just as he turned to extricate the garment from that dilemma, Rosalie sprang upon him, and naturally lifting her hands to that height where she fancied the human face divine, took another extremity of Monsieur Goupille's graceful frame thus exposed, by surprise.

"I don't know who this is. Quelle drole de visage!" muttered Rosalie.

"Mais, madame," faltered Monsieur Goupille, looking greatly disconcerted.

The gentle Adele, who did not seem to relish this adventure, came to the relief of her wooer, and pinched Rosalie very sharply in the arm.

"That's not fair. But I will know who this is," cried Rosalie, angrily; "you sha'n't escape!"

A sudden and universal burst of laughter roused her suspicions—she drew back—and exclaiming, "Mais quelle mauvaise plaisanterie; c'est trop fort!" applied her fair hand to the place in dispute, with so hearty a good-will, that Monsieur Goupille uttered a dolorous cry, and sprang from the chair leaving the coat-tail (the cause of all his woe) suspended upon the hook.

It was just at this moment, and in the midst of the excitement caused by Monsieur Goupille's misfortune, that the door opened, and the attendant reappeared, followed by a young man in a large cloak.

The new-comer paused at the threshold, and gazed around him in evident surprise.

"Diable!" said Mr. Love, approaching, and gazing hard at the stranger. "Is it possible?—You are come at last? Welcome!"

"But," said the stranger, apparently still bewildered, "there is some mistake; you are not—"

"Yes, I am Mr. Love!—Love all the world over. How is our friend Gregg?—told you to address yourself to Mr. Love,—eh?—Mum!—Ladies and gentlemen, an acquisition to our party. Fine fellow, eh?—Five feet eleven without his shoes,—and young enough to hope to be thrice married before he dies. When did you arrive?"

"To-day."

And thus, Philip Morton and Mr. William Gawtrey met once more.

CHAPTER II

"Happy the man who, void of care and strife,
In silken or in leathern purse retains A splendid shilling!"—The Splendid Shilling.

"And wherefore should they take or care for thought, The unreasoning vulgar willingly obey, And leaving toil and poverty behind. Run forth by different ways, the blissful boon to find." WEST'S Education.

"Poor, boy! your story interests me. The events are romantic, but the moral is practical, old, everlasting—life, boy, life. Poverty by itself is no such great curse; that is, if it stops short of starving. And passion by itself is a noble thing, sir; but poverty and passion together—poverty and feeling—poverty and pride—the poverty one is not born to,—but falls into;—and the man who ousts you out of your easy-chair, kicking you with every turn he takes, as he settles himself more comfortably—why there's no romance in that—hard every-day life, sir! Well, well:—so after your brother's letter you resigned yourself to that fellow Smith."

"No; I gave him my money, not my soul. I turned from his door, with a few shillings that he himself thrust into my hand, and walked on—I cared not whither—out of the town, into the fields—till night came; and then, just as I suddenly entered on the high-road, many miles away, the moon rose; and I saw, by the hedge-side, something that seemed like a corpse; it was an old beggar, in the last state of raggedness, disease, and famine. He had laid himself down to die. I shared with him what I had, and helped him to a little inn. As he crossed the threshold, he turned round and blessed me. Do you know, the moment I heard that blessing a stone seemed rolled away from my heart? I said to myself, 'What then! even I can be of use to some one; and I am better off than that old man, for I have youth and health.' As these thoughts stirred in me, my limbs, before heavy with fatigue, grew light; a strange kind of excitement seized me. I ran on gaily beneath the moonlight that smiled over the crisp, broad road. I felt as if no house, not even a palace, were large enough for me that night. And when, at last, wearied out, I crept into a wood, and laid myself down to sleep, I still murmured to myself, 'I have youth and health.' But, in the morning, when I rose, I stretched out my arms, and missed my brother!... In two or three days I found employment with a farmer; but we quarrelled after a few weeks; for once he wished to strike me; and somehow or other I could work, but not serve. Winter had begun when we parted.—Oh, such a winter!—Then—then I knew what it was to be houseless. How I lived for some months—if to live it can be called—it would pain you to hear, and humble me to tell. At last, I found myself again in London; and one evening, not many days since, I resolved at last—for nothing else seemed left, and I had not touched food for two days—to come to you."

"And why did that never occur to you before?"!

"Because," said Philip, with a deep blush,—"because I trembled at the power over my actions and my future life that I was to give to one, whom I was to bless as a benefactor, yet distrust as a guide."

"Well," said Love, or Gawtrey, with a singular mixture of irony and compassion in his voice; "and it was hunger, then, that terrified you at last even more than I?"

"Perhaps hunger—or perhaps rather the reasoning that comes from hunger. I had not, I say, touched food for two days; and I was standing on that bridge, from which on one side you see the palace of a head of the Church, on the other the towers of the Abbey, within which the men I have read of in history lie buried. It was a cold, frosty evening, and the river below looked bright with the lamps and stars. I leaned, weak and sickening, against the wall of the bridge; and in one of the arched recesses beside me a cripple held out his hat for pence. I envied him!—he had a livelihood; he was inured to it, perhaps bred to it; he had no shame. By a sudden impulse, I, too, turned abruptly round—held out my hand to the first passenger, and started at the shrillness of my own voice, as it cried 'Charity.'"

Gawtrey threw another log on the fire, looked complacently round the comfortable room, and rubbed his hands. The young man continued,—

"'You should be ashamed of yourself—I've a great mind to give you to the police,' was the answer, in a pert and sharp tone. I looked up, and saw the livery my father's menials had worn. I had been begging my bread from Robert Beaufort's lackey! I said nothing; the man went on his business on tiptoe, that the mud might not splash above the soles of his shoes. Then, thoughts so black that they seemed to blot out every star from the sky—thoughts I had often wrestled against, but to which I now gave myself up with a sort of mad joy—seized me: and I remembered you. I had still preserved the address you gave me; I went straight to the house. Your friend, on naming you, received me kindly, and without question placed food before me—pressed on me clothing and money—procured me a passport—gave me your address—and now I am beneath your roof. Gawtrey, I know nothing yet of the world but the dark side of it. I know not what to deem you—but as you alone have been kind to me, so it is to your kindness rather than your aid, that I now cling—your kind words and kind looks—yet—" he stopped short, and breathed hard.

"Yet you would know more of me. Faith, my boy, I cannot tell you more at this moment. I believe, to speak fairly, I don't live exactly within the pale of the law. But I'm not a villain! I never plundered my friend and called it play!—I never murdered my friend and called it honour!—I never seduced my friend's wife and called it gallantry!" As Gawtrey said this, he drew the words out, one by one, through his grinded teeth, paused and resumed more gaily: "I struggle with Fortune; voila tout! I am not what you seem to suppose—not exactly a swindler, certainly not a robber! But, as I before told you, I am a charlatan, so is every man who strives to be richer or greater than he is.

"I, too, want kindness as much as you do. My bread and my cup are at your service. I will try and keep you unsullied, even by the clean dirt that now and then sticks to me. On the other hand, youth, my young friend, has no right to play the censor; and you must take me as you take the world, without being over-scrupulous and dainty. My present vocation pays well; in fact, I am beginning to lay by. My real name and past life are thoroughly unknown, and as yet unsuspected, in this quartier; for though I have seen much of Paris, my career hitherto has passed in other parts of the city;—and for the rest, own that I am well disguised! What a benevolent air this bald forehead gives me—eh? True," added Gawtrey, somewhat more seriously, "if I saw how you could support yourself in a broader path of life than that in which I pick out my own way, I might say to you, as a gay man of fashion might say to some sober stripling—nay, as many a dissolute father says (or ought to say) to his son, 'It is no reason you should be a sinner, because I am not a saint.' In a word, if you were well off in a respectable profession, you might have safer acquaintances than myself. But, as it is, upon my word as a plain man, I don't see what you can do better." Gawtrey made this speech with so much frankness and ease, that it seemed greatly to relieve the listener, and when he wound up with, "What say you? In fine, my life is that of a great schoolboy, getting into scrapes for the fun of it, and fighting his way out as he best can!—Will you see how you like it?" Philip, with a confiding and grateful impulse, put his hand into Gawtrey's. The host shook it cordially, and, without saying another word, showed his guest into a little cabinet where there was a sofa-bed, and they parted for the night. The new life upon which Philip Morton entered was so odd, so grotesque, and so amusing, that at his age it was, perhaps, natural that he should not be clear-sighted as to its danger.

William Gawtrey was one of those men who are born to exert a certain influence and ascendency wherever they may be thrown; his vast strength, his redundant health, had a power of themselves—a moral as well as physical power. He naturally possessed high animal spirits, beneath the surface of which, however, at times, there was visible a certain undercurrent of malignity and scorn. He had evidently received a superior education, and could command at will the manner of a man not unfamiliar with a politer class of society. From the first hour that Philip had seen him on the top of the coach on the R— road, this man had attracted his curiosity and interest; the conversation he had heard in the churchyard, the obligations he owed to Gawtrey in his escape from the officers of justice, the time afterwards passed in his society till they separated at the little inn, the rough and hearty kindliness Gawtrey had shown him at that period, and the hospitality extended to him now,—all contributed to excite his fancy, and in much, indeed very much, entitled this singular person to his gratitude. Morton, in a word, was fascinated; this man was the only friend he had made. I have not thought it necessary to detail to the reader the conversations that had taken place between them, during that passage of Morton's life when he was before for some days Gawtrey's companion; yet those conversations had sunk deep in his mind. He was struck, and almost awed, by the profound gloom which lurked under Gawtrey's broad humour—a gloom, not of temperament, but of knowledge. His views of life, of human justice and human virtue, were (as, to be sure, is commonly the case with men who have had reason to quarrel with the world) dreary and despairing; and Morton's own experience had been so sad, that these opinions were more influential than they could ever have been with the happy. However in this, their second reunion, there was a greater gaiety than in their first; and under his host's roof Morton insensibly, but rapidly, recovered something of the early and natural tone of his impetuous and ardent spirits. Gawtrey himself was generally a boon companion; their society, if not select, was merry. When their evenings were disengaged, Gawtrey was fond of haunting cafes and theatres, and Morton was his companion; Birnie (Mr. Gawtrey's partner) never accompanied them. Refreshed by this change of life, the very person of this young man regained its bloom and vigour, as a plant, removed from some choked atmosphere and unwholesome soil, where it had struggled for light and air, expands on transplanting; the graceful leaves burst from the long-drooping boughs, and the elastic crest springs upward to the sun in the glory of its young prime. If there was still a certain fiery sternness in his aspect, it had ceased, at least, to be haggard and savage, it even suited the character of his dark and expressive features. He might not have lost the something of the tiger in his fierce temper, but in the sleek hues and the sinewy symmetry of the frame he began to put forth also something of the tiger's beauty.

Mr. Birnie did not sleep in the house, he went home nightly to a lodging at some little distance. We have said but little about this man, for, to all appearance, there was little enough to say; he rarely opened his own mouth except to Gawtrey, with whom Philip often observed him engaged in whispered conferences, to which he was not admitted. His eye, however, was less idle than his lips; it was not a bright eye: on the contrary, it was dull, and, to the unobservant, lifeless, of a pale blue, with a dim film over it—the eye of a vulture; but it had in it a calm, heavy, stealthy watchfulness, which inspired Morton with great distrust and aversion. Mr. Birnie not only spoke French like a native, but all his habits, his gestures, his tricks of manner, were French; not the French of good society, but more idiomatic, as it were, and popular. He was not exactly a vulgar person, he was too silent for that, but he was evidently of low extraction and coarse breeding; his accomplishments were of a mechanical nature; he was an extraordinary arithmetician, he was a very skilful chemist, and kept a laboratory at his lodgings—he mended his own clothes and linen with incomparable neatness. Philip suspected him of blacking his own shoes, but that was prejudice. Once he found Morton sketching horses' heads—pour se desennuyer; and he made some short criticisms on the drawings, which showed him well acquainted with the art. Philip, surprised, sought to draw him into conversation; but Birnie eluded the attempt, and observed that he had once been an engraver.

Gawtrey himself did not seem to know much of the early life of this person, or at least he did not seem to like much to talk of him. The footstep of Mr. Birnie was gliding, noiseless, and catlike; he had no sociality in him—enjoyed nothing—drank hard—but was never drunk. Somehow or other, he had evidently over Gawtrey an influence little less than that which Gawtrey had over Morton, but it was of a different nature: Morton had conceived an extraordinary affection for his friend, while Gawtrey seemed secretly to dislike Birnie, and to be glad whenever he quitted his presence. It was, in truth, Gawtrey's custom when Birnie retired for the night, to rub his hands, bring out the punchbowl, squeeze the lemons, and while Philip, stretched on the sofa, listened to him, between sleep and waking, to talk on for the hour together, often till daybreak, with that bizarre mixture of knavery and feeling, drollery and sentiment, which made the dangerous charm of his society.

One evening as they thus sat together, Morton, after listening for some time to his companion's comments on men and things, said abruptly,—

"Gawtrey! there is so much in you that puzzles me, so much which I find it difficult to reconcile with your present pursuits, that, if I ask no indiscreet confidence, I should like greatly to hear some account of your early life. It would please me to compare it with my own; when I am your age, I will then look back and see what I owed to your example."

"My early life! well—you shall hear it. It will put you on your guard, I hope, betimes against the two rocks of youth—love and friendship." Then, while squeezing the lemon into his favourite beverage, which Morton observed he made stronger than usual, Gawtrey thus commenced:

THE HISTORY OF A GOOD-FOR-NOTHING.

CHAPTER III

"All his success must on himself depend,
He had no money, counsel, guide, or friend;
With spirit high John learned the world to brave,
And in both senses was a ready knave."—CRABBE.

"My grandfather sold walking-sticks and umbrellas in the little passage by Exeter 'Change; he was a man of genius and speculation. As soon as he had scraped together a little money, he lent it to some poor devil with a hard landlord, at twenty per cent., and made him take half the loan in umbrellas or bamboos. By these means he got his foot into the ladder, and climbed upward and upward, till, at the age of forty, he had amassed £5,000. He then looked about for a wife. An honest trader in the Strand, who dealt largely in cotton prints, possessed an only daughter; this young lady had a legacy, from a great-aunt, of £3,220., with a small street in St. Giles's, where the tenants paid weekly (all thieves or rogues—all, so their rents were sure). Now my grandfather conceived a great friendship for the father of this young lady; gave him a hint as to a new pattern in spotted cottons; enticed him to take out a patent, and lent him £700. for the speculation; applied for the money at the very moment cottons were at their worst, and got the daughter instead of the money,—by which exchange, you see, he won £2,520., to say nothing of the young lady. My grandfather then entered into partnership with the worthy trader, carried on the patent with spirit, and begat two sons. As he grew older, ambition seized him; his sons should be gentlemen—one was sent to College, the other put into a marching regiment. My grandfather meant to die worth a plum; but a fever he caught in visiting his tenants in St. Giles's prevented him, and he only left £20,000. equally divided between the sons. My father, the College man" (here Gawtrey paused a moment, took a large draught of the punch, and resumed with a visible effort)—"my father, the College man, was a person of rigid principles—bore an excellent character—had a great regard for the world. He married early and respectably. I am the sole fruit of that union; he lived soberly, his temper was harsh and morose, his home gloomy; he was a very severe father, and my mother died before I was ten years old. When I was fourteen, a little old Frenchman came to lodge with us; he had been persecuted under the old regime for being a philosopher; he filled my head with odd crotchets which, more or less, have stuck there ever since. At eighteen I was sent to St. John's College, Cambridge. My father was rich enough to have let me go up in the higher rank of a pensioner, but he had lately grown avaricious; he thought that I was extravagant; he made me a sizar, perhaps to spite me. Then, for the first time, those inequalities in life which the Frenchman had dinned into my ears met me practically. A sizar! another name for a dog! I had such strength, health, and spirits, that I had more life in my little finger than half the fellow-commoners—genteel, spindle-shanked striplings, who might have passed for a collection of my grandfather's walking-canes—bad in their whole bodies. And I often think," continued Gawtrey, "that health and spirits have a great deal to answer for! When we are young we so far resemble savages who are Nature's young people—that we attach prodigious value to physical advantages. My feats of strength and activity—the clods I thrashed—and the railings I leaped—and the boat-races I won—are they not written in the chronicle of St. John's? These achievements inspired me with an extravagant sense of my own superiority; I could not but despise the rich fellows whom I could have blown down with a sneeze. Nevertheless, there was an impassable barrier between me and them—a sizar was not a proper associate for the favourites of fortune! But there was one young man, a year younger myself, of high birth, and the heir to considerable wealth, who did not regard me with the same supercilious insolence as the rest; his very rank, perhaps, made him indifferent to the little conventional formalities which influence persons who cannot play at football with this round world; he was the wildest youngster in the university—lamp-breaker—tandem-driver—mob-fighter—a very devil in short—clever, but not in the reading line—small and slight, but brave as a lion. Congenial habits made us intimate, and I loved him like a brother—better than a brother—as a dog loves his master. In all our rows I covered him with my body. He had but to say to me, 'Leap into the water,' and I would not have stopped to pull off my coat. In short, I loved him as a proud man loves one who stands betwixt him and contempt,—as an affectionate man loves one who stands between him and solitude. To cut short a long story: my friend, one dark night, committed an outrage against discipline, of the most unpardonable character. There was a sanctimonious, grave old fellow of the College, crawling home from a tea-party; my friend and another of his set seized, blindfolded, and handcuffed this poor wretch, carried him, vi et armis, back to the house of an old maid whom he had been courting for the last ten years, fastened his pigtail (he wore a long one) to the knocker, and so left him. You may imagine the infernal hubbub which his attempts to extricate himself caused in the whole street; the old maid's old maidservant, after emptying on his head all the vessels of wrath she could lay her hand to, screamed, 'Rape and murder!' The proctor and his bull-dogs came up, released the prisoner, and gave chase to the delinquents, who had incautiously remained near to enjoy the sport. The night was dark and they reached the College in safety, but they had been tracked to the gates. For this offence I was expelled."

"Why, you were not concerned in it?" said Philip.

"No; but I was suspected and accused. I could have got off by betraying the true culprits, but my friend's father was in public life—a stern, haughty old statesman; my friend was mortally afraid of him—the only person he was afraid of. If I had too much insisted on my innocence, I might have set inquiry on the right track. In fine, I was happy to prove my friendship for him. He shook me most tenderly by the hand on parting, and promised never to forget my generous devotion. I went home in disgrace: I need not tell you what my father said to me: I do not think he ever loved me from that hour. Shortly after this my uncle, George Gawtrey, the captain, returned from abroad; he took a great fancy to me, and I left my father's house (which had grown insufferable) to live with him. He had been a very handsome man—a gay spendthrift; he had got through his fortune, and now lived on his wits—he was a professed gambler. His easy temper, his lively humour, fascinated me; he knew the world well; and, like all gamblers, was generous when the dice were lucky,—which, to tell you the truth, they generally were, with a man who had no scruples. Though his practices were a little suspected, they had never been discovered. We lived in an elegant apartment, mixed familiarly with men of various ranks, and enjoyed life extremely. I brushed off my college rust, and conceived a taste for expense: I knew not why it was, but in my new existence every one was kind to me; and I had spirits that made me welcome everywhere. I was a scamp—but a frolicsome scamp—and that is always a popular character. As yet I was not dishonest, but saw dishonesty round me, and it seemed a very pleasant, jolly mode of making money; and now I again fell into contact with the young heir. My college friend was as wild in London as he had been at Cambridge; but the boy-ruffian, though not then twenty years of age, had grown into the man-villain."

Here Gawtrey paused, and frowned darkly.

"He had great natural parts, this young man—much wit, readiness, and cunning, and he became very intimate with my uncle. He learned of him how to play the dice, and a pack the cards—he paid him £1,000. for the knowledge!"

"How! a cheat? You said he was rich."

"His father was very rich, and he had a liberal allowance, but he was very extravagant; and rich men love gain as well as poor men do! He had no excuse but the grand excuse of all vice—SELFISHNESS. Young as he was he became the fashion, and he fattened upon the plunder of his equals, who desired the honour of his acquaintance. Now, I had seen my uncle cheat, but I had never imitated his example; when the man of fashion cheated, and made a jest of his earnings and my scruples—when I saw him courted, flattered, honoured, and his acts unsuspected, because his connections embraced half the peerage, the temptation grew strong, but I still resisted it. However, my father always said I was born to be a good-for-nothing, and I could not escape my destiny. And now I suddenly fell in love—you don't know what that is yet—so much the better for you. The girl was beautiful, and I thought she loved me—perhaps she did—but I was too poor, so her friends said, for marriage. We courted, as the saying is, in the meanwhile. It was my love for her, my wish to deserve her, that made me iron against my friend's example. I was fool enough to speak to him of Mary—to present him to her—this ended in her seduction." (Again Gawtrey paused, and breathed hard.) "I discovered the treachery—I called out the seducer—he sneered, and refused to fight the low-born adventurer. I struck him to the earth—and then we fought. I was satisfied by a ball through my side! but he," added Gawtrey, rubbing his hands, and with a vindictive chuckle,—"He was a cripple for life! When I recovered I found that my foe, whose sick-chamber was crowded with friends and comforters, had taken advantage of my illness to ruin my reputation. He, the swindler, accused me of his own crime: the equivocal character of my uncle confirmed the charge. Him, his own high-born pupil was enabled to unmask, and his disgrace was visited on me. I left my bed to find my uncle (all disguise over) an avowed partner in a hell, and myself blasted alike in name, love, past, and future. And then, Philip—then I commenced that career which I have trodden since—the prince of good-fellows and good-for-nothings, with ten thousand aliases, and as many strings to my bow. Society cast me off when I was innocent. Egad, I have had my revenge on society since!—Ho! ho! ho!"

The laugh of this man had in it a moral infection. There was a sort of glorying in its deep tone; it was not the hollow hysteric of shame and despair—it spoke a sanguine joyousness! William Gawtrey was a man whose animal constitution had led him to take animal pleasure in all things: he had enjoyed the poisons he had lived on.

"But your father—surely your father—"

"My father," interrupted Gawtrey, "refused me the money (but a small sum) that, once struck with the strong impulse of a sincere penitence, I begged of him, to enable me to get an honest living in a humble trade. His refusal soured the penitence—it gave me an excuse for my career and conscience grapples to an excuse as a drowning wretch to a straw. And yet this hard father—this cautious, moral, money-loving man, three months afterwards, suffered a rogue—almost a stranger—to decoy him into a speculation that promised to bring him fifty per cent. He invested in the traffic of usury what had sufficed to save a hundred such as I am from perdition, and he lost it all. It was nearly his whole fortune; but he lives and has his luxuries still: he cannot speculate, but he can save: he cared not if I starved, for he finds an hourly happiness in starving himself."

"And your friend," said Philip, after a pause in which his young sympathies went dangerously with the excuses for his benefactor; "what has become of him, and the poor girl?"

"My friend became a great man; he succeeded to his father's peerage—a very ancient one—and to a splendid income. He is living still. Well, you shall hear about the poor girl! We are told of victims of seduction dying in a workhouse or on a dunghill, penitent, broken-hearted, and uncommonly ragged and sentimental. It may be a frequent case, but it is not the worst. It is worse, I think, when the fair, penitent, innocent, credulous dupe becomes in her turn the deceiver—when she catches vice from the breath upon which she has hung—when she ripens, and mellows, and rots away into painted, blazing, staring, wholesale harlotry—when, in her turn, she ruins warm youth with false smiles and long bills—and when worse—worse than all—when she has children, daughters perhaps, brought up to the same trade, cooped, plumper, for some hoary lecher, without a heart in their bosoms, unless a balance for weighing money may be called a heart. Mary became this; and I wish to Heaven she had rather died in an hospital! Her lover polluted her soul as well as her beauty: he found her another lover when he was tired of her. When she was at the age of thirty-six I met her in Paris, with a daughter of sixteen. I was then flush with money, frequenting salons, and playing the part of a fine gentleman. She did not know me at first; and she sought my acquaintance. For you must know, my young friend," said Gawtrey, abruptly breaking off the thread of his narrative, "that I am not altogether the low dog you might suppose in seeing me here. At Paris—ah! you don't know Paris—there is a glorious ferment in society in which the dregs are often uppermost! I came here at the Peace, and here have I resided the greater part of each year ever since. The vast masses of energy and life, broken up by the great thaw of the Imperial system, floating along the tide, are terrible icebergs for the vessel of the state. Some think Napoleonism over—its effects are only begun. Society is shattered from one end to the other, and I laugh at the little rivets by which they think to keep it together.

[This passage was written at a period when the dynasty of Louis Philippe seemed the most assured, and Napoleonism was indeed considered extinct.]

"But to return. Paris, I say, is the atmosphere for adventurers—new faces and new men are so common here that they excite no impertinent inquiry, it is so usual to see fortunes made in a day and spent in a month; except in certain circles, there is no walking round a man's character to spy out where it wants piercing! Some lean Greek poet put lead in his pockets to prevent being blown away;—put gold in your pockets, and at Paris you may defy the sharpest wind in the world,—yea, even the breath of that old AEolus—Scandal! Well, then, I had money—no matter how I came by it—and health, and gaiety; and I was well received in the coteries that exist in all capitals, but mostly in France, where pleasure is the cement that joins many discordant atoms. Here, I say, I met Mary and her daughter, by my old friend—the daughter, still innocent, but, sacra! in what an element of vice! We knew each other's secrets, Mary and I, and kept them: she thought me a greater knave than I was, and she intrusted to me her intention of selling her child to a rich English marquis. On the other hand, the poor girl confided to me her horror of the scenes she witnessed and the snares that surrounded her. What do you think preserved her pure from all danger? Bah! you will never guess! It was partly because, if example corrupts, it as often deters, but principally because she loved. A girl who loves one man purely has about her an amulet which defies the advances of the profligate. There was a handsome young Italian, an artist, who frequented the house—he was the man. I had to choose, then, between mother and daughter: I chose the last."

Philip seized hold of Gawtrey's hand, grasped it warmly, and the good-for-nothing continued—

"Do you know, that I loved that girl as well as I had ever loved the mother, though in another way; she was what I fancied the mother to be; still more fair, more graceful, more winning, with a heart as full of love as her mother's had been of vanity. I loved that child as if she had been my own daughter. I induced her to leave her mother's house—I secreted her—I saw her married to the man she loved—I gave her away, and saw no more of her for several months."

"Why?"

"Because I spent them in prison! The young people could not live upon air; I gave them what I had, and in order to do more I did something which displeased the police; I narrowly escaped that time; but I am popular—very popular, and with plenty of witnesses, not over-scrupulous, I got off! When I was released, I would not go to see them, for my clothes were ragged: the police still watched me, and I would not do them harm in the world! Ay, poor wretches! they struggled so hard: he could get very little by his art, though, I believe, he was a cleverish fellow at it, and the money I had given them could not last for ever. They lived near the Champs Elysees, and at night I used to steal out and look at them through the window. They seemed so happy, and so handsome, and so good; but he looked sickly, and I saw that, like all Italians, he languished for his own warm climate. But man is born to act as well as to contemplate," pursued Gawtrey, changing his tone into the allegro; "and I was soon driven into my old ways, though in a lower line. I went to London, just to give my reputation an airing, and when I returned, pretty flush again, the poor Italian was dead, and Fanny was a widow, with one boy, and enceinte with a second child. So then I sought her again, for her mother had found her out, and was at her with her devilish kindness; but Heaven was merciful, and took her away from both of us: she died in giving birth to a girl, and her last words were uttered to me, imploring me—the adventurer—the charlatan—the good-for-nothing—to keep her child from the clutches of her own mother. Well, sir, I did what I could for both the children; but the boy was consumptive, like his father, and sleeps at Pere-la-Chaise. The girl is here—you shall see her some day. Poor Fanny! if ever the devil will let me, I shall reform for her sake. Meanwhile, for her sake I must get grist for the mill. My story is concluded, for I need not tell you all of my pranks—of all the parts I have played in life. I have never been a murderer, or a burglar, or a highway robber, or what the law calls a thief. I can only say, as I said before, I have lived upon my wits, and they have been a tolerable capital on the whole. I have been an actor, a money-lender, a physician, a professor of animal magnetism (that was lucrative till it went out of fashion, perhaps it will come in again); I have been a lawyer, a house-agent, a dealer in curiosities and china; I have kept a hotel; I have set up a weekly newspaper; I have seen almost every city in Europe, and made acquaintance with some of its gaols; but a man who has plenty of brains generally falls on his legs."

"And your father?" said Philip; and here he spoke to Gawtrey of the conversation he had overheard in the churchyard, but on which a scruple of natural delicacy had hitherto kept him silent.

"Well, now," said his host, while a slight blush rose to his cheeks, "I will tell you, that though to my father's sternness and avarice I attribute many of my faults, I yet always had a sort of love for him; and when in London I accidentally heard that he was growing blind, and living with an artful old jade of a housekeeper, who might send him to rest with a dose of magnesia the night after she had coaxed him to make a will in her favour. I sought him out—and—but you say you heard what passed."

"Yes; and I heard him also call you by name, when it was too late, and I saw the tears on his cheeks."

"Did you? Will you swear to that?" exclaimed Gawtrey, with vehemence: then, shading his brow with his band, he fell into a reverie that lasted some moments.

"If anything happen to me, Philip," he said, abruptly, "perhaps he may yet be a father to poor Fanny; and if he takes to her, she will repay him for whatever pain I may, perhaps, have cost him. Stop! now I think of it, I will write down his address for you—never forget it—there! It is time to go to bed."

Gawtrey's tale made a deep impression on Philip. He was too young, too inexperienced, too much borne away by the passion of the narrator, to see that Gawtrey had less cause to blame Fate than himself. True, he had been unjustly implicated in the disgrace of an unworthy uncle, but he had lived with that uncle, though he knew him to be a common cheat; true, he had been betrayed by a friend, but he had before known that friend to be a man without principle or honour. But what wonder that an ardent boy saw nothing of this—saw only the good heart that had saved a poor girl from vice, and sighed to relieve a harsh and avaricious parent? Even the hints that Gawtrey unawares let fall of practices scarcely covered by the jovial phrase of "a great schoolboy's scrapes," either escaped the notice of Philip, or were charitably construed by him, in the compassion and the ignorance of a young, hasty, and grateful heart.

CHAPTER IV

"And she's a stranger
Women—beware women."—MIDDLETON.

"As we love our youngest children best,
So the last fruit of our affection,

Wherever we bestow it, is most strong;
Since 'tis indeed our latest harvest-home,
Last merriment 'fore winter!"
WEBSTER, Devil's Law Case.

"I would fain know what kind of thing a man's heart is?
I will report it to you; 'tis a thing framed
With divers corners!"—ROWLEY.

I have said that Gawtrey's tale made a deep impression on Philip;—that impression was increased by subsequent conversations, more frank even than their talk had hitherto been. There was certainly about this man a fatal charm which concealed his vices. It arose, perhaps, from the perfect combinations of his physical frame—from a health which made his spirits buoyant and hearty under all circumstances—and a blood so fresh, so sanguine, that it could not fail to keep the pores of the heart open. But he was not the less—for all his kindly impulses and generous feelings, and despite the manner in which, naturally anxious to make the least unfavourable portrait of himself to Philip, he softened and glossed over the practices of his life—a thorough and complete rogue, a dangerous, desperate, reckless daredevil. It was easy to see when anything crossed him, by the cloud on his shaggy brow, by the swelling of the veins on the forehead, by the dilation of the broad nostril, that he was one to cut his way through every obstacle to an end,—choleric, impetuous, fierce, determined. Such, indeed, were the qualities that made him respected among his associates, as his more bland and humorous ones made him beloved. He was, in fact, the incarnation of that great spirit which the laws of the world raise up against the world, and by which the world's injustice on a large scale is awfully chastised; on a small scale, merely nibbled at and harassed, as the rat that gnaws the hoof of the elephant:—the spirit which, on a vast theatre, rises up, gigantic and sublime, in the heroes of war and revolution—in Mirabeaus, Marats, Napoleons: on a minor stage, it shows itself in demagogues, fanatical philosophers, and mob-writers; and on the forbidden boards, before whose reeking lamps outcasts sit, at once audience and actors, it never produced a knave more consummate in his part, or carrying it off with more buskined dignity, than William Gawtrey. I call him by his aboriginal name; as for his other appellations, Bacchus himself had not so many!

One day, a lady, richly dressed, was ushered by Mr. Birnie into the bureau of Mr. Love, alias Gawtrey. Philip was seated by the window, reading, for the first time, the Candide,—that work, next to Rasselas, the most hopeless and gloomy of the sports of genius with mankind. The lady seemed rather embarrassed when she perceived Mr. Love was not alone. She drew back, and, drawing her veil still more closely round her, said, in French:

"Pardon me, I would wish a private conversation." Philip rose to withdraw, when the lady, observing him with eyes whose lustre shone through the veil, said gently: "But perhaps the young gentleman is discreet."

"He is not discreet, he is discretion!—my adopted son. You may confide in him—upon my honour you may, madam!" and Mr. Love placed his hand on his heart.

"He is very young," said the lady, in a tone of involuntary compassion, as, with a very white hand, she unclasped the buckle of her cloak.

"He can the better understand the curse of celibacy," returned Mr. Love, smiling.

The lady lifted part of her veil, and discovered a handsome mouth, and a set of small, white teeth; for she, too, smiled, though gravely, as she turned to Morton, and said—

"You seem, sir, more fitted to be a votary of the temple than one of its officers. However, Monsieur Love, let there be no mistake between us; I do not come here to form a marriage, but to prevent one. I understand that Monsieur the Vicomte de Vaudemont has called into request your services. I am one of the Vicomte's family; we are all anxious that he should not contract an engagement of the strange and, pardon me, unbecoming character, which must stamp a union formed at a public office."

"I assure you, madam," said Mr. Love, with dignity, "that we have contributed to the very first—"

"Mon Dieu!" interrupted the lady, with much impatience, "spare me a eulogy on your establishment: I have no doubt it is very respectable; and for grisettes and epiciers may do extremely well. But the Vicomte is a man of birth and connections. In a word, what he contemplates is preposterous. I know not what fee Monsieur Love expects; but if he contrive to amuse Monsieur de Vaudemont, and to frustrate every connection he proposes to form, that fee, whatever it may be, shall be doubled. Do you understand me?"

"Perfectly, madam; yet it is not your offer that will bias me, but the desire to oblige so charming a lady."

"It is agreed, then?" said the lady, carelessly; and as she spoke she again glanced at Philip.

"If madame will call again, I will inform her of my plans," said Mr. Love.

"Yes, I will call again. Good morning!" As she rose and passed Philip, she wholly put aside her veil, and looked at him with a gaze entirely free from coquetry, but curious, searching, and perhaps admiring—the look that an artist may give to a picture that seems of more value than the place where he finds it would seem to indicate. The countenance of the lady herself was fair and noble, and Philip felt a strange thrill at his heart as, with a slight inclination of her head, she turned from the room.

"Ah!" said Gawtrey, laughing, "this is not the first time I have been paid by relations to break off the marriages I had formed. Egad! if one could open a bureau to make married people single, one would soon be a Croesus! Well, then, this decides me to complete the union between Monsieur Goupille and Mademoiselle de Courval. I had balanced a little hitherto between the epicier and the Vicomte. Now I will conclude matters. Do you know, Phil, I think you have made a conquest?"

"Pooh!" said Philip, colouring.

In effect, that very evening Mr. Love saw both the epicier and Adele, and fixed the marriage-day. As Monsieur Goupille was a person of great distinction in the Faubourg, this wedding was one upon which Mr. Love congratulated himself greatly; and he cheerfully accepted an invitation for himself and his partners to honour the noces with their presence.

A night or two before the day fixed for the marriage of Monsieur Goupille and the aristocratic Adele, when Mr. Birnie had retired, Gawtrey made his usual preparations for enjoying himself. But this time the cigar and the punch seemed to fail of their effect. Gawtrey remained moody and silent; and Morton was thinking of the bright eyes of the lady who was so much interested against the amours of the Vicomte de Vaudemont.

At last, Gawtrey broke silence:

"My young friend," said he, "I told you of my little protege; I have been buying toys for her this morning; she is a beautiful creature; to-morrow is her birthday—she will then be six years old. But—but—" here Gawtrey sighed—"I fear she is not all right here," and he touched his forehead.

"I should like much to see her," said Philip, not noticing the latter remark.

"And you shall—you shall come with me to-morrow. Heigho! I should not like to die, for her sake!"

"Does her wretched relation attempt to regain her?"

"Her relation! No; she is no more—she died about two years since! Poor Mary! I—well, this is folly. But Fanny is at present in a convent; they are all kind to her, but then I pay well; if I were dead, and the pay stopped,—again I ask, what would become of her, unless, as I before said, my father—"

"But you are making a fortune now?"

"If this lasts—yes; but I live in fear—the police of this cursed city are lynx-eyed; however, that is the bright side of the question."

"Why not have the child with you, since you love her so much? She would be a great comfort to you."

"Is this a place for a child—a girl?" said Gawtrey, stamping his foot impatiently. "I should go mad if I saw that villainous deadman's eye bent upon her!"

"You speak of Birnie. How can you endure him?"

"When you are my age you will know why we endure what we dread—why we make friends of those who else would be most horrible foes: no, no—nothing can deliver me of this man but Death. And—and—" added Gawtrey, turning pale, "I cannot murder a man who eats my bread. There are stronger ties, my lad, than affection, that bind men, like galley-slaves, together. He who can hang you puts the halter round your neck and leads you by it like a dog."

A shudder came over the young listener. And what dark secrets, known only to those two, had bound, to a man seemingly his subordinate and tool, the strong will and resolute temper of William Gawtrey?

"But, begone, dull care!" exclaimed Gawtrey, rousing himself. "And, after all, Birnie is a useful fellow, and dare no more turn against me than I against him! Why don't you drink more?

"Oh! have you e'er heard of the famed Captain Wattle?"

and Gawtrey broke out into a loud Bacchanalian hymn, in which Philip could find no mirth, and from which the songster suddenly paused to exclaim:—

"Mind you say nothing about Fanny to Birnie; my secrets with him are not of that nature. He could not hurt her, poor lamb! it is true—at least, as far as I can foresee. But one can never feel too sure of one's lamb, if one once introduces it to the butcher!"

The next day being Sunday, the bureau was closed, and Philip and Gawtrey repaired to the convent. It was a dismal-looking place as to the exterior; but, within, there was a large garden, well kept, and, notwithstanding the winter, it seemed fair and refreshing, compared with the polluted streets. The window of the room into which they were shown looked upon the green sward, with walls covered with ivy at the farther end. And Philip's own childhood came back to him as he gazed on the quiet of the lonely place.

The door opened—an infant voice was heard, a voice of glee—of rapture; and a child, light and beautiful as a fairy, bounded to Gawtrey's breast.

Nestling there, she kissed his face, his hands, his clothes, with a passion that did not seem to belong to her age, laughing and sobbing almost at a breath.

On his part, Gawtrey appeared equally affected: he stroked down her hair with his huge hand, calling her all manner of pet names, in a tremulous voice that vainly struggled to be gay.

At length he took the toys he had brought with him from his capacious pockets, and strewing them on the floor, fairly stretched his vast bulk along; while the child tumbled over him, sometimes grasping at the toys, and then again returning to his bosom, and laying her head there, looked up quietly into his eyes, as if the joy were too much for her.

Morton, unheeded by both, stood by with folded arms. He thought of his lost and ungrateful brother, and muttered to himself:

"Fool! when she is older, she will forsake him!"

Fanny betrayed in her face the Italian origin of her father. She had that exceeding richness of complexion which, though not common even in Italy, is only to be found in the daughters of that land, and which harmonised well with the purple lustre of her hair, and the full, clear iris of the dark eyes. Never were parted cherries brighter than her dewy lips; and the colour of the open neck and the rounded arms was of a whiteness still more dazzling, from the darkness of the hair and the carnation of the glowing cheek.

Suddenly Fanny started from Gawtrey's arms, and running up to Morton, gazed at him wistfully, and said, in French:

"Who are you? Do you come from the moon? I think you do." Then, stopping abruptly, she broke into a verse of a nursery-song, which she chaunted with a low, listless tone, as if she were not conscious of the sense. As she thus sang, Morton, looking at her, felt a strange and painful doubt seize him. The child's eyes, though soft, were so vacant in their gaze.

"And why do I come from the moon?" said he.

"Because you look sad and cross. I don't like you—I don't like the moon; it gives me a pain here!" and she put her hand to her temples. "Have you got anything for Fanny—poor, poor Fanny?" and, dwelling on the epithet, she shook her head mournfully.

"You are rich, Fanny, with all those toys."

"Am I? Everybody calls me poor Fanny—everybody but papa;" and she ran again to Gawtrey, and laid her head on his shoulder.

"She calls me papa!" said Gawtrey, kissing her; "you hear it? Bless her!"

"And you never kiss any one but Fanny—you have no other little girl?" said the child, earnestly, and with a look less vacant than that which had saddened Morton.

"No other—no—nothing under heaven, and perhaps above it, but you!" and he clasped her in his arms. "But," he added, after a pause—"but mind me, Fanny, you must like this gentleman. He will be always good to you: and he had a little brother whom he was as fond of as I am of you."

"No, I won't like him—I won't like anybody but you and my sister!"

"Sister!—who is your sister?"

The child's face relapsed into an expression almost of idiotcy. "I don't know—I never saw her. I hear her sometimes, but I don't understand what she says.—Hush! come here!" and she stole to the window on tiptoe. Gawtrey followed and looked out.

"Do you hear her, now?" said Fanny. "What does she say?"

As the girl spoke, some bird among the evergreens uttered a shrill, plaintive cry, rather than song—a sound which the thrush occasionally makes in the winter, and which seems to express something of fear, and pain, and impatience. "What does she say?—can you tell me?" asked the child.

"Pooh! that is a bird; why do you call it your sister?"

"I don't know!—because it is—because it—because—I don't know—is it not in pain?—do something for it, papa!"

Gawtrey glanced at Morton, whose face betokened his deep pity, and creeping up to him, whispered,—

"Do you think she is really touched here? No, no,—she will outgrow it—I am sure she will!"

Morton sighed.

Fanny by this time had again seated herself in the middle of the floor, and arranged her toys, but without seeming to take pleasure in them.

At last Gawtrey was obliged to depart. The lay sister, who had charge of Fanny, was summoned into the parlour; and then the child's manner entirely changed; her face grew purple—she sobbed with as much anger as grief. "She would not leave papa—she would not go—that she would not!"

"It is always so," whispered Gawtrey to Morton, in an abashed and apologetic voice. "It is so difficult to get away from her. Just go and talk with her while I steal out."

Morton went to her, as she struggled with the patient good-natured sister, and began to soothe and caress her, till she turned on him her large humid eyes, and said, mournfully,

"Tu es mechant, tu. Poor Fanny!"

"But this pretty doll—" began the sister. The child looked at it joylessly.

"And papa is going to die!"

"Whenever Monsieur goes," whispered the nun, "she always says that he is dead, and cries herself quietly to sleep; when Monsieur returns, she says he is come to life again. Some one, I suppose, once talked to her about death; and she thinks when she loses sight of any one, that that is death."

"Poor child!" said Morton, with a trembling voice.

The child looked up, smiled, stroked his cheek with her little hand, and said:

"Thank you!—Yes! poor Fanny! Ah, he is going—see!—let me go too—tu es mechant."

"But," said Morton, detaining her gently, "do you know that you give him pain?—you make him cry by showing pain yourself. Don't make him so sad!"

The child seemed struck, hung down her head for a moment, as if in thought, and then, jumping from Morton's lap, ran to Gawtrey, put up her pouting lips, and said:

"One kiss more!"

Gawtrey kissed her, and turned away his head.

"Fanny is a good girl!" and Fanny, as she spoke, went back to Morton, and put her little fingers into her eyes, as if either to shut out Gawtrey's retreat from her sight, or to press back her tears.

"Give me the doll now, sister Marie."

Morton smiled and sighed, placed the child, who struggled no more, in the nun's arms, and left the room; but as he closed the door he looked back, and saw that Fanny had escaped from the sister, thrown herself on the floor, and was crying, but not loud.

"Is she not a little darling?" said Gawtrey, as they gained the street.

"She is, indeed, a most beautiful child!"

"And you will love her if I leave her penniless," said Gawtrey, abruptly. "It was your love for your mother and your brother that made me like you from the first. Ay," continued Gawtrey, in a tone of great earnestness, "ay, and whatever may happen to me, I will strive and keep you, my poor lad, harmless; and what is better, innocent even of such matters as sit light enough on my own well-seasoned conscience. In turn, if ever you have the power, be good to her,—yes, be good to her! and I won't say a harsh word to you if ever you like to turn king's evidence against myself."

"Gawtrey!" said Morton, reproachfully, and almost fiercely.

"Bah!—such things are! But tell me honestly, do you think she is very strange—very deficient?"

"I have not seen enough of her to judge," answered Morton, evasively.

"She is so changeful," persisted Gawtrey. "Sometimes you would say that she was above her age, she comes out with such thoughtful, clever things; then, the next moment, she throws me into despair. These nuns are very skilful in education—at least they are said to be so. The doctors give me hope, too. You see, her poor mother was very unhappy at the time of her birth—delirious, indeed: that may account for it. I often fancy that it is the constant excitement which her state occasions me that makes me love her so much. You see she is one who can never shift for herself. I must get money for her; I have left a little already with the superior, and I would not touch it to save myself from famine! If she has money people will be kind enough to her. And then," continued Gawtrey, "you must perceive that she loves nothing in the world but me—me, whom nobody else loves! Well—well, now to the shop again!"

On returning home the bonne informed them that a lady had called, and asked both for Monsieur Love and the young gentleman, and seemed much chagrined at missing both. By the description, Morton guessed she was the fair incognita, and felt disappointed at having lost the interview.

CHAPTER V

"The cursed carle was at his wonted trade,
Still tempting heedless men into his snare,
In witching wise, as I before have said;
But when he saw, in goodly gear array'd,
The grave majestic knight approaching nigh,
His countenance fell."—THOMSON, Castle of Indolence.

The morning rose that was to unite Monsieur Goupille with Mademoiselle Adele de Courval. The ceremony was performed, and bride and bridegroom went through that trying ordeal with becoming gravity. Only the elegant Adele seemed more unaffectedly agitated than Mr. Love could well account for; she was very nervous in church, and more often turned her eyes to the door than to the altar. Perhaps she wanted to run away; but it was either too late or too early for the proceeding. The rite performed, the happy pair and their friends adjourned to the Cadran Bleu, that restaurant so celebrated in the festivities of the good citizens of Paris. Here Mr. Love had ordered, at the epicier's expense, a most tasteful entertainment.

"Sacre! but you have not played the economist, Monsieur Lofe," said Monsieur Goupille, rather querulously, as he glanced at the long room adorned with artificial flowers, and the table a cingitante couverts.

"Bah!" replied Mr. Love, "you can retrench afterwards. Think of the fortune she brought you."

"It is a pretty sum, certainly," said Monsieur Goupille, "and the notary is perfectly satisfied."

"There is not a marriage in Paris that does me more credit," said Mr. Love; and he marched off to receive the compliments and congratulations that awaited him among such of the guests as were aware of his good offices. The Vicomte de Vaudemont was of course not present. He had not been near Mr. Love since Adele had accepted the epicier. But Madame Beavor, in a white bonnet lined with lilac, was hanging, sentimentally, on the arm of the Pole, who looked very grand with his white favour; and Mr. Higgins had been introduced, by Mr. Love, to a little dark Creole, who wore paste diamonds, and had very languishing eyes; so that Mr. Love's heart might well swell with satisfaction at the prospect of the various blisses to come, which might owe their origin to his benevolence. In fact, that archpriest of the Temple of Hymen was never more great than he was that day; never did his establishment seem more solid, his reputation more popular, or his fortune more sure. He was the life of the party.

The banquet over, the revellers prepared for a dance. Monsieur Goupille, in tights, still tighter than he usually wore, and of a rich nankeen, quite new, with striped silk stockings, opened the ball with the lady of a rich patissier in the same Faubourg; Mr. Love took out the bride. The evening advanced; and after several other dances of ceremony, Monsieur Goupille conceived himself entitled to dedicate one to connubial affection. A country-dance was called, and the epicier claimed the fair hand of the gentle Adele. About this time, two persons not hitherto perceived had quietly entered the room, and, standing near the doorway, seemed examining the dancers, as if in search for some one. They bobbed their heads up and down, to and fro stopped—now stood on tiptoe. The one was a tall, large-whiskered, fair-haired man; the other, a little, thin, neatly-dressed person, who kept his hand on the arm of his companion, and whispered to him from time to time. The whiskered gentleman replied in a guttural tone, which proclaimed his origin to be German. The busy dancers did not perceive the strangers. The bystanders did, and a hum of curiosity circled round; who could they be?—who had invited them?—they were new faces in the Faubourg—perhaps relations to Adele?

In high delight the fair bride was skipping down the middle, while Monsieur Goupille, wiping his forehead with care, admired her agility; when, to and behold! the whiskered gentleman I have described abruptly advanced from his companion, and cried:

"La voila!—sacre tonnerre!"

At that voice—at that apparition, the bride halted; so suddenly indeed, that she had not time to put down both feet, but remained with one high in the air, while the other sustained itself on the light fantastic toe. The company naturally imagined this to be an operatic flourish, which called for approbation. Monsieur Love, who was thundering down behind her, cried, "Bravo!" and as the well-grown gentleman had to make a sweep to avoid disturbing her equilibrium, he came full against the whiskered stranger, and sent him off as a bat sends a ball.

"Mon Dieu!" cried Monsieur Goupille. "Ma douce amie—she has fainted away!" And, indeed, Adele had no sooner recovered her, balance, than she resigned it once more into the arms of the startled Pole, who was happily at hand.

In the meantime, the German stranger, who had saved himself from falling by coming with his full force upon the toes of Mr. Higgins, again advanced to the spot, and, rudely seizing the fair bride by the arm, exclaimed,—

"No sham if you please, madame—speak! What the devil have you done with the money?"

"Really, sir," said Monsieur Goupille, drawing tip his cravat, "this is very extraordinary conduct! What have you got to say to this lady's money?—it is my money now, sir!"

"Oho! it is, is it? We'll soon see that. Approchez donc, Monsieur Favart, faites votre devoir."

At these words the small companion of the stranger slowly sauntered to the spot, while at the sound of his name and the tread of his step, the throng gave way to the right and left. For Monsieur Favart was one of the most renowned chiefs of the great Parisian police—a man worthy to be the contemporary of the illustrious Vidocq.

"Calmez vous, messieurs; do not be alarmed, ladies," said this gentleman, in the mildest of all human voices; and certainly no oil dropped on the waters ever produced so tranquillising an effect as that small, feeble, gentle tenor. The Pole, in especial, who was holding the fair bride with both his arms, shook all over, and seemed about to let his burden gradually slide to the floor, when Monsieur Favart, looking at him with a benevolent smile, said—

"Aha, mon brave! c'est toi. Restez donc. Restez, tenant toujours la dame!"

The Pole, thus condemned, in the French idiom, "always to hold the dame," mechanically raised the arms he had previously dejected, and the police officer, with an approving nod of the head, said,—

"Bon! ne bougez point,—c'est ca!"

Monsieur Goupille, in equal surprise and indignation to see his better half thus consigned, without any care to his own marital feelings, to the arms of another, was about to snatch her from the Pole, when Monsieur Favart, touching him on the breast with his little finger, said, in the suavest manner,—

"Mon bourgeois, meddle not with what does not concern you!"

"With what does not concern me!" repeated Monsieur Goupille, drawing himself up to so great a stretch that he seemed pulling off his tights the wrong way. "Explain yourself, if you please! This lady is my wife!"

"Say that again,—that's all!" cried the whiskered stranger, in most horrible French, and with a furious grimace, as he shook both his fists just under the nose of the epicier.

"Say it again, sir," said Monsieur Goupille, by no means daunted; "and why should not I say it again? That lady is my wife!"

"You lie!—she is mine!" cried the German; and bending down, he caught the fair Adele from the Pole with as little ceremony as if she had never had a great-grandfather a marquis, and giving her a shake that might have roused the dead, thundered out,—

"Speak! Madame Bihl! Are you my wife or not?"

"Monstre!" murmured Adele, opening her eyes.

"There—you hear—she owns me!" said the German, appealing to the company with a triumphant air.

"C'est vrai!" said the soft voice of the policeman. "And now, pray don't let us disturb your amusements any longer. We have a fiacre at the door. Remove your lady, Monsieur Bihl."

"Monsieur Lofe!—Monsieur Lofe!" cried, or rather screeched the epicier, darting across the room, and seizing the chef by the tail of his coat, just as he was half way through the door, "come back! Quelle mauvaise plaisanterie me faites-vous ici? Did you not tell me that lady was single? Am I married or not: Do I stand on my head or my heels?"

"Hush-hush! mon bon bourgeois!" whispered Mr. Love; "all shall be explained to-morrow!"

"Who is this gentleman?" asked Monsieur Favart, approaching Mr. Love, who, seeing himself in for it, suddenly jerked off the epicier, thrust his hands down into his breeches' pockets, buried his chin in his cravat, elevated his eyebrows, screwed in his eyes, and puffed out his cheeks, so that the astonished Monsieur Goupille really thought himself bewitched, and literally did not recognise the face of the match-maker.

"Who is this gentleman?" repeated the little officer, standing beside, or rather below, Mr. Love, and looking so diminutive by the contrast that you might have fancied that the Priest of Hymen had only to breathe to blow him away.

"Who should he be, monsieur?" cried, with great pertness, Madame Rosalie Caumartin, coming to the relief, with the generosity of her sex.—"This is Monsieur Lofe—Anglais celebre. What have you to say against him?"

"He has got five hundred francs of mine!" cried the epicier.

The policeman scanned Mr. Love, with great attention. "So you are in Paris again?—Hein!—vous jouez toujours votre role!

"Ma foi!" said Mr. Love, boldly; "I don't understand what monsieur means; my character is well known—go and inquire it in London—ask the Secretary of Foreign Affairs what is said of me—inquire of my Ambassador—demand of my—"

"Votre passeport, monsieur?"

"It is at home. A gentleman does not carry his passport in his pocket when he goes to a ball!"

"I will call and see it—au revoir! Take my advice and leave Paris; I think I have seen you somewhere!"

"Yet I have never had the honour to marry monsieur!" said Mr. Love, with a polite bow.

In return for his joke, the policeman gave Mr. Love one look—it was a quiet look, very quiet; but Mr. Love seemed uncommonly affected by it; he did not say another word, but found himself outside the house in a twinkling. Monsieur Favart turned round and saw the Pole making himself as small as possible behind the goodly proportions of Madame Beavor.

"What name does that gentleman go by?"

"So—vo—lofski, the heroic Pole," cried Madame Beavor, with sundry misgivings at the unexpected cowardice of so great a patriot.

"Hein! take care of yourselves, ladies. I have nothing against that person this time. But Monsieur Latour has served his apprenticeship at the galleys, and is no more a Pole than I am a Jew."

"And this lady's fortune!" cried Monsieur Groupille, pathetically; "the settlements are all made—the notaries all paid. I am sure there must be some mistake."

Monsieur Bihl, who had by this time restored his lost Helen to her senses, stalked up to the epicier, dragging the lady along with him.

"Sir, there is no mistake! But, when I have got the money, if you like to have the lady you are welcome to her."

"Monstre!" again muttered the fair Adele.

"The long and the short of it," said Monsieur Favart, "is that Monsieur Bihl is a brave garcon, and has been half over the world as a courier."

"A courier!" exclaimed several voices.

"Madame was nursery-governess to an English milord. They married, and quarrelled—no harm in that, mes amis; nothing more common. Monsieur Bihl is a very faithful fellow; nursed his last master in an illness that ended fatally, because he travelled with his doctor. Milord left him a handsome legacy—he retired from service, and fell ill, perhaps from idleness or beer. Is not that the story, Monsieur Bihl?"

"He was always drunk—the wretch!" sobbed Adele. "That was to drown my domestic sorrows," said the German; "and when I was sick in my bed, madame ran off with my money. Thanks to monsieur, I have found both, and I wish you a very good night."

"Dansez-vous toujours, mes amis," said the officer, bowing. And following Adele and her spouse, the little man left the room—where he had caused, in chests so broad and limbs so doughty, much the same consternation as that which some diminutive ferret occasions in a burrow of rabbits twice his size.

Morton had outstayed Mr. Love. But he thought it unnecessary to linger long after that gentleman's departure; and, in the general hubbub that ensued, he crept out unperceived, and soon arrived at the bureau. He found Mr. Love and Mr. Birnie already engaged in packing up their effects.

"Why—when did you leave?" said Morton to Mr. Birnie.

"I saw the policeman enter."

"And why the deuce did not you tell us?" said Gawtrey.

"Every man for himself. Besides, Mr. Love was dancing," replied Mr. Birnie, with a dull glance of disdain. "Philosophy," muttered Gawtrey, thrusting his dresscoat into his trunk; then, suddenly changing his voice, "Ha! ha! it was a very good joke after all—own I did it well. Ecod! if he had not given me that look, I think I should have turned the tables on him. But those d—d fellows learn of the mad doctors how to tame us. Faith, my heart went down to my shoes—yet I'm no coward!"

"But, after all, he evidently did not know you," said Morton; "and what has he to say against you? Your trade is a strange one, but not dishonest. Why give up as if—"

"My young friend," interrupted Gawtrey, "whether the officer comes after us or not, our trade is ruined; that infernal Adele, with her fabulous grandmaman, has done for us. Goupille will blow the temple about our ears. No help for it—eh, Birnie?"

"None."

"Go to bed, Philip: we'll call thee at daybreak, for we must make clear work before our neighbours open their shutters."

Reclined, but half undressed, on his bed in the little cabinet, Morton revolved the events of the evening. The thought that he should see no more of that white hand and that lovely mouth, which still haunted his recollection as appertaining to the incognita, greatly indisposed him towards the abrupt flight intended by Gawtrey, while (so much had his faith in that person depended upon respect for his confident daring, and so thoroughly fearless was Morton's own nature) he felt himself greatly shaken in his allegiance to the chief, by recollecting the effect produced on his valour by a single glance from the instrument of law. He had not yet lived long enough to be aware that men are sometimes the Representatives of Things; that what the scytale was to the Spartan hero, a sheriff's writ often is to a Waterloo medallist: that a Bow Street runner will enter the foulest den where Murder sits with his fellows, and pick out his prey with the beck of his forefinger. That, in short, the thing called LAW, once made tangible and present, rarely fails to palsy the fierce heart of the thing called CRIME. For Law is the symbol of all mankind reared against One Foe—the Man of Crime. Not yet aware of this truth, nor, indeed, in the least suspecting Gawtrey of worse offences than those of a charlatanic and equivocal profession, the young man mused over his protector's cowardice in disdain and wonder: till, wearied with conjectures, distrust, and shame at his own strange position of obligation to one whom he could not respect, he fell asleep.

When he woke, he saw the grey light of dawn that streamed cheerlessly through his shutterless window, struggling with the faint ray of a candle that Gawtrey, shading with his hand, held over the sleeper. He started up, and, in the confusion of waking and the imperfect light by which he beheld the strong features of Gawtrey, half imagined it was a foe who stood before him.

"Take care, man," said Gawtrey, as Morton, in this belief, grasped his arm. "You have a precious rough gripe of your own. Be quiet, will you? I have a word to say to you." Here Gawtrey, placing the candle on a chair, returned to the door and closed it.

"Look you," he said in a whisper, "I have nearly run through my circle of invention, and my wit, fertile as it is, can present to me little encouragement in the future. The eyes of this Favart once on me, every disguise and every double will not long avail. I dare not return to London: I am too well known in Brussels, Berlin, and Vienna—"

"But," interrupted Morton, raising himself on his arm, and fixing his dark eyes upon his host,—"but you have told me again and again that you have committed no crime; why then be so fearful of discovery?"

"Why," repeated Gawtrey, with a slight hesitation which he instantly overcame, "why! have not you yourself learned that appearances have the effect of crimes?—were you not chased as a thief when I rescued you from your foe, the law?—are you not, though a boy in years, under an alias, and an exile from your own land? And how can you put these austere questions to me, who am growing grey in the endeavour to extract sunbeams from cucumbers—subsistence from poverty? I repeat that there are reasons why I must avoid, for the present, the great capitals. I must sink in life, and take to the provinces. Birnie is sanguine as ever; but he is a terrible sort of comforter! Enough of that. Now to yourself: our savings are less than you might expect; to be sure, Birnie has been treasurer, and I have laid by a little for Fanny, which I will rather starve than touch. There remain, however, 150 napoleons, and our effects, sold at a fourth their value, will fetch 150 more. Here is your share. I have compassion on you. I told you I would bear you harmless and innocent. Leave us while yet time."

It seemed, then, to Morton that Gawtrey had divined his thoughts of shame and escape of the previous night; perhaps Gawtrey had: and such is the human heart, that, instead of welcoming the very release he had half contemplated, now that it was offered him, Philip shrank from it as a base desertion.

"Poor Gawtrey!" said he, pushing back the canvas bag of gold held out to him, "you shall not go over the world, and feel that the orphan you fed and fostered left you to starve with your money in his pocket. When you again assure me that you have committed no crime, you again remind me that gratitude has no right to be severe upon the shifts and errors of its benefactor. If you do not conform to society, what has society done for me? No! I will not forsake you in a reverse. Fortune has given you a fall. What, then, courage, and at her again!"

These last words were said so heartily and cheerfully as Morton sprang from the bed, that they inspirited Gawtrey, who had really desponded of his lot.

"Well," said he, "I cannot reject the only friend left me; and while I live—. But I will make no professions. Quick, then, our luggage is already gone, and I hear Birnie grunting the rogue's march of retreat."

Morton's toilet was soon completed, and the three associates bade adieu to the bureau.

Birnie, who was taciturn and impenetrable as ever, walked a little before as guide. They arrived, at length, at a serrurier's shop, placed in an alley near the Porte St. Denis. The serrurier himself, a tall, begrimed, blackbearded man, was taking the shutters from his shop as they approached. He and Birnie exchanged silent nods; and the former, leaving his work, conducted them up a very filthy flight of stairs to an attic, where a bed, two stools, one table, and an old walnut-tree bureau formed the sole articles of furniture. Gawtrey looked rather ruefully round the black, low, damp walls, and said in a crestfallen tone:

"We were better off at the Temple of Hymen. But get us a bottle of wine, some eggs, and a frying-pan. By Jove, I am a capital hand at an omelet!"

The serrurier nodded again, grinned, and withdrew.

"Rest here," said Birnie, in his calm, passionless voice, that seemed to Morton, however, to assume an unwonted tone of command. "I will go and make the best bargain I can for our furniture, buy fresh clothes, and engage our places for Tours."

"For Tours?" repeated Morton.

"Yes, there are some English there; one can live wherever there are English," said Gawtrey.

"Hum!" grunted Birnie, drily, and, buttoning up his coat, he walked slowly away.

About noon he returned with a bundle of clothes, which Gawtrey, who always regained his elasticity of spirit wherever there was fair play to his talents, examined with great attention, and many exclamations of "Bon!—c'est va."

"I have done well with the Jew," said Birnie, drawing from his coat pocket two heavy bags. "One hundred and eighty napoleons. We shall commence with a good capital."

"You are right, my friend," said Gawtrey.

The serrurier was then despatched to the best restaurant in the neighbourhood, and the three adventurers made a less Socratic dinner than might have been expected.

CHAPTER VI

"Then out again he flies to wing his marry round."
THOMPSON'S Castle of Indolence.

"Again he gazed, 'It is,' said he, 'the same;
There sits he upright in his seat secure,
As one whose conscience is correct and pure.'"—CRABBE.

The adventurers arrived at Tours, and established themselves there in a lodging, without any incident worth narrating by the way.

At Tours Morton had nothing to do but take his pleasure and enjoy himself. He passed for a young heir; Gawtrey for his tutor—a doctor in divinity; Birnie for his valet. The task of maintenance fell on Gawtrey, who hit off his character to a hair; larded his grave jokes with university scraps of Latin; looked big and well-fed; wore knee-breeches and a shovel hat; and played whist with the skill of a veteran vicar. By his science in that game he made, at first, enough; at least, to defray their weekly expenses. But, by degrees, the good people at Tours, who, under pretence of health, were there for economy, grew shy of so excellent a player; and though Gawtrey always swore solemnly that he played with the most scrupulous honour (an asseveration which Morton, at least, implicitly believed), and no proof to the contrary was ever detected, yet a first-rate card-player is always a suspicious character, unless the losing parties know exactly who he is. The market fell off, and Gawtrey at length thought it prudent to extend their travels.

"Ah!" said Mr. Gawtrey, "the world nowadays has grown so ostentatious that one cannot travel advantageously without a post-chariot and four horses." At length they found themselves at Milan, which at that time was one of the El Dorados for gamesters. Here, however, for want of introductions, Mr. Gawtrey found it difficult to get into society. The nobles, proud and rich, played high, but were circumspect in their company; the bourgeoisie, industrious and energetic, preserved much of the old Lombard shrewdness; there were no tables d'hote and public reunions. Gawtrey saw his little capital daily diminishing, with the Alps at the rear and Poverty in the van. At length, always on the qui vive, he contrived to make acquaintance with a Scotch family of great respectability. He effected this by picking up a snuff-box which the Scotchman had dropped in taking out his handkerchief. This politeness paved the way to a conversation in which Gawtrey made himself so agreeable, and talked with such zest of the Modern Athens, and the tricks practised upon travellers, that he was presented to Mrs. Macgregor; cards were interchanged, and, as Mr. Gawtrey lived in tolerable style, the Macgregors pronounced him "a vara genteel mon." Once in the house of a respectable person, Gawtrey contrived to turn himself round and round, till he burrowed a hole into the English circle then settled in Milan. His whist-playing came into requisition, and once more Fortune smiled upon Skill.

To this house the pupil one evening accompanied the tutor. When the whist party, consisting of two tables, was formed, the young man found himself left out with an old gentleman, who seemed loquacious and good-natured, and who put many questions to Morton, which he found it difficult to answer. One of the whist tables was now in a state of revolution, viz., a lady had cut out and a gentleman cut in, when the door opened, and Lord Lilburne was announced.

Mr. Macgregor, rising, advanced with great respect to this personage.

"I scarcely ventured to hope you would coom, Lord Lilburne, the night is so cold."

"You did not allow sufficiently, then, for the dulness of my solitary inn and the attractions of your circle. Aha! whist, I see."

"You play sometimes?"

"Very seldom, now; I have sown all my wild oats, and even the ace of spades can scarcely dig them out again."

"Ha! ha! vara gude."

"I will look on;" and Lord Lilburne drew his chair to the table, exactly opposite to Mr. Gawtrey.

The old gentleman turned to Philip.

"An extraordinary man, Lord Lilburne; you have heard of him, of course?"

"No, indeed; what of him?" asked the young man, rousing himself.

"What of him?" said the old gentleman, with a smile; "why the newspapers, if you ever read them, will tell you enough of the elegant, the witty Lord Lilburne; a man of eminent talent, though indolent. He was wild in his youth, as clever men often are; but, on attaining his title and fortune, and marrying into the family of the then premier, he became more sedate. They say he might make a great figure in politics if he would. He has a very high reputation—very. People do say that he is still fond of pleasure; but that is a common failing amongst the aristocracy. Morality is only found in the middle classes, young gentleman. It is a lucky family, that of Lilburne; his sister, Mrs. Beaufort—"

"Beaufort!" exclaimed Morton, and then muttered to himself, "Ah, true—true; I have heard the name of Lilburne before."

"Do you know the Beauforts? Well, you remember how luckily Robert, Lilburne's brother-in-law, came into that fine property just as his predecessor was about to marry a—"

Morton scowled at his garrulous acquaintance, and stalked abruptly to the card table.

Ever since Lord Lilburne had seated himself opposite to Mr. Gawtrey, that gentleman had evinced a perturbation of manner that became obvious to the company. He grew deadly pale, his hands trembled, he moved uneasily in his seat, he missed deal, he trumped his partner's best diamond; finally he revoked, threw down his money, and said, with a forced smile, "that the heat of the room overcame him." As he rose Lord Lilburne rose also, and the eyes of both met. Those of Lilburne were calm, but penetrating and inquisitive in their gaze; those of Gawtrey were like balls of fire. He seemed gradually to dilate in his height, his broad chest expanded, he breathed hard.

"Ah, Doctor," said Mr. Macgregor, "let me introduce you to Lord Lilburne."

The peer bowed haughtily; Mr. Gawtrey did not return the salutation, but with a sort of gulp, as if he were swallowing some burst of passion, strode to the fire, and then, turning round, again fixed his gaze upon the new guest.

Lilburne, however, who had never lost his self-composure at this strange rudeness, was now quietly talking with their host.

"Your Doctor seems an eccentric man—a little absent—learned, I suppose. Have you been to Como, yet?"

Mr. Gawtrey remained by the fire beating the devil's tattoo upon the chimney-piece, and ever and anon turning his glance towards Lilburne, who seemed to have forgotten his existence.

Both these guests stayed till the party broke up; Mr. Gawtrey apparently wishing to outstay Lord Lilburne; for, when the last went down-stairs, Mr. Gawtrey, nodding to his comrade and giving a hurried bow to the host, descended also. As they passed the porter's lodge, they found Lilburne on the step of his carriage; he turned his head abruptly, and again met Mr. Gawtrey's eye; paused a moment, and whispered over his shoulder:

"So we remember each other, sir? Let us not meet again; and, on that condition, bygones are bygones."

"Scoundrel!" muttered Gawtrey, clenching his fists; but the peer had sprung into his carriage with a lightness scarcely to be expected from his lameness, and the wheels whirled within an inch of the soi-disant doctor's right pump.

Gawtrey walked on for some moments in great excitement; at length he turned to his companion,—

"Do you guess who Lord Lilburne is? I will tell you my first foe and Fanny's grandfather! Now, note the justice of Fate: here is this man—mark well—this man who commenced life by putting his faults on my own shoulders! From that little boss has fungused out a terrible hump. This man who seduced my affianced bride, and then left her whole soul, once fair and blooming—I swear it—with its leaves fresh from the dews of heaven, one rank leprosy, this man who, rolling in riches, learned to cheat and pilfer as a boy learns to dance and play the fiddle, and (to damn me, whose happiness he had blasted) accused me to the world of his own crime!—here is this man who has not left off one vice, but added to those of his youth the bloodless craft of the veteran knave;—here is this man, flattered, courted, great, marching through lanes of bowing parasites to an illustrious epitaph and a marble tomb, and I, a rogue too, if you will, but rogue for my bread, dating from him my errors and my ruin! I—vagabond—outcast—skulking through tricks to avoid crime—why the difference? Because one is born rich and the other poor—because he has no excuse for crime, and therefore no one suspects him!"

The wretched man (for at that moment he was wretched) paused breathless from his passionate and rapid burst, and before him rose in its marble majesty, with the moon full upon its shining spires—the wonder of Gothic Italy—the Cathedral Church of Milan.

"Chafe not yourself at the universal fate," said the young man, with a bitter smile on his lips and pointing to the cathedral; "I have not lived long, but I have learned already enough to know this,— he who could raise a pile like that, dedicated to Heaven, would be honoured as a saint; he who knelt to God by the roadside under a hedge would be sent to the house of correction as a vagabond. The difference between man and man is money, and will be, when you, the despised charlatan, and Lilburne, the honoured cheat, have not left as much dust behind you as will fill a snuff-box. Comfort yourself, you are in the majority."

CHAPTER VII

"A desert wild
Before them stretched bare, comfortless, and vast,
With gibbets, bones, and carcasses defiled."
THOMPSON'S *Castle of Indolenece.*

Mr. Gawtrey did not wish to give his foe the triumph of thinking he had driven him from Milan; he resolved to stay and brave it out; but when he appeared in public, he found the acquaintances he had formed bow politely, but cross to the other side of the way. No more invitations to tea and cards showered in upon the jolly parson. He was puzzled, for people, while they shunned him, did not appear uncivil. He found out at last that a report was circulated that he was deranged; though he could not trace this rumour to Lord Lilburne, he was at no loss to guess from whom it had emanated. His own eccentricities, especially his recent manner at Mr. Macgregor's, gave confirmation to the charge. Again the funds began to sink low in the canvas bags, and at length, in despair, Mr. Gawtrey was obliged to quit the field. They returned to France through Switzerland—a country too poor for gamesters; and ever since the interview with Lilburne, a great change had come over Gawtrey's gay spirit: he grew moody and thoughtful, he took no pains to replenish the common stock, he talked much and seriously to his young friend of poor Fanny, and owned that he yearned to see her again. The desire to return to Paris haunted him like a fatality; he saw the danger that awaited him there, but it only allured him the more, as the candle does the moth whose wings it has singed. Birnie, who, in all their vicissitudes and wanderings, their ups and downs, retained the same tacit, immovable demeanour, received with a sneer the orders at last to march back upon the French capital. "You would never have left it, if you had taken my advice," he said, and quitted the room.

Mr. Gawtrey gazed after him and muttered, "Is the die then cast?"

"What does he mean?" said Morton.

"You will know soon," replied Gawtrey, and he followed Birnie; and from that time the whispered conferences with that person, which had seemed suspended during their travels, were renewed.

One morning, three men were seen entering Paris on foot through the Porte St. Denis. It was a fine day in spring, and the old city looked gay with its loitering passengers and gaudy shops, and under that clear blue exhilarating sky so peculiar to France.

Two of these men walked abreast, the other preceded them a few steps. The one who went first—thin, pale, and threadbare—yet seemed to suffer the least from fatigue; he walked with a long, swinging, noiseless stride, looking to the right and left from the corners of his eyes. Of the two who followed, one was handsome and finely formed, but of swarthy complexion, young, yet with a look of care; the other, of sturdy frame, leaned on a thick stick, and his eyes were gloomily cast down.

"Philip," said the last, "in coming back to Paris—I feel that I am coming back to my grave!"

"Pooh—you were equally despondent in our excursions elsewhere."

"Because I was always thinking of poor Fanny, and because—because—Birnie was ever at me with his horrible temptations!"

"Birnie! I loathe the man! Will you never get rid of him?"

"I cannot! Hush! he will hear us. How unlucky we have been! and now without a sou in our pockets—here the dunghill—there the gaol! We are in his power at last!"

"His power! what mean you?"

"What ho! Birnie!" cried Gawtrey, unheeding Morton's question. "Let us halt and breakfast: I am tired."

"You forget!—we have no money till we make it," returned Birnie, coldly.—"Come to the serrurier's he will trust us."

CHAPTER VIII

"Gaunt Beggary and Scorn with many bell-hounds more."
THOMSON'S *Castle of Indolence.*

"The other was a fell, despiteful fiend."—Ibid.

"Your happiness behold! then straight a wand
He waved, an anti-magic power that hath
Truth from illusive falsehood to command."—Ibid.

"But what for us, the children of despair,
Brought to the brink of hell—what hope remains?
RESOLVE, RESOLVE!"—Ibid.

It may be observed that there are certain years in which in a civilised country some particular crime comes into vogue. It flares its season, and then burns out. Thus at one time we have Burking—at another, Swingism—now, suicide is in vogue—now, poisoning tradespeople in apple-dumplings—now, little boys stab each other with penknives—now, common soldiers shoot at their sergeants. Almost every year there is one crime peculiar to it; a sort of annual which overruns the country but does not bloom again. Unquestionably the Press has a great deal to do with these epidemics. Let a newspaper once give an account of some out-of-the-way atrocity that has the charm of being novel, and certain depraved minds fasten to it like leeches. They brood over and revolve it—the idea grows up, a horrid phantasmalian monomania; and all of a sudden, in a hundred different places, the one seed sown by the leaden types springs up into foul flowering.

[An old Spanish writer, treating of the Inquisition, has some very striking remarks on the kind of madness which, whenever some terrible notoriety is given to a particular offence, leads persons of distempered fancy to accuse themselves of it. He observes that when the cruelties of the Inquisition against the imaginary crime of sorcery were the most barbarous, this singular frenzy led numbers to accuse themselves of sorcery. The publication and celebrity of the crime begat the desire of the crime.]

But if the first reported aboriginal crime has been attended with impunity, how much more does the imitative faculty cling to it. Ill-judged mercy falls, not like dew, but like a great heap of manure, on the rank deed.

Now it happened that at the time I write of, or rather a little before, there had been detected and tried in Paris a most redoubted coiner. He had carried on the business with a dexterity that won admiration even for the offence; and, moreover, he had served previously with some distinction at Austerlitz and Marengo. The consequence was that the public went with instead of against him, and his sentence was transmuted to three years' imprisonment by the government. For all governments in free countries aspire rather to be popular than just.

No sooner was this case reported in the journals—and even the gravest took notice, of it (which is not common with the scholastic journals of France)—no sooner did it make a stir and a sensation, and cover the criminal with celebrity, than the result became noticeable in a very large issue of false money.

Coining in the year I now write of was the fashionable crime. The police were roused into full vigour: it became known to them that there was one gang in especial who cultivated this art with singular success. Their coinage was, indeed, so good, so superior to all their rivals, that it was often unconsciously preferred by the public to the real mintage. At the same time they carried on their calling with such secrecy that they utterly baffled discovery.

An immense reward was offered by the bureau to any one who would betray his accomplices, and Monsieur Favart was placed at the head of a commission of inquiry. This person had himself been a faux monnoyer, and was an adept in the art, and it was he who had discovered the redoubted coiner who had brought the crime into such notoriety. Monsieur Favart was a man of the most vigilant acuteness, the most indefatigable research, and of a courage which; perhaps, is more common than we suppose. It is a popular error to suppose that courage means courage in everything. Put a hero on board ship at a five-barred gate, and, if he is not used to hunting, he will turn pale; put a fox-hunter on one of the Swiss chasms, over which the mountaineer springs like a roe, and his knees will knock under him. People are brave in the dangers to which they accustom themselves, either in imagination or practice.

Monsieur Favart, then, was a man of the most daring bravery in facing rogues and cut-throats. He awed them with his very eye; yet he had been known to have been kicked down-stairs by his wife, and when he was drawn into the grand army, he deserted the eve of his first battle. Such, as moralists say, is the inconsistency of man!

But Monsieur Favart was sworn to trace the coiners, and he had never failed yet in any enterprise he undertook. One day he presented himself to his chief with a countenance so elated that that penetrating functionary said to him at once—

"You have heard of our messieurs!"

"I have: I am to visit them to-night."

"Bravo! How many men will you take?"

"From twelve to twenty to leave without on guard. But I must enter alone. Such is the condition: an accomplice who fears his own throat too much to be openly a betrayer will introduce me to the house—nay, to the very room. By his description it is necessary I should know the exact locale in order to cut off retreat; so to-morrow night I shall surround the beehive and take the honey."

"They are desperate fellows, these coiners, always; better be cautious."

"You forget I was one of them, and know the masonry." About the same time this conversation was going on at the bureau of the police, in another part of the town Morton and Gawtrey were seated alone. It is some weeks since they entered Paris, and spring has mellowed into summer.

The house in which they lodged was in the lordly quartier of the Faubourg St. Germain; the neighbouring streets were venerable with the ancient edifices of a fallen noblesse; but their tenement was in a narrow, dingy lane, and the building itself seemed beggarly and ruinous. The apartment was in an attic on the sixth story, and the window, placed at the back of the lane, looked upon another row of houses of a better description, that communicated with one of the great streets of the quartier. The space between their abode and their opposite neighbours was so narrow that the sun could scarcely pierce between. In the height of summer might be found there a perpetual shade.

The pair were seated by the window. Gawtrey, well-dressed, smooth-shaven, as in his palmy time; Morton, in the same garments with which he had entered Paris, weather-stained and ragged. Looking towards the casements of the attic in the opposite house, Gawtrey said, mutteringly, "I wonder where Birnie has been, and why he has not returned. I grow suspicious of that man."

"Suspicious of what?" asked Morton. "Of his honesty? Would he rob you?"

"Rob me! Humph—perhaps! but you see I am in Paris, in spite of the hints of the police; he may denounce me."

"Why, then, suffer him to lodge away from you?"

"Why? because, by having separate houses there are two channels of escape. A dark night, and a ladder thrown across from window to window, he is with us, or we with him."

"But wherefore such precautions? You blind—you deceive me; what have you done?—what is your employment now? You are mute. Hark you, Gawtrey. I have pinned my fate to you—I am fallen from hope itself! At times it almost makes me mad to look back—and yet you do not trust me. Since your return to Paris you are absent whole nights—often days; you are moody and thoughtful—yet, whatever your business, it seems to bring you ample returns."

"You think that," said Gawtrey, mildly, and with a sort of pity in his voice; "yet you refuse to take even the money to change those rags."

"Because I know not how the money was gained. Ah, Gawtrey, I am not too proud for charity, but I am for—" He checked the word uppermost in his thoughts, and resumed—

"Yes; your occupations seem lucrative. It was but yesterday Birnie gave me fifty napoleons, for which he said you wished change in silver."

"Did he? The ras— Well! and you got change for them?"

"I know not why, but I refused."

"That was right, Philip. Do nothing that man tells you."

"Will you, then, trust me? You are engaged in some horrible traffic! it may be blood! I am no longer a boy—I have a will of my own—I will not be silently and blindly entrapped to perdition. If I march thither, it shall be with my own consent. Trust me, and this day, or we part to-morrow."

"Be ruled. Some secrets it is better not to know."

"It matters not. I have come to my decision—I ask yours."

Gawtrey paused for some moments in deep thought. At last he lifted his eyes to Philip, and replied:

"Well, then, if it must be. Sooner or later it must have been so; and I want a confidant. You are bold, and will not shrink. You desire to know my occupation—will you witness it to-night?"

"I am prepared: to-night!"

Here a step was heard on the stairs—a knock at the door—and Birnie entered.

He drew aside Gawtrey, and whispered him, as usual, for some moments.

Gawtrey nodded his head, and then said aloud—

"To-morrow we shall talk without reserve before my young friend. To-night he joins us."

"To-night!—very well," said Birnie, with his cold sneer. "He must take the oath; and you, with your life, will be responsible for his honesty?"

"Ay! it is the rule."

"Good-bye, then, till we meet," said Birnie, and withdrew.

"I wonder," said Gawtrey, musingly, and between his grinded teeth, "whether I shall ever have a good fair shot at that fellow? Ho! ho!" and his laugh shook the walls.

Morton looked hard at Gawtrey, as the latter now sank down in his chair, and gazed with a vacant stare, that seemed almost to partake of imbecility, upon the opposite wall. The careless, reckless, jovial expression, which usually characterised the features of the man, had for some weeks given place to a restless, anxious, and at times ferocious aspect, like the beast that first finds a sport while the hounds are yet afar, and his limbs are yet strong, in the chase which marks him for his victim, but grows desperate with rage and fear as the day nears its close, and the death-dogs pant hard upon his track. But at that moment the strong features, with their gnarled muscle and iron sinews, seemed to have lost every sign both of passion and the will, and to be locked in a stolid and dull repose. At last he looked up at Morton, and said, with a smile like that of an old man in his dotage—

"I'm thinking that my life has been one mistake! I had talents—you would not fancy it—but once I was neither a fool nor a villain! Odd, isn't it? Just reach me the brandy."

But Morton, with a slight shudder, turned and left the room.

He walked on mechanically, and gained, at last, the superb Quai that borders the Seine; there, the passengers became more frequent; gay equipages rolled along; the white and lofty mansions looked fair and stately in the clear blue sky of early summer; beside him flowed the sparkling river, animated with the painted baths that floated on its surface: earth was merry and heaven serene his heart was dark through all: Night within—Morning beautiful without! At last he paused by that bridge, stately with the statues of those whom the caprice of time honours with a name; for though Zeus and his gods be overthrown, while earth exists will live the worship of Dead Men;—the bridge by which you pass from the royal Tuileries, or the luxurious streets beyond the Rue de Rivoli, to the Senate of the emancipated People, and the gloomy and desolate grandeur of the Faubourg St. Germain, in whose venerable haunts the impoverished descendants of the old feudal tyrants, whom the birth of the Senate overthrew, yet congregate;—the ghosts of departed powers proud of the shadows of great names. As the English outcast paused midway on the bridge, and for the first time lifting his head from his bosom, gazed around, there broke at once on his remembrance that terrible and fatal evening, when, hopeless, friendless, desperate, he had begged for charity of his uncle's hireling, with all the feelings that then (so imperfectly and lightly touched on in his brief narrative to Gawtrey) had raged and blackened in his breast, urging to the resolution he had adopted, casting him on the ominous friendship of the man whose guidance he even then had suspected and distrusted. The spot in either city had a certain similitude and correspondence each with each: at the first he had consummated his despair of human destinies—he had dared to forget the Providence of God—he had arrogated his fate to himself: by the first bridge he had taken his resolve; by the last he stood in awe at the result—stood no less poor—no less abject—equally in rags and squalor; but was his crest as haughty and his eye as fearless, for was his conscience as free and his honour as unstained? Those arches of stone—those rivers that rolled between, seemed to him then to take a more mystic and typical sense than belongs to the outer world—they were the bridges to the Rivers of his Life. Plunged in thoughts so confused and dim that he could scarcely distinguish, through the chaos, the one streak of light which, perhaps, heralded the reconstruction or regeneration of the elements of his soul;—two passengers halted, also by his side.

"You will be late for the debate," said one of them to the other. "Why do you stop?"

"My friend," said the other, "I never pass this spot without recalling the time when I stood here without a son, or, as I thought, a chance of one, and impiously meditated self-destruction."

"You!—now so rich—so fortunate in repute and station—is it possible? How was it? A lucky chance?—a sudden legacy?"

"No: Time, Faith, and Energy—the three Friends God has given to the Poor!"

The men moved on; but Morton, who had turned his face towards them, fancied that the last speaker fixed on him his bright, cheerful eye, with a meaning look; and when the man was gone, he repeated those words, and hailed them in his heart of hearts as an augury from above.

Quickly, then, and as if by magic, the former confusion of his mind seemed to settle into distinct shapes of courage and resolve. "Yes," he muttered; "I will keep this night's appointment—I will learn the secret of these men's life. In my inexperience and destitution, I have suffered myself to be led hitherto into a partnership, if not with vice and crime, at least with subterfuge and trick. I awake from my reckless boyhood—my unworthy palterings with my better self. If Gawtrey be as I dread to find him—if he be linked in some guilty and hateful traffic; with that loathsome accomplice—I will—" He paused, for his heart whispered, "Well, and even so,—the guilty man clothed and fed thee!" "I will," resumed his thought, in answer to his heart—"I will go on my knees to him to fly while there is yet time, to work—beg—starve—perish even—rather than lose the right to look man in the face without a blush, and kneel to his God without remorse!"

And as he thus ended, he felt suddenly as if he himself were restored to the perception and the joy of the Nature and the World around him; the NIGHT had vanished from his soul—he inhaled the balm and freshness of the air—he comprehended the delight which the liberal June was scattering over the earth—he looked above, and his eyes were suffused with pleasure, at the smile of the soft blue skies. The MORNING became, as it were, a part of his own being; and he felt that as the world in spite of the storms is fair, so in spite of evil God is good. He walked on—he passed the bridge, but his step was no more the same,—he forgot his rags. Why should he be ashamed? And thus, in the very flush of this new and strange elation and elasticity of spirit, he came unawares upon a group of young men, lounging before the porch of one of the chief hotels in that splendid Rue de Rivoli, wherein Wealth and the English have made their homes. A groom, mounted, was leading another horse up and down the road, and the young men were making their comments of approbation upon both the horses, especially the one led, which was, indeed, of uncommon beauty and great value. Even Morton, in whom the boyish passion of his earlier life yet existed, paused to turn his experienced and admiring eye upon the stately shape and pace of the noble animal, and as he did so, a name too well remembered came upon his ear.

"Certainly, Arthur Beaufort is the most enviable fellow in Europe."

"Why, yes," said another of the young men; "he has plenty of money—is good-looking, devilish good-natured, clever, and spends like a prince."

"Has the best horses!"

"The best luck at roulette!"

"The prettiest girls in love with him!"

"And no one enjoys life more. Ah! here he is!"

The group parted as a light, graceful figure came out of a jeweller's shop that adjoined the hotel, and halted gaily amongst the loungers. Morton's first impulse was to hurry from the spot; his second impulse arrested his step, and, a little apart, and half-hid beneath one of the arches of the colonnade which adorns the street, the Outcast gazed upon the Heir. There was no comparison in the natural personal advantages of the two young men; for Philip Morton, despite all the hardships of his rough career, had now grown up and ripened into a rare perfection of form and feature. His broad chest, his erect air, his lithe and symmetrical length of limb, united, happily, the attributes of activity and strength; and though there was no delicacy of youthful bloom upon his dark cheek, and though lines which should have come later marred its smoothness with the signs of care and thought, yet an expression of intelligence and daring, equally beyond his years, and the evidence of hardy, abstemious, vigorous health, served to show to the full advantage the outline of features which, noble and regular, though stern and masculine, the artist might have borrowed for his ideal of a young Spartan arming for his first battle. Arthur, slight to feebleness, and with the paleness, partly of constitution, partly of gay excess, on his fair and clear complexion, had features far less symmetrical and impressive than his cousin: but what then? All that are bestowed by elegance of dress, the refinements of luxurious habit, the nameless grace that comes from a mind and a manner polished, the one by literary culture, the other by social intercourse, invested the person of the heir with a fascination that rude Nature alone ever fails to give. And about him there was a gaiety, an airiness of spirit, an atmosphere of enjoyment which bespoke one who is in love with life.

"Why, this is lucky! I'm so glad to see you all!" said Arthur Beaufort, with that silver-ringing tone and charming smile which are to the happy spring of man what its music and its sunshine are to the spring of earth. "You must dine with me at Verey's. I want something to rouse me to-day; for I did not get home from the Salon* till four this morning."

*[The most celebrated gaming-house in Paris in the day before gaming-houses were suppressed by the well-directed energy of the government.]

"But you won?"

"Yes, Marsden. Hang it! I always win: I who could so well afford to lose: I'm quite ashamed of my luck!"

"It is easy to spend what one wins," observed Mr. Marsden, sententiously; "and I see you have been at the jeweller's! A present for Cecile? Well, don't blush, my dear fellow. What is life without women?"

"And wine?" said a second. "And play?" said a third. "And wealth?" said a fourth.

"And you enjoy them all! Happy fellow!" said a fifth. The Outcast pulled his hat over his brows, and walked away.

"This dear Paris," said Beaufort, as his eye carelessly and unconsciously followed the dark form retreating through the arches;—"this dear Paris! I must make the most of it while I stay! I have only been here a few weeks, and next week I must go."

"Pooh—your health is better: you don't look like the same man."

"You think so really? Still I don't know: the doctors say that I must either go to the German waters—the season is begun—or—"

"Or what?"

"Live less with such pleasant companions, my dear fellow! But as you say, what is life without—"

"Women!"

"Wine!"

"Play!"

"Wealth!"

"Ha! ha. 'Throw physic to the dogs: I'll none of it!'"

And Arthur leaped lightly on his saddle, and as he rode gaily on, humming the favourite air of the last opera, the hoofs of his horse splashed the mud over a foot-passenger halting at the crossing. Morton checked the fiery exclamation rising to his lips; and gazing after the brilliant form that hurried on towards the Champs Elysees, his eye caught the statues on the bridge, and a voice, as of a cheering angel, whispered again to his heart, "TIME, FAITH, ENERGY!"

The expression of his countenance grew calm at once, and as he continued his rambles it was with a mind that, casting off the burdens of the past, looked serenely and steadily on the obstacles and hardships of the future. We have seen that a scruple of conscience or of pride, not without its nobleness, had made him refuse the importunities of Gawtrey for less sordid raiment; the same feeling made it his custom to avoid sharing the luxurious and dainty food with which Gawtrey was wont to regale himself. For that strange man, whose wonderful felicity of temperament and constitution rendered him, in all circumstances, keenly alive to the hearty and animal enjoyments of life, would still emerge, as the day declined, from their wretched apartment, and, trusting to his disguises, in which indeed he possessed a masterly art, repair to one of the better description of restaurants, and feast away his cares for the moment. William Gawtrey would not have cared three straws for the curse of Damocles. The sword over his head would never have spoiled his appetite! He had lately, too, taken to drinking much more deeply than he had been used to do—the fine intellect of the man was growing thickened and dulled; and this was a spectacle that Morton could not bear to contemplate. Yet so great was Gawtrey's vigour of health, that, after draining wine and spirits enough to have despatched a company of fox-hunters, and after betraying, sometimes in uproarious glee, sometimes in maudlin self-bewailings, that he himself was not quite invulnerable to the thyrsus of the god, he would—on any call on his energies, or especially before departing on those mysterious expeditions which kept him from home half, and sometimes all, the night—plunge his head into cold water—drink as much of the lymph as a groom would have shuddered to bestow on a horse—close his eyes in a doze for half an hour, and wake, cool, sober, and collected, as if he had lived according to the precepts of Socrates or Cornaro!

But to return to Morton. It was his habit to avoid as much as possible sharing the good cheer of his companion; and now, as he entered the Champs Elysees, he saw a little family, consisting of a young mechanic, his wife, and two children, who, with that love of harmless recreation which yet characterises the French, had taken advantage of a holiday in the craft, and were enjoying their simple meal under the shadow of the trees. Whether in hunger or in envy, Morton paused and contemplated the happy group. Along the road rolled the equipages and trampled the steeds of those to whom all life is a holiday. There, was Pleasure—under those trees was Happiness. One of the children, a little boy of about six years old, observing the attitude and gaze of the pausing wayfarer, ran to him, and holding up a fragment of a coarse kind of cake, said to him, willingly, "Take it—I have had enough!" The child reminded Morton of his brother—his heart melted within him—he lifted the young Samaritan in his arms, and as he kissed him, wept.

The mother observed and rose also. She laid her hand on his own: "Poor boy! why do you weep?—can we relieve you?"

Now that bright gleam of human nature, suddenly darting across the sombre recollections and associations of his past life, seemed to Morton as if it came from Heaven, in approval and in blessing of this attempt at reconciliation to his fate.

"I thank you," said he, placing the child on the ground, and passing his hand over his eyes,—"I thank you—yes! Let me sit down amongst you." And he sat down, the child by his side, and partook of their fare, and was merry with them,—the proud Philip!—had he not begun to discover the "precious jewel" in the "ugly and venomous" Adversity?

The mechanic, though a gay fellow on the whole, was not without some of that discontent of his station which is common with his class; he vented it, however, not in murmurs, but in jests. He was satirical on the carriages and the horsemen that passed; and, lolling on the grass, ridiculed his betters at his ease.

"Hush!" said his wife, suddenly; "here comes Madame de Merville;" and rising as she spoke, she made a respectful inclination of her head towards an open carriage that was passing very slowly towards the town.

"Madame de Merville!" repeated the husband, rising also, and lifting his cap from his head. "Ah! I have nothing to say against her!"

Morton looked instinctively towards the carriage, and saw a fair countenance turned graciously to answer the silent salutations of the mechanic and his wife—a countenance that had long haunted his dreams, though of late it had faded away beneath harsher thoughts—the countenance of the stranger whom he had seen at the bureau of Gawtrey, when that worthy personage had borne a more mellifluous name. He started and changed colour: the lady herself now seemed suddenly to recognise him; for their eyes met, and she bent forward eagerly. She pulled the check-string—the carriage halted—she beckoned to the mechanic's wife, who went up to the roadside.

"I worked once for that lady," said the man with a tone of feeling; "and when my wife fell ill last winter she paid the doctors. Ah, she is an angel of charity and kindness!"

Morton scarcely heard this eulogium, for he observed, by something eager and inquisitive in the face of Madame de Merville, and by the sudden manner in which the mechanic's helpmate turned her head to the spot in which he stood, that he was the object of their conversation. Once more he became suddenly aware of his ragged dress, and with a natural shame—a fear that charity might be extended to him from her—he muttered an abrupt farewell to the operative, and without another glance at the carriage, walked away.

Before he had got many paces, the wife however came up to him, breathless. "Madame de Merville would speak to you, sir!" she said, with more respect than she had hitherto thrown into her manner. Philip paused an instant, and again strode on—

"It must be some mistake," he said, hurriedly: "I have no right to expect such an honour."

He struck across the road, gained the opposite side, and had vanished from Madame de Merville's eyes, before the woman regained the carriage. But still that calm, pale, and somewhat melancholy face, presented itself before him; and as he walked again through the town, sweet and gentle fancies crowded confusedly on his heart. On that soft summer day, memorable for so many silent but mighty events in that inner life which prepares the catastrophes of the outer one; as in the region, of which Virgil has sung, the images of men to be born hereafter repose or glide—on that soft summer day, he felt he had reached the age when Youth begins to clothe in some human shape its first vague ideal of desire and love.

In such thoughts, and still wandering, the day wore away, till he found himself in one of the lanes that surround that glittering Microcosm of the vices, the frivolities, the hollow show, and the real beggary of the gay City—the gardens and the galleries of the Palais Royal. Surprised at the lateness of the hour, it was then on the stroke of seven, he was about to return homewards, when the loud voice of Gawtrey sounded behind, and that personage, tapping him on the back, said,—

"Hollo, my young friend, well met! This will be a night of trial to you. Empty stomachs produce weak nerves. Come along! you must dine with me. A good dinner and a bottle of old wine—come! nonsense, I say you shall come! Vive la joie!"

While speaking, he had linked his arm in Morton's, and hurried him on several paces in spite of his struggles; but just as the words Vive la joie left his lips, he stood still and mute, as if a thunderbolt had fallen at his feet; and Morton felt that heavy arm shiver and tremble like a leaf. He looked up, and just at the entrance of that part of the Palais Royal in which are situated the restaurants of Verey and Vefour, he saw two men standing but a few paces before them, and gazing full on Gawtrey and himself.

"It is my evil genius," muttered Gawtrey, grinding his teeth.

"And mine!" said Morton.

The younger of the two men thus apostrophised made a step towards Philip, when his companion drew him back and whispered,—"What are you about—do you know that young man?"

"He is my cousin; Philip Beaufort's natural son!"

"Is he? then discard him for ever. He is with the most dangerous knave in Europe!"

As Lord Lilburne—for it was he—thus whispered his nephew, Gawtrey strode up to him; and, glaring full in his face, said in a deep and hollow tone,—"There is a hell, my lord,—I go to drink to our meeting!" Thus saying, he took off his hat with a ceremonious mockery, and disappeared within the adjoining restaurant, kept by Vefour.

"A hell!" said Lilburne, with his frigid smile; "the rogue's head runs upon gambling-houses!"

"And I have suffered Philip again to escape me," said Arthur, in self-reproach: for while Gawtrey had addressed Lord Lilburne, Morton had plunged back amidst the labyrinth of alleys. "How have I kept my oath?"

"Come! your guests must have arrived by this time. As for that wretched young man, depend upon it that he is corrupted body and soul."

"But he is my own cousin."

"Pooh! there is no relationship in natural children: besides, he will find you out fast enough. Ragged claimants are not long too proud to beg."

"You speak in earnest?" said Arthur, irresolutely. "Ay! trust my experience of the world—Allons!"

And in a cabinet of the very restaurant, adjoining that in which the solitary Gawtrey gorged his conscience, Lilburne, Arthur, and their gay friends, soon forgetful of all but the roses of the moment, bathed their airy spirits in the dews of the mirthful wine. Oh, extremes of life! Oh, Night! Oh, Morning!

CHAPTER IX

"Meantime a moving scene was open laid,
That lazar house."—THOMSON'S *Castle of Indolence.*

It was near midnight. At the mouth of the lane in which Gawtrey resided there stood four men. Not far distant, in the broad street at angles with the lane, were heard the wheels of carriages and the sound of music. A lady, fair in form, tender of heart, stainless in repute, was receiving her friends!

"Monsieur Favart," said one of the men to the smallest of the four; "you understand the conditions—20,000 francs and a free pardon?"

"Nothing more reasonable—it is understood. Still I confess that I should like to have my men close at hand. I am not given to fear; but this is a dangerous experiment."

"You knew the danger beforehand and subscribed to it: you must enter alone with me, or not at all. Mark you, the men are sworn to murder him who betrays them. Not for twenty times 20,000 francs would I have them know me as the informer. My life were not worth a day's purchase. Now, if you feel secure in your disguise, all is safe. You will have seen them at their work—you will recognise their persons—you can depose against them at the trial—I shall have time to quit France."

"Well, well! as you please."

"Mind, you must wait in the vault with them till they separate. We have so planted your men that whatever street each of the gang takes in going home, he can be seized quietly and at once. The bravest and craftiest of all, who, though he has but just joined, is already their captain;—him, the man I told you of, who lives in the house, you must take after his return, in his bed. It is the sixth story to the right, remember: here is the key to his door. He is a giant in strength; and will never be taken alive if up and armed."

"Ah, I comprehend!—Gilbert" (and Favart turned to one of his companions who had not yet spoken) "take three men besides yourself, according to the directions I gave you,—the porter will admit you, that's arranged. Make no noise. If I don't return by four o'clock, don't wait for me, but proceed at once. Look well to your primings. Take him alive, if possible—at the worst, dead. And now—mon ami—lead on!"

The traitor nodded, and walked slowly down the street. Favart, pausing, whispered hastily to the man whom he had called Gilbert,—

"Follow me close—get to the door of the cellar-place eight men within hearing of my whistle—recollect the picklocks, the axes. If you hear the whistle, break in; if not, I'm safe, and the first orders to seize the captain in his room stand good."

So saying, Favart strode after his guide. The door of a large, but ill-favoured-looking house stood ajar—they entered-passed unmolested through a court-yard—descended some stairs; the guide unlocked the door of a cellar, and took a dark lantern from under his cloak. As he drew up the slide, the dim light gleamed on barrels and wine-casks, which appeared to fill up the space. Rolling aside one of these, the guide lifted a trap-door, and lowered his lantern. "Enter," said he; and the two men disappeared.

The coiners were at their work. A man, seated on a stool before a desk, was entering accounts in a large book. That man was William Gawtrey. While, with the rapid precision of honest mechanics, the machinery of the Dark Trade went on in its several departments. Apart—alone—at the foot of a long table, sat Philip Morton. The truth had exceeded his darkest suspicions. He had consented to take the oath not to divulge what was to be given to his survey; and when, led into that vault, the bandage was taken from his eyes, it was some minutes before he could fully comprehend the desperate and criminal occupations of the wild forms amidst which towered the burly stature of his benefactor. As the truth slowly grew upon him, he shrank from the side of Gawtrey; but, deep compassion for his friend's degradation swallowing up the horror of the trade, he flung himself on one of the rude seats, and felt that the bond between them was indeed broken, and that the next morning he should be again alone in the world. Still, as the obscene jests, the fearful oaths, that from time to time rang through the vault, came on his ear, he cast his haughty eye in such disdain over the groups, that Gawtrey, observing him, trembled for his safety; and nothing but Philip's sense of his own impotence, and the brave, not timorous, desire not to perish by such hands, kept silent the fiery denunciations of a nature still proud and honest, that quivered on his lips. All present were armed with pistols and cutlasses except Morton, who suffered the weapons presented to him to lie unheeded on the table.

"Courage, mes amis!" said Gawtrey, closing his book,—"Courage!—a few months more, and we shall have made enough to retire upon, and enjoy ourselves for the rest of the days. Where is Birnie?"

"Did he not tell you?" said one of the artisans, looking up. "He has found out the cleverest hand in France, the very fellow who helped Bouchard in all his five-franc pieces. He has promised to bring him to-night."

"Ay, I remember," returned Gawtrey, "he told me this morning,—he is a famous decoy!"

"I think so, indeed!" quoth a coiner; "for he caught you, the best head to our hands that ever les industriels were blessed with—sacre fichtre!"

"Flatterer!" said Gawtrey, coming from the desk to the table, and pouring out wine from one of the bottles into a huge flagon—"To your healths!"

Here the door slid back, and Birnie glided in.

"Where is your booty, mon brave?" said Gawtrey. "We only coin money; you coin men, stamp with your own seal, and send them current to the devil!"

The coiners, who liked Birnie's ability (for the ci-devant engraver was of admirable skill in their craft), but who hated his joyless manners, laughed at this taunt, which Birnie did not seem to heed, except by a malignant gleam of his dead eye.

"If you mean the celebrated coiner, Jacques Giraumont, he waits without. You know our rules. I cannot admit him without leave."

"Bon! we give it,—eh, messieurs?" said Gawtrey. "Ay-ay," cried several voices. "He knows the oath, and will hear the penalty."

"Yes, he knows the oath," replied Birnie, and glided back.

In a moment more he returned with a small man in a mechanic's blouse. The new comer wore the republican beard and moustache—of a sandy grey—his hair was the same colour; and a black patch over one eye increased the ill-favoured appearance of his features.

"Diable! Monsieur Giraumont! but you are more like Vulcan than Adonis!" said Gawtrey.

"I don't know anything about Vulcan, but I know how to make five-franc pieces," said Monsieur Giraumont, doggedly.

"Are you poor?"

"As a church mouse! The only thing belonging to a church, since the Bourbons came back, that is poor!"

At this sally, the coiners, who had gathered round the table, uttered the shout with which, in all circumstances, Frenchmen receive a bon mot.

"Humph!" said Gawtrey. "Who responds with his own life for your fidelity?"

"I," said Birnie.

"Administer the oath to him."

Suddenly four men advanced, seized the visitor, and bore him from the vault into another one within. After a few moments they returned.

"He has taken the oath and heard the penalty."

"Death to yourself, your wife, your son, and your grandson, if you betray us!"

"I have neither son nor grandson; as for my wife, Monsieur le Capitaine, you offer a bribe instead of a threat when you talk of her death."

"Sacre! but you will be an addition to our circle, mon brave!" said Gawtrey, laughing; while again the grim circle shouted applause.

"But I suppose you care for your own life."

"Otherwise I should have preferred starving to coming here," answered the laconic neophyte.

"I have done with you. Your health!"

On this the coiners gathered round Monsieur Giraumont, shook him by the hand, and commenced many questions with a view to ascertain his skill.

"Show me your coinage first; I see you use both the die and the furnace. Hem! this piece is not bad—you have struck it from an iron die?—right—it makes the impression sharper than plaster of Paris. But you take the poorest and the most dangerous part of the trade in taking the home market. I can put you in a way to make ten times as much—and with safety. Look at this!"—and Monsieur Giraumont took a forged Spanish dollar from his pocket, so skilfully manufactured that the connoisseurs were lost in admiration—"you may pass thousands of these all over Europe, except France, and who is ever to detect you? But it will require better machinery than you have here."

Thus conversing, Monsieur Giraumont did not perceive that Mr. Gawtrey had been examining him very curiously and minutely. But Birnie had noted their chief's attention, and once attempted to join his new ally, when Gawtrey laid his hand on his shoulder, and stopped him.

"Do not speak to your friend till I bid you, or—" he stopped short, and touched his pistols.

Birnie grew a shade more pale, but replied with his usual sneer:

"Suspicious!—well, so much the better!" and seating himself carelessly at the table, lighted his pipe.

"And now, Monsieur Giraumont," said Gawtrey, as he took the head of the table, "come to my right hand. A half-holiday in your honour. Clear these infernal instruments; and more wine, mes amis!"

The party arranged themselves at the table. Among the desperate there is almost invariably a tendency to mirth. A solitary ruffian, indeed, is moody, but a gang of ruffians are jovial. The coiners talked and laughed loud. Mr. Birnie, from his dogged silence, seemed apart from the rest, though in the centre. For in a noisy circle a silent tongue builds a wall round its owner. But that respectable personage kept his furtive watch upon Giraumont and Gawtrey, who appeared talking together, very amicably. The younger novice of that night, equally silent, seated towards the bottom of the table, was not less watchful than Birnie. An uneasy, undefinable foreboding had come over him since the entrance of Monsieur Giraumont; this had been increased by the manner of Mr. Gawtrey. His faculty of observation, which was very acute, had detected something false in the chief's blandness to their guest—something dangerous in the glittering eye that Gawtrey ever, as he spoke to Giraumont, bent on that person's lips as he listened to his reply. For, whenever William Gawtrey suspected a man, he watched not his eyes, but his lips.

Waked from his scornful reverie, a strange spell chained Morton's attention to the chief and the guest, and he bent forward, with parted mouth and straining ear, to catch their conversation.

"It seems to me a little strange," said Mr. Gawtrey, raising his voice so as to be heard by the party, "that a coiner so dexterous as Monsieur Giraumont should not be known to any of us except our friend Birnie."

"Not at all," replied Giraumont; "I worked only with Bouchard and two others since sent to the galleys. We were but a small fraternity—everything has its commencement."

"C'est juste: buvez, donc, cher ami!"

The wine circulated. Gawtrey began again:

"You have had a bad accident, seemingly, Monsieur Giraumont. How did you lose your eye?"

"In a scuffle with the gens d' armes the night Bouchard was taken and I escaped. Such misfortunes are on the cards."

"C'est juste: buvez, donc, Monsieur Giraumont!"

Again there was a pause, and again Gawtrey's deep voice was heard.

"You wear a wig, I think, Monsieur Giraumont? To judge by your eyelashes your own hair has been a handsomer colour."

"We seek disguise, not beauty, my host; and the police have sharp eyes."

"C'est juste: buvez, donc-vieux Renard! When did we two meet last?"

"Never, that I know of."

"Ce n'est pas vrai! buvez, donc, MONSIEUR FAVART!"

At the sound of that name the company started in dismay and confusion, and the police officer, forgetting himself for the moment, sprang from his seat, and put his right hand into his blouse.

"Ho, there!—treason!" cried Gawtrey, in a voice of thunder; and he caught the unhappy man by the throat. It was the work of a moment. Morton, where he sat, beheld a struggle—he heard a death-cry. He saw the huge form of the master-coiner rising above all the rest, as cutlasses gleamed and eyes sparkled round. He saw the quivering and powerless frame of the unhappy guest raised aloft in those mighty arms, and presently it was hurled along the table-bottles crashing—the board shaking beneath its weight—and lay before the very eyes of Morton, a distorted and lifeless mass. At the same instant Gawtrey sprang upon the table, his black frown singling out from the group the ashen, cadaverous face of the shrinking traitor. Birnie had darted from the table—he was half-way towards the sliding door—his face, turned over his shoulder, met the eyes of the chief.

"Devil!" shouted Gawtrey, in his terrible voice, which the echoes of the vault gave back from side to side. "Did I not give thee up my soul that thou mightest not compass my death? Hark ye! thus die my slavery and all our secrets!" The explosion of his pistol half swallowed up the last word, and with a single groan the traitor fell on the floor, pierced through the brain—then there was a dead and grim hush as the smoke rolled slowly along the roof of the dreary vault.

Morton sank back on his seat, and covered his face with his hands. The last seal on the fate of THE MAN OF CRIME was set; the last wave in the terrible and mysterious tide of his destiny had dashed on his soul to the shore whence there is no return. Vain, now and henceforth, the humour, the sentiment, the kindly impulse, the social instincts which had invested that stalwart shape with dangerous fascination, which had implied the hope of ultimate repentance, of redemption even in this world. The HOUR and the CIRCUMSTANCE had seized their prey; and the self-defence, which a lawless career rendered a necessity, left the eternal die of blood upon his doom!

"Friends, I have saved you," said Gawtrey, slowly gazing on the corpse of his second victim, while he turned the pistol to his belt. "I have not quailed before this man's eye" (and he spurned the clay of the officer as he spoke with a revengeful scorn) "without treasuring up its aspect in my heart of hearts. I knew him when he entered—knew him through his disguise—yet, faith, it was a clever one! Turn up his face and gaze on him now; he will never terrify us again, unless there be truth in ghosts!"

Murmuring and tremulous the coiners scrambled on the table and examined the dead man. From this task Gawtrey interrupted them, for his quick eye detected, with the pistols under the policeman's blouse, a whistle of metal of curious construction, and he conjectured at once that danger was at hand.

"I have saved you, I say, but only for the hour. This deed cannot sleep. See, he had help within call! The police knew where to look for their comrade—we are dispersed. Each for himself. Quick, divide the spoils! Sauve qui peat!"

Then Morton heard where he sat, his hands still clasped before his face, a confused hubbub of voices, the jingle of money, the scrambling of feet, the creaking of doors. All was silent!

A strong grasp drew his hands from his eyes.

"Your first scene of life against life," said Gawtrey's voice, which seemed fearfully changed to the ear that heard it. "Bah! what would you think of a battle? Come to our eyrie: the carcasses are gone."

Morton looked fearfully round the vault. He and Gawtrey were alone. His eyes sought the places where the dead had lain—they were removed—no vestige of the deeds, not even a drop of blood.

"Come, take up your cutlass, come!" repeated the voice of the chief, as with his dim lantern—now the sole light of the vault—he stood in the shadow of the doorway.

Morton rose, took up the weapon mechanically, and followed that terrible guide, mute and unconscious, as a Soul follows a Dream through the House of Sleep!

CHAPTER X

"Sleep no more!"—Macbeth

After winding through gloomy and labyrinthine passages, which conducted to a different range of cellars from those entered by the unfortunate Favart, Gawtrey emerged at the foot of a flight of stairs, which, dark, narrow, and in many places broken, had been probably appropriated to servants of the house in its days of palmier glory. By these steps the pair regained their attic. Gawtrey placed the lantern on the table and seated himself in silence. Morton, who had recovered his self-possession and formed his resolution, gazed on him for some moments, equally taciturn. At length he spoke:

"Gawtrey!"

"I bade you not call me by that name," said the coiner; for we need scarcely say that in his new trade he had assumed a new appellation.

"It is the least guilty one by which I have known you," returned Morton, firmly. "It is for the last time I call you by it! I demanded to see by what means one to whom I had entrusted my fate supported himself. I have seen," continued the young man, still firmly, but with a livid cheek and lip, "and the tie between us is rent for ever. Interrupt me not! it is not for me to blame you. I have eaten of your bread and drunk of your cup. Confiding in you too blindly, and believing that you were at least free from those dark and terrible crimes for which there is no expiation—at least in this life—my conscience seared by distress, my very soul made dormant by despair, I surrendered myself to one leading a career equivocal, suspicious, dishonourable perhaps, but still not, as I believed, of atrocity and bloodshed. I wake at the brink of the abyss—my mother's hand beckons to me from the grave; I think I hear her voice while I address you—I recede while it is yet time—we part, and for ever!"

Gawtrey, whose stormy passion was still deep upon his soul, had listened hitherto in sullen and dogged silence, with a gloomy frown on his knitted brow; he now rose with an oath—

"Part! that I may let loose on the world a new traitor! Part! when you have seen me fresh from an act that, once whispered, gives me to the guillotine! Part—never! at least alive!"

"I have said it," said Morton, folding his arms calmly; "I say it to your face, though I might part from you in secret. Frown not on me, man of blood! I am fearless as yourself! In another minute I am gone."

"Ah! is it so?" said Gawtrey; and glancing round the room, which contained two doors, the one concealed by the draperies of a bed, communicating with the stairs by which they had entered, the other with the landing of the principal and common flight: he turned to the former, within his reach, which he locked, and put the key into his pocket, and then, throwing across the latter a heavy swing bar, which fell into its socket with a harsh noise,—before the threshold he placed his vast bulk, and burst into his loud, fierce laugh: "Ho! ho! Slave and fool, once mine, you were mine body and soul for ever!"

"Tempter, I defy you! stand back!" And, firm and dauntless, Morton laid his hand on the giant's vest.

Gawtrey seemed more astonished than enraged. He looked hard at his daring associate, on whose lip the down was yet scarcely dark.

"Boy," said he, "off! do not rouse the devil in me again! I could crush you with a hug."

"My soul supports my body, and I am armed," said Morton, laying hand on his cutlass. "But you dare not harm me, nor I you; bloodstained as you are, you gave me shelter and bread; but accuse me not that I will save my soul while it is yet time!—Shall my mother have blessed me in vain upon her death-bed?"

Gawtrey drew back, and Morton, by a sudden impulse, grasped his hand.

"Oh! hear me—hear me!" he cried, with great emotion. "Abandon this horrible career; you have been decoyed and betrayed to it by one who can deceive or terrify you no more! Abandon it, and I will never desert you. For her sake—for your Fanny's sake—pause, like me, before the gulf swallow us. Let us fly!—far to the New World—to any land where our thews and sinews, our stout hands and hearts, can find an honest mart. Men, desperate as we are, have yet risen by honest means. Take her, your orphan, with us. We will work for her, both of us. Gawtrey! hear me. It is not my voice that speaks to you—it is your good angel's!"

Gawtrey fell back against the wall, and his chest heaved.

"Morton," he said, with choked and tremulous accent, "go now; leave me to my fate! I have sinned against you—shamefully sinned. It seemed to me so sweet to have a friend; in your youth and character of mind there was so much about which the tough strings of my heart wound themselves, that I could not bear to lose you—to suffer you to know me for what I was. I blinded—I deceived you as to my past deeds; that was base in me: but I swore to my own heart to keep you unexposed to every danger, and free from every vice that darkened my own path. I kept that oath till this night, when, seeing that you began to recoil from me, and dreading that you should desert me, I thought to bind you to me for ever by implicating you in this fellowship of crime. I am punished, and justly. Go, I repeat—leave me to the fate that strides nearer and nearer to me day by day. You are a boy still—I am no longer young. Habit is a second nature. Still—still I could repent—I could begin life again. But repose!—to look back—to remember—to be haunted night and day with deeds that shall meet me bodily and face to face on the last day—"

"Add not to the spectres! Come—fly this night—this hour!"

Gawtrey paused, irresolute and wavering, when at that moment he heard steps on the stairs below. He started—as starts the boar caught in his lair—and listened, pale and breathless.

"Hush!—they are on us!—they come!" as he whispered, the key from without turned in the wards—the door shook. "Soft! the bar preserves us both—this way." And the coiner crept to the door of the private stairs. He unlocked and opened it cautiously. A man sprang through the aperture:

"Yield!—you are my prisoner!"

"Never!" cried Gawtrey, hurling back the intruder, and clapping to the door, though other and stout men were pressing against it with all their power.

"Ho! ho! Who shall open the tiger's cage?"

At both doors now were heard the sound of voices. "Open in the king's name, or expect no mercy!"

"Hist!" said Gawtrey. "One way yet—the window—the rope."

Morton opened the casement—Gawtrey uncoiled the rope. The dawn was breaking; it was light in the streets, but all seemed quiet without. The doors reeled and shook beneath the pressure of the pursuers. Gawtrey flung the rope across the street to the opposite parapet; after two or three efforts, the grappling-hook caught firm hold—the perilous path was made.

"On!—quick!—loiter not!" whispered Gawtrey; "you are active—it seems more dangerous than it is—cling with both hands—shut your eyes. When on the other side—you see the window of Birnie's room,—enter it—descend the stairs—let yourself out, and you are safe."

"Go first," said Morton, in the same tone: "I will not leave you now: you will be longer getting across than I shall. I will keep guard till you are over."

"Hark! hark!—are you mad? You keep guard! what is your strength to mine? Twenty men shall not move that door, while my weight is against it. Quick, or you destroy us both! Besides, you will hold the rope for me, it may not be strong enough for my bulk in itself. Stay!—stay one moment. If you escape, and I fall—Fanny—my father, he will take care of her,—you remember—thanks! Forgive me all! Go; that's right!"

With a firm impulse, Morton threw himself on the dreadful bridge; it swung and crackled at his weight. Shifting his grasp rapidly—holding his breath—with set teeth-with closed eyes—he moved on—he gained the parapet—he stood safe on the opposite side. And now, straining his eyes across, he saw through the open casement into the chamber he had just quitted. Gawtrey was still standing against the door to the principal staircase, for that of the two was the weaker and the more assailed. Presently the explosion of a fire-arm was heard; they had shot through the panel. Gawtrey seemed wounded, for he staggered forward, and uttered a fierce cry; a moment more, and he gained the window—he seized the rope—he hung over the tremendous depth! Morton knelt by the parapet, holding the grappling-hook in its place, with convulsive grasp, and fixing his eyes, bloodshot with fear and suspense, on the huge bulk that clung for life to that slender cord!

"Le voiles! Le voiles!" cried a voice from the opposite side. Morton raised his gaze from Gawtrey; the casement was darkened by the forms of his pursuers—they had burst into the room—an officer sprang upon the parapet, and Gawtrey, now aware of his danger, opened his eyes, and as he moved on, glared upon the foe. The policeman deliberately raised his pistol—Gawtrey arrested himself—from a wound in his side the blood trickled slowly and darkly down, drop by drop, upon the stones below; even the officers of law shuddered as they eyed him—his hair bristling—his cheek white—his lips drawn convulsively from his teeth, and his eyes glaring from beneath the frown of agony and menace in which yet spoke the indomitable power and fierceness of the man. His look, so fixed—so intense—so stern, awed the policeman; his hand trembled as he fired, and the ball struck the parapet an inch below the spot where Morton knelt. An indistinct, wild, gurgling sound-half-laugh, half-yell of scorn and glee, broke from Gawtrey's lips. He swung himself on—near—near—nearer—a yard from the parapet.

"You are saved!" cried Morton; when at the moment a volley burst from the fatal casement—the smoke rolled over both the fugitives—a groan, or rather howl, of rage, and despair, and agony, appalled even the hardest on whose ear it came. Morton sprang to his feet and looked below. He saw on the rugged stones far down, a dark, formless, motionless mass—the strong man of passion and levity—the giant who had played with life and soul, as an infant with the baubles that it prizes and breaks—was what the Caesar and the leper alike are, when the clay is without God's breath—what glory, genius, power, and beauty, would be for ever and for ever, if there were no God!

"There is another!" cried the voice of one of the pursuers. "Fire!"

"Poor Gawtrey!" muttered Philip. "I will fulfil your last wish;" and scarcely conscious of the bullet that whistled by him, he disappeared behind the parapet.

CHAPTER XI

"Gently moved
By the soft wind of whispering silks."—DECKER.

The reader may remember that while Monsieur Favart and Mr. Birnie were holding commune in the lane, the sounds of festivity were heard from a house in the adjoining street. To that house we are now summoned.

At Paris, the gaieties of balls, or soirees, are, I believe, very rare in that period of the year in which they are most frequent in London. The entertainment now given was in honour of a christening; the lady who gave it, a relation of the new-born.

Madame de Merville was a young widow; even before her marriage she had been distinguished in literature; she had written poems of more than common excellence; and being handsome, of good family, and large fortune, her talents made her an object of more interest than they might otherwise have done. Her poetry showed great sensibility and tenderness. If poetry be any index to the heart, you would have thought her one to love truly and deeply. Nevertheless, since she married—as girls in France do—not to please herself, but her parents, she made a mariage de convenance. Monsieur de Merville was a sober, sensible man, past middle age. Not being fond of poetry, and by no means coveting a professional author for his wife, he had during their union, which lasted four years, discouraged his wife's liaison with Apollo. But her mind, active and ardent, did not the less prey upon itself. At the age of four-and-twenty she became a widow, with an income large even in England for a single woman, and at Paris constituting no ordinary fortune. Madame de Merville, however, though a person of elegant taste, was neither ostentatious nor selfish; she had no children, and she lived quietly in apartments, handsome, indeed, but not more than adequate to the small establishment which—where, as on the Continent, the costly convenience of an entire house is not usually incurred—sufficed for her retinue. She devoted at least half her income, which was entirely at her own disposal, partly to the aid of her own relations, who were not rich, and partly to the encouragement of the literature she cultivated. Although she shrank from the ordeal of publication, her poems and sketches of romance were read to her own friends, and possessed an eloquence seldom accompanied with so much modesty. Thus, her reputation, though not blown about the winds, was high in her own circle, and her position in fashion and in fortune made her looked up to by her relations as the head of her family; they regarded her as femme superieure, and her advice with them was equivalent to a command. Eugenie de Merville was a strange mixture of qualities at once feminine and masculine. On the one hand, she had a strong will, independent views, some contempt for the world, and followed her own inclinations without servility to the opinion of others; on the other hand, she was susceptible, romantic, of a sweet, affectionate, kind disposition. Her visit to M. Love, however indiscreet, was not less in accordance with her character than her charity to the mechanic's wife; masculine and careless where an eccentric thing was to be done—curiosity satisfied, or some object in female diplomacy achieved—womanly, delicate, and gentle, the instant her benevolence was appealed to or her heart touched. She had now been three years a widow, and was consequently at the age of twenty-seven. Despite the tenderness of her poetry and her character, her reputation was unblemished. She had never been in love. People who are much occupied do not fall in love easily; besides, Madame de Merville was refining, exacting, and wished to find heroes where she only met handsome dandies or ugly authors. Moreover, Eugenie was both a vain and a proud person—vain of her celebrity and proud of her birth. She was one whose goodness of heart made her always active in promoting the happiness of others. She was not only generous and charitable, but willing to serve people by good offices as well as money. Everybody loved her. The new-born infant, to whose addition to the Christian community the fete of this night was dedicated, was the pledge of a union which Madame de Merville had managed to effect between two young persons, first cousins to each other, and related to herself. There had been scruples of parents to remove—money matters to adjust—Eugenie had smoothed all. The husband and wife, still lovers, looked up to her as the author, under Heaven, of their happiness.

The gala of that night had been, therefore, of a nature more than usually pleasurable, and the mirth did not sound hollow, but wrung from the heart. Yet, as Eugenie from time to time contemplated the young people, whose eyes ever sought each other—so fair, so tender, and so joyous as they seemed—a melancholy shadow darkened her brow, and she sighed involuntarily. Once the young wife, Madame d'Anville, approaching her timidly, said:

"Ah! my sweet cousin, when shall we see you as happy as ourselves? There is such happiness," she added, innocently, and with a blush, "in being a mother!—that little life all one's own—it is something to think of every hour!"

"Perhaps," said Eugenie, smiling, and seeking to turn the conversation from a subject that touched too nearly upon feelings and thoughts her pride did not wish to reveal—"perhaps it is you, then, who have made our cousin, poor Monsieur de Vaudemont, so determined to marry? Pray, be more cautious with him. How difficult I have found it to prevent his bringing into our family some one to make us all ridiculous!"

"True," said Madame d'Anville, laughing. "But then, the Vicomte is so poor, and in debt. He would fall in love, not with the demoiselle, but the dower. A propos of that, how cleverly you took advantage of his boastful confession to break off his liaisons with that bureau de mariage."

"Yes; I congratulate myself on that manoeuvre. Unpleasant as it was to go to such a place (for, of course, I could not send for Monsieur Love here), it would have been still more unpleasant to have received such a Madame de Vaudemont as our cousin would have presented to us. Only think—he was the rival of an epicier! I heard that there was some curious denouement to the farce of that establishment; but I could never get from Vaudemont the particulars. He was ashamed of them, I fancy."

"What droll professions there are in Paris!" said Madame d'Anville. "As if people could not marry without going to an office for a spouse as we go for a servant! And so the establishment is broken up? And you never again saw that dark, wild-looking boy who so struck your fancy that you have taken him as the original for the Murillo sketch of the youth in that charming tale you read to us the other evening? Ah! cousin, I think you were a little taken with him. The bureau de mariage had its allurements for you as well as for our poor cousin!" The young mother said this laughingly and carelessly.

"Pooh!" returned Madame de Merville, laughing also; but a slight blush broke over her natural paleness. "But a propos of the Vicomte. You know how cruelly he has behaved to that poor boy of his by his English wife—never seen him since he was an infant—kept him at some school in England; and all because his vanity does not like the world to know that he has a son of nineteen! Well, I have induced him to recall this poor youth."

"Indeed! and how?"

"Why," said Eugenie, with a smile, "he wanted a loan, poor man, and I could therefore impose conditions by way of interest. But I also managed to conciliate him to the proposition, by representing that, if the young man were good-looking, he might, himself, with our connections, &c., form an advantageous marriage; and that in such a case, if the father treated him now justly and kindly, he would naturally partake with the father whatever benefits the marriage might confer."

"Ah! you are an excellent diplomatist, Eugenie; and you turn people's heads by always acting from your heart. Hush! here comes the Vicomte!"

"A delightful ball," said Monsieur de Vaudemont, approaching the hostess. "Pray, has that young lady yonder, in the pink dress, any fortune? She is pretty—eh? You observe she is looking at me—I mean at us!"

"My dear cousin, what a compliment you pay to marriage! You have had two wives, and you are ever on the qui vive for a third!"

"What would you have me do?—we cannot resist the overtures of your bewitching sex. Hum—what fortune has she?"

"Not a sou; besides, she is engaged."

"Oh! now I look at her, she is not pretty—not at all. I made a mistake. I did not mean her; I meant the young lady in blue."

"Worse and worse—she is married already. Shall I present you?"

"Ah, Monsieur de Vaudemont," said Madame d'Anville; "have you found out a new bureau de mariage?"

The Vicomte pretended not to hear that question. But, turning to Eugenie, took her aside, and said, with an air in which he endeavoured to throw a great deal of sorrow, "You know, my dear cousin, that, to oblige you, I consented to send for my son, though, as I always said, it is very unpleasant for a man like me, in the prime of life, to hawk about a great boy of nineteen or twenty. People soon say, 'Old Vaudemont and young Vaudemont.' However, a father's feelings are never appealed to in vain." (Here the Vicomte put his handkerchief to his eyes, and after a pause, continued,)—"I sent for him—I even went to your old bonne, Madame Dufour, to make a bargain for her lodgings, and this day—guess my grief—I received a letter sealed with black. My son is dead!—a sudden fever—it is shocking!"

"Horrible! dead!—your own son, whom you hardly ever saw—never since he was an Infant!"

"Yes, that softens the blow very much. And now you see I must marry. If the boy had been good-looking, and like me, and so forth, why, as you observed, he might have made a good match, and allowed me a certain sum, or we could have all lived together."

"And your son is dead, and you come to a ball!"

"Je suis philosophe," said the Vicomte, shrugging his shoulders. "And, as you say, I never saw him. It saves me seven hundred francs a-year. Don't say a word to any one—I sha'n't give out that he is dead, poor fellow! Pray be discreet: you see there are some ill-natured people who might think it odd I do not shut myself up. I can wait till Paris is quite empty. It would be a pity to lose any opportunity at present, for now, you see, I must marry!" And the philosophe sauntered away.

CHAPTER XII

GUIOMAR.
"Those devotions I am to pay
Are written in my heart, not in this book."

Enter RUTILIO.
"I am pursued—all the ports are stopped too,
Not any hope to escape—behind, before me,
On either side, I am beset."

BEAUMONT AND FLETCHER, *The Custom of the Country*

The party were just gone—it was already the peep of day—the wheels of the last carriage had died in the distance.

Madame de Merville had dismissed her woman, and was seated in her own room, leaning her head musingly on her hand.

Beside her was the table that held her MSS. and a few books, amidst which were scattered vases of flowers. On a pedestal beneath the window was placed a marble bust of Dante. Through the open door were seen in perspective two rooms just deserted by her guests; the lights still burned in the chandeliers and girandoles, contending with the daylight that came through the half-closed curtains. The person of the inmate was in harmony with the apartment. It was characterised by a certain grace which, for want of a better epithet, writers are prone to call classical or antique. Her complexion, seeming paler than usual by that light, was yet soft and delicate—the features well cut, but small and womanly. About the face there was that rarest of all charms, the combination of intellect with sweetness; the eyes, of a dark blue, were thoughtful, perhaps melancholy, in their expression; but the long dark lashes, and the shape of the eyes, themselves more long than full, gave to their intelligence a softness approaching to languor, increased, perhaps, by that slight shadow round and below the orbs which is common with those who have tasked too much either the mind or the heart. The contour of the face, without being sharp or angular, had yet lost a little of the roundness of earlier youth; and the hand on which she leaned was, perhaps, even too white, too delicate, for the beauty which belongs to health; but the throat and bust were of exquisite symmetry.

"I am not happy," murmured Eugenie to herself; "yet I scarce know why. Is it really, as we women of romance have said till the saying is worn threadbare, that the destiny of women is not fame but love. Strange, then, that while I have so often pictured what love should be, I have never felt it. And now,—and now," she continued, half rising, and with a natural pang—"now I am no longer in my first youth. If I loved, should I be loved again? How happy the young pair seemed—they are never alone!"

At this moment, at a distance, was heard the report of fire-arms—again! Eugenie started, and called to her servant, who, with one of the waiters hired for the night, was engaged in removing, and nibbling as he removed, the remains of the feast. "What is that, at this hour?—open the window and look out!"

"I can see nothing, madame."

"Again—that is the third time. Go into the street and look—some one must be in danger."

The servant and the waiter, both curious, and not willing to part company, ran down the stairs, and thence into the street.

Meanwhile, Morton, after vainly attempting Birnie's window, which the traitor had previously locked and barred against the escape of his intended victim, crept rapidly along the roof, screened by the parapet not only from the shot but the sight of the foe. But just as he gained the point at which the lane made an angle with the broad street it adjoined, he cast his eyes over the parapet, and perceived that one of the officers had ventured himself to the fearful bridge; he was pursued—detection and capture seemed inevitable. He paused, and breathed hard. He, once the heir to such fortunes, the darling of such affections!—he, the hunted accomplice of a gang of miscreants! That was the thought that paralysed—the disgrace, not the danger. But he was in advance of the pursuer—he hastened on—he turned the angle—he heard a shout behind from the opposite side—the officer had passed the bridge: "it is but one man as yet," thought he, and his nostrils dilated and his hands clenched as he glided on, glancing at each casement as he passed.

Now as youth and vigour thus struggled against Law for life, near at hand Death was busy with toil and disease. In a miserable grabat, or garret, a mechanic, yet young, and stricken by a lingering malady contracted by the labour of his occupation, was slowly passing from that world which had frowned on his cradle, and relaxed not the gloom of its aspect to comfort his bed of Death. Now this man had married for love, and his wife had loved him; and it was the cares of that early marriage which had consumed him to the bone. But extreme want, if long continued, eats up love when it has nothing else to eat. And when people are very long dying, the people they fret and trouble begin to think of that too often hypocritical prettiness of phrase called "a happy release." So the worn-out and half-famished wife did not care three straws for the dying husband, whom a year or two ago she had vowed to love and cherish in sickness and in health. But still she seemed to care, for she moaned, and pined, and wept, as the man's breath grew fainter and fainter.

"Ah, Jean!" said she, sobbing, "what will become of me, a poor lone widow, with nobody to work for my bread?" And with that thought she took on worse than before.

"I am stifling," said the dying man, rolling round his ghastly eyes. "How hot it is! Open the window; I should like to see the light—daylight once again."

"Mon Dieu! what whims he has, poor man!" muttered the woman, without stirring.

The poor wretch put out his skeleton hand and clutched his wife's arm.

"I sha'n't trouble you long, Marie! Air—air!"

"Jean, you will make yourself worse—besides, I shall catch my death of cold. I have scarce a rag on, but I will just open the door."

"Pardon me," groaned the sufferer; "leave me, then." Poor fellow! perhaps at that moment the thought of unkindness was sharper than the sharp cough which brought blood at every paroxysm. He did not like her so near him, but he did not blame her. Again, I say,—poor fellow! The woman opened the door, went to the other side of the room, and sat down on an old box and began darning an old neck-handkerchief. The silence was soon broken by the moans of the fast-dying man, and again he muttered, as he tossed to and fro, with baked white lips:

"Je m'etoufee!—Air!"

There was no resisting that prayer, it seemed so like the last. The wife laid down the needle, put the handkerchief round her throat, and opened the window.

"Do you feel easier now?"

"Bless you, Marie—yes; that's good—good. It puts me in mind of old days, that breath of air, before we came to Paris. I wish I could work for you now, Marie."

"Jean! my poor Jean!" said the woman, and the words and the voice took back her hardening heart to the fresh fields and tender thoughts of the past time. And she walked up to the bed, and he leaned his temples, damp with livid dews, upon her breast.

"I have been a sad burden to you, Marie; we should not have married so soon; but I thought I was stronger. Don't cry; we have no little ones, thank God. It will be much better for you when I am gone."

And so, word after word gasped out—he stopped suddenly, and seemed to fall asleep.

The wife then attempted gently to lay him once more on his pillow—the head fell back heavily—the jaw had dropped—the teeth were set—the eyes were open and like the stone—the truth broke on her!

"Jean—Jean! My God, he is dead! and I was unkind to him at the last!" With these words she fell upon the corpse, happily herself insensible.

Just at that moment a human face peered in at the window. Through that aperture, after a moment's pause, a young man leaped lightly into the room. He looked round with a hurried glance, but scarcely noticed the forms stretched on the pallet. It was enough for him that they seemed to sleep, and saw him not. He stole across the room, the door of which Marie had left open, and descended the stairs. He had almost gained the courtyard into which the stairs had conducted, when he heard voices below by the porter's lodge.

"The police have discovered a gang of coiners!"

"Coiners!"

"Yes, one has been shot dead! I have seen his body in the kennel; another has fled along the roofs—a desperate fellow! We were to watch for him. Let us go up-stairs and get on the roof and look out."

By the hum of approval that followed this proposition, Morton judged rightly that it had been addressed to several persons whom curiosity and the explosion of the pistols had drawn from their beds, and who were grouped round the porter's lodge. What was to be done?—to advance was impossible: and was there yet time to retreat?—it was at least the only course left him; he sprang back up the stairs; he had just gained the first flight when he heard steps descending; then, suddenly, it flashed across him that he had left open the window above—that, doubtless, by that imprudent oversight the officer in pursuit had detected a clue to the path he had taken. What was to be done?—die as Gawtrey had done!—death rather than the galleys. As he thus resolved, he saw to the right the open door of an apartment in which lights still glimmered in their sockets. It seemed deserted—he entered boldly and at once, closing the door after him. Wines and viands still left on the table; gilded mirrors, reflecting the stern face of the solitary intruder; here and there an artificial flower, a knot of riband on the floor, all betokening the gaieties and graces of luxurious life—the dance, the revel, the feast—all this in one apartment!—above, in the same house, the pallet—the corpse—the widow—famine and woe! Such is a great city! such, above all, is Paris! where, under the same roof, are gathered such antagonist varieties of the social state! Nothing strange in this; it is strange and sad that so little do people thus neighbours know of each other, that the owner of those rooms had a heart soft to every distress, but she did not know the distress so close at hand. The music that had charmed her guests had mounted gaily to the vexed ears of agony and hunger. Morton passed the first room—a second—he came to a third, and Eugenie de Merville, looking up at that instant, saw before her an apparition that might well have alarmed the boldest. His head was uncovered—his dark hair shadowed in wild and disorderly profusion the pale face and features, beautiful indeed, but at that moment of the beauty which an artist would impart to a young gladiator—stamped with defiance, menace, and despair. The disordered garb—the fierce aspect—the dark eyes, that literally shone through the shadows of the room—all conspired to increase the terror of so abrupt a presence.

"What are you?—What do you seek here?" said she, falteringly, placing her hand on the bell as she spoke. Upon that soft hand Morton laid his own.

"I seek my life! I am pursued! I am at your mercy! I am innocent! Can you save me?"

As he spoke, the door of the outer room beyond was heard to open, and steps and voices were at hand.

"Ah!" he exclaimed, recoiling as he recognised her face. "And is it to you that I have fled?"

Eugenie also recognised the stranger; and there was something in their relative positions—the suppliant, the protectress—that excited both her imagination and her pity. A slight colour mantled to her cheeks—her look was gentle and compassionate.

"Poor boy! so young!" she said. "Hush!"

She withdrew her hand from his, retired a few steps, lifted a curtain drawn across a recess—and pointing to an alcove that contained one of those sofa-beds common in French houses, added in a whisper,—

"Enter—you are saved."

Morton obeyed, and Eugenie replaced the curtain.

CHAPTER XIII

GUIOMAR. *"Speak! What are you?"*

RUTILIO. *"Gracious woman, hear me. I am a stranger:*
And in that I answer all your demands."
Custom of the Country.

Eugenie replaced the curtain. And scarcely had she done so ere the steps in the outer room entered the chamber where she stood. Her servant was accompanied by two officers of the police.

"Pardon, madame," said one of the latter; "but we are in pursuit of a criminal. We think he must have entered this house through a window above while your servant was in the street. Permit us to search?"

"Without doubt," answered Eugenie, seating herself. "If he has entered, look in the other apartments. I have not quitted this room."

"You are right. Accept our apologies."

And the officers turned back to examine every corner where the fugitive was not. For in that, the scouts of Justice resembled their mistress: when does man's justice look to the right place?

The servant lingered to repeat the tale he had heard—the sight he had seen. When, at that instant, he saw the curtain of the alcove slightly stirred. He uttered an exclamation—sprung to the bed—his hand touched the curtain—Eugenie seized his arm. She did not speak; but as he turned his eyes to her, astonished, he saw that she trembled, and that her cheek was as white as marble.

"Madame," he said, hesitating, "there is some one hid in the recess."

"There is! Be silent!"

A suspicion flashed across the servant's mind. The pure, the proud, the immaculate Eugenie!

"There is!—and in madame's chamber!" he faltered unconsciously.

Eugenie's quick apprehensions seized the foul thought. Her eyes flashed—her cheek crimsoned. But her lofty and generous nature conquered even the indignant and scornful burst that rushed to her lips. The truth!—could she trust the man? A doubt—and the charge of the human life rendered to her might be betrayed. Her colour fell—tears gushed to her eyes.

"I have been kind to you, Francois. Not a word."

"Madame confides in me—it is enough," said the Frenchman, bowing, with a slight smile on his lips; and he drew back respectfully.

One of the police officers re-entered.

"We have done, madame; he is not here. Aha! that curtain!"

"It is madame's bed," said Francois. "But I have looked behind."

"I am most sorry to have disarranged you," said the policeman, satisfied with the answer; "but we shall have him yet." And he retired.

The last footsteps died away, the last door of the apartments closed behind the officers, and Eugenie and her servant stood alone gazing on each other.

"You may retire," said she at last; and taking her purse from the table, she placed it in his hands.

The man took it, with a significant look. "Madame may depend on my discretion."

Eugenie was alone again. Those words rang in her ear,—Eugenie de Merville dependent on the discretion of her lackey! She sunk into her chair, and, her excitement succeeded by exhaustion, leaned her face on her hands, and burst into tears. She was aroused by a low voice; she looked up, and the young man was kneeling at her feet.

"Go—go!" she said: "I have done for you all I can."

"You heard—you heard—my own hireling, too! At the hazard of my own good name you are saved. Go!"

"Of your good name!"—for Eugenie forgot that it was looks, not words, that had so wrung her pride—"Your good name," he repeated: and glancing round the room—the toilette, the curtain, the recess he had quitted—all that bespoke that chastest sanctuary of a chaste woman, which for a stranger to enter is, as it were, to profane—her meaning broke on him. "Your good name—your hireling! No, madame,—no!" And as he spoke, he rose to his feet. "Not for me, that sacrifice! Your humanity shall not cost you so dear. Ho, there! I am the man you seek." And he strode to the door.

Eugenie was penetrated with the answer. She sprung to him—she grasped his garments.

"Hush! hush!—for mercy's sake! What would you do? Think you I could ever be happy again, if the confidence you placed in me were betrayed? Be calm—be still. I knew not what I said. It will be easy to undeceive the man—later—when you are saved. And you are innocent,—are you not?"

"Oh, madame," said Morton, "from my soul I say it, I am innocent—not of poverty—wretchedness—error—shame; I am innocent of crime. May Heaven bless you!"

And as he reverently kissed the hand laid on his arm, there was something in his voice so touching, in his manner something so above his fortunes, that Eugenie was lost in her feelings of compassion, surprise, and something, it might be, of admiration in her wonder.

"And, oh!" he said, passionately, gazing on her with his dark, brilliant eyes, liquid with emotion, "you have made my life sweet in saving it. You—you—of whom, ever since the first time, almost the sole time, I beheld you—I have so often mused and dreamed. Henceforth, whatever befall me, there will be some recollections that will—that—"

He stopped short, for his heart was too full for words; and the silence said more to Eugenie than if all the eloquence of Rousseau had glowed upon his tongue.

"And who, and what are you?" she asked, after a pause.

"An exile—an orphan—an outcast! I have no name! Farewell!"

"No—stay yet—the danger is not past. Wait till my servant is gone to rest; I hear him yet. Sit down—sit down. And whither would you go?"

"I know not."

"Have you no friends?"

"Gone."

"No home?"

"None."

"And the police of Paris so vigilant!" cried Eugenie, wringing her hands. "What is to be done? I shall have saved you in vain—you will be discovered! Of what do they charge you? Not robbery—not—"

And she, too, stopped short, for she did not dare to breathe the black word, "Murder!"

"I know not," said Morton, putting his hand to his forehead, "except of being friends with the only man who befriended me—and they have killed him!"

"Another time you shall tell me all."

"Another time!" he exclaimed, eagerly—"shall I see you again?"

Eugenie blushed beneath the gaze and the voice of joy. "Yes," she said; "yes. But I must reflect. Be calm be silent. Ah!—a happy thought!"

She sat down, wrote a hasty line, sealed, and gave it to Morton.

"Take this note, as addressed, to Madame Dufour; it will provide you with a safe lodging. She is a person I can depend on—an old servant who lived with my mother, and to whom I have given a small pension. She has a lodging—it is lately vacant—I promised to procure her a tenant—go—say nothing of what has passed. I will see her, and arrange all. Wait!—hark!—all is still. I will go first, and see that no one watches you. Stop," (and she threw open the window, and looked into the court.) "The porter's door is open—that is fortunate! Hurry on, and God be with you!"

In a few minutes Morton was in the streets. It was still early—the thoroughfares deserted-none of the shops yet open. The address on the note was to a street at some distance, on the other side of the Seine. He passed along the same Quai which he had trodden but a few hours since—he passed the same splendid bridge on which he had stood despairing, to quit it revived—he gained the Rue Faubourg St. Honore. A young man in a cabriolet, on whose fair cheek burned the hectic of late vigils and lavish dissipation, was rolling leisurely home from the gaming-house, at which he had been more than usually fortunate—his pockets were laden with notes and gold. He bent forwards as Morton passed him. Philip, absorbed in his reverie, perceived him not, and continued his way. The gentleman turned down one of the streets to the left, stopped, and called to the servant dozing behind his cabriolet.

"Follow that passenger! quietly—see where he lodges; be sure to find out and let me know. I shall go home without you." With that he drove on.

Philip, unconscious of the espionage, arrived at a small house in a quiet but respectable street, and rang the bell several times before at last he was admitted by Madame Dufour herself, in her nightcap. The old woman looked askant and alarmed at the unexpected apparition. But the note seemed at once to satisfy her. She conducted him to an apartment on the first floor, small, but neatly and even elegantly furnished, consisting of a sitting-room and a bedchamber, and said, quietly,—

"Will they suit monsieur?"

To monsieur they seemed a palace. Morton nodded assent.

"And will monsieur sleep for a short time?"

"Yes."

"The bed is well aired. The rooms have only been vacant three days since. Can I get you anything till your luggage arrives?"

"No."

The woman left him. He threw off his clothes—flung himself on the bed—and did not wake till noon.

When his eyes unclosed—when they rested on that calm chamber, with its air of health, and cleanliness, and comfort, it was long before he could convince himself that he was yet awake. He missed the loud, deep voice of Gawtrey—the smoke of the dead man's meerschaum—the gloomy garret—the distained walls—the stealthy whisper of the loathed Birnie; slowly the life led and the life gone within the last twelve hours grew upon his struggling memory. He groaned, and turned uneasily round, when the door slightly opened, and he sprung up fiercely,—

"Who is there?"

"It is only I, sir," answered Madame Dufour. "I have been in three times to see if you were stirring. There is a letter I believe for you, sir; though there is no name to it," and she laid the letter on the chair beside him. Did it come from her—the saving angel? He seized it. The cover was blank; it was sealed with a small device, as of a ring seal. He tore it open, and found four billets de banque for 1,000 francs each,—a sum equivalent in our money to about £160.

"Who sent this, the—the lady from whom I brought the note?"

"Madame de Merville? certainly not, sir," said Madame Dufour, who, with the privilege of age, was now unscrupulously filling the water-jugs and settling the toilette-table. "A young man called about two hours after you had gone to bed; and, describing you, inquired if you lodged here, and what your name was. I said you had just arrived, and that I did not yet know your name. So he went away, and came again half an hour afterwards with this letter, which he charged me to deliver to you safely."

"A young man—a gentleman?"

"No, sir; he seemed a smart but common sort of lad." For the unsophisticated Madame Dufour did not discover in the plain black frock and drab gaiters of the bearer of that letter the simple livery of an English gentleman's groom.

Whom could it come from, if not from Madame de Merville? Perhaps one of Gawtrey's late friends. A suspicion of Arthur Beaufort crossed him, but he indignantly dismissed it. Men are seldom credulous of what they are unwilling to believe. What kindness had the Beauforts hitherto shown him?—Left his mother to perish broken-hearted—stolen from him his brother, and steeled, in that brother, the only heart wherein he had a right to look for gratitude and love! No, it must be Madame de Merville. He dismissed Madame Dufour for pen and paper—rose—wrote a letter to Eugenie—grateful, but proud, and inclosed the notes. He then summoned Madame Dufour, and sent her with his despatch.

"Ah, madame," said the ci-devant bonne, when she found herself in Eugenie's presence. "The poor lad! how handsome he is, and how shameful in the Vicomte to let him wear such clothes!"

"The Vicomte!"

"Oh, my dear mistress, you must not deny it. You told me, in your note, to ask him no questions, but I guessed at once. The Vicomte told me himself that he should have the young gentleman over in a few days. You need not be ashamed of him. You will see what a difference clothes will make in his appearance; and I have taken it on myself to order a tailor to go to him. The Vicomte—must pay me."

"Not a word to the Vicomte as yet. We will surprise him," said Eugenie, laughing.

Madame de Merville had been all that morning trying to invent some story to account for her interest in the lodger, and now how Fortune favoured her!

"But is that a letter for me?"

"And I had almost forgot it," said Madame Dufour, as she extended the letter.

Whatever there had hitherto been in the circumstances connected with Morton, that had roused the interest and excited the romance of Eugenie de Merville, her fancy was yet more attracted by the tone of the letter she now read. For though Morton, more accustomed to speak than to write French, expressed himself with less precision, and a less euphuistic selection of phrase, than the authors and elegans who formed her usual correspondents; there was an innate and rough nobleness—a strong and profound feeling in every line of his letter, which increased her surprise and admiration.

"All that surrounds him—all that belongs to him, is strangeness and mystery!" murmured she; and she sat down to reply.

When Madame Dufour departed with that letter, Eugenie remained silent and thoughtful for more than an hour, Morton's letter before her; and sweet, in their indistinctness, were the recollections and the images that crowded on her mind.

Morton, satisfied by the earnest and solemn assurances of Eugenie that she was not the unknown donor of the sum she reinclosed, after puzzling himself in vain to form any new conjectures as to the quarter whence it came, felt that under his present circumstances it would be an absurd Quixotism to refuse to apply what the very Providence to whom he had anew consigned himself seemed to have sent to his aid. And it placed him, too, beyond the offer of all pecuniary assistance from one from whom he could least have brooked to receive it. He consented, therefore, to all that the loquacious tailor proposed to him. And it would have been difficult to have recognised the wild and frenzied fugitive in the stately form, with its young beauty and air of well-born pride, which the next day sat by the side of Eugenie. And that day he told his sad and troubled story, and Eugenie wept: and from that day he came daily; and two weeks—happy, dreamlike, intoxicating to both—passed by; and as their last sun set, he was kneeling at her feet, and breathing to one to whom the homage of wit, and genius, and complacent wealth had hitherto been vainly proffered, the impetuous, agitated, delicious secrets of the First Love. He spoke, and rose to depart for ever—when the look and sigh detained him.

The next day, after a sleepless night, Eugenie de Merville sent for the Vicomte de Vaudemont.

CHAPTER XIV

"A silver river small
In sweet accents
Its music vents;
The warbling virginal
To which the merry birds do sing,
Timed with stops of gold the silver string."
Sir Richard Fanshawe.

One evening, several weeks after the events just commemorated, a stranger, leading in his hand, a young child, entered the churchyard of H—. The sun had not long set, and the short twilight of deepening summer reigned in the tranquil skies; you might still hear from the trees above the graves the chirp of some joyous bird;—what cared he, the denizen of the skies, for the dead that slept below?—what did he value save the greenness and repose of the spot,—to him alike the garden or the grave! As the man and the child passed, the robin, scarcely scared by their tread from the long grass beside one of the mounds, looked at them with its bright, blithe eye. It was a famous plot for the robin—the old churchyard! That domestic bird—"the friend of man," as it has been called by the poets—found a jolly supper among the worms!

The stranger, on reaching the middle of the sacred ground, paused and looked round him wistfully. He then approached, slowly and hesitatingly, an oblong tablet, on which were graven, in letters yet fresh and new, these words:—

TO THE
MEMORY OF ONE CALUMNIATED AND WRONGED
THIS BURIAL-STONE IS DEDICATED
BY HER SON.

Such, with the addition of the dates of birth and death, was the tablet which Philip Morton had directed to be placed over his mother's bones; and around it was set a simple palisade, which defended it from the tread of the children, who sometimes, in defiance of the beadle, played over the dust of the former race.

"Thy son!" muttered the stranger, while the child stood quietly by his side, pleased by the trees, the grass, the song of the birds, and reeking not of grief or death,—"thy son!—but not thy favoured son—thy darling—thy youngest born; on what spot of earth do thine eyes look down on him? Surely in heaven thy love has preserved the one whom on earth thou didst most cherish, from the sufferings and the trials that have visited the less-favoured outcast. Oh, mother—mother!—it was not his crime—not Philip's—that he did not fulfil to the last the trust bequeathed to him! Happier, perhaps, as it is! And, oh, if thy memory be graven as deeply in my brother's heart as my own, how often will it warn and save him! That memory!—it has been to me the angel of my life! To thee—to thee, even in death, I owe it, if, though erring, I am not criminal,—if I have lived with the lepers, and am still undefiled!" His lips then were silent—not his heart!

After a few minutes thus consumed he turned to the child, and said, gently and in a tremulous voice, "Fanny, you have been taught to pray—you will live near this spot,—will you come sometimes here and pray that you may grow up good and innocent, and become a blessing to those who love you?"

"Will papa ever come to hear me pray?"

That sad and unconscious question went to the heart of Morton. The child could not comprehend death. He had sought to explain it, but she had been accustomed to consider her protector dead when he was absent from her, and she still insisted that he must come again to life. And that man of turbulence and crime, who had passed unrepentant, unabsolved, from sin to judgment: it was an awful question, "If he should hear her pray?"

"Yes!" said he, after a pause,—"yes, Fanny, there is a Father who will hear you pray; and pray to Him to be merciful to those who have been kind to you. Fanny, you and I may never meet again!"

"Are you going to die too? Mechant, every one dies to Fanny!" and, clinging to him endearingly, she put up her lips to kiss him. He took her in his arms: and, as a tear fell upon her rosy cheek, she said, "Don't cry, brother, for I love you."

"Do you, dear Fanny? Then, for my sake, when you come to this place, if any one will give you a few flowers, scatter them on that stone. And now we will go to one whom you must love also, and to whom, as I have told you, he sends you; he who—Come!"

As he thus spoke, and placed Fanny again on the ground, he was startled to see: precisely on the spot where he had seen before the like apparition—on the same spot where the father had cursed the son, the motionless form of an old man. Morton recognised, as if by an instinct rather than by an effort of the memory, the person to whom he was bound.

He walked slowly towards him; but Fanny abruptly left his side, lured by a moth that flitted duskily over the graves.

"Your name, sir, I think, is Simon Gawtrey?" said Morton. "I have came to England in quest of you."

"Of me?" said the old man, half rising, and his eyes, now completely blind, rolled vacantly over Morton's person—"Of me?—for what?—Who are you?—I don't know your voice!"

"I come to you from your son!"

"My son!" exclaimed the old man, with great vehemence,—"the reprobate!—the dishonoured!—the infamous!—the accursed—"

"Hush! you revile the dead!"

"Dead!" muttered the wretched father, tottering back to the seat he had quitted,—"dead!" and the sound of his voice was so full of anguish, that the dog at his feet, which Morton had not hitherto perceived, echoed it with a dismal cry, that recalled to Philip the awful day in which he had seen the son quit the father for the last time on earth.

The sound brought Fanny to the spot; and, with a laugh of delight, which made to it a strange contrast, she threw herself on the grass beside the dog and sought to entice it to play. So there, in that place of death, were knit together the four links in the Great Chain;—lusty and blooming life—desolate and doting age—infancy, yet scarce conscious of a soul—and the dumb brute, that has no warrant of a Hereafter!

"Dead!—dead!" repeated the old man, covering his sightless balls with his withered hands. "Poor William!"

"He remembered you to the last. He bade me seek you out—he bade me replace the guilty son with a thing pure and innocent, as he had been had he died in his cradle—a child to comfort your old age! Kneel, Fanny, I have found you a father who will cherish you—(oh! you will, sir, will you not?)—as he whom you may see no more!"

There was something in Morton's voice so solemn, that it awed and touched both the old man and the infant; and Fanny, creeping to the protector thus assigned to her, and putting her little hands confidingly on his knees, said—

"Fanny will love you if papa wished it. Kiss Fanny."

"Is it his child—his?" said the blind man, sobbing. "Come to my heart; here—here! O God, forgive me!" Morton did not think it right at that moment to undeceive him with regard to the poor child's true connexion with the deceased: and he waited in silence till Simon, after a burst of passionate grief and tenderness, rose, and still clasping the child to his breast, said—

"Sir, forgive me!—I am a very weak old man—I have many thanks to give—I have much, too, to learn. My poor son! he did not die in want,—did he?"

The particulars of Gawtrey's fate, with his real name and the various aliases he had assumed, had appeared in the French journals, had been partially copied into the English; and Morton had expected to have been saved the painful narrative of that fearful death; but the utter seclusion of the old man, his infirmity, and his estranged habits, had shut him out from the intelligence that it now devolved on Philip to communicate. Morton hesitated a little before he answered:

"It is late now; you are not yet prepared to receive this poor infant at your home, nor to hear the details I have to state. I arrived in England but to-day. I shall lodge in the neighbourhood, for it is dear to me. If I may feel sure, then, that you will receive and treasure this sacred and last deposit bequeathed to you by your unhappy son, I will bring my charge to you to-morrow, and we will then, more calmly than we can now, talk over the past."

"You do not answer my question," said Simon, passionately; "answer that, and I will wait for the rest. They call me a miser! Did I send out my only child to starve? Answer that!"

"Be comforted. He did not die in want; and he has even left some little fortune for Fanny, which I was to place in your hands."

"And he thought to bribe the old miser to be human! Well—well—well—I will go home."

"Lean on me!"

The dog leapt playfully on his master as the latter rose, and Fanny slid from Simon's arms to caress and talk to the animal in her own way. As they slowly passed through the churchyard Simon muttered incoherently to himself for several paces, and Morton would not disturb, since he could not comfort, him.

At last he said abruptly, "Did my son repent?"

"I hoped," answered Morton, evasively, "that, had his life been spared, he would have amended!"

"Tush, sir!—I am past seventy; we repent!—we never amend!" And Simon again sunk into his own dim and disconnected reveries.

At length they arrived at the blind man's house. The door was opened to them by an old woman of disagreeable and sinister aspect, dressed out much too gaily for the station of a servant, though such was her reputed capacity; but the miser's affliction saved her from the chance of his comment on her extravagance. As she stood in the doorway with a candle in her hand, she scanned curiously, and with no welcoming eye, her master's companions.

"Mrs. Boxer, my son is dead!" said Simon, in a hollow voice.

"And a good thing it is, then, sir!"

"For shame, woman!" said Morton, indignantly.

"Hey-dey! sir! whom have we got here?"

"One," said Simon, sternly, "whom you will treat with respect. He brings me a blessing to lighten my loss. One harsh word to this child, and you quit my house!"

The woman looked perfectly thunderstruck; but, recovering herself, she said, whiningly—

"I! a harsh word to anything my dear, kind master cares for. And, Lord, what a sweet pretty creature it is! Come here, my dear!"

But Fanny shrunk back, and would not let go Philip's hand.

"To-morrow, then," said Morton; and he was turning away, when a sudden thought seemed to cross the old man,—

"Stay, sir—stay! I—I—did my son say I was rich? I am very, very poor—nothing in the house, or I should have been robbed long ago!"

"Your son told me to bring money, not to ask for it!"

"Ask for it! No; but," added the old man, and a gleam of cunning intelligence shot over his face,—"but he had got into a bad set. Ask!—No!—Put up the door-chain, Mrs. Boxer!"

It was with doubt and misgivings that Morton, the next day, consigned the child, who had already nestled herself into the warmest core of his heart, to the care of Simon. Nothing short of that superstitious respect, which all men owe to the wishes of the dead, would have made him select for her that asylum; for Fate had now, in brightening his own prospects, given him an alternative in the benevolence of Madame de Merville. But Gawtrey had been so earnest on the subject, that he felt as if he had no right to hesitate. And was it not a sort of atonement to any faults the son might have committed against the parent, to place by the old man's hearth so sweet a charge?

The strange and peculiar mind and character of Fanny made him, however, yet more anxious than otherwise he might have been. She certainly deserved not the harsh name of imbecile or idiot, but she was different from all other children; she felt more acutely than most of her age, but she could not be taught to reason. There was something either oblique or deficient in her intellect, which justified the most melancholy apprehensions; yet often, when some disordered, incoherent, inexplicable train of ideas most saddened the listener, it would be followed by fancies so exquisite in their strangeness, or feelings so endearing in their tenderness, that suddenly she seemed as much above, as before she seemed below, the ordinary measure of infant comprehension. She was like a creature to which Nature, in some cruel but bright caprice, has given all that belongs to poetry, but denied all that belongs to the common understanding necessary to mankind; or, as a fairy changeling, not, indeed, according to the vulgar superstition, malignant and deformed, but lovelier than the children of men, and haunted by dim and struggling associations of a gentler and fairer being, yet wholly incapable to learn the dry and hard elements which make up the knowledge of actual life.

Morton, as well as he could, sought to explain to Simon the peculiarities in Fanny's mental constitution. He urged on him the necessity of providing for her careful instruction, and Simon promised to send her to the best school the neighbourhood could afford; but, as the old man spoke, he dwelt so much on the supposed fact that Fanny was William's daughter, and with his remorse, or affection, there ran so interwoven a thread of selfishness and avarice, that Morton thought it would be dangerous to his interest in the child to undeceive his error. He, therefore,—perhaps excusably enough—remained silent on that subject.

Gawtrey had placed with the superior of the convent, together with an order to give up the child to any one who should demand her in his true name, which he confided to the superior, a sum of nearly £300., which he solemnly swore had been honestly obtained, and which, in all his shifts and adversities, he had never allowed himself to touch. This sum, with the trifling deduction made for arrears due to the convent, Morton now placed in Simon's hands. The old man clutched the money, which was for the most in French gold, with a convulsive gripe: and then, as if ashamed of the impulse, said—

"But you, sir—will any sum—that is, any reasonable sum—be of use to you?"

"No! and if it were, it is neither yours nor mine—it is hers. Save it for her, and add to it what you can."

While this conversation took place, Fanny had been consigned to the care of Mrs. Boxer, and Philip now rose to see and bid her farewell before he departed.

"I may come again to visit you, Mr. Gawtrey; and I pray Heaven to find that you and Fanny have been a mutual blessing to each other. Oh, remember how your son loved her!"

"He had a good heart, in spite of all his sins. Poor William!" said Simon.

Philip Morton heard, and his lip curled with a sad and a just disdain.

If when, at the age of nineteen, William Gawtrey had quitted his father's roof, the father had then remembered that the son's heart was good,—the son had been alive still, an honest and a happy man. Do ye not laugh, O ye all-listening Fiends! when men praise those dead whose virtues they discovered not when alive? It takes much marble to build the sepulchre—how little of lath and plaster would have repaired the garret!

On turning into a small room adjoining the parlour in which Gawtrey sat, Morton found Fanny standing gloomily by a dull, soot-grimed window, which looked out on the dead walls of a small yard. Mrs. Boxer, seated by a table, was employed in trimming a cap, and putting questions to Fanny in that falsetto voice of endearment in which people not used to children are apt to address them.

"And so, my dear, they've never taught you to read or write? You've been sadly neglected, poor thing!"

"We must do our best to supply the deficiency," said Morton, as he entered.

"Bless me, sir, is that you?" and the gouvernante bustled up and dropped a low courtesy; for Morton, dressed then in the garb of a gentleman, was of a mien and person calculated to strike the gaze of the vulgar.

"Ah, brother!" cried Fanny, for by that name he had taught her to call him; and she flew to his side. "Come away—it's ugly there—it makes me cold."

"My child, I told you you must stay; but I shall hope to see you again some day. Will you not be kind to this poor creature, ma'am? Forgive me, if I offended you last night, and favour me by accepting this, to show that we are friends." As he spoke, he slid his purse into the woman's hand. "I shall feel ever grateful for whatever you can do for Fanny."

"Fanny wants nothing from any one else; Fanny wants her brother."

"Sweet child! I fear she don't take to me. Will you like me, Miss Fanny?"

"No! get along!"

"Fie, Fanny—you remember you did not take to me at first. But she is so affectionate, ma'am; she never forgets a kindness."

"I will do all I can to please her, sir. And so she is really master's grandchild?" The woman fixed her eyes, as she spoke, so intently on Morton, that he felt embarrassed, and busied himself, without answering, in caressing and soothing Fanny, who now seemed to awake to the affliction about to visit her; for though she did not weep—she very rarely wept—her slight frame trembled—her eyes closed—her cheeks, even her lips, were white—and her delicate hands were clasped tightly round the neck of the one about to abandon her to strange breasts.

Morton was greatly moved. "One kiss, Fanny! and do not forget me when we meet again."

The child pressed her lips to his cheek, but the lips were cold. He put her down gently; she stood mute and passive.

"Remember that he wished me to leave you here," whispered Morton, using an argument that never failed. "We must obey him; and so—God bless you, Fanny!"

He rose and retreated to the door; the child unclosed her eyes, and gazed at him with a strained, painful, imploring gaze; her lips moved, but she did not speak. Morton could not bear that silent woe. He sought to smile on her consolingly; but the smile would not come. He closed the door, and hurried from the house.

From that day Fanny settled into a kind of dreary, inanimate stupor, which resembled that of the somnambulist whom the magnetiser forgets to waken. Hitherto, with all the eccentricities or deficiencies of her mind, had mingled a wild and airy gaiety. That was vanished. She spoke little—she never played—no toys could lure her—even the poor dog failed to win her notice. If she was told to do anything she stared vacantly and stirred not. She evinced, however, a kind of dumb regard to the old blind man; she would creep to his knees and sit there for hours, seldom answering when he addressed her, but uneasy, anxious, and restless, if he left her.

"Will you die too?" she asked once; the old man understood her not, and she did not try to explain. Early one morning, some days after Morton was gone, they missed her: she was not in the house, nor the dull yard where she was sometimes dismissed and told to play—told in vain. In great alarm the old man accused Mrs. Boxer of having spirited her away, and threatened and stormed so loudly that the woman, against her will, went forth to the search. At last she found the child in the churchyard, standing wistfully beside a tomb.

"What do you here, you little plague?" said Mrs. Boxer, rudely seizing her by the arm.

"This is the way they will both come back some day! I dreamt so!"

"If ever I catch you here again!" said the housekeeper, and, wiping her brow with one hand, she struck the child with the other. Fanny had never been struck before. She recoiled in terror and amazement, and, for the first time since her arrival, burst into tears.

"Come—come, no crying! and if you tell master I'll beat you within an inch of your life!" So saying, she caught Fanny in her arms, and, walking about, scolding and menacing, till she had frightened back the child's tears, she returned triumphantly to the house, and bursting into the parlour, exclaimed, "Here's the little darling, sir!"

When old Simon learned where the child had been found he was glad; for it was his constant habit, whenever the evening was fine, to glide out to that churchyard—his dog his guide—and sit on his one favourite spot opposite the setting sun. This, not so much for the sanctity of the place, or the meditations it might inspire, as because it was the nearest, the safest, and the loneliest spot in the neighbourhood of his home, where the blind man could inhale the air and bask in the light of heaven. Hitherto, thinking it sad for the child, he had never taken her with him; indeed, at the hour of his monotonous excursion she had generally been banished to bed. Now she was permitted to accompany him; and the old man and the infant would sit there side by side, as Age and Infancy rested side by side in the graves below. The first symptom of childlike interest and curiosity that Fanny betrayed was awakened by the affliction of her protector. One evening, as they thus sat, she made him explain what the desolation of blindness is. She seemed to comprehend him, though he did not seek to adapt his complaints to her understanding.

"Fanny knows," said she, touchingly; "for she, too, is blind here;" and she pressed her hands to her temples. Notwithstanding her silence and strange ways, and although he could not see the exquisite loveliness which Nature, as in remorseful pity, had lavished on her outward form, Simon soon learned to love her better than he had ever loved yet: for they most cold to the child are often dotards to the grandchild. For her even his avarice slept. Dainties, never before known at his sparing board, were ordered to tempt her appetite, toy-shops ransacked to amuse her indolence. He was long, however, before he could prevail on himself to fulfil his promise to Morton, and rob himself of her presence. At length, however, wearied with Mrs. Boxer's lamentations at her ignorance, and alarmed himself at some evidences of helplessness, which made him dread to think what her future might be when left alone in life, he placed her at a day-school in the suburb. Here Fanny, for a considerable time, justified the harshest assertions of her stupidity. She could not even keep her eyes two minutes together on the page from which she was to learn the mysteries of reading; months passed before she mastered the alphabet, and, a month after, she had again forgot it, and the labour was renewed. The only thing in which she showed ability, if so it might be called, was in the use of the needle. The sisters of the convent had already taught her many pretty devices in this art; and when she found that at the school they were admired—that she was praised instead of blamed—her vanity was pleased, and she learned so readily all that they could teach in this not unprofitable accomplishment, that Mrs. Boxer slyly and secretly turned her tasks to account and made a weekly perquisite of the poor pupil's industry. Another faculty she possessed, in common with persons usually deficient, and with the lower species—viz., a most accurate and faithful recollection of places. At first Mrs. Boxer had been duly sent, morning, noon, and evening, to take her to, or bring her from, the school; but this was so great a grievance to Simon's solitary superintendent, and Fanny coaxed the old man so endearingly to allow her to go and return alone, that the attendance, unwelcome to both, was waived. Fanny exulted in this liberty; and she never, in going or in returning, missed passing through the burial-ground, and gazing wistfully at the tomb from which she yet believed Morton would one day reappear. With his memory she cherished also that of her earlier and more guilty protector; but they were separate feelings, which she distinguished in her own way.

"Papa had given her up. She knew that he would not have sent her away, far—far over the great water, if he had meant to see Fanny again; but her brother was forced to leave her—he would come to life one day, and then they should live together!"

One day, towards the end of autumn, as her schoolmistress, a good woman on the whole, but who had not yet had the wit to discover by what chords to tune the instrument, over which so wearily she drew her unskilful hand—one day, we say, the schoolmistress happened to be dressed for a christening party to which she was invited in the suburb; and, accordingly, after the morning lessons, the pupils were to be dismissed to a holiday. As Fanny now came last, with the hopeless spelling-book, she stopped suddenly short, and her eyes rested with avidity upon a large bouquet of exotic flowers, with which the good lady had enlivened the centre of the parted kerchief, whose yellow gauze modestly veiled that tender section of female beauty which poets have likened to hills of snow—a chilling simile! It was then autumn; and field, and even garden flowers were growing rare.

"Will you give me one of those flowers?" said Fanny, dropping her book.

"One of these flowers, child! why?"

Fanny did not answer; but one of the elder and cleverer girls said—

"Oh! she comes from France, you know, ma'am, and the Roman Catholics put flowers, and ribands, and things, over the graves; you recollect, ma'am, we were reading yesterday about Pere-la-Chaise?"

"Well! what then?"

"And Miss Fanny will do any kind of work for us if we will give her flowers."

"My brother told me where to put them;—but these pretty flowers, I never had any like them; they may bring him back again! I'll be so good if you'll give me one, only one!"

"Will you learn your lesson if I do, Fanny?"

"Oh! yes! Wait a moment!"

And Fanny stole back to her desk, put the hateful book resolutely before her, pressed both hands tightly on her temples,—Eureka! the chord was touched; and Fanny marched in triumph through half a column of hostile double syllables!

From that day the schoolmistress knew how to stimulate her, and Fanny learned to read: her path to knowledge thus literally strewn with flowers! Catherine, thy children were far off, and thy grave looked gay!

It naturally happened that those short and simple rhymes, often sacred, which are repeated in schools as helps to memory, made a part of her studies; and no sooner had the sound of verse struck upon her fancy than it seemed to confuse and agitate anew all her senses. It was like the music of some breeze, to which dance and tremble all the young leaves of a wild plant. Even when at the convent she had been fond of repeating the infant rhymes with which they had sought to lull or to amuse her, but now the taste was more strongly developed. She confounded, however, in meaningless and motley disorder, the various snatches of song that came to her ear, weaving them together in some form which she understood, but which was jargon to all others; and often, as she went alone through the green lanes or the bustling streets, the passenger would turn in pity and fear to hear her half chant—half murmur—ditties that seemed to suit only a wandering and unsettled imagination. And as Mrs. Boxer, in her visits to the various shops in the suburb, took care to bemoan her hard fate in attending to a creature so evidently moon-stricken, it was no wonder that the manner and habits of the child, coupled with that strange predilection to haunt the burial-ground, which is not uncommon with persons of weak and disordered intellect; confirmed the character thus given to her.

So, as she tripped gaily and lightly along the thoroughfares, the children would draw aside from her path, and whisper with superstitious fear mingled with contempt, "It's the idiot girl!"—Idiot—how much more of heaven's light was there in that cloud than in the rushlights that, flickering in sordid chambers, shed on dull things the dull ray—esteeming themselves as stars!

Months—years passed—Fanny was thirteen, when there dawned a new era to her existence. Mrs. Boxer had never got over her first grudge to Fanny. Her treatment of the poor girl was always harsh, and sometimes cruel. But Fanny did not complain, and as Mrs. Boxer's manner to her before Simon was invariably cringing and caressing, the old man never guessed the hardships his supposed grandchild underwent. There had been scandal some years back in the suburb about the relative connexion of the master and the housekeeper; and the flaunting dress of the latter, something bold in her regard, and certain whispers that her youth had not been vowed to Vesta, confirmed the suspicion. The only reason why we do not feel sure that the rumour was false is this,—Simon Gawtrey had been so hard on the early follies of his son! Certainly, at all events, the woman had exercised great influence over the miser before the arrival of Fanny, and she had done much to steel his selfishness against the ill-fated William. And, as certainly, she had fully calculated on succeeding to the savings, whatever they might be, of the miser, whenever Providence should be pleased to terminate his days. She knew that Simon had, many years back, made his will in her favour; she knew that he had not altered that will: she believed, therefore, that in spite of all his love for Fanny, he loved his gold so much more, that he could not accustom himself to the thought of bequeathing it to hands too helpless to guard the treasure. This had in some measure reconciled the housekeeper to the intruder; whom, nevertheless, she hated as a dog hates another dog, not only for taking his bone, but for looking at it.

But suddenly Simon fell ill. His age made it probable he would die. He took to his bed—his breathing grew fainter and fainter—he seemed dead. Fanny, all unconscious, sat by his bedside as usual, holding her breath not to waken him. Mrs. Boxer flew to the bureau—she unlocked it—she could not find the will; but she found three bags of bright gold guineas: the sight charmed her. She tumbled them forth on the distained green cloth of the bureau—she began to count them; and at that moment, the old man, as if there were a secret magnetism between himself and the guineas, woke from his trance. His blindness saved him the pain that might have been fatal, of seeing the unhallowed profanation; but he heard the chink of the metal. The very sound restored his strength. But the infirm are always cunning—he breathed not a suspicion. "Mrs. Boxer," said he, faintly, "I think I could take some broth." Mrs. Boxer rose in great dismay, gently re-closed the bureau, and ran down-stairs for the broth. Simon took the occasion to question Fanny; and no sooner had he learnt the operation of the heir-expectant, than he bade the girl first lock the bureau and bring him the key, and next run to a lawyer (whose address he gave her), and fetch him instantly.

With a malignant smile the old man took the broth from his handmaid,—"Poor Boxer, you are a disinterested creature," said he, feebly; "I think you will grieve when I go."

Mrs. Boxer sobbed, and before she had recovered, the lawyer entered. That day a new will was made; and the lawyer politely informed Mrs. Boxer that her services would be dispensed with the next morning, when he should bring a nurse to the house. Mrs. Boxer heard, and took her resolution. As soon as Simon again fell asleep, she crept into the room—led away Fanny—locked her up in her own chamber—returned—searched for the key of the bureau, which she found at last under Simon's pillow—possessed herself of all she could lay her hands on—and the next morning she had disappeared forever! Simon's loss was greater than might have been supposed; for, except a trifling sum in the savings bank, he, like many other misers, kept all he had, in notes or specie, under his own lock and key. His whole fortune, indeed, was far less than was supposed: for money does not make money unless it is put out to interest,—and the miser cheated himself. Such portion as was in bank-notes Mrs. Boxer probably had the prudence to destroy; for those numbers which Simon could remember were never traced; the gold, who could swear to? Except the pittance in the savings bank, and whatever might be the paltry worth of the house he rented, the father who had enriched the menial to exile the son was a beggar in his dotage. This news, however, was carefully concealed from him by the advice of the doctor, whom, on his own responsibility, the lawyer introduced, till he had recovered sufficiently to bear the shock without danger; and the delay naturally favoured Mrs. Boxer's escape.

Simon remained for some moments perfectly stunned and speechless when the news was broken to him. Fanny, in alarm at his increasing paleness, sprang to his breast. He pushed her away,—"Go—go—go, child," he said; "I can't feed you now. Leave me to starve."

"To starve!" said Fanny, wonderingly; and she stole away, and sat herself down as if in deep thought. She then crept up to the lawyer as he was about to leave the room, after exhausting his stock of commonplace consolation; and putting her hand in his, whispered, "I want to talk to you—this way:"—She led him through the passage into the open air. "Tell me," she said, "when poor people try not to starve, don't they work?"

"My dear, yes."

"For rich people buy poor people's work?"

"Certainly, my dear; to be sure."

"Very well. Mrs. Boxer used to sell my work. Fanny will feed grandpapa! Go and tell him never to say 'starve' again."

The good-natured lawyer was moved. "Can you work, indeed, my poor girl? Well, put on your bonnet, and come and talk to my wife."

And that was the new era in Fanny's existence! Her schooling was stopped. But now life schooled her. Necessity ripened her intellect. And many a hard eye moistened,—as, seeing her glide with her little basket of fancy work along the streets, still murmuring her happy and bird-like snatches of unconnected song—men and children alike said with respect, in which there was now no contempt, "It's the idiot girl who supports her blind grandfather!" They called her idiot still!

BOOK IV

CHAPTER I

"O that sweet gleam of sunshine on the lake!"
WILSON'S City of the Plague

If, reader, you have ever looked through a solar microscope at the monsters in a drop of water, perhaps you have wondered to yourself how things so terrible have been hitherto unknown to you—you have felt a loathing at the limpid element you hitherto deemed so pure—you have half fancied that you would cease to be a water-drinker; yet, the next day you have forgotten the grim life that started before you, with its countless shapes, in that teeming globule; and, if so tempted by your thirst, you have not shrunk from the lying crystal, although myriads of the horrible Unseen are mangling, devouring, gorging each other in the liquid you so tranquilly imbibe; so is it with that ancestral and master element called Life. Lapped in your sleek comforts, and lolling on the sofa of your patent conscience—when, perhaps for the first time, you look through the glass of science upon one ghastly globule in the waters that heave around, that fill up, with their succulence, the pores of earth, that moisten every atom subject to your eyes or handled by your touch—you are startled and dismayed; you say, mentally, "Can such things be? I never dreamed of this before! I thought what was invisible to me was non-existent in itself—I will remember this dread experiment." The next day the experiment is forgotten.—The Chemist may purify the Globule—can Science make pure the World?

Turn we now to the pleasant surface, seen in the whole, broad and fair to the common eye. Who would judge well of God's great designs, if he could look on no drop pendent from the rose-tree, or sparkling in the sun, without the help of his solar microscope?

It is ten years after the night on which William Gawtrey perished:—I transport you, reader, to the fairest scenes in England,—scenes consecrated by the only true pastoral poetry we have known to Contemplation and Repose.

Autumn had begun to tinge the foliage on the banks of Winandermere. It had been a summer of unusual warmth and beauty; and if that year you had visited the English lakes, you might, from time to time, amidst the groups of happy idlers you encountered, have singled out two persons for interest, or, perhaps, for envy. Two who might have seemed to you in peculiar harmony with those serene and soft retreats, both young—both beautiful. Lovers you would have guessed them to be; but such lovers as Fletcher might have placed under the care of his "Holy Shepherdess"—forms that might have reclined by

"The virtuous well, about whose flowery banks
The nimble-footed fairies dance their rounds
By the pale moonshine."

For in the love of those persons there seemed a purity and innocence that suited well their youth and the character of their beauty. Perhaps, indeed, on the girl's side, love sprung rather from those affections which the spring of life throws upward to the surface, as the spring of earth does its flowers, than from that concentrated and deep absorption of self in self, which alone promises endurance and devotion, and of which first love, or rather the first fancy, is often less susceptible than that which grows out of the more thoughtful fondness of maturer years. Yet he, the lover, was of so rare and singular a beauty, that he might well seem calculated to awake, to the utmost, the love which wins the heart through the eyes.

But to begin at the beginning. A lady of fashion had, in the autumn previous to the year in which our narrative re-opens, taken, with her daughter, a girl then of about eighteen, the tour of the English lakes. Charmed by the beauty of Winandermere, and finding one of the most commodious villas on its banks to be let, they had remained there all the winter. In the early spring a severe illness had seized the elder lady, and finding herself, as she slowly recovered, unfit for the gaieties of a London season, nor unwilling, perhaps,—for she had been a beauty in her day—to postpone for another year the debut of her daughter, she had continued her sojourn, with short intervals of absence, for a whole year. Her husband, a busy man of the world, with occupation in London, and fine estates in the country, joined them only occasionally, glad to escape the still beauty of landscapes which brought him no rental, and therefore afforded no charm to his eye.

In the first month of their arrival at Winandermere, the mother and daughter had made an eventful acquaintance in the following manner.

One evening, as they were walking on their lawn, which sloped to the lake, they heard the sound of a flute, played with a skill so exquisite as to draw them, surprised and spellbound, to the banks. The musician was a young man, in a boat, which he had moored beneath the trees of their demesne. He was alone, or, rather, he had one companion, in a large Newfoundland dog, that sat watchful at the helm of the boat, and appeared to enjoy the music as much as his master. As the ladies approached the spot, the dog growled, and the young man ceased, though without seeing the fair causes of his companion's displeasure. The sun, then setting, shone full on his countenance as he looked round; and that countenance was one that might have haunted the nymphs of Delos; the face of Apollo, not as the hero, but the shepherd—not of the bow, but of the lute—not the Python-slayer, but the young dreamer by shady places—he whom the sculptor has portrayed leaning idly against the tree—the boy-god whose home is yet on earth, and to whom the Oracle and the Spheres are still unknown.

At that moment the dog leaped from the boat, and the elder lady uttered a faint cry of alarm, which, directing the attention of the musician, brought him also ashore. He called off his dog, and apologised, with a not ungraceful mixture of diffidence and ease, for his intrusion. He was not aware the place was inhabited—it was a favourite haunt of his—he lived near. The elder lady was pleased with his address, and struck with his appearance. There was, indeed, in his manner that indefinable charm, which is more attractive than mere personal appearance, and which can never be imitated or acquired. They parted, however, without establishing any formal acquaintance. A few days after, they met at dinner at a neighbouring house, and were introduced by name. That of the young man seemed strange to the ladies; not so theirs to him. He turned pale when he heard it, and remained silent and aloof the rest of the evening. They met again and often; and for some weeks—nay, even for months—he appeared to avoid, as much as possible, the acquaintance so auspiciously begun; but, by little and little, the beauty of the younger lady seemed to gain ground on his diffidence or repugnance. Excursions among the neighbouring mountains threw them together, and at last he fairly surrendered himself to the charm he had at first determined to resist.

This young man lived on the opposite side of the lake, in a quiet household, of which he was the idol. His life had been one of almost monastic purity and repose; his tastes were accomplished, his character seemed soft and gentle; but beneath that calm exterior, flashes of passion—the nature of the poet, ardent and sensitive—would break forth at times. He had scarcely ever, since his earliest childhood, quitted those retreats; he knew nothing of the world, except in books—books of poetry and romance. Those with whom he lived—his relations, an old bachelor, and the cold bachelor's sisters, old maids—seemed equally innocent and inexperienced. It was a family whom the rich respected and the poor loved—inoffensive, charitable, and well off. To whatever their easy fortune might be, he appeared the heir. The name of this young man was Charles Spencer; the ladies were Mrs. Beaufort, and Camilla her daughter.

Mrs. Beaufort, though a shrewd woman, did not at first perceive any danger in the growing intimacy between Camilla and the younger Spencer. Her daughter was not her favourite—not the object of her one thought or ambition. Her whole heart and soul were wrapped in her son Arthur, who lived principally abroad. Clever enough to be considered capable, when he pleased, of achieving distinction, good-looking enough to be thought handsome by all who were on the qui vive for an advantageous match, good-natured enough to be popular with the society in which he lived, scattering to and fro money without limit,—Arthur Beaufort, at the age of thirty, had established one of those brilliant and evanescent reputations, which, for a few years, reward the ambition of the fine gentleman. It was precisely the reputation that the mother could appreciate, and which even the more saving father secretly admired, while, ever respectable in phrase, Mr. Robert Beaufort seemed openly to regret it. This son was, I say, everything to them; they cared little, in comparison, for their daughter. How could a daughter keep up the proud name of Beaufort? However well she might marry, it was another house, not theirs, which her graces and beauty would adorn. Moreover, the better she might marry the greater her dowry would naturally be,—the dowry, to go out of the family! And Arthur, poor fellow! was so extravagant, that really he would want every sixpence. Such was the reasoning of the father. The mother reasoned less upon the matter. Mrs. Beaufort, faded and meagre, in blonde and cashmere, was jealous of the charms of her daughter; and she herself, growing sentimental and lachrymose as she advanced in life, as silly women often do, had convinced herself that Camilla was a girl of no feeling.

Miss Beaufort was, indeed, of a character singularly calm and placid; it was the character that charms men in proportion, perhaps, to their own strength and passion. She had been rigidly brought up—her affections had been very early chilled and subdued; they moved, therefore, now, with ease, in the serene path of her duties. She held her parents, especially her father, in reverential fear, and never dreamed of the possibility of resisting one of their wishes, much less their commands. Pious, kind, gentle, of a fine and never-ruffled temper, Camilla, an admirable daughter, was likely to make no less admirable a wife; you might depend on her principles, if ever you could doubt her affection. Few girls were more calculated to inspire love. You would scarcely wonder at any folly, any madness, which even a wise man might commit for her sake. This did not depend on her beauty alone, though she was extremely lovely rather than handsome, and of that style of loveliness which is universally fascinating: the figure, especially as to the arms, throat, and bust, was exquisite; the mouth dimpled; the teeth dazzling; the eyes of that velvet softness which to look on is to love. But her charm was in a certain prettiness of manner, an exceeding innocence, mixed with the most captivating, because unconscious, coquetry. With all this, there was a freshness, a joy, a virgin and bewitching candour in her voice, her laugh—you might almost say in her very movements. Such was Camilla Beaufort at that age. Such she seemed to others. To her parents she was only a great girl rather in the way. To Mrs. Beaufort a rival, to Mr. Beaufort an encumbrance on the property.

CHAPTER II

—"The moon
Saddening the solemn night, yet with that sadness
Mingling the breath of undisturbed Peace."
WILSON: City of the Plague

—"Tell me his fate.
Say that he lives, or say that he is dead
But tell me—tell me!
I see him not—some cloud envelopes him."—Ibid.

One day (nearly a year after their first introduction) as with a party of friends Camilla and Charles Spencer were riding through those wild and romantic scenes which lie between the sunny Winandermere and the dark and sullen Wastwater, their conversation fell on topics more personal than it had hitherto done, for as yet, if they felt love, they had never spoken of it.

The narrowness of the path allowed only two to ride abreast, and the two to whom I confine my description were the last of the little band.

"How I wish Arthur were here!" said Camilla; "I am sure you would like him."

"Are you? He lives much in the world—the world of which I know nothing. Are we then characters to suit each other?"

"He is the kindest—the best of human beings!" said Camilla, rather evasively, but with more warmth than usually dwelt in her soft and low voice.

"Is he so kind?" returned Spencer, musingly. "Well, it may be so. And who would not be kind to you? Ah! it is a beautiful connexion that of brother and sister—I never had a sister!"

"Have you then a brother?" asked Camilla, in some surprise, and turning her ingenuous eyes full on her companion.

Spencer's colour rose—rose to his temples: his voice trembled as he answered, "No;—no brother!" then, speaking in a rapid and hurried tone, he continued, "My life has been a strange and lonely one. I am an orphan. I have mixed with few of my own age: my boyhood and youth have been spent in these scenes; my education such as Nature and books could bestow, with scarcely any guide or tutor save my guardian—the dear old man! Thus the world, the stir of cities, ambition, enterprise,—all seem to me as things belonging to a distant land to which I shall never wander. Yet I have had my dreams, Miss Beaufort; dreams of which these solitudes still form a part—but solitudes not unshared. And lately I have thought that those dreams might be prophetic. And you—do you love the world?"

"I, like you, have scarcely tried it," said Camilla, with a sweet laugh. "but I love the country better,—oh! far better than what little I have seen of towns. But for you," she continued with a charming hesitation, "a man is so different from us,—for you to shrink from the world—you, so young and with talents too—nay, it is true!—it seems to me strange."

"It may be so, but I cannot tell you what feelings of dread—what vague forebodings of terror seize me if I carry my thoughts beyond these retreats. Perhaps my good guardian—"

"Your uncle?" interrupted Camilla.

"Ay, my uncle—may have contributed to engender feelings, as you say, strange at my age; but still—"

"Still what!"

"My earlier childhood," continued Spencer, breathing hard and turning pale, "was not spent in the happy home I have now; it was passed in a premature ordeal of suffering and pain. Its recollections have left a dark shadow on my mind, and under that shadow lies every thought that points towards the troublous and labouring career of other men. But," he resumed after a pause, and in a deep, earnest, almost solemn voice,—"but after all, is this cowardice or wisdom? I find no monotony—no tedium in this quiet life. Is there not a certain morality—a certain religion in the spirit of a secluded and country existence? In it we do not know the evil passions which ambition and strife are said to arouse. I never feel jealous or envious of other men; I never know what it is to hate; my boat, my horse, our garden, music, books, and, if I may dare to say so, the solemn gladness that comes from the hopes of another life,—these fill up every hour with thoughts and pursuits, peaceful, happy, and without a cloud, till of late, when—when—"

"When what?" said Camilla, innocently.

"When I have longed, but did not dare to ask another, if to share such a lot would content her!"

He bent, as he spoke, his soft blue eyes full upon the blushing face of her whom he addressed, and Camilla half smiled and half sighed:

"Our companions are far before us," said she, turning away her face, "and see, the road is now smooth." She quickened her horse's pace as she said this; and Spencer, too new to women to interpret favourably her evasion of his words and looks, fell into a profound silence which lasted during the rest of their excursion.

As towards the decline of day he bent his solitary way home, emotions and passions to which his life had hitherto been a stranger, and which, alas! he had vainly imagined a life so tranquil would everlastingly restrain, swelled his heart.

"She does not love me," he muttered, half aloud; "she will leave me, and what then will all the beauty of the landscape seem in my eyes? And how dare I look up to her? Even if her cold, vain mother—her father, the man, they say, of forms and scruples, were to consent, would they not question closely of my true birth and origin? And if the one blot were overlooked, is there no other? His early habits and vices, his?—a brother's—his unknown career terminating at any day, perhaps, in shame, in crime, in exposure, in the gibbet,—will they overlook this?" As he spoke, he groaned aloud, and, as if impatient to escape himself, spurred on his horse and rested not till he reached the belt of trim and sober evergreens that surrounded his hitherto happy home.

Leaving his horse to find its way to the stables, the young man passed through rooms, which he found deserted, to the lawn on the other side, which sloped to the smooth waters of the lake.

Here, seated under the one large tree that formed the pride of the lawn, over which it cast its shadow broad and far, he perceived his guardian poring idly over an oft-read book, one of those books of which literary dreamers are apt to grow fanatically fond—books by the old English writers, full of phrases and conceits half quaint and half sublime, interspersed with praises of the country, imbued with a poetical rather than orthodox religion, and adorned with a strange mixture of monastic learning and aphorisms collected from the weary experience of actual life.

To the left, by a greenhouse, built between the house and the lake, might be seen the white dress and lean form of the eldest spinster sister, to whom the care of the flowers—for she had been early crossed in love—was consigned; at a little distance from her, the other two were seated at work, and conversing in whispers, not to disturb their studious brother, no doubt upon the nephew, who was their all in all. It was the calmest hour of eve, and the quiet of the several forms, their simple and harmless occupations—if occupations they might be called—the breathless foliage rich in the depth of summer; behind, the old-fashioned house, unpretending, not mean, its open doors and windows giving glimpses of the comfortable repose within; before, the lake, without a ripple and catching the gleam of the sunset clouds,—all made a picture of that complete tranquillity and stillness, which sometimes soothes and sometimes saddens us, according as we are in the temper to woo CONTENT.

The young man glided to his guardian and touched his shoulder,—"Sir, may I speak to you?—Hush! they need not see us now! it is only you I would speak with."

The elder Spencer rose; and, with his book still in his hand, moved side by side with his nephew under the shadow of the tree and towards a walk to the right, which led for a short distance along the margin of the lake, backed by the interlaced boughs of a thick copse.

"Sir!" said the young man, speaking first, and with a visible effort, "your cautions have been in vain! I love this girl—this daughter of the haughty Beauforts! I love her—better than life I love her!"

"My poor boy," said the uncle tenderly, and with a simple fondness passing his arm over the speaker's shoulder, "do not think I can chide you—I know what it is to love in vain!"

"In vain!—but why in vain?" exclaimed the younger Spencer, with a vehemence that had in it something of both agony and fierceness. "She may love me—she shall love me!" and almost for the first time in his life, the proud consciousness of his rare gifts of person spoke in his kindled eye and dilated stature. "Do they not say that Nature has been favourable to me?—What rival have I here?—Is she not young?—And (sinking his voice till it almost breathed like music) is not love contagious?"

"I do not doubt that she may love you—who would not?—but—but—the parents, will they ever consent?"

"Nay!" answered the lover, as with that inconsistency common to passion, he now argued stubbornly against those fears in another to which he had just before yielded in himself,—"Nay!—after all, am I not of their own blood?—Do I not come from the elder branch?—Was I not reared in equal luxury and with higher hopes?—And my mother—my poor mother—did she not to the last maintain our birthright—her own honour?—Has not accident or law unjustly stripped us of our true station?—Is it not for us to forgive spoliation?—Am I not, in fact, the person who descends, who forgets the wrongs of the dead—the heritage of the living?"

The young man had never yet assumed this tone—had never yet shown that he looked back to the history connected with his birth with the feelings of resentment and the remembrance of wrong. It was a tone contrary to his habitual calm and contentment—it struck forcibly on his listener—and the elder Spencer was silent for some moments before he replied, "If you feel thus (and it is natural), you have yet stronger reason to struggle against this unhappy affection."

"I have been conscious of that, sir," replied the young man, mournfully. "I have struggled!—and I say again it is in vain! I turn, then, to face the obstacles! My birth—let us suppose that the Beauforts overlook it. Did you not tell me that Mr. Beaufort wrote to inform you of the abrupt and intemperate visit of my brother—of his determination never to forgive it? I think I remember something of this years ago."

"It is true!" said the guardian; "and the conduct of that brother is, in fact, the true cause why you never ought to reassume your proper name!—never to divulge it, even to the family with whom you connect yourself by marriage; but, above all, to the Beauforts, who for that cause, if that cause alone, would reject your suit."

The young man groaned—placed one hand before his eyes, and with the other grasped his guardian's arm convulsively, as if to check him from proceeding farther; but the good man, not divining his meaning, and absorbed in his subject, went on, irritating the wound he had touched.

"Reflect!—your brother in boyhood—in the dying hours of his mother, scarcely saved from the crime of a thief, flying from a friendly pursuit with a notorious reprobate; afterwards implicated in some discreditable transaction about a horse, rejecting all—every hand that could save him, clinging by choice to the lowest companions and the meanest-habits, disappearing from the country, and last seen, ten years ago—the beard not yet on his chin—with that same reprobate of whom I have spoken, in Paris; a day or so only before his companion, a coiner—a murderer—fell by the hands of the police! You remember that when, in your seventeenth year, you evinced some desire to retake your name—nay, even to re-find that guilty brother—I placed before you, as a sad and terrible duty, the newspaper that contained the particulars of the death and the former adventures of that wretched accomplice, the notorious Gawtrey. And,—telling you that Mr. Beaufort had long since written to inform me that his own son and Lord Lilburne had seen your brother in company with the miscreant just before his fate—nay, was, in all probability, the very youth described in the account as found in his chamber and escaping the pursuit—I asked you if you would now venture to leave that disguise—that shelter under which you would for ever be safe from the opprobrium of the world—from the shame that, sooner or later, your brother must bring upon your name!"

"It is true—it is true!" said the pretended nephew, in a tone of great anguish, and with trembling lips which the blood had forsaken. "Horrible to look either to his past or his future! But—but—we have heard of him no more—no one ever has learned his fate. Perhaps—perhaps" (and he seemed to breathe more freely)—"my brother is no more!"

And poor Catherine—and poor Philip—had it come to this? Did the one brother feel a sentiment of release, of joy, in conjecturing the death—perhaps the death of violence and shame—of his fellow-orphan? Mr. Spencer shook his head doubtingly, but made no reply. The young man sighed heavily, and strode on for several paces in advance of his protector, then, turning back, he laid his hand on his shoulder.

"Sir," he said in a low voice and with downcast eyes, "you are right: this disguise—this false name—must be for ever borne! Why need the Beauforts, then, ever know who and what I am? Why not as your nephew—nephew to one so respected and exemplary—proffer my claims and plead my cause?"

"They are proud—so it is said—and worldly;—you know my family was in trade—still—but—" and here Mr. Spencer broke off from a tone of doubt into that of despondency, "but, recollect, though Mrs. Beaufort may not remember the circumstance, both her husband and her son have seen me—have known my name. Will they not suspect, when once introduced to you, the stratagem that has been adopted?—Nay, has it not been from that very fear that you have wished me to shun the acquaintance of the family? Both Mr. Beaufort and Arthur saw you in childhood, and their suspicion once aroused, they may recognise you at once; your features are developed, but not altogether changed. Come, come!—my adopted, my dear son, shake off this fantasy betimes: let us change the scene: I will travel with you—read with you—go where—"

"Sir—sir!" exclaimed the lover, smiting his breast, "you are ever kind, compassionate, generous; but do not—do not rob me of hope. I have never—thanks to you—felt, save in a momentary dejection, the curse of my birth. Now how heavily it falls! Where shall I look for comfort?"

As he spoke, the sound of a bell broke over the translucent air and the slumbering lake: it was the bell that every eve and morn summoned that innocent and pious family to prayer. The old man's face changed as he heard it—changed from its customary indolent, absent, listless aspect, into an expression of dignity, even of animation.

"Hark!" he said, pointing upwards; "Hark! it chides you. Who shall say, 'Where shall I look for comfort' while God is in the heavens?"

The young man, habituated to the faith and observance of religion, till they had pervaded his whole nature, bowed his head in rebuke; a few tears stole from his eyes.

"You are right, father—," he said tenderly, giving emphasis to the deserved and endearing name. "I am comforted already!"

So, side by side, silently and noiselessly, the young and the old man glided back to the house. When they gained the quiet room in which the family usually assembled, the sisters and servants were already gathered round the table. They knelt as the loiterers entered. It was the wonted duty of the younger Spencer to read the prayers; and, as he now did so, his graceful countenance more hushed, his sweet voice more earnest than usual, in its accents: who that heard could have deemed the heart within convulsed by such stormy passions? Or was it not in that hour—that solemn commune—soothed from its woe? O beneficent Creator! thou who inspirest all the tribes of earth with the desire to pray, hast Thou not, in that divinest instinct, bestowed on us the happiest of Thy gifts?

CHAPTER III

"Bertram. I mean the business is not ended, as fearing to hear of it hereafter.

"1st Soldier. Do you know this Captain Dumain?"
All's Well that Ends Well.

One evening, some weeks after the date of the last chapter, Mr. Robert Beaufort sat alone in his house in Berkeley Square. He had arrived that morning from Beaufort Court, on his way to Winandermere, to which he was summoned by a letter from his wife. That year was an agitated and eventful epoch in England; and Mr. Beaufort had recently gone through the bustle of an election—not, indeed, contested; for his popularity and his property defied all rivalry in his own county.

The rich man had just dined, and was seated in lazy enjoyment by the side of the fire, which he had had lighted, less for the warmth—though it was then September—than for the companionship;—engaged in finishing his madeira, and, with half-closed eyes, munching his devilled biscuits. "I am sure," he soliloquised while thus employed, "I don't know exactly what to do,—my wife ought to decide matters where the girl is concerned; a son is another affair—that's the use of a wife. Humph!"

"Sir," said a fat servant, opening the door, "a gentleman wishes to see you upon very particular business."

"Business at this hour! Tell him to go to Mr. Blackwell."

"Yes, sir."

"Stay! perhaps he is a constituent, Simmons. Ask him if he belongs to the county."

"Yes, Sir."

"A great estate is a great plague," muttered Mr. Beaufort; "so is a great constituency. It is pleasanter, after all, to be in the House of Lords. I suppose I could if I wished; but then one must rat—that's a bore. I will consult Lilburne. Humph!"

The servant re-appeared. "Sir, he says he does belong to the county."

"Show him in!—What sort of a person?"

"A sort of gentleman, sir; that is," continued the butler, mindful of five shillings just slipped within his palm by the stranger, "quite the gentleman."

"More wine, then—stir up the fire."

In a few moments the visitor was ushered into the apartment. He was a man between fifty and sixty, but still aiming at the appearance of youth. His dress evinced military pretensions; consisting of a blue coat, buttoned up to the chin, a black stock, loose trousers of the fashion called Cossacks, and brass spurs. He wore a wig, of great luxuriance in curl and rich auburn in hue; with large whiskers of the same colour slightly tinged with grey at the roots. By the imperfect light of the room it was not perceptible that the clothes were somewhat threadbare, and that the boots, cracked at the side, admitted glimpses of no very white hosiery within. Mr. Beaufort, reluctantly rising from his repose and gladly sinking back to it, motioned to a chair, and put on a doleful and doubtful semi-smile of welcome. The servant placed the wine and glasses before the stranger;—the host and visitor were alone.

"So, sir," said Mr. Beaufort, languidly, "you are from —shire; I suppose about the canal,—may I offer you a glass of wine?"

"Most hauppy, sir—your health!" and the stranger, with evident satisfaction, tossed off a bumper to so complimentary a toast.

"About the canal?" repeated Mr. Beaufort.

"No, sir, no! You parliament gentlemen must hauve a vaust deal of trouble on your haunds—very foine property I understaund yours is, sir. Sir, allow me to drink the health of your good lady!"

"I thank you, Mr.—, Mr.—, what did you say your name was?—I beg you a thousand pardons."

"No offaunce in the least, sir; no ceremony with me—this is perticler good madeira!"

"May I ask how I can serve you?" said Mr. Beaufort, struggling between the sense of annoyance and the fear to be uncivil. "And pray, had I the honour of your vote in the last election!"

"No, sir, no! It's mauny years since I have been in your part of the world, though I was born there."

"Then I don't exactly see—" began Mr. Beaufort, and stopped with dignity.

"Why I call on you," put in the stranger, tapping his boots with his cane; and then recognising the rents, he thrust both feet under the table.

"I don't say that; but at this hour I am seldom at leisure—not but what I am always at the service of a constituent, that is, a voter! Mr.—, I beg your pardon, I did not catch your name."

"Sir," said the stranger, helping himself to a third glass of wine; "here's a health to your young folk! And now to business." Here the visitor, drawing his chair nearer to his host, assuming a more grave aspect, and dropping something of his stilted pronunciation, continued, "You had a brother?"

"Well, sir," said Mr. Beaufort, with a very changed countenance.

"And that brother had a wife!"

Had a cannon gone off in the ear of Mr. Robert Beaufort, it could not have shocked or stunned him more than that simple word with which his companion closed his sentence. He fell back in his chair—his lips apart, his eyes fixed on the stranger. He sought to speak, but his tongue clove to his mouth.

"That wife had two sons, born in wedlock!"

"It is false!" cried Mr. Beaufort, finding a voice at length, and springing to his feet. "And who are you, sir? and what do you mean by—"

"Hush!" said the stranger, perfectly unconcerned, and regaining the dignity of his haw-haw enunciation, "better not let the servants hear aunything. For my pawt, I think servants hauve the longest pair of ears of auny persons, not excepting jauckasses; their ears stretch from the pauntry to the parlour. Hush, sir!—perticler good madeira, this!"

"Sir!" said Mr. Beaufort, struggling to preserve, or rather recover, his temper, "your conduct is exceedingly strange; but allow me to say that you are wholly misinformed. My brother never did marry; and if you have anything to say on behalf of those young men—his natural sons—I refer you to my solicitor, Mr. Blackwell, of Lincoln's Inn. I wish you a good evening."

"Sir!—the same to you—I won't trouble you auny farther; it was only out of koindness I called—I am not used to be treated so—sir, I am in his maujesty's service—sir, you will foind that the witness of the marriage is forthcoming; you will think of me then, and, perhaps, be sorry. But I've done, 'Your most obedient humble, sir!'" And the stranger, with a flourish of his hand, turned to the door. At the sight of this determination on the part of his strange guest, a cold, uneasy, vague presentiment seized Mr. Beaufort. There, not flashed, but rather froze, across him the recollection of his brother's emphatic but disbelieved assurances—of Catherine's obstinate assertion of her son's alleged rights—rights which her lawsuit, undertaken on her own behalf, had not compromised;—a fresh lawsuit might be instituted by the son, and the evidence which had been wanting in the former suit might be found at last. With this remembrance and these reflections came a horrible train of shadowy fears,—witnesses, verdict, surrender, spoliation—arrears—ruin!

The man, who had gained the door, turned back and looked at him with a complacent, half-triumphant leer upon his impudent, reckless face.

"Sir," then said Mr. Beaufort, mildly, "I repeat that you had better see Mr. Blackwell."

The tempter saw his triumph. "I have a secret to communicate which it is best for you to keep snug. How mauny people do you wish me to see about it? Come, sir, there is no need of a lawyer; or, if you think so, tell him yourself. Now or never, Mr. Beaufort."

"I can have no objection to hear anything you have to say, sir," said the rich man, yet more mildly than before; and then added, with a forced smile, "though my rights are already too confirmed to admit of a doubt."

Without heeding the last assertion, the stranger coolly walked back, resumed his seat, and, placing both arms on the table and looking Mr. Beaufort full in the face, thus proceeded,—

"Sir, of the marriage between Philip Beaufort and Catherine Morton there were two witnesses: the one is dead, the other went abroad—the last is alive still!"

"If so," said Mr. Beaufort, who, not naturally deficient in cunning and sense, felt every faculty now prodigiously sharpened, and was resolved to know the precise grounds for alarm,—"if so, why did not the man—it was a servant, sir, a man-servant, whom Mrs. Morton pretended to rely on—appear on the trial?"

"Because, I say, he was abroad and could not be found; or, the search after him miscaurried, from clumsy management and a lack of the rhino."

"Hum!" said Mr. Beaufort—"one witness—one witness, observe, there is only one!—does not alarm me much. It is not what a man deposes, it is what a jury believe, sir! Moreover, what has become of the young men? They have never been heard of for years. They are probably dead; if so, I am heir-at-law!"

"I know where one of them is to be found at all events."

"The elder?—Philip?" asked Mr. Beaufort anxiously, and with a fearful remembrance of the energetic and vehement character prematurely exhibited by his nephew.

"Pawdon me! I need not aunswer that question."

"Sir! a lawsuit of this nature, against one in possession, is very doubtful, and," added the rich man, drawing himself up—"and, perhaps very expensive!"

"The young man I speak of does not want friends, who will not grudge the money."

"Sir!" said Mr. Beaufort, rising and placing his back to the fire—"sir! what is your object in this communication? Do you come, on the part of the young man, to propose a compromise? If so, be plain!"

"I come on my own pawt. It rests with you to say if the young men shall never know it!"

"And what do you want?"

"Five hundred a year as long as the secret is kept."

"And how can you prove that there is a secret, after all?"

"By producing the witness if you wish."

"Will he go halves in the £500. a year?" asked Mr. Beaufort artfully.

"That is moy affair, sir," replied the stranger.

"What you say," resumed Mr. Beaufort, "is so extraordinary—so unexpected, and still, to me, seems so improbable, that I must have time to consider. If you will call on me in a week, and produce your facts, I will give you my answer. I am not the man, sir, to wish to keep any one out of his true rights, but I will not yield, on the other hand, to imposture."

"If you don't want to keep them out of their rights, I'd best go and tell my young gentlemen," said the stranger, with cool impudence.

"I tell you I must have time," repeated Beaufort, disconcerted. "Besides, I have not myself alone to look to, sir," he added, with dignified emphasis—"I am a father!"

"This day week I will call on you again. Good evening, Mr. Beaufort!"

And the man stretched out his hand with an air of amicable condescension. The respectable Mr. Beaufort changed colour, hesitated, and finally suffered two fingers to be enticed into the grasp of the visitor, whom he ardently wished at that bourne whence no visitor returns.

The stranger smiled, stalked to the door, laid his finger on his lip, winked knowingly, and vanished, leaving Mr. Beaufort a prey to such feelings of uneasiness, dread, and terror, as may be experienced by a man whom, on some inch or two of slippery rock, the tides have suddenly surrounded.

He remained perfectly still for some moments, and then glancing round the dim and spacious room, his eyes took in all the evidences of luxury and wealth which it betrayed. Above the huge sideboard, that on festive days groaned beneath the hoarded weight of the silver heirlooms of the Beauforts, hung, in its gilded frame, a large picture of the family seat, with the stately porticoes—the noble park—the groups of deer; and around the wall, interspersed here and there with ancestral portraits of knight and dame, long since gathered to their rest, were placed masterpieces of the Italian and Flemish art, which generation after generation had slowly accumulated, till the Beaufort Collection had become the theme of connoisseurs and the study of young genius.

The still room, the dumb pictures—even the heavy sideboard seemed to gain voice, and speak to him audibly. He thrust his hand into the folds of his waistcoat, and griped his own flesh convulsively; then, striding to and fro the apartment, he endeavoured to re-collect his thoughts.

"I dare not consult Mrs. Beaufort," he muttered; "no—no,—she is a fool! Besides, she's not in the way. No time to lose—I will go to Lilburne."

Scarce had that thought crossed him than he hastened to put it into execution. He rang for his hat and gloves and sallied out on foot to Lord Lilburne's house in Park Lane,—the distance was short, and impatience has long strides.

He knew Lord Lilburne was in town, for that personage loved London for its own sake; and even in September he would have said with the old Duke of Queensberry, when some one observed that London was very empty—"Yes; but it is fuller than the country."

Mr. Beaufort found Lord Lilburne reclined on a sofa, by the open window of his drawing-room, beyond which the early stars shone upon the glimmering trees and silver turf of the deserted park. Unlike the simple dessert of his respectable brother-in-law, the costliest fruits, the richest wines of France, graced the small table placed beside his sofa; and as the starch man of forms and method entered the room at one door, a rustling silk, that vanished through the aperture of another, seemed to betray tokens of a tete-a-tete, probably more agreeable to Lilburne than the one with which only our narrative is concerned.

It would have been a curious study for such men as love to gaze upon the dark and wily features of human character, to have watched the contrast between the reciter and the listener, as Beaufort, with much circumlocution, much affected disdain and real anxiety, narrated the singular and ominous conversation between himself and his visitor.

The servant, in introducing Mr. Beaufort, had added to the light of the room; and the candles shone full on the face and form of Mr. Beaufort. All about that gentleman was so completely in unison with the world's forms and seemings, that there was something moral in the very sight of him! Since his accession of fortune he had grown less pale and less thin; the angles in his figure were filled up. On his brow there was no trace of younger passion. No able vice had ever sharpened the expression—no exhausting vice ever deepened the lines. He was the beau-ideal of a county member,—so sleek, so staid, so business-like; yet so clean, so neat, so much the gentleman. And now there was a kind of pathos in his grey hairs, his nervous smile, his agitated hands, his quick and uneasy transition of posture, the tremble of his voice. He would have appeared to those who saw, but heard not, The Good Man in trouble. Cold, motionless, speechless, seemingly apathetic, but in truth observant, still reclined on the sofa, his head thrown back, but one eye fixed on his companion, his hands clasped before him, Lord Lilburne listened; and in that repose, about his face, even about his person, might be read the history of how different a life and character! What native acuteness in the stealthy eye! What hardened resolve in the full nostril and firm lips! What sardonic contempt for all things in the intricate lines about the mouth. What animal enjoyment of all things so despised in that delicate nervous system, which, combined with original vigour of constitution, yet betrayed itself in the veins on the hands and temples, the occasional quiver of the upper lip! His was the frame above all others the most alive to pleasure—deep-chested, compact, sinewy, but thin to leanness—delicate in its texture and extremities, almost to effeminacy. The indifference of the posture, the very habit of the dress—not slovenly, indeed, but easy, loose, careless—seemed to speak of the man's manner of thought and life—his profound disdain of externals.

Not till Beaufort had concluded did Lord Lilburne change his position or open his lips; and then, turning to his brother-in-law his calm face, he said drily,—

"I always thought your brother had married that woman; he was the sort of man to do it. Besides, why should she have gone to law without a vestige of proof, unless she was convinced of her rights? Imposture never proceeds without some evidence. Innocence, like a fool as it is, fancies it has only to speak to be believed. But there is no cause for alarm."

"No cause!—And yet you think there was a marriage."

"It is quite clear," continued Lilburne, without heeding this interruption; "that the man, whatever his evidence, has not got sufficient proofs. If he had, he would go to the young men rather than you: it is evident that they would promise infinitely larger rewards than he could expect from yourself. Men are always more generous with what they expect than with what they have. All rogues know this. 'Tis the way Jews and usurers thrive upon heirs rather than possessors; 'tis the philosophy of post-obits. I dare say the man has found out the real witness of the marriage, but ascertained, also, that the testimony of that witness would not suffice to dispossess you. He might be discredited—rich men have a way sometimes of discrediting poor witnesses. Mind, he says nothing of the lost copy of the register—whatever may be the value of that document, which I am not lawyer enough to say—of any letters of your brother avowing the marriage. Consider, the register itself is destroyed—the clergyman dead. Pooh! make yourself easy."

"True," said Mr. Beaufort, much comforted; "what a memory you have!"

"Naturally. Your wife is my sister—I hate poor relations—and I was therefore much interested in your accession and your lawsuit. No—you may feel—at rest on this matter, so far as a successful lawsuit is concerned. The next question is, Will you have a lawsuit at all? and is it worth while buying this fellow? That I can't say unless I see him myself."

"I wish to Heaven you would!"

"Very willingly: 'tis a sort of thing I like—I'm fond of dealing with rogues—it amuses me. This day week? I'll be at your house—your proxy; I shall do better than Blackwell. And since you say you are wanted at the Lakes, go down, and leave all to me."

"A thousand thanks. I can't say how grateful I am. You certainly are the kindest and cleverest person in the world."

"You can't think worse of the world's cleverness and kindness than I do," was Lilburne's rather ambiguous answer to the compliment. "But why does my sister want to see you?"

"Oh, I forgot!—here is her letter. I was going to ask your advice in this too."

Lord Lilburne took the letter, and glanced over it with the rapid eye of a man accustomed to seize in everything the main gist and pith.

"An offer to my pretty niece—Mr. Spencer—requires no fortune—his uncle will settle all his own—(poor silly old man!) All! Why that's only £1000. a year. You don't think much of this, eh? How my sister can even ask you about it puzzles me."

"Why, you see, Lilburne," said Mr. Beaufort, rather embarrassed, "there is no question of fortune—nothing to go out of the family; and, really, Arthur is so expensive, and, if she were to marry well, I could not give her less than fifteen or twenty thousand pounds."

"Aha!—I see—every man to his taste: here a daughter—there a dowry. You are devilish fond of money, Beaufort. Any pleasure in avarice,—eh?"

Mr. Beaufort coloured very much at the remark and the question, and, forcing a smile, said,—

"You are severe. But you don't know what it is to be father to a young man."

"Then a great many young women have told me sad fibs! But you are right in your sense of the phrase. No, I never had an heir apparent, thank Heaven! No children imposed upon me by law—natural enemies, to count the years between the bells that ring for their majority, and those that will toll for my decease. It is enough for me that I have a brother and a sister—that my brother's son will inherit my estates—and that, in the meantime, he grudges me every tick in that clock. What then? If he had been my uncle, I had done the same. Meanwhile, I see as little of him as good breeding will permit. On the face of a rich man's heir is written the rich man's memento mori! But revenons a nos moutons. Yes, if you give your daughter no fortune, your death will be so much the more profitable to Arthur!"

"Really, you take such a very odd view of the matter," said Mr. Beaufort, exceedingly shocked. "But I see you don't like the marriage; perhaps you are right."

"Indeed, I have no choice in the matter; I never interfere between father and children. If I had children myself, I will, however, tell you, for your comfort, that they might marry exactly as they pleased—I would never thwart them. I should be too happy to get them out of my way. If they married well, one would have all the credit; if ill, one would have an excuse to disown them. As I said before, I dislike poor relations. Though if Camilla lives at the Lakes when she is married, it is but a letter now and then; and that's your wife's trouble, not yours. But, Spencer—what Spencer!—what family? Was there not a Mr. Spencer who lived at Winandermere—who—"

"Who went with us in search of these boys, to be sure. Very likely the same—nay, he must be so. I thought so at the first."

"Go down to the Lakes to-morrow. You may hear something about your nephews;" at that word Mr. Beaufort winced.

"'Tis well to be forearmed."

"Many thanks for all your counsel," said Beaufort, rising, and glad to escape; for though both he and his wife held the advice of Lord Lilburne in the highest reverence, they always smarted beneath the quiet and careless stings which accompanied the honey. Lord Lilburne was singular in this,—he would give to any one who asked it, but especially a relation, the best advice in his power; and none gave better, that is, more worldly advice. Thus, without the least benevolence, he was often of the greatest service; but he could not help mixing up the draught with as much aloes and bitter-apple as possible. His intellect delighted in exhibiting itself even gratuitously. His heart equally delighted in that only cruelty which polished life leaves to its tyrants towards their equals,—thrusting pins into the feelings and breaking self-love upon the wheel. But just as Mr. Beaufort had drawn on his gloves and gained the doorway, a thought seemed to strike Lord Lilburne:

"By the by," he said, "you understand that when I promised I would try and settle the matter for you, I only meant that I would learn the exact causes you have for alarm on the one hand, or for a compromise with this fellow on the other. If the last be advisable you are aware that I cannot interfere. I might get into a scrape; and Beaufort Court is not my property."

"I don't quite understand you."

"I am plain enough, too. If there is money to be given it is given in order to defeat what is called justice—to keep these nephews of yours out of their inheritance. Now, should this ever come to light, it would have an ugly appearance. They who risk the blame must be the persons who possess the estate."

"If you think it dishonourable or dishonest—" said Beaufort, irresolutely.

"I! I never can advise as to the feelings; I can only advise as to the policy. If you don't think there ever was a marriage, it may, still, be honest in you to prevent the bore of a lawsuit."

"But if he can prove to me that they were married?"

"Pooh!" said Lilburne, raising his eyebrows with a slight expression of contemptuous impatience; "it rests on yourself whether or not he prove it to YOUR satisfaction! For my part, as a third person, I am persuaded the marriage did take place. But if I had Beaufort Court, my convictions would be all the other way. You understand. I am too happy to serve you. But no man can be expected to jeopardise his character, or coquet with the law, unless it be for his own individual interest. Then, of course, he must judge for himself. Adieu! I expect some friends foreigners—Carlists—to whist. You won't join them?"

"I never play, you know. You will write to me at Winandermere: and, at all events, you will keep off the man till I return?"

"Certainly."

Beaufort, whom the latter part of the conversation had comforted far less than the former, hesitated, and turned the door-handle three or four times; but, glancing towards his brother-in-law, he saw in that cold face so little sympathy in the struggle between interest and conscience, that he judged it best to withdraw at once.

As soon as he was gone, Lilburne summoned his valet, who had lived with him many years, and who was his confidant in all the adventurous gallantries with which he still enlivened the autumn of his life.

"Dykeman," said he, "you have let out that lady?"

"Yes, my lord."

"I am not at home if she calls again. She is stupid; she cannot get the girl to come to her again. I shall trust you with an adventure, Dykeman—an adventure that will remind you of our young days, man. This charming creature—I tell you she is irresistible—her very oddities bewitch me. You must—well, you look uneasy. What would you say?"

"My lord, I have found out more about her—and—and—"

"Well, well."

The valet drew near and whispered something in his master's ear.

"They are idiots who say it, then," answered Lilburne. "And," faltered the man, with the shame of humanity on his face, "she is not worthy your lordship's notice—a poor—"

"Yes, I know she is poor; and, for that reason, there can be no difficulty, if the thing is properly managed. You never, perhaps, heard of a certain Philip, king of Macedon; but I will tell you what he once said, as well as I can remember it: 'Lead an ass with a pannier of gold; send the ass through the gates of a city, and all the sentinels will run away.' Poor!—where there is love, there is charity also, Dykeman. Besides—"

Here Lilburne's countenance assumed a sudden aspect of dark and angry passion,—he broke off abruptly, rose, and paced the room, muttering to himself. Suddenly he stopped, and put his hand to his hip, as an expression of pain again altered the character of his face.

"The limb pains me still! Dykeman—I was scarce twenty-one—when I became a cripple for life." He paused, drew a long breath, smiled, rubbed his hands gently, and added: "Never fear—you shall be the ass; and thus Philip of Macedon begins to fill the pannier." And he tossed his purse into the hands of the valet, whose face seemed to lose its anxious embarrassment at the touch of the gold. Lilburne glanced at him with a quiet sneer: "Go!—I will give you my orders when I undress."

"Yes!" he repeated to himself, "the limb pains me still. But he died!—shot as a man would shoot a jay or a polecat!

"I have the newspaper still in that drawer. He died an outcast—a felon—a murderer! And I blasted his name—and I seduced his mistress—and I—am John Lord Lilburne!"

About ten o'clock, some half-a-dozen of those gay lovers of London, who, like Lilburne, remain faithful to its charms when more vulgar worshippers desert its sunburnt streets—mostly single men—mostly men of middle age—dropped in. And soon after came three or four high-born foreigners, who had followed into England the exile of the unfortunate Charles X. Their looks, at once proud and sad—their moustaches curled downward—their beards permitted to grow—made at first a strong contrast with the smooth gay Englishmen. But Lilburne, who was fond of French society, and who, when he pleased, could be courteous and agreeable, soon placed the exiles at their ease; and, in the excitement of high play, all differences of mood and humour speedily vanished. Morning was in the skies before they sat down to supper.

"You have been very fortunate to-night, milord," said one of the Frenchmen, with an envious tone of congratulation.

"But, indeed," said another, who, having been several times his host's partner, had won largely, "you are the finest player, milord, I ever encountered."

"Always excepting Monsieur Deschapelles and—," replied Lilburne, indifferently. And, turning the conversation, he asked one of the guests why he had not introduced him to a French officer of merit and distinction; "With whom," said Lord Lilburne, "I understand that you are intimate, and of whom I hear your countrymen very often speak."

"You mean De Vaudemont. Poor fellow!" said a middle-aged Frenchman, of a graver appearance than the rest.

"But why 'poor fellow!' Monsieur de Liancourt?"

"He was rising so high before the revolution. There was not a braver officer in the army. But he is but a soldier of fortune, and his career is closed."

"Till the Bourbons return," said another Carlist, playing with his moustache.

"You will really honour me much by introducing me to him," said Lord Lilburne. "De Vaudemont—it is a good name,—perhaps, too, he plays at whist."

"But," observed one of the Frenchmen, "I am by no means sure that he has the best right in the world to the name. 'Tis a strange story."

"May I hear it?" asked the host.

"Certainly. It is briefly this: There was an old Vicomte de Vaudemont about Paris; of good birth, but extremely poor—a mauvais sujet. He had already had two wives, and run through their fortunes. Being old and ugly, and men who survive two wives having a bad reputation among marriageable ladies at Paris, he found it difficult to get a third. Despairing of the noblesse he went among the bourgeoisie with that hope. His family were kept in perpetual fear of a ridiculous mesalliance. Among these relations was Madame de Merville, whom you may have heard of."

"Madame de Merville! Ah, yes! Handsome, was she not?"

"It is true. Madame de Merville, whose failing was pride, was known more than once to have bought off the matrimonial inclinations of the amorous vicomte. Suddenly there appeared in her circles a very handsome young man. He was presented formally to her friends as the son of the Vicomte de Vaudemont by his second marriage with an English lady, brought up in England, and now for the first time publicly acknowledged. Some scandal was circulated—"

"Sir," interrupted Monsieur de Liancourt, very gravely, "the scandal was such as all honourable men must stigmatise and despise—it was only to be traced to some lying lackey—a scandal that the young man was already the lover of a woman of stainless reputation the very first day that he entered Paris! I answer for the falsity of that report. But that report I own was one that decided not only Madame de Merville, who was a sensitive—too sensitive a person, but my friend young Vaudemont, to a marriage, from the pecuniary advantages of which he was too high-spirited not to shrink."

"Well," said Lord Lilburne, "then this young De Vaudemont married Madame de Merville?"

"No," said Liancourt somewhat sadly, "it was not so decreed; for Vaudemont, with a feeling which belongs to a gentleman, and which I honour, while deeply and gratefully attached to Madame de Merville, desired that he might first win for himself some honourable distinction before he claimed a hand to which men of fortunes so much higher had aspired in vain. I am not ashamed," he added, after a slight pause, "to say that I had been one of the rejected suitors, and that I still revere the memory of Eugenie de Merville. The young man, therefore, was to have entered my regiment. Before, however, he had joined it, and while yet in the full flush of a young man's love for a woman formed to excite the strongest attachment, she—she—" The Frenchman's voice trembled, and he resumed with affected composure: "Madame de Merville, who had the best and kindest heart that ever beat in a human breast, learned one day that there was a poor widow in the garret of the hotel she inhabited who was dangerously ill—without medicine and without food—having lost her only friend and supporter in her husband some time before. In the impulse of the moment, Madame de Merville herself attended this widow—caught the fever that preyed upon her—was confined to her bed ten days—and died as she had lived, in serving others and forgetting self.—And so much, sir, for the scandal you spoke of!"

"A warning," observed Lord Lilburne, "against trifling with one's health by that vanity of parading a kind heart, which is called charity. If charity, mon cher, begins at home, it is in the drawing-room, not the garret!"

The Frenchman looked at his host in some disdain, bit his lip, and was silent.

"But still," resumed Lord Lilburne, "still it is so probable that your old vicomte had a son; and I can so perfectly understand why he did not wish to be embarrassed with him as long as he could help it, that I do not understand why there should be any doubt of the younger De Vaudemont's parentage."

"Because," said the Frenchman who had first commenced the narrative,—"because the young man refused to take the legal steps to proclaim his birth and naturalise himself a Frenchman; because, no sooner was Madame de Merville dead than he forsook the father he had so newly discovered—forsook France, and entered with some other officers, under the brave, &m— in the service of one of the native princes of India."

"But perhaps he was poor," observed Lord Lilburne. "A father is a very good thing, and a country is a very good thing, but still a man must have money; and if your father does not do much for you, somehow or other, your country generally follows his example."

"My lord," said Liancourt, "my friend here has forgotten to say that Madame de Merville had by deed of gift; (though unknown to her lover), before her death, made over to young Vaudemont the bulk of her fortune; and that, when he was informed of this donation after her decease, and sufficiently recovered from the stupor of his grief, he summoned her relations round him, declared that her memory was too dear to him for wealth to console him for her loss, and reserving to himself but a modest and bare sufficiency for the common necessaries of a gentleman, he divided the rest amongst them, and repaired to the East; not only to conquer his sorrow by the novelty and stir of an exciting life, but to carve out with his own hand the reputation of an honourable and brave man. My friend remembered the scandal long buried—he forgot the generous action."

"Your friend, you see, my dear Monsieur de Liancourt," remarked Lilburne, "is more a man of the world than you are!"

"And I was just going to observe," said the friend thus referred to, "that that very action seemed to confirm the rumour that there had been some little manoeuvring as to this unexpected addition to the name of De Vaudemont; for, if himself related to Madame de Merville, why have such scruples to receive her gift?"

"A very shrewd remark," said Lord Lilburne, looking with some respect at the speaker; "and I own that it is a very unaccountable proceeding, and one of which I don't think you or I would ever have been guilty. Well, and the old Vicomte?"

"Did not live long!" said the Frenchman, evidently gratified by his host's compliment, while Liancourt threw himself back in his chair in grave displeasure. "The young man remained some years in India, and when he returned to Paris, our friend here, Monsieur de Liancourt (then in favour with Charles X.), and Madame de Merville's relations took him up. He had already acquired a reputation in this foreign service, and he obtained a place at the court, and a commission in the king's guards. I allow that he would certainly have made a career, had it not been for the Three Days. As it is, you see him in London, like the rest of us, an exile!"

"And I suppose, without a sous."

"No, I believe that he had still saved, and even augmented, in India, the portion he allotted to himself from Madame de Merville's bequest."

"And if he don't play whist, he ought to play it," said Lilburne. "You have roused my curiosity; I hope you will let me make his acquaintance, Monsieur de Liancourt. I am no politician, but allow me to propose this toast, 'Success to those who have the wit to plan, and the strength to execute.' In other words, 'the Right Divine!'"

Soon afterwards the guests retired.

CHAPTER IV

"Ros. Happily, he's the second time come to them."—Hamlet.

It was the evening after that in which the conversations recorded in our last chapter were held;—evening in the quiet suburb of H—. The desertion and silence of the metropolis in September had extended to its neighbouring hamlets;—a village in the heart of the country could scarcely have seemed more still; the lamps were lighted, many of the shops already closed, a few of the sober couples and retired spinsters of the place might, here and there, be seen slowly wandering homeward after their evening walk: two or three dogs, in spite of the prohibitions of the magistrates placarded on the walls,—(manifestoes which threatened with death the dogs, and predicted more than ordinary madness to the public,)—were playing in the main road, disturbed from time to time as the slow coach, plying between the city and the suburb, crawled along the thoroughfare, or as the brisk mails whirled rapidly by, announced by the cloudy dust and the guard's lively horn. Gradually even these evidences of life ceased—the saunterers disappeared, the mails had passed, the dogs gave place to the later and more stealthy perambulations of their feline successors "who love the moon." At unfrequent intervals, the more important shops—the linen-drapers', the chemists', and the gin-palace—still poured out across the shadowy road their streams of light from windows yet unclosed: but with these exceptions, the business of the place stood still.

At this time there emerged from a milliner's house (shop, to outward appearance, it was not, evincing its gentility and its degree above the Capelocracy, to use a certain classical neologism, by a brass plate on an oak door, whereon was graven, "Miss Semper, Milliner and Dressmaker, from Madame Devy,")—at this time, I say, and from this house there emerged the light and graceful form of a young female. She held in her left hand a little basket, of the contents of which (for it was empty) she had apparently just disposed; and, as she stepped across the road, the lamplight fell on a face in the first bloom of youth, and characterised by an expression of childlike innocence and candour. It was a face regularly and exquisitely lovely, yet something there was in the aspect that saddened you; you knew not why, for it was not sad itself; on the contrary, the lips smiled and the eyes sparkled. As she now glided along the shadowy street with a light, quick step, a man, who had hitherto been concealed by the portico of an attorney's house, advanced stealthily, and followed her at a little distance. Unconscious that she was dogged, and seemingly fearless of all danger, the girl went lightly on, swinging her basket playfully to and fro, and chaunting, in a low but musical tone, some verses that seemed rather to belong to the nursery than to that age which the fair singer had attained.

As she came to an angle which the main street formed with a lane, narrow and partially lighted, a policeman, stationed there, looked hard at her, and then touched his hat with an air of respect, in which there seemed also a little of compassion.

"Good night to you," said the girl, passing him, and with a frank, gay tone.

"Shall I attend you home, Miss?" said the man.

"What for? I am very well!" answered the young woman, with an accent and look of innocent surprise.

Just at this time the man, who had hitherto followed her, gained the spot, and turned down the lane.

"Yes," replied the policeman; "but it is getting dark, Miss."

"So it is every night when I walk home, unless there's a moon.—Good-bye.—The moon," she repeated to herself, as she walked on, "I used to be afraid of the moon when I was a little child;" and then, after a pause, she murmured, in a low chaunt:

"'The moon she is a wandering ghost,
That walks in penance nightly;
How sad she is, that wandering moon,
For all she shines so brightly!

"'I watched her eyes when I was young,
Until they turned my brain,
And now I often weep to think
'Twill ne'er be right again.'"

As the murmur of these words died at a distance down the lane in which the girl had disappeared, the policeman, who had paused to listen, shook his head mournfully, and said, while he moved on,—

"Poor thing! they should not let her always go about by herself; and yet, who would harm her?"

Meanwhile the girl proceeded along the lane, which was skirted by small, but not mean houses, till it terminated in a cross-stile that admitted into a church yard. Here hung the last lamp in the path, and a few dim stars broke palely over the long grass, and scattered gravestones, without piercing the deep shadow which the church threw over a large portion of the sacred ground. Just as she passed the stile, the man, whom we have before noticed, and who had been leaning, as if waiting for some one, against the pales, approached, and said gently,—

"Ah, Miss! it is a lone place for one so beautiful as you are to be alone. You ought never to be on foot."

The girl stopped, and looked full, but without any alarm in her eyes, into the man's face.

"Go away!" she said, with a half-peevish, half-kindly tone of command. "I don't know you."

"But I have been sent to speak to you by one who does know you, Miss—one who loves you to distraction—he has seen you before at Mrs. West's. He is so grieved to think you should walk—you ought, he says, to have every luxury—that he has sent his carriage for you. It is on the other side of the yard. Do come now;" and he laid his hand, though very lightly, on her arm.

"At Mrs. West's!" she said; and, for the first time, her voice and look showed fear. "Go away directly! How dare you touch me!"

"But, my dear Miss, you have no idea how my employer loves you, and how rich he is. See, he has sent you all this money; it is gold—real gold. You may have what you like, if you will but come. Now, don't be silly, Miss." The girl made no answer, but, with a sudden spring, passed the man, and ran lightly and rapidly along the path, in an opposite direction from that to which the tempter had pointed, when inviting her to the carriage. The man, surprised, but not baffled, reached her in an instant, and caught hold of her dress.

"Stay! you must come—you must!" he said, threateningly; and, loosening his grasp on her shawl, he threw his arm round her waist.

"Don't!" cried the girl, pleadingly, and apparently subdued, turning her fair, soft face upon her pursuer, and clasping her hands. "Be quiet! Fanny is silly! No one is ever rude to poor Fanny!"

"And no one will be rude to you, Miss," said the man, apparently touched; "but I dare not go without you. You don't know what you refuse. Come;" and he attempted gently to draw her back.

"No, no!" said the girl, changing from supplication to anger, and raising her voice into a loud shriek, "No! I will—"

"Nay, then," interrupted the man, looking round anxiously, and, with a quick and dexterous movement he threw a large handkerchief over her face, and, as he held it fast to her lips with one hand, he lifted her from the ground. Still violently struggling, the girl contrived to remove the handkerchief, and once more her shriek of terror rang through the violated sanctuary.

At that instant a loud deep voice was heard, "Who calls?" And a tall figure seemed to rise, as from the grave itself, and emerge from the shadow of the church. A moment more, and a strong gripe was laid on the shoulder of the ravisher. "What is this? On God's ground, too! Release her, wretch!"

The man, trembling, half with superstitious, half with bodily fear, let go his captive, who fell at once at the knees of her deliverer. "Don't you hurt me too," she said, as the tears rolled down her eyes. "I am a good girl—and my grandfather's blind."

The stranger bent down and raised her; then looking round for the assailant with an eye whose dark fire shone through the gloom, he perceived the coward stealing off. He disdained to pursue.

"My poor child," said he, with that voice which the strong assume to the weak—the man to some wounded infant—the voice of tender superiority and compassion, "there is no cause for fear now. Be soothed. Do you live near? Shall I see you home?"

"Thank you! That's kind. Pray do!" And, with an infantine confidence she took his hand, as a child does that of a grown-up person;—so they walked on together.

"And," said the stranger, "do you know that man? Has he insulted you before?"

"No—don't talk of him: ce me fait mal!" And she put her hand to her forehead.

The French was spoken with so French an accent, that, in some curiosity, the stranger cast his eye over her plain dress.

"You speak French well."

"Do I? I wish I knew more words—I only recollect a few. When I am very happy or very sad they come into my head. But I am happy now. I like your voice—I like you—Oh! I have dropped my basket!"

"Shall I go back for it, or shall I buy you another?"

"Another!—Oh, no! come back for it. How kind you are!—Ah! I see it!" and she broke away and ran forward to pick it up.

When she had recovered it, she laughed—she spoke to it—she kissed it.

Her companion smiled as he said: "Some sweetheart has given you that basket—it seems but a common basket too."

"I have had it—oh, ever since—since—I don't know how long! It came with me from France—it was full of little toys. They are gone—I am so sorry!"

"How old are you?"

"I don't know."

"My pretty one," said the stranger, with deep pity in his rich voice, "your mother should not let you go out alone at this hour."

"Mother!—mother!" repeated the girl, in a tone of surprise.

"Have you no mother?"

"No! I had a father once. But he died, they say. I did not see him die. I sometimes cry when I think that I shall never, never see him again! But," she said, changing her accent from melancholy almost to joy, "he is to have a grave here like the other girl's fathers—a fine stone upon it—and all to be done with my money!"

"Your money, my child?"

"Yes; the money I make. I sell my work and take the money to my grandfather; but I lay by a little every week for a gravestone for my father."

"Will the gravestone be placed in that churchyard?" They were now in another lane; and, as he spoke, the stranger checked her, and bending down to look into her face, he murmured to himself, "Is it possible?—it must be—it must!"

"Yes! I love that churchyard—my brother told me to put flowers there; and grandfather and I sit there in the summer, without speaking. But I don't talk much, I like singing better:—

"'All things that good and harmless are
Are taught, they say, to sing
The maiden resting at her work,
The bird upon the wing;
The little ones at church, in prayer;
The angels in the sky
The angels less when babes are born
Than when the aged die.'"

And unconscious of the latent moral, dark or cheering, according as we estimate the value of this life, couched in the concluding rhyme, Fanny turned round to the stranger, and said, "Why should the angels be glad when the aged die?"

"That they are released from a false, unjust, and miserable world, in which the first man was a rebel, and the second a murderer!" muttered the stranger between his teeth, which he gnashed as he spoke.

The girl did not understand him: she shook her head gently, and made no reply. A few moments, and she paused before a small house.

"This is my home."

"It is so," said her companion, examining the exterior of the house with an earnest gaze; "and your name is Fanny."

"Yes—every one knows Fanny. Come in;" and the girl opened the door with a latch-key.

The stranger bowed his stately height as he crossed the low threshold and followed his guide into a little parlour. Before a table on which burned dimly, and with unheeded wick, a single candle, sat a man of advanced age; and as he turned his face to the door, the stranger saw that he was blind.

The girl bounded to his chair, passed her arms round the old man's neck, and kissed his forehead; then nestling herself at his feet, and leaning her clasped hands caressingly on his knee, she said,—

"Grandpapa, I have brought you somebody you must love. He has been so kind to Fanny."

"And neither of you can remember me!" said the guest.

The old man, whose dull face seemed to indicate dotage, half raised himself at the sound of the stranger's voice. "Who is that?" said he, with a feeble and querulous voice. "Who wants me?"

"I am the friend of your lost son. I am he who, ten years go, brought Fanny to your roof, and gave her to your care—your son's last charge. And you blessed your son, and forgave him, and vowed to be a father to his Fanny." The old man, who had now slowly risen to his feet, trembled violently, and stretched out his hands.

"Come near—near—let me put my hands on your head. I cannot see you; but Fanny talks of you, and prays for you; and Fanny—she has been an angel to me!"

The stranger approached and half knelt as the old man spread his hands over his head, muttering inaudibly. Meanwhile Fanny, pale as death—her lips apart—an eager, painful expression on her face—looked inquiringly on the dark, marked countenance of the visitor, and creeping towards him inch by inch, fearfully touched his dress—his arms—his countenance.

"Brother," she said at last, doubtingly and timidly, "Brother, I thought I could never forget you! But you are not like my brother; you are older;—you are—you are!—no! no! you are not my brother!"

"I am much changed, Fanny; and you too!"

He smiled as he spoke; and the smile—sweet and pitying—thoroughly changed the character of his face, which was ordinarily stern, grave, and proud.

"I know you now!" exclaimed Fanny, in a tone of wild joy. "And you come back from that grave! My flowers have brought you back at last! I knew they would! Brother! Brother!"

And she threw herself on his breast and burst into passionate tears. Then, suddenly drawing herself back, she laid her finger on his arm, and looked up at him beseechingly.

"Pray, now, is he really dead? He, my father!—he, too, was lost like you. Can't he come back again as you have done?"

"Do you grieve for him still, then? Poor girl!" said the stranger, evasively, and seating himself. Fanny continued to listen for an answer to her touching question; but finding that none was given, she stole away to a corner of the room, and leaned her face on her hands, and seemed to think—till at last, as she so sat, the tears began to flow down her cheeks, and she wept, but silently and unnoticed.

"But, sir," said the guest, after a short pause, "how is this? Fanny tells me she supports you by her work. Are you so poor, then? Yet I left you your son's bequest; and you, too, I understood, though not rich, were not in want!"

"There was a curse on my gold," said the old man, sternly. "It was stolen from us."

There was another pause. Simon broke it.

"And you, young man—how has it fared with you? You have prospered, I hope."

"I am as I have been for years—alone in the world, without kindred and without friends. But, thanks to Heaven, I am not a beggar!"

"No kindred and no friends!" repeated the old man. "No father—no brother—no wife—no sister!"

"None! No one to care whether I live or die," answered the stranger, with a mixture of pride and sadness in his voice. "But, as the song has it—

"'I care for nobody—no, not I,
For nobody cares for me!'"

There was a certain pathos in the mockery with which he repeated the homely lines, although, as he did, he gathered himself up, as if conscious of a certain consolation and reliance on the resources not dependent on others which he had found in his own strong limbs and his own stout heart.

At that moment he felt a soft touch upon his hand, and he saw Fanny looking at him through the tears that still flowed.

"You have no one to care for you? Don't say so! Come and live with us, brother; we'll care for you. I have never forgotten the flowers—never! Do come! Fanny shall love you. Fanny can work for three!"

"And they call her an idiot!" mumbled the old man, with a vacant smile on his lips.

"My sister! You shall be my sister! Forlorn one—whom even Nature has fooled and betrayed! Sister!—we, both orphans! Sister!" exclaimed that dark, stern man, passionately, and with a broken voice; and he opened his arms, and Fanny, without a blush or a thought of shame, threw herself on his breast. He kissed her forehead with a kiss that was, indeed, pure and holy as a brother's: and Fanny felt that he had left upon her cheek a tear that was not her own.

"Well," he said, with an altered voice, and taking the old man's hand, "what say you? Shall I take up my lodging with you? I have a little money; I can protect and aid you both. I shall be often away—in London or else where—and will not intrude too much on you. But you blind, and she—(here he broke off the sentence abruptly and went on)—you should not be left alone. And this neighbourhood, that burial-place, are dear to me. I, too, Fanny, have lost a parent; and that grave—"

He paused, and then added, in a trembling voice, "And you have placed flowers over that grave?"

"Stay with us," said the blind man; "not for our sake, but your own. The world is a bad place. I have been long sick of the world. Yes! come and live near the burial-ground—the nearer you are to the grave, the safer you are;—and you have a little money, you say!"

"I will come to-morrow, then. I must return now. Tomorrow, Fanny, we shall meet again."

"Must you go?" said Fanny, tenderly. "But you will come again; you know I used to think every one died when he left me. I am wiser now. Yet still, when you do leave me, it is true that you die for Fanny!"

At this moment, as the three persons were grouped, each had assumed a posture of form, an expression of face, which a painter of fitting sentiment and skill would have loved to study. The visitor had gained the door; and as he stood there, his noble height—the magnificent strength and health of his manhood in its full prime—contrasted alike the almost spectral debility of extreme age and the graceful delicacy of Fanny—half girl, half child. There was something foreign in his air—and the half military habit, relieved by the red riband of the Bourbon knighthood. His complexion was dark as that of a Moor, and his raven hair curled close to the stately head. The soldier-moustache—thick, but glossy as silk-shaded the firm lip; and the pointed beard, assumed by the exiled Carlists, heightened the effect of the strong and haughty features and the expression of the martial countenance.

But as Fanny's voice died on his ear, he half averted that proud face; and the dark eyes—almost Oriental in their brilliancy and depth of shade—seemed soft and humid. And there stood Fanny, in a posture of such unconscious sadness—such childlike innocence; her arms drooping—her face wistfully turned to his—and a half smile upon the lips, that made still more touching the tears not yet dried upon her cheeks. While thin, frail, shadowy, with white hair and furrowed cheeks, the old man fixed his sightless orbs on space; and his face, usually only animated from the lethargy of advancing dotage by a certain querulous cynicism, now grew suddenly earnest, and even thoughtful, as Fanny spoke of Death!

CHAPTER V

"*Ulyss. Time hath a wallet at his back*
Wherein he puts alms for oblivion.
Perseverance, dear my lord,
Keeps honour bright."—*Troilus and Cressida.*

I have not sought—as would have been easy, by a little ingenuity in the earlier portion of this narrative—whatever source of vulgar interest might be derived from the mystery of names and persons. As in Charles Spencer the reader is allowed at a glance to detect Sidney Morton, so in Philip de Vaudemont (the stranger who rescued Fanny) the reader at once recognises the hero of my tale; but since neither of these young men has a better right to the name resigned than to the name adopted, it will be simpler and more convenient to designate them by those appellations by which they are now known to the world. In truth, Philip de Vaudemont was scarcely the same being as Philip Morton. In the short visit he had paid to the elder Gawtrey, when he consigned Fanny to his charge, he had given no name; and the one he now took (when, towards the evening of the next day he returned to Simon's house) the old man heard for the first time. Once more sunk into his usual apathy, Simon did not express any surprise that a Frenchman should be so well acquainted with English—he scarcely observed that the name was French. Simon's age seemed daily to bring him more and more to that state when life is mere mechanism, and the soul, preparing for its departure, no longer heeds the tenement that crumbles silently and neglected into its lonely dust. Vaudemont came with but little luggage (for he had an apartment also in London), and no attendant,—a single horse was consigned to the stables of an inn at hand, and he seemed, as soldiers are, more careful for the comforts of the animal than his own. There was but one woman servant in the humble household, who did all the ruder work, for Fanny's industry could afford it. The solitary servant and the homely fare sufficed for the simple and hardy adventurer.

Fanny, with a countenance radiant with joy, took his hand and led him to his room. Poor child! with that instinct of woman which never deserted her, she had busied herself the whole day in striving to deck the chamber according to her own notions of comfort. She had stolen from her little hoard wherewithal to make some small purchases, on which the Dowbiggin of the suburb had been consulted. And what with flowers on the table, and a fire at the hearth, the room looked cheerful.

She watched him as he glanced around, and felt disappointed that he did not utter the admiration she expected. Angry at last with the indifference which, in fact, as to external accommodation, was habitual to him, she plucked his sleeve, and said,—

"Why don't you speak? Is it not nice?—Fanny did her best."

"And a thousand thanks to Fanny! It is all I could wish."

"There is another room, bigger than this, but the wicked woman who robbed us slept there; and besides, you said you liked the churchyard. See!" and she opened the window and pointed to the church-tower rising dark against the evening sky.

"This is better than all!" said Vaudemont; and he looked out from the window in a silent reverie, which Fanny did not disturb.

And now he was settled! From a career so wild, agitated, and various, the adventurer paused in that humble resting-nook. But quiet is not repose—obscurity is not content. Often as, morn and eve, he looked forth upon the spot, where his mother's heart, unconscious of love and woe, mouldered away, the indignant and bitter feelings of the wronged outcast and the son who could not clear the mother's name swept away the subdued and gentle melancholy into which time usually softens regret for the dead, and with which most of us think of the distant past, and the once joyous childhood!

In this man's breast lay, concealed by his external calm, those memories and aspirations which are as strong as passions. In his earlier years, when he had been put to hard shifts for existence, he had found no leisure for close and brooding reflection upon that spoliation of just rights—that calumny upon his mother's name, which had first brought the Night into his Morning. His resentment towards the Beauforts, it is true, had ever been an intense but a fitful and irregular passion. It was exactly in proportion as, by those rare and romantic incidents which Fiction cannot invent, and which Narrative takes with diffidence from the great Store-house of Real Life, his steps had ascended in the social ladder—that all which his childhood had lost—all which the robbers of his heritage had gained, the grandeur and the power of WEALTH—above all, the hourly and the tranquil happiness of a stainless name, became palpable and distinct. He had loved Eugenie as a boy loves for the first time an accomplished woman. He regarded her, so refined—so gentle—so gifted, with the feelings due to a superior being, with an eternal recollection of the ministering angel that had shone upon him when he stood on the dark abyss. She was the first that had redeemed his fate—the first that had guided aright his path—the first that had tamed the savage at his breast:—it was the young lion charmed by the eyes of Una. The outline of his story had been truly given at Lord Lilburne's. Despite his pride, which revolted from such obligations to another, and a woman—which disliked and struggled against a disguise which at once and alone saved him from the detection of the past and the terrors of the future—he had yielded to her, the wise and the gentle, as one whose judgment he could not doubt; and, indeed, the slanderous falsehoods circulated by the lackey, to whose discretion, the night of Gawtrey's death, Eugenie had preferred to confide her own honour, rather than another's life, had (as Liancourt rightly stated) left Philip no option but that which Madame de Merville deemed the best, whether for her happiness or her good name. Then had followed a brief season—the holiday of his life—the season of young hope and passion, of brilliancy and joy, closing by that abrupt death which again left him lonely in the world.

When, from the grief that succeeded to the death of Eugenie, he woke to find himself amidst the strange faces and exciting scenes of an Oriental court, he turned with hard and disgustful contempt from Pleasure, as an infidelity to the dead. Ambition crept over him—his mind hardened as his cheek bronzed under those burning suns—his hardy frame, his energies prematurely awakened, his constitutional disregard to danger,—made him a brave and skilful soldier. He acquired reputation and rank. But, as time went on, the ambition took a higher flight—he felt his sphere circumscribed; the Eastern indolence that filled up the long intervals between Eastern action chafed a temper never at rest: he returned to France: his reputation, Liancourt's friendship, and the relations of Eugenie—grateful, as has before been implied, for the generosity with which he surrendered the principal part of her donation—opened for him a new career, but one painful and galling. In the Indian court there was no question of his birth—one adventurer was equal with the rest. But in Paris, a man attempting to rise provoked all the sarcasm of wit, all the cavils of party; and in polished and civil life, what valour has weapons against a jest? Thus, in civilisation, all the passions that spring from humiliated self-love and baffled aspiration again preyed upon his breast. He saw, then, that the more he struggled from obscurity, the more acute would become research into his true origin; and his writhing pride almost stung to death his ambition. To succeed in life by regular means was indeed difficult for this man; always recoiling from the name he bore—always strong in the hope yet to regain that to which he conceived himself entitled—cherishing that pride of country which never deserts the native of a Free State, however harsh a parent she may have proved; and, above all, whatever his ambition and his passions, taking, from the very misfortunes he had known, an indomitable belief in the ultimate justice of Heaven;—he had refused to sever the last ties that connected him with his lost heritage and his forsaken land—he refused to be naturalised—to make the name he bore legally undisputed—he was contented to be an alien. Neither was Vaudemont fitted exactly for that crisis in the social world when the men of journals and talk bustle aside the men of action. He had not cultivated literature, he had no book-knowledge—the world had been his school, and stern life his teacher. Still, eminently skilled in those physical accomplishments which men admire and soldiers covet, calm and self-possessed in manner, of great personal advantages, of much ready talent and of practised observation in character, he continued to breast the obstacles around him, and to establish himself in the favour of those in power. It was natural to a person so reared and circumstanced to have no sympathy with what is called the popular cause. He was no citizen in the state—he was a stranger in the land. He had suffered and still suffered too much from mankind to have that philanthropy, sometimes visionary but always noble, which, in fact, generally springs from the studies we cultivate, not in the forum, but the closet. Men, alas! too often lose the Democratic Enthusiasm in proportion as they find reason to suspect or despise their kind. And if there were not hopes for the Future, which this hard, practical daily life does not suffice to teach us, the vision and the glory that belong to the Great Popular Creed, dimmed beneath the injustice, the follies, and the vices of the world as it is, would fade into the lukewarm sectarianism of temporary Party. Moreover, Vaudemont's habits of thought and reasoning were those of the camp, confirmed by the systems familiar to him in the East: he regarded the populace as a soldier enamoured of discipline and order usually does. His theories, therefore, or rather his ignorance of what is sound in theory, went with Charles the Tenth in his excesses, but not with the timidity which terminated those excesses by dethronement and disgrace. Chafed to the heart, gnawed with proud grief, he obeyed the royal mandates, and followed the exiled monarch: his hopes overthrown, his career in France annihilated forever. But on entering England, his temper, confident and ready of resource, fastened itself on new food. In the land where he had no name he might yet rebuild his fortunes. It was an arduous effort—an improbable hope; but the words heard by the bridge of Paris—words that had often cheered him in his exile through hardships and through dangers which it is unnecessary to our narrative to detail—yet rung again in his ear, as he leaped on his native land,—"Time, Faith, Energy."

While such his character in the larger and more distant relations of life, in the closer circles of companionship many rare and noble qualities were visible. It is true that he was stern, perhaps imperious—of a temper that always struggled for command; but he was deeply susceptible of kindness, and, if feared by those who opposed, loved by those who served him. About his character was that mixture of tenderness and fierceness which belonged, of old, to the descriptions of the warrior. Though so little unlettered, Life had taught him a certain poetry of sentiment and idea—More poetry, perhaps, in the silent thoughts that, in his happier moments, filled his solitude, than in half the pages that his brother had read and written by the dreaming lake. A certain largeness of idea and nobility of impulse often made him act the sentiments of which bookmen write. With all his passions, he held licentiousness in disdain; with all his ambition for the power of wealth, he despised its luxury. Simple, masculine, severe, abstemious, he was of that mould in which, in earlier times, the successful men of action have been cast. But to successful action, circumstance is more necessary than to triumphant study.

It was to be expected that, in proportion as he had been familiar with a purer and nobler life, he should look with great and deep self-humiliation at his early association with Gawtrey. He was in this respect more severe on himself than any other mind ordinarily just and candid would have been,—when fairly surveying the circumstances of penury, hunger, and despair, which had driven him to Gawtrey's roof, the imperfect nature of his early education, the boyish trust and affection he had felt for his protector, and his own ignorance of, and exemption from, all the worst practices of that unhappy criminal. But still, when, with the knowledge he had now acquired, the man looked calmly back, his cheek burned with remorseful shame at his unreflecting companionship in a life of subterfuge and equivocation, the true nature of which, the boy (so circumstanced as we have shown him) might be forgiven for not at that time comprehending. Two advantages resulted, however, from the error and the remorse: first, the humiliation it brought curbed, in some measure, a pride that might otherwise have been arrogant and unamiable, and, secondly, as I have before intimated, his profound gratitude to Heaven for his deliverance from the snares that had beset his youth gave his future the guide of an earnest and heartfelt faith. He acknowledged in life no such thing as accident. Whatever his struggles, whatever his melancholy, whatever his sense of worldly wrong, he never despaired; for nothing now could shake his belief in one directing Providence.

The ways and habits of Vaudemont were not at discord with those of the quiet household in which he was now a guest. Like most men of strong frames, and accustomed to active, not studious pursuits, he rose early;—and usually rode to London, to come back late at noon to their frugal meal. And if again, perhaps after the hour when Fanny and Simon retired, he would often return to London, his own pass-key re-admitted him, at whatever time he came back, without disturbing the sleep of the household. Sometimes, when the sun began to decline, if the air was warm, the old man would crawl out, leaning on that strong arm, through the neighbouring lanes, ever returning through the lonely burial-ground; or when the blind host clung to his fireside, and composed himself to sleep, Philip would saunter forth along with Fanny; and on the days when she went to sell her work, or select her purchases, he always made a point of attending her. And her cheek wore a flush of pride when she saw him carrying her little basket, or waiting without, in musing patience, while she performed her commissions in the shops. Though in reality Fanny's intellect was ripening within, yet still the surface often misled the eye as to the depths. It was rather that something yet held back the faculties from their growth than that the faculties themselves were wanting. Her weakness was more of the nature of the infant's than of one afflicted with incurable imbecility. For instance, she managed the little household with skill and prudence; she could calculate in her head, as rapidly as Vaudemont himself, the arithmetic necessary to her simple duties; she knew the value of money, which is more than some of us wise folk do. Her skill, even in her infancy so remarkable, in various branches of female handiwork, was carried, not only by perseverance, but by invention and peculiar talent, to a marvellous and exquisite perfection. Her embroidery, especially in what was then more rare than at present, viz., flowers on silk, was much in request among the great modistes of London, to whom it found its way through the agency of Miss Semper. So that all this had enabled her, for years, to provide every necessary comfort of life for herself and her blind protector. And her care for the old man was beautiful in its minuteness, its vigilance. Wherever her heart was interested, there never seemed a deficiency of mind. Vaudemont was touched to see how much of affectionate and pitying respect she appeared to enjoy in the neighbourhood, especially among the humbler classes—even the beggar who swept the crossings did not beg of her, but bade God bless her as she passed; and the rude, discontented artisan would draw himself from the wall and answer, with a softened brow, the smile with which the harmless one charmed his courtesy. In fact, whatever attraction she took from her youth, her beauty, her misfortune, and her affecting industry, was heightened, in the eyes of the poorer neighbours, by many little traits of charity and kindness; many a sick child had she tended, and many a breadless board had stolen something from the stock set aside for her father's grave.

"Don't you think," she once whispered to Vaudemont, "that God attends to us more if we are good to those who are sick and hungry?"

"Certainly we are taught to think so."

"Well, I'll tell you a secret—don't tell again. Grandpapa once said that my father had done bad things; now, if Fanny is good to those she can help, I think that God will hear her more kindly when she prays him to forgive what her father did. Do you think so too? Do say—you are so wise!"

"Fanny, you are wiser than all of us; and I feel myself better and happier when I hear you speak."

There were, indeed, many moments when Vaudemont thought that her deficiencies of intellect might have been repaired, long since, by skilful culture and habitual companionship with those of her own age; from which companionship, however, Fanny, even when at school, had shrunk aloof. At other moments there was something so absent and distracted about her, or so fantastic and incoherent, that Vaudemont, with the man's hard, worldly eye, read in it nothing but melancholy confusion. Nevertheless, if the skein of ideas was entangled, each thread in itself was a thread of gold.

Fanny's great object—her great ambition—her one hope—was a tomb for her supposed father. Whether from some of that early religion attached to the grave, which is most felt in Catholic countries, and which she had imbibed at the convent; or from her residence so near the burial ground, and the affection with which she regarded the spot;—whatever the cause, she had cherished for some years, as young maidens usually cherish the desire of the Altar—the dream of the Gravestone. But the hoard was amassed so slowly;—now old Gawtrey was attacked by illness;—now there was some little difficulty in the rent; now some fluctuation in the price of work; and now, and more often than all, some demand on her charity, which interfered with, and drew from, the pious savings. This was a sentiment in which her new friend sympathised deeply; for he, too, remembered that his first gold had bought that humble stone which still preserved upon the earth the memory of his mother.

Meanwhile, days crept on, and no new violence was offered to Fanny. Vaudemont learned, then, by little and little—and Fanny's account was very confused—the nature of the danger she had run.

It seemed that one day, tempted by the fineness of the weather up the road that led from the suburb farther into the country, Fanny was stopped by a gentleman in a carriage, who accosted her, as she said, very kindly: and after several questions, which she answered with her usual unsuspecting innocence, learned her trade, insisted on purchasing some articles of work which she had at the moment in her basket, and promised to procure her a constant purchaser, upon much better terms than she had hitherto obtained, if she would call at the house of a Mrs. West, about a mile from the suburb towards London. This she promised to do, and this she did, according to the address he gave her. She was admitted to a lady more gaily dressed than Fanny had ever seen a lady before,—the gentleman was also present,—they both loaded her with compliments, and bought her work at a price which seemed about to realise all the hopes of the poor girl as to the gravestone for William Gawtrey,—as if his evil fate pursued that wild man beyond the grave, and his very tomb was to be purchased by the gold of the polluter! The lady then appointed her to call again; but, meanwhile, she met Fanny in the streets, and while she was accosting her, it fortunately chanced that Miss Semper the milliner passed that way—turned round, looked hard at the lady, used very angry language to her, seized Fanny's hand, led her away while the lady slunk off; and told her that the said lady was a very bad woman, and that Fanny must never speak to her again. Fanny most cheerfully promised this. And, in fact, the lady, probably afraid, whether of the mob or the magistrates, never again came near her.

"And," said Fanny, "I gave the money they had both given to me to Miss Semper, who said she would send it back."

"You did right, Fanny; and as you made one promise to Miss Semper, so you must make me one—never to stir from home again without me or some other person. No, no other person—only me. I will give up everything else to go with you."

"Will you? Oh, yes. I promise! I used to like going alone, but that was before you came, brother."

And as Fanny kept her promise, it would have been a bold gallant indeed who would have ventured to molest her by the side of that stately and strong protector.

CHAPTER VI

"Timon. Each thing's a thief
The laws, your curb and whip, in their rough power
Have unchecked theft.

The sweet degrees that this brief world affords,
To such as may the passive drugs of it
Freely command."—Timon of Athens.

On the day and at the hour fixed for the interview with the stranger who had visited Mr. Beaufort, Lord Lilburne was seated in the library of his brother-in-law; and before the elbow-chair, on which he lolled carelessly, stood our old friend Mr. Sharp, of Bow Street notability.

"Mr. Sharp," said the peer, "I have sent for you to do me a little favour. I expect a man here who professes to give Mr. Beaufort, my brother-in-law, some information about a lawsuit. It is necessary to know the exact value of his evidence. I wish you to ascertain all particulars about him. Be so good as to seat yourself in the porter's chair in the hall; note him when he enters, unobserved yourself—but as he is probably a stranger to you, note him still more when he leaves the house; follow him at a distance; find out where he lives, whom he associates with, where he visits, their names and directions, what his character and calling are;—in a word, everything you can, and report to me each evening. Dog him well, never lose sight of him—you will be handsomely paid. You understand?"

"Ah!" said Mr. Sharp, "leave me alone, my lord. Been employed before by your lordship's brother-in-law. We knows what's what."

"I don't doubt it. To your post—I expect him every moment."

And, in fact, Mr. Sharp had only just ensconced himself in the porter's chair when the stranger knocked at the door—in another moment he was shown in to Lord Lilburne.

"Sir," said his lordship, without rising, "be so good as to take a chair. Mr. Beaufort is obliged to leave town—he has asked me to see you—I am one of his family—his wife is my sister—you may be as frank with me as with him,—more so, perhaps."

"I beg the fauvour of your name, sir," said the stranger, adjusting his collar.

"Yours first—business is business."

"Well, then, Captain Smith."

"Of what regiment?"

"Half-pay."

"I am Lord Lilburne. Your name is Smith—humph!" added the peer, looking over some notes before him. "I see it is also the name of the witness appealed to by Mrs. Morton—humph!"

At this remark, and still more at the look which accompanied it, the countenance, before impudent and complacent, of Captain Smith fell into visible embarrassment; he cleared his throat and said, with a little hesitation,—

"My lord, that witness is living!"

"No doubt of it—witnesses never die where property is concerned and imposture intended."

At this moment the servant entered, and placed a little note, quaintly folded, before Lord Lilburne. He glanced at it in surprise—opened, and read as follows, in pencil,—

"My LORD,—I knows the man; take caer of him; he is as big a roge as ever stept; he was transported some three year back, and unless his time has been shortened by the Home, he's absent without leve.

We used to call him Dashing Jerry. That ere youngster we went arter, by Mr. Bofort's wish, was a pall of his. Scuze the liberty I take.

"J. SHARP."

While Lord Lilburne held this effusion to the candle, and spelled his way through it, Captain Smith, recovering his self-composure, thus proceeded:

"Imposture, my lord! imposture! I really don't understand. Your lordship really seems so suspicious, that it is quite uncomfortable. I am sure it is all the same to me; and if Mr. Beaufort does not think proper to see me himself, why I'd best make my bow."

And Captain Smith rose.

"Stay a moment, sir. What Mr. Beaufort may yet do, I cannot say; but I know this, you stand charged of a very grave offence, and if your witness or witnesses—you may have fifty, for what I care—are equally guilty, so much the worse for them."

"My lord, I really don't comprehend."

"Then I will be more plain. I accuse you of devising an infamous falsehood for the purpose of extorting money. Let your witnesses appear in court, and I promise that you, they, and the young man, Mr. Morton, whose claim they set up, shall be indicted for conspiracy—conspiracy, if accompanied (as in the case of your witnesses) with perjury, of the blackest die. Mr. Smith, I know you; and, before ten o'clock to-morrow, I shall know also if you had his majesty's leave to quit the colonies! Ah! I am plain enough now, I see."

And Lord Lilburne threw himself back in his chair, and coldly contemplated the white face and dismayed expression of the crestfallen captain. That most worthy person, after a pause of confusion, amaze, and fear, made an involuntary stride, with a menacing gesture, towards Lilburne; the peer quietly placed his hand on the bell.

"One moment more," said the latter; "if I ring this bell, it is to place you in custody. Let Mr. Beaufort but see you here once again—nay, let him but hear another word of this pretended lawsuit—and you return to the colonies. Pshaw! Frown not at me, sir! A Bow Street officer is in the hall. Begone!—no, stop one moment, and take a lesson in life. Never again attempt to threaten people of property and station. Around every rich man is a wall—better not run your head against it."

"But I swear solemnly," cried the knave, with an emphasis so startling that it carried with it the appearance of truth, "that the marriage did take place."

"And I say, no less solemnly, that any one who swears it in a court of law shall be prosecuted for perjury! Bah! you are a sorry rogue, after all!"

And with an air of supreme and half-compassionate contempt, Lord Lilburne turned away and stirred the fire. Captain Smith muttered and fumbled a moment with his gloves, then shrugged his shoulders and sneaked out.

That night Lord Lilburne again received his friends, and amongst his guests came Vaudemont. Lilburne was one who liked the study of character, especially the character of men wrestling against the world. Wholly free from every species of ambition, he seemed to reconcile himself to his apathy by examining into the disquietude, the mortification, the heart's wear and tear, which are the lot of the ambitious. Like the spider in his hole, he watched with hungry pleasure the flies struggling in the web; through whose slimy labyrinth he walked with an easy safety. Perhaps one reason why he loved gaming was less from the joy of winning than the philosophical complacency with which he feasted on the emotions of those who lost; always serene, and, except in debauch, always passionless,—Majendie, tracing the experiments of science in the agonies of some tortured dog, could not be more rapt in the science, and more indifferent to the dog, than Lord Lilburne, ruining a victim, in the analysis of human passions,—stoical in the writhings of the wretch whom he tranquilly dissected. He wished to win money of Vaudemont—to ruin this man, who presumed to be more generous than other people—to see a bold adventurer submitted to the wheel of the Fortune which reigns in a pack of cards;—and all, of course, without the least hate to the man whom he then saw for the first time. On the contrary, he felt a respect for Vaudemont. Like most worldly men, Lord Lilburne was prepossessed in favour of those who seek to rise in life: and like men who have excelled in manly and athletic exercises, he was also prepossessed in favour of those who appeared fitted for the same success.

Liancourt took aside his friend, as Lord Lilburne was talking with his other guests:—

"I need not caution you, who never play, not to commit yourself to Lord Lilburne's tender mercies; remember, he is an admirable player."

"Nay," answered Vaudemont, "I want to know this man: I have reasons, which alone induce me to enter his house. I can afford to venture something, because I wish to see if I can gain something for one dear to me. And for the rest (he muttered)—I know him too well not to be on my guard." With that he joined Lord Lilburne's group, and accepted the invitation to the card-table. At supper, Vaudemont conversed more than was habitual to him; he especially addressed himself to his host, and listened, with great attention, to Lilburne's caustic comments upon every topic successively started. And whether it was the art of De Vaudemont, or from an interest that Lord Lilburne took in studying what was to him a new character,—or whether that, both men excelling peculiarly in all masculine accomplishments, their conversation was of a nature that was more attractive to themselves than to others; it so happened that they were still talking while the daylight already peered through the window-curtains.

"And I have outstayed all your guests," said De Vaudemont, glancing round the emptied room.

"It is the best compliment you could pay me. Another night we can enliven our tete-a-tete with ecarte; though at your age, and with your appearance, I am surprised, Monsieur de Vaudemont, that you are fond of play: I should have thought that it was not in a pack of cards that you looked for hearts. But perhaps you are blase betimes of the beau sexe."

"Yet your lordship's devotion to it is, perhaps, as great now as ever?"

"Mine?—no, not as ever. To different ages different degrees. At your age I wooed; at mine I purchase—the better plan of the two: it does not take up half so much time."

"Your marriage, I think, Lord Lilburne, was not blessed with children. Perhaps sometimes you feel the want of them?"

"If I did, I could have them by the dozen. Other ladies have been more generous in that department than the late Lady Lilburne, Heaven rest her!"

"And," said Vaudemont, fixing his eyes with some earnestness on his host, "if you were really persuaded that you had a child, or perhaps a grandchild—the mother one whom you loved in your first youth—a child affectionate, beautiful, and especially needing your care and protection, would you not suffer that child, though illegitimate, to supply to you the want of filial affection?"

"Filial affection, mon cher!" repeated Lord Lilburne, "needing my care and protection! Pshaw! In other words, would I give board and lodging to some young vagabond who was good enough to say he was son to Lord Lilburne?"

"But if you were convinced that the claimant were your son, or perhaps your daughter—a tenderer name of the two, and a more helpless claimant?"

"My dear Monsieur de Vaudemont, you are doubtless a man of gallantry and of the world. If the children whom the law forces on one are, nine times out of ten, such damnable plagues, judge if one would father those whom the law permits us to disown! Natural children are the pariahs of the world, and I—am one of the Brahmans."

"But," persisted Vaudemont, "forgive me if I press the question farther. Perhaps I seek from your wisdom a guide to my own conduct;—suppose, then, a man had loved, had wronged, the mother;—suppose that in the child he saw one who, without his aid, might be exposed to every curse with which the pariahs (true, the pariahs!) of the world are too often visited, and who with his aid might become, as age advanced, his companion, his nurse, his comforter—"

"Tush!" interrupted Lilburne, with some impatience; "I know not how our conversation fell on such a topic—but if you really ask my opinion in reference to any case in practical life, you shall have it. Look you, then Monsieur de Vaudemont, no man has studied the art of happiness more than I have; and I will tell you the great secret—have as few ties as possible. Nurse!—pooh! you or I could hire one by the week a thousand times more useful and careful than a bore of a child. Comforter!—a man of mind never wants comfort. And there is no such thing as sorrow while we have health and money, and don't care a straw for anybody in the world. If you choose to love people, their health and circumstances, if either go wrong, can fret you: that opens many avenues to pain. Never live alone, but always feel alone. You think this unamiable: possibly. I am no hypocrite, and, for my part, I never affect to be anything but what I am—John Lilburne."

As the peer thus spoke, Vaudemont, leaning against the door, contemplated him with a strange mixture of interest and disgust. "And John Lilburne is thought a great man, and William Gawtrey was a great rogue. You don't conceal your heart?—no, I understand. Wealth and power have no need of hypocrisy: you are the man of vice—Gawtrey, the man of crime. You never sin against the law—he was a felon by his trade. And the felon saved from vice the child, and from want the grandchild (Your flesh and blood) whom you disown: which will Heaven consider the worse man? No, poor Fanny, I see I am wrong. If he would own you, I would not give you up to the ice of such a soul:—better the blind man than the dead heart!"

"Well, Lord Lilburne," said De Vaudemont aloud, shaking off his reverie, "I must own that your philosophy seems to me the wisest for yourself. For a poor man it might be different—the poor need affection."

"Ay, the poor, certainly," said Lord Lilburne, with an air of patronising candour.

"And I will own farther," continued De Vaudemont, "that I have willingly lost my money in return for the instruction I have received in hearing you converse."

"You are kind: come and take your revenge next Thursday. Adieu."

As Lord Lilburne undressed, and his valet attended him, he said to that worthy functionary,—

"So you have not been able to make out the name of the stranger—the new lodger you tell me of?"

"No, my lord. They only say he is a very fine-looking man."

"You have not seen him?"

"No, my lord. What do you wish me now to do?"

"Humph! Nothing at this moment! You manage things so badly, you might get me into a scrape. I never do anything which the law or the police, or even the news papers, can get hold of. I must think of some other way—humph! I never give up what I once commence, and I never fail in what I undertake! If life had been worth what fools trouble it with—business and ambition—I suppose I should have been a great man with a very bad liver—ha ha! I alone, of all the world, ever found out what the world was good for! Draw the curtains, Dykeman."

CHAPTER VII

"Org. Welcome, thou ice that sitt'st about his heart
No heat can ever thaw thee!"—FORD: Broken Heart.

"Nearch. Honourable infamy!"—Ibid.

"Amye. Her tenderness hath yet deserved no rigour,
So to be crossed by fate!"

"Arm. You misapply, sir,
With favour let me speak it, what Apollo
Hath clouded in dim sense!"—Ibid.

If Vaudemont had fancied that, considering the age and poverty of Simon, it was his duty to see whether Fanny's not more legal, but more natural protector were, indeed, the unredeemed and unmalleable egotist which Gawtrey had painted him, the conversation of one night was sufficient to make him abandon for ever the notion of advancing her claims upon Lord Lilburne. But Philip had another motive in continuing his acquaintance with that personage. The sight of his mother's grave had recalled to him the image of that lost brother over whom he had vowed to watch. And, despite the deep sense of wronged affection with which he yet remembered the cruel letter that had contained the last tidings of Sidney, Philip's heart clung with undying fondness to that fair shape associated with all the happy recollections of childhood; and his conscience as well as his love asked him, each time that he passed the churchyard, "Will you make no effort to obey that last prayer of the mother who consigned her darling to your charge?" Perhaps, had Philip been in want, or had the name he now bore been sullied by his conduct, he might have shrunk from seeking one whom he might injure, but could not serve. But though not rich, he had more than enough for tastes as hardy and simple as any to which soldier of fortune ever limited his desires. And he thought, with a sentiment of just and noble pride, that the name which Eugenie had forced upon him had been borne spotless as the ermine through the trials and vicissitudes he had passed since he had assumed it. Sidney could give him nothing, and therefore it was his duty to seek Sidney out. Now, he had always believed in his heart that the Beauforts were acquainted with a secret which he more and more pined to penetrate. He would, for Sidney's sake, smother his hate to the Beauforts; he would not reject their acquaintance if thrown in his way; nay, secure in his change of name and his altered features, from all suspicion on their part, he would seek that acquaintance in order to find his brother and fulfil Catherine's last commands. His intercourse with Lilburne would necessarily bring him easily into contact with Lilburne's family. And in this thought he did not reject the invitations pressed on him. He felt, too, a dark and absorbing interest in examining a man who was in himself the incarnation of the World—the World of Art—the World as the Preacher paints it—the hollow, sensual, sharp-witted, self-wrapped WORLD—the World that is all for this life, and thinks of no Future and no God!

Lord Lilburne was, indeed, a study for deep contemplation. A study to perplex the ordinary thinker, and task to the utmost the analysis of more profound reflection. William Gawtrey had possessed no common talents; he had discovered that his life had been one mistake; Lord Lilburne's intellect was far keener than Gawtrey's, and he had never made, and if he had lived to the age of Old Parr, never would have made a similar discovery. He never wrestled against a law, though he slipped through all laws! And he knew no remorse, for he knew no fear. Lord Lilburne had married early, and long survived, a lady of fortune, the daughter of the then Premier—the best match, in fact, of his day. And for one very brief period of his life he had suffered himself to enter into the field of politics the only ambition common with men of equal rank. He showed talents that might have raised one so gifted by circumstance to any height, and then retired at once into his old habits and old system of pleasure. "I wished to try," said he once, "if fame was worth one headache, and I have convinced myself that the man who can sacrifice the bone in his mouth to the shadow of the bone in the water is a fool." From that time he never attended the House of Lords, and declared himself of no political opinions one way or the other. Nevertheless, the world had a general belief in his powers, and Vaudemont reluctantly subscribed to the world's verdict. Yet he had done nothing, he had read but little, he laughed at the world to its face,—and that last was, after all, the main secret of his ascendancy over those who were drawn into his circle. That contempt of the world placed the world at his feet. His sardonic and polished indifference, his professed code that there was no life worth caring for but his own life, his exemption from all cant, prejudice, and disguise, the frigid lubricity with which he glided out of the grasp of the Conventional, whenever it so pleased him, without shocking the Decorums whose sense is in their ear, and who are not roused by the deed but by the noise,—all this had in it the marrow and essence of a system triumphant with the vulgar; for little minds give importance to the man who gives importance to nothing. Lord Lilburne's authority, not in matters of taste alone, but in those which the world calls judgment and common sense, was regarded as an oracle. He cared not a straw for the ordinary baubles that attract his order; he had refused both an earldom and the garter, and this was often quoted in his honour. But you only try a man's virtue when you offer him something that he covets. The earldom and the garter were to Lord Lilburne no more tempting inducements than a doll or a skipping-rope; had you offered him an infallible cure for the gout, or an antidote against old age, you might have hired him as your lackey on your own terms. Lord Lilburne's next heir was the son of his only brother, a person entirely dependent on his uncle. Lord Lilburne allowed him £1000. a year and kept him always abroad in a diplomatic situation. He looked upon his successor as a man who wanted power, but not inclination, to become his assassin.

Though he lived sumptuously and grudged himself nothing, Lord Lilburne was far from an extravagant man; he might, indeed, be considered close; for he knew how much of comfort and consideration he owed to his money, and valued it accordingly; he knew the best speculations and the best investments. If he took shares in an American canal, you might be sure that the shares would soon be double in value; if he purchased an estate, you might be certain it was a bargain. This pecuniary tact and success necessarily augmented his fame for wisdom.

He had been in early life a successful gambler, and some suspicions of his fair play had been noised abroad; but, as has been recently seen in the instance of a man of rank equal to Lilburne's, though, perhaps, of less acute if more cultivated intellect, it is long before the pigeon will turn round upon a falcon of breed and mettle. The rumours, indeed, were so vague as to carry with them no weight. During the middle of his career, when in the full flush of health and fortune, he had renounced the gaming-table. Of late years, as advancing age made time more heavy, he had resumed the resource, and with all his former good luck. The money-market, the table, the sex, constituted the other occupations and amusements with which Lord Lilburne filled up his rosy leisure.

Another way by which this man had acquired reputation for ability was this,—he never pretended to any branch of knowledge of which he was ignorant, any more than to any virtue in which he was deficient. Honesty itself was never more free from quackery or deception than was this embodied and walking Vice. If the world chose to esteem him, he did not buy its opinion by imposture. No man ever saw Lord Lilburne's name in a public subscription, whether for a new church, or a Bible Society, or a distressed family, no man ever heard of his doing one generous, benevolent, or kindly action,—no man was ever startled by one philanthropic, pious, or amiable sentiment from those mocking lips. Yet, in spite of all this, John Lord Lilburne was not only esteemed but liked by the world, and set up in the chair of its Rhadamanthuses. In a word, he seemed to Vaudemont, and he was so in reality, a brilliant example of the might of Circumstance—an instance of what may be done in the way of reputation and influence by a rich, well-born man to whom the will a kingdom is. A little of genius, and Lord Lilburne would have made his vices notorious and his deficiencies glaring; a little of heart, and his habits would have led him into countless follies and discreditable scrapes. It was the lead and the stone that he carried about him that preserved his equilibrium, no matter which way the breeze blew. But all his qualities, positive or negative, would have availed him nothing without that position which enabled him to take his ease in that inn, the world—which presented, to every detection of his want of intrinsic nobleness, the irreproachable respectability of a high name, a splendid mansion, and a rent-roll without a flaw. Vaudemont drew comparisons between Lilburne and Gawtrey, and he comprehended at last, why one was a low rascal and the other a great man.

Although it was but a few days after their first introduction to each other, Vaudemont had been twice to Lord Lilburne's, and their acquaintance was already on an easy footing—when one afternoon as the former was riding through the streets towards H—, he met the peer mounted on a stout cob, which, from its symmetrical strength, pure English breed, and exquisite grooming, showed something of those sporting tastes for which, in earlier life, Lord Lilburne had been noted.

"Why, Monsieur de Vaudemont, what brings you to this part of the town?—curiosity and the desire to explore?"

"That might be natural enough in me; but you, who know London so well; rather what brings you here?"

"Why I am returned from a long ride. I have had symptoms of a fit of the gout, and been trying to keep it off by exercise. I have been to a cottage that belongs to me, some miles from the town—a pretty place enough, by the way—you must come and see me there next month. I shall fill the house for a battue! I have some tolerable covers—you are a good shot, I suppose?"

"I have not practised, except with a rifle, for some years."

"That's a pity; for as I think a week's shooting once a year quite enough, I fear that your visit to me at Fernside may not be sufficiently long to put your hand in."

"Fernside!"

"Yes; is the name familiar to you?"

"I think I have heard it before. Did your lordship purchase or inherit it?"

"I bought it of my brother-in-law. It belonged to his brother—a gay, wild sort of fellow, who broke his neck over a six-barred gate; through that gate my friend Robert walked the same day into a very fine estate!"

"I have heard so. The late Mr. Beaufort, then, left no children?"

"Yes; two. But they came into the world in the primitive way in which Mr. Owen wishes us all to come—too naturally for the present state of society, and Mr. Owen's parallelogram was not ready for them. By the way, one of them disappeared at Paris—you never met with him, I suppose?"

"Under what name?"

"Morton."

"Morton! hem! What Christian name?"

"Philip."

"Philip! no. But did Mr. Beaufort do nothing for the young men? I think I have heard somewhere that he took compassion on one of them."

"Have you? Ah, my brother-in-law is precisely one of those excellent men of whom the world always speaks well. No; he would very willingly have served either or both the boys, but the mother refused all his overtures and went to law, I fancy. The elder of these bastards turned out a sad fellow, and the younger,—I don't know exactly where he is, but no doubt with one of his mother's relations. You seem to interest yourself in natural children, my dear Vaudemont?"

"Perhaps you have heard that people have doubted if I were a natural son?"

"Ah! I understand now. But are you going?—I was in hopes you would have turned back my way, and—"

"You are very good; but I have a particular appointment, and I am now too late. Good morning, Lord Lilburne." Sidney with one of his mother's relations! Returned, perhaps, to the Mortons! How had he never before chanced on a conjecture so probable? He would go at once!—that very night he would go to the house from which he had taken his brother. At least, and at the worst, they might give him some clue.

Buoyed with this hope and this resolve, he rode hastily to H—, to announce to Simon and Fanny that he should not return to them, perhaps, for two or three days. As he entered the suburb, he drew up by the statuary of whom he had purchased his mother's gravestone.

The artist of the melancholy trade was at work in his yard.

"Ho! there!" said Vaudemont, looking over the low railing; "is the tomb I have ordered nearly finished?"

"Why, sir, as you were so anxious for despatch, and as it would take a long time to get a new one ready, I thought of giving you this, which is finished all but the inscription. It was meant for Miss Deborah Primme; but her nephew and heir called on me yesterday to say, that as the poor lady died worth less by £5,000. than he had expected, he thought a handsome wooden tomb would do as well, if I could get rid of this for him. It is a beauty, sir. It will look so cheerful—"

"Well, that will do: and you can place it now where I told you."

"In three days, sir."

"So be it." And he rode on, muttering, "Fanny, your pious wish will be fulfilled. But flowers,—will they suit that stone?"

He put up his horse, and walked through the lane to Simon's.

As he approached the house, he saw Fanny's bright eyes at the window. She was watching his return. She hastened to open the door to him, and the world's wanderer felt what music there is in the footstep, what summer there is in the smile, of Welcome!

"My dear Fanny," he said, affected by her joyous greeting, "it makes my heart warm to see you. I have brought you a present from town. When I was a boy, I remember that my poor mother was fond of singing some simple songs, which often, somehow or other, come back to me, when I see and hear you. I fancied you would understand and like them as well at least as I do—for Heaven knows (he added to himself) my ear is dull enough generally to the jingle of rhyme." And he placed in her hands a little volume of those exquisite songs, in which Burns has set Nature to music.

"Oh! you are so kind, brother," said Fanny, with tears swimming in her eyes, and she kissed the book.

After their simple meal, Vaudemont broke to Fanny and Simon the intelligence of his intended departure for a few days. Simon heard it with the silent apathy into which, except on rare occasions, his life had settled. But Fanny turned away her face and wept.

"It is but for a day or two, Fanny."

"An hour is very—very long sometimes," said the girl, shaking her head mournfully.

"Come, I have a little time yet left, and the air is mild, you have not been out to-day, shall we walk—"

"Hem!" interrupted Simon, clearing his throat, and seeming to start into sudden animation; "had not you better settle the board and lodging before you go?"

"Oh, grandfather!" cried Fanny, springing to her feet, with such a blush upon her face.

"Nay, child," said Vaudemont, laughingly; "your grandfather only anticipates me. But do not talk of board and lodging; Fanny is as a sister to me, and our purse is in common."

"I should like to feel a sovereign—just to feel it," muttered Simon, in a sort of apologetic tone, that was really pathetic; and as Vaudemont scattered some coins on the table, the old man clawed them up, chuckling and talking to himself; and, rising with great alacrity, hobbled out of the room like a raven carrying some cunning theft to its hiding-place.

This was so amusing to Vaudemont that he burst out fairly into an uncontrollable laughter. Fanny looked at him, humbled and wondering for some moments; and then, creeping to him, put her hand gently on his arm and said—

"Don't laugh—it pains me. It was not nice in grand papa; but—but, it does not mean anything. It—it—don't laugh—Fanny feels so sad!"

"Well, you are right. Come, put on your bonnet, we will go out."

Fanny obeyed; but with less ready delight than usual. And they took their way through lanes over which hung, still in the cool air, the leaves of the yellow autumn.

Fanny was the first to break silence.

"Do you know," she said, timidly, "that people here think me very silly?—do you think so too?"

Vaudemont was startled by the simplicity of the question, and hesitated. Fanny looked up in his dark face anxiously and inquiringly.

"Well," she said, "you don't answer?"

"My dear Fanny, there are some things in which I could wish you less childlike and, perhaps, less charming. Those strange snatches of song, for instance!"

"What! do you not like me to sing? It is my way of talking."

"Yes; sing, pretty one! But sing something that we can understand,—sing the songs I have given you, if you will. And now, may I ask why you put to me that question?"

"I have forgotten," said Fanny, absently, and looking down.

Now, at that instant, as Philip Vaudemont bent over the exceeding sweetness of that young face, a sudden thrill shot through his heart, and he, too, became silent, and lost in thought. Was it possible that there could creep into his breast a wilder affection for this creature than that of tenderness and pity? He was startled as the idea crossed him. He shrank from it as a profanation—as a crime—as a frenzy. He with his fate so uncertain and chequered—he to link himself with one so helpless—he to debase the very poetry that clung to the mental temperament of this pure being, with the feelings which every fair face may awaken to every coarse heart—to love Fanny! No, it was impossible! For what could he love in her but beauty, which the very spirit had forgotten to guard? And she—could she even know what love was? He despised himself for even admitting such a thought; and with that iron and hardy vigour which belonged to his mind, resolved to watch closely against every fancy that would pass the fairy boundary which separated Fanny from the world of women.

He was roused from this self-commune by an abrupt exclamation from his companion.

"Oh! I recollect now why I asked you that question. There is one thing that always puzzles me—I want you to explain it. Why does everything in life depend upon money? You see even my poor grandfather forgot how good you are to us both, when—when Ah! I don't understand—it pains—it puzzles me!"

"Fanny, look there—no, to the left—you see that old woman, in rags, crawling wearily along; turn now to the right—you see that fine house glancing through the trees, with a carriage and four at the gates? The difference between that old woman and the owner of that house is—Money; and who shall blame your grandfather for liking Money?"

Fanny understood; and while the wise man thus moralised, the girl, whom his very compassion so haughtily contemned, moved away to the old woman to do her little best to smooth down those disparities from which wisdom and moralising never deduct a grain! Vaudemont felt this as he saw her glide towards the beggar; but when she came bounding back to him, she had forgotten his dislike to her songs, and was chaunting, in the glee of the heart that a kind act had made glad, one of her own impromptu melodies.

Vaudemont turned away. Poor Fanny had unconsciously decided his self-conquest; she guessed not what passed within him, but she suddenly recollected—what he had said to her about her songs, and fancied him displeased.

"Ah I will never do it again. Brother, don't turn away!"

"But we must go home. Hark! the clock strikes seven—I have no time to lose. And you will promise me never to stir out till I return?"

"I shall have no heart to stir out," said Fanny, sadly; and then in a more cheerful voice, she added, "And I shall sing the songs you like before you come back again!"

CHAPTER VIII

"Well did they know that service all by rote;

Some singing loud as if they had complained,
Some with their notes another manner feigned."
CHAUCER: Pie Cuckoo and the Nightingale,
modernised by WORDSWORTH.—HORNE's Edition.

And once more, sweet Winandermere, we are on the banks of thy happy lake! The softest ray of the soft clear sun of early autumn trembled on the fresh waters, and glanced through the leaves of the limes and willows that were reflected—distinct as a home for the Naiads—beneath the limpid surface. You might hear in the bushes the young blackbirds trilling their first untutored notes. And the graceful dragon-fly, his wings glittering in the translucent sunshine, darted to and fro—the reeds gathered here and there in the mimic bays that broke the shelving marge of the grassy shore.

And by that grassy shore, and beneath those shadowy limes, sat the young lovers. It was the very place where Spencer had first beheld Camilla. And now they were met to say, "Farewell!"

"Oh, Camilla!" said he, with great emotion, and eyes that swam in tears, "be firm—be true. You know how my whole life is wrapped up in your love. You go amidst scenes where all will tempt you to forget me. I linger behind in those which are consecrated by your remembrance, which will speak to me every hour of you. Camilla, since you do love me—you do—do you not?—since you have confessed it—since your parents have consented to our marriage, provided only that your love last (for of mine there can be no doubt) for one year—one terrible year—shall I not trust you as truth itself? And yet how darkly I despair at times!"

Camilla innocently took the hands that, clasped together, were raised to her, as if in supplication, and pressed them kindly between her own.

"Do not doubt me—never doubt my affection. Has not my father consented? Reflect, it is but a year's delay!"

"A year!—can you speak thus of a year—a whole year? Not to see—not to hear you for a whole year, except in my dreams! And, if at the end your parents waver? Your father—I distrust him still. If this delay is but meant to wean you from me,—if, at the end, there are new excuses found,—if they then, for some cause or other not now foreseen, still refuse their assent? You—may I not still look to you?"

Camilla sighed heavily; and turning her meek face on her lover, said, timidly, "Never think that so short a time can make me unfaithful, and do not suspect that my father will break his promise."

"But, if he does, you will still be mine."

"Ah, Charles, how could you esteem me as a wife if I were to tell you I could forget I am a daughter?"

This was said so touchingly, and with so perfect a freedom from all affectation, that her lover could only reply by covering her hand with his kisses. And it was not till after a pause that he continued passionately,—

"You do but show me how much deeper is my love than yours. You can never dream how I love you. But I do not ask you to love me as well—it would be impossible. My life from my earliest childhood has been passed in these solitudes;—a happy life, though tranquil and monotonous, till you suddenly broke upon it. You seemed to me the living form of the very poetry I had worshipped—so bright—so heavenly—I loved you from the very first moment that we met. I am not like other men of my age. I have no pursuit—no occupation—nothing to abstract me from your thought. And I love you so purely—so devotedly, Camilla. I have never known even a passing fancy for another. You are the first—the only woman—it ever seemed to me possible to love. You are my Eve—your presence my paradise! Think how sad I shall be when you are gone—how I shall visit every spot your footstep has hallowed—how I shall count every moment till the year is past!"

While he thus spoke, he had risen in that restless agitation which belongs to great emotion; and Camilla now rose also, and said soothingly, as she laid her hand on his shoulder with tender but modest frankness:

"And shall I not also think of you? I am sad to feel that you will be so much alone—no sister—no brother!"

"Do not grieve for that. The memory of you will be dearer to me than comfort from all else. And you will be true!"

Camilla made no answer by words, but her eyes and her colour spoke. And in that moment, while plighting eternal truth, they forgot that they were about to part!

Meanwhile, in a room in the house which, screened by the foliage, was only partially visible where the lovers stood, sat Mr. Robert Beaufort and Mr. Spencer.

"I assure you, sir," said the former, "that I am not insensible to the merits of your nephew and to the very handsome proposals you make, still I cannot consent to abridge the time I have named. They are both very young. What is a year?"

"It is a long time when it is a year of suspense," said the recluse, shaking his head.

"It is a longer time when it is a year of domestic dissension and repentance. And it is a very true proverb, 'Marry in haste and repent at leisure.' No! If at the end of the year the young people continue of the same mind, and no unforeseen circumstances occur—"

"No unforeseen circumstances, Mr. Beaufort!—that is a new condition—it is a very vague phrase."

"My dear sir, it is hard to please you. Unforeseen circumstances," said the wary father, with a wise look, "mean circumstances that we don't foresee at present. I assure you that I have no intention to trifle with you, and I shall be sincerely happy in so respectable a connexion."

"The young people may write to each other?"

"Why, I'll consult Mrs. Beaufort. At all events, it must not be very often, and Camilla is well brought up, and will show all the letters to her mother. I don't much like a correspondence of that nature. It often leads to unpleasant results; if, for instance—"

"If what?"

"Why, if the parties change their minds, and my girl were to marry another. It is not prudent in matters of business, my dear sir, to put down anything on paper that can be avoided."

Mr. Spencer opened his eyes. "Matters of business, Mr. Beaufort!"

"Well, is not marriage a matter of business, and a very grave matter too? More lawsuits about marriage and settlements, &c., than I like to think of. But to change the subject. You have never heard anything more of those young men, you say?"

"No," said Mr. Spencer, rather inaudibly, and looking down.

"And it is your firm impression that the elder one, Philip, is dead?"

"I don't doubt it."

"That was a very vexatious and improper lawsuit their mother brought against me. Do you know that some wretched impostor, who, it appears, is a convict broke loose before his time, has threatened me with another, on the part of one of those young men? You never heard anything of it—eh?"

"Never, upon my honour."

"And, of course, you would not countenance so villanous an attempt?"

"Certainly not."

"Because that would break off our contract at once. But you are too much a gentleman and a man of honour. Forgive me so improper a question. As for the younger Mr. Morton, I have no ill-feeling against him. But the elder! Oh, a thorough reprobate! a very alarming character! I could have nothing to do with any member of the family while the elder lived; it would only expose me to every species of insult and imposition. And now I think we have left our young friends alone long enough.

"But stay, to prevent future misunderstanding, I may as well read over again the heads of the arrangement you honour me by proposing. You agree to settle your fortune after your decease, amounting to £23,000. and your house, with twenty-five acres one rood and two poles, more or less, upon your nephew and my daughter, jointly—remainder to their children. Certainly, without offence, in a worldly point of view, Camilla might do better; still, you are so very respectable, and you speak so handsomely, that I cannot touch upon that point; and I own, that though there is a large nominal rent-roll attached to Beaufort Court (indeed, there is not a finer property in the county), yet there are many incumbrances, and ready money would not be convenient to me. Arthur—poor fellow, a very fine young man, sir,—is, as I have told you in perfect confidence, a little imprudent and lavish; in short, your offer to dispense with any dowry is extremely liberal, and proves your nephew is actuated by no mercenary feelings: such conduct prepossesses me highly in your favour and his too."

Mr. Spencer bowed, and the great man rising, with a stiff affectation of kindly affability, put his arm into the uncle's, and strolled with him across the lawn towards the lovers. And such is life—love on the lawn and settlements in the parlour.

The lover was the first to perceive the approach of the elder parties. And a change came over his face as he saw the dry aspect and marked the stealthy stride of his future father-in-law; for then there flashed across him a dreary reminiscence of early childhood; the happy evening when, with his joyous father, that grave and ominous aspect was first beheld; and then the dismal burial, the funereal sables, the carriage at the door, and he himself clinging to the cold uncle to ask him to say a word of comfort to the mother, who now slept far away. "Well, my young friend," said Mr. Beaufort, patronisingly, "your good uncle and myself are quite agreed—a little time for reflection, that's all. Oh! I don't think the worse of you for wishing to abridge it. But papas must be papas."

There was so little jocular about that sedate man, that this attempt at jovial good humour seemed harsh and grating—the hinges of that wily mouth wanted oil for a hearty smile.

"Come, don't be faint-hearted, Mr. Charles. 'Faint heart,'—you know the proverb. You must stay and dine with us. We return to-morrow to town. I should tell you, that I received this morning a letter from my son Arthur, announcing his return from Baden, so we must give him the meeting—a very joyful one you may guess. We have not seen him these three years. Poor fellow! he says he has been very ill and the waters have ceased to do him any good. But a little quiet and country air at Beaufort Court will set him up, I hope."

Thus running on about his son, then about his shooting—about Beaufort Court and its splendours—about parliament and its fatigues—about the last French Revolution, and the last English election—about Mrs. Beaufort and her good qualities and bad health—about, in short, everything relating to himself, some things relating to the public, and nothing that related to the persons to whom his conversation was directed, Mr. Robert Beaufort wore away half an hour, when the Spencer's took their leave, promising to return to dinner.

"Charles," said Mr. Spencer, as the boat, which the young man rowed, bounded over the water towards their quiet home; "Charles, I dislike these Beauforts!"

"Not the daughter?"

"No, she is beautiful, and seems good; not so handsome as your poor mother, but who ever was?"—here Mr. Spencer sighed, and repeated some lines from Shenstone.

"Do you think Mr. Beaufort suspects in the least who I am?"

"Why, that puzzles me; I rather think he does."

"And that is the cause of the delay? I knew it."

"No, on the contrary, I incline to think he has some kindly feeling to you, though not to your brother, and that it is such a feeling that made him consent to your marriage. He sifted me very closely as to what I knew of the young Mortons—observed that you were very handsome, and that he had fancied at first that he had seen you before."

"Indeed!"

"Yes: and looked hard at me while he spoke; and said more than once, significantly, 'So his name is Charles?' He talked about some attempt at imposture and litigation, but that was, evidently, merely invented to sound me about your brother—whom, of course, he spoke ill of—impressing on me three or four times that he would never have anything to say to any of the family while Philip lived."

"And you told him," said the young man, hesitatingly, and with a deep blush of shame over his face, "that you were persuaded—that is, that you believed Philip was—was—"

"Was dead! Yes—and without confusion. For the more I reflect, the more I think he must be dead. At all events, you may be sure that he is dead to us, that we shall never hear more of him."

"Poor Philip!"

"Your feelings are natural; they are worthy of your excellent heart; but remember, what would have become of you if you had stayed with him!"

"True!" said the brother, with a slight shudder—"a career of suffering—crime—perhaps the gibbet! Ah! what do I owe you?"

The dinner-party at Mr. Beaufort's that day was constrained and formal, though the host, in unusual good humour, sought to make himself agreeable. Mrs. Beaufort, languid and afflicted with headache, said little. The two Spencers were yet more silent. But the younger sat next to her he loved; and both hearts were full: and in the evening they contrived to creep apart into a corner by the window, through which the starry heavens looked kindly on them. They conversed in whispers, with long pauses between each: and at times Camilla's tears flowed silently down her cheeks, and were followed by the false smiles intended to cheer her lover.

Time did not fly, but crept on breathlessly and heavily. And then came the last parting—formal, cold—before witnesses. But the lover could not restrain his emotion, and the hard father heard his suppressed sob as he closed the door.

It will now be well to explain the cause of Mr. Beaufort's heightened spirits, and the motives of his conduct with respect to his daughter's suitor.

This, perhaps, can be best done by laying before the reader the following letters that passed between Mr. Beaufort and Lord Lilburne.

From LORD LILBURNE to ROBERT BEAUFORT, ESQ., M.P.

"DEAR BEAUFORT,—I think I have settled, pretty satisfactorily, your affair with your unwelcome visitor. The first thing it seemed to me necessary to do, was to learn exactly what and who he was, and with what parties that could annoy you he held intercourse. I sent for Sharp, the Bow Street officer, and placed him in the hall to mark, and afterwards to dog and keep watch on your new friend. The moment the latter entered I saw at once, from his dress and his address, that he was a 'scamp;' and thought it highly inexpedient to place you in his power by any money transactions. While talking with him, Sharp sent in a billet containing his recognition of our gentleman as a transported convict.

"I acted accordingly; soon saw, from the fellow's manner, that he had returned before his time; and sent him away with a promise, which you may be sure he believes will be kept, that if he molest you farther, he shall return to the colonies, and that if his lawsuit proceed, his witness or witnesses shall be indicted for conspiracy and perjury. Make your mind easy so far. For the rest, I own to you that I think what he says probable enough: but my object in setting Sharp to watch him is to learn what other parties he sees. And if there be really anything formidable in his proofs or witnesses, it is with those other parties I advise you to deal. Never transact business with the go between, if you can with the principal. Remember, the two young men are the persons to arrange with after all. They must be poor, and therefore easily dealt with. For, if poor, they will think a bird in the hand worth two in the bush of a lawsuit.

"If, through Mr. Spencer, you can learn anything of either of the young men, do so; and try and open some channel, through which you can always establish a communication with them, if necessary. Perhaps, by learning their early history, you may learn something to put them into your power.

"I have had a twinge of the gout this morning, and am likely, I fear, to be laid up for some weeks.

"Yours truly,

"LILBURNE.

"P.S.—Sharp has just been here. He followed the man who calls himself 'Captain Smith' to a house in Lambeth, where he lodges, and from which he did not stir till midnight, when Sharp ceased his watch. On renewing it this morning, he found that the captain had gone off, to what place Sharp has not yet discovered.

"Burn this immediately."

From ROBERT BEAUFORT, ESQ., M.P., to the LORD LILBURNE.

"DEAR, LILBURNE,—Accept my warmest thanks for your kindness; you have done admirably, and I do not see that I have anything further to apprehend. I suspect that it was an entire fabrication on that man's part, and your firmness has foiled his wicked designs. Only think, I have discovered—I am sure of it—one of the Mortons; and he, too, though the younger, yet, in all probability, the sole pretender the fellow could set up. You remember that the child Sidney had disappeared mysteriously,—you remember also, how much that Mr. Spencer had interested himself in finding out the same Sidney. Well,—this gentleman at the Lakes is, as we suspected, the identical Mr. Spencer, and his soi-disant nephew, Camilla's suitor, is assuredly no other than the lost Sidney. The moment I saw the young man I recognised him, for he is very little altered, and has a great look of his mother into the bargain. Concealing my more than suspicions, I, however, took care to sound Mr. Spencer (a very poor soul), and his manner was so embarrassed as to leave no doubt of the matter; but in asking him what he had heard of the brothers, I had the satisfaction of learning that, in all human probability, the elder is dead: of this

Mr. Spencer seems convinced. I also assured myself that neither Spencer nor the young man had the remotest connection with our Captain Smith, nor any idea of litigation. This is very satisfactory, you will allow. And now, I hope you will approve of what I have done. I find that young Morton, or Spencer, as he is called, is desperately enamoured of Camilla; he seems a meek, well-conditioned, amiable young man; writes poetry;—in short, rather weak than otherwise. I have demanded a year's delay, to allow mutual trial and reflection. This gives us the channel for constant information which you advise me to establish, and I shall have the opportunity to learn if the impostor makes any communication to them, or if there be any news of the brother. If by any trick or chicanery (for I will never believe that there was a marriage) a lawsuit that might be critical or hazardous can be cooked up, I can, I am sure, make such terms with Sidney, through his love for my daughter, as would effectively and permanently secure me from all further trouble and machinations in regard to my property. And if, during the year, we convince ourselves that, after all, there is not a leg of law for any claimant to stand on, I may be guided by other circumstances how far I shall finally accept or reject the suit. That must depend on any other views we may then form for Camilla; and I shall not allow a hint of such an engagement to get abroad. At the worst, as Mr. Spencer's heir, it is not so very bad a match, seeing that they dispense with all marriage portion, &c.—a proof how easily they can be managed. I have not let Mr. Spencer see that I have discovered his secret—I can do that or not, according to circumstances hereafter; neither have I said anything of my discovery to Mrs. B., or Camilla. At present, 'Least said soonest mended.' I heard from Arthur to-day. He is on his road home, and we hasten to town, sooner than we expected, to meet him. He complains still of his health. We shall all go down to Beaufort Court. I write this at night, the pretended uncle and sham nephew having just gone. But though we start to-morrow, you will get this a day or two before we arrive, as Mrs. Beaufort's health renders short stages necessary. I really do hope that Arthur, also, will not be an invalid, poor fellow! one in a family is quite enough; and I find Mrs. Beaufort's delicacy very inconvenient, especially in moving about and in keeping up one's county connexions. A young man's health, however, is soon restored. I am very sorry to hear of your gout, except that it carries off all other complaints. I am very well, thank Heaven; indeed, my health has been much better of late years: Beaufort Court agrees with me so well! The more I reflect, the more I am astonished at the monstrous and wicked impudence of that fellow—to defraud a man out of his own property! You are quite right,—certainly a conspiracy.

"Yours truly, "R. B."

"P. S.—I shall keep a constant eye on the Spencers.

"Burn this immediately."

After he had written and sealed this letter, Mr. Beaufort went to bed and slept soundly.

And the next day that place was desolate, and the board on the lawn announced that it was again to be let. But thither daily, in rain or sunshine, came the solitary lover, as a bird that seeks its young in the deserted nest:—Again and again he haunted the spot where he had strayed with the lost one,—and again and again murmured his passionate vows beneath the fast-fading limes. Are those vows destined to be ratified or annulled? Will the absent forget, or the lingerer be consoled? Had the characters of that young romance been lightly stamped on the fancy where once obliterated they are erased for ever,—or were they graven deep in those tablets where the writing, even when invisible, exists still, and revives, sweet letter by letter, when the light and the warmth borrowed from the One Bright Presence are applied to the faithful record? There is but one Wizard to disclose that secret, as all others,—the old Grave-digger, whose Churchyard is the Earth,—whose trade is to find burial-places for Passions that seemed immortal,—disinterring the ashes of some long-crumbling Memory—to hollow out the dark bed of some new-perished Hope:—He who determines all things, and prophesies none,—for his oracles are uncomprehended till the doom is sealed—He who in the bloom of the fairest affection detects the hectic that consumes it, and while the hymn rings at the altar, marks with his joyless eye the grave for the bridal vow.—Wherever is the sepulchre, there is thy temple, O melancholy Time!

BOOK V

CHAPTER I

"Per ambages et ministeria deorum."—PETRONTUS.

[Through the mysteries and ministerings of the gods.]

Mr. Roger Morton was behind his counter one drizzling, melancholy day. Mr. Roger Morton, alderman, and twice mayor of his native town, was a thriving man. He had grown portly and corpulent. The nightly potations of brandy and water, continued year after year with mechanical perseverance, had deepened the roses on his cheek. Mr. Roger Morton was never intoxicated—he "only made himself comfortable." His constitution was strong; but, somehow or other, his digestion was not as good as it might be. He was certain that something or other disagreed with him. He left off the joint one day—the pudding another. Now he avoided vegetables as poison—and now he submitted with a sigh to the doctor's interdict of his cigar. Mr. Roger Morton never thought of leaving off the brandy and water: and he would have resented as the height of impertinent insinuation any hint upon that score to a man of so sober and respectable a character.

Mr. Roger Morton was seated—for the last four years, ever since his second mayoralty, he had arrogated to himself the dignity of a chair. He received rather than served his customers. The latter task was left to two of his sons. For Tom, after much cogitation, the profession of an apothecary had been selected. Mrs. Morton observed, that it was a genteel business, and Tom had always been a likely lad. And Mr. Roger considered that it would be a great comfort and a great saving to have his medical adviser in his own son.

The other two sons and the various attendants of the shop were plying the profitable trade, as customer after customer, with umbrellas and in pattens, dropped into the tempting shelter—when a man, meanly dressed, and who was somewhat past middle age, with a careworn, hungry face, entered timidly. He waited in patience by the crowded counter, elbowed by sharp-boned and eager spinsters—and how sharp the elbows of spinsters are, no man can tell who has not forced his unwelcome way through the agitated groups in a linendraper's shop!—the man, I say, waited patiently and sadly, till the smallest of the shopboys turned from a lady, who, after much sorting and shading, had finally decided on two yards of lilac-coloured penny riband, and asked, in an insinuating professional tone,—

"What shall I show you, sir?"

"I wish to speak to Mr. Morton. Which is he?"

"Mr. Morton is engaged, sir. I can give you what you want."

"No—it is a matter of business—important business." The boy eyed the napless and dripping hat, the gloveless hands, and the rusty neckcloth of the speaker; and said, as he passed his fingers through a profusion of light curls "Mr. Morton don't attend much to business himself now; but that's he. Any cravats, sir?"

The man made no answer, but moved where, near the window, and chatting with the banker of the town (as the banker tried on a pair of beaver gloves), sat still—after due apology for sitting—Mr. Roger Morton.

The alderman lowered his spectacles as he glanced grimly at the lean apparition that shaded the spruce banker, and said,—

"Do you want me, friend?"

"Yes, sir, if you please;" and the man took off his shabby hat, and bowed low.

"Well, speak out. No begging petition, I hope?"

"No, sir! Your nephews—"

The banker turned round, and in his turn eyed the newcomer. The linendraper started back.

"Nephews!" he repeated, with a bewildered look. "What does the man mean? Wait a bit."

"Oh, I've done!" said the banker, smiling. "I am glad to find we agree so well upon this question: I knew we should. Our member will never suit us if he goes on in this way. Trade must take care of itself. Good day to You!"

"Nephews!" repeated Mr. Morton, rising, and beckoning to the man to follow him into the back parlour, where Mrs. Morton sat casting up the washing bills.

"Now," said the husband, closing the door, "what do you mean, my good fellow?"

"Sir, what I wish to ask you is—if you can tell me what has become of—of the young Beau—, that is, of your sister's sons. I understand there were two—and I am told that—that they are both dead. Is it so?"

"What is that to you, friend?"

"An please you, sir, it is a great deal to them!"

"Yes—ha! ha! it is a great deal to everybody whether they are alive or dead!" Mr. Morton, since he had been mayor, now and then had his joke. "But really—"

"Roger!" said Mrs. Morton, under her breath—"Roger!"

"Yes, my dear."

"Come this way—I want to speak to you about this bill." The husband approached, and bent over his wife. "Who's this man?"

"I don't know."

"Depend on it, he has some claim to make—some bills or something. Don't commit yourself—the boys are dead for what we know!"

Mr. Morton hemmed and returned to his visitor.

"To tell you the truth, I am not aware of what has become of the young men."

"Then they are not dead—I thought not!" exclaimed the man, joyously.

"That's more than I can say. It's many years since I lost sight of the only one I ever saw; and they may be both dead for what I know."

"Indeed!" said the man. "Then you can give me no kind of—of—hint like, to find them out?"

"No. Do they owe you anything?"

"It does not signify talking now, sir. I beg your pardon."

"Stay—who are you?"

"I am a very poor man, sir."

Mr. Morton recoiled.

"Poor! Oh, very well—very well. You have done with me now. Good day—good day. I'm busy."

The stranger pecked for a moment at his hat—turned the handle of the door—peered under his grey eyebrows at the portly trader, who, with both hands buried in his pockets, his mouth pursed up, like a man about to say "No" fidgeted uneasily behind Mrs. Morton's chair. He sighed, shook his head, and vanished.

Mrs. Morton rang the bell—the maid-servant entered. "Wipe the carpet, Jenny;—dirty feet! Mr. Morton, it's a Brussels!"

"It was not my fault, my dear. I could not talk about family matters before the whole shop. Do you know, I'd quite forgot those poor boys. This unsettles me. Poor Catherine! she was so fond of them. A pretty boy that Sidney, too. What can have become of them? My heart rebukes me. I wish I had asked the man more."

"More!—why he was just going to beg."

"Beg—yes—very true!" said Mr. Morton, pausing irresolutely; and then, with a hearty tone, he cried out, "And, damme, if he had begged, I could afford him a shilling! I'll go after him." So saying, he hastened back through the shop, but the man was gone—the rain was falling, Mr. Morton had his thin shoes on—he blew his nose, and went back to the counter. But, there, still rose to his memory the pale face of his dead sister; and a voice murmured in his ear, "Brother, where is my child?"

"Pshaw! it is not my fault if he ran away. Bob, go and get me the county paper."

Mr. Morton had again settled himself, and was deep in a trial for murder, when another stranger strode haughtily into the shop. The new-comer, wrapped in a pelisse of furs, with a thick moustache, and an eye that took in the whole shop, from master to boy, from ceiling to floor, in a glance, had the air at once of a foreigner and a soldier. Every look fastened on him, as he paused an instant, and then walking up to the alderman, said,—

"Sir, you are doubtless Mr. Morton?"

"At your commands, sir," said Roger, rising involuntarily.

"A word with you, then, on business."

"Business!" echoed Mr. Morton, turning rather pale, for he began to think himself haunted; "anything in my line, sir? I should be—"

The stranger bent down his tall stature, and hissed into Mr. Morton's foreboding ear:

"Your nephews!"

Mr. Morton was literally dumb-stricken. Yes, he certainly was haunted! He stared at this second questioner, and fancied that there was something very supernatural and unearthly about him. He was so tall, and so dark, and so stern, and so strange. Was it the Unspeakable himself come for the linendraper? Nephews again! The uncle of the babes in the wood could hardly have been more startled by the demand!

"Sir," said Mr. Morton at last, recovering his dignity and somewhat peevishly,—"sir, I don't know why people should meddle with my family affairs. I don't ask other folks about their nephews. I have no nephew that I know of."

"Permit me to speak to you, alone, for one instant." Mr. Morton sighed, hitched up his trousers, and led the way to the parlour, where Mrs. Morton, having finished the washing bills, was now engaged in tying certain pieces of bladder round certain pots of preserves. The eldest Miss Morton, a young woman of five or six-and-twenty, who was about to be very advantageously married to a young gentleman who dealt in coals and played the violin (for N— was a very musical town), had just joined her for the purpose of extorting "The Swiss Boy, with variations," out of a sleepy little piano, that emitted a very painful cry under the awakening fingers of Miss Margaret Morton.

Mr. Morton threw open the door with a grunt, and the stranger pausing at the threshold, the full flood of sound (key C) upon which "the Swiss Boy" was swimming along, "kine" and all, for life and death, came splash upon him.

"Silence! can't you?" cried the father, putting one hand to his ear, while with the other he pointed to a chair; and as Mrs. Morton looked up from the preserves with that air of indignant suffering with which female meekness upbraids a husband's wanton outrage, Mr. Roger added, shrugging his shoulders,—

"My nephews again, Mrs. K!"

Miss Margaret turned round, and dropped a courtesy. Mrs. Morton gently let fall a napkin over the preserves, and muttered a sort of salutation, as the stranger, taking off his hat, turned to mother and daughter one of those noble faces in which Nature has written her grant and warranty of the lordship of creation.

"Pardon me," he said, "if I disturb you. But my business will be short. I have come to ask you, sir, frankly, and as one who has a right to ask it, what tidings you can give me of Sidney Morton?"

"Sir, I know nothing whatever about him. He was taken from my house, about twelve years since, by his brother. Myself, and the two Mr. Beauforts, and another friend of the family, went in search of them both. My search failed."

"And theirs?"

"I understood from Mr. Beaufort that they had not been more successful. I have had no communication with those gentlemen since. But that's neither here nor there. In all probability, the elder of the boys—who, I fear, was a sad character—corrupted and ruined his brother; and, by this time, Heaven knows what and where they are."

"And no one has inquired of you since—no one has asked the brother of Catherine Morton, nay, rather of Catherine Beaufort—where is the child intrusted to your care?"

This question, so exactly similar to that which his superstition had rung on his own ears, perfectly appalled the worthy alderman. He staggered back-stared at the marked and stern face that lowered upon him—and at last cried,—

"For pity's sake, sir, be just! What could I do for one who left me of his own accord?—"

"The day you had beaten him like a dog. You see, Mr. Morton, I know all."

"And what are you?" said Mr. Morton, recovering his English courage, and feeling himself strangely browbeaten in his own house;—"What and who are you, that you thus take the liberty to catechise a man of my character and respectability?"

"Twice mayor—" began Mrs. Morton.

"Hush, mother!" whispered Miss Margaret,—"don't work him up."

"I repeat, sir, what are you?"

"What am I?—your nephew! Who am I? Before men, I bear a name that I have assumed, and not dishonoured—before Heaven I am Philip Beaufort!"

Mrs. Morton dropped down upon her stool. Margaret murmured "My cousin!" in a tone that the ear of the musical coal-merchant might not have greatly relished. And Mr. Morton, after a long pause, came up with a frank and manly expression of joy, and said:—

"Then, sir, I thank Heaven, from my heart, that one of my sister's children stands alive before me!"

"And now, again, I—I whom you accuse of having corrupted and ruined him—him for whom I toiled and worked—him, who was to me, then, as a last surviving son to some anxious father—I, from whom he was reft and robbed—I ask you again for Sidney—for my brother!"

"And again, I say, that I have no information to give you—that—Stay a moment—stay. You must pardon what I have said of you before you made yourself known. I went but by the accounts I had received from Mr. Beaufort. Let me speak plainly; that gentleman thought, right or wrong, that it would be a great thing to separate your brother from you. He may have found him—it must be so—and kept his name and condition concealed from us all, lest you should detect it. Mrs. M., don't you think so?"

"I'm sure I'm so terrified I don't know what to think," said Mrs. Morton, putting her hand to her forehead, and see-sawing herself to and fro upon her stool.

"But since they wronged you—since you—you seem so very—very—"

"Very much the gentleman," suggested Miss Margaret. "Yes, so much the gentleman;—well off, too, I should hope, sir,"—and the experienced eye of Mr. Morton glanced at the costly sables that lined the pelisse,—"there can be no difficulty in your learning from Mr. Beaufort all that you wish to know. And pray, sir, may I ask, did you send any one here to-day to make the very inquiry you have made?"

"I?—No. What do you mean?"

"Well, well—sit down—there may be something in all this that you may make out better than I can."

And as Philip obeyed, Mr. Morton, who was really and honestly rejoiced to see his sister's son alive and apparently thriving, proceeded to relate pretty exactly the conversation he had held with the previous visitor. Philip listened earnestly and with attention. Who could this questioner be? Some one who knew his birth—some one who sought him out?—some one, who—Good Heavens! could it be the long-lost witness of the marriage?

As soon as that idea struck him, he started from his seat and entreated Morton to accompany him in search of the stranger. "You know not," he said, in a tone impressed with that energy of will in which lay the talent of his mind,—"you know not of what importance this may be to my prospects—to your sister's fair name. If it should be the witness returned at last! Who else, of the rank you describe, would be interested in such inquiries? Come!"

"What witness?" said Mrs. Morton, fretfully. "You don't mean to come over us with the old story of the marriage?"

"Shall your wife slander your own sister, sir? A marriage there was—God yet will proclaim the right—and the name of Beaufort shall be yet placed on my mother's gravestone. Come!"

"Here are your shoes and umbrella, pa," cried Miss Margaret, inspired by Philip's earnestness.

"My fair cousin, I guess," and as the soldier took her hand, he kissed the unreluctant cheek—turned to the door—Mr. Morton placed his arm in his, and the next moment they were in the street.

When Catherine, in her meek tones, had said, "Philip Beaufort was my husband," Roger Morton had disbelieved her. And now one word from the son, who could, in comparison, know so little of the matter, had almost sufficed to convert and to convince the sceptic. Why was this? Because—Man believes the Strong!

CHAPTER II

"—Quid Virtus et quid Sapientia possit
Utile proposuit nobis exemplar Ulssem." HOR.

["He has proposed to us Ulysses as a useful example of how much may be accomplished by Virtue and Wisdom."]

Meanwhile the object of their search, on quitting Mr. Morton's shop, had walked slowly and sadly on, through the plashing streets, till he came to a public house in the outskirts and on the high road to London. Here he took shelter for a short time, drying himself by the kitchen fire, with the license purchased by fourpenny-worth of gin; and having learned that the next coach to London would not pass for some hours, he finally settled himself in the Ingle, till the guard's horn should arouse him. By the same coach that the night before had conveyed Philip to N—, had the very man he sought been also a passenger!

The poor fellow was sickly and wearied out: he had settled into a doze, when he was suddenly wakened by the wheels of a coach and the trampling of horses. Not knowing how long he had slept, and imagining that the vehicle he had awaited was at the door, he ran out. It was a coach coming from London, and the driver was joking with a pretty barmaid who, in rather short petticoats, was fielding up to him the customary glass. The man, after satisfying himself that his time was not yet come, was turning back to the fire, when a head popped itself out of the window, and a voice cried, "Stars and garters! Will—so that's you!" At the sound of the voice the man halted abruptly, turned very pale, and his limbs trembled. The inside passenger opened the door, jumped out with a little carpet-bag in his hand, took forth a long leathern purse from which he ostentatiously selected the coins that paid his fare and satisfied the coachman, and then, passing his arm through that of the acquaintance he had discovered, led him back into the house.

"Will—Will," he whispered, "you have been to the Mortons. Never moind—let's hear all. Jenny or Dolly, or whatever your sweet praetty name is—a private room and a pint of brandy, my dear. Hot water and lots of the grocery. That's right."

And as soon as the pair found themselves, with the brandy before them, in a small parlour with a good fire, the last comer went to the door, shut it cautiously, flung his bag under the table, took off his gloves, spread himself wider and wider before the fire, until he had entirely excluded every ray from his friend, and then suddenly turning so that the back might enjoy what the front had gained, he exclaimed.

"Damme, Will, you're a praetty sort of a broather to give me the slip in that way. But in this world every man for his-self!"

"I tell you," said William, with something like decision in his voice, "that I will not do any wrong to these young men if they live."

"Who asks you to do a wrong to them?—booby! Perhaps I may be the best friend they may have yet—ay, or you too, though you're the ungratefulest whimsicallist sort of a son of a gun that ever I came across. Come, help yourself, and don't roll up your eyes in that way, like a Muggletonian asoide of a Fye-Fye!"

Here the speaker paused a moment, and with a graver and more natural tone of voice proceeded:

"So you did not believe me when I told you that these brothers were dead, and you have been to the Mortons to learn more?"

"Yes."

"Well, and what have you learned?"

"Nothing. Morton declares that he does not know that they are alive, but he says also that he does not know that they are dead."

"Indeed," said the other, listening with great attention; "and you really think that he does not know anything about them?"

"I do, indeed."

"Hum! Is he a sort of man who would post down the rhino to help the search?"

"He looked as if he had the yellow fever when I said I was poor," returned William, turning round, and trying to catch a glimpse at the fire, as he gulped his brandy and water.

"Then I'll be d—d if I run the risk of calling. I have done some things in this town by way of business before now; and though it's a long time ago, yet folks don't forget a haundsome man in a hurry—especially if he has done 'em! Now, then, listen to me. You see, I have given this matter all the 'tention in my power. 'If the lads be dead,' said I to you, 'it is no use burning one's fingers by holding a candle to bones in a coffin. But Mr. Beaufort need not know they are dead, and we'll see what we can get out of him; and if I succeeds, as I think I shall, you and I may hold up our heads for the rest of our life.' Accordingly, as I told you, I went to Mr. Beaufort, and—'Gad, I thought we had it all our own way. But since I saw you last, there's been the devil and all. When I called again, Will, I was shown in to an old lord, sharp as a gimblet. Hang me, William, if he did not frighten me out of my seven senses!"

Here Captain Smith (the reader has, no doubt, already discovered that the speaker was no less a personage) took three or four nervous strides across the room, returned to the table, threw himself in a chair, placed one foot on one hob, and one on the other, laid his finger on his nose, and, with a significant wink, said in a whisper, "Will, he knew I had been lagged! He not only refused to hear all I had to say, but threatened to prosecute—persecute, hang, draw, and quarter us both, if we ever dared to come out with the truth."

"But what's the good of the truth if the boys are dead?" said William, timidly.

The captain, without heeding this question, continued, as he stirred the sugar in his glass, "Well, out I sneaked, and as soon as I had got to my own door I turned round and saw Sharp the runner on the other side of the way—I felt deuced queer. However, I went in, sat down, and began to think. I saw that it was up with us, so far as the old uns were concerned; and it might be worth while to find out if the young uns really were dead."

"Then you did not know that after all! I thought so. Oh, Jerry!"

"Why, look you, man, it was not our interest to take their side if we could make our bargain out of the other. 'Cause why? You are only one witness—you are a good fellow, but poor, and with very shaky nerves, Will. You does not know what them big wigs are when a man's caged in a witness-box—they flank one up, and they flank one down, and they bully and bother, till one's like a horse at Astley's dancing on hot iron. If your testimony broke down, why it would be all up with the case, and what then would become of us? Besides," added the captain, with dignified candour, "I have been lagged, it's no use denying it; I am back before my time. Inquiries about your respectability would soon bring the bulkies about me. And you would not have poor Jerry sent back to that d—d low place on t'other side of the herring-pond, would you?"

"Ah, Jerry!" said William, kindly placing his hand in his brother's, "you know I helped you to escape; I left all to come over with you."

"So you did, and you're a good fellow; though as to leaving all, why you had got rid of all first. And when you told me about the marriage, did not I say that I saw our way to a snug thing for life? But to return to my story. There is a danger in going with the youngsters. But since, Will,—since nothing but hard words is to be got on the other side, we'll do our duty, and I'll find them out, and do the best I can for us—that is, if they be yet above ground. And now I'll own to you that I think I knows that the younger one is alive."

"You do?"

"Yes! But as he won't come in for anything unless his brother is dead, we must have a hunt for the heir. Now I told you that, many years ago, there was a lad with me, who, putting all things together—seeing how the Beauforts came after him, and recollecting different things he let out at the time—I feel pretty sure is your old master's Hopeful. I know that poor Will Gawtrey gave this lad the address of Old Gregg, a friend of mine. So after watching Sharp off the sly, I went that very night, or rather at two in the morning, to Gregg's house, and, after brushing up his memory, I found that the lad had been to him, and gone over afterwards to Paris in search of Gawtrey, who was then keeping a matrimony shop. As I was not rich enough to go off to Paris in a pleasant, gentlemanlike way, I allowed Gregg to put me up to a noice quiet little bit of business. Don't shake your head—all safe—a rural affair! That took some days. You see it has helped to new rig me," and the captain glanced complacently over a very smart suit of clothes. "Well, on my return I went to call on you, but you had flown. I half suspected you might have gone to the mother's relations here; and I thought, at all events, that I could not do better than go myself and see what they knew of the matter. From what you say I feel I had better now let that alone, and go over to Paris at once; leave me alone to find out. And faith, what with Sharp and the old lord, the sooner I quit England the better."

"And you really think you shall get hold of them after all? Oh, never fear my nerves if I'm once in the right; it's living with you, and seeing you do wrong, and hearing you talk wickedly, that makes me tremble."

"Bother!" said the captain, "you need not crow over me. Stand up, Will; there now, look at us two in the glass! Why, I look ten years younger than you do, in spite of all my troubles. I dress like a gentleman, as I am; I have money in my pocket; I put money in yours; without me you'd starve. Look you, you carried over a little fortune to Australia—you married—you farmed—you lived honestly, and yet that d—d shilly-shally disposition of yours, 'ticed into one speculation to-day, and scared out of another to-morrow, ruined you!"

"Jerry! Jerry!" cried William, writhing; "don't—don't."

"But it's all true, and I wants to cure you of preaching. And then, when you were nearly run out, instead of putting a bold face on it, and setting your shoulder to the wheel, you gives it up—you sells what you have—you bolts over, wife and all, to Boston, because some one tells you you can do better in America—you are out of the way when a search is made for you—years ago when you could have benefited yourself and your master's family without any danger to you or me—nobody can find you; 'cause why, you could not bear that your old friends in England, or in the colony either, should know that you were turned a slave-driver in Kentucky. You kick up a mutiny among the niggers by moaning over them, instead of keeping 'em to it—you get kicked out yourself—your wife begs you to go back to Australia, where her relations will do something for you—you work your passage out, looking as ragged as a colt from grass—wife's uncle don't like ragged nephews-in-law—wife dies broken-hearted—and you might be breaking stones on the roads with the convicts, if I, myself a convict, had not taken compassion on you. Don't cry, Will, it is all for your own good—I hates cant! Whereas I, my own master from eighteen, never stooped to serve any other—have dressed like a gentleman—kissed the pretty girls—drove my pheaton—been in all the papers as 'the celebrated Dashing Jerry'—never wanted a guinea in my pocket, and even when lagged at last, had a pretty little sum in the colonial bank to lighten my misfortunes. I escape,—I bring you over—and here I am, supporting you, and in all probability, the one on whom depends the fate of one of the first families in the country. And you preaches at me, do you? Look you, Will;—in this world, honesty's nothing without force of character! And so your health!"

Here the captain emptied the rest of the brandy into his glass, drained it at a draught, and, while poor William was wiping his eyes with a ragged blue pocket-handkerchief, rang the bell, and asked what coaches would pass that way to —, a seaport town at some distance. On hearing that there was one at six o'clock, the captain ordered the best dinner the larder would afford to be got ready as soon as possible; and, when they were again alone, thus accosted his brother:—

"Now you go back to town—here are four shiners for you. Keep quiet—don't speak to a soul—don't put your foot in it, that's all I beg, and I'll find out whatever there is to be found. It is damnably out of my way embarking at —, but I had best keep clear of Lunnon. And I tell you what, if these youngsters have hopped the twig, there's another bird on the bough that may prove a goldfinch after all—Young Arthur

Beaufort: I hear he is a wild, expensive chap, and one who can't live without lots of money. Now, it's easy to frighten a man of that sort, and I sha'n't have the old lord at his elbow."

"But I tell you, that I only care for my poor master's children."

"Yes; but if they are dead, and by saying they are alive, one can make old age comfortable, there's no harm in it—eh?"

"I don't know," said William, irresolutely. "But certainly it is a hard thing to be so poor at my time of life; and so honest a man as I've been, too!"

Captain Smith went a little too far when he said that "honesty's nothing without force of character." Still, Honesty has no business to be helpless and draggle-tailed;—she must be active and brisk, and make use of her wits; or, though she keep clear or the prison, 'tis no very great wonder if she fall on the parish.

CHAPTER III

"Mitis.—This Macilente, signior, begins to be more sociable on a sudden." Every Man out of his Humour.

"Punt. Signior, you are sufficiently instructed.

"Fast. Who, I, sir?"—Ibid.

After spending the greater part of the day in vain inquiries and a vain search, Philip and Mr. Morton returned to the house of the latter.

"And now," said Philip, "all that remains to be done is this: first give to the police of the town a detailed description of the man; and secondly, let us put an advertisement both in the county journal and in some of the London papers, to the effect, that if the person who called on you will take the trouble to apply again, either personally or by letter, he may obtain the information sought for. In case he does, I will trouble you to direct him to—yes—to Monsieur de Vaudemont, according to this address."

"Not to you, then?"

"It is the same thing," replied Philip, drily. "You have confirmed my suspicions, that the Beauforts know some thing of my brother. What did you say of some other friend of the family who assisted in the search?"

"Oh,—a Mr. Spencer! an old acquaintance of your mother's." Here Mr. Morton smiled, but not being encouraged in a joke, went on, "However, that's neither here nor there; he certainly never found out your brother. For I have had several letters from him at different times, asking if any news had been heard of either of you."

And, indeed, Spencer had taken peculiar pains to deceive the Mortons, whose interposition he feared little less than that of the Beauforts.

"Then it can be of no use to apply to him," said Philip, carelessly, not having any recollection of the name of Spencer, and therefore attaching little importance to the mention of him.

"Certainly, I should think not. Depend on it, Mr. Beaufort must know."

"True," said Philip. "And I have only to thank you for your kindness, and return to town."

"But stay with us this day—do—let me feel that we are friends. I assure you poor Sidney's fate has been a load on my mind ever since he left. You shall have the bed he slept in, and over which your mother bent when she left him and me for the last time."

These words were said with so much feeling, that the adventurer wrung his uncle's hand, and said, "Forgive me, I wronged you—I will be your guest."

Mrs. Morton, strange to say, evinced no symptoms of ill-humour at the news of the proffered hospitality. In fact, Miss Margaret had been so eloquent in Philip's praise during his absence, that she suffered herself to be favourably impressed. Her daughter, indeed, had obtained a sort of ascendency over Mrs. M. and the whole house, ever since she had received so excellent an offer. And, moreover, some people are like dogs—they snarl at the ragged and fawn on the well-dressed. Mrs. Morton did not object to a nephew de facto, she only objected to a nephew in forma pauperis. The evening, therefore, passed more cheerfully than might have been anticipated, though Philip found some difficulty in parrying the many questions put to him on the past. He contented himself with saying, as briefly as possible, that he had served in a foreign service, and acquired what sufficed him for an independence; and then, with the ease which a man picks up in the great world, turned the conversation to the prospects of the family whose guest he was. Having listened with due attention to Mrs. Morton's eulogies on Tom, who had been sent for, and who drank the praises on his own gentility into a very large pair of blushing ears,—also, to her self-felicitations on Miss Margaret's marriage,—item, on the service rendered to the town by Mr. Roger, who had repaired the town-hall in his first mayoralty at his own expense,—item, to a long chronicle of her own genealogy, how she had one cousin a clergyman, and how her great-grandfather had been knighted,—item, to the domestic virtues of all her children,—item, to a confused explanation of the chastisement inflicted on Sidney, which Philip cut short in the middle; he asked, with a smile, what had become of the Plaskwiths. "Oh!" said Mrs. Morton, "my brother Kit has retired from business. His son-in-law, Mr. Plimmins, has succeeded."

"Oh, then, Plimmins married one of the young ladies?"

"Yes, Jane—she had a sad squint!—Tom, there is nothing to laugh at,—we are all as God made us,—'Handsome is as handsome does,'—she has had three little uns!"

"Do they squint too?" asked Philip; and Miss Margaret giggled, and Tom roared, and the other young men roared too. Philip had certainly said something very witty.

This time Mrs. Morton administered no reproof; but replied pensively

"Natur is very mysterious—they all squint!"

Mr. Morton conducted Philip to his chamber. There it was, fresh, clean, unaltered—the same white curtains, the same honeysuckle paper as when Catherine had crept across the threshold.

"Did Sidney ever tell you that his mother placed a ring round his neck that night?" asked Mr. Morton.

"Yes; and the dear boy wept when he said that he had slept too soundly to know that she was by his side that last, last time. The ring—oh, how well I remember it! she never put it off till then; and often in the fields—for we were wild wanderers together in that day—often when his head lay on my shoulder, I felt that ring still resting on his heart, and fancied it was a talisman—a blessing. Well, well-good night to you!" And he shut the door on his uncle, and was alone.

CHAPTER IV

"The Man of Law,........
And a great suit is like to be between them."
BEN JONSON: *Staple of News.*

On arriving in London, Philip went first to the lodging he still kept there, and to which his letters were directed; and, among some communications from Paris, full of the politics and the hopes of the Carlists, he found the following note from Lord Lilburne:—

"DEAR SIR,—When I met you the other day I told you I had been threatened with the gout. The enemy has now taken possession of the field. I am sentenced to regimen and the sofa. But as it is my rule in life to make afflictions as light as possible, so I have asked a few friends to take compassion on me, and help me 'to shuffle off this mortal coil' by dealing me, if they can, four by honours. Any time between nine and twelve to-night, or to-morrow night, you will find me at home; and if you are not better engaged, suppose you dine with me to-day—or rather dine opposite to me—and excuse my Spartan broth. You will meet (besides any two or three friends whom an impromptu invitation may find disengaged) my sister, with Beaufort and their daughter: they only arrived in town this morning, and are kind enough 'to nurse me,' as they call it,—that is to say, their cook is taken ill!

"Yours,

"LILBURNE "Park Lane, Sept. —"

"The Beauforts. Fate favors me—I will go. The date is for to-day."

He sent off a hasty line to accept the invitation, and finding he had a few hours yet to spare, he resolved to employ them in consultation with some lawyer as to the chances of ultimately regaining his inheritance—a hope which, however wild, he had, since his return to his native shore, and especially since he had heard of the strange visit made to Roger Morton, permitted himself to indulge. With this idea he sallied out, meaning to consult Liancourt, who, having a large acquaintance among the English, seemed the best person to advise him as to the choice of a lawyer at once active and honest,—when he suddenly chanced upon that gentleman himself.

"This is lucky, my dear Liancourt. I was just going to your lodgings."

"And I was coming to yours to know if you dine with Lord Lilburne. He told me he had asked you. I have just left him. And, by the sofa of Mephistopheles, there was the prettiest Margaret you ever beheld."

"Indeed!—Who?"

"He called her his niece; but I should doubt if he had any relation on this side the Styx so human as a niece."

"You seem to have no great predilection for our host."

"My dear Vaudemont, between our blunt, soldierly natures, and those wily, icy, sneering intellects, there is the antipathy of the dog to the cat."

"Perhaps so on our side, not on his—or why does he invite us?"

"London is empty; there is no one else to ask. We are new faces, new minds to him. We amuse him more than the hackneyed comrades he has worn out. Besides, he plays—and you, too. Fie on you!"

"Liancourt, I had two objects in knowing that man, and I pay to the toll for the bridge. When I cease to want the passage, I shall cease to pay the toll."

"But the bridge may be a draw-bridge, and the moat is devilish deep below. Without metaphor, that man may ruin you before you know where you are."

"Bah! I have my eyes open. I know how much to spend on the rogue whose service I hire as a lackey's; and I know also where to stop. Liancourt," he added, after a short pause, and in a tone deep with suppressed passion, "when I first saw that man, I thought of appealing to his heart for one who has a claim on it. That was a vain hope. And then there came upon me a sterner and deadlier thought—the scheme of the Avenger! This Lilburne—this rogue whom the world sets up to worship—ruined, body and soul ruined—one whose name the world gibbets with scorn! Well, I thought to avenge that man. In his own house—amidst you all—I thought to detect the sharper, and brand the cheat!"

"You startle me!—It has been whispered, indeed, that Lord Lilburne is dangerous,—but skill is dangerous. To cheat!—an Englishman!—a nobleman!—impossible!"

"Whether he do or not," returned Vaudemont, in a calmer tone, "I have foregone the vengeance, because he is—"

"Is what?"

"No matter," said Vaudemont aloud, but he added to himself,—"Because he is the grandfather of Fanny!"

"You are very enigmatical to-day."

"Patience, Liancourt; I may solve all the riddles that make up my life, yet. Bear with me a little longer. And now can you help me to a lawyer?—a man experienced, indeed, and of repute, but young, active, not overladen with business;—I want his zeal and his time, for a hazard that your monopolists of clients may not deem worth their devotion."

"I can recommend you, then, the very man you require. I had a suit some years ago at Paris, for which English witnesses were necessary. My avocat employed a solicitor here whose activity in collecting my evidence gained my cause. I will answer for his diligence and his honesty."

"His address?"

"Mr. Barlow—somewhere by the Strand—let me see—Essex-yes, Essex Street."

"Then good-bye to you for the present.—You dine at Lord Lilburne's too?"

"Yes. Adieu till then."

Vaudemont was not long before he arrived at Mr. Barlow's; a brass-plate announced to him the house. He was shown at once into a parlour, where he saw a man whom lawyers would call young, and spinsters middle-aged—viz., about two-and-forty; with a bold, resolute, intelligent countenance, and that steady, calm, sagacious eye, which inspires at once confidence and esteem.

Vaudemont scanned him with the look of one who has been accustomed to judge mankind—as a scholar does books—with rapidity because with practice. He had at first resolved to submit to him the heads of his case without mentioning names, and, in fact, he so commenced his narrative; but by degrees, as he perceived how much his own earnestness arrested and engrossed the interest of his listener, he warmed into fuller confidence, and ended by a full disclosure, and a caution as to the profoundest secrecy in case, if there were no hope to recover his rightful name, he might yet wish to retain, unannoyed by curiosity or suspicion, that by which he was not discreditably known.

"Sir," said Mr. Barlow, after assuring him of the most scrupulous discretion,—"sir, I have some recollection of the trial instituted by your mother, Mrs. Beaufort"—and the slight emphasis he laid on that name was the most grateful compliment he could have paid to the truth of Philip's recital. "My impression is, that it was managed in a very slovenly manner by her lawyer; and some of his oversights we may repair in a suit instituted by yourself. But it would be absurd to conceal from you the great difficulties that beset us—your mother's suit, designed to establish her own rights, was far easier than that which you must commence—viz., an action for ejectment against a man who has been some years in undisturbed possession. Of course, until the missing witness is found out, it would be madness to commence litigation. And the question, then, will be, how far that witness will suffice? It is true, that one witness of a marriage, if the others are dead, is held sufficient by law. But I need not add, that that witness must be thoroughly credible. In suits for real property, very little documentary or secondary evidence is admitted. I doubt even whether the certificate of the marriage on which—in the loss or destruction of the register—you lay so much stress, would be available in itself. But if an examined copy, it becomes of the last importance, for it will then inform us of the name of the person who extracted and examined it. Heaven grant it may not have been the clergyman himself who performed the ceremony, and who, you say, is dead; if some one else, we should then have a second, no doubt credible and most valuable witness. The document would thus become available as proof, and, I think, that we should not fail to establish our case."

"But this certificate, how is it ever to be found? I told you we had searched everywhere in vain."

"True; but you say that your mother always declared that the late Mr. Beaufort had so solemnly assured her, even just prior to his decease, that it was in existence, that I have no doubt as to the fact. It may be possible, but it is a terrible insinuation to make, that if Mr. Robert Beaufort, in examining the papers of the deceased, chanced upon a document so important to him, he abstracted or destroyed it. If this should not have been the case (and Mr. Robert Beaufort's moral character is unspotted—and we have no right to suppose it), the probability is, either that it was intrusted to some third person, or placed in some hidden drawer or deposit, the secret of which your father never disclosed. Who has purchased the house you lived in?"

"Fernside? Lord Lilburne. Mrs. Robert Beaufort's brother."

"Humph—probably, then, he took the furniture and all. Sir, this is a matter that requires some time for close consideration. With your leave, I will not only insert in the London papers an advertisement to the effect that you suggested to Mr. Roger Morton (in case you should have made a right conjecture as to the object of the man who applied to him), but I will also advertise for the witness himself. William Smith, you say, his name is. Did the lawyer employed by Mrs. Beaufort send to inquire for him in the colony?"

"No; I fear there could not have been time for that. My mother was so anxious and eager, and so convinced of the justice of her case—"

"That's a pity; her lawyer must have been a sad driveller."

"Besides, now I remember, inquiry was made of his relations in England. His father, a farmer, was then alive; the answer was that he had certainly left Australia. His last letter, written two years before that date, containing a request for money, which the father, himself made a bankrupt by reverses, could not give, had stated that he was about to seek his fortune elsewhere—since then they had heard nothing of him."

"Ahem! Well, you will perhaps let me know where any relations of his are yet to be found, and I will look up the former suit, and go into the whole case without delay. In the meantime, you do right, sir—if you will allow me to say it—not to disclose either your own identity or a hint of your intentions. It is no use putting suspicion on its guard. And my search for this certificate must be managed with the greatest address. But, by the way—speaking of identity—there can be no difficulty, I hope, in proving yours."

Philip was startled. "Why, I am greatly altered."

"But probably your beard and moustache may contribute to that change; and doubtless, in the village where you lived, there would be many with whom you were in sufficient intercourse, and on whose recollection, by recalling little anecdotes and circumstances with which no one but yourself could be acquainted, your features would force themselves along with the moral conviction that the man who spoke to them could be no other but Philip Morton—or rather Beaufort."

"You are right; there must be many such. There was not a cottage in the place where I and my dogs were not familiar and half domesticated."

"All's right, so far, then. But I repeat, we must not be too sanguine. Law is not justice—"

"But God is," said Philip; and he left the room.

CHAPTER V

"Volpone. A little in a mist, but not dejected;
Never—but still myself."
BEN JONSON: *Volpone.*

"Peregrine. Am I enough disguised?
Mer. Ay. I warrant you.
Per. Save you, fair lady."—Ibid.

It is an ill wind that blows nobody good. The ill wind that had blown gout to Lord Lilburne had blown Lord Lilburne away from the injury he had meditated against what he called "the object of his attachment." How completely and entirely, indeed, the state of Lord Lilburne's feelings depended on the state of his health, may be seen in the answer he gave to his valet, when, the morning after the first attack of the gout, that worthy person, by way of cheering his master, proposed to ascertain something as to the movements of one with whom Lord Lilburne professed to be so violently in love,—"Confound you, Dykeman!" exclaimed the invalid,—"why do you trouble me about women when I'm in this condition? I don't care if they were all at the bottom of the sea! Reach me the colchicum! I must keep my mind calm."

Whenever tolerably well, Lord Lilburne was careless of his health; the moment he was ill, Lord Lilburne paid himself the greatest possible attention. Though a man of firm nerves, in youth of remarkable daring, and still, though no longer rash, of sufficient personal courage, he was by no means fond of the thought of death—that is, of his own death. Not that he was tormented by any religious apprehensions of the Dread Unknown, but simply because the only life of which he had any experience seemed to him a peculiarly pleasant thing. He had a sort of instinctive persuasion that John Lord Lilburne would not be better off anywhere else. Always disliking solitude, he disliked it more than ever when he was ill, and he therefore welcomed the visit of his sister and the gentle hand of his pretty niece. As for Beaufort, he bored the sufferer; and when that gentleman, on his arrival, shutting out his wife and daughter, whispered to Lilburne, "Any more news of that impostor?" Lilburne answered peevishly, "I never talk about business when I have the gout! I have set Sharp to keep a lookout for him, but he has learned nothing as yet. And now go to your club. You are a worthy creature, but too solemn for my spirits just at this moment. I have a few people coming to dine with me, your wife will do the honors, and—you can come in the evening." Though Mr. Robert Beaufort's sense of importance swelled and chafed at this very unceremonious conge, he forced a smile, and said:—

"Well, it is no wonder you are a little fretful with the gout. I have plenty to do in town, and Mrs. Beaufort and Camilla can come back without waiting for me."

"Why, as your cook is ill, and they can't dine at a club, you may as well leave them here till I am a little better; not that I care, for I can hire a better nurse than either of them."

"My dear Lilburne, don't talk of hiring nurses; certainly, I am too happy if they can be of comfort to you."

"No! on second thoughts, you may take back your wife, she's always talking of her own complaints, and leave me Camilla: you can't want her for a few days."

"Just as you like. And you really think I have managed as well as I could about this young man,—eh?"

"Yes—yes! And so you go to Beaufort Court in a few days?"

"I propose doing so. I wish you were well enough to come."

"Um! Chambers says that it would be a very good air for me—better than Fernside; and as to my castle in the north, I would as soon go to Siberia. Well, if I get better, I will pay you a visit, only you always have such a stupid set of respectable people about you. I shock them, and they oppress me."

"Why, as I hope soon to see Arthur, I shall make it as agreeable to him as I can, and I shall be very much obliged to you if you would invite a few of your own friends."

"Well, you are a good fellow, Beaufort, and I will take you at your word; and, since one good turn deserves another, I have now no scruples in telling you that I feel quite sure that you will have no further annoyance from this troublesome witness-monger."

"In that case," said Beaufort, "I may pick up a better match for Camilla! Good-bye, my dear Lilburne."

"Form and Ceremony of the world!" snarled the peer, as the door closed on his brother-in-law, "ye make little men very moral, and not a bit the better for being so."

It so happened that Vaudemont arrived before any of the other guests that day, and during the half hour which Dr. Chambers assigned to his illustrious patient, so that, when he entered, there were only Mrs. Beaufort and Camilla in the drawing-room.

Vaudemont drew back involuntarily as he recognized in the faded countenance of the elder lady, features associated with one of the dark passages in his earlier life; but Mrs. Beaufort's gracious smile, and urbane, though languid welcome, sufficed to assure him that the recognition was not mutual. He advanced, and again stopped short, as his eye fell upon that fair and still childlike form, which had once knelt by his side and pleaded, with the orphan, for his brother. While he spoke to her, many recollections, some dark and stern—but those, at least, connected with Camilla, soft and gentle—thrilled through his heart. Occupied as her own thoughts and feelings necessarily were with Sidney, there was something in Vaudemont's appearance—his manner, his voice—which forced upon Camilla a strange and undefined interest; and even Mrs. Beaufort was roused from her customary apathy, as she glanced at that dark and commanding face with something between admiration and fear. Vaudemont had scarcely, however, spoken ten words, when some other guests were announced, and Lord Lilburne was wheeled in upon his sofa shortly afterwards. Vaudemont continued, however, seated next to Camilla, and the embarrassment he had at first felt disappeared. He possessed, when he pleased, that kind of eloquence which belongs to men who have seen much and felt deeply, and whose talk has not been frittered down to the commonplace jargon of the world. His very phraseology was distinct and peculiar, and he had that rarest of all charms in polished life, originality both of thought and of manner. Camilla blushed, when she found at dinner that he placed himself by her side. That evening De Vaudemont excused himself from playing, but the table was easily made without him, and still he continued to converse with the daughter of the man whom he held as his worst foe. By degrees, he turned the conversation into a channel that might lead him to the knowledge he sought.

"It was my fate," said he, "once to become acquainted with an intimate friend of the late Mr. Beaufort. Will you pardon me if I venture to fulfil a promise I made to him, and ask you to inform me what has become of a—a—that is, of Sidney Morton?"

"Sidney Morton! I don't even remember the name. Oh, yes! I have heard it," added Camilla, innocently, and with a candour that showed how little she knew of the secrets of the family; "he was one of two poor boys in whom my brother felt a deep interest—some relations to my uncle. Yes—yes! I remember now. I never knew Sidney, but I once did see his brother."

"Indeed! and you remember—"

"Yes! I was very young then. I scarcely recollect what passed, it was all so confused and strange; but, I know that I made papa very angry, and I was told never to mention the name of Morton again. I believe they behaved very ill to papa."

"And you never learned—never!—the fate of either—of Sidney?"

"Never!"

"But your father must know?"

"I think not; but tell me,"—said Camilla, with girlish and unaffected innocence, "I have always felt anxious to know,—what and who were those poor boys?"

What and who were they? So deep, then, was the stain upon their name, that the modest mother and the decorous father had never even said to that young girl, "They are your cousins—the children of the man in whose gold we revel!"

Philip bit his lip, and the spell of Camilla's presence seemed vanished. He muttered some inaudible answer, turned away to the card-table, and Liancourt took the chair he had left vacant.

"And how does Miss Beaufort like my friend Vaudemont? I assure you that I have seldom seen him so alive to the fascination of female beauty!"

"Oh!" said Camilla, with her silver laugh, "your nation spoils us for our own countrymen. You forget how little we are accustomed to flattery."

"Flattery! what truth could flatter on the lips of an exile? But you don't answer my question—what think you of Vaudemont? Few are more admired. He is handsome!"

"Is he?" said Camilla, and she glanced at Vaudemont, as he stood at a little distance, thoughtful and abstracted. Every girl forms to herself some untold dream of that which she considers fairest. And Vaudemont had not the delicate and faultless beauty of Sidney. There was nothing that corresponded to her ideal in his marked features and lordly shape! But she owned, reluctantly to herself, that she had seldom seen, among the trim gallants of everyday life, a form so striking and impressive. The air, indeed, was professional—the most careless glance could detect the soldier. But it seemed the soldier of an elder age or a wilder clime. He recalled to her those heads which she had seen in the Beaufort Gallery and other Collections yet more celebrated—portraits by Titian of those warrior statesman who lived in the old Republics of Italy in a perpetual struggle with their kind—images of dark, resolute, earnest men. Even whatever was intellectual in his countenance spoke, as in those portraits, of a mind sharpened rather in active than in studious life;—intellectual, not from the pale hues, the worn exhaustion, and the sunken cheek of the bookman and dreamer, but from its collected and stern repose, the calm depth that lay beneath the fire of the eyes, and the strong will that spoke in the close full lips, and the high but not cloudless forehead.

And, as she gazed, Vaudemont turned round—her eyes fell beneath his, and she felt angry with herself that she blushed. Vaudemont saw the downcast eye, he saw the blush, and the attraction of Camilla's presence was restored. He would have approached her, but at that moment Mr. Beaufort himself entered, and his thoughts went again into a darker channel.

"Yes," said Liancourt, "you must allow Vaudemont looks what he is—a noble fellow and a gallant soldier. Did you never hear of his battle with the tigress? It made a noise in India. I must tell it you as I have heard it."

And while Laincourt was narrating the adventure, whatever it was, to which he referred, the card-table was broken up, and Lord Lilburne, still reclining on his sofa, lazily introduced his brother-in-law to such of the guests as were strangers to him—Vaudemont among the rest. Mr. Beaufort had never seen Philip Morton more than three times; once at Fernside, and the other times by an imperfect light, and when his features were convulsed by passion, and his form disfigured by his dress. Certainly, therefore, had Robert Beaufort even possessed that faculty of memory which is supposed to belong peculiarly to kings and princes, and which recalls every face once seen, it might have tasked the gift to the utmost to have detected, in the bronzed and decorated foreigner to whom he was now presented, the features of the wild and long-lost boy. But still some dim and uneasy presentiment, or some struggling and painful effort of recollection, was in his mind, as he spoke to Vaudemont, and listened to the cold calm tone of his reply.

"Who do you say that Frenchman is?" he whispered to his brother-in-law, as Vaudemont turned away.

"Oh! a cleverish sort of adventurer—a gentleman; he plays.—He has seen a good deal of the world—he rather amuses me—different from other people. I think of asking him to join our circle at Beaufort Court."

Mr. Beaufort coughed huskily, but not seeing any reasonable objection to the proposal, and afraid of rousing the sleeping hyaena of Lord Lilburne's sarcasm, he merely said:—

"Any one you like to invite:" and looking round for some one on whom to vent his displeasure, perceived Camilla still listening to Liancourt. He stalked up to her, and as Liancourt, seeing her rise, rose also and moved away, he said peevishly, "You will never learn to conduct yourself properly; you are to be left here to nurse and comfort your uncle, and not to listen to the gibberish of every French adventurer. Well, Heaven be praised, I have a son—girls are a great plague!"

"So they are, Mr. Beaufort," sighed his wife, who had just joined him, and who was jealous of the preference Lilburne had given to her daughter.

"And so selfish," added Mrs. Beaufort; "they only care for their own amusements, and never mind how uncomfortable their parents are for want of them."

"Oh! dear mamma, don't say so—let me go home with you—I'll speak to my uncle!"

"Nonsense, child! Come along, Mr. Beaufort;" and the affectionate parents went out arm in arm. They did not perceive that Vaudemont had been standing close behind them; but Camilla, now looking up with tears in her eyes, again caught his gaze: he had heard all.

"And they ill-treat her," he muttered: "that divides her from them!—she will be left here—I shall see her again." As he turned to depart, Lilburne beckoned to him.

"You do not mean to desert our table?"

"No: but I am not very well to-night—to-morrow, if you will allow me."

"Ay, to-morrow; and if you can spare an hour in the morning it will be a charity. You see," he added in a whisper, "I have a nurse, though I have no children. D'ye think that's love? Bah! sir—a legacy! Good night."

"No—no—no!" said Vaudemont to himself, as he walked through the moonlit streets. "No! though my heart burns,—poor murdered felon!—to avenge thy wrongs and thy crimes, revenge cannot come from me—he is Fanny's grandfather and—Camilla's uncle!"

And Camilla, when that uncle had dismissed her for the night, sat down thoughtfully in her own room. The dark eyes of Vaudemont seemed still to shine on her; his voice yet rung in her ear; the wild tales of daring and danger with which Liancourt had associated his name yet haunted her bewildered fancy—she started, frightened at her own thoughts. She took from her bosom some lines that Sidney had addressed to her, and, as she read and re-read, her spirit became calmed to its wonted and faithful melancholy. Vaudemont was forgotten, and the name of Sidney yet murmured on her lips, when sleep came to renew the image of the absent one, and paint in dreams the fairy land of a happy Future!

CHAPTER VI

"Ring on, ye bells—most pleasant is your chime!"
WILSON. *Isle of Palms.*

"O fairy child! What can I wish for thee?"—Ibid.

Vaudemont remained six days in London without going to H—, and on each of those days he paid a visit to Lord Lilburne. On the seventh day, the invalid being much better, though still unable to leave his room, Camilla returned to Berkeley Square. On the same day, Vaudemont went once more to see Simon and poor Fanny.

As he approached the door, he heard from the window, partially opened, for the day was clear and fine, Fanny's sweet voice. She was chaunting one of the simple songs she had promised to learn by heart; and Vaudemont, though but a poor judge of the art, was struck and affected by the music of the voice and the earnest depth of the feeling. He paused opposite the window and called her by her name. Fanny looked forth joyously, and ran, as usual, to open the door to him.

"Oh! you have been so long away; but I already know many of the songs: they say so much that I always wanted to say!"

Vaudemont smiled, but languidly.

"How strange it is," said Fanny, musingly, "that there should be so much in a piece of paper! for, after all," pointing to the open page of her book, "this is but a piece of paper—only there is life in it!"

"Ay," said Vaudemont, gloomily, and far from seizing the subtle delicacy of Fanny's thought—her mind dwelling upon Poetry, and his upon Law,—"ay, and do you know that upon a mere scrap of paper, if I could but find it, may depend my whole fortune, my whole happiness, all that I care for in life?"

"Upon a scrap of paper? Oh! how I wish I could find it! Ah! you look as if you thought I should never be wise enough for that!"

Vaudemont, not listening to her, uttered a deep sigh. Fanny approached him timidly.

"Do not sigh, brother,—I can't bear to hear you sigh. You are changed. Have you, too, not been happy?"

"Happy, Fanny! yes, lately very happy—too happy!"

"Happy, have you? and I—" the girl stopped short—her tone had been that of sadness and reproach, and she stopped—why, she knew not, but she felt her heart sink within her. Fanny suffered him to pass her, and he went straight to his room. Her eyes followed him wistfully: it was not his habit to leave her thus abruptly. The family meal of the day was over; and it was an hour before Vaudemont descended to the parlour. Fanny had put aside the songs; she had no heart to recommence those gentle studies that had been so sweet,—they had drawn no pleasure, no praise from him. She was seated idly and listlessly beside the silent old man, who every day grew more and more silent still. She turned her head as Vaudemont entered, and her pretty lip pouted as that of a neglected child. But he did not heed it, and the pout vanished, and tears rushed to her eyes.

Vaudemont was changed. His countenance was thoughtful and overcast. His manner abstracted. He addressed a few words to Simon, and then, seating himself by the window, leant his cheek on his hand, and was soon lost in reverie. Fanny, finding that he did not speak, and after stealing many a long and earnest glance at his motionless attitude and gloomy brow, rose gently, and gliding to him with her light step, said, in a trembling voice,—

"Are you in pain, brother?"

"No, pretty one!"

"Then why won't you speak to Fanny? Will you not walk with her? Perhaps my grandfather will come too."

"Not this evening. I shall go out; but it will be alone."

"Where? Has not Fanny been good? I have not been out since you left us. And the grave—brother!—I sent Sarah with the flowers—but—"

Vaudemont rose abruptly. The mention of the grave brought back his thoughts from the dreaming channel into which they had flowed. Fanny, whose very childishness had once so soothed him, now disturbed; he felt the want of that complete solitude which makes the atmosphere of growing passion: he muttered some scarcely audible excuse, and quitted the house. Fanny saw him no more that evening. He did not return till midnight. But Fanny did not sleep till she heard his step on the stairs, and his chamber door close: and when she did sleep, her dreams were disturbed and painful. The next morning, when they met at breakfast (for Vaudemont did not return to London), her eyes were red and heavy, and her cheek pale. And, still buried in meditation, Vaudemont's eye, usually so kind and watchful, did not detect those signs of a grief that Fanny could not have explained. After breakfast, however, he asked her to walk out; and her face brightened as she hastened to put on her bonnet, and take her little basket full of fresh flowers which she had already sent Sarah forth to purchase.

"Fanny," said Vaudemont, as leaving the house, he saw the basket on her arm, "to-day you may place some of those flowers on another tombstone!—Poor child, what natural goodness there is in that heart!—what pity that—"

He paused. Fanny looked delightedly in his face. "You were praising me—you! And what is a pity, brother?"

While she spoke, the sound of the joy-bells was heard near at hand.

"Hark!" said Vaudemont, forgetting her question—and almost gaily—"Hark!—I accept the omen. It is a marriage peal!"

He quickened his steps, and they reached the churchyard.

There was a crowd already assembled, and Vaudemont and Fanny paused; and, leaning over the little gate, looked on.

"Why are these people here, and why does the bell ring so merrily?"

"There is to be a wedding, Fanny."

"I have heard of a wedding very often," said Fanny, with a pretty look of puzzlement and doubt, "but I don't know exactly what it means. Will you tell me?—and the bells, too!"

"Yes, Fanny, those bells toll but three times for man! The first time, when he comes into the world; the last time, when he leaves it; the time between when he takes to his side a partner in all the sorrows—in all the joys that yet remain to him; and who, even when the last bell announces his death to this earth, may yet, for ever and ever, be his partner in that world to come—that heaven, where they who are as innocent as you, Fanny, may hope to live and to love each other in a land in which there are no graves!"

"And this bell?"

"Tolls for that partnership—for the wedding!"

"I think I understand you;—and they who are to be wed are happy?"

"Happy, Fanny, if they love, and their love continue. Oh! conceive the happiness to know some one person dearer to you than your own self—some one breast into which you can pour every thought, every grief, every joy! One person, who, if all the rest of the world were to calumniate or forsake you, would never wrong you by a harsh thought or an unjust word,—who would cling to you the closer in sickness, in poverty, in care,—who would sacrifice all things to you, and for whom you would sacrifice all—from whom, except by death, night or day, you must be never divided—whose smile is ever at your hearth—who has no tears while you are well and happy, and your love the same. Fanny, such is marriage, if they who marry have hearts and souls to feel that there is no bond on earth so tender and so sublime. There is an opposite picture;—I will not draw that! And as it is, Fanny, you cannot understand me!"

He turned away:—and Fanny's tears were falling like rain upon the grass below;—he did not see them! He entered the churchyard; for the bell now ceased. The ceremony was to begin. He followed the bridal party into the church, and Fanny, lowering her veil, crept after him, awed and trembling.

They stood, unobserved, at a little distance, and heard the service.

The betrothed were of the middle class of life, young, both comely; and their behaviour was such as suited the reverence and sanctity of the rite. Vaudemont stood looking on intently, with his arms folded on his breast. Fanny leant behind him, and apart from all, against one of the pews. And still in her hand, while the priest was solemnising Marriage, she held the flowers intended for the Grave. Even to that MORNING—hushed, calm, earliest, with her mysterious and unconjectured heart—her shape brought a thought of NIGHT!

When the ceremony was over—when the bride fell on her mother's breast and wept; and then, when turning thence, her eyes met the bridegroom's, and the tears were all smiled away—when, in that one rapid interchange of looks, spoke all that holy love can speak to love, and with timid frankness she placed her hand in his to whom she had just vowed her life,—a thrill went through the hearts of those present. Vaudemont sighed heavily. He heard his sigh echoed; but by one that had in its sound no breath of pain; he turned; Fanny had raised her veil; her eyes met his, moistened, but bright, soft, and her cheeks were rosy-red. Vaudemont recoiled before that gaze, and turned from the church. The persons interested retired to the vestry to sign their names in the registry; the crowd dispersed, and Vaudemont and Fanny stood alone in the burial-ground.

"Look, Fanny," said the former, pointing to a tomb that stood far from his mother's (for those ashes were too hallowed for such a neighbourhood). "Look yonder; it is a new tomb. Fanny, let us approach it. Can you read what is there inscribed?"

The inscription was simply this:

TO W— G—
MAN SEES THE DEED
GOD THE CIRCUMSTANCE.
JUDGE NOT,
THAT YE BE NOT JUDGED.

"Fanny, this tomb fulfils your pious wish: it is to the memory of him whom you called your father. Whatever was his life here—whatever sentence it hath received, Heaven, at least, will not condemn your piety, if you honour one who was good to you, and place flowers, however idle, even over that grave."

"It is his—my father's—and you have thought of this for me!" said Fanny, taking his hand, and sobbing. "And I have been thinking that you were not so kind to me as you were!"

"Have I not been so kind to you? Nay, forgive me, I am not happy."

"Not?—you said yesterday you had been too happy."

"To remember happiness is not to be happy, Fanny."

"That's true—and—"

Fanny stopped; and, as she bent over the tomb, musing, Vaudemont, willing to leave her undisturbed, and feeling bitterly how little his conscience could vindicate, though it might find palliation for, the dark man who slept not there—retired a few paces.

At this time the new-married pair, with their witnesses, the clergyman, &c., came from the vestry, and crossed the path. Fanny, as she turned from the tomb, saw them, and stood still, looking earnestly at the bride.

"What a lovely face!" said the mother. "Is it—yes it is—the poor idiot girl."

"Ah!" said the bridegroom, tenderly, "and she, Mary, beautiful as she is, she can never make another as happy as you have made me."

Vaudemont heard, and his heart felt sad. "Poor Fanny!—And yet, but for that affliction—I might have loved her, ere I met the fatal face of the daughter of my foe!" And with a deep compassion, an inexpressible and holy fondness, he moved to Fanny.

"Come, my child; now let us go home."

"Stay," said Fanny—"you forget." And she went to strew the flowers still left over Catherine's grave.

"Will my mother," thought Vaudemont, "forgive me, if I have other thoughts than hate and vengeance for that house which builds its greatness over her slandered name?" He groaned:—and that grave had lost its melancholy charm.

CHAPTER VII

"Of all men, I say,
That dare, for 'tis a desperate adventure,
Wear on their free necks the yoke of women,
Give me a soldier."—Knight of Malta.

"So lightly doth this little boat
Upon the scarce-touch'd billows float;
So careless doth she seem to be,
Thus left by herself on the homeless sea,
To lie there with her cheerful sail,
Till Heaven shall send some gracious gale."
WILSON: Isle of Palms.

Vaudemont returned that evening to London, and found at his lodgings a note from Lord Lilburne, stating that as his gout was now somewhat mitigated, his physician had recommended him to try change of air—that Beaufort Court was in one of the western counties, in a genial climate—that he was therefore going thither the next day for a short time—that he had asked some of Monsieur de Vaudemont's countrymen, and a few other friends, to enliven the circle of a dull country-house—that Mr. and Mrs. Beaufort would be delighted to see Monsieur de Vaudemont also—and that his compliance with their invitation would be a charity to Monsieur de Vaudemont's faithful and obliged, LILBURNE.

The first sensation of Vaudemont on reading this effusion was delight. "I shall see her," he cried; "I shall be under the same roof!" But the glow faded at once from his cheek;—the roof!—what roof? Be the guest where he held himself the lord!—be the guest of Robert Beaufort!—Was that all? Did he not meditate the deadliest war which civilised life admits of—the War of Law—war for name, property, that very hearth, with all its household gods, against this man—could he receive his hospitality? "And what then!" he exclaimed, as he paced to and fro the room,—"because her father wronged me, and because I would claim mine own—must I therefore exclude from my thoughts, from my sight, an image so fair and gentle;—the one who knelt by my side, an infant, to that hard man?—Is hate so noble a passion that it is not to admit one glimpse of Love?—Love! what word is that? Let me beware in time!" He paused in fierce self-contest, and, throwing open the window, gasped for air. The street in which he lodged was situated in the neighbourhood of St. James's; and, at that very moment, as if to defeat all opposition, and to close the struggle, Mrs. Beaufort's barouche drove by, Camilla at her side. Mrs. Beaufort, glancing up; languidly bowed; and Camilla herself perceived him, and he saw her change colour as she inclined her head. He gazed after them almost breathless, till the carriage disappeared; and then reclosing the window, he sat down to collect his thoughts, and again to reason with himself. But still, as he reasoned, he saw ever before him that blush and that smile. At last he sprang up, and a noble and bright expression elevated the character of his face,—"Yes, if I enter that house, if I eat that man's bread, and drink of his cup, I must forego, not justice—not what is due to my mother's name—but whatever belongs to hate and vengeance. If I enter that house—and if Providence permit me the means whereby to regain my rights, why she—the innocent one—she may be the means of saving her father from ruin, and stand like an angel by that boundary where justice runs into revenge!—Besides, is it not my duty to discover Sidney? Here is the only clue I shall obtain." With these thoughts he hesitated no more—he decided he would not reject this hospitality, since it might be in his power to pay it back ten thousandfold. "And who knows," he murmured again, "if Heaven, in throwing this sweet being in my way, might not have designed to subdue and chasten in me the angry passions I have so long fed on? I have seen her,—can I now hate her father?"

He sent off his note accepting the invitation. When he had done so, was he satisfied? He had taken as noble and as large a view of the duties thereby imposed on him as he well could take: but something whispered at his heart, "There is weakness in thy generosity—Darest thou love the daughter of Robert Beaufort?" And his heart had no answer to this voice.

The rapidity with which love is ripened depends less upon the actual number of years that have passed over the soil in which the seed is cast, than upon the freshness of the soil itself. A young man who lives the ordinary life of the world, and who fritters away, rather than exhausts, his feelings upon a variety of quick succeeding subjects—the Cynthias of the minute—is not apt to form a real passion at the first sight. Youth is inflammable only when the heart is young!

There are certain times of life when, in either sex, the affections are prepared, as it were, to be impressed with the first fair face that attracts the fancy and delights the eye. Such times are when the heart has been long solitary, and when some interval of idleness and rest succeeds to periods of harsher and more turbulent excitement. It was precisely such a period in the life of Vaudemont. Although his ambition had been for many years his dream, and his sword his mistress, yet naturally affectionate, and susceptible of strong emotion, he had often repined at his lonely lot. By degrees the boy's fantasy and reverence which had wound themselves round the image of Eugenie subsided into that gentle and tender melancholy which, perhaps by weakening the strength of the sterner thoughts, leaves us inclined rather to receive, than to resist, a new attachment;—and on the verge of the sweet Memory trembles the sweet Hope. The suspension of his profession, his schemes, his struggles, his career, left his passions unemployed. Vaudemont was thus unconsciously prepared to love. As we have seen, his first and earliest feelings directed themselves to Fanny. But he had so immediately detected the clanger, and so immediately recoiled from nursing those thoughts and fancies, without which love dies for want of food, for a person to whom he ascribed the affliction of an imbecility which would give to such a sentiment all the attributes either of the weakest rashness or of dishonour approaching to sacrilege—that the wings of the deity were scared away the instant their very shadow fell upon his mind. And thus, when Camilla rose upon him his heart was free to receive her image. Her graces, her accomplishments, a certain nameless charm that invested her, pleased him even more than her beauty; the recollections connected with that first time in which he had ever beheld her, were also grateful and endearing; the harshness with which her parents spoke to her moved his compassion, and addressed itself to a temper peculiarly alive to the generosity that leans towards the weak and the wronged; the engaging mixture of mildness and gaiety with which she tended her peevish and sneering uncle, convinced him of her better and more enduring qualities of disposition and womanly heart. And even—so strange and contradictory are our feelings—the very remembrance that she was connected with a family so hateful to him made her own image the more bright from the darkness that surrounded it. For was it not with the daughter of his foe that the lover of Verona fell in love at first sight? And is not that a common type of us all—as if Passion delighted in contradictions? As the Diver, in Schiller's exquisite ballad, fastened upon the rock of coral in the midst of the gloomy sea, so we cling the more gratefully to whatever of fair thought and gentle shelter smiles out to us in the depths of Hate and Strife.

But, perhaps, Vaudemont would not so suddenly and so utterly have rendered himself to a passion that began, already, completely to master his strong spirit, if he had not, from Camilla's embarrassment, her timidity, her blushes, intoxicated himself with the belief that his feelings were not unshared. And who knows not that such a belief, once cherished, ripens our own love to a development in which hours are as years?

It was, then, with such emotions as made him almost insensible to every thought but the luxury of breathing the same air as his cousin, which swept from his mind the Past, the Future—leaving nothing but a joyous, a breathless PRESENT on the Face of Time, that he repaired to Beaufort Court. He did not return to H— before he went, but he wrote to Fanny a short and hurried line to explain that he might be absent for some days at least, and promised to write again, if he should be detained longer than he anticipated.

In the meanwhile, one of those successive revolutions which had marked the eras in Fanny's moral existence took its date from that last time they had walked and conversed together.

The very evening of that day, some hours after Philip was gone, and after Simon had retired to rest, Fanny was sitting before the dying fire in the little parlour in an attitude of deep and pensive reverie. The old woman-servant, Sarah, who, very different from Mrs. Boxer, loved Fanny with her whole heart, came into the room as was her wont before going to bed, to see that the fire was duly out, and all safe: and as she approached the hearth, she started to see Fanny still up.

"Dear heart alive!" she said; "why, Miss Fanny, you will catch your death of cold,—what are you thinking about?"

"Sit down, Sarah; I want to speak to you." Now, though Fanny was exceedingly kind, and attached to Sarah, she was seldom communicative to her, or indeed to any one. It was usually in its own silence and darkness that that lovely mind worked out its own doubts.

"Do you, my sweet young lady? I'm sure anything I can do—" and Sarah seated herself in her master's great chair, and drew it close to Fanny. There was no light in the room but the expiring fire, and it threw upward a pale glimmer on the two faces bending over it,—the one so strangely beautiful, so smooth, so blooming, so exquisite in its youth and innocence,—the other withered, wrinkled, meagre, and astute. It was like the Fairy and the Witch together.

"Well, miss," said the crone, observing that, after a considerable pause, Fanny was still silent,—"Well—"

"Sarah, I have seen a wedding!"

"Have you?" and the old woman laughed. "Oh! I heard it was to be to-day!—young Waldron's wedding! Yes, they have been long sweethearts."

"Were you ever married, Sarah?"

"Lord bless you,—yes! and a very good husband I had, poor man! But he's dead these many years; and if you had not taken me, I must have gone to the workhus."

"He is dead! Wasn't it very hard to live after that, Sarah?"

"The Lord strengthens the hearts of widders!" observed Sarah, sanctimoniously.

"Did you marry your brother, Sarah?" said Fanny, playing with the corner of her apron.

"My brother!" exclaimed the old woman, aghast. "La! miss, you must not talk in that way,—it's quite wicked and heathenish! One must not marry one's brother!"

"No!" said Fanny, tremblingly, and turning very pale, even by that light. "No!—are you sure of that?"

"It is the wickedest thing even to talk about, my dear young mistress;—but you're like a babby unborn!"

Fanny was silent for some moments. At length she said, unconscious that she was speaking aloud, "But he is not my brother, after all!"

"Oh, miss, fie! Are you letting your pretty head run on the handsome gentleman. You, too,—dear, dear! I see we're all alike, we poor femel creturs! You! who'd have thought it? Oh, Miss Fanny!—you'll break your heart if you goes for to fancy any such thing."

"Any what thing?"

"Why, that that gentleman will marry you!—I'm sure, tho' he's so simple like, he's some great gentleman! They say his hoss is worth a hundred pounds! Dear, dear! why didn't I ever think of this before? He must be a very wicked man. I see, now, why he comes here. I'll speak to him, that I will!—a very wicked man!"

Sarah was startled from her indignation by Fanny's rising suddenly, and standing before her in the flickering twilight, almost like a shape transformed,—so tall did she seem, so stately, so dignified.

"Is it of him that you are speaking?" said she, in a voice of calm but deep resentment—"of him! If so, Sarah, we two can live no more in the same house."

And these words were said with a propriety and collectedness that even, through all her terrors, showed at once to Sarah how much they now wronged Fanny who had suffered their lips to repeat the parrot-cry of the "idiot girl!"

"O! gracious me!—miss—ma'am—I am so sorry—I'd rather bite out my tongue than say a word to offend you; it was only my love for you, dear innocent creature that you are!" and the honest woman sobbed with real passion as she clasped Fanny's hand. "There have been so many young persons, good and harmless, yes, even as you are, ruined. But you don't understand me. Miss Fanny! hear me; I must try and say what I would say. That man, that gentleman—so proud, so well-dressed, so grand-like, will never marry you, never—never. And if ever he says he does love you, and you say you love him, and you two don't marry, you will be ruined and wicked, and die—die of a broken heart!"

The earnestness of Sarah's manner subdued and almost awed Fanny. She sank down again in her chair, and suffered the old woman to caress and weep over her hand for some moments in a silence that concealed the darkest and most agitated feelings Fanny's life had hitherto known. At length she said:—

"Why may he not marry me if he loves me?—he is not my brother,—indeed he is not! I'll never call him so again."

"He cannot marry you," said Sarah, resolved, with a sort of rude nobleness, to persevere in what she felt to be a duty; "I don't say anything about money, because that does not always signify. But he cannot marry you, because—because people who are hedicated one way never marry those who are hedicated and brought up in another. A gentleman of that kind requires a wife to know—oh—to know ever so much; and you—"

"Sarah," interrupted Fanny, rising again, but this time with a smile on her face, "don't say anything more about it; I forgive you, if you promise never to speak unkindly of him again—never—never—never, Sarah!"

"But may I just tell him that—that—"

"That what?"

"That you are so young and innocent, and has no pertector like; and that if you were to love him it would be a shame in him—that it would!"

And then (oh, no, Fanny, there was nothing clouded now in your reason!)—and then the woman's alarm, the modesty, the instinct, the terror came upon her:—

"Never! never! I will not love him, I do not love him, indeed, Sarah. If you speak to him, I will never look you in the face again. It is all past—all, dear Sarah!"

She kissed the old woman; and Sarah, fancying that her sagacity and counsel had prevailed, promised all she was asked; so they went up-stairs together—friends.

CHAPTER VIII

"As the wind
Sobs, an uncertain sweetness comes from out
The orange-trees.

Rise up, Olympia.—She sleeps soundly. Ho!
Stirring at last." BARRY CORNWALL.

The next day, Fanny was seen by Sarah counting the little hoard that she had so long and so painfully saved for her benefactor's tomb. The money was no longer wanted for that object. Fanny had found another; she said nothing to Sarah or to Simon. But there was a strange complacent smile upon her lip as she busied herself in her work, that puzzled the old woman. Late at noon came the postman's unwonted knock at the door. A letter!—a letter for Miss Fanny. A letter!—the first she had ever received in her life! And it was from him!—and it began with "Dear Fanny." Vaudemont had called her "dear Fanny" a hundred times, and the expression had become a matter of course. But "Dear Fanny" seemed so very different when it was written. The letter could not well be shorter, nor, all things considered, colder. But the girl found no fault with it. It began with "Dear Fanny," and it ended with "yours truly." "—Yours truly—mine truly—and how kind to write at all!" Now it so happened that Vaudemont, having never merged the art of the penman into that rapid scrawl into which people, who are compelled to write hurriedly and constantly, degenerate, wrote a remarkably good hand,—bold, clear, symmetrical—almost too good a hand for one who was not to make money by caligraphy. And after Fanny had got the words by heart, she stole gently to a cupboard and took forth some specimens of her own hand, in the shape of house and work memoranda, and extracts which, the better to help her memory, she had made from the poem-book Vaudemont had given her. She gravely laid his letter by the side of these specimens, and blushed at the contrast; yet, after all, her own writing, though trembling and irresolute, was far from a bad or vulgar hand. But emulation was now fairly roused within her. Vaudemont, pre-occupied by more engrossing thoughts, and indeed, forgetting a danger which had seemed so thoroughly to have passed away, did not in his letter caution Fanny against going out alone. She remarked this; and having completely recovered her own alarm at the attempt that had been made on her liberty, she thought she was now released from her promise to guard against a past and imaginary peril. So after dinner she slipped out alone, and went to the mistress of the school where she had received her elementary education. She had ever since continued her acquaintance with that lady, who, kindhearted, and touched by her situation, often employed her industry, and was far from blind to the improvement that had for some time been silently working in the mind of her old pupil.

Fanny had a long conversation with this lady, and she brought back a bundle of books. The light might have been seen that night, and many nights after, burning long and late from her little window. And having recovered her old freedom of habits, which Simon, poor man, did not notice, and which Sarah, thinking that anything was better than moping at home, did not remonstrate against, Fanny went out regularly for two hours, or sometimes for even a longer period, every evening after old Simon had composed himself to the nap that filled up the interval between dinner and tea.

In a very short time—a time that with ordinary stimulants would have seemed marvellously short—Fanny's handwriting was not the same thing; her manner of talking became different; she no longer called herself "Fanny" when she spoke; the music of her voice was more quiet and settled; her sweet expression of face was more thoughtful; the eyes seemed to have deepened in their very colour; she was no longer heard chaunting to herself as she tripped along. The books that she nightly fed on had passed into her mind; the poetry that had ever unconsciously sported round her young years began now to create poetry in herself. Nay, it might almost have seemed as if that restless disorder of the intellect, which the dullards had called Idiotcy, had been the wild efforts, not of Folly, but of GENIUS seeking to find its path and outlet from the cold and dreary solitude to which the circumstances of her early life had compelled it.

Days, even weeks, passed—she never spoke of Vaudemont. And once, when Sarah, astonished and bewildered by the change in her young mistress, asked:

"When does the gentleman come back?"

Fanny answered, with a mysterious smile, "Not yet, I hope,—not quite yet!"

CHAPTER IX

"Thierry. I do begin
To feel an alteration in my nature,

And in his full-sailed confidence a shower
Of gentle rain, that falling on the fire
Hath quenched it.

How is my heart divided
Between the duty of a son and love!"
BEAUMONT AND FLETCHER: Thierry and Theodorat.

Vaudemont had now been a month at Beaufort Court. The scene of a country-house, with the sports that enliven it, and the accomplishments it calls forth, was one in which he was well fitted to shine. He had been an excellent shot as a boy; and though long unused to the fowling-piece, had, in India, acquired a deadly precision with the rifle; so that a very few days of practice in the stubbles and covers of Beaufort Court made his skill the theme of the guests and the admiration of the keepers. Hunting began, and—this pursuit, always so strong a passion in the active man, and which, to the turbulence and agitation of his half-tamed breast, now excited by a kind of frenzy of hope and fear, gave a vent and release—was a sport in which he was yet more fitted to excel. His horsemanship, his daring, the stone walls he leaped and the floods through which he dashed, furnished his companions with wondering tale and comment on their return home. Mr. Marsden, who, with some other of Arthur's early friends, had been invited to Beaufort Court, in order to welcome its expected heir, and who retained all the prudence which had distinguished him of yore, when having ridden over old Simon he dismounted to examine the knees of his horse;—Mr. Marsden, a skilful huntsman, who rode the most experienced horses in the world, and who generally contrived to be in at the death without having leaped over anything higher than a hurdle, suffering the bolder quadruped (in case what is called the "knowledge of the country"—that is, the knowledge of gaps and gates—failed him) to perform the more dangerous feats alone, as he quietly scrambled over or scrambled through upon foot, and remounted the well-taught animal when it halted after the exploit, safe and sound;—Mr. Marsden declared that he never saw a rider with so little judgment as Monsieur de Vaudemont, and that the devil was certainly in him.

This sort of reputation, commonplace and merely physical as it was in itself, had a certain effect upon Camilla; it might be an effect of fear. I do not say, for I do not know, what her feelings towards Vaudemont exactly were. As the calmest natures are often those the most hurried away by their contraries, so, perhaps, he awed and dazzled rather than pleased her;—at least, he certainly forced himself on her interest. Still she would have started in terror if any one had said to her, "Do you love your betrothed less than when you met by that happy lake?"—and her heart would have indignantly rebuked the questioner. The letters of her lover were still long and frequent; hers were briefer and more subdued. But then there was constraint in the correspondence—it was submitted to her mother. Whatever might be Vaudemont's manner to Camilla whenever occasion threw them alone together, he certainly did not make his attentions glaring enough to be remarked. His eye watched her rather than his lip addressed; he kept as much aloof as possible from the rest of her family, and his customary bearing was silent even to gloom. But there were moments when he indulged in a fitful exuberance of spirits, which had something strained and unnatural. He had outlived Lord Lilburne's short liking; for since he had resolved no longer to keep watch on that noble gamester's method of play, he played but little himself; and Lord Lilburne saw that he had no chance of ruining him—there was, therefore, no longer any reason to like him. But this was not all; when Vaudemont had been at the house somewhat more than two weeks, Lilburne, petulant and impatient, whether at his refusals to join the card-table, or at the moderation with which, when he did, he confined his ill-luck to petty losses, one day limped up to him, as he stood at the embrasure of the window, gazing on the wide lands beyond, and said:—

"Vaudemont, you are bolder in hunting, they tell me, than you are at whist."

"Honours don't tell against one—over a hedge!"

"What do you mean?" said Lilburne, rather haughtily.

Vaudemont was, at that moment, in one of those bitter moods when the sense of his situation, the sight of the usurper in his home, often swept away the gentler thoughts inspired by his fatal passion. And the tone of Lord Lilburne, and his loathing to the man, were too much for his temper.

"Lord Lilburne," he said, and his lip curled, "if you had been born poor, you would have made a great fortune—you play luckily."

"How am I to take this, sir?"

"As you please," answered Vaudemont, calmly, but with an eye of fire. And he turned away.

Lilburne remained on the spot very thoughtful: "Hum! he suspects me. I cannot quarrel on such ground—the suspicion itself dishonours me—I must seek another."

The next day, Lilburne, who was familiar with Mr. Harsden (though the latter gentleman never played at the same table), asked that prudent person after breakfast if he happened to have his pistols with him.

"Yes; I always take them into the country—one may as well practise when one has the opportunity. Besides, sportsmen are often quarrelsome; and if it is known that one shoots well,—it keeps one out of quarrels!"

"Very true," said Lilburne, rather admiringly. "I have made the same remark myself when I was younger. I have not shot with a pistol for some years. I am well enough now to walk out with the help of a stick. Suppose we practise for half-an-hour or so."

"With all my heart," said Mr. Marsden.

The pistols were brought, and they strolled forth;—Lord Lilburne found his hand out.

"As I never hunt now," said the peer, and he gnashed his teeth, and glanced at his maimed limb; "for though lameness would not prevent my keeping my seat, violent exercise hurts my leg; and Brodie says any fresh accident might bring on tic douloureux;—and as my gout does not permit me to join the shooting parties at present, it would be a kindness in you to lend me your pistols—it would while away an hour or so; though, thank Heaven, my duelling days are over!"

"Certainly," said Mr. Marsden; and the pistols were consigned to Lord Lilburne.

Four days from the date, as Mr. Marsden, Vaudemont, and some other gentlemen were making for the covers, they came upon Lord Lilburne, who, in a part of the park not within sight or sound of the house, was amusing himself with Mr. Marsden's pistols, which Dykeman was at hand to load for him.

He turned round, not at all disconcerted by the interruption.

"You have no idea how I've improved, Marsden:—just see!" and he pointed to a glove nailed to a tree. "I've hit that mark twice in five times; and every time I have gone straight enough along the line to have killed my man."

"Ay, the mark itself does not so much signify," said Mr. Marsden, "at least, not in actual duelling—the great thing is to be in the line."

While he spoke, Lord Lilburne's ball went a third time through the glove. His cold bright eye turned on Vaudemont, as he said, with a smile,—

"They tell me you shoot well with a fowling-piece, my dear Vaudemont—are you equally adroit with a pistol?"

"You may see, if you like; but you take aim, Lord Lilburne; that would be of no use in English duelling. Permit me."

He walked to the glove, and tore from it one of the fingers, which he fastened separately to the tree, took the pistol from Dykeman as he walked past him, gained the spot whence to fire, turned at once round, without apparent aim, and the finger fell to the ground.

Lilburne stood aghast.

"That's wonderful!" said Marsden; "quite wonderful. Where the devil did you get such a knack?—for it is only knack after all!"

"I lived for many years in a country where the practice was constant, where all that belongs to rifle-shooting was a necessary accomplishment—a country in which man had often to contend against the wild beast. In civilised states, man himself supplies the place of the wild beast—but we don't hunt him!—Lord Lilburne" (and this was added with a smiling and disdainful whisper), "you must practise a little more."

But, disregardful of the advice, from that day Lord Lilburne's morning occupation was gone. He thought no longer of a duel with Vaudemont. As soon as the sportsman had left him, he bade Dykeman take up the pistols, and walked straight home into the library, where Robert Beaufort, who was no sportsman, generally spent his mornings.

He flung himself into an arm-chair, and said, as he stirred the fire with unusual vehemence,—

"Beaufort, I'm very sorry I asked you to invite Vaudemont. He's a very ill-bred, disagreeable fellow!" Beaufort threw down his steward's account-book, on which he was employed, and replied,—

"Lilburne, I have never had an easy moment since that man has been in the house. As he was your guest, I did not like to speak before, but don't you observe—you must observe—how like he is to the old family portraits? The more I have examined him, the more another resemblance grows upon me. In a word," said Robert, pausing and breathing hard, "if his name were not Vaudemont—if his history were not, apparently, so well known, I should say—I should swear, that it is Philip Morton who sleeps under this roof!"

"Ha!" said Lilburne, with an earnestness that surprised Beaufort, who expected to have heard his brother-in-law's sneering sarcasm at his fears; "the likeness you speak of to the old portraits did strike me; it struck Marsden, too, the other day, as we were passing through the picture-gallery; and Marsden remarked it aloud to Vaudemont. I remember now that he changed countenance and made no answer. Hush! hush! hold your tongue, let me think—let me think. This Philip—yes—yes—I and Arthur saw him with—with Gawtrey—in Paris—"

"Gawtrey! was that the name of the rogue he was said to—"

"Yes—yes—yes. Ah! now I guess the meaning of those looks—those words," muttered Lilburne between his teeth. "This pretension to the name of Vaudemont was always apocryphal—the story always but half believed—the invention of a woman in love with him—the claim on your property is made at the very time he appears in England. Ha! Have you a newspaper there? Give it me. No! 'tis not in this paper. Ring the bell for the file!"

"What's the matter? you terrify me!" gasped out Mr. Beaufort, as he rang the bell.

"Why! have you not seen an advertisement repeated several times within the last month?"

"I never read advertisements; except in the county paper, if land is to be sold."

"Nor I often; but this caught my eye. John" (here the servant entered), "bring the file of the newspapers. The name of the witness whom Mrs. Morton appealed to was Smith, the same name as the captain; what was the Christian name?"

"I don't remember."

"Here are the papers—shut the door—and here is the advertisement: 'If Mr. William Smith, son of Jeremiah Smith, who formerly rented the farm of Shipdale-Bury, under the late Right Hon. Charles Leopold Beaufort (that's your uncle), and who emigrated in the year 18— to Australia, will apply to Mr. Barlow, Solicitor, Essex Street, Strand, he will hear of something to his advantage.'"

"Good Heavens! why did not you mention this to me before?"

"Because I did not think it of any importance. In the first place, there might be some legacy left to the man, quite distinct from your business. Indeed, that was the probable supposition;—or even if connected with the claim, such an advertisement might be but a despicable attempt to frighten you. Never mind—don't look so pale—after all, this is a proof that the witness is not found—that Captain Smith is neither the Smith, nor has discovered where the Smith is!"

"True!" observed Mr. Beaufort: "true—very true!"

"Humph!" said Lord Lilburne, who was still rapidly glancing over the file—"Here is another advertisement which I never saw before: this looks suspicious: 'If the person who called on the — of September, on Mr. Morton, linendraper, &c., of N—, will renew his application personally or by letter, he may now obtain the information he sought for.'"

"Morton!—the woman's brother! their uncle! it is too clear!"

"But what brings this man, if he be really Philip Morton, what brings him here!—to spy or to threaten?"

"I will get him out of the house this day."

"No—no; turn the watch upon himself. I see now; he is attracted by your daughter; sound her quietly; don't tell her to discourage his confidences; find out if he ever speaks of these Mortons. Ha! I recollect—he has spoken to me of the Mortons, but vaguely—I forget what. Humph! this is a man of spirit and daring—watch him, I say,—watch him! When does Arthur came back?"

"He has been travelling so slowly, for he still complains of his health, and has had relapses; but he ought to be in Paris this week, perhaps he is there now. Good Heavens! he must not meet this man!"

"Do what I tell you! get out all from your daughter. Never fear: he can do nothing against you except by law. But if he really like Camilla—"

"He!—Philip Morton—the adventurer—the—"

"He is the eldest son: remember you thought even of accepting the second. He—nay find the witness—he may win his suit; if he likes Camilla, there may be a compromise."

Mr. Beaufort felt as if turned to ice.

"You think him likely to win this infamous suit, then?" he faltered.

"Did not you guard against the possibility by securing the brother? More worth while to do it with this man. Hark ye! the politics of private are like those of public life,—when the state can't crush a demagogue, it should entice him over. If you can ruin this dog" (and Lilburne stamped his foot fiercely, forgetful of the gout), "ruin him! hang him! If you can't" (and here with a wry face he caressed the injured foot), "if you can't ['sdeath, what a twinge!], and he can ruin you,—bring him into the family, and make his secret ours! I must go and lie down—I have overexcited myself."

In great perplexity Beaufort repaired at once to Camilla. His nervous agitation betrayed itself, though he smiled a ghastly smile, and intended to be exceeding cool and collected. His questions, which confused and alarmed her, soon drew out the fact that the very first time Vaudemont had been introduced to her he had spoken of the Mortons; and that he had often afterwards alluded to the subject, and seemed at first strongly impressed with the notion that the younger brother was under Beaufort's protection; though at last he appeared reluctantly convinced of the contrary. Robert, however agitated, preserved at least enough of his natural slyness not to let out that he suspected Vaudemont to be Philip Morton himself, for he feared lest his daughter should betray that suspicion to its object.

"But," he said, with a look meant to win confidence, "I dare say he knows these young men. I should like myself to know more about them. Learn all you can, and tell me, and, I say—I say, Camilla,—he! he! he!—you have made a conquest, you little flirt, you! Did he, this Vaudemont, ever say how much he admired you?"

"He!—never!" said Camilla, blushing, and then turning pale.

"But he looks it. Ah! you say nothing, then. Well, well, don't discourage him; that is to say,—yes, don't discourage him. Talk to him as much as you can,—ask him about his own early life. I've a particular wish to know—'tis of great importance to me."

"But, my dear father," said Camilla, trembling and thoroughly bewildered, "I fear this man,—I fear—I fear—"

Was she going to add, "I fear myself?" I know not; but she stopped short, and burst into tears.

"Hang these girls!" muttered Mr. Beaufort, "always crying when they ought to be of use to one. Go down, dry your eyes, do as I tell you,—get all you can from him. Fear him!—yes, I dare say she does!" muttered the poor man, as he closed the door.

From that time what wonder that Camilla's manner to Vaudemont was yet more embarrassed than ever: what wonder that he put his own heart's interpretation on that confusion. Beaufort took care to thrust her more often than before in his way; he suddenly affected a creeping, fawning civility to Vaudemont; he was sure he was fond of music; what did he think of that new air Camilla was so fond of? He must be a judge of scenery, he who had seen so much: there were beautiful landscapes in the neighbourhood, and, if he would forego his sports, Camilla drew prettily, had an eye for that sort of thing, and was so fond of riding.

Vaudemont was astonished at this change, but his delight was greater than the astonishment. He began to perceive that his identity was suspected; perhaps Beaufort, more generous than he had deemed him, meant to repay every early wrong or harshness by one inestimable blessing. The generous interpret motives in extremes—ever too enthusiastic or too severe. Vaudemont felt as if he had wronged the wronger; he began to conquer even his dislike to Robert Beaufort. For some days he was thus thrown much with Camilla; the questions her father forced her to put to him, uttered tremulously and fearfully, seemed to him proof of her interest in his fate. His feelings to Camilla, so sudden in their growth—so ripened and so favoured by the Sub-Ruler of the world—CIRCUMSTANCE—might not, perhaps, have the depth and the calm completeness of that, One True Love, of which there are many counterfeits,—and which in Man, at least, possibly requires the touch and mellowness, if not of time, at least of many memories—of perfect and tried conviction of the faith, the worth, the value and the beauty of the heart to which it clings;—but those feelings were, nevertheless, strong, ardent, and intense. He believed himself beloved—he was in Elysium. But he did not yet declare the passion that beamed in his eyes. No! he would not yet claim the hand of Camilla Beaufort, for he imagined the time would soon come when he could claim it, not as the inferior or the suppliant, but as the lord of her father's fate.

CHAPTER X

"Here's something got amongst us!"—Knight of Malta.

Two or three nights after his memorable conversation with Robert Beaufort, as Lord Lilburne was undressing, he said to his valet:

"Dykeman, I am getting well."

"Indeed, my lord, I never saw your lordship look better."

"There you lie. I looked better last year—I looked better the year before—and I looked better and better every year back to the age of twenty-one! But I'm not talking of looks, no man with money wants looks. I am talking of feelings. I feel better. The gout is almost gone. I have been quiet now for a month—that's a long time—time wasted when, at my age, I have so little time to waste. Besides, as you know, I am very much in love!"

"In love, my lord? I thought that you told me never to speak of—"

"Blockhead! what the deuce was the good of speaking about it when I was wrapped in flannels! I am never in love when I am ill—who is? I am well now, or nearly so; and I've had things to vex me—things to make this place very disagreeable; I shall go to town, and before this day week, perhaps, that charming face may enliven the solitude of Fernside. I shall look to it myself now. I see you're going to say something. Spare yourself the trouble! nothing ever goes wrong if I myself take it in hand."

The next day Lord Lilburne, who, in truth, felt himself uncomfortable and gene in the presence of Vaudemont; who had won as much as the guests at Beaufort Court seemed inclined to lose; and who made it the rule of his life to consult his own pleasure and amusement before anything else, sent for his post-horses, and informed his brother-in-law of his departure.

"And you leave me alone with this man just when I am convinced that he is the person we suspected! My dear Lilburne, do stay till he goes."

"Impossible! I am between fifty and sixty—every moment is precious at that time of life. Besides, I've said all I can say; rest quiet—act on the defensive—entangle this cursed Vaudemont, or Morton, or whoever he be, in the mesh of your daughter's charms, and then get rid of him, not before. This can do no harm, let the matter turn out how it will. Read the papers; and send for Blackwell if you want advice on any new advertisements. I don't see that anything more is to be done at present. You can write to me; I shall be at Park Lane or Fernside. Take care of yourself. You're a lucky fellow—you never have the gout! Good-bye."

And in half an hour Lord Lilburne was on the road to London.

The departure of Lilburne was a signal to many others, especially and naturally to those he himself had invited. He had not announced to such visitors his intention of going till his carriage was at the door. This might be delicacy or carelessness, just as people chose to take it: and how they did take it, Lord Lilburne, much too selfish to be well-bred, did not care a rush. The next day half at least of the guests were gone; and even Mr. Marsden, who had been specially invited on Arthur's account, announced that he should go after dinner! he always travelled by night—he slept well on the road—a day was not lost by it.

"And it is so long since you saw Arthur," said Mr. Beaufort, in remonstrance, "and I expect him every day."

"Very sorry—best fellow in the world—but the fact is, that I am not very well myself. I want a little sea air; I shall go to Dover or Brighton. But I suppose you will have the house full again about Christmas; in that case I shall be delighted to repeat my visit."

The fact was, that Mr. Marsden, without Lilburne's intellect on the one hand, or vices on the other, was, like that noble sensualist, one of the broken pieces of the great looking-glass "SELF." He was noticed in society as always haunting the places where Lilburne played at cards, carefully choosing some other table, and as carefully betting upon Lilburne's side. The card-tables were now broken up; Vaudemont's superiority in shooting, and the manner in which he engrossed the talk of the sportsmen, displeased him. He was bored—he wanted to be off—and off he went. Vaudemont felt that the time was come for him to depart, too; Robert Beaufort—who felt in his society the painful fascination of the bird with the boa, who hated to see him there, and dreaded to see him depart, who had not yet extracted all the confirmation of his persuasions that he required, for Vaudemont easily enough parried the artless questions of Camilla—pressed him to stay with so eager a hospitality, and made Camilla herself falter out, against her will, and even against her remonstrances—(she never before had dared to remonstrate with either father or mother),—"Could not you stay a few days longer?"—that Vaudemont was too contented to yield to his own inclinations; and so for some little time longer he continued to move before the eyes of Mr. Beaufort—stern, sinister, silent, mysterious—like one of the family pictures stepped down from its frame. Vaudemont wrote, however, to Fanny, to excuse his delay; and anxious to hear from her as to her own and Simon's health, bade her direct her letter to his lodging in London (of which he gave her the address), whence, if he still continued to defer his departure, it would be forwarded to him. He did not do this, however, till he had been at Beaufort Court several days after Lilburne's departure, and till, in fact, two days before the eventful one which closed his visit.

The party, now greatly diminished; were at breakfast, when the servant entered, as usual, with the letter-bag. Mr. Beaufort, who was always important and pompous in the small ceremonials of life, unlocked the precious deposit with slow dignity, drew forth the newspapers, which he threw on the table, and which the gentlemen of the party eagerly seized; then, diving out one by one, jerked first a letter to Camilla, next a letter to Vaudemont, and, thirdly, seized a letter for himself.

"I beg that there may be no ceremony, Monsieur de Vaudemont: pray excuse me and follow my example: I see this letter is from my son;" and he broke the seal.

The letter ran thus:

"MY DEAR FATHER,—Almost as soon as you receive this, I shall be with you. Ill as I am, I can have no peace till I see and consult you. The most startling—the most painful intelligence has just been conveyed to me. It is of a nature not to bear any but personal communication.

"Your affectionate son,
"ARTHUR BEAUFORT. "Boulogne.

"P.S.—This will go by the same packet-boat that I shall take myself, and can only reach you a few hours before I arrive."

Mr. Beaufort's trembling hand dropped the letter—he grasped the elbow of the chair to save himself from falling. It was clear!—the same visitor who had persecuted himself had now sought his son! He grew sick, his son might have heard the witness—might be convinced. His son himself now appeared to him as a foe—for the father dreaded the son's honour! He glanced furtively round the table, till his eye rested on Vaudemont, and his terror was redoubled, for Vaudemont's face, usually so calm, was animated to an extraordinary degree, as he now lifted it from the letter he had just read. Their eyes met.

Robert Beaufort looked on him as a prisoner at the bar looks on the accusing counsel, when he first commences his harangue.

"Mr. Beaufort," said the guest, "the letter you have given me summons me to London on important business, and immediately. Suffer me to send for horses at your earliest convenience."

"What's the matter?" said the feeble and seldom heard voice of Mrs. Beaufort. "What's the matter, Robert?—is Arthur coming?"

"He comes to-day," said the father, with a deep sigh; and Vaudemont, at that moment rising from his half-finished breakfast, with a bow that included the group, and with a glance that lingered on Camilla, as she bent over her own unopened letter (a letter from Winandermere, the seal of which she dared not yet to break), quitted the room. He hastened to his own chamber, and strode to and fro with a stately step—the step of the Master—then, taking forth the letter, he again hurried over its contents. They ran thus:

DEAR, Sir,—At last the missing witness has applied to me. He proves to be, as you conjectured, the same person who had called on Mr. Roger Morton; but as there are some circumstances on which I wish to take your instructions without a moment's delay, I shall leave London by the mail, and wait you at D— (at the principal inn), which is, I understand, twenty miles on the high road from Beaufort Court.

"I have the honor to be, sir,
"Yours, &c.,
"JOHN BARLOW.

Vaudemont was yet lost in the emotions that this letter aroused, when they came to announce that his chaise was arrived. As he went down the stairs he met Camilla, who was on the way to her own room.

"Miss Beaufort," said he, in a low and tremulous voice, "in wishing you farewell I may not now say more. I leave you, and, strange to say, I do not regret it, for I go upon an errand that may entitle me to return again, and speak those thoughts which are uppermost in my soul even at this moment."

He raised her hand to his lips as he spoke, and at that moment Mr. Beaufort looked from the door of his own room, and cried, "Camilla." She was too glad to escape. Philip gazed after her light form for an instant, and then hurried down the stairs.

CHAPTER XI

"Longueville.—What! are you married, Beaufort?
Beaufort.—Ay, as fast
As words, and hands, and hearts, and priest,
Could make us."—BEAUMONT AND FLETCHER: Noble Gentleman.

In the parlour of the inn at D— sat Mr. John Barlow. He had just finished his breakfast, and was writing letters and looking over papers connected with his various business—when the door was thrown open, and a gentleman entered abruptly.

"Mr. Beaufort," said the lawyer rising, "Mr. Philip Beaufort—for such I now feel you are by right—though," he added, with his usual formal and quiet smile, "not yet by law; and much—very much, remains to be done to make the law and the right the same;—I congratulate you on having something at last to work on. I had begun to despair of finding our witness, after a month's advertising; and had commenced other investigations, of which I will speak to you presently, when yesterday, on my return to town from an errand on your business, I had the pleasure of a visit from William Smith himself.—My dear sir, do not yet be too sanguine.—It seems that this poor fellow, having known misfortune, was in America when the first fruitless inquiries were made. Long after this he returned to the colony, and there met with a brother, who, as I drew from him, was a convict. He helped the brother to escape. They both came to England. William learned from a distant relation, who lent him some little money, of the inquiry that had been set on foot for him; consulted his brother, who desired him to leave all to his management. The brother afterwards assured him that you and Mr. Sidney were both dead; and it seems (for the witness is simple enough to allow me to extract all) this same brother then went to Mr. Beaufort to hold out the threat of a lawsuit, and to offer the sale of the evidence yet existing—"

"And Mr. Beaufort?"

"I am happy to say, seems to have spurned the offer. Meanwhile William, incredulous of his brother's report, proceeded to N—, learned nothing from Mr. Morton, met his brother again—and the brother (confessing that he had deceived him in the assertion that you and Mr. Sidney were dead) told him that he had known you in earlier life, and set out to Paris to seek you—"

"Known me?—To Paris?"

"More of this presently. William returned to town, living hardly and penuriously on the little his brother bestowed on him, too melancholy and too poor for the luxury of a newspaper, and never saw our advertisement, till, as luck would have it, his money was out; he had heard nothing further of his brother, and he went for new assistance to the same relation who had before aided him. This relation, to his surprise, received the poor man very kindly, lent him what he wanted, and then asked him if he had not seen our advertisement. The newspaper shown him contained both the advertisements—that relating to Mr. Morton's visitor, that containing his own name. He coupled them both together—called on me at once. I was from town on your business. He returned to his own home; the next morning (yesterday morning) came a letter from his brother, which I obtained from him at last, and with promises that no harm should happen to the writer on account of it."

Vaudemont took the letter and read as follows:

"DEAR WILLIAM,—No go about the youngster I went after: all researches in vane. Paris develish expensive. Never mind, I have sene the other—the young B—; different sort of fellow from his father—very ill—frightened out of his wits—will go off to the governor, take me with him as far as Bullone. I think we shall settel it now. Mind as I saide before, don't put your foot in it. I send you a Nap in the Seele—all I can spare.

"Yours,
"JEREMIAH SMITH.

"Direct to me, Monsieur Smith—always a safe name—Ship Inn, Bullone."

"Jeremiah—Smith—Jeremiah!"

"Do you know the name then?" said Mr. Barlow. "Well; the poor man owns that he was frightened at his brother—that he wished to do what is right—that he feared his brother would not let him—that your father was very kind to him—and so he came off at once to me; and I was very luckily at home to assure him that the heir was alive, and prepared to assert his rights. Now then, Mr. Beaufort, we have the witness, but will that suffice us? I fear not. Will the jury believe him with no other testimony at his back? Consider!—When he was gone I put myself in communication with some officers at Bow Street about this brother of his—a most notorious character, commonly called in the police slang Dashing Jerry—"

"Ah! Well, proceed!"

"Your one witness, then, is a very poor, penniless man, his brother a rogue, a convict: this witness, too, is the most timid, fluctuating, irresolute fellow I ever saw; I should tremble for his testimony against a sharp, bullying lawyer. And that, sir, is all at present we have to look to."

"I see—I see. It is dangerous—it is hazardous. But truth is truth; justice—justice! I will run the risk."

"Pardon me, if I ask, did you ever know this brother?—were you ever absolutely acquainted with him—in the same house?"

"Many years since—years of early hardship and trial—I was acquainted with him—what then?"

"I am sorry to hear it," and the lawyer looked grave. "Do you not see that if this witness is browbeat—is disbelieved, and if it be shown that you, the claimant, was—forgive my saying it—intimate with a brother of such a character, why the whole thing might be made to look like perjury and conspiracy. If we stop here it is an ugly business!"

"And is this all you have to say to me? The witness is found—the only surviving witness—the only proof I ever shall or ever can obtain, and you seek to terrify me—me too—from using the means for redress Providence itself vouchsafes me—Sir, I will not hear you!"

"Mr. Beaufort, you are impatient—it is natural. But if we go to law—that is, should I have anything to do with it, wait—wait till your case is good. And hear me yet. This is not the only proof—this is not the only witness; you forget that there was an examined copy of the register; we may yet find that copy, and the person who copied it may yet be alive to attest it. Occupied with this thought, and weary of waiting the result of our advertisement, I resolved to go into the neighbourhood of Fernside; luckily, there was a gentleman's seat to be sold in the village. I made the survey of this place my apparent business. After going over the house, I appeared anxious to see how far some alterations could be made—alterations to render it more like Lord Lilburne's villa. This led me to request a sight of that villa—a crown to the housekeeper got me admittance. The housekeeper had lived with your father, and been retained by his lordship. I soon, therefore, knew which were the rooms the late Mr. Beaufort had principally occupied; shown into his study, where it was probable he would keep his papers, I inquired if it were the same furniture (which seemed likely enough from its age and fashion) as in your father's time: it was so; Lord Lilburne had bought the house just as it stood, and, save a few additions in the drawing-room, the general equipment of the villa remained unaltered. You look impatient!—I'm coming to the point. My eye fell upon an old-fashioned bureau—"

"But we searched every drawer in that bureau!"

"Any secret drawers?"

"Secret drawers! No! there were no secret drawers that I ever heard of!"

Mr. Barlow rubbed his hands and mused a moment.

"I was struck with that bureau; for any father had had one like it. It is not English—it is of Dutch manufacture."

"Yes, I have heard that my father bought it at a sale, three or four years after his marriage."

"I learned this from the housekeeper, who was flattered by my admiring it. I could not find out from her at what sale it had been purchased, but it was in the neighbourhood she was sure. I had now a date to go upon; I learned, by careless inquiries, what sales near Fernside had taken place in a certain year. A gentleman had died at that date whose furniture was sold by auction. With great difficulty, I found that his widow was still alive, living far up the country: I paid her a visit; and, not to fatigue you with too long an account, I have only to say that she not only assured me that she perfectly remembered the bureau, but that it had secret drawers and wells, very curiously contrived; nay, she showed me the very catalogue in which the said receptacles are noticed in capitals, to arrest the eye of the bidder, and increase the price of the bidding. That your father should never have revealed where he stowed this document is natural enough, during the life of his uncle; his own life was not spared long enough to give him much opportunity to explain afterwards, but I feel perfectly persuaded in my mind—that unless Mr. Robert Beaufort discovered that paper amongst the others he examined—in one of those drawers will be found all we want to substantiate your claims. This is the more likely from your father never mentioning, even to your mother apparently, the secret receptacles in the bureau. Why else such mystery? The probability is that he received the document either just before or at the time he purchased the bureau, or that he bought it for that very purpose: and, having once deposited the paper in a place he deemed secure from curiosity—accident, carelessness, policy, perhaps, rather shame itself (pardon me) for the doubt of your mother's discretion, that his secrecy seemed to imply, kept him from ever alluding to the circumstance, even when the intimacy of after years made him more assured of your mother's self-sacrificing devotion to his interests. At his uncle's death he thought to repair all!"

"And how, if that be true—if that Heaven which has delivered me hitherto from so many dangers, has, in the very secrecy of my poor father, saved my birthright front the gripe of the usurper—how, I say, is—"

"The bureau to pass into our possession? That is the difficulty. But we must contrive it somehow, if all else fail us; meanwhile, as I now feel sure that there has been a copy of that register made, I wish to know whether I should not immediately cross the country into Wales, and see if I can find any person in the neighbourhood of A— who did examine the copy taken: for, mark you, the said copy is only of importance as leading to the testimony of the actual witness who took it."

"Sir," said Vaudemont, heartily shaking Mr. Barlow by the hand, "forgive my first petulance. I see in you the very man I desired and wanted—your acuteness surprises and encourages me. Go to Wales, and God speed you!"

"Very well!—in five minutes I shall be off. Meanwhile, see the witness yourself; the sight of his benefactor's son will do more to keep him steady than anything else. There's his address, and take care not to give him money. And now I will order my chaise—the matter begins to look worth expense. Oh! I forgot to say that Monsieur Liancourt called on you yesterday about his own affairs. He wishes much to consult you. I told him you would probably be this evening in town, and he said he would wait you at your lodging."

"Yes—I will lose not a moment in going to London, and visiting our witness. And he saw my mother at the altar! My poor mother—Ah, how could my father have doubted her!" and as he spoke, he blushed for the first time with shame at that father's memory. He could not yet conceive that one so frank, one usually so bold and open, could for years have preserved from the woman who had sacrificed all to him, a secret to her so important! That was, in fact, the only blot on his father's honour—a foul and grave blot it was. Heavily had the punishment fallen on those whom the father loved best! Alas, Philip had not yet learned what terrible corrupters are the Hope and the Fear of immense Wealthy, even to men reputed the most honourable, if they have been reared and pampered in the belief that wealth is the Arch blessing of life. Rightly considered, in Philip Beaufort's solitary meanness lay the vast moral of this world's darkest truth!

Mr. Barlow was gone. Philip was about to enter his own chaise, when a dormeuse-and-four drove up to the inn-door to change horses. A young man was reclining, at his length, in the carriage, wrapped in cloaks, and with a ghastly paleness—the paleness of long and deep disease upon his cheeks. He turned his dim eye with, perhaps, a glance of the sick man's envy on that strong and athletic, form, majestic with health and vigour, as it stood beside the more humble vehicle. Philip did not, however, notice the new arrival; he sprang into the chaise, it rattled on, and thus, unconsciously, Arthur Beaufort and his cousin had again met. To which was now the Night—to which the Morning?

CHAPTER XII

"Bakam. Let my men guard the walls.
Syana. And mine the temple."—The Island Princess.

While thus eventfully the days and the weeks had passed for Philip, no less eventfully, so far as the inner life is concerned, had they glided away for Fanny. She had feasted in quiet and delighted thought on the consciousness that she was improving—that she was growing worthier of him—that he would perceive it on his return. Her manner was more thoughtful, more collected—less childish, in short, than it had been. And yet, with all the stir and flutter of the aroused intellect, the charm of her strange innocence was not scared away. She rejoiced in the ancient liberty she had regained of going out and coming back when she pleased; and as the weather was too cold ever to tempt Simon from his fireside, except, perhaps, for half-an-hour in the forenoon, so the hours of dusk, when he least missed her, were those which she chiefly appropriated for stealing away to the good school-mistress, and growing wiser and wiser every day in the ways of God and the learning of His creatures. The schoolmistress was not a brilliant woman. Nor was it accomplishments of which Fanny stood in need, so much as the opening of her thoughts and mind by profitable books and rational conversation. Beautiful as were all her natural feelings, the schoolmistress had now little difficulty in educating feelings up to the dignity of principles.

At last, hitherto patient under the absence of one never absent from her heart, Fanny received from him the letter he had addressed to her two days before he quitted Beaufort Court;—another letter—a second letter—a letter to excuse himself for not coming before—a letter that gave her an address that asked for a reply. It was a morning of unequalled delight approaching to transport. And then the excitement of answering the letter—the pride of showing how she was improved, what an excellent hand she now wrote! She shut herself up in her room: she did not go out that day. She placed the paper before her, and, to her astonishment, all that she had to say vanished from her mind at once. How was she even to begin? She had always hitherto called him "Brother." Ever since her conversation with Sarah she felt that she could not call him that name again for the world—no, never! But what should she call him—what could she call him? He signed himself "Philip." She knew that was his name. She thought it a musical name to utter, but to write it! No! some instinct she could not account for seemed to whisper that it was improper—presumptuous, to call him "Dear Philip." Had Burns's songs—the songs that unthinkingly he had put into her hand, and told her to read—songs that comprise the most beautiful love-poems in the world—had they helped to teach her some of the secrets of her own heart? And had timidity come with knowledge? Who shall say—who guess what passed within her? Nor did Fanny herself, perhaps, know her own feelings: but write the words "Dear Philip" she could not. And the whole of that day, though she thought of nothing else, she could not even get through the first line to her satisfaction. The next morning she sat down again. It would be so unkind if she did not answer immediately: she must answer. She placed his letter before her—she resolutely began. But copy after copy was made and torn. And Simon wanted her—and Sarah wanted her—and there were bills to be paid; and dinner was over before her task was really begun. But after dinner she began in good earnest.

"How kind in you to write to me" (the difficulty of any name was dispensed with by adopting none), "and to wish to know about my dear grandfather! He is much the same, but hardly ever walks out now, and I have had a good deal of time to myself. I think something will surprise you, and make you smile, as you used to do at first, when you come back. You must not be angry with me that I have gone out by myself very often—every day, indeed. I have been so safe. Nobody has ever offered to be rude again to Fanny" (the word "Fanny" was carefully scratched out with a penknife, and me substituted). "But you shall know all when you come. And are you sure you are well—quite—quite well? Do you never have the headaches you complained of sometimes? Do say this! Do you walk out—every day? Is there any pretty churchyard near you now? Whom do you walk with?

"I have been so happy in putting the flowers on the two graves. But I still give yours the prettiest, though the other is so dear to me. I feel sad when I come to the last, but not when I look at the one I have looked at so long. Oh, how good you were! But you don't like me to thank you."

"This is very stupid!" cried Fanny, suddenly throwing down her pen; "and I don't think I am improved at it;" and she half cried with vexation. Suddenly a bright idea crossed her. In the little parlour where the schoolmistress privately received her, she had seen among the books, and thought at the time how useful it might be to her if ever she had to write to Philip, a little volume entitled, The Complete Letter Writer. She knew by the title-page that it contained models for every description of letter—no doubt it would contain the precise thing that would suit the present occasion. She started up at the notion. She would go—she could be back to finish the letter before post-time. She put on her bonnet—left the letter, in her haste, open on the table—and just looking into the parlour in her way to the street door, to convince herself that Simon was asleep, and the wire-guard was on the fire, she hurried to the kind schoolmistress.

One of the fogs that in autumn gather sullenly over London and its suburbs covered the declining day with premature dimness. It grew darker and darker as she proceeded, but she reached the house in safety. She spent a quarter of an hour in timidly consulting her friend about all kinds of letters except the identical one that she intended to write, and having had it strongly impressed on her mind that if the letter was to a gentleman at all genteel, she ought to begin "Dear Sir," and end with "I have the honour to remain;" and that he would be everlastingly offended if she did not in the address affix "Esquire" to his name (that, was a great discovery),—she carried off the precious volume, and quitted the house. There was a wall that, bounding the demesnes of the school, ran for some short distance into the main street. The increasing fog, here, faintly struggled against the glimmer of a single lamp at some little distance. Just in this spot, her eye was caught by a dark object in the road, which she could scarcely perceive to be a carriage, when her hand was seized, and a voice said in her ear:—

"Ah! you will not be so cruel to me, I hope, as you were to my messenger! I have come myself for you."

She turned in great alarm, but the darkness prevented her recognising the face of him who thus accosted her. "Let me go!" she cried,—"let me go!"

"Hush! hush! No—no. Come with me. You shall have a house—carriage—servants! You shall wear silk gowns and jewels! You shall be a great lady!"

As these various temptations succeeded in rapid course each new struggle of Fanny, a voice from the coach-box said in a low tone,—

"Take care, my lord, I see somebody coming—perhaps a policeman!"

Fanny heard the caution, and screamed for rescue.

"Is it so?" muttered the molester. And suddenly Fanny felt her voice checked—her head mantled—her light form lifted from the ground. She clung—she struggled it was in vain. It was the affair of a moment: she felt herself borne into the carriage—the door closed—the stranger was by her side, and his voice said:—

"Drive on, Dykeman. Fast! fast!"

Two or three minutes, which seemed to her terror as ages, elapsed, when the gag and the mantle were gently removed, and the same voice (she still could not see her companion) said in a very mild tone:—

"Do not alarm yourself; there is no cause,—indeed there is not. I would not have adopted this plan had there been any other—any gentler one. But I could not call at your own house—I knew no other where to meet you.

"This was the only course left to me—indeed it was. I made myself acquainted with your movements. Do not blame me, then, for prying into your footsteps. I watched for you all last night—you did not come out. I was in despair. At last I find you. Do not be so terrified: I will not even touch your hand if you do not wish it."

As he spoke, however, he attempted to touch it, and was repulsed with an energy that rather disconcerted him. The poor girl recoiled from him into the farthest corner of that prison in speechless horror—in the darkest confusion of ideas. She did not weep—she did not sob—but her trembling seemed to shake the very carriage. The man continued to address, to expostulate, to pray, to soothe.

His manner was respectful. His protestations that he would not harm her for the world were endless.

"Only just see the home I can give you; for two days—for one day. Only just hear how rich I can make you and your grandfather, and then if you wish to leave me, you shall."

More, much more, to this effect, did he continue to pour forth, without extracting any sound from Fanny but gasps as for breath, and now and then a low murmur:

"Let me go, let me go! My grandfather, my blind grandfather!"

And finally tears came to her relief, and she sobbed with a passion that alarmed, and perhaps even touched her companion, cynical and icy as he was. Meanwhile the carriage seemed to fly. Fast as two horses, thorough-bred, and almost at full speed, could go, they were whirled along, till about an hour, or even less, from the time in which she had been thus captured, the carriage stopped.

"Are we here already?" said the man, putting his head out of the window. "Do then as I told you. Not to the front door; to my study."

In two minutes more the carriage halted again, before a building which looked white and ghostlike through the mist. The driver dismounted, opened with a latch-key a window-door, entered for a moment to light the candles in a solitary room from a fire that blazed on the hearth, reappeared, and opened the carriage-door. It was with a difficulty for which they were scarcely prepared that they were enabled to get Fanny from the carriage. No soft words, no whispered prayers could draw her forth; and it was with no trifling address, for her companion sought to be as gentle as the force necessary to employ would allow, that he disengaged her hands from the window-frame, the lining, the cushions, to which they clung; and at last bore her into the house. The driver closed the window again as he retreated, and they were alone. Fanny then cast a wild, scarce conscious glance over the apartment. It was small and simply furnished. Opposite to her was an old-fashioned bureau, one of those quaint, elaborate monuments of Dutch ingenuity, which, during the present century, the audacious spirit of curiosity-vendors has transplanted from their native receptacles, to contrast, with grotesque strangeness, the neat handiwork of Gillow and Seddon. It had a physiognomy and character of its own—this fantastic foreigner! Inlaid with mosaics, depicting landscapes and animals; graceless in form and fashion, but still picturesque, and winning admiration, when more closely observed, from the patient defiance of all rules of taste which had formed its cumbrous parts into one profusely ornamented and eccentric whole. It was the more noticeable from its total want of harmony with the other appurtenances of the room, which bespoke the tastes of the plain English squire. Prints of horses and hunts, fishing-rods and fowling-pieces, carefully suspended, decorated the walls. Not, however, on this notable stranger from the sluggish land rested the eye of Fanny. That, in her hurried survey, was arrested only by a portrait placed over the bureau—the portrait of a female in the bloom of life; a face so fair, a brow so candid, and eyes so pure, a lip so rich in youth and joy—that as her look lingered on the features Fanny felt comforted, felt as if some living protectress were there. The fire burned bright and merrily; a table, spread as for dinner, was drawn near it. To any other eye but Fanny's the place would have seemed a picture of English comfort. At last her looks rested on her companion. He had thrown himself, with a long sigh, partly of fatigue, partly of satisfaction, on one of the chairs, and was contemplating her as she thus stood and gazed, with an expression of mingled curiosity and admiration;

she recognised at once her first, her only persecutor. She recoiled, and covered her face with her hands. The man approached her:—

"Do not hate me, Fanny,—do not turn away. Believe me, though I have acted thus violently, here all violence will cease. I love you, but I will not be satisfied till you love me in return. I am not young, and I am not handsome, but I am rich and great, and I can make those whom I love happy,—so happy, Fanny!"

But Fanny had turned away, and was now busily employed in trying to re-open the door at which she had entered. Failing in this, she suddenly darted away, opened the inner door, and rushed into the passage with a loud cry. Her persecutor stifled an oath, and sprung after and arrested her. He now spoke sternly, and with a smile and a frown at once:—

"This is folly;—come back, or you will repent it! I have promised you, as a gentleman—as a nobleman, if you know what that is—to respect you. But neither will I myself be trifled with nor insulted. There must be no screams!"

His look and his voice awed Fanny in spite of her bewilderment and her loathing, and she suffered herself passively to be drawn into the room. He closed and bolted the door. She threw herself on the ground in one corner, and moaned low but piteously. He looked at her musingly for some moments, as he stood by the fire, and at last went to the door, opened it, and called "Harriet" in a low voice. Presently a young woman, of about thirty, appeared, neatly but plainly dressed, and of a countenance that, if not very winning, might certainly be called very handsome. He drew her aside for a few moments, and a whispered conference was exchanged. He then walked gravely up to Fanny "My young friend," said he, "I see my presence is too much for you this evening. This young woman will attend you—will get you all you want. She can tell you, too, that I am not the terrible sort of person you seem to suppose. I shall see you to-morrow." So saying, he turned on his heel and walked out.

Fanny felt something like liberty, something like joy, again. She rose, and looked so pleadingly, so earnestly, so intently into the woman's face, that Harriet turned away her bold eyes abashed; and at this moment Dykeman himself looked into the room.

"You are to bring us in dinner here yourself, uncle; and then go to my lord in the drawing-room."

Dykeman looked pleased, and vanished. Then Harriet came up and took Fanny's hand, and said, kindly,—

"Don't be frightened. I assure you, half the girls in London would give I don't know what to be in your place. My lord never will force you to do anything you don't like—it's not his way; and he's the kindest and best man,—and so rich; he does not know what to do with his money!"

To all this Fanny made but one answer,—she threw herself suddenly upon the woman's breast, and sobbed out: "My grandfather is blind, he cannot do without me—he will die—die. Have you nobody you love, too? Let me go—let me out! What can they want with me?—I never did harm to any one."

"And no one will harm you;—I swear it!" said Harriet, earnestly. "I see you don't know my lord. But here's the dinner; come, and take a bit of something, and a glass of wine."

Fanny could not touch anything except a glass of water, and that nearly choked her. But at last, as she recovered her senses, the absence of her tormentor—the presence of a woman—the solemn assurances of Harriet that, if she did not like to stay there, after a day or two, she should go back, tranquillised her in some measure. She did not heed the artful and lengthened eulogiums that the she-tempter then proceeded to pour forth upon the virtues, and the love, and the generosity, and, above all, the money of my lord. She only kept repeating to herself, "I shall go back in a day or two." At length, Harriet, having eaten and drunk as much as she could by her single self, and growing wearied with efforts from which so little resulted, proposed to Fanny to retire to rest. She opened a door to the right of the fireplace, and lighted her up a winding staircase to a pretty and comfortable chamber, where she offered to help her to undress. Fanny's complete innocence, and her utter ignorance of the precise nature of the danger that awaited her, though she fancied it must be very great and very awful, prevented her quite comprehending all that Harriet meant to convey by her solemn assurances that she should not be disturbed. But she understood, at least, that she was not to see her hateful gaoler till the next morning; and when Harriet, wishing her "good night," showed her a bolt to her door, she was less terrified at the thought of being alone in that strange place. She listened till Harriet's footsteps had died away, and then, with a beating heart, tried to open the door; it was locked from without. She sighed heavily. The window?—alas! when she had removed the shutter, there was another one barred from without, which precluded all hope there; she had no help for it but to bolt her door, stand forlorn and amazed at her own condition, and, at last, falling on her knees, to pray, in her own simple fashion, which since her recent visits to the schoolmistress had become more intelligent and earnest, to Him from whom no bolts and no bars can exclude the voice of the human heart.

CHAPTER XIII

"In te omnis domus inclinata recumbit."—VIRGIL.

[On thee the whole house rests confidingly.]

Lord Lilburne, seated before a tray in the drawing-room, was finishing his own solitary dinner, and Dykeman was standing close behind him, nervous and agitated. The confidence of many years between the master and the servant—the peculiar mind of Lilburne, which excluded him from all friendship with his own equals—had established between the two the kind of intimacy so common with the noble and the valet of the old French regime, and indeed, in much Lilburne more resembled the men of that day and land, than he did the nobler and statelier being which belongs to our own. But to the end of time, whatever is at once vicious, polished, and intellectual, will have a common likeness.

"But, my lord," said Dykeman, "just reflect. This girl is so well known in the place; she will be sure to be missed; and if any violence is done to her, it's a capital crime, my lord—a capital crime. I know they can't hang a great lord like you, but all concerned in it may—"

Lord Lilburne interrupted the speaker by, "Give me some wine and hold your tongue!" Then, when he had emptied his glass, he drew himself nearer to the fire, warmed his hands, mused a moment, and turned round to his confidant:—

"Dykeman," said he, "though you're an ass and a coward, and you don't deserve that I should be so condescending, I will relieve your fears at once. I know the law better than you can, for my whole life has been spent in doing exactly as I please, without ever putting myself in the power of LAW, which interferes with the pleasures of other men. You are right in saying violence would be a capital crime. Now the difference between vice and crime is this: Vice is what parsons write sermons against, Crime is what we make laws against. I never committed a crime in all my life,—at an age between fifty and sixty—I am not going to begin. Vices are safe things; I may have my vices like other men: but crimes are dangerous things—illegal things—things to be carefully avoided. Look you" (and here the speaker, fixing his puzzled listener with his eye, broke into a grin of sublime mockery), "let me suppose you to be the World—that cringing valet of valets, the WORLD! I should say to you this, 'My dear World, you and I understand each other well,—we are made for each other,—I never come in your way, nor you in mine. If I get drunk every day in my own room, that's vice, you can't touch me; if I take an extra glass for the first time in my life, and knock down the watchman, that's a crime which, if I am rich, costs me one pound—perhaps five pounds; if I am poor, sends me to the treadmill. If I break the hearts of five hundred old fathers, by buying with gold or flattery the embraces of five hundred young daughters, that's vice,—your servant, Mr. World! If one termagant wench scratches my face, makes a noise, and goes brazen-faced to the Old Bailey to swear to her shame, why that's crime, and my friend, Mr. World, pulls a hemp-rope out of his pocket.' Now, do you understand? Yes, I repeat," he added, with a change of voice, "I never committed a crime in my life,—I have never even been accused of one,—never had an action of crim. con.—of seduction against me. I know how to manage such matters better. I was forced to carry off this girl, because I had no other means of courting her. To court her is all I mean to do now. I am perfectly aware that an action for violence, as you call it, would be the more disagreeable, because of the very weakness of intellect which the girl is said to possess, and of which report I don't believe a word. I shall most certainly avoid even the remotest appearance that could be so construed. It is for that reason that no one in the house shall attend the girl except yourself and your niece. Your niece I can depend on, I know; I have been kind to her; I have got her a good husband; I shall get her husband a good place;—I shall be godfather to her first child. To be sure, the other servants will know there's a lady in the house, but to that they are accustomed; I don't set up for a Joseph. They need know no more, unless you choose to blab it out. Well, then, supposing that at the end of a few days, more or less, without any rudeness on my part, a young woman, after seeing a few jewels, and fine dresses, and a pretty house, and being made very comfortable, and being convinced that her grandfather shall be taken care of without her slaving herself to death, chooses of her own accord to live with me, where's the crime, and who can interfere with it?"

"Certainly, my lord, that alters the case," said Dykeman, considerably relieved. "But still," he added, anxiously, "if the inquiry is made,—if before all this is settled, it is found out where she is?"

"Why then no harm will be done—no violence will be committed. Her grandfather,—drivelling and a miser, you say—can be appeased by a little money, and it will be nobody's business, and no case can be made of it. Tush! man! I always look before I leap! People in this world are not so charitable as you suppose. What more natural than that a poor and pretty girl—not as wise as Queen Elizabeth—should be tempted to pay a visit to a rich lover!

"All they can say of the lover is, that he is a very gay man or a very bad man, and that's saying nothing new of me. But don't think it will be found out. Just get me that stool; this has been a very troublesome piece of business—rather tried me. I am not so young as I was. Yes, Dykeman, something which that Frenchman Vaudemont, or Vautrien, or whatever his name is, said to me once, has a certain degree of truth. I felt it in the last fit of the gout, when my pretty niece was smoothing my pillows. A nurse, as we grow older, may be of use to one. I wish to make this girl like me, or be grateful to me. I am meditating a longer and more serious attachment than usual,—a companion!"

"A companion, my lord, in that poor creature!—so ignorant—so uneducated!"

"So much the better. This world palls upon me," said Lilburne, almost gloomily. "I grow sick of the miserable quackeries—of the piteous conceits that men, women, and children call 'knowledge,' I wish to catch a glimpse of nature before I die. This creature interests me, and that is something in this life. Clear those things away, and leave me."

"Ay!" muttered Lilburne, as he bent over the fire alone, "when I first heard that that girl was the granddaughter of Simon Gawtrey, and, therefore, the child of the man whom I am to thank that I am a cripple, I felt as if love to her were a part of that hate which I owe to him; a segment in the circle of my vengeance. But now, poor child!

"I forget all this. I feel for her, not passion, but what I never felt before, affection. I feel that if I had such a child, I could understand what men mean when they talk of the tenderness of a father. I have not one impure thought for that girl—not one. But I would give thousands if she could love me. Strange! strange! in all this I do not recognise myself!"

Lord Lilburne retired to rest betimes that night; he slept sound; rose refreshed at an earlier hour than usual; and what he considered a fit of vapours of the previous night was passed away. He looked with eagerness to an interview with Fanny. Proud of his intellect, pleased in any of those sinister exercises of it which the code and habits of his life so long permitted to him, he regarded the conquest of his fair adversary with the interest of a scientific game. Harriet went to Fanny's room to prepare her to receive her host; and Lord Lilburne now resolved to make his own visit the less unwelcome by reserving for his especial gift some showy, if not valuable, trinkets, which for similar purposes never failed the depositories of the villa he had purchased for his pleasures. He, recollected that these gewgaws were placed in the bureau in the study; in which, as having a lock of foreign and intricate workmanship, he usually kept whatever might tempt cupidity in those frequent absences when the house was left guarded but by two women servants. Finding that Fanny had not yet quitted her own chamber, while Harriet went up to attend and reason with her, he himself limped into the study below, unlocked the bureau, and was searching in the drawers, when he heard the voice of Fanny above, raised a little as if in remonstrance or entreaty; and he paused to listen. He could not, however, distinguish what was said; and in the meanwhile, without attending much to what he was about, his hands were still employed in opening and shutting the drawers, passing through the pigeon-holes, and feeling for a topaz brooch, which he thought could not fail of pleasing the unsophisticated eyes of Fanny. One of the recesses was deeper than the rest; he fancied the brooch was there; he stretched his hand into the recess; and, as the room was partially darkened by the lower shutters from without, which were still unclosed to prevent any attempted escape of his captive, he had only the sense of touch to depend on; not finding the brooch, he stretched on till he came to the extremity of the recess, and was suddenly sensible of a sharp pain; the flesh seemed caught as in a trap; he drew back his finger with sudden force and a half-suppressed exclamation, and he perceived the bottom or floor of the pigeon-hole recede, as if sliding back. His curiosity was aroused; he again felt warily and cautiously, and discovered a very slight inequality and roughness at the extremity of the recess. He was aware instantly that there was some secret spring; he pressed with some force on the spot, and he felt the board give way; he pushed it back towards him, and it slid suddenly with a whirring noise, and left a cavity below exposed to his sight. He peered in, and drew forth a paper; he opened it at first carelessly, for he was still trying to listen to Fanny. His eye ran rapidly over a few preliminary lines till it rested on what follows:

"Marriage. The year 18—

"No. 83, page 21.

"Philip Beaufort, of this parish of A—, and Catherine Morton, of the parish of St. Botolph, Aldgate, London, were married in this church by banns, this 12th day of November, in the year one thousand eight hundred and —' by me,

"CALEB PRICE, Vicar.

"This marriage was solemnised between us,

"PHILIP BEAUFORT.
"CATHERINE MORTON.

"In the presence of
"DAVID APREECE.
"WILLIAM SMITH.

"The above is a true copy taken from the registry of marriages, in A—parish, this 19th day of March, 18—, by me,

"MORGAN JONES, Curate of C—."

[This is according to the form customary at the date at which the copy was made. There has since been an alteration.]

Lord Lilburne again cast his eye over the lines prefixed to this startling document, which, being those written at Caleb's desire, by Mr. Jones to Philip Beaufort, we need not here transcribe to the reader. At that instant Harriet descended the stairs, and came into the room; she crept up on tiptoe to Lilburne, and whispered,—

"She is coming down, I think; she does not know you are here."

"Very well—go!" said Lord Lilburne. And scarce had Harriet left the room, when a carriage drove furiously to the door, and Robert Beaufort rushed into the study.

CHAPTER XIV

"Gone, and none know it.

How now?—What news, what hopes and steps discovered!"
BEAUMONT AND FLETCHER: The Pilgrim.

When Philip arrived at his lodgings in town it was very late, but he still found Liancourt waiting the chance of his arrival. The Frenchman was full of his own schemes and projects. He was a man of high repute and connections; negotiations for his recall to Paris had been entered into; he was divided between a Quixotic loyalty and a rational prudence; he brought his doubts to Vaudemont. Occupied as he was with thoughts of so important and personal a nature, Philip could yet listen patiently to his friend, and weigh with him the pros and cons. And after having mutually agreed that loyalty and prudence would both be best consulted by waiting a little, to see if the nation, as the Carlists yet fondly trusted, would soon, after its first fever, offer once more the throne and the purple to the descendant of St. Louis, Liancourt, as he lighted his cigar to walk home, said, "A thousand thanks to you, my dear friend: and how have you enjoyed yourself in your visit? I am not surprised or jealous that Lilburne did not invite me, as I do not play at cards, and as I have said some sharp things to him!"

"I fancy I shall have the same disqualifications for another invitation," said Vaudemont, with a severe smile. "I may have much to disclose to you in a few days. At present my news is still unripe. And have you seen anything of Lilburne? He left us some days since. Is he in London?"

"Yes; I was riding with our friend Henri, who wished to try a new horse off the stones, a little way into the country yesterday. We went through—and H—. Pretty places, those. Do you know them?"

"Yes; I know H—."

"And just at dusk, as we were spurring back to town, whom should I see walking on the path of the high-road but Lord Lilburne himself! I could hardly believe my eyes. I stopped, and, after asking him about you, I could not help expressing my surprise to see him on foot at such a place. You know the man's sneer. 'A Frenchman so gallant as Monsieur de Liancourt,' said he, 'need not be surprised at much greater miracles; the iron moves to the magnet: I have a little adventure here. Pardon me if I ask you to ride on.' Of course I wished him good day; and a little farther up the road I saw a dark plain chariot, no coronet, no arms, no footman only the man on the box, but the beauty of the horses assured me it must belong to Lilburne. Can you conceive such absurdity in a man of that age—and a very clever fellow too? Yet, how is it that one does not ridicule it in Lilburne, as one would in another man between fifty and sixty?"

"Because one does not ridicule,—one loathes-him."

"No; that's not it. The fact is that one can't fancy Lilburne old. His manner is young—his eye is young. I never saw any one with so much vitality. 'The bad heart and the good digestion'—the twin secrets for wearing well, eh!"

"Where did you meet him—not near H—?"

"Yes; close by. Why? Have you any adventure there too? Nay, forgive me; it was but a jest. Good night!"

Vaudemont fell into an uneasy reverie: he could not divine exactly why he should be alarmed; but he was alarmed at Lilburne being in the neighbourhood of H—. It was the foot of the profane violating the sanctuary. An undefined thrill shot through him, as his mind coupled together the associations of Lilburne and Fanny; but there was no ground for forebodings. Fanny did not stir out alone. An adventure, too—pooh! Lord Lilburne must be awaiting a willing and voluntary appointment, most probably from some one of the fair but decorous frailties of London. Lord Lilburne's more recent conquests were said to be among those of his own rank; suburbs are useful for such assignations. Any other thought was too horrible to be contemplated. He glanced to the clock; it was three in the morning. He would go to H— early, even before he sought out Mr. William Smith. With that resolution, and even his hardy frame worn out by the excitement of the day, he threw himself on his bed and fell asleep.

He did not wake till near nine, and had just dressed, and hurried over his abstemious breakfast, when the servant of the house came to tell him that an old woman, apparently in great agitation, wished to see him. His head was still full of witnesses and lawsuits; and he was vaguely expecting some visitor connected with his primary objects, when Sarah broke into the room. She cast a hurried, suspicious look round her, and then throwing herself on her knees to him, "Oh!" she cried, "if you have taken that poor young thing away, God forgive you. Let her come back again. It shall be all hushed up. Don't ruin her! don't, that's a dear good gentleman!"

"Speak plainly, woman—what do you mean?" cried Philip, turning pale.

A very few words sufficed for an explanation: Fanny's disappearance the previous night; the alarm of Sarah at her non-return; the apathy of old Simon, who did not comprehend what had happened, and quietly went to bed; the search Sarah had made during half the night; the intelligence she had picked up, that the policeman, going his rounds, had heard a female shriek near the school; but that all he could perceive through the mist was a carriage driving rapidly past him; Sarah's suspicions of Vaudemont confirmed in the morning, when, entering Fanny's room, she perceived the poor girl's unfinished letter with his own, the clue to his address that the letter gave her; all this, ere she well understood what she herself was talking about,—Vaudemont's alarm seized, and the reflection of a moment construed: the carriage; Lilburne seen lurking in the neighbourhood the previous day; the former attempt;—all flashed on him with an intolerable glare. While Sarah was yet speaking, he rushed from the house, he flew to Lord Lilburne's in Park Lane; he composed his manner, he inquired calmly. His lordship had slept from home; he was, they believed, at Fernside: Fernside! H— was on the direct way to that villa. Scarcely ten minutes had elapsed since he heard the story ere he was on the road, with such speed as the promise of a guinea a mile could extract from the spurs of a young post-boy applied to the flanks of London post-horses.

CHAPTER XV

"Ex humili magna ad fastigia rerum
Extollit."—JUVENAL.

[Fortune raises men from low estate to the very summit of prosperity.]

When Harriet had quitted Fanny, the waiting-woman, craftily wishing to lure her into Lilburne's presence, had told her that the room below was empty; and the captive's mind naturally and instantly seized on the thought of escape. After a brief breathing pause, she crept noiselessly down the stairs, and gently opened the door; and at the very instant she did so, Robert Beaufort entered from the other door; she drew back in terror, when, what was her astonishment in hearing a name uttered that spell-bound her—the last name she could have expected to hear; for Lilburne, the instant he saw Beaufort, pale, haggard, agitated, rush into the room, and bang the door after him, could only suppose that something of extraordinary moment had occurred with regard to the dreaded guest, and cried:

"You come about Vaudemont! Something has happened about Vaudemont! about Philip! What is it? Calm yourself."

Fanny, as the name was thus abruptly uttered, actually thrust her face through the door; but she again drew back, and, all her senses preternaturally quickened at that name, while she held the door almost closed, listened with her whole soul in her ears.

The faces of both the men were turned from her, and her partial entry had not been perceived.

"Yes," said Robert Beaufort, leaning his weight, as if ready to sink to the ground, upon Lilburne's shoulder, "Yes; Vaudemont, or Philip, for they are one,—yes, it is about that man I have come to consult you. Arthur has arrived."

"Well?"

"And Arthur has seen the wretch who visited us, and the rascal's manner has so imposed on him, so convinced him that Philip is the heir to all our property, that he has come over-ill, ill—I fear" (added Beaufort, in a hollow voice), "dying, to—to—"

"To guard against their machinations?"

"No, no, no—to say that if such be the case, neither honour nor conscience will allow us to resist his rights. He is so obstinate in this matter; his nerves so ill bear reasoning and contradiction, that I know not what to do—"

"Take breath—go on."

"Well, it seems that this man found out Arthur almost as soon as my son arrived at Paris—that he has persuaded Arthur that he has it in his power to prove the marriage—that he pretended to be very impatient for a decision—that Arthur, in order to gain time to see me, affected irresolution—took him to Boulogne, for the rascal does not dare to return to England—left him there; and now comes back, my own son, as my worst enemy, to conspire against me for my property! I could not have kept my temper if I had stayed. But that's not all—that's not the worst: Vaudemont left me suddenly in the morning on the receipt of a letter. In taking leave of Camilla he let fall hints which fill me with fear. Well, I inquired his movements as I came along; he had stopped at D—, had been closeted for above an hour with a man whose name the landlord of the inn knew, for it was on his carpet-bag—the name was Barlow. You remember the advertisements! Good Heavens! what is to be done? I would not do anything unhandsome or dishonest. But there never was a marriage. I never will believe there was a marriage—never!"

"There was a marriage, Robert Beaufort," said Lord Lilburne, almost enjoying the torture he was about to inflict; "and I hold here a paper that Philip Vaudemont—for so we will yet call him—would give his right hand to clutch for a moment. I have but just found it in a secret cavity in that bureau. Robert, on this paper may depend the fate, the fortune, the prosperity, the greatness of Philip Vaudemont;—or his poverty, his exile, his ruin. See!"

Robert Beaufort glanced over the paper held out to him—dropped it on the floor—and staggered to a seat. Lilburne coolly replaced the document in the bureau, and, limping to his brother-in-law, said with a smile,—

"But the paper is in my possession—I will not destroy it. No; I have no right to destroy it. Besides, it would be a crime; but if I give it to you, you can do with it as you please."

"O Lilburne, spare me—spare me. I meant to be an honest man. I—I—" And Robert Beaufort sobbed. Lilburne looked at him in scornful surprise.

"Do not fear that I shall ever think worse of you; and who else will know it? Do not fear me. No;—I, too, have reasons to hate and to fear this Philip Vaudemont; for Vaudemont shall be his name, and not Beaufort, in spite of fifty such scraps of paper! He has known a man—my worst foe—he has secrets of mine—of my past—perhaps of my present: but I laugh at his knowledge while he is a wandering adventurer;—I should tremble at that knowledge if he could thunder it out to the world as Philip Beaufort of Beaufort Court! There, I am candid with you. Now hear my plan. Prove to Arthur that his visitor is a convicted felon, by sending the officers of justice after him instantly—off with him again to the Settlements. Defy a single witness—entrap Vaudemont back to France and prove him (I think I will prove him such)—I think so—with a little money and a little pains)—prove him the accomplice of William Gawtrey, a coiner and a murderer! Pshaw! take yon paper. Do with it as you will—keep it—give it to Arthur—let Philip Vaudemont have it, and Philip Vaudemont will be rich and great, the happiest man between earth and paradise! On the other hand, come and tell me that you have lost it, or that I never gave you such a paper, or that no such paper ever existed; and Philip Vaudemont may live a pauper, and die, perhaps, a slave at the galleys! Lose it, I say,—lose it,—and advise with me upon the rest."

Horror-struck, bewildered, the weak man gazed upon the calm face of the Master-villain, as the scholar of the old fables might have gazed on the fiend who put before him worldly prosperity here and the loss of his soul hereafter. He had never hitherto regarded Lilburne in his true light. He was appalled by the black heart that lay bare before him.

"I can't destroy it—I can't," he faltered out; "and if I did, out of love for Arthur,—don't talk of galleys,—of vengeance—I—I—"

"The arrears of the rents you have enjoyed will send you to gaol for your life. No, no; don't destroy the paper."

Beaufort rose with a desperate effort; he moved to the bureau. Fanny's heart was on her lips;—of this long conference she had understood only the one broad point on which Lilburne had insisted with an emphasis that could have enlightened an infant; and he looked on Beaufort as an infant then—On that paper rested Philip Vaudemont's fate—happiness if saved, ruin if destroyed; Philip—her Philip! And Philip himself had said to her once—when had she ever forgotten his words? and now how those words flashed across her—Philip himself had said to her once, "Upon a scrap of paper, if I could but find it, may depend my whole fortune, my whole happiness, all that I care for in life."—Robert Beaufort moved to the bureau—he seized the document—he looked over it again, hurriedly, and ere Lilburne, who by no means wished to have it destroyed in his own presence, was aware of his intention—he hastened with tottering steps to the hearth-averted his eyes, and cast it on the fire. At that instant something white—he scarce knew what, it seemed to him as a spirit, as a ghost—darted by him, and snatched the paper, as yet uninjured, from the embers! There was a pause for the hundredth part of a moment:—a gurgling sound of astonishment and horror from Beaufort—an exclamation from Lilburne—a laugh from Fanny, as, her eyes flashing light, with a proud dilation of stature, with the paper clasped tightly to her bosom, she turned her looks of triumph from one to the other. The two men were both too amazed, at the instant, for rapid measures. But Lilburne, recovering himself first, hastened to her; she eluded his grasp—she made towards the door to the passage; when Lilburne, seriously alarmed, seized her arm;—

"Foolish child!—give me that paper!"

"Never but with my life!" And Fanny's cry for help rang through the house.

"Then—" the speech died on his lips, for at that instant a rapid stride was heard without—a momentary scuffle—voices in altercation;—the door gave way as if a battering ram had forced it;—not so much thrown forward as actually hurled into the room, the body of Dykeman fell heavily, like a dead man's, at the very feet of Lord Lilburne—and Philip Vaudemont stood in the doorway!

The grasp of Lilburne on Fanny's arm relaxed, and the girl, with one bound, sprung to Philip's breast. "Here, here!" she cried, "take it—take it!" and she thrust the paper into his hand. "Don't let them have it—read it—see it—never mind me!" But Philip, though his hand unconsciously closed on the precious document, did mind Fanny; and in that moment her cause was the only one in the world to him.

"Foul villain!" he said, as he strode to Lilburne, while Fanny still clung to his breast: "Speak!—speak!—is—she—is she?—man—man, speak!—you know what I would say!—She is the child of your own daughter—the grandchild of that Mary whom you dishonoured—the child of the woman whom William Gawtrey saved from pollution! Before he died, Gawtrey commended her to my care!—O God of Heaven!—speak!—I am not too late!"

The manner, the words, the face of Philip left Lilburne terror-stricken with conviction. But the man's crafty ability, debased as it was, triumphed even over remorse for the dread guilt meditated,—over gratitude for the dread guilt spared. He glanced at Beaufort—at Dykeman, who now, slowly recovering, gazed at him with eyes that seemed starting from their sockets; and lastly fixed his look on Philip himself. There were three witnesses—presence of mind was his great attribute.

"And if, Monsieur de Vaudemont, I knew, or, at least, had the firmest persuasion that Fanny was my grandchild, what then? Why else should she be here?—Pooh, sir! I am an old man."

Philip recoiled a step in wonder; his plain sense was baffled by the calm lie. He looked down at Fanny, who, comprehending nothing of what was spoken, for all her faculties, even her very sense of sight and hearing, were absorbed in her impatient anxiety for him, cried out:

"No harm has come to Fanny—none: only frightened. Read!—Read!—Save that paper!—You know what you once said about a mere scrap of paper! Come away! Come!"

He did now cast his eyes on the paper he held. That was an awful moment for Robert Beaufort—even for Lilburne! To snatch the fatal document from that gripe! They would as soon have snatched it from a tiger! He lifted his eyes—they rested on his mother's picture! Her lips smiled on him! He turned to Beaufort in a state of emotion too exulting, too blest for vulgar vengeance—for vulgar triumph—almost for words.

"Look yonder, Robert Beaufort—look!" and he pointed to the picture. "Her name is spotless! I stand again beneath a roof that was my father's,—the Heir of Beaufort! We shall meet before the justice of our country. For you, Lord Lilburne, I will believe you: it is too horrible to doubt even your intentions. If wrong had chanced to her, I would have rent you where you stand, limb from limb. And thank her",—(for Lilburne recovered at this language the daring of his youth, before calculation, indolence, and excess had dulled the edge of his nerves; and, unawed by the height, and manhood, and strength of his menacer, stalked haughtily up to him)—"and thank your relationship to her," said Philip, sinking his voice into a whisper, "that I do not brand you as a pilferer and a cheat! Hush, knave!—hush, pupil of George Gawtrey!—there are no duels for me but with men of honour!"

Lilburne now turned white, and the big word stuck in his throat. In another instant Fanny and her guardian had quitted the house.

"Dykeman," said Lord Lilburne after a long silence, "I shall ask you another time how you came to admit that impertinent person. At present, go and order breakfast for Mr. Beaufort."

As soon as Dykeman, more astounded, perhaps, by his lord's coolness than even by the preceding circumstances, had left the study, Lilburne came up to Beaufort,—who seemed absolutely stricken as if by palsy,—and touching him impatiently and rudely, said,—

"'Sdeath, man!—rouse yourself! There is not a moment to be lost! I have already decided on what you are to do. This paper is not worth a rush, unless the curate who examined it will depose to that fact. He is a curate—a Welsh curate;—you are yet Mr. Beaufort, a rich and a great man. The curate, properly managed, may depose to the contrary; and then we will indict them all for forgery and conspiracy. At the worst, you can, no doubt, get the parson to forget all about it—to stay away. His address was on the certificate:

"—C—. Go yourself into Wales without an instant's delay— Then, having arranged with Mr. Jones, hurry back, cross to Boulogne, and buy this convict and his witnesses, buy them! That, now, is the only thing. Quick! quick!—quick! Zounds, man! if it were my affair, my estate, I would not care a pin for that fragment of paper; I should rather rejoice at it. I see how it could be turned against them! Go!"

"No, no; I am not equal to it! Will you manage it? will you? Half my estate!—all! Take it: but save—"

"Tut!" interrupted Lord Lilburne, in great disdain. "I am as rich as I want to be. Money does not bribe me. I manage this! I! Lord Lilburne. I! Why, if found out, it is subornation of witnesses. It is exposure—it is dishonour—it is ruin. What then? You should take the risk—for you must meet ruin if you do not. I cannot. I have nothing to gain!"

"I dare not!—I dare not!" murmured Beaufort, quite spirit-broken. "Subornation, dishonour, exposure!—and I, so respectable—my character!—and my son against me, too!—my son, in whom I lived again! No, no; let them take all! Let them take it! Ha! ha! let them take it! Good-day to you."

"Where are you going?"

"I shall consult Mr. Blackwell, and I'll let you know." And Beaufort walked tremulously back to his carriage. "Go to his lawyer!" growled Lilburne. "Yes, if his lawyer can help him to defraud men lawfully, he'll defraud them fast enough. That will be the respectable way of doing it! Um!—This may be an ugly business for me—the paper found here—if the girl can depose to what she heard, and she must have heard something.—No, I think the laws of real property will hardly allow her evidence; and if they do—Um!—My granddaughter—is it possible!—And Gawtrey rescued her mother, my child, from her own mother's vices! I thought my liking to that girl different from any other I have ever felt: it was pure—it was!—it was pity—affection. And I must never see her again—must forget the whole thing! And I am growing old—and I am childless—and alone!" He paused, almost with a groan: and then the expression of his face changing to rage, he cried out, "The man threatened me, and I was a coward! What to do?—Nothing! The defensive is my line. I shall play no more.—I attack no one. Who will accuse Lord Lilburne? Still, Robert is a fool. I must not leave him to himself. Ho! there! Dykeman!—the carriage! I shall go to London."

Fortunate, no doubt, it was for Philip that Mr. Beaufort was not Lord Lilburne. For all history teaches us—public and private history—conquerors—statesmen—sharp hypocrites and brave designers—yes, they all teach us how mighty one man of great intellect and no scruple is against the justice of millions! The One Man moves—the Mass is inert. Justice sits on a throne. Roguery never rests,—Activity is the lever of Archimedes.

CHAPTER XVI

"Quam inulta injusta ac prava fiunt moribus."—TULL.

[How many unjust and vicious actions are perpetrated   under the name of morals.]

*"Volat ambiguis
Mobilis alis Hera."—SENECA.*

[The hour flies moving with doubtful wings.]

Mr. Robert Beaufort sought Mr. Blackwell, and long, rambling, and disjointed was his narrative. Mr. Blackwell, after some consideration, proposed to set about doing the very things that Lilburne had proposed at once to do. But the lawyer expressed himself legally and covertly, so that it did not seem to the sober sense of Mr. Beaufort at all the same plan. He was not the least alarmed at what Mr. Blackwell proposed, though so shocked at what Lilburne dictated. Blackwell would go the next day into Wales—he would find out Mr. Jones—he would sound him! Nothing was more common with people of the nicest honour, than just to get a witness out of the way! Done in election petitions, for instance, every day.

"True," said Mr. Beaufort, much relieved.

Then, after having done that, Mr. Blackwell would return to town, and cross over to Boulogne to see this very impudent person whom Arthur (young men were so apt to be taken in!) had actually believed. He had no doubt he could settle it all. Robert Beaufort returned to Berkeley Square actually in spirits. There he found Lilburne, who, on reflection, seeing that Blackwell was at all events more up to the business than his brother, assented to the propriety of the arrangement.

Mr. Blackwell accordingly did set off the next day. That next day, perhaps, made all the difference. Within two hours from his gaining the document so important, Philip, without any subtler exertion of intellect than the decision of a plain, bold sense, had already forestalled both the peer and the lawyer. He had sent down Mr. Barlow's head clerk to his master in Wales with the document, and a short account of the manner in which it had been discovered. And fortunate, indeed, was it that the copy had been found; for all the inquiries of Mr. Barlow at A— had failed, and probably would have failed, without such a clue, in fastening upon any one probable person to have officiated as Caleb Price's amanuensis. The sixteen hours' start Mr. Barlow gained over Blackwell enabled the former to see Mr. Jones—to show him his own handwriting—to get a written and witnessed attestation from which the curate, however poor, and however tempted, could never well have escaped (even had he been dishonest, which he was not), of his perfect recollection of the fact of making an extract from the registry at Caleb's desire, though he owned he had quite forgotten the names he extracted till they were again placed before him. Barlow took care to arouse Mr. Jones's interest in the case—quitted Wales—hastened over to Boulogne—saw Captain Smith, and without bribes, without threats, but by plainly proving to that worthy person that he could not return to England nor see his brother without being immediately arrested; that his brother's evidence was already pledged on the side of truth; and that by the acquisition of new testimony there could be no doubt that the suit would be successful—he diverted the captain from all disposition towards perfidy, convinced him on which side his interest lay, and saw him return to Paris, where very shortly afterwards he disappeared for ever from this world, being forced into a duel, much against his will (with a Frenchman whom he had attempted to defraud), and shot through the lungs. Thus verifying a favourite maxim of Lord Lilburne's, viz. that it does not do, in the long run, for little men to play the Great Game!

On the same day that Blackwell returned, frustrated in his half-and-half attempts to corrupt Mr. Jones, and not having been able even to discover Mr. Smith, Mr. Robert Beaufort received a notice of an Action for Ejectment to be brought by Philip Beaufort at the next Assizes. And, to add to his afflictions, Arthur, whom he had hitherto endeavoured to amuse by a sort of ambiguous shilly-shally correspondence, became so alarmingly worse, that his mother brought him up to town for advice. Lord Lilburne was, of course, sent for; and on learning all, his counsel was prompt.

"I told you before that this man loves your daughter. See if you can effect a compromise. The lawsuit will be ugly, and probably ruinous. He has a right to claim six years' arrears—that is above £100,000. Make yourself his father-in-law, and me his uncle-in-law; and, since we can't kill the wasp, we may at least soften the venom of his sting."

Beaufort, still perplexed, irresolute, sought his son; and, for the first time, spoke to him frankly—that is, frankly for Robert Beaufort! He owned that the copy of the register had been found by Lilburne in a secret drawer. He made the best of the story Lilburne himself furnished him with (adhering, of course, to the assertion uttered or insinuated to Philip) in regard to Fanny's abduction and interposition; he said nothing of his attempt to destroy the paper. Why should he? By admitting the copy in court—if so advised—he could get rid of Fanny's evidence altogether; even without such concession, her evidence might possibly be objected to or eluded. He confessed that he feared the witness who copied the register and the witness to the marriage were alive. And then he talked pathetically of his desire to do what was right, his dread of slander and misinterpretation. He said nothing of Sidney, and his belief that Sidney and Charles Spencer were the same; because, if his daughter were to be the instrument for effecting a compromise, it was clear that her engagement with Spencer must be cancelled and concealed. And luckily Arthur's illness and Camilla's timidity, joined now to her father's injunctions not to excite Arthur in his present state with any additional causes of anxiety, prevented the confidence that might otherwise have ensued between the brother and sister. And Camilla, indeed, had no heart for such a conference. How, when she looked on Arthur's glassy eye, and listened to his hectic cough, could she talk to him of love and marriage? As to the automaton, Mrs. Beaufort, Robert made sure of her discretion.

Arthur listened attentively to his father's communication; and the result of that interview was the following letter from Arthur to his cousin:

"I write to you without fear of misconstruction; for I write to you unknown to all my family, and I am the only one of them who can have no personal interest in the struggle about to take place between my father and yourself. Before the law can decide between you, I shall be in my grave. I write this from the Bed of Death. Philip, I write this—I, who stood beside a deathbed more sacred to you than mine—I, who received your mother's last sigh. And with that sigh there was a smile that lasted when the sigh was gone: for I promised to befriend her children. Heaven knows how anxiously I sought to fulfil that solemn vow! Feeble and sick myself, I followed you and your brother with no aim, no prayer, but this,—to embrace you and say, 'Accept a new brother in me.' I spare you the humiliation, for it is yours, not mine, of recalling what passed between us when at last we met. Yet, I still sought to save, at least, Sidney,—more especially confided to my care by his dying mother. He mysteriously eluded our search; but we had reason, by a letter received from some unknown hand, to believe him saved and provided for. Again I met you at Paris. I saw you were poor. Judging from your associate, I might with justice think you depraved. Mindful of your declaration never to accept bounty from a Beaufort, and remembering with natural resentment the outrage I had before received from you, I judged it vain to seek and remonstrate with you, but I did not judge it vain to aid. I sent you, anonymously, what at least would suffice, if absolute poverty had subjected you to evil courses, to rescue you from them if your heart were so disposed. Perhaps that sum, trifling as it was, may have smoothed your path and assisted your career. And why tell you all this now? To dissuade from asserting rights you conceive to be just?—Heaven forbid! If justice is with you, so also is the duty due to your mother's name. But simply for this: that in asserting such rights, you content yourself with justice, not revenge—that in righting yourself, you do not wrong others. If the law should decide for you, the arrears you could demand would leave my father and sister beggars. This may be law—it would not be justice; for my father solemnly believed himself, and had every apparent probability in his favour, the true heir of the wealth that devolved upon him. This is not all. There may be circumstances connected with the discovery of a certain document that, if authentic, and I do not presume to question it, may decide the contest so far as it rests on truth; circumstances which might seem to bear hard upon my father's good name and faith. I do not know sufficiently of law to say how far these could be publicly urged, or, if urged, exaggerated and tortured by an advocate's calumnious ingenuity. But again, I say justice, and not revenge! And with this I conclude, inclosing to you these lines, written in your own hand, and leaving you the arbiter of their value.

"ARTHUR BEAUFORT."

The lines inclosed were these, a second time placed before the reader

"I cannot guess who you are. They say that you call yourself a relation; that must be some mistake. I knew not that my poor mother had relations so kind. But, whoever you be, you soothed her last hours—she died in your arms; and if ever—years, long years, hence—we should chance to meet, and I can do anything to aid another, my blood, and my life, and my heart, and my soul, all are slaves to your will! If you be really of her kindred I commend to you my brother; he is at — with Mr. Morton. If you can serve him, my mother's soul will watch over you as a guardian angel. As for me, I ask no help from any one; I go into the world, and will carve out my own way. So much do I shrink from the thought of charity from others, that I do not believe I could bless you as I do now, if your kindness to me did not close with the stone upon my mother's grave.

PHILIP."

This letter was sent to the only address of Monsieur de Vaudemont which the Beauforts knew, viz., his apartments in town, and he did not receive it the day it was sent.

Meanwhile Arthur Beaufort's malady continued to gain ground rapidly. His father, absorbed in his own more selfish fears (though, at the first sight of Arthur, overcome by the alteration of his appearance), had ceased to consider his illness fatal. In fact, his affection for Arthur was rather one of pride than love: long absence had weakened the ties of early custom. He prized him as an heir rather than treasured him as a son. It almost seemed that as the Heritage was in danger, so the Heir became less dear: this was only because he was less thought of. Poor Mrs. Beaufort, yet but partially acquainted with the terrors of her husband, still clung to hope for Arthur. Her affection for him brought out from the depths of her cold and insignificant character qualities that had never before been apparent. She watched—she nursed—she tended him. The fine lady was gone; nothing but the mother was left behind.

With a delicate constitution, and with an easy temper, which yielded to the influence of companions inferior to himself, except in bodily vigour and more sturdy will, Arthur Beaufort had been ruined by prosperity. His talents and acquirements, if not first-rate, at least far above mediocrity, had only served to refine his tastes, not to strengthen his mind. His amiable impulses, his charming disposition and sweet temper, had only served to make him the dupe of the parasites that feasted on the lavish heir. His heart, frittered away in the usual round of light intrigues and hollow pleasures, had become too sated and exhausted for the redeeming blessings of a deep and a noble love. He had so lived for Pleasure that he had never known Happiness. His frame broke by excesses in which his better nature never took delight, he came home—to hear of ruin and to die!

It was evening in the sick-room. Arthur had risen from the bed to which, for some days, he had voluntarily taken, and was stretched on the sofa before the fire. Camilla was leaning over him, keeping in the shade, that he might not see the tears which she could not suppress. His mother had been endeavouring to amuse him, as she would have amused herself, by reading aloud one of the light novels of the hour; novels that paint the life of the higher classes as one gorgeous holyday.

"My dear mother," said the patient querulously, "I have no interest in these false descriptions of the life I have led. I know that life's worth. Ah! had I been trained to some employment, some profession! had I—well—it is weak to repine. Mother, tell me, you have seen Mons. de Vaudemont: is he strong and healthy?"

"Yes; too much so. He has not your elegance, dear Arthur."

"And do you admire him, Camilla? Has no other caught your heart or your fancy?"

"My dear Arthur," interrupted Mrs. Beaufort, "you forget that Camilla is scarcely out; and of course a young girl's affections, if she's well brought up, are regulated by the experience of her parents. It is time to take the medicine: it certainly agrees with you; you have more colour to-day, my dear, dear son."

While Mrs. Beaufort was pouring out the medicine, the door gently opened, and Mr. Robert Beaufort appeared; behind him there rose a taller and a statelier form, but one which seemed more bent, more humbled, more agitated. Beaufort advanced. Camilla looked up and turned pale. The visitor escaped from Mr. Beaufort's grasp on his arm; he came forward, trembling, he fell on his knees beside Arthur, and seizing his hand, bent over, it in silence. But silence so stormy! silence more impressive than all words his breast heaved, his whole frame shook. Arthur guessed at once whom he saw, and bent down gently as if to raise his visitor.

"Oh! Arthur! Arthur!" then cried Philip; "forgive me! My mother's comforter—my cousin—my brother! Oh! brother, forgive me!"

And as he half rose, Arthur stretched out his arms, and Philip clasped him to his breast.

It is in vain to describe the different feelings that agitated those who beheld; the selfish congratulations of Robert, mingled with a better and purer feeling; the stupor of the mother; the emotions that she herself could not unravel, which rooted Camilla to the spot.

"You own me, then,—you own me!" cried Philip. "You accept the brotherhood that my mad passions once rejected! And you, too—you, Camilla—you who once knelt by my side, under this very roof—do you remember me now? Oh, Arthur! that letter—that letter!—yes, indeed, that aid which I ascribed to any one—rather than to you—made the date of a fairer fortune. I may have owed to that aid the very fate that has preserved me till now; the very name which I have not discredited. No, no; do not think you can ask me a favour; you can but claim your due. Brother! my dear brother!"

CHAPTER XVII

"Warwick.—Exceeding well! his cares are now all over."—Henry IV.

The excitement of this interview soon overpowering Arthur, Philip, in quitting the room with Mr. Beaufort, asked a conference with that gentleman; and they went into the very parlour from which the rich man had once threatened to expel the haggard suppliant. Philip glanced round the room, and the whole scene came again before him. After a pause, he thus began,—

"Mr. Beaufort, let the Past be forgotten. We may have need of mutual forgiveness, and I, who have so wronged your noble son, am willing to suppose that I misjudged you. I cannot, it is true, forego this lawsuit."

Mr. Beaufort's face fell.

"I have no right to do so. I am the trustee of my father's honour and my mother's name: I must vindicate both: I cannot forego this lawsuit. But when I once bowed myself to enter your house—then only with a hope, where now I have the certainty of obtaining my heritage—it was with the resolve to bury in oblivion every sentiment that would transgress the most temperate justice. Now, I will do more. If the law decide against me, we are as we were; if with me—listen: I will leave you the lands of Beaufort, for your life and your son's. I ask but for me and for mine such a deduction from your wealth as will enable me, should my brother be yet living, to provide for him; and (if you approve the choice, which out of all earth I would desire to make) to give whatever belongs to more refined or graceful existence than I myself care for,—to her whom I would call my wife. Robert Beaufort, in this room I once asked you to restore to me the only being I then loved: I am now again your suppliant; and this time you have it in your power to grant my prayer. Let Arthur be, in truth, my brother: give me, if I prove myself, as I feel assured, entitled to hold the name my father bore, give me your daughter as my wife; give me Camilla, and I will not envy you the lands I am willing for myself to resign; and if they pass to any children, those children will be your daughter's!"

The first impulse of Mr. Beaufort was to grasp the hand held out to him; to pour forth an incoherent torrent of praise and protestation, of assurances that he could not hear of such generosity, that what was right was right, that he should be proud of such a son-in-law, and much more in the same key. And in the midst of this, it suddenly occurred to Mr. Beaufort, that if Philip's case were really as good as he said it was, he could not talk so coolly of resigning the property it would secure him for the term of a life (Mr. Beaufort thought of his own) so uncommonly good, to say nothing of Arthur's. At this notion, he thought it best not to commit himself too far; drew in as artfully as he could, until he could consult Lord Lilburne and his lawyer; and recollecting also that he had a great deal to manage with respect to Camilla and her prior attachment, he began to talk of his distress for Arthur, of the necessity of waiting a little before Camilla was spoken to, while so agitated about her brother, of the exceedingly strong case which his lawyer advised him he possessed—not but what he would rather rest the matter on justice than law—and that if the law should be with him, he would not the less (provided he did not force his daughter's inclinations, of which, indeed, he had no fear) be most happy to bestow her hand on his brother's nephew, with such a portion as would be most handsome to all parties.

It often happens to us in this world, that when we come with our heart in our hands to some person or other,—when we pour out some generous burst of feeling so enthusiastic and self-sacrificing, that a bystander would call us fool and Quixote;—it often, I say, happens to us, to find our warm self suddenly thrown back upon our cold self; to discover that we are utterly uncomprehended, and that the swine who would have munched up the acorn does not know what to make of the pearl. That sudden ice which then freezes over us, that supreme disgust and despair almost of the whole world, which for the moment we confound with the one worldling—they who have felt, may reasonably ascribe to Philip. He listened to Mr. Beaufort in utter and contemptuous silence, and then replied only,—

"Sir, at all events this is a question for law to decide. If it decide as you think, it is for you to act; if as I think, it is for me. Till then I will speak to you no more of your daughter, or my intentions. Meanwhile, all I ask is the liberty to visit your son. I would not be banished from his sick-room!"

"My dear nephew!" cried Mr. Beaufort, again alarmed, "consider this house as your home."

Philip bowed and retreated to the door, followed obsequiously by his uncle.

It chanced that both Lord Lilburne and Mr. Blackwell were of the same mind as to the course advisable for Mr. Beaufort now to pursue. Lord Lilburne was not only anxious to exchange a hostile litigation for an amicable lawsuit, but he was really eager to put the seal of relationship upon any secret with regard to himself that a man who might inherit £20,000. a year—a dead shot, and a bold tongue—might think fit to disclose. This made him more earnest than he otherwise might have been in advice as to other people's affairs. He spoke to Beaufort as a man of the world—to Blackwell as a lawyer.

"Pin the man down to his generosity," said Lilburne, "before he gets the property. Possession makes a great change in a man's value of money. After all, you can't enjoy the property when you're dead: he gives it next to Arthur, who is not married; and if anything happen to Arthur, poor fellow, why, in devolving on your daughter's husband and children, it goes in the right line. Pin him down at once: get credit with the world for the most noble and disinterested conduct, by letting your counsel state that the instant you discovered the lost document you wished to throw no obstacle in the way of proving the marriage, and that the only thing to consider is, if the marriage be proved; if so, you will be the first to rejoice, &c. &c. You know all that sort of humbug as well as any man!"

Mr. Blackwell suggested the same advice, though in different words—after taking the opinions of three eminent members of the bar; those opinions, indeed, were not all alike—one was adverse to Mr. Robert Beaufort's chance of success, one was doubtful of it, the third maintained that he had nothing to fear from the action—except, possibly, the ill-natured construction of the world. Mr. Robert Beaufort disliked the idea of the world's ill-nature, almost as much as he did that of losing his property. And when even this last and more encouraging authority, learning privately from Mr. Blackwell that Arthur's illness was of a nature to terminate fatally, observed, "that a compromise with a claimant, who was at all events Mr. Beaufort's nephew, by which Mr. Beaufort could secure the enjoyment of the estates to himself for life, and to his son for life also, should not (whatever his probabilities of legal success) be hastily rejected—unless he had a peculiar affection for a very distant relation—who, failing Mr. Beaufort's male issue and Philip's claim, would be heir-at-law, but whose rights would cease if Arthur liked to cut off the entail."

Mr. Beaufort at once decided. He had a personal dislike to that distant heir-at-law; he had a strong desire to retain the esteem of the world; he had an innate conviction of the justice of Philip's claim; he had a remorseful recollection of his brother's generous kindness to himself; he preferred to have for his heir, in case of Arthur's decease, a nephew who would marry his daughter, than a remote kinsman. And should, after all, the lawsuit fail to prove Philip's right, he was not sorry to have the estate in his own power by Arthur's act in cutting off the entail. Brief; all these reasons decided him. He saw Philip—he spoke to Arthur—and all the preliminaries, as suggested above, were arranged between the parties. The entail was cut off, and Arthur secretly prevailed upon his father, to whom, for the present, the fee-simple thus belonged, to make a will, by which he bequeathed the estates to Philip, without reference to the question of his legitimacy. Mr. Beaufort felt his conscience greatly eased after this action—which, too, he could always retract if he pleased; and henceforth the lawsuit became but a matter of form, so far as the property it involved was concerned.

While these negotiations went on, Arthur continued gradually to decline. Philip was with him always. The sufferer took a strange liking to this long-dreaded relation, this man of iron frame and thews. In Philip there was so much of life, that Arthur almost felt as if in his presence itself there was an antagonism to death. And Camilla saw thus her cousin, day by day, hour by hour, in that sick chamber, lending himself, with the gentle tenderness of a woman, to soften the pang, to arouse the weariness, to cheer the dejection. Philip never spoke to her of love: in such a scene that had been impossible. She overcame in their mutual cares the embarrassment she had before felt in his presence; whatever her other feelings, she could not, at least, but be grateful to one so tender to her brother. Three letters of Charles Spencer's had been, in the afflictions of the house, only answered by a brief line. She now took the occasion of a momentary and delusive amelioration in Arthur's disease to write to him more at length. She was carrying, as usual, the letter to her mother, when Mr. Beaufort met her, and took the letter from her hand. He looked embarrassed for a moment, and bade her follow him into his study. It was then that Camilla learned, for the first time, distinctly, the claims and rights of her cousin; then she learned also at what price those rights were to be enforced with the least possible injury to her father. Mr. Beaufort naturally put the case before her in the strongest point of the dilemma. He was to be ruined—utterly ruined; a pauper, a beggar, if Camilla did not save him. The master of his fate demanded his daughter's hand. Habitually subservient to even a whim of her parents, this intelligence, the entreaty, the command with which it was accompanied, overwhelmed her. She answered but by tears; and Mr. Beaufort, assured of her submission, left her, to consider of the tone of the letter he himself should write to Mr. Spencer. He had sat down to this very task when he was summoned to Arthur's room. His son was suddenly taken worse: spasms that threatened immediate danger convulsed and exhausted him, and when these were allayed, he continued for three days so feeble that Mr. Beaufort, his eyes now thoroughly opened to the loss that awaited him, had no thoughts even for worldly interests.

On the night of the third day, Philip, Robert Beaufort, his wife, his daughter, were grouped round the death-bed of Arthur. The sufferer had just wakened from sleep, and he motioned to Philip to raise him. Mr. Beaufort started, as by the dim light he saw his son in the arms of Catherine's! and another Chamber of Death seemed, shadow-like, to replace the one before him. Words, long since uttered, knelled in his ear: "There shall be a death-bed yet beside which you shall see the spectre of her, now so calm, rising for retribution from the grave!" His blood froze, his hair stood erect; he cast a hurried, shrinking glance round the twilight of the darkened room: and with a feeble cry covered his white face with his trembling hands! But on Arthur's lips there was a serene smile; he turned his eyes from Philip to Camilla, and murmured, "She will repay you!" A pause, and the mother's shriek rang through the room! Robert Beaufort raised his face from his hands. His son was dead!

CHAPTER XVIII

"Jul. And what reward do you propose?

It must be my love."— BEAUMONT AND FLETCHER: The Double Marriage.

While these events, dark, hurried, and stormy, had befallen the family of his betrothed, Sidney Beaufort continued his calm life by the banks of the lovely lake. After a few weeks, his confidence in Camilla's fidelity overbore all his apprehensions and forebodings. Her letters, though constrained by the inspection to which they were submitted, gave him inexpressible consolation and delight. He began, however, early to fancy that there was a change in their tone. The letters seemed to shun the one subject to which all others were as nought; they turned rather upon the guests assembled at Beaufort Court; and why I know not,—for there was nothing in them to authorise jealousy—the brief words devoted to Monsieur de Vaudemont filled him with uneasy and terrible suspicion. He gave vent to these feelings, as fully as he dared do, under the knowledge that his letter would be seen; and Camilla never again even mentioned the name of Vaudemont. Then there was a long pause; then her brother's arrival and illness were announced; then, at intervals, but a few hurried lines; then a complete, long, dreadful silence, and lastly, with a deep black border and a solemn black seal, came the following letter from Mr. Beaufort:

"MY DEAR SIR,—I have the unutterable grief to announce to you and your worthy uncle the irreparable loss I have sustained in the death of my only son. It is a month to day since he departed this life. He died, sir, as a Christian should die—humbly, penitently—exaggerating the few faults of his short life, but—(and here the writer's hypocrisy, though so natural to him—was it, that he knew not that he was hypocritical?—fairly gave way before the real and human anguish, for which there is no dictionary!) but I cannot pursue this theme!

"Slowly now awakening to the duties yet left me to discharge, I cannot but be sensible of the material difference in the prospects of my remaining child. Miss Beaufort is now the heiress to an ancient name and a large fortune. She subscribes with me to the necessity of consulting those new considerations which so melancholy an event forces upon her mind. The little fancy—or liking—(the acquaintance was too short for more) that might naturally spring up between two amiable young persons thrown together in the country, must be banished from our thoughts. As a friend, I shall be always happy to hear of your welfare; and should you ever think of a profession in which I can serve you, you may command my utmost interest and exertions. I know, my young friend, what you will feel at first, and how disposed you will be to call me mercenary and selfish. Heaven knows if that be really my character! But at your age, impressions are easily effaced; and any experienced friend of the world will assure you that, in the altered circumstances of the case, I have no option. All intercourse and correspondence, of course, cease with this letter,—until, at least, we may all meet, with no sentiments but those of friendship and esteem. I desire my compliments to your worthy uncle, in which Mrs. and Miss Beaufort join; and I am sure you will be happy to hear that my wife and daughter, though still in great affliction, have suffered less in health than I could have ventured to anticipate.

"Believe me, dear Sir,

"Yours sincerely,

"ROBERT BEAUFORT.

"To C. SPENCER, Esq., Jun."

When Sidney received this letter, he was with Mr. Spencer, and the latter read it over the young man's shoulder, on which he leant affectionately. When they came to the concluding words, Sidney turned round with a vacant look and a hollow smile. "You see, sir," he said, "you see—"

"My boy—my son—you bear this as you ought. Contempt will soon efface—"

Sidney started to his feet, and his whole countenance was changed.

"Contempt—yes, for him! But for her—she knows it not—she is no party to this—I cannot believe it—I will not! I—I—" and he rushed out of the room. He was absent till nightfall, and when he returned, he endeavoured to appear calm—but it was in vain.

The next day brought him a letter from Camilla, written unknown to her parents,—short, it is true (confirming the sentence of separation contained in her father's), and imploring him not to reply to it,—but still so full of gentle and of sorrowful feeling, so evidently worded in the wish to soften the anguish she inflicted, that it did more than soothe—it even administered hope.

Now when Mr. Robert Beaufort had recovered the ordinary tone of his mind sufficiently to indite the letter Sidney had just read, he had become fully sensible of the necessity of concluding the marriage between Philip and Camilla before the publicity of the lawsuit. The action for the ejectment could not take place before the ensuing March or April. He would waive the ordinary etiquette of time and mourning to arrange all before. Indeed, he lived in hourly fear lest Philip should discover that he had a rival in his brother, and break off the marriage, with its contingent advantages. The first announcement of such a suit in the newspapers might reach the Spencers; and if the young man were, as he doubted not, Sidney Beaufort, would necessarily bring him forward, and ensure the dreaded explanation. Thus apprehensive and ever scheming, Robert Beaufort spoke to Philip so much, and with such apparent feeling, of his wish to gratify, at the earliest possible period, the last wish of his son, in the union now arranged—he spoke, with such seeming consideration and good sense, of the avoidance of all scandal and misinterpretation in the suit itself, which suit a previous marriage between the claimant and his daughter would show at once to be of so amicable a nature,—that Philip, ardently in love as he was, could not but assent to any hastening of his expected happiness compatible with decorum. As to any previous publicity by way of newspaper comment, he agreed with Mr. Beaufort in deprecating it. But then came the question, What name was he to bear in the interval?

"As to that," said Philip, somewhat proudly, "when, after my mother's suit in her own behalf, I persuaded her not to bear the name of Beaufort, though her due—and for my own part, I prized her own modest name, which under such dark appearances was in reality spotless—as much as the loftier one which you bear and my father bore;—so I shall not resume the name the law denies me till the law restores it to me. Law alone can efface the wrong which law has done me."

Mr. Beaufort was pleased with this reasoning (erroneous though it was), and he now hoped that all would be safely arranged.

That a girl so situated as Camilla, and of a character not energetic or profound, but submissive, dutiful, and timid, should yield to the arguments of her father, the desire of her dying brother—that she should not dare to refuse to become the instrument of peace to a divided family, the saving sacrifice to her father's endangered fortunes—that, in fine, when, nearly a month after Arthur's death, her father, leading her into the room, where Philip waited her footstep with a beating heart, placed her hand in his—and Philip falling on his knees said, "May I hope to retain this hand for life?"—she should falter out such words as he might construe into not reluctant acquiescence; that all this should happen is so natural that the reader is already prepared for it. But still she thought with bitter and remorseful feelings of him thus deliberately and faithlessly renounced. She felt how deeply he had loved her—she knew how fearful would be his grief. She looked sad and thoughtful; but her brother's death was sufficient in Philip's eyes to account for that. The praises and gratitude of her father, to whom she suddenly seemed to become an object of even greater pride and affection than ever Arthur had been—the comfort of a generous heart, that takes pleasure in the very sacrifice it makes—the acquittal of her conscience as to the motives of her conduct—began, however, to produce their effect. Nor, as she had lately seen more of Philip, could she be insensible of his attachment—of his many noble qualities—of the pride which most women might have felt in his addresses, when his rank was once made clear; and as she had ever been of a character more regulated by duty than passion, so one who could have seen what was passing in her mind would have had little fear for Philip's future happiness in her keeping—little fear but that, when once married to him, her affections would have gone along with her duties; and that if the first love were yet recalled, it would be with a sigh due rather to some romantic recollection than some continued regret. Few of either sex are ever united to their first love; yet married people jog on, and call each other "my dear" and "my darling" all the same. It might be, it is true, that Philip would be scarcely loved with the intenseness with which he loved; but if Camilla's feelings were capable of corresponding to the ardent and impassioned ones of that strong and vehement nature—such feelings were not yet developed in her. The heart of the woman might still be half concealed in the vale of the virgin innocence. Philip himself was satisfied—he believed that he was beloved: for it is the property of love, in a large and noble heart, to reflect itself, and to see its own image in the eyes on which it looks. As the Poet gives ideal beauty and excellence to some ordinary child of Eve, worshipping less the being that is than the being he imagines and conceives—so Love, which makes us all poets for a while, throws its own divine light over a heart perhaps really cold; and becomes dazzled into the joy of a false belief by the very lustre with which it surrounds its object.

The more, however, Camilla saw of Philip, the more (gradually overcoming her former mysterious and superstitious awe of him) she grew familiarised to his peculiar cast of character and thought, so the more she began to distrust her father's assertion, that he had insisted on her hand as a price—a bargain—an equivalent for the sacrifice of a dire revenge. And with this thought came another. Was she worthy of this man?—was she not deceiving him? Ought she not to say, at least, that she had known a previous attachment, however determined she might be to subdue it? Often the desire for this just and honourable confession trembled on her lips, and as often was it checked by some chance circumstance or some maiden fear. Despite their connection, there was not yet between them that delicious intimacy which ought to accompany the affiance of two hearts and souls. The gloom of the house; the restraint on the very language of love imposed by a death so recent and so deplored, accounted in much for this reserve. And for the rest, Robert Beaufort prudently left them very few and very brief opportunities to be alone.

In the meantime, Philip (now persuaded that the Beauforts were ignorant of his brother's fate) had set Mr. Barlow's activity in search of Sidney; and his painful anxiety to discover one so dear and so mysteriously lost was the only cause of uneasiness apparent in the brightening Future. While these researches, hitherto fruitless, were being made, it so happened, as London began now to refill, and gossip began now to revive, that a report got abroad, no one knew how (probably from the servants) that Monsieur de Vaudemont, a distinguished French officer, was shortly to lead the daughter and sole heiress of Robert Beaufort, Esq., M.P., to the hymeneal altar; and that report very quickly found its way into the London papers: from the London papers it spread to the provincial—it reached the eyes of Sidney in his now gloomy and despairing solitude. The day that he read it he disappeared.

CHAPTER XIX

"Jul.... Good lady, love him!
You have a noble and an honest gentleman.
I ever found him so.
Love him no less than I have done, and serve him,
And Heaven shall bless you—you shall bless my ashes."
BEAUMONT AND FLETCHER: *The Double Marriage.*

We have been too long absent from Fanny; it is time to return to her. The delight she experienced when Philip made her understand all the benefits, the blessings, that her courage, nay, her intellect, had bestowed upon him, the blushing ecstasy with which she heard (as they returned to H—, the eventful morning of her deliverance, side by side, her hand clasped in his, and often pressed to his grateful lips) his praises, his thanks, his fear for her safety, his joy at regaining her—all this amounted to a bliss, which, till then, she could not have conceived that life was capable of bestowing. And when he left her at H—, to hurry to his lawyer's with the recovered document, it was but for an hour. He returned, and did not quit her for several days. And in that time he became sensible of her astonishing, and, to him, it seemed miraculous, improvement in all that renders Mind the equal to Mind; miraculous, for he guessed not the Influence that makes miracles its commonplace. And now he listened attentively to her when she conversed; he read with her (though reading was never much in his vocation), his unfastidious ear was charmed with her voice, when it sang those simple songs; and his manner (impressed alike by gratitude for the signal service rendered to him, and by the discovery that Fanny was no longer a child, whether in mind or years), though not less gentle than before, was less familiar, less superior, more respectful, and more earnest. It was a change which raised her in her own self-esteem. Ah, those were rosy days for Fanny!

A less sagacious judge of character than Lilburne would have formed doubts perhaps of the nature of Philip's interest in Fanny. But he comprehended at once the fraternal interest which a man like Philip might well take in a creature like Fanny, if commended to his care by a protector whose doom was so awful as that which had ingulfed the life of William Gawtrey. Lilburne had some thoughts at first of claiming her, but as he had no power to compel her residence with him, he did not wish, on consideration, to come again in contact with Philip upon ground so full of humbling recollections as that still overshadowed by the images of Gawtrey and Mary. He contented himself with writing an artful letter to Simon, stating that from Fanny's residence with Mr. Gawtrey, and from her likeness to her mother, whom he had only seen as a child, he had conjectured the relationship she bore to himself; and having obtained other evidence of that fact (he did not say what or where), he had not scrupled to remove her to his roof, meaning to explain all to Mr. Simon Gawtrey the next day. This letter was accompanied by one from a lawyer, informing Simon Gawtrey that Lord Lilburne would pay £200. a year, in quarterly payments, to his order; and that he was requested to add, that when the young lady he had so benevolently reared came of age, or married, an adequate provision would be made for her. Simon's mind blazed up at this last intelligence, when read to him, though he neither comprehended nor sought to know why Lord Lilburne should be so generous, or what that noble person's letter to himself was intended to convey. For two days, he seemed restored to vigorous sense; but when he had once clutched the first payment made in advance, the touch of the money seemed to numb him back to his lethargy: the excitement of desire died in the dull sense of possession.

And just at that time Fanny's happiness came to a close. Philip received Arthur Beaufort's letter; and now ensued long and frequent absences; and on his return, for about an hour or so at a time, he spoke of sorrow and death; and the books were closed and the songs silenced. All fear for Fanny's safety was, of course, over; all necessity for her work; their little establishment was increased. She never stirred out without Sarah; yet she would rather that there had been some danger on her account for him to guard against, or some trial that his smile might soothe. His prolonged absences began to prey upon her—the books ceased to interest—no study filled up the dreary gap—her step grew listless—her cheek pale—she was sensible at last that his presence had become necessary to her very life. One day, he came to the house earlier than usual, and with a much happier and serener expression of countenance than he had worn of late.

Simon was dozing in his chair, with his old dog, now scarce vigorous enough to bark, curled up at his feet. Neither man nor dog was more as a witness to what was spoken than the leathern chair, or the hearth-rug, on which they severally reposed.

There was something which, in actual life, greatly contributed to the interest of Fanny's strange lot, but which, in narration, I feel I cannot make sufficiently clear to the reader. And this was her connection and residence with that old man. Her character forming, as his was completely gone; here, the blank becoming filled—there, the page fading to a blank. It was the utter, total Deathliness-in-Life of Simon, that, while so impressive to see, renders it impossible to bring him before the reader in his full force of contrast to the young Psyche. He seldom spoke—often, not from morning till night; he now seldom stirred. It is in vain to describe the indescribable: let the reader draw the picture for himself. And whenever (as I sometimes think he will, after he has closed this book) he conjures up the idea he attaches to the name of its heroine, let him see before her, as she glides through the humble room—as she listens to the voice of him she loves—as she sits musing by the window, with the church spire just visible—as day by day the soul brightens and expands within her—still let the reader see within the same walls, greyhaired, blind, dull to all feeling, frozen to all life, that stony image of Time and Death! Perhaps then he may understand why they who beheld the real and living Fanny blooming under that chill and mass of shadow, felt that her grace, her simplicity, her charming beauty, were raised by the contrast, till they grew associated with thoughts and images, mysterious and profound, belonging not more to the lovely than to the sublime.

So there sat the old man; and Philip, though aware of his presence, speaking as if he were alone with Fanny, after touching on more casual topics, thus addressed her:

"My true and my dear friend, it is to you that I shall owe, not only my rights and fortune, but the vindication of my mother's memory. You have not only placed flowers upon that gravestone, but it is owing to you, under Providence, that it will be inscribed at last with the Name which refutes all calumny. Young and innocent as you now are, my gentle and beloved benefactress, you cannot as yet know what a blessing it will be to me to engrave that Name upon that simple stone. Hereafter, when you yourself are a wife, a mother, you will comprehend the service you have rendered to the living and the dead!"

He stopped—struggling with the rush of emotions that overflowed his heart. Alas, THE DEAD! what service can we render to them?—what availed it now, either to the dust below, or to the immortality above, that the fools and knaves of this world should mention the Catherine whose life was gone, whose ears were deaf, with more or less respect? There is in calumny that poison that, even when the character throws off the slander, the heart remains diseased beneath the effect. They say that truth comes sooner or later; but it seldom comes before the soul, passing from agony to contempt, has grown callous to men's judgments. Calumniate a human being in youth—adulate that being in age;—what has been the interval? Will the adulation atone either for the torture, or the hardness which the torture leaves at last? And if, as in Catherine's case (a case, how common!), the truth come too late—if the tomb is closed—if the heart you have wrung can be wrung no more—why the truth is as valueless as the epitaph on a forgotten Name! Some such conviction of the hollowness of his own words, when he spoke of service to the dead, smote upon Philip's heart, and stopped the flow of his words.

Fanny, conscious only of his praise, his thanks, and the tender affection of his voice, stood still silent—her eyes downcast, her breast heaving.

Philip resumed:

"And now, Fanny, my honoured sister, I would thank you for more, were it possible, even than this. I shall owe to you not only name and fortune, but happiness. It is from the rights to which you have assisted me, and which will shortly be made clear, that I am able to demand a hand I have so long coveted—the hand of one as dear to me as you are. In a word, the time has, this day, been fixed, when I shall have a home to offer to you and to this old man—when I can present to you a sister who will prize you as I do: for I love you so dearly—I owe you so much—that even that home would lose half its smiles if you were not there. Do you understand me, Fanny? The sister I speak of will be my wife!"

The poor girl who heard this speech of most cruel tenderness did not fall, or faint, or evince any outward emotion, except in a deadly paleness. She seemed like one turned to stone. Her very breath forsook her for some moments, and then came back with a long deep sigh. She laid her hand lightly on his arm, and said calmly:

"Yes—I understand. We once saw a wedding. You are to be married—I shall see yours!"

"You shall; and, later, perhaps, I may see your own."

"I have a brother. Ah! if I could but find him—younger than I am—beautiful almost as you!"

"You will be happy," said Fanny, still calmly.

"I have long placed my hopes of happiness in such a union! Stay, where are you going?"

"To pray for you," said Fanny, with a smile, in which there was something of the old vacancy, as she walked gently from the room. Philip followed her with moistened eyes. Her manner might have deceived one more vain. He soon after quitted the house, and returned to town.

Three hours after, Sarah found Fanny stretched on the floor of her own room—so still—so white—that, for some moments, the old woman thought life was gone. She recovered, however, by degrees; and, after putting her hands to her eyes, and muttering some moments, seemed much as usual, except that she was more silent, and that her lips remained colourless, and her hands cold like stone.

CHAPTER XX.

"Vec. Ye see what follows.
Duke. O gentle sir! this shape again!"—The Chances.

That evening Sidney Beaufort arrived in London. It is the nature of solitude to make passions calm on the surface—agitated in the deeps. Sidney had placed his whole existence in one object. When the letter arrived that told him to hope no more, he was at first rather sensible of the terrible and dismal blank—the "void abyss"—to which all his future was suddenly changed, than roused to vehement and turbulent emotion. But Camilla's letter had, as we have seen, raised his courage and animated his heart. To the idea of her faith he still clung with the instinct of hope in the midst of despair. The tidings that she was absolutely betrothed to another, and in so short a time since her rejection of him, let loose from all restraint his darker and more tempestuous passions. In a state of mind bordering upon frenzy, he hurried to London—to seek her—to see her; with what intent—what hope, if hope there were—he himself could scarcely tell. But what man who has loved with fervour and trust will be contented to receive the sentence of eternal separation except from the very lips of the one thus worshipped and thus foresworn?

The day had been intensely cold. Towards evening the snow fell fast and heavily. Sidney had not, since a child, been before in London; and the immense City, covered with a wintry and icy mist, through which the hurrying passengers and the slow-moving vehicles passed, spectre-like, along the dismal and slippery streets—opened to the stranger no hospitable arms. He knew not a step of the way—he was pushed to and fro—his scarce intelligible questions impatiently answered—the snow covered him—the frost pierced to his veins. At length a man, more kindly than the rest, seeing that he was a stranger to London, procured him a hackney-coach, and directed the driver to the distant quarter of Berkeley Square. The snow balled under the hoofs of the horses—the groaning vehicle proceeded at the pace of a hearse. At length, and after a period of such suspense, and such emotion, as Sidney never in after-life could recall without a shudder, the coach stopped—the benumbed driver heavily descended—the sound of the knocker knelled loud through the muffled air—and the light from Mr. Beaufort's hall glared full upon the dizzy eyes of the visitor. He pushed aside the porter, and sprang into the hall. Luckily, one of the footmen who had attended Mrs. Beaufort to the Lakes recognised him; and, in answer to his breathless inquiry, said,—

"Why, indeed, Mr. Spencer, Miss Beaufort is at home—up-stairs in the drawing-room, with master and mistress, and Monsieur de Vaudemont; but—"

Sidney waited no more. He bounded up the stairs—he opened the first door that presented itself to him, and burst, unannounced and unlooked-for, upon the eyes of the group seated within. He saw not the terrified start of Mr. Robert Beaufort—he heeded not the faint, nervous exclamation of the mother—he caught not the dark and wondering glace of the stranger seated beside Camilla—he saw but Camilla herself, and in a moment he was at her feet.

"Camilla, I am here!—I, who love you so—I, who have nothing in the world but you! I am here—to learn from you, and you alone, if I am indeed abandoned—if you are indeed to be another's!"

He had dashed his hat from his brow as he sprang forward; his long fair hair, damp with the snows, fell disordered over his forehead; his eyes were fixed, as for life and death, upon the pale face and trembling lips of Camilla. Robert Beaufort, in great alarm, and well aware of the fierce temper of Philip, anticipative of some rash and violent impulse, turned his glance upon his destined son-in-law. But there was no angry pride in the countenance he there beheld. Philip had risen, but his frame was bent—his knees knocked together—his lips were parted—his eyes were staring full upon the face of the kneeling man.

Suddenly Camilla, sharing her father's fear, herself half rose, and with an unconscious pathos, stretched one hand, as if to shelter, over Sidney's head, and looked to Philip. Sidney's eyes followed hers. He sprang to his feet.

"What, then, it is true! And this is the man for whom I am abandoned! But unless you—you, with your own lips, tell me that you love me no more—that you love another—I will not yield you but with life."

He stalked sternly and impetuously up to Philip, who recoiled as his rival advanced. The characters of the two men seemed suddenly changed. The timid dreamer seemed dilated into the fearless soldier. The soldier seemed shrinking—quailing—into nameless terror. Sidney grasped that strong arm, as Philip still retreated, with his slight and delicate fingers, grasped it with violence and menace; and frowning into the face from which the swarthy blood was scared away, said, in a hollow whisper:

"Do you hear me? Do you comprehend me? I say that she shall not be forced into a marriage at which I yet believe her heart rebels. My claim is holier than yours. Renounce her, or win her but with my blood."

Philip did not apparently hear the words thus addressed to him. His whole senses seemed absorbed in the one sense of sight. He continued to gaze upon the speaker, till his eye dropped on the hand that yet griped his arm. And as he thus looked, he uttered an inarticulate cry. He caught the hand in his own, and pointed to a ring on the finger, but remained speechless. Mr. Beaufort approached, and began some stammered words of soothing to Sidney, but Philip motioned him to be silent, and, at last, as if by a violent effort, gasped forth, not to Sidney, but to Beaufort,—

"His name?—his name?"

"It is Mr. Spencer—Mr. Charles Spencer," cried Beaufort. "Listen to me, I will explain all—I—"

"Hush, hush! cried Philip; and turning to Sidney, he put his hand on his shoulder, and looking him full in the face, said,—

"Have you not known another name? Are you not—yes, it is so—it is—it is! Follow me—follow!"

And still retaining his grasp, and leading Sidney, who was now subdued, awed, and a prey to new and wild suspicions, he moved on gently, stride by stride—his eyes fixed on that fair face—his lips muttering—till the closing door shut both forms from the eyes of the three there left.

It was the adjoining room into which Philip led his rival. It was lit but by a small reading-lamp, and the bright, steady blaze of the fire; and by this light they both continued to gaze on each other, as if spellbound, in complete silence. At last Philip, by an irresistible impulse, fell upon Sidney's bosom, and, clasping him with convulsive energy, gasped out:

"Sidney!—Sidney!—my mother's son!"

"What!" exclaimed Sidney, struggling from the embrace, and at last freeing himself; "it is you, then!—you, my own brother! You, who have been hitherto the thorn in my path, the cloud in my fate! You, who are now come to make me a wretch for life! I love that woman, and you tear her from me! You, who subjected my infancy to hardship, and, but for Providence, might have degraded my youth, by your example, into shame and guilt!"

"Forbear!—forbear!" cried Philip, with a voice so shrill in its agony, that it smote the hearts of those in the adjoining chamber like the shriek of some despairing soul. They looked at each other, but not one had the courage to break upon the interview.

Sidney himself was appalled by the sound. He threw himself on a seat, and, overcome by passions so new to him, by excitement so strange, hid his face, and sobbed as a child.

Philip walked rapidly to and fro the room for some moments; at length he paused opposite to Sidney, and said, with the deep calmness of a wronged and goaded spirit:

"Sidney Beaufort, hear me! When my mother died she confided you to my care, my love, and my protection. In the last lines that her hand traced, she bade me think less of myself than of you; to be to you as a father as well as brother. The hour that I read that letter I fell on my knees, and vowed that I would fulfil that injunction—that I would sacrifice my very self, if I could give fortune or happiness to you. And this not for your sake alone, Sidney; no! but as my mother—our wronged, our belied, our broken-hearted mother!—O Sidney, Sidney! have you no tears for her, too?" He passed his hand over his own eyes for a moment, and resumed: "But as our mother, in that last letter, said to me, 'let my love pass into your breast for him,' so, Sidney, so, in all that I could do for you, I fancied that my mother's smile looked down upon me, and that in serving you it was my mother whom I obeyed. Perhaps, hereafter, Sidney, when we talk over that period of my earlier life when I worked for you, when the degradation you speak of (there was no crime in it!)—was borne cheerfully for your sake, and yours the holiday though mine the task—perhaps, hereafter, you will do me more justice. You left me, or were reft from me, and I gave all the little fortune that my mother had bequeathed us, to get some tidings from you. I received your letter—that bitter letter—and I cared not then that I was a beggar, since I was alone. You talk of what I have cost you—you talk! and you now ask me to—to—Merciful Heaven! let me understand you—do you love Camilla? Does she love you? Speak—speak—explain—what, new agony awaits me?"

It was then that Sidney, affected and humbled, amidst all his more selfish sorrows, by his brother's language and manner, related, as succinctly as he could, the history of his affection for Camilla, the circumstances of their engagement, and ended by placing before him the letter he had received from Mr. Beaufort.

In spite of all his efforts for self-control, Philip's anguish was so great, so visible, that Sidney, after looking at his working features, his trembling hands, for a moment, felt all the earlier parts of his nature melt in a flow of generous sympathy and remorse. He flung himself on the breast from which he had shrunk before, and cried,—

"Brother, brother! forgive me; I see how I have wronged you. If she has forgotten me, if she love you, take her and be happy!"

Philip returned his embrace, but without warmth, and then moved away; and, again, in great disorder, paced the room. His brother only heard disjointed exclamations that seemed to escape him unawares: "They said she loved me! Heaven give me strength! Mother—mother! let me fulfil my vow! Oh, that I had died ere this!" He stopped at last, and the large dews rolled down his forehead. "Sidney!" said he, "there is a mystery here that I comprehend not. But my mind now is very confused. If she loves you—if!—is it possible for a woman to love two? Well, well, I go to solve the riddle: wait here!"

He vanished into the next room, and for nearly half an hour Sidney was alone. He heard through the partition murmured voices; he caught more clearly the sound of Camilla's sobs. The particulars of that interview between Philip and Camilla, alone at first (afterwards Mr. Robert Beaufort was re-admitted), Philip never disclosed, nor could Sidney himself ever obtain a clear account from Camilla, who could not recall it, even years after, without great emotion. But at last the door was opened, and Philip entered, leading Camilla by the hand. His face was calm, and there was a smile on his lips; a greater dignity than even that habitual to him was diffused over his whole person. Camilla was holding her handkerchief to her eyes and weeping passionately. Mr. Beaufort followed them with a mortified and slinking air.

"Sidney," said Philip, "it is past. All is arranged. I yield to your earlier, and therefore better, claim. Mr. Beaufort consents to your union. He will tell you, at some fitter time, that our birthright is at last made clear, and that there is no blot on the name we shall hereafter bear. Sidney, embrace your bride!"

Amazed, delighted, and still half incredulous, Sidney seized and kissed the hand of Camilla; and as he then drew her to his breast, she said, as she pointed to Philip:—

"Oh! if you do love me as you say, see in him the generous, the noble—" Fresh sobs broke off her speech; but as Sidney sought again to take her hand, she whispered, with a touching and womanly sentiment, "Ah! respect him: see!—" and Sidney, looking then at his brother, saw, that though he still attempted to smile, his lip writhed, and his features were drawn together, as one whose frame is wrung by torture, but who struggles not to groan.

He flew to Philip, who, grasping his hand, held him back, and said,—

"I have fulfilled my vow! I have given you up the only blessing my life has known. Enough, you are happy, and I shall be so too, when God pleases to soften this blow. And now you must not wonder or blame me, if, though so lately found, I leave you for a while. Do me one kindness,—you, Sidney—you, Mr. Beaufort. Let the marriage take place at H—, in the village church by which my mother sleeps; let it be delayed till the suit is terminated: by that time I shall hope to meet you all—to meet you, Camilla, as I ought to meet my brother's wife; till then, my presence will not sadden your happiness. Do not seek to see me; do not expect to hear from me. Hist! be silent, all of you; my heart is yet bruised and sore. O THOU," and here, deepening his voice, he raised his arms, "Thou who hast preserved my youth from such snares and such peril, who hast guided my steps from the abyss to which they wandered, and beneath whose hand I now bow, grateful if chastened, receive this offering, and bless that union! Fare ye well."

CHAPTER XXI

"Heaven's airs amid the harpstrings dwell;
And we wish they ne'er may fade;
They cease; and the soul is a silent cell,
Where music never played.
Dream follows dream through the long night-hours."
WILSON: The Past, a poem.

The self-command which Philip had obtained for a while deserted him when he was without the house. His mind felt broken up into chaos; he hurried on, mechanically, on foot; he passed street upon street, now solitary and deserted, as the lamps gleamed upon the thick snow. The city was left behind him. He paused not, till, breathless, and exhausted in spirit if not in frame, he reached the churchyard where Catherine's dust reposed. The snow had ceased to fall, but it lay deep over the graves; the yew-trees, clad in their white shrouds, gleamed ghost-like through the dimness. Upon the rail that fenced the tomb yet hung a wreath that Fanny's hand had placed there. But the flowers were hid; it was a wreath of snow! Through the intervals of the huge and still clouds, there gleamed a few melancholy stars. The very calm of the holy spot seemed unutterably sad. The Death of the year overhung the Death of man. And as Philip bent over the tomb, within and without all was ICE and NIGHT!

For hours he remained on that spot, alone with his grief and absorbed in his prayer. Long past midnight Fanny heard his step on the stairs, and the door of his chamber close with unwonted violence. She heard, too, for some time, his heavy tread on the floor, till suddenly all was silent. The next morning, when, at the usual hour, Sarah entered to unclose the shutters and light the fire, she was startled by wild exclamations and wilder laughter. The fever had mounted to the brain—he was delirious.

For several weeks Philip Beaufort was in imminent danger; for a considerable part of that time he was unconscious; and when the peril was past, his recovery was slow and gradual. It was the only illness to which his vigorous frame had ever been subjected: and the fever had perhaps exhausted him more than it might have done one in whose constitution the disease had encountered less resistance. His brother; imagining he had gone abroad, was unacquainted with his danger. None tended his sick-bed save the hireling nurse, the feed physician, and the unpurchasable heart of the only being to whom the wealth and rank of the Heir of Beaufort Court were as nothing. Here was reserved for him Fate's crowning lesson, in the vanity of those human wishes which anchor in gold and power. For how many years had the exile and the outcast pined indignantly for his birthright?—Lo! it was won: and with it came the crushed heart and the smitten frame. As he slowly recovered sense and reasoning, these thoughts struck him forcibly. He felt as if he were rightly punished in having disdained, during his earlier youth, the enjoyments within his reach. Was there nothing in the glorious health—the unconquerable hope—the heart, if wrung, and chafed, and sorely tried, free at least from the direst anguish of the passions, disappointed and jealous love? Though now certain, if spared to the future, to be rich, powerful, righted in name and honour, might he not from that sick-bed envy his earlier past? even when with his brother orphan he wandered through the solitary fields, and felt with what energies we are gifted when we have something to protect; or when, loving and beloved, he saw life smile out to him in the eyes of Eugenie; or when, after that melancholy loss, he wrestled boldly, and breast to breast with Fortune, in a far land, for honour and independence? There is something in severe illness, especially if it be in violent contrast to the usual strength of the body, which has often the most salutary effect upon the mind; which often, by the affliction of the frame, roughly wins us from the too morbid pains of the heart! which makes us feel that, in mere LIFE, enjoyed as the robust enjoy it, God's Great Principle of Good breathes and moves. We rise thus from the sick-bed softened and humbled, and more disposed to look around us for such blessings as we may yet command.

The return of Philip, his danger, the necessity of exertion, of tending him, had roused Fanny from a state which might otherwise have been permanently dangerous to the intellect so lately ripened within her. With what patience, with what fortitude, with what unutterable thought and devotion, she fulfilled that best and holiest woman's duty—let the man whose struggle with life and death has been blessed with the vigil that wakes and saves, imagine to himself. And in all her anxiety and terror, she had glimpses of a happiness which it seemed to her almost criminal to acknowledge. For, even in his delirium, her voice seemed to have some soothing influence over him, and he was calmer while she was by. And when at last he was conscious, her face was the first he saw, and her name the first which his lips uttered. As then he grew gradually stronger, and the bed was deserted for the sofa, he took more than the old pleasure in hearing her read to him; which she did with a feeling that lecturers cannot teach. And once, in a pause from this occupation, he spoke to her frankly,—he sketched his past history—his last sacrifice. And Fanny, as she wept, learned that he was no more another's!

It has been said that this man, naturally of an active and impatient temperament, had been little accustomed to seek those resources which are found in books. But somehow in that sick chamber—it was Fanny's voice—the voice of her over whose mind he had once so haughtily lamented, that taught him how much of aid and solace the Herd of Men derive from the Everlasting Genius of the Few.

Gradually, and interval by interval, moment by moment, thus drawn together, all thought beyond shut out (for, however crushing for the time the blow that had stricken Philip from health and reason, he was not that slave to a guilty fancy, that he could voluntarily indulge—that he would not earnestly seek to shun—all sentiments that yet turned with unholy yearning towards the betrothed of his brother);—gradually, I say, and slowly, came those progressive and delicious epochs which mark a revolution in the affections:—unspeakable gratitude, brotherly tenderness, the united strength of compassion and respect that he had felt for Fanny seemed, as he gained health, to mellow into feelings yet more exquisite and deep. He could no longer delude himself with a vain and imperious belief that it was a defective mind that his heart protected; he began again to be sensible to the rare beauty of that tender face—more lovely, perhaps, for the paleness that had replaced its bloom. The fancy that he had so imperiously checked before—before he saw Camilla, returned to him, and neither pride nor honour had now the right to chase the soft wings away. One evening, fancying himself alone, he fell into a profound reverie; he awoke with a start, and the exclamation, "was it true love that I ever felt for Camilla, or a passion, a frenzy, a delusion?"

His exclamation was answered by a sound that seemed both of joy and grief. He looked up, and saw Fanny before him; the light of the moon, just risen, fell full on her form, but her hands were clasped before her face; he heard her sob.

"Fanny, dear Fanny!" he cried, and sought to throw himself from the sofa to her feet. But she drew herself away, and fled from the chamber silent as a dream.

Philip rose, and, for the first time since his illness, walked, but with feeble steps, to and fro the room. With what different emotions from those in which last, in fierce and intolerable agony, he had paced that narrow boundary! Returning health crept through his veins—a serene, a kindly, a celestial joy circumfused his heart. Had the time yet come when the old Florimel had melted into snow; when the new and the true one, with its warm life, its tender beauty, its maiden wealth of love, had risen before his hopes? He paused before the window; the spot within seemed so confined, the night without so calm and lovely, that he forgot his still-clinging malady, and unclosed the casement: the air came soft and fresh upon his temples, and the church-tower and spire, for the first time, did not seem to him to rise in gloom against the heavens. Even the gravestone of Catherine, half in moonlight, half in shadow, appeared to him to wear a smile. His mother's memory was become linked with the living Fanny.

"Thou art vindicated—thy Sidney is happy," he murmured: "to her the thanks!"

Fair hopes, and soft thoughts busy within him, he remained at the casement till the increasing chill warned him of the danger he incurred.

The next day, when the physician visited him, he found the fever had returned. For many days, Philip was again in danger—dull, unconscious even of the step and voice of Fanny.

He woke at last as from a long and profound sleep; woke so refreshed, so revived, that he felt at once that some great crisis had been passed, and that at length he had struggled back to the sunny shores of Life.

By his bedside sat Liancourt, who, long alarmed at his disappearance, had at last contrived, with the help of Mr. Barlow, to trace him to Gawtrey's house, and had for several days taken share in the vigils of poor Fanny.

While he was yet explaining all this to Philip, and congratulating him on his evident recovery, the physician entered to confirm the congratulation. In a few days the invalid was able to quit his room, and nothing but change of air seemed necessary for his convalescence. It was then that Liancourt, who had for two days seemed impatient to unburden himself of some communication, thus addressed him:—

"My—My dear friend, I have learned now your story from Barlow, who called several times during your relapse; and who is the more anxious about you, as the time for the decision of your case now draws near. The sooner you quit this house the better."

"Quit this house! and why? Is there not one in this house to whom I owe my fortune and my life?"

"Yes; and for that reason I say, 'Go hence:' it is the only return you can make her."

"Pshaw!—speak intelligibly."

"I will," said Liancourt, gravely. "I have been a watcher with her by your sick-bed, and I know what you must feel already:—nay, I must confess that even the old servant has ventured to speak to me. You have inspired that poor girl with feelings dangerous to her peace."

"Ha!" cried Philip, with such joy that Liancourt frowned, and said, "Hitherto I have believed you too honourable to—"

"So you think she loves me?" interrupted Philip. "Yes; what then? You, the heir of Beaufort Court, of a rental of £20,000. a year,—of an historical name,—you cannot marry this poor girl?"

"Well!—I will consider what you say, and, at all events, I will leave the house to attend the result of the trial. Let us talk no more on the subject now."

Philip had the penetration to perceive that Liancourt, who was greatly moved by the beauty, the innocence, and the unprotected position of Fanny, had not confined caution to himself; that with his characteristic well-meaning bluntness, and with the license of a man somewhat advanced in years, he had spoken to Fanny herself: for Fanny now seemed to shun Philip,—her eyes were heavy, her manner was embarrassed. He saw the change, but it did not grieve him; he hailed the omens which he drew from it.

And at last he and Liancourt went. He was absent three weeks, during which time the formality of the friendly lawsuit was decided in the plaintiff's favour; and the public were in ecstasies at the noble and sublime conduct of Mr. Robert Beaufort: who, the moment he had discovered a document which he might so easily have buried for ever in oblivion, voluntarily agreed to dispossess himself of estates he had so long enjoyed, preferring conscience to lucre. Some persons observed that it was reported that Mr. Philip Beaufort had also been generous—that he had agreed to give up the estates for his uncle's life, and was only in the meanwhile to receive a fourth of the revenues. But the universal comment was, "He could not have done less!" Mr. Robert Beaufort was, as Lord Lilburne had once observed, a man who was born, made, and reared to be spoken well of by the world; and it was a comfort to him now, poor man, to feel that his character was so highly estimated. If Philip should live to the age of one hundred, he will never become so respectable and popular a man with the crowd as his worthy uncle.

But does it much matter? Philip returned to H— the eve before the day fixed for the marriage of his brother and Camilla.

CHAPTER XII

From Night, Sunshine and Day arose—HES

The sun of early May shone cheerfully over the quiet suburb of H—. In the thoroughfares life was astir. It was the hour of noon—the hour at which commerce is busy, and streets are full. The old retired trader, eying wistfully the rolling coach or the oft-pausing omnibus, was breathing the fresh and scented air in the broadest and most crowded road, from which, afar in the distance, rose the spires of the metropolis. The boy let loose from the day-school was hurrying home to dinner, his satchel on his back: the ballad-singer was sending her cracked whine through the obscurer alleys, where the baker's boy, with puddings on his tray, and the smart maid-servant, despatched for porter, paused to listen. And round the shops where cheap shawls and cottons tempted the female eye, many a loitering girl detained her impatient mother, and eyed the tickets and calculated her hard-gained savings for the Sunday gear. And in the corners of the streets steamed the itinerant kitchens of the piemen, and rose the sharp cry, "All hot! all hot!" in the ear of infant and ragged hunger. And amidst them all rolled on some lazy coach of ancient merchant or withered maiden, unconscious of any life but that creeping through their own languid veins. And before the house in which Catherine died, there loitered many stragglers, gossips, of the hamlet, subscribers to the news-room hard by, to guess, and speculate, and wonder why, from the church behind, there rose the merry peal of the marriage-bell!

At length along the broad road leading from the great city, there were seen rapidly advancing three carriages of a very different fashion from those familiar to the suburb. On they came; swiftly they whirled round the angle that conducted to the church; the hoofs of the gay steeds ringing cheerily on the ground; the white favours of the servants gleaming in the sun. Happy is the bride the sun shines on! And when the carriages had thus vanished, the scattered groups melted into one crowd, and took their way to the church. They stood idling without in the burial-ground; many of them round the fence that guarded from their footsteps Catherine's lonely grave. All in nature was glad, exhilarating, and yet serene; a genial freshness breathed through the soft air; not a cloud was to be seen in the smiling azure; even the old dark yews seemed happy in their everlasting verdure. The bell ceased, and then even the crowd grew silent; and not a sound was heard in that solemn spot to whose demesnes are consecrated alike the Birth, the Marriage, and the Death.

At length there came forth from the church door the goodly form of a rosy beadle. Approaching the groups, he whispered the better-dressed and commanded the ragged, remonstrated with the old and lifted his cane against the young; and the result of all was, that the churchyard, not without many a murmur and expostulation, was cleared, and the crowd fell back in the space behind the gates of the principal entrance, where they swayed and gaped and chattered round the carriages, which were to bear away the bridal party.

Within the church, as the ceremony was now concluded, Philip Beaufort conducted, hand-in-hand, silently along the aisle, his brother's wife.

Leaning on his stick, his cold sneer upon his thin lip, Lord Lilburne limped, step by step, with the pair, though a little apart from them, glancing from moment to moment at the face of Philip Beaufort, where he had hoped to read a grief that he could not detect. Lord Lilburne had carefully refrained from an interview with Philip till that day, and he now only came to the wedding as a surgeon goes to an hospital, to examine a disease he had been told would be great and sore: he was disappointed. Close behind followed Sidney, radiant with joy, and bloom, and beauty; and his kind guardian, the tears rolling down his eyes, murmured blessings as he looked upon him. Mrs. Beaufort had declined attending the ceremony—her nerves were too weak—but, behind, at a longer interval, came Robert Beaufort, sober, staid, collected as ever to outward seeming; but a close observer might have seen that his eye had lost its habitual complacent cunning, that his step was more heavy, his stoop more joyless. About his air there was a some thing crestfallen. The consciousness of acres had passed away from his portly presence. He was no longer a possessor, but a pensioner. The rich man, who had decided as he pleased on the happiness of others, was a cipher; he had ceased to have any interest in anything. What to him the marriage of his daughter now? Her children would not be the heirs of Beaufort. As Camilla kindly turned round, and through happy tears waited for his approach, to clasp his hand, he forced a smile, but it was sickly and piteous. He longed to creep away, and be alone.

"My father!" said Camilla, in her sweet low voice; and she extricated herself from Philip, and threw herself on his breast.

"She is a good child," said Robert Beaufort vacantly, and, turning his dry eyes to the group, he caught instinctively at his customary commonplaces;—"and a good child, Mr. Sidney, makes a good wife!"

The clergyman bowed as if the compliment were addressed to himself: he was the only man there whom Robert Beaufort could now deceive.

"My sister," said Philip Beaufort, as once more leaning on his arm, they paused before the church door, "may Sidney love and prize you as—as I would have done; and believe me, both of you, I have no regret, no memory, that wounds me now."

He dropped the hand, and motioned to her father to load her to the carriage. Then winding his arm into Sidney's, he said,—

"Wait till they are gone: I have one word yet with you. Go on, gentlemen."

The clergyman bowed, and walked through the churchyard. But Lilburne, pausing and surveying Philip Beaufort, said to him, whisperingly,—

"And so much for feeling—the folly! So much for generosity—the delusion! Happy man!"

"I am thoroughly happy, Lord Lilburne."

"Are you?—Then, it was neither feeling nor generosity; and we were taken in! Good day." With that he limped slowly to the gate.

Philip answered not the sarcasm even by a look. For at that moment a loud shout was set up by the mob without—they had caught a glimpse of the bride.

"Come, Sidney, this way." he said; "I must not detain you long."

Arm in arm they passed out of the church, and turned to the spot hard by, where the flowers smiled up to them from the stone on their mother's grave.

The old inscription had been effaced, and the name of CATHERINE BEAUFORT was placed upon the stone. "Brother," said Philip, "do not forget this grave: years hence, when children play around your own hearth. Observe, the name of Catherine Beaufort is fresher on the stone than the dates of birth and death—the name was only inscribed there to-day—your wedding-day. Brother, by this grave we are now indeed united."

"Oh, Philip!" cried Sidney, in deep emotion, clasping the hand stretched out to him; "I feel, I feel how noble, how great you are—that you have sacrificed more than I dreamed of—"

"Hush!" said Philip, with a smile. "No talk of this. I am happier than you deem me. Go back now—she waits you."

"And you?—leave you!—alone!"

"Not alone," said Philip, pointing to the grave.

Scarce had he spoken when, from the gate, came the shrill, clear voice of Lord Lilburne,—

"We wait for Mr. Sidney Beaufort."

Sidney passed his hand over his eyes, wrung the hand of his brother once more, and in a moment was by Camilla's side.

Another shout—the whirl of the wheels—the trampling of feet—the distant hum and murmur—and all was still. The clerk returned to lock up the church—he did not observe where Philip stood in the shadow of the wall—and went home to talk of the gay wedding, and inquire at what hour the funeral of the young woman; his next-door neighbour, would take place the next day.

It might be a quarter of an hour after Philip was thus left—nor had he moved from the spot—when he felt his sleeve pulled gently. He turned round and saw before him the wistful face of Fanny!

"So you would not come to the wedding?" said he.

"No. But I fancied you might be here alone—and sad."

"And you will not even wear the dress I gave you?"

"Another time. Tell me, are you unhappy?"

"Unhappy, Fanny! No; look around. The very burial-ground has a smile. See the laburnums clustering over the wall, listen to the birds on the dark yews above, and yonder see even the butterfly has settled upon her grave!

"I am not unhappy." As he thus spoke he looked at her earnestly, and taking both her hands in his, drew her gently towards him, and continued: "Fanny, do you remember, that, leaning over that gate, I once spoke to you of the happiness of marriage where two hearts are united? Nay, Fanny, nay, I must go on. It was here in this spot,—it was here that I first saw you on my return to England. I came to seek the dead, and I have thought since, it was my mother's guardian spirit that drew me hither to find you—the living! And often afterwards, Fanny, you would come with me here, when, blinded and dull as I was, I came to brood and to repine, insensible of the treasures even then perhaps within my reach. But, best as it was: the ordeal through which I have passed has made me more grateful for the prize I now dare to hope for. On this grave your hand daily renewed the flowers. By this grave, the link between the Time and the Eternity, whose lessons we have read together, will you consent to record our vows? Fanny, dearest, fairest, tenderest, best, I love you, and at last as alone you should be loved!—I woo you as my wife! Mine, not for a season, but for ever—for ever, even when these graves are open, and the World shrivels like a scroll. Do you understand me?—do you heed me?—or have I dreamed that that—"

He stopped short—a dismay seized him at her silence. Had he been mistaken in his divine belief!—the fear was momentary: for Fanny, who had recoiled as he spoke, now placing her hands to her temples, gazing on him, breathlessly and with lips apart, as if, indeed, with great effort and struggle her modest spirit conceived the possibility of the happiness that broke upon it, advanced timidly, her face suffused in blushes; and, looking into his eyes, as if she would read into his very soul, said, with an accent, the intenseness of which showed that her whole fate hung on his answer,—

"But this is pity?—they have told you that I—in short, you are generous—you—you—Oh, deceive me not! Do you love her still?—Can you—do you love the humble, foolish Fanny?"

"As God shall judge me, sweet one, I am sincere! I have survived a passion—never so deep, so tender, so entire as that I now feel for you! And, oh, Fanny, hear this true confession. It was you—you to whom my heart turned before I saw Camilla!—against that impulse I struggled in the blindness of a haughty error!"

Fanny uttered a low and suppressed cry of delight and rapture. Philip passionately continued,—

"Fanny, make blessed the life you have saved. Fate destined us for each other. Fate for me has ripened your sweet mind. Fate for you has softened this rugged heart. We may have yet much to bear and much to learn. We will console and teach each other!"

He drew her to his breast as he spoke—drew her trembling, blushing, confused, but no more reluctant; and there, by the GRAVE that had been so memorable a scene in their common history, were murmured those vows in which all this world knows of human happiness is treasured and recorded—love that takes the sting from grief, and faith that gives eternity to love. All silent, yet all serene around them! Above, the heaven,—at their feet, the grave:—For the love, the grave!—for the faith, the heaven!

CHAPTER THE LAST

"A labore reclinat otium."—HORAT.

[Leisure unbends itself from labour.]

I feel that there is some justice in the affection the general reader entertains for the old-fashioned and now somewhat obsolete custom, of giving to him, at the close of a work, the latest news of those who sought his acquaintance through its progress.

The weak but well-meaning Smith, no more oppressed by the evil influence of his brother, has continued to pass his days in comfort and respectability on the income settled on him by Philip Beaufort. Mr. and Mrs. Roger Morton still live, and have just resigned their business to their eldest son; retiring themselves to a small villa adjoining the town in which they had made their fortune. Mrs. Morton is very apt, when she goes out to tea, to talk of her dear deceased sister-in-law, the late Mrs. Beaufort, and of her own remarkable kindness to her nephew when a little boy. She observes that, in fact, the young men owe everything to Mr. Roger and herself; and, indeed, though Sidney was never of a grateful disposition, and has not been near her since, yet the elder brother, the Mr. Beaufort, always evinces his respect to them by the yearly present of a fat buck. She then comments on the ups and downs of life; and observes that it is a pity her son Tom preferred the medical profession to the church. Their cousin, Mr. Beaufort, has two livings. To all this Mr. Roger says nothing, except an occasional "Thank Heaven, I want no man's help! I am as well to do as my neighbours. But that's neither here nor there."

There are some readers—they who do not thoroughly consider the truths of this life—who will yet ask, "But how is Lord Lilburne punished?" Punished?—ay, and indeed, how? The world, and not the poet, must answer that question. Crime is punished from without. If Vice is punished, it must be from within. The Lilburnes of this hollow world are not to be pelted with the soft roses of poetical justice. They who ask why he is not punished may be the first to doff the hat to the equipage in which my lord lolls through the streets! The only offence he habitually committed of a nature to bring the penalties of detection, he renounced the moment he perceived there was clanger of discovery! he gambled no more after Philip's hint. He was one of those, some years after, most bitter upon a certain nobleman charged with unfair play—one of those who took the accusation as proved; and whose authority settled all disputes thereon.

But, if no thunderbolt falls on Lord Lilburne's head—if he is fated still to eat, and drink, and to die on his bed, he may yet taste the ashes of the Dead Sea fruit which his hands have culled. He is grown old. His infirmities increase upon him; his sole resources of pleasure—the senses—are dried up. For him there is no longer savour in the viands, or sparkle in the wine,—man delights him not, nor woman neither. He is alone with Old Age, and in the sight of Death.

With the exception of Simon, who died in his chair not many days after Sidney's marriage, Robert Beaufort is the only one among the more important agents left at the last scene of this history who has passed from our mortal stage.

After the marriage of his daughter he for some time moped and drooped. But Philip learned from Mr. Blackwell of the will that Robert had made previously to the lawsuit; and by which, had the lawsuit failed, his rights would yet have been preserved to him. Deeply moved by a generosity he could not have expected from his uncle, and not pausing to inquire too closely how far it was to be traced to the influence of Arthur, Philip so warmly expressed his gratitude, and so surrounded Mr. Beaufort with affectionate attentions, that the poor man began to recover his self-respect,—began even to regard the nephew he had so long dreaded, as a son,—to forgive him for not marrying Camilla. And, perhaps, to his astonishment, an act in his life for which the customs of the world (that never favour natural ties not previously sanctioned by the legal) would have rather censured than praised, became his consolation; and the memory he was most proud to recall. He gradually recovered his spirits; he was very fond of looking over that will: he carefully preserved it: he even flattered himself that it was necessary to preserve Philip from all possible litigation hereafter; for if the estates were not legally Philip's, why, then, they were his to dispose of as he pleased. He was never more happy than when his successor was by his side; and was certainly a more cheerful and, I doubt not, a better man—during the few years in which he survived the law-suit—than ever he had been before. He died—still member for the county, and still quoted as a pattern to county members—in Philip's arms; and on his lips there was a smile that even Lilburne would have called sincere.

Mrs. Beaufort, after her husband's death, established herself in London; and could never be persuaded to visit Beaufort Court. She took a companion, who more than replaced, in her eyes, the absence of Camilla.

And Camilla-Spencer-Sidney. They live still by the gentle Lake, happy in their own serene joys and graceful leisure; shunning alike ambition and its trials, action and its sharp vicissitudes; envying no one, covetous of nothing; making around them, in the working world, something of the old pastoral and golden holiday. If Camilla had at one time wavered in her allegiance to Sidney, her good and simple heart has long since been entirely regained by his devotion; and, as might be expected from her disposition, she loved him better after marriage than before.

Philip had gone through severer trials than Sidney. But, had their earlier fates been reversed, and that spirit, in youth so haughty and self-willed, been lapped in ease and luxury, would Philip now be a better or a happier man? Perhaps, too, for a less tranquil existence than his brother, Philip yet may be reserved; but, in proportion to the uses of our destiny, do we repose or toil: he who never knows pain knows but the half of pleasure. The lot of whatever is most noble on the earth below falls not amidst the rosy Gardels of the Epicurean. We may envy the man who enjoys and rests; but the smile of Heaven settles rather on the front of him who labours and aspires.

And did Philip ever regret the circumstances that had given him Fanny for the partner of his life? To some who take their notions of the Ideal from the conventional rules of romance, rather than from their own perceptions of what is true, this narrative would have been more pleasing had Philip never loved but Fanny. But all that had led to that love had only served to render it more enduring and concentred. Man's strongest and worthiest affection is his last—is the one that unites and embodies all his past dreams of what is excellent—the one from which Hope springs out the brighter from former disappointments—the one in which the MEMORIES are the most tender and the most abundant—the one which, replacing all others, nothing hereafter can replace.

And now ere the scene closes, and the audience, whom perhaps the actors may have interested for a while, disperse, to forget amidst the pursuits of actual life the Shadows that have amused an hour, or beguiled a care, let the curtain fall on one happy picture:—

It is some years after the marriage of Philip and Fanny. It is a summer morning. In a small old-fashioned room at Beaufort Court, with its casements open to the gardens, stood Philip, having just entered; and near the window sat Fanny, his boy by her side. She was at the mother's hardest task—the first lessons to the first-born child; and as the boy looked up at her sweet earnest face with a smile of intelligence on his own, you might have seen at a glance how well understood were the teacher and the pupil. Yes: whatever might have been wanting in the Virgin to the full development of mind, the cares of the mother had supplied. When a being was born to lean on her alone—dependent on her providence for life—then hour after hour, step after step, in the progress of infant destinies, had the reason of the mother grown in the child's growth, adapting itself to each want that it must foresee, and taking its perfectness and completion from the breath of the New Love!

The child caught sight of Philip and rushed to embrace him.

"See!" whispered Fanny, as she also hung upon him, and strange recollections of her own mysterious childhood crowded upon her,—"See," whispered she, with a blush half of shame and half of pride, "the poor idiot girl is the teacher of your child!"

"And," answered Philip, "whether for child or mother, what teacher is like Love?"

Thus saying, he took the boy into his arms; and, as he bent over those rosy cheeks, Fanny saw, from the movement of his lips and the moisture in his eyes, that he blessed God. He looked upon the mother's face, he glanced round on the flowers and foliage of the luxurious summer, and again he blessed God: And without and within, it was Light and MORNING!

Edward Bulwer-Lytton – A Short Biography

Edward George Earle Bulwer-Lytton was born on May 25th, 1803 to General William Earle Bulwer and Elizabeth Barbara Lytton, and was the youngest of three sons.

When Edward was four his father died and his mother moved the family to London. As a child he was delicate and neurotic and failed to fit in at any number of boarding schools. However, he was academically and creatively precocious and, as a teenager, he published his first work; Ishmael and Other Poems in 1820.

In 1822 he entered Trinity College, Cambridge, but shortly afterwards moved to Trinity Hall. He continued to write poetry and in 1825 he won the Chancellor's Gold Medal for English verse for Sculpture. The following year he received his B.A. degree and printed, for private circulation, the small volume of poems, Weeds and Wild Flowers.

He appears to have briefly considered a career in the Army and purchased a commission, but sold it without serving.

In August 1827, much against his mother's wishes, he married Rosina Doyle Wheeler, a 25 year old and famous Irish beauty. His mother withdrew his allowance and he was forced to work for a living. The couple had two children, Emily Elizabeth (1828), and Edward Robert (1831) who later became Governor-General and Viceroy of British India (1876–1880).

During his career he was to be extremely prolific and write across a number of genres; historical fiction, mystery, romance, the occult, and science fiction as well as poetry. His personal life style was extravagant but his works sold well enabling him to continue to write in varied styles. Sometimes he would publish anonymously.

In 1828 his novel, Pelham, brought him an income, as well as a commercial and critical reputation. The books intricate plot and humorous, intimate portrayals kept many a gossip busy trying to pair up public figures with characters in the book.

At the time there was a suggestion that it was similar in vein to Benjamin Disraeli's first novel, Vivian Grey, published the previous year. In fact, Bulwer-Lytton admired Disraeli's father, Isaac D'Israeli, who was himself a noted author. Correspondence between them began in the late 1820s and they met for the first time in March 1830, when Isaac D'Israeli dined at Bulwer-Lytton's house. Among the other diners present were Charles Pelham Villiers, who was to enjoy a long parliamentary career, and Alexander Cockburn who would become Lord Chief Justice of England in 1859.

Bulwer-Lytton took a keen interest in and quickly became a follower of Jeremy Bentham, an English philosopher, jurist, and social reformer. Bentham was the founder of modern utilitarianism, which is best described in Bentham's own words as "the sum of all pleasure that results from an action, minus the suffering of anyone involved in the action".

In 1831 Bulwer-Lytton became the editor of the New Monthly magazine but he resigned the following year.

Bulwer-Lytton was elected the Member of Parliament for St Ives in Cornwall, in 1831, after which he was returned for the Lincoln seat in 1832. He sat in Parliament for that city for nine years. He spoke in favour of the Reform Bill, and took the leading part in securing the reduction, after vainly essaying the repeal, of the newspaper stamp duties. His influence was perhaps most keenly felt when, on the Whigs' dismissal from office in 1834, he issued a pamphlet entitled A Letter to a Late Cabinet Minister on the Crisis.

Lord Melbourne, the then Prime Minister, offered Bulwer-Lytton a lordship of the admiralty, which he declined as he had no wish for anything further to deflect him from his writing.

Indeed beginning with the publication of Falkland in 1827 Bulwer-Lytton had kept up a writing schedule that was both prolific and very well received. His income grew as did his reputation.

Bulwer-Lytton reached perhaps the height of his popularity with the publication of Godolphin (1833), followed by The Pilgrims of the Rhine (1834), The Last Days of Pompeii (1834), Rienzi, Last of the Roman Tribunes (1835), and continued until Harold, the Last of the Saxons (1848).

Unfortunately for Bulwer-Lytton his writing and political work had strained his marriage to Rosina. Undoubtedly his infidelity also embittered Rosina and in 1833 they separated acrimoniously with the separation becoming legal in 1836. Three years after that Rosina published Cheveley, or the Man of Honour (1839), a near-libelous fiction bitterly satirising her husband's alleged hypocrisy.

His play Money (1840) was first produced at the Theatre Royal, Haymarket, London, on December 8th, 1840. Its success merited an opening on the other side of the Atlantic and on February 1st, 1841 it opened at the Old Park Theater in New York.

In 1841, he left Parliament and would not return to politics for another 11 years. However that year he started the Monthly Chronicle, a semi-scientific magazine. The Victorian era was filled with many magazines and periodicals all of whom had a great fascination to chronicle and publish the many things that the Empire and Industrial Revolution were discovering, inventing and changing.

The death of Bulwer-Lytton's mother in 1843 was a great sadness to him despite their difference over his marriage. His own "exhaustion of toil and study had been completed by great anxiety and grief", and by "about the January of 1844, I was thoroughly shattered". In his mother's room, Bulwer-Lytton "had inscribed above the mantelpiece a request that future generations preserve the room as his beloved mother had used it"; that request is still essentially honoured to this day.

On 20th February 1844, in accordance with his mother's will, he changed his surname from 'Bulwer' to 'Bulwer-Lytton' and assumed the arms of Lytton by royal licence. His widowed mother had done the same in 1811. But, his brothers would remain plain 'Bulwer'.

Bulwer-Lytton was very interested in the latest medical advances and practices. He happened upon a copy of "Captain Claridge's work on the 'Water Cure', as practised by Priessnitz, at Graefenberg", and "making allowances for certain exaggerations therein", pondered the option of travelling to Graefenberg, but preferred to find something closer to home, with access to his own doctors in case of failure: "I who scarcely lived through a day without leech or potion!"

After reading a pamphlet by Doctor James Wilson, who operated a hydropathic establishment with James Manby Gully at Malvern, he stayed there for "some nine or ten weeks", after which he "continued the system some seven weeks longer under Doctor Weiss, at Petersham", then again at "Doctor Schmidt's magnificent hydropathic establishment at Boppart" (at the former Marienberg Convent at Boppard), after developing a cold and fever upon his return home.

He returned to Parliament in 1852, when, having differed from the policy of Lord John Russell over the Corn Laws, he stood for Hertfordshire as a Conservative, a seat he would now hold until 1866.

In 1858 he entered Lord Derby's government as Secretary of State for the Colonies, thus serving alongside his old friend Disraeli. He took an active interest in the development of the Crown Colony of British Columbia and wrote with great passion to the Royal Engineers upon assigning them their duties there. The former Hudson Bay's Company Fort Dallas at Camchin, the confluence of the Thompson and Fraser Rivers, was renamed in his honour by Governor Sir James Douglas in 1858 as Lytton, British Columbia.

In June 1858, when her husband was standing as parliamentary candidate for Hertfordshire, his ex-wife Rosina sought him out and denounced him from the crowd. It was humiliating but his actions seemed only to further inflame the situation. He threatened her publishers, withheld her allowance, and denied her access to her children. Finally, he had her committed to a mental asylum. There ensued a public outcry at her treatment and she was released a few weeks later. Rosina chronicled the incident in her memoir, A Blighted Life (1880).

By this time, Bulwer-Lytton's great and prolific literary output was essentially over. He did write a few pieces, now and then usually with a horror or supernatural theme including "The Haunted and the Haunters" or "The House and the Brain" (1859) and a novel, A Strange Story (1862), said to have been an influence for Bram Stoker's Dracula.

When King Otto of Greece abdicated in 1862, Bulwer-Lytton was apparently offered the crown of Greece, which he declined.

In 1866 Bulwer-Lytton was raised to the peerage as Baron Lytton of Knebworth in the County of Hertford but his passion for politics now somewhat dimmed.

The English Rosicrucian society, founded in 1867 by Robert Wentworth Little, claimed Bulwer-Lytton as their 'Grand Patron', but he wrote to the society complaining that he was 'extremely surprised' by their use of the title, as he had 'never sanctioned such'. Nevertheless, a number of esoteric groups continued to claim Bulwer-Lytton as their own, chiefly because some of his writings—such as the 1842 book Zanoni—have included Rosicrucian and other esoteric notions.

Bulwer-Lytton continued to pen several other works, including The Coming Race or Vril: The Power of the Coming Race (1871), which drew heavily on his interest in the occult and contributed to the early growth of the science fiction genre. Its story of a subterranean race waiting to reclaim the surface of the Earth is an early science fiction theme. The book popularised the prevailing Hollow Earth theory. His term "vril" lent its name to Bovril meat extract. Adopted by theosophists and occultists since the 1870s, "vril" would develop into a major esoteric topic, and eventually become closely associated with the ideas of an esoteric neo-Nazism after 1945.

Bulwer-Lytton had long suffered with a disease of the ear and for the last two or three years of his life he lived in Torquay nursing his health.

An operation to cure his deafness resulted in an abscess forming in his ear which later burst.

Edward George Earle Bulwer-Lytton endured intense pain for a week and died at 2am on January 18th, 1873, in Torquay, just short of his 70th birthday. The cause of death was not clear but it was thought at the time that the infection had spread to his brain and caused a fit.

Bulwer-Lytton's last novel was Kenelm Chillingly, which at the time of his death was being serialised in Blackwood's Magazine.

He was buried at Westminster Abbey, though this was against his own wishes.

Among his much-used phrases are "the great unwashed", "pursuit of the almighty dollar", "the pen is mightier than the sword", and the classic opening line "It was a dark and stormy night".

Edward Bulwer-Lytton – A Concise Bibliography

Novels
Falkland (1827)
Pelham: or The Adventures of a Gentleman (1828)
The Disowned (1829)
Devereux (1829)
Paul Clifford (1830)
Eugene Aram (1832)

Godolphin (1833)
The Pilgrims of the Rhine (1834)
The Last Days of Pompeii (1834)
Rienzi, the last of the Roman tribunes (1835)
The Student (1835)
Ernest Maltravers (1837)
Alice, or The Mysteries (1838) A sequel to Ernest Maltravers
Leila: or The Siege of Granada (1838)
Calderon, the Courtier (1838)
Zicci: A Tale (1838)
Night and Morning (1841)
Zanoni (1842)
The Last of the Barons (1843)
Lucretia (1846)
Harold, the Last of the Saxons (1848)
The Caxtons: A Family Picture (1849)
My Novel, or Varieties in English Life (1853)
What Will He Do With It? (1858)
The Haunted and the Haunters or The House and the Brain, a short story (1859)
A Strange Story (1862)
The Coming Race (1871), republished as Vril: The Power of the Coming Race
Kenelm Chillingly (1873)
The Parisians (1873 unfinished)

Verse
Ismael: An Oriental Tale, with Other Poems (1820)
Delmour; or, A Tale of a Sylphid, and Other Poems, (1823)
Sculpture (1825)
Weeds and Wildflowers (1826)
Collected Poems (1831)
The New Timon (1846), an attack on Tennyson published anonymously
King Arthur (1848–9)

Plays
The Duchess de la Vallière (1837)
The Lady of Lyons (1838)
The Sea Captain; or, The Birthright [drama], 1839
Richelieu (1839), A five-act play in blank verse
Money (1840)
Not So Bad as We Seem, or, Many Sides to a Character: A Comedy in Five Acts (1851)
The Rightful Heir (1868), based on The Sea Captain
Walpole, or Every Man Has His Price (1869)
Darnley (unfinished)

Miscellaneous

History of England, (1833)
Letter to a Late Cabinet Minister on the Present Crisis (pamphlet), (1834)
Athens, Its Rise and Fall, (5 Books. Book 1 was published in 1837 and Book 5 posthumously)
A Word to the Public, (1847)
The Odes and Epodes of Horace (Translation), (1869)

Manufactured by Amazon.ca
Bolton, ON

37542900R00188